praise for M
THE NEWIRTI

"This author has a gift."
—*Books! Books! Books!*

"Must read for the summer! It's part adventure, part fantasy, a bit of mystery, and all fun."
—*Times Weekly*

"Sure to be on the shelves with Tolkien, Gaiman and others for a very long time."
—*Paper Safari Reviews*

"It is nice to have an author come up with a new concept when it comes to fiction. And Koep has done just that."
—*Reading Is A Way Of Life BLOG-USA*

"If *The Stand* and the *DaVinci Code* had a baby. Smart and the language is beautiful. 12 out of 10 stars!"

"Not only does Koep have a beautiful writing style and a flare for language—the book resurrects the imponderables of youth, bringing them yet again into the forefront of thought. That is a very good thing, indeed."
—*Netgalley Reviews*

"The most unique book I've read all year--wholly original."

"Full of tricks, turns and slight of hand. A roller coaster ride right from the beginning."
—*Goodreads Reviews*

"Pulse quickening, blockbuster perfection. Masterfully creative!"
—*Nspire Magazine*

"Wow, just WOW!"

"I can honestly say that the ending shocked me. I have not seen a twist like the one in this book since the movie *The Sixth Sense*. That alone makes this a 5 Star book for me."

"I highly recommend this book to lovers of suspense, thrillers, and paranormal!"

"This book is totally WOW! A roller-coaster ride right from the beginning!"

"It's almost difficult to put into words how strongly this book affected me. It is filled with surprises, turns, twists and honestly, the end blew me away."

"If you enjoy a touch of the supernatural and art mysteries, then you will enjoy this. Great Read."

"A remarkably inventive story told in an imaginative way. A story within a story. Looking forward to reading more in this series."
—*Netgalley Reviews*

"Highly addictive! You will LOVE this book."
—*Roger Nichols, Cover to Cover*

"This author has a gift."
—*Books! Books! Books!*

FIVE STAR REVIEWS

from
Readers' Favorite

"The writing is powerful, filled with descriptions that immerse the reader in the action, it offers clear and sweeping visuals, and allow the reader to easily get into the beautiful setting."

"You will want to get in on the ground floor of this series because people are going to be talking about it."

"This is the kind of book that one finishes and has to take a walk afterward, trying to feel the air, to touch things, to talk to the neighbor, just to ensure one isn't still in a dream."

"The fruit of genius, of rich imagination, and sheer madness. Readers will love every page of this engaging story."

—*Readers' Favorite Reviews*

PART THREE

THE NEWIRTH MYTHOLOGY

The SHAPE of RAIN

MICHAEL B. KOEP

FIRST EDITION

Trade Paperback ISBN: 978-0-9976234-2-0
Hardcover ISBN: 978-09976234-3-7

Designed by Will Dreamly Arts Publishing.
Cover art, maps and text illustrations by Michael B. Koep
Author portraits by Brady Campbell
The Newirth Mythology, Part Three, The Shape of Rain
is also available in EBook formats.

Library of Congress Cataloging-in-Publication Data has been applied for.

For Dad

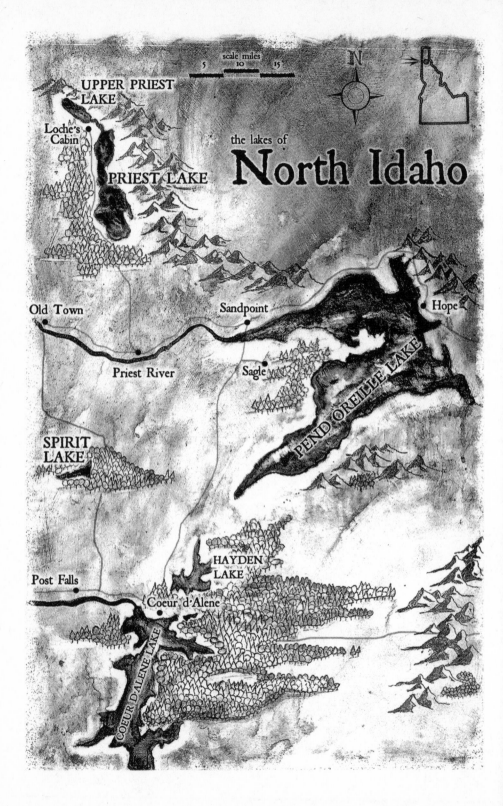

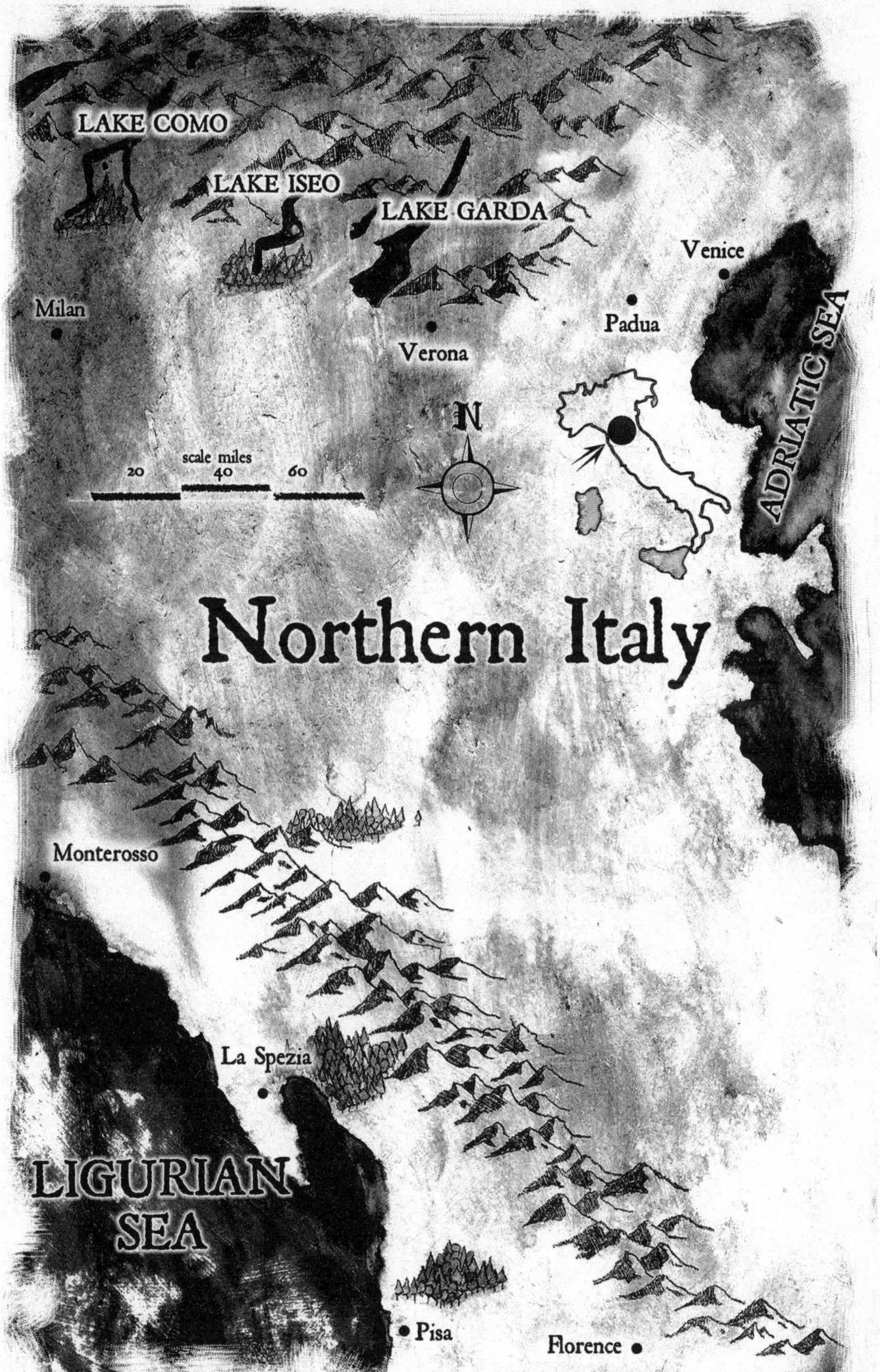
LAKE COMO
LAKE ISEO
LAKE GARDA
Venice
Milan
Padua
Verona
ADRIATIC SEA
N
scale miles
20
40
60
Northern Italy
Monterosso
La Spezia
LIGURIAN SEA
Pisa
Florence

Wyn Avuqua

Hope Tree

Aldyar

southern dike

armory   Shar Temple

Tiris Avu

Sharfiris

Aunald Ven

Vas Temple

Carn Sethqua

William H Greenhame
14, November, 1010 AD

ifae Temple

Vifaetiris

northern dike

book houses

Heron Atheneum

Falio Fethequa

Vastiris

Keptiris

playhouse

N →

Omivide Dellithion

Wyn Avugua
and Fethequa
(Upper Priest Lake)

lat 48 48' 20.92" N
long 116 55' 2.42" W

N

Wyn Avugua

Godrethion

Fethequa

Omivide Mellithion

Gillian K. Greenlane
14. November 1010 AD

Synopsis

This is the third part of THE NEWIRTH MYTHOLOGY.

THE FIRST PART, of the *Newirth Mythology*, *The Invasion of Heaven,* tells of how Loche Newirth discovers that his mentor, criminal psychologist Marcus Rearden, is a murderer, and how Loche journals an imaginative and mythical story to capture him. It also tells of Loche's terrifying and supernatural incident in writing the tale, and how his words have altered the very fabric of existence. Throughout his narrative, Loche raises the question, *"This is really happening, isn't it?"*

The journal, left by Loche for Rearden to read, portrays Loche, and painter Basil Fenn, as brothers and artists with the ability, through their art, to open pathways between this life and the Hereafter. Basil's paintings and Loche's writings are of great interest to an ancient society of immortals called the *Orathom Wis*, whose mission is to guard the doors between this life and the next and prevent the crossing of spirits into our world. One of that Order, William Greenhame, had been keeping a secret watch over the two and protecting them since they were children.

Another immortal, Albion Ravistelle, succeeds in luring Loche, along with his wife Helen, and their young son, Edwin, and Basil to Italy and proposes that by sharing Basil's paintings they could cure mental illness, and the darker elements of the human condition. The brothers discover that Albion's intention is instead to contaminate the afterlife with human fallibility, sin and imperfection.

At the intimation of Loche, Basil takes his own life to stop the invasion of Heaven and protect the natural order of existence. His death begins a war between the *Orathom Wis* and Albion Ravistelle. The journal ends with Loche's life falling further into the surreal when he learns that the immortal William Greenhame is his father. He also discovers that his wife, Helen, has betrayed him for the love of Albion Ravistelle.

Once Rearden completes reading the journal he tests the story's validity by contacting a character within the narrative, the love of Loche Newirth, Julia Iris. When she joins Rearden on a journey to find Loche, she also reads the incredible events depicted in the journal. Convinced the afterlife exists, that an immortal order of men and women protect it, and that the fate of humankind hangs in the balance, both Rearden and Julia are enmeshed in Loche's snare. During the final confrontation between Rearden and Loche, Julia is mortally wounded, Rearden's crime is exposed and he is arrested. Soon after, Loche meets the real life characters from out of his imagination: William Greenhame, Samuel Lifeson and Corey Thomas, and he is forced to come to terms with the anomalous and supernatural quality of his writing. *The Invasion of Heaven* concludes with the discovery that Julia Iris is an immortal.

THE SECOND PART of the *Newirth Mythology*, *Leaves of Fire*, is comprised of four interwoven tales that take place over three different time periods.

THE FIRST TALE traces the early life of six year old William of Leaves (William Greenhame) in fourteenth century, England. After being mortally wounded while unsuccessfully trying to defend his mother from witch hunter, Stephen

Gravesend, Bishop of London, and his group of Sentinel Monks, William and his father, Radulphus Grenehamer, escape into the English countryside with immortal, Albion Ravistelle. William miraculously recovers from his injury before his father's eyes, and Albion promises Radulphus and the boy a chance at revenge.

Before the journey north to Stephen Gravesend's house in Strotford, William sneaks away to the site where his mother was burned with the vain hope that she is still alive. There, growing around her ashes, is a luminous wreath of green leaves and stems. Before Radulphus and Albion pull the crying boy away and back to the road, William takes three leaves and plants them in a leather pouch full of soil.

On the journey north, Albion begins to instruct William in the ways of the *Itonalya*, the ancient Order of the *Orathom Wis*, and their solemn purpose to hunt and eliminate divine beings trespassing into the human, mortal world. According to the Order, all deities were to be dispatched; however, some would be allowed to live if their actions were deemed virtuous. William learns that his mother was indeed a god on earth, and Albion admits that he and the Order had been keeping an eye on her. Albion believes that the villainous Bishop Stephen Gravesend is indeed a bridging god and vows to both eliminate the crossing spirit and to provide William vengeance.

The trio stops to resupply at Albion's house in London. There they meet Albion's steward, Alice of Bath. They also learn about one of Albion's vocations as a known apothecary.

As they set out to Strotford, both father and son struggle with the task before them, weighing vengeance against love. Through Albion's influence, as well as accepting the supernatural reality of their plight, the killing of Gravesend proves to be a necessary choice, and it is decided that William will poison the Bishop.

The attempt to poison Gravesend at his house fails and the assassins are revealed. A fight ensues. William learns, along with Albion, that the true bridging deity is not the bishop, but instead, one of the Sentinel Monks, Father Cyrus. It also comes to light that William's father, Radulphus, is a god on earth. Bishop Gravesend claims that Cyrus is behind the killings and burnings, and names the monk as the Devil himself. The fray leaves Albion incapacitated, the other monks dead and Radulphus pitted against Satan. The dying bishop presses a dagger into the boy's hand and opens a secret escape passage through the wall. Before William runs, his father is killed by Cyrus.

The young boy is chased by Cyrus through a long, underground tunnel. In despair, William loses courage and decides there is no escape from the terror that pursues him. He lies down in the shadowed mouth of the tunnel. As a final, desperate gesture, William raises the dagger and directs its point back into the tunnel. The dagger slices into Cyrus' abdomen as he rushes over the unseen boy. Filled with confusion, William plucks one of his mother's leaves and presses it to the Devil's mortal wound, and Cyrus revives. The Devil then rises up and stares into the eyes of the boy. Before Cyrus can reconcile the nature of William's actions, Albion Ravistelle deals the monk a killing blow.

From that day on, William's leaves are of great interest to Albion Ravistelle.

THE SECOND TALE examines the early life, training and development of the immortal, Helen Storm (later, the wife of Loche Newirth, Helen Newirth).

Helen discovers her immortality in the early summer of 1972. While attempting to gain the favor of the rock star Jimmy Page, she accidentally falls from the fourteenth story of a Los Angeles hotel rooftop. She not only survives but emerges completely unscathed from the event. The serendipitous supernatural occurrence prompts Page to contact his friend (whom Page knows to have a keen interest in such matters), Albion Ravistelle.

Helen's love affair with Albion begins on the first day of their meeting. But Helen feels wholly inadequate to be the companion of the sophisticated and centuries old Ravistelle.

Albion removes Helen from her abusive, alcoholic step father, her poverty and her hopeless future on the Sunset Strip. Before long, Helen is living in Venice, Italy, longing to become the object of Albion's affection.

To achieve his love, Helen determines that she must learn the ways of her kind. She devours the opportunity. Albion provides education, experience and travel. Helen becomes the most dangerous and cold-hearted assassin the *Orathom Wis* has ever produced.

Over two decades, Albion is purposefully absent in her life while Helen pines for him. It isn't until Helen meets Nicolas Cythe (the resurrected Cyrus—the Devil, himself), that Albion reappears. He explains to Helen that before he will take her hand in marriage there is one final trial she must complete.

Albion explains the importance of an ancient prophecy: the coming of two brothers, painter, Basil Fenn and poet, Loche Newirth. She must infiltrate their lives, become their muse and inspire the art that will open the door to the Hereafter.

This account of Helen ends the day she meets Basil Fenn in 1988 in a high school class room.

THE THIRD AND FOURTH TALES take place in present day after the events told in *The Invasion of Heaven.*

In Padua, Italy, William Greenhame assists Loche Newirth and Julia Iris to realize how Loche's journal has changed the course of history. Julia is violently kidnapped by Helen Newirth and taken to Albion Ravistelle. Helen contacts Loche and proposes a trade: Julia for their son, Edwin. William Greenhame suggests that he himself will confront Albion and return with both Julia and Helen. Greenhame then insists that Loche travel to the *Orathom Wis* stronghold, *Mel Tiris*, and enter into Basil Fenn's paintings to learn how to stop what Albion has begun. With great hesitancy, Loche agrees.

Leonaie Echelle is a 95 year-old resident at the Greenhaven's Community Home in Coeur d'Alene, Idaho. She suffers from Alzheimer's. She and the immortal, Samuel Lifeson, have been lovers for well over half a century.

When Samuel arrives to escort her to Europe for a new treatment that will reverse her aging process and infuse her blood with immortal qualities, a procedure that has been developed by Albion Ravistelle and secretly arranged through Corey Thomas who is still deep within Albion's trust, the son of Emil Wishfeill attempts to assassinate the couple. He fails, but before he escapes he vows to kill Samuel.

While a prisoner, Julia Iris is educated by Albion Ravistelle on her immortal condition. Albion shares his reasons for the war he's started against the *Orathom Wis* as well as the Divinities. Through the art of Basil Fenn he plans to defeat the gods; through the experiments using William's leaves he has discovered a way to give the gift of immortality to humankind. Albion intends to create a heaven on earth populated by immortals.

Samuel and Leonaie join William, Loche and Edwin at *Mel Tiris,* north of Italy, along the Rhine River. Mustered there to repel Albion Ravistelle's new faction, the *Endale Gen,* are the remaining immortals and soldiers of the *Orathom Wis*. A high tower houses the remaining paintings of Basil Fenn, and the *Orathom Wis* prepare to defend them from being captured.

Loche is taken to the paintings. He then enters into Basil's surreal and seraphic Center, searching for both his sanity and his brother.

Corey Thomas guides Julia through Basil Fenn's deserted studio within Albion's compound. Julia discovers a cryptic message that only she could find, one that she believes Basil intended to direct her to the pyramids at the Giza Plateau, Egypt.

Within Basil's painting, Loche's quest takes him across a macabre ocean of death. When he reaches the shore he finds his brother, Basil. A deathly vision of darkness, hate and war dims the light around them. It is determined that the ills of humanity are strangling the realm of the gods. The brothers struggle to discover a way to stop the invasion.

Samuel, Leonaie, William and his grandson, Edwin, strike out together for Venice. Just outside of the city, William leaves Edwin in the care of Alice of Bath. When the company arrives at Albion's door, Leonaie and Samuel join Corey and begin her treatment. William confronts Albion and demands the release of Julia and Helen.

Leonaie's procedure is simply the eating of a fruit cultivated through a leaf from William's plant and Albion's alchemy. Shortly after, Leonaie awakes to her new immortal self. As Samuel celebrates that his love now shares the same blood, he is tragically beheaded by the assassin Emil Wishfeill before Leonaie's very eyes. Emil then forces the grief stricken Leonaie to meet Albion.

The *Orathom Wis* fail in their defense of *Mel Tiris*. Before Loche is pulled out of the Center, he and Basil witness the final battle and fall of the ancient city of *Wyn Avuqua* (the city of immortals). Loche leaves Basil at the edge of a pyramid near the city.

Meanwhile, William challenges Albion to a duel. Helen, Julia and others of Albion's charge witness the exchange. Psychologist Marcus Rearden is also a part of the audience. When Leonaie is brought into the chamber, William defeats Albion but does not destroy him. Leaving Albion injured, but still very much alive, William escapes into the underground tunnels with Julia, as does Leonaie with the aid of Corey Thomas. They capture Helen.

Before the company can board the boat that will take them to safety, William must bargain with not only Albion and his host of *Endale Gen* soldiers, but with the Devil, Nicholas Cythe, now an immortal on Earth. Nicholas and Albion produce hostages, Loche's son, Edwin, and Alice of Bath. For the safe passage of the boy and Alice, William offers in return the leaves of everlasting life, the small plant that he harvested as a boy from his mother's ashes. Through a sleight of hand trick, William manages to sneak the plant aboard the boat with Edwin. As the boat speeds away, Julia watches the Devil behead William Greenhame.

The unconscious Loche, along with George Eversman, Julia, Helen, Corey Thomas and the surviving *Orathom Wis,* retreat to the Azores, a cluster of islands in the middle of the Atlantic ocean. On the plane, in a kind of dream-state, the near-to-death Loche Newirth pens several pages of entries into a Red Notebook. No one has yet read what he's written for fear of another history-altering anomaly.

Part Two ends with Loche and Julia preparing to set out to the pyramids of Giza with the hope of deciphering Basil's message.

Imagine there's no heaven.
It's easy if you try.
No hell below us.
Above us only sky.

I wonder if you can.

—John Lennon

The Newirth Mythology

part three of three

The Shape of Rain

Prologue

November 9, this year.
Venice, Italy

"The most important act of my life was driving a jagged piece of ceramic into the throat of the man that put me in chains. And if you do not understand the beauty of that, you do not understand the power of choice." Albion Ravistelle squeezes the knot of his tie as if pinching the stem of a delicate flower.

"So, what shall we become? It is my favorite question of all." November sunlight on the Venetian waterway reflects a spectrum of color across the boardroom ceiling. He smiles at the twenty-three gathered international dignitaries. No face in the room smiles back at Ravistelle. "It is my favorite because we get to choose. And to me, this choice is simple. I say we become gods. I say, we survive and flourish—take the next natural step in our evolution. This is why this Board was formed. This is why we will not falter now. As we all know, to accomplish The Board's goals, we must do two things.

"First, let us eat of the fruit of life. Let us end old age and death and allow the wisdom of millennia to instruct us—not the haste and barbarism a single century teaches. We shall become an immortal race. We will live forever—we will save our planet— we will become gods ourselves. We possess the genetic data, the technology to propel evolution. The fruit is heavy on the bough.

"Second, let us retire and end the false gods that have bred fear and scarcity. Come now, the disease is easy to see. Is it not? The monster that is humankind wallows in pools of its own excrement: religions, monetary systems, geopolitical agendas, war, misguided and irresponsible activity."

He holds up Loche Newirth's leather bound Priest Lake Journal as if it were a visual aid, waggles it and then sets it on the table. "Admittedly, your kind have made progress in recent years —easing the pain of the human condition. Famine is not what it once was (though by some monstrous lack of mental function on humanity's part, it still exists). Medical advances have extended lives and ended plagues, save the ones with the higher financial gains. And even war has lessened. Amazing. Well met, humanity."

Albion places both palms down on the long oak table, presses and slowly stands. He lifts his fountain pen and waves it in the air like a conductor's baton.

"But at what cost? The human condition? As if such a thing outweighs all else? While attempting to ease its own suffering, and increase its pleasure and comfort humanity will desolate the ecosystem. Animals, land and sea, subjugated by human *progress* is holocaust. The destruction of the environment and the killing and/or enslavement of the other inhabitants of this world negates true progress. It is the path that will lead to the destruction of all. The systems of humankind are the disease that we must eliminate. Obvious, I know. Ladies and gentlemen, the pieces are on the board and the time is now. We can create from the ashes." He waits. His fingers rattle a drum roll on the Journal's cover.

Andi Hartson, a woman from the British Secret Service, four seats down the table says, "It appears that you've already started, Mr. Ravistelle. And without the Board's approval." Her tone is sharp with a trace of condescension.

"I have," Albion states. "And you are all aware of our progress. Let me stress that it is our progress, for all of you have aided in the authorship of this plan."

"Yes, but Mr. Ravistelle," Miss Hartson says, "there is research to be done and there are projections to be made. We've been through this Frankenstein scenario before. We know all too well that playing god is a dangerous business. Careless gods create monsters." Albion watches her attractive mouth speak. He has always liked the bright and talented, Miss Hartson, despite her haughty manner. *Young,* Albion thinks, *so very young.*

"I concur," the United States senator seated next to her says, "monsters."

"Ah," Albion says, "But who are the monsters, I wonder?"

"We may have been involved in planning stages, but that is all," Senator Hannazil continues. "No one in this room approved moving forward. And you say that the true saboteur is a psychologist from the Northwest of the United States, a Loche Newirth—"

"Correct. It is feared that Loche Newirth has the ability to undermine everything we've worked for. But the problem of Loche Newirth is being dealt with."

"As you have said many times," the senator sneers. "Haven't you had several opportunities to handle him already?"

Albion does not answer. He searches for something genuinely attractive about the middle-aged senator's appearance. *There is nothing,* he thinks. Hannazil's suit and tie are navy blue and his eyes match. His hair style is perfect American politician —a 1950s above-the-collar cut. And his face is a manufactured handsome, white male.

"And the mistakes of Ravistelle keep on coming," the senator continues. "Since the Uffizi debacle, the political maneuvering and media favors that were needed to cover up the —"

Albion interrupts and points his pen, "Joining us all the way from Washington DC, Utah Senator Hannazil. We all know his conservative and cautionary stance when it comes to changing policy. Senator, the Uffizi official report and the media coverage married into the terrorism chorus without fail—in fact, I found the tune to be rather sublime." He opens his arms and welcomingly asks, "Wasn't it someone on your staff that spun the biological weapon piece? What was the headline, an American Islamic Extremist detonates a biological weapon at Florence art opening. . . or something of the sort? Certainly not the first time you have used such a story. Killing and maiming in the name of Allah never seems to lose its ratings appeal, nor does it weaken your grip on a frightened public—your *America* is not only getting used to it, they crave the fear. Quite the story, Hannazil. Making Newirth a terrorist was quite an ingenious twist. I appreciate your talent as does the Board."

"Someone had to do something to repair the damage you've done, Ravistelle. It is a marvel how a simple story can change the fate of an endeavor."

"Indeed," Albion muses. "I think Dr. Newirth might agree. Stories are powerful."

The senator smiles. He sighs at Albion. "Do be careful, Ravistelle," he says. "We control the mechanism. The Board holds the strings—you're well aware. The Board has been put in place to make sure our collective goals—human and immortal— are met." Hannazil appeals to the group, "And what else were we to say about the Uffizi events? Those that survived seeing those *paintings* or whatever they were, could not explain—Christ, they couldn't speak. You have overstepped your bounds without consulting us. You promised transparency. Now my people tell me there are some kind of underground experiments taking place. Something to do with the suicide victim, that painter Basil Fenn, or rather, his art? Monsters? Frankenstein? I dare say Miss Hartson has a point. This is moving too fast. Too fast."

All the dignitaries mutter their affirmation. Albion's focus moves from face to face.

The British Secret Service's Andi Hartson says, "I'm afraid, Mr. Ravistelle, that the senator is justified in his trepidation. As a body we have discussed the *Melgia* Gene and its significance. Packaging immortality will take some time, as will preparing the strategies and forward progress of humankind. But the ramifications of implementing our plans are still unclear. I move that we suspend operations until we have the transparency we've agreed upon—and the research to support the stratagem—from all levels, social, political and scientific."

Senator Hannazil says, "The sweet lady from Britton is right. Ravistelle, you've gone too far, and you've made too many mistakes. I second her motion—and I suggest new leadership from here on out."

The room is silent. Albion Ravistelle lets his stare rest on Andi for several, long uncomfortable seconds. He is delighted and surprised that she holds eye contact with him. *Impressive*, he thinks.

"A first," he says releasing her. "Never have I been accused of being *hasty*. Of course there is a difference between impetuousness and the hazards of briskly executing a plan long in the making." He laughs, lightly, "A plan conceived well before many of your countries were founded, I might add. My lady," he says to Andi, "research, you beg? Transparency? How will we capture Loche Newirth? Some reassurance our path is provisioned and properly lit? That it is all going to be okay?"

Albion stands and starts a slow circle around the seated board. "Success does not spontaneously combust, ladies and gentlemen. We must set ourselves on fire.

"Many of you know the man seated next to Senator Hannizil. Not only is he one of our Board's top advisors, but his research and personal experience in our long story are perhaps the reasons we are gathered even now. And there is nothing quite as accurate as saying that he has been around since the very beginning." Albion stops and places his hand on Nicolas Cythe's shoulder. "Mr. Cythe has agreed to demonstrate one side of the dynamic that we face in moving forward. But we need a volunteer to give the demonstration its full weight." Albion waits a moment until he moves his hand to Senator Hannazil's shoulder. "Thank you, Senator." Hannazil twists and looks up at Albion standing over him. His expression is amused with a tinge of impatience. "The kind Andi Hartson from the Queen's England is correct. We do not want monsters among us, but distinguishing monsters from men is of the upmost importance. As a body, we agreed to retire monsters and, with this experiment, all of you shall judge which is the monster. Please observe closely."

Albion twirls the fountain pen in his fingers like a drummer might spin a drumstick. With lightning quickness he stabs the point into Nicolas Cythe's windpipe. Jets of blood surge from the wound and splash heavily upon the oak table. Andi reels back with a cry. The senator, his eyes horror wide, freezes at the sight. Hannazil watches Cythe's glittery irises darken as his body slumps forward. Albion then twirls the pen between his fingers again and lifts it high in the air.

Hannazil's eyes tick from Cythe to Albion's raised arm. Albion suddenly punches the pen three times into Hannazil's throat. On the fourth, Albion angles the weapon downward and leaves it embedded deep between the man's ribs.

The room fills with the sound of choking. The senator's fingertips dig at the final insertion point. A moment later he topples to his left, crashes down into Andi Hartson's lap and then collapses to the floor. The torn fissures gush blood in throes, as the dying man's heart stops. Albion's assistant hands him a white towel. He wipes a small amount of blood from his fingers—dabs at a tiny stain on his suit jacket. He sighs and shakes his head. "Must improve my speed," he says. The assistant moves behind him and removes the jacket, folds it over his arm and exits the room.

"Both are dead in my estimation, Andi. What do you say?" No answer. Andi's hand is over her mouth and her eyes are encased in tears.

"What shall we become? The theme of this experiment. . . Should we, do you think, remain on the floor there with *good* Senator Hannazil? For that is where humankind and the world hurtle toward—finality, death and destruction. Shall we continue to be like dear Senator Hannazil with his corrupt policies, his appetite for sordid pleasures—his failure to understand longevity, his ignorance? Or, I wonder, should we join the likes of Mr. Nicolas Cythe here?" Albion gestures to the slumped figure face down on the table in a pool of blood. "Andi, what do you think?"

She is weeping, looking at Cythe. Her body is rigid. Fear fueling her sobs. Over the side of the table, blood drizzles. The tap, tap, tap of heavy drops on the wood floor.

"Mr. Nicholas Cythe?" Albion says. "Are you quite all right?" Cythe's hand twitches and he pushes against the table lifting his torso back into the chair. A thick, white foam is caked around the stab point. He does not answer. With delicate movements he gingerly rubs at the visibly closing wound. He nods a moment later and smiles. "Judgement!" yells Albion. The Board flinches at his voice. "I say we join Mr. Cythe. I say we live the life immortal. We will carry on what we have started—we will weather the storms we have summoned.

"All roads lead to Dr. Loche Newirth, ladies and gentlemen. I assure you that if he is allowed to live, we risk not only everything we've worked for, but our very existence. Why did I not eliminate him when that opportunity knocked? I suppose that is a justified question. I did not kill him because, at that time, I shared the same perspective as my colleague here, Mr. Nicholas Cythe. Nicolas still believes that Loche has the potential to be made to create what we want him to create. And that strategy has been supported and augmented by none other than Loche's mentor and psychologist, Dr. Marcus Rearden." Albion's lips break a grim smile, "Rearden. . . If we give Rearden his way, he will deliver a tortured poet beyond our wildest dreams." He shakes his head. "Dr. Rearden is our best chance at either killing or capturing the Poet. I have given him access to our collected knowledge and resources—what's more, I have allowed him access to the paintings of Basil Fenn. He assures me that he has laid the groundwork—a kind of authorship of his own—that will solve the problem we know as Loche Newirth. Now, for my own part, I feel that we've positioned ourselves to complete the task we have begun without the supernatural hand of Dr. Loche Newirth. I believe he should be eliminated. Our genetic experiments have taken fruit, literally. Basil Fenn's paintings have torn a breech in the fabric of Heaven, and we are sending the sickness that is humanity into a dimension that cannot combat its presence. We shall be victorious. We do not need, nor should we risk what he may eventually write." Ravistelle nods at the journal, "Make no mistake—the Poet's gift is terrifyingly complex and much more powerful than imagined." His eyes rest on the worn leather cover for a moment. "He started this whole affair, but we shall end it. If there is such a thing as endings. . ."

Albion's voice picks up a trace of comfort and ease, "So fear not! Loche Newirth will be killed or he will be made to do what we ask of him. As I've said, the pieces are on the board. We will find him, so be comforted. Our greatest weapon against Newirth is Dr. Marcus Rearden. Dr. Rearden assures us that he knows every weakness there is to know within the Poet. And he tells me that when he finishes with Newirth, we will need only ask, *What shall we become?* and the tortured Poet shall write it, and it shall be."

Pocket Diary Entry # 1

November 11, this year
Terciera Island, Azores, Portugal
10:10 am AZOT
(Loche Newirth's Pocket Diary)

How will it end ?

This first entry in a new pocket diary. I am a little frightened. Everything in my being tells me not to write—for who knows what will come of it? Disaster? Salvation? Nothing? But I will write. I must try to keep track of what has transpired—to somehow find the end. . .

—We are in the middle of the Atlantic. The Azores.

—Terciera is purple — floating lilac on the sea.

—Green plots framed in stone from my feet to the horizon.

—Edwin and I on a Vespa — his helmet is too big—he wants ice cream, I want espresso.

—Bruised clouds stumble over the Atlantic.

—A sweet pipe tobacco haze in the cafe. Tweed jackets - hats hang on pegs.

—Outside, a horse pulls a cart—an orange triangle tacked to the   back. The driver wears yellow gloves.

Describe! Pay attention. Everything is extraordinary. See this world! This light! Forget the Center, the Orathom! Stay here. Stay here!!

I watch Edwin sleep. He holds the blanket to his chest with a fist. An empty, chocolate stained cup with a pink plastic spoon is abandoned on his bedside table. I should have had the Bug brush his teeth, I think. At the foot of the bed are his clothes. Grey sky is framed in the window. The furnace fan hushes the room - a lulling white noise. I set our book, The Lion, The Witch and the Wardrobe down next to the ice cream cup and lean my head into my hands.

Where am I? What am I?

I hold my head to keep my hands from trembling—to keep from going mad. Perhaps to keep my skull from cracking and my mind from clawing its way out. Deep breaths. Many of them. Each time I look out at the sea, I feel like something is searching for us. Something is coming.

I breathe. I think.

Focus.

We have been in the Azores for two days. We're hiding here. I find it difficult to believe that Albion and his Order of Endale Gen, haven't already found us. George Eversman assures me that we are safe, for a time, anyway.

What little I have seen of the Azores is beautiful. If only there was time to explore. I'm told there are nine islands in this once volcanic cluster positioned in the middle of the Atlantic. Its primary industries are agriculture, dairy farming and tourism. I wonder what it would be like to live here. Maybe one day, I will.

The Red Notebook, supposedly containing my handwritten entry, lies on the dresser. I understand that I penned it while I was in a trancelike state on the flight to where we are now. I have not read it. No one has read it. When my eyes linger on the notebook, I think I see a pale glow from under the cover—as if it contains some kind of Center. George and the remaining Orathom Wis fear

*that something frightening lurks within it—The Red Notebook—
something that could alter a long settled past and warp a forming
present. The future? Well, thankfully it still remains a mystery. So
far.*

*Apparently, I wrote it on the eight hour flight across the
Atlantic. I have no memory of this. Julia has shared her
recollection: "You woke from your experience at Mel Tiris and
staggered to the forward cabin—rummaged through a number of
drawers until you found a pen and the red spiral notebook. You
staggered through a little turbulence, bent over the counter and
started writing furiously, mumbling over and over, 'Cold, I'm so
cold. Cold.'"*

*Cold. Perhaps I remember feeling cold. It might be that I
remember the deathly chill of the October water of Priest Lake
some ten days ago.*

*Edwin's eyes swim beneath his lids. His breathing is soft
—hair is still damp from the bath. The sweet scent of the
shampoo rises from the pillow.*

*I think of the birds that woke us both earlier this morning.
They were perched above the window on the roof. High pitched
chirps and long melodic calls as the sun climbed out of the sea.
Hearing the song, Edwin had rushed to the glass and peered up
but could not catch a glimpse of them. Even after all that had
happened over the last days, the sound of a bird and the chance
of seeing it was enough to pull him out of dreams, out of sleep,
onto his feet and to the glass to discover. A bird. A simple bird.
And its song.*

*When they fluttered up and out of sight, Edwin had
tumbled back to his pillow and his slumber.*

*I hope they sing us awake— when we do wake. After all
that has happened, it seems as if nothing now can stop sleep.*

A purple smear of clouds is over the sea. It is near mid day in the center of the Atlantic ocean. Cold.

I must try to rest. I will try to sleep.

The Hell Between

November 11, this year
Terciera Island, Azores, Portugal
1:20pm AZOT

Loche Newirth wakes. He stares up. The thin glowing streak from the drapes cuts the ceiling into two panels of deep grey. He is at the *Orathom Wis* compound in the Azores. It all comes back: Basil's paintings in the castle tower, the death of William Greenhame and so many others, the Red Notebook—it is all his doing. It is he that brought these things to pass. His heart rate quickens. Sweat beads. Tears burn his eyes. There is no peace—nothing between the two hells of sleep and consciousness. He must do something, but what?

His breathing is heavy. He sits up and feels for Julia beside him. He then remembers her desire to take some time to herself—to process, she had said. Loche thankfully agreed knowing that he, too, needed time to himself. Though, right now, in the throes of this terrifying anxiety attack, he wishes someone would come.

He falls back into the sweat chilled sheets, and shivers through halting gasps for air. Time slows. Seconds seem to last for hours as his thoughts race—flashing fears—from Rearden murdering Beth Winship, to Edwin, to Julia, to William, to Helen, to writing the damned Journal. . .

He struggles to catch the words of the song Julia's father sang to her when she was a girl. *That Single Star*, he thinks it was called. He searches for the first line. If only to find a single star amid the trillion sparks of eternity glittering in his head. The boy god is standing in the shadow of his mind. He looks like Edwin.

Lying beside him is his sleeping son. He is motionless save for his eyelids and the gentle rise and fall of his chest. Loche can hear the light puffs of his breathing. The empty ice cream cup lies near the bed. The clock reads 1:20pm.

Loche sits up, places his feet on the wood floor, stands and ties his robe. He walks to the window. Outside, there is a pale grey light under a dark canopy of clouds. He scratches his chin and scans the gloomy ocean horizon. He turns and stares at Edwin. Then, after a few moments he moves to the door, opens it and steps into the hallway.

He walks a short distance to a window encased boardroom with a long marble conference table and comfortable leather chairs on wheels. The ceiling-to-floor glass walls provide a stunning view of the plotted green-lands that stretch to the cliff edge, and then to the ocean maybe two-hundred meters away. Loche rolls a chair to the window and sits. The light is flat and dull. Outside there is no wind. He tries to recall the melody of Julia's song, *That Single Star*. He strains to see through the overcast, wishing to see her star pulse through the grey. He squints. The heater vent blows a warm draft. He feels his eyes close as he listens to the gentle rush of air. Loche believes he sees the star—there, just there!

Then cool finger tips caress his brow.

The star, there. Just above the black silhouette of the mountain against the grey. The fingers move slowly, grazing his forehead, bringing chills to his upper arms and neck. He feels a calm settling over him. The star blinks.

"Husband," a voice whispers into his ear and Loche vaults into consciousness again. "Breathe, Loche. Breathe." His body freezes. Two bare arms are embracing him from behind— Helen's arms. She is warm. For an instant, he hesitates from pulling away. Her hands now gripping his chest.

"W-what are you doing, Helen?" Loche says, startled. "How did you get in here?"

Helen sighs. "Same way you did. The door, Loche. I came in through the door. What did you expect—through the bathroom window? And what am I doing?" She gives him a squeeze, "I'm holding my husband."

Loche doesn't move. The scent of her skin—the sound of her voice—his heart breaks as it did the moment he learned that she and Albion Ravistelle were lovers, partners, husband and wife. Soul mates. Loche scowls and attempts to put up a wall in his mind against Helen's *other* life. Her *real* life. Immortal. A soldier. Deceiver. Murderer. Assassin. A woman with an agenda that he was never privy to.

And he grapples at just how and why *he* created her to be just what she had become. This story—this frightful power of his. . .

As if in answer to his thought, she says, "To think that I could be capable of such treachery, such horrors." Her hushed breath heats the back of his neck. He can imagine her nearly perfect face—a sad smile as she whispers. "How could I do such things? Kill. Lie. Appear to be the loving, and the sometimes inconsolable, wife? Use my mind and body as emotional weapons against the very powers that move the world, the Painter and the Poet?" She pauses. Grief enters her voice. "And Albion." She pulls Loche close. "I am not what you think I am. I am not what you have made me." Loche remains silent. His body tenses. "I have done what was necessary. I know you can't yet understand that."

"What do you want, Helen?" Loche hisses through his teeth. Anger. The fear of her lessening. The familiar pattern of speech between them blurs the extreme circumstances. He pulls away and swivels his chair before he stands up.

Helen looks up at him. "Wait—"

"Please, Helen."

Helen sits in a chair. She lets her arms drape on the rests. "I know that I've said some terrible things. Hurtful things. Done things that are—" she stops speaking and looks at Loche. The start of tears—she shakes her head, unable to find words.

Rain taps at the glass. Helen glances to the window then back to Loche. "W-why did you make us god killers, Loche? Why did you make *me* a god killer?"

Loche has no response. Helen stands up, tosses her hair behind her shoulders and faces him. Then, questions fall out of her like a sudden storm. "Loche, what have you done? Can you tell me how this has happened? Why do I feel as if there is another *me* out there somewhere?" She shakes her head. Again, her focus flits to the window. "How many mistakes can we make before there's no returning?" She asked. "Is there a final number?" She looks down at her hands as she wrings them in her lap and whispers, "How will it end?"

"It is a story I wrote, Helen. A story to trap Rearden." There is a thread of apology in his tone. "Something happened that made it—true." He shakes his head in frustration, "I never meant—I mean—I needed to use my real life, you, Edwin, William Greenhame—so Rearden would at least begin to believe." Loche squeezes his eyes shut and exhales angrily. "I keep hoping that I will wake up soon—that this is all a freakish nightmare."

"To trap Rearden you risked your family," she says. "Your wife! Your son!"

"Helen," again he notes his apologetic tone, "the Journal's purpose was meant to deceive my mentor—it was a lie! How could I have known the horror—known the tale would come to be? Come. . . true?"

Helen glares at him. "Look at what you've done to Edwin and me. Behold, your wife." Helen walks toward him, closing the distance between them. She pushes one hand heavily against his sternum and presses his body against the glass wall. Her other hand raises below his chin with her sharp thumb nail poised to stab upward into his jugular. She brings her face close to his. The heat of her stare, and her strength and speed send a sudden electric chill.

"I may not have been a perfect wife to you, Loche— before you made me into what I am now. They want you dead, Loche. Do you know that yet?" Her thumb digs upward. Adrenaline floods through his body. The dagger like point draws blood. He can feel his airway pinching off. "But, Rearden. . . Rearden wants. . . he wants you. . . tortured. Killing you will save you. Save those that surround you. . ."

"Helen," he says.

"Albion, the *Endale Gen*—they no longer have an interest in controlling you—they think it safer to kill you. It must be why Albion allowed me to be taken. It *must* be." A storm rages in her grey eyes. "I believe that is why I'm here now." Her gaze ticks to Loche's cheek, to his nose, to his mouth, as if searching. "None of us knew what kind of power you were to bring. We thought you would have a craft similar to Basil. They are just now figuring out what you've done—and what it means. The impossibility of it. The chaos of it. You are dangerous to them, Loche. Dangerous to everyone and everything. You can change the fabric of existence through your writing. The great myths of the *Oläthion* prophesied your coming. Like the Painter, we thought you, the Poet, would be just another door. Turns out—" He can feel her body tense. The tip of her nail pushing in. "But Rearden—Nicholas Cythe—they will do far worse than kill you." She meets his eyes, "Loche, we think you are a god."

Astrid

November 11, this year
Gonzaga University, Spokane, WA
8:20 am PST

"The lost city of *Wyn Avuqua*, city of immortals, you say? Right up there with Atlantis, the Loch Ness Monster and Area 51. What's next, Professor? Tell me that you've not uncovered *Hobbiton?*"

Astrid Finnley looks at her notes on the podium. Amid this horrible criticism, sweat dribbles down her neck. She hopes it doesn't show through her blouse. *And how could I be sweating now? Good God, it's just after 7AM and I'm sweating?* she thinks.

After a deep breath and a straightening of her shoulders she smiles. With an agreeable nod she offers, "Yes, of course much of this must sound well outside of the grant's requirements, but I assure you—"

"Professor," Chairman Chad Molmer interrupts. He flashes his irritated face to the other five members of the board. "This is not merely outside of our expectations, this is outside of *sanity*—and frankly, insulting! The funding given to you over the last three years was for research based on. . ." he pauses, wrinkles his nose at the freshly printed manuscript open before him, then hisses, "*evidence.*"

The woman beside him, Dr. Charlotte Tuzass, shakes her head as she flips through the pages of the book, looking for something that makes sense. She says, "We asked for a book on the evolution of ancient Sumerian, Celtic and Egyptian languages and how they are connected, not *this*—what *you believe* came before. Not some fairy story of an ancient culture of immortals that influenced language itself. What you're proposing here—a redefining of the historical record? *Wyn Avuqua?*" she nearly spits, and shakes her head again. "I am stunned, Professor. Just stunned. This is crazy."

Don't look like a crazy woman, Astrid recalls thinking when she had readied herself in the mirror earlier that morning. She had decided to wear a conservative blue top with a rather boring, slate grey skirt—but there was a slight trace of sexy in the way it fit. Not too much. And not too much makeup either. It would be a mistake for a middle aged academic to appear too fashionable, after all, especially in front of the Washington University Grant Board. *Act your age—and most importantly, dress your age.* And today of all days, she needed credibility. Before leaving her bathroom she had pushed her glasses up, brushed away a lone thread at her sleeve, and studied herself. Over half of her life has been spent reading, teaching and writing about mythology—studying the stories that have shaped human behavior—the belief systems that people cling to in order to quell their fear of the unknown—their fear of death and what comes after. All of that must add up to the ability to do at least one thing well, and that's looking like she knows her subject. Or, perhaps, hiding her own kind of crazy.

Florescent lights buzz above. There's the sound of shuffling paper. A board member coughs. She tastes the bad, brown water coffee from the boardroom's 1970s Mr. Coffee maker.

Astrid drops her gaze back down to her notes, clears her throat and quickly decides to carry on with the presentation. Her finger taps the slide advance button on the laptop. Her clear and articulate professor's voice says, "On June 29th, 1873, a magnitude 6.3 earthquake killed nearly one hundred people and did considerable damage to the city of Venice. It also uncovered a view into history that was heretofore hidden from us." Two black and white photos appear on the screen behind her. The first is of the basilica domes of Santa Maria Della Salute in Venice. A hand-drawn red circle directs the eye to the lower foundation. The other picture is a close up of the cornerstone. Carved into the rock at the building's base are two figures of armored men, both holding spears aimed up to a single star. Below are chiseled letters in both Latin and a rune-like script known as *Elliqui.*

Astrid continues, "The damage cracked away portions of stone, revealing this engraving. It is the original dedication to the Santa Maria Della Salute itself. Both the Latin—" she pauses and looks quickly up from her notes and then back down, "and Elliqui read, *For the love of Man, we await the Poet, we await the Painter, until then we shall destroy the plague of gods among us.* You can also see the carved insignia below of the single Eye, including the symbols for the Four Households of *Wyn Avuqua: Shar, Kep, Vas and Vifae.* That is, Talons, Mind, Heart and Wings."

The board member at the far end of the panel raises up another book. The cover Astrid recognizes immediately. The man says, "Professor, really? You must have read *Wyn Avuqua and the Historical Hoax,* by Geoff Bilner."

Another of the board says, "If I am not mistaken, Professor, have you not already made these claims?" He holds up copies of Astrid's two self-published works. "Conspiracy theory meets myth. That stone inscription has long been debunked, along with hundreds of other such claims." He pauses and looks around the room. "I got up early for this?"

Chairman Molmer says, "Professor Finnley, I'm afraid you've not produced the kind of research we have requested, nor have you used the administered funds under the agreed upon requisites. What you have given us is yet another wild chase into rewriting history. *Wyn Avuqua* and the city of immortals, like Atlantis, like Camelot, like the face on Mars, should be left where they belong: in the fantasy section at the library—"

"This man is said to have had the inscription placed," Astrid interrupts, turning to the screen and pointing. She advances to the next slide. It is another split screen with two photographs. On the right a sepia toned, grainy picture of a man's face. Behind him is London at what looks like the turn of the nineteenth century. The other photo is the same face, in crisp color. Behind is the sparkling skyline of modern London. "His name is Albion Ravis—"

A board member blurts out, "You're not saying that he's one of your fabled *immortals*, are you?"

"Not exactly," Astrid replies, "but there is evidence to suggest that he or his family is in some way involved in—"

"As a professor of mythology and linguistics, you surprise me by your effort to blur the lines of what is real and what is not."

Astrid feels her face scowl. She then relaxes and tries to smile, "Isn't that what mythology is?"

The board member waves his hand, "Come now, you know what I mean. *Wyn Avuqua* is not Delphi. It is not Troy. It is not the Giza Plateau. Not Jerusalem. Those are real places and real cultures with substantial historical relevance—with realities that have had an impact on human history. Please, do not enter the invented *ancient city of immortals* into the canon of established giants. It is simply insulting, Dr. Finnley."

Another of the panel says, "And especially after what happened up there, Professor." He waves randomly toward the ceiling, clears his throat and shifts his tone, "While you have our sympathies, I cannot help but think that these revelations that you outline here aren't in some way associated with your boating accident at Priest Lake. . ."

Astrid can still feel the ache in her knee and the chill of the icy water. The deep thunk of the hull crashing into a deadhead. The headache is still there, too. The headache that never seems to fade—and a wall. A wall she placed back there.

No one speaks for a moment. The panel member's comment hovers in the air for an uncomfortable few seconds. Someone coughs.

"Professor, I apologize," Molmer says finally.

Astrid shakes her head. Tears of frustration rise. Her voice quavers, "It was a long time ago. I'm fine now— so if you'll let me finish— there, there's more to the story. Of course I've been through a lot."

"And you've made great progress," Molmer offers.

"Yes," she nods. "I still have my moments, but I have come a long way—"

"Indeed you have, Professor. But I'm afraid your personal trials are not the reason we meet here this morning. What is under scrutiny is your work. I move that Dr. Finnley's manuscript be rejected and that litigation be implemented for breach of contract," Dr. Charlotte Tuzass states.

The motion is seconded.

Molmer asks, "All in favor?"

The entire board replies, "Aye."

Molmer gives a slight nod at the papers on his desk and looks up at Astrid.

Astrid Finnley closes her notebook and stares at the cover. On it is a faded image that she had sketched the day she began her research, some eight years ago—the image of a solitary eye.

The Water's Eye #2

November 11, this year
Terciera Island, Azores, Portugal
1:45pm AZOT

Helen holds the spike of her finger at his throat and pauses. Loche can see her struggling—her pupils flitting—seeking some reason not to murder.

Loche closes his eyes and wonders if his death would be the best option. And what better way than at the hand of his estranged wife, a woman he never truly knew. Was it his fault for not understanding her, or has she deceived him all these years? Why did he make her a god-killer?

Then, Edwin fills his mind. His only son. His eyes snap open and he feels flame stabbing out. For a split second Loche sees that his anger causes Helen to tremble and fall back. And to his surprise the sharp nail drops down and away, and Helen cries as if the wind had been knocked from her lungs. Her chin drops and her legs weaken. She catches herself by grasping Loche's arms.

Loche, shocked at this sudden turn, catches her waist and lowers her to the floor.

"What, what is the matter?" Loche asks.

"It's *Rathinalya,*" she manages to breathe out. "I've never —never felt it so powerful. I cannot stand. You—you are a god after all."

"What are you talking about?"

The *Rathinalya.* Loche recalls the sensation described as an immortal's innate dexterity. But also, their instinctive reaction to a celestial on earth. William Greenhame had told of overwhelming chills, like a thousand needles pricking the skin, a cascade of ice crystals ticking down the spine. This is how an immortal knows a god had bridged—how an immortal knows that a god is near—the purpose of their existence—god killer.

Loche positions her so that she can lean her body against the wall of glass. Her breathing is heavy. Sweat mats the hair around her face. Her hands are still clamped to Loche's upper arms.

"I've never. . . felt it like this. . . even with Cythe. . . this can't be possible. . . *you*. . ."

"I don't understand, Helen," Loche says. "It is not me you're sensing." She raises her face to his and searches.

"Albion, Nicholas Cythe—Rearden—they must be right. You're. . ." She breaks off again, unable to breathe. Fear blackens the grey of her irises. Her hands grip tighter. "I didn't want to believe it."

Loche studies her. He is confused. She is clinging to him, and he cannot decide if she is yearning to hold him for comfort, or to raise her hands to his throat and strangle the life from him.

"Make it stop, Loche. Make it stop!" she cries.

"It is not me," Loche tells her. "It must be something else."

Heavy, uneven footsteps thump behind him. Loche turns and sees Julia Iris leaning unsteadily in the passageway. She is grappling for the door frame and the wall to balance herself. Like Helen, Julia's face is blurred by fear.

"Loche," she cries. "Edwin! Edwin is—" Loche pulls away from Helen and rushes to Julia. He catches her as her legs give way. "He's outside, Loche."

"What? What are you saying?"

"Edwin! Stop Edwin!" Julia raises her arm and points. Loche follows the line of her arm to the huge window, out across the green to the sea. "Edwin! Stop him!" she cries again.

With an awkward, feeble push, Helen turns her body and looks out the window. She then slaps her hand to the glass and screams, "Edwin! Edwin!"

Loche rushes to the window and scans the lawn. The afternoon is a flat metal wash. A small figure is running across the center of the grass plot toward the sea—toward the cliff. It is six-year-old Edwin Newirth.

Loche's fist beats repeatedly against the glass as his voice screams "Edwin! Edwin!"

The little boy stops in the middle of the green field, turns around and looks up. He waves at his father. Silence. Despite the distance of fifty meters and the grey light, Loche can see a grin upon his son's face. Edwin lowers his hand, looks back toward the sea and then back to Loche. He waves one more time, and as if he were being called, he spins his little body toward the sea and runs.

"Edwin! Stop!" The glass walls clatter. Loche knocks harder. "What are you doing?"

"Go after him! Bring him back!" Helen cries. Loche looks down at her and then to Julia. Both are overcome and crippled with some power he can only guess at. He lunges for the door, through the hall and vaults himself down three floors of stairs.

Near the exit, two armed *Orathom Wis* are visibly struggling with the powerful *Rathinalya*. They note Loche but say nothing as he rushes through. One is slumped in his chair, the other is on his knees just outside with his hands over his mouth. Looking over his shoulder as he passes, Loche identifies the same shadow of horror in their faces that he saw on Helen— upon Julia. He squints, dashing out under the steel sky. He trains his eyes on his son. In his periphery a puff of white birds swirl down below the cliff line. The raw chill in the air cuts into his chest. A quickening throb booms in his ears.

"Edwin!" He yells. The sound is muffled in the stillness. His breath is an icy fume. The boy is running far ahead. His legs running to the cliff. "Edwin!"

Distance is closing between them. Behind, Helen's weakened voice is calling, "Edwin! Loche!" He glances back. Both his wife and Julia are staggering out of the building, trying to follow.

When he faces forward again, he sees Edwin stopped at the cliff edge. He turns toward his father and smiles. The smile is genuine and beautiful, as if the boy has rediscovered a loved missing toy. Loche tries to run faster. "Careful, son!" he manages to blurt between heaves. Edwin's grin grows, then he turns away and looks down.

When the little boy's body disappears, dropping fast below the cliff-line, Loche is nearly an arms reach. Helen's defeated scream scrapes at Loche's soul. Loche leaps forward and lands on his chest, arms stretched out and down, his hands splayed wide, but empty. He watches helplessly as his son plunges from the high cliff to the mirrored water below.

Then he understands.

Spreading out upon the surface of the water beneath Edwin, like spilled black ink, is a massive, widening pupil. Around its diameter an ice blue iris forms. Loche's breathing halts. Edwin tumbles down. He descends well below the waterline but there is no splash. The surface does not cover over him. Loche sees him plummet to a tiny speck then disappear into the black.

Helen and Julia drop to their knees beside Loche. Helen is shrieking, "No! No! No!" Julia attempts to peer down into the eye; then cries out as if in pain. She covers her face with her hands.

Loche stands, takes three steps backward and then rushes forward, hurling himself out into the sky above the sea. Arms rotate and thread through the air to keep his body from tumbling head over foot—he keeps his glare latched to the massive eye.

He does not look away.
He does not blink.
This time he will make it blink.
He will drive a lance through it.
This time it will fear him.

Silence.
Flash.
Gone.

An Apology

November 11, this year
Gonzaga University, Spokane, WA
8:45am PST

Astrid Finnley is a forty-seven-year-old professor of mythology and linguistics at Whitworth University in Washington State. She has shoulder-length, dark brown hair with a thick swathe of grey draping over her left eye, full shapely lips, crisp blue eyes and too-much-time-in-the-library pale skin. Striking. She's not overweight and yet she's not athletic. *Maybe a little exercise would be good*, she often thinks. She's been called gorgeous, mostly by her mother and a few friends, but she does not believe it. Or more accurately, she doesn't give two shits. She's smart, thorough and has a tireless insistence on follow-through. Her father had given her a copy of *Bulfinch's Mythology* when she was twelve. And that damn book started it all. The telling of human truth through gods and goddesses, through heroes and monsters, from Olympus veiled in the clouds above to the pits of Pluto and the underworld of Hell—and humans trapped between. Myth obsessed her. She received her doctoral degree in May of her 29th year. A month later she stood on the Giza Plateau in Egypt in the bright sun with a pencil behind her ear, a book under her arm and a whining British tour guide describing the medieval punishments for those caught trying to climb the Great Pyramid without permission. (Astrid ended up hiring a short, brown skinned Egyptian tout to guide her to the top later that night.) The year that followed was a tour through antiquity. She visited as many ancient sites and known mythological attractions as she could. The places that filled her days. The stories that haunted her dreams.

Professor Finnley's expertise is primarily focused on Greek and Roman myths. But she has discovered folk-tales, whether Asian, Middle Eastern or, of late, the legends and beliefs of the indigenous peoples of the Americas. She even loves some of the invented mythologies from her favorite authors such as Tolkien, King and many others. Game of Thrones, *not so much—* too needlessly peaceful.

Astrid closes the door behind her and turns toward the stairs. She imagines the Washington Grant Board continuing to scoff at her research. Tears threaten to appear. Cold air drafts through the hall and she's reminded of wearing three layers during her time here as an undergrad. *The place still needs to be insulated*, she thinks. Gonzaga's administration building, or more recently renamed College Hall, was built in 1898. Old, in relative terms. The Pacific Northwest of the United States isn't particularly known for its ancient cathedrals or centuries of culture. Certainly the indigenous tribes of the Northwest Plateau left behind a wealth of artifacts and tradition, but no Great Pyramid, or cliff dwellings like those found in the American Southwest. So a hundred-plus-year-old building in the center of Spokane, Washington is kind of a big deal. As long as Astrid could remember, she wanted to go to a school that had the feel of something solid. Halls with ghosts in the walls. Stone, mortar, old. A structure that possessed character—a living past. Beyond the brick building on all sides, in this young part of the world, is urban sprawl, strip malls and structures devoid of art.

She pauses a moment and allows the familiar atmosphere of the hallway to fill her head with memories—hot coffee, early morning hunger pangs, chilled to the bone, sleepy from late night study group. Fletcher Cowling, musician, the college boyfriend enters her thought. She put an expiration date on him moments after their first kiss. Though they were together for nearly two years, and the sex was knee-weakening-magnificent (the conversation not so much), she knew he would never outlast her academic ambition. Besides, he was too pretty—tall, athletic, angelic face, and she always felt she did not match up to his aesthetic, especially in social settings. She wasn't fond of make-up and the latest fashion. Better stated, she did not want to try. She knew he loved her, perhaps too much. Astrid recognized his sincerity, but even back then she was all too aware of his limited understanding of her—of even himself—never mind love. She nicknamed him Pothos after one of the Greek gods of love. Fletcher considered the title both sweet and appropriate. After all, what boyfriend wouldn't appreciate being elevated to god status by his beloved. Astrid shakes her head. Pothos in Greek means desire, but more accurately, the god represented man's yearning beyond what he is capable of—beyond understanding. Astrid smiles sadly, hoping that he never looked further into myth and discovered her sardonic irony. Perhaps he is, to this day, still delighted with the thought of the short and nerdy lover-girl in college who proclaimed him a god.

She misses him. Ghosts. This building has ghosts indeed.

And today—today must be her punishment for her overly pedantic, far reaching aspirations—for using her head and not her heart. Years of research into an ancient culture that the world has not recognized—and could very well change the direction of humankind—and she's branded a fool. Sacrificing her personal happiness for the expansion of her learning, all for what? Today it ended.

Midway down the stairs she hears the tap of footsteps above and then her name, "Professor Finnley? Professor, may I have a word?"

Chairman Molmer.

Astrid stops and without turning she says, "Dr. Molmer, I think I've had enough embarrassment for today."

"I dare say you have," he replies, his voice almost a whisper. "And for good reason."

Astrid still does not look at him. An angry smile, then, "Fuck you, Chairman. You people are sheep." She turns and glares, giving up on holding back her tears, "Thank you for funding my project and the opportunity to study a world-changing culture, but you and your board can remain in the dark and ignorant. I'm through for today." Astrid straightens the strap of her heavy bag on her shoulder and begins to descend again.

Molmer says, "Professor Finnley, please, don't mistake me—there is much more to share with you." His voice is urgent and quiet. He takes a few steps down the stairs toward her. "I know you've been through a lot over the last few years while working on this project. I don't know how you managed to keep going after the horrible accident." He pauses. His expression winces slightly, as if he wishes he had not mentioned the event. "Please forgive me, Professor. Won't you please accompany me to my office?" Astrid stops and looks up. Molmer's plaid blue bow tie is crooked. His coat is the color of weak coffee. Astrid's manuscript is under his arm. "The day is still young and there's much to share." She looks at his greying beard and horn-rimmed glasses. Molmer then whispers with a gentle smile, "Please, a few short minutes. And an apology."

Only Begotten Son

November 11, this year
Terciera Island, Azores, Portugal
1:52pm AZOT

Loche bursts through the surface. His lungs suck in the cold air, salt, fear. Limbs are numb.

Circling, Loche scans the surface. Edwin is not there.

Crowding into Loche's mind is an overwhelming déjà vu. Several meters away, a hand shoots up. His son's hand. It reaches for some hold in the air that does not exist. Then, his face appears, his mouth agape, struggling for breath. Loche swings his arms through the water, lugging his body toward the boy. When he grabs hold of the hand, it goes limp. Edwin floats up on his back, face skyward, eyes closed— he is not breathing.

Two heavy splashes thump and mist beside him. As Loche pulls the little boy toward the shore, Helen's face appears to his right. She lays hold of his shoulder. Julia grasps his other shoulder. The three kick and pull through the freezing water.

Having reached a rocky inlet, Helen stands and yanks the boy up, cradles him in her arms, and rushes toward a flat sand bar. She lays him down and kneels. Julia and Loche follow.

"Edwin!" Helen shouts. The boy does not respond. She leans her ear to his mouth and nose, tips his head back, pinches his nostrils shut and breathes into his mouth. After two breaths, Helen reels and pulls her face and hands away. Her eyes dart toward Julia. Loche watches the two women connect through a fearful stare—an unspoken knowing.

"What is it?" Loche shrieks. "What?"

Helen shakes her head and attempts to lean toward her son and begin CPR. She is visibly shaking and fighting pain.

"It's Edwin! It's the *Rathinalya*," Julia whispers. She wraps her arms around herself and cowers into a ball. "It is *Edwin*. I can't— I can't. Oh Christ, I can't—"

Loche shoves Helen aside and begins CPR on his son. He breathes five times into the boy's mouth, rises and begins chest compressions. Edwin's face is blue and frozen in sleep. Strangely translucent. Loche watches for any sign of life. He thinks of the faceless boy god.

He drops down and forces air into Edwin's chest again. After the second breath, Edwin coughs. Water gurgles up. Loche rolls him to the side, letting the liquid flow out. A moment later he lifts the child into his arms and holds him close.

Helen's hands are holding her head, her eyes streaming with tears. "My sweet boy," she cries. "What is happening?"

Julia still has her arms wrapped around her midsection.

"Loche," Helen cries, "did you see the Eye?"

He nods, ruefully.

Helen looks to Julia. She, too, nods.

"Dad," Edwin mumbles, "I'm cold." Loche leans the boy back so he can get a look at his face. "I'm cold." The small boy lays the flat of his palm along his father's cheek. Edwin's eyes appear to swirl and glisten.

Loche flinches. The image of the boy god from Basil's Center haunts his sight. For a flash of an instant, Loche does not recognize his son.

The boy smiles, untroubled. Calm.

Tea

November 11, this year
Gonzaga University, Spokane, WA
8:50am PST

"Tea?" Professor Chad Molmer asks.

Astrid does not answer. Her mind wontedly pings to the word *tu* and the Chinese character 茶, both meaning *tea*. A drink first referenced in Chinese mythology nearly five thousand years ago, it is said to have been invented by the deity, Shennong, a particularly astute alchemist of medicinal plants as well as agricultural educator to humankind. Her mind tacks to a London tea room and a discussion with colleagues about cultural tea ceremonies around the world. Used as medicine, as an aesthetic centerpiece for social gatherings, as a way to wake the senses up after a long day, tea is the second most consumed drink after water. *Even the Itonalya,* Astrid muses, *had their tea ceremonies.*

"Astrid?" Molmer asks. "Tea?"

Astrid glares at him and remains silent.

November's final leaves tumble across the window. A grandfather clock ticks. Below a wall exhibiting awards and certifications is a chess board. Old, by the look of it. Her mind pings to the etymology of the game and she cannot help but think of the *Wyn Avuquain* game, *Shtan*—the earliest influence on the games Go and Chess. Molmer pours hot water into a dainty, pearl colored teacup for himself. The plink of the delicate china infuriates her.

In the corner, she notes a man whose age she cannot determine. Somewhere between late fifty and mid seventy. Quite an age spread, she thinks—hard to tell—he appears spry despite the age that weighs around his eyes. He wears a black suit that fits his gaunt frame well. His legs are crossed. Something familiar about him, but she can't quite figure out just what.

Would either of you care for tea?

"I am quite content," the man says.

"No," Astrid says.

"Very well." He rounds his desk and sits. Piles of paperwork and books crowd for space. He clears a spot for his teacup and saucer. He takes a sip. A drop of cream clings to his beard.

"So," he says after a moment, "how did you gather so much material on a subject that has joined the ranks of *Bigfoot* and *Area 51*?"

"You read it?" Astrid nods to her book on his desk.

"Of course I did."

"Why ask then? It's all there."

Molmer's eyes tick to the manuscript, to the man behind her and then back to Astrid. "Not quite."

"Not quite?" Astrid repeats. "What is that supposed to mean?"

"Professor Finnley," Dr. Molmer's voice is laced with humor, "please forgive my comments during your review. I can only imagine the disappointment and humiliation you must have felt while the board shredded your life's work."

"One can't count on capturing every reader," Astrid says. She then adds with indignation, "After all, I've read one of *your* books, so I now know how you feel. Can't win 'em all."

Molmer smiles and looks into his tea. "Chair of the Philosophy department and thirty-five years teaching does not a popular author make."

"Nor does it give you any authority to judge the validity of my research," Astrid almost spits, "and marshal my career to crucifixion."

Dr. Molmer sits up and places the cup onto its saucer. Another maddening plink. "I'm sorry, Astrid. I should tell you that I found your research to be captivating beyond measure. In fact, the work is teeming with merit." Molmer is now leaning toward her and his face is earnest.

Astrid watches him. The drop still dangling there. A flurry of wind presses the window.

"You see, I was forced to put on an act during the review. In that formal setting it was best that the matter of *Wyn Avuqua* remain where it should: in legend, in myth," he stifles a laugh.

Astrid wonders at him. "What are you talking about?"

Molmer nods to the man behind her. Astrid turns.

The man's hands are folded in his lap and his long legs are crossed. His short greying hair is neatly trimmed. Astrid rethinks his age. He looks younger than he did when she first entered the room.

"Professor Finnley," the man says, "it is a marvel that you've managed to put together such an impressive view into the past. Quite frankly, I'm stunned and wonder-filled as to how you did it." He then shifts in his chair, and in a kind of aside to himself says, "though she's missed the mark at many points—" he looks at her, "you've written things that, well," he looks at Molmer, "should be impossible for anyone to know."

"Is that so?" Astrid says. "I don't know what the two of you are trying to do, but today I've been told that everything I've presented is nonsense—my life's work has been discredited and I no longer own it. So if you've got something to say before I go home and drink a bottle of wine, say it!"

"Well, Astrid," Molmer says gently, "you can remove *money* from your list of worries."

"Tell that to my mortgage company."

"Astrid," Molmer continues, "I don't think you'll want to go home right now." He shakes his head and sighs. "I'm afraid I am doing a very poor job at this apology."

"I'll say."

"Astrid—" There is a knock on the door. Molmer says, "Yes?"

The door opens and a dark haired man dressed in all black leans in. "The van is waiting," he says.

"Good," Molmer says standing.

"Van?" Astrid asks still sitting.

Molmer reaches for his coat and pushes one arm into a sleeve. "You want funding, doctor? You've got funding. You want to own your work? Ownership is yours." He pushes his other arm in, flips the collar up around his ears. "If you want validation beyond your wildest dreams— come with us."

Astrid watches Molmer move to the door. The man behind her stands to put on his overcoat.

"Professor Molmer," Astrid says, "you've failed to introduce—"

"Oh my word," Dr. Molmer says. "My apologies, Professor Astrid Finnley, may I introduce an old friend from college and colleague, psychologist Dr. Marcus Rearden."

"A pleasure," Rearden says.

Eggs Benediction

November 11, this year
Terciera Island, Azores, Portugal
2:25pm AZOT

"The house buzzes, no?"

George Eversman sets a small cup and saucer on the counter as Loche enters the kitchen. Bacon hisses in a skillet. A pot of water boils, quietly huffing steam. The windows are fogged. Loche sits. He smells the coffee. He can feel tears pressing upward from just below the surface.

"Edwin warm now? Bug asleep?" George says.

Loche's answer is a slight nod. Confusion and uncertainty cloud his skull. "Yes. He is sleeping."

"My hands tingle," George says. "The *Rathinalya*. First it came from the Eye rising in the water— now it comes from Edwin. Even when he is on the other side of the house, I feel his power. He okay, yes?"

Another nod to some vague notion of *okay*.

"Are you warming up?"

"Trying." Loche feels cold. He feels complete helplessness. "You wanted to see me?"

"Busy day already, yes? Edwin. . . And Albion Ravistelle wants you dead? And wife Helen is his assassin? Sounds like a most unhappy marriage, yes?"

Loche shivers at the thought of Edwin's body disappearing into a black hole. "She could have killed me many times, I think."

"Yes, but now she say that you no longer wanted alive. Better dead?"

"Because of my writing—I suppose I could potentially challenge Albion's plans. But I can't simply write him out of the story." Text illuminates behind his lids when he blinks. As does a mirrored eye. "It appears that I must be near death, suffering or completely removed from reality to compose in a way that can change history—change the world."

George chuckles nudging a strip of bacon in the pan. "What most writers say. The usual excuses, yes?"

Loche thinks of the Red Notebook. He shudders.

"They tried once before, you know?" George says. "To stop the prophecy—to kill you—you and your brother. Your father, William, and Samuel Lifeson, and believe it or not, Albion Ravistelle save you. You children then."

Loche remembers writing in the Journal about the file box —provided by Albion Ravistelle in Venice, or does Loche recall reading through it? He squints. The memories mix. The car accident—assassination attempt. His entire life outlined and documented by a character he had created.

"Helen we will watch closer now. Talan will go where she goes." Loche recalls meeting Talan Adamsman before the siege of *Mel Tiris*. The huge man resembled several gangster film hit men: intimidating bulk, thick neck, dark eyebrows, a jaw forged to fracture fists. Scary. Very scary. "Talan will keep her from harming anyone."

"I do not think Helen would have killed me."

"No? Maybe no. He will watch her anyway. Much still ahead for wife, Helen. For mother, wife, Helen. Much."

George exhales a deep sigh. "And now," his voice lowers to a solemn whisper, "Edwin—a god walks among us. A god sleeps a room away. God is here."

For Loche, no words come. He watches the leader of the *Orathom Wis* chop onions on a board. Flashes of Italy, Monterosso. A memory? Perhaps. Perhaps now. Seemingly, as each day passes, his written fiction, the events therein, become more like memory. His first meeting of the long-limbed, orange-haired George was in a kitchen. He was preparing fresh pesto.

Loche's mind battles between images. He sees his own hand scribbling out the affair—words on a page—then images of meeting George in Monterosso, the wood table with family photos in frames, the wine glasses, George's eyes like bowls of amber-brown paint. He recalls the little girl, Elainya.

"Well done," George says. He gestures out the window to the cliffs beyond the field. "Saving your boy. Brave. Brave leaping into death and returning—bringing with you your son."

Loche does not answer. George adds, "But you and death have been becoming better acquainted over these last days, yes?"

"What does this mean?" Loche asks. "What does this mean for my son?"

George looks up and laughs. "What a question! What, indeed. I do not know. . . yet." The edge of the bowl rings as he cracks another egg. "Tell me, Poet, what did you see at *Mel Tiris*, in the castle tower, in the paintings, the *Orathom*? You see Basil there?"

"Yes."

"You see others there?"

"I saw Samuel Lifeson's face." Loche flinches and tries to erase the image of the severed head at his feet. George frowns and sighs. "And the boy god was there again. Only this time, it felt as if Edwin and *It* were one and the same."

George's odd grin stretches out across his face and he glances at Loche, "Now they *are* same, yes?"

Tears rise. Between sobs Loche manages to get out, "What of my son? What does this mean for my son?"

George's smile disappears. He looks at the egg in his hand and then holds it up. "The *Itonalya* have a story about an egg— other peoples heard it, changed it, made it theirs. You might know the Hindu version. You know the tale?"

Loche shakes his head.

With his index finger on the tip and his thumb supporting the bottom of the oval, he holds it up to one eye. "Hindu say, like *Itonalya*, this egg—this egg is everything that is. Gods and stars, trees and bees, love and fear, man and sea, words and pictures. All existence. They call it Vishnu, but *Itonalya* call it *Thi*. Crazy, yes?

"Mighty *Thi* wanted to tell stories, but *It* had no listeners. So, *Thi* broke, became two parts." George tosses the egg to his other hand, cracks it open and slowly drools its contents into the bowl. "This part," he swirls the yolk and white, "all spirit, all heaven, all god, all *Orathom*. All things we cannot see." He raises the broken egg shell, "And this is earth, and flesh. The world of physical. You, me, all this, caught in between." George then reaches for another from the carton. He lifts it again to his eye, "Edwin, I think, is egg. Both he and *Thi* unbroken. Inside him is god and man. He is everything that is. Just as a parent's child should be, yes?" The rim of the bowl chimes again. "Your son is *Thi*. *Thi* is your son. Stupid crazy." He tips the white and the yolk into the bowl and tosses the shell into the wastebasket. "Trouble for Edwin is that we, *Orathom Wis,* eat the gods." He fires a quick scowl at Loche. "But not Edwin. Something different now. Something very different this time. So, I make afternoon breakfast and eat omelette instead."

He pours the egg batter into the hot pan. The two watch as the gold sizzles and thickens. Loche is suddenly hungry. It feels as if breakfast is the right meal for his internal clock.

"Julia tells me she believes Basil calls her to Egypt. To Menkaure pyramid."

"Yes," Loche says, recalling Julia's story of what she found in Basil's studio in Venice—some cryptic message of a paint splattered constellation, characters of Greek mythology tacked to the wall, leading to a photograph of the Menkaure pyramid on the Giza plateau. He shakes his head. Was it a message? Was it a warning?

George flips the omelette into the air and catches it in the pan. It hisses and pops as he lowers it back to the stove. "And you—you see Basil at pyramid, too, yes? In painting?"

"Yes," he answers, "but the pyramid was different. I do not think it was Menkaure."

"Different?"

"It was white. As if made of frosted glass—beside a lake. And there was a horrifying battle surrounding us."

The immortal's face seems suddenly ancient and pained—and then shifts back. "*Wyn Avuqua*," he whispers. "You saw streams of light stabbing from sky, yes? A city breaking?"

Loche nods.

"You saw the gods of *Thi,* the *Godrethion* destroy the *Itonalya*. You saw the fall of our only home." A single tear forms and slips over his high cheekbones. "My home. . ."

"The *Godrethion,*" Loche says, his tone lost in thought.

"Yes. The disloyal gods—summoned by *Thi, Itself.* The bridging spirits. Lawless gods. The true enemy of the *Itonalya* and the *Orathom Wis*. But you know this already, yes?"

Loche sees the open Journal on the table in his Priest Lake Cabin. He sees the volumes of writings in what were once locked cabinets in his office tower. The name *Godrethion* flickers like a faraway light at dusk on the sea. These tiny lights seem to become more familiar as each new vexing day unfolds.

George watches the eggs cook. His expression is troubled. "And now you go with *Thi* to Menkaure." He whispers to himself, "Menkaure. Why Menkaure?"

Corey Thomas enters the kitchen along with a man Loche recognizes as Athelstan, Loche's protector and door warden at *Mel Tiris*. "*Angofal*." He bows and rises before George. "There are thirty-five confirmed *Orathom Wis* still living. Twenty-seven living in remote locations have not yet reported in."

"News may not have reached them," Athelstan says.

George does not respond. Worry still darkens his face. "And our Samuel and William?"

"They are gone," Corey replies, his gaze falling to the floor.

George inhales the grief. His chest rises, sorrow tugs, and he breathes out a sigh.

"Menkaure," George says to Loche, "is mystery. We do not know where it leads. Those that have crossed it, no return." He laughs, "But maybe that will change. Maybe sometime we will learn. The changes in past change the times at hand."

"I don't understand," Loche says.

"No mind," he says, "we eat, then I talk with Edwin. After we talk, we leave here. We leave here and find Basil. We find Basil in Egypt at the pyramid." George slides a spatula under the omelette and flips it, "Or the pyramid will take you to him."

"I don't know what Basil can do. He didn't seem to have any answers."

"Answers?" George says. "They do not exist. We don't need answers. We must add to the story. Or take it away. I think you are being pulled to the beginning of the tale."

The Lie In Belief

November 11, this year
2 Newport Highway, Washington State
9:00am PST

And why not? What else was there to do today? She could have declined and bade these two a hearty fuck off and right now be a third into a bottle of red, soaking in a bath of Epsom salts and lavender. But something about validation and your wildest dreams had a nice ring to it. Not to mention ownership and financial security.

A light rain falls. Astrid's stomach growls. She wonders about breakfast. The driver turns the passenger van north.

"Where are we going?"

"North to Sandpoint," Molmer answers wrestling with removing his coat, which he manages to remove. He folds it. He exhales and offers Astrid a kind smile. "So, Professor Finnley," he says, "what's *your* story?"

"My story?"

"Yes. I know a bit about you, given our academic dealings —very little about your personal life."

"I—"

"You're still teaching, yes? You're quite known for your love of mythology— but what more? Surely you've got a story."

Astrid wonders. She draws a blank. Her first thought is *lonely*. But that is not entirely true. She has her career and the respect and acclaim it has garnered. That is, at least, something. Colleagues and students have been her primary social outlet, and she has forged what she thinks are relationships worth mentioning—but she does not mention them. She has traveled extensively, all over the world, many times. Especially over the last few years. She has heard her students express their envy when seeing her travel photos in class, or when reading her bio, or the travel logs printed in one of the university publications, or her self-published titles. She would hear her student's marvel: *there's Professor Finnley in the crumbling terraced ruins at Machu Picchu, Prof at Easter Island, Prof studying Greek letters carved into a stone at Delphi, Prof with her hands in the soil at a dig near Carthage.* Their voices were some comfort. Occasionally she traveled with students, other times with educators or archeologists and their teams, but most of the time, she was alone.

She has enjoyed treasure hunting—especially for her best friend Sadie, and her kids, Prudence and Jude (names chosen from Beatle songs, of course—Sadie and her husband being crazy Beatle fans). Much of her free time during her journeys has been spent searching for rare stones and action figures for Jude, silk scarves and old maps for Prue. The two had become increasingly dear to her over the last few years, especially since the boating accident. She has found it nice to be their crazy Aunt Astrid without having to juggle soccer, ballet and stomach flu. Jude and Prue's mother, Sadie (another name lifted from the Beatle canon —*her* parents were crazy Beatle fans, too), tried to talk Astrid out of having her tubes tied. "What if you change your mind? What if one day you decide it's time."

Astrid's wonted reply was, "Meh."

Her divorce sucked. And as with most divorces, there were many parts and pieces. Certainly Astrid's unyielding work ethic, long hours and dedication to her career played a part. Her ex, Zachary, used to say, "I always come second to your job. Second to everything." Astrid's seemingly endless travel schedule didn't help either. She took Zachary along with her once to a dig near the Black Sea when they were newly married. It turned out to be a disaster. Zach, bless his heart, was impossibly slow, packed too heavy and was overly vocal about the dust, the heat and the food at the dig site. "Let's get a nice hotel when you're done," he would suggest with enthusiasm—which prompted, "When will that be?" nudge. Of course there were wonderful memories, too. But most of those had been eclipsed by the insatiable appetite for her work. His take: she gave up. Her take: he doesn't understand. There were darker things back there, too. Things shoved aside. Things that make no sense to wallow in. Their disparate interests aside, she loved him, and he loved her, but it wasn't until she needed to tell him that she was going to get her tubes tied that the relationship broke. One afternoon a year later she entered their house to discover Zach had excavated his presence. He left a note. She put it on the refrigerator door. It is still there and it flutters at her every time the heat wafts into the room from the downstairs furnace.

"If I could change what happened, I would. Beginning again is all I can do—make a new story. I wish it was with you— Z" As she sips her coffee nearly every morning, her eyes find the message. Nearly every morning after reading it she hears her voice say, "Meh."

"Would you like to hear about my failed marriage, or what?" she asks. Molmer's eyebrows scrunch together. Astrid shrugs, "There's not much to tell. I don't like the past."

"I doubt that very much," Molmer replies. "Isn't that where you reside most of the time?"

Astrid's smile is dry, "Good try. Not in *my* past. You sound like my ex."

Dr. Marcus Rearden's voice enters the conversation. Astrid notes it is the first time he's joined in. "Ah, the past. . . difficult to overcome bad memories."

Astrid's head tilts at the psychologist. Her eyes narrow. "I don't think my past is any of your business."

"Forgive me," Rearden says. "I am well versed in human tragedy—and I understand that you've suffered the worst possible—"

"Molmer?" Astrid nearly spits, "what is this all about? Is there a shrink here for a reason? Because of what happened? If so, we're done here. This is ridiculous!"

"No, no," Molmer says apologetically. "Marcus, please. Let us stay on the subject—"

Astrid speaks over him, "Because I've had my share of fucking therapy—and I'm through—"

"Forgive me," Rearden says again. "My mistake. I simply offer my sympathy."

"Noted," Astrid says.

"Well," Molmer says in an attempt to lighten the mood, "the past is the past is the past. Now, Astrid, the distant past is about to come thundering into the present."

"Let's cut to the validation part, okay? Why Sandpoint, Idaho?"

"Please, Doctor," Molmer says, "be patient. Because we've funded you for over three years, you can afford us an hour of patience. Besides, I'd hate to spoil the surprise—or at least, the opportunity of seeing your face when we arrive."

"Arrive where?"

"Professor Finnley," Rearden says. His voice is quiet and thoughtful. "Will you tell me about *Wyn Avuqua* in brief? There is much to learn, I'm sure, about this ancient city, and I know a few things from my own sources—your book I've not yet had the pleasure—"

Molmer says, "I'm sorry to interrupt, Doctor. Professor Finnley, I called Marcus yesterday after I had completed reading your submission." He looks at the psychologist, "We've been friends for a good number of years, and I felt that his presence on this little field trip would be beneficial to both you and him."

"How so?" Astrid asks.

"Tell me about your work," Rearden interrupts, "and I will then tell you about mine." He laces his fingers and lowers them to his lap.

Astrid sighs and scowls. "*Wyn Avuqua* in brief?" she says. "I'm sure you've already heard a few versions of that."

Rearden nods. "I have. The ancient city of immortals that is said to have been founded over seven thousand years ago, maybe longer—and was destroyed by the gods sometime around 1000 AD." He smiles and repeats, "Destroyed by the gods. . ."

"That's the tale," she agrees.

"The gods?" Rearden asks solemnly.

"The old rebellion tale, Doctor. *The* god, *Thi* gave the *Wyn Avuquains* immortal bodies in return for guarding Earth."

"Guarding the Earth from what?" Rearden asks.

"From the lesser gods, the *Godrethion*. It was believed that these lesser gods coveted the creation of *Thi*: humans— particularly. Our nature. These deities interfered in human affairs —altering the creation, as it were. Immortals called them *Godrethion*. And despite *Thi's* forbidding their coming here, the *Godrethion* found ways. The *Itonalya,* the immortals, were *Thi's* first line of defense. The *Wyn Avuquain* immortals at first were content with their charge—and extremely effective. But over time they felt that immortality was not enough compensation for the burden placed upon them."

Rearden shifts in his seat and says with some incredulity, "Immortality was not enough? What greater gift could there be?"

Astrid looks absently out the window and then back to the psychologist. She wonders why this man is along for the ride. After the accident, she has had to deal with a few psychologists over the last few years. They can be so incredibly tedious. She takes a deep breath and answers. "Immortal, yes. But with the minds of human beings—of mortals—accounts of their suffering are profound—extremely moving. A greater gift would be an afterlife. The *Itonalya* were not allowed a life beyond their immortal mandate. Over time, they wanted to be released from their charge and so they rebelled. After the city was destroyed, *Thi* sent a peace offering— a prophecy."

"A prophecy?" Rearden repeats. "How very mythical."

"Indeed," Astrid replies blithely.

A few moments of silence pass before Rearden asks, "What do you know of this, as you call it, prophecy? It must be of some import?" It seems to Astrid that Rearden poses the question with a kind of indifference. Midway through the asking, he turned his head and looked out the window. She feels her forehead scrunch.

"We know that it augured two brothers, a Poet and a Painter. Both of which would enable and allow gods, through the brothers' works, to look in on us and feel the human condition— without interfering. The *Itonalya* would then no longer be tasked as guardians. They would be free. But that's about all we know."

"And how do you we know this?" Rearden says turning back to her.

"The belief has been heavily documented."

"Documented?"

"Yes, within what little *Itonalya* literature we've uncovered. But we do not know the direct source."

"Source?"

"The circumstances surrounding the prophecy—just when, where and how the Prophecy came into the culture."

"I see," Marcus says. Astrid cannot read this man.

"It's a myth, doctor. It is meant to keep the population in line. You know, the old *if you're not happy with what you've been given, tough shit. If you don't follow the rules, God will come and sack your city.*" Astrid sighs. "Do you know much about myth, Dr. Rearden?" He does not answer. "Myth exists to make sense of what we can't understand—life and after death, et cetera. And to control. That's it. Mostly to control. An imagined construct to organize humanity—surely you must know that."

Marcus shrugs, "So none of the stories are true?"

"Believers believe them to be true—or rather, folks you're probably used to dealing with professionally—the delusional."

"I see."

A subtle wash of frustration enters her tone. *Here we go again,* she thinks. "Okay, let's make this simple," she says. "Humankind's historical record begins with hunter gatherer bands—groups of say twelve to fifty or so moving from place to place and eating what they can scratch up. These small bands governed themselves without too much difficulty. But once a group multiplied over a hundred, rules needed to be established. It is really quite elementary. The more people, the more difficult it is to maintain order. Government, right?"

"Okay," Rearden agrees.

"Fast forward to the agricultural revolution, a little less than 10,000 years ago, humans figured out how to grow food. With that came a farming culture—settling down in one place, villages, cooperation—the beginnings of society. Now laws are needed. A kind of government naturally rises. But the most important and powerful construct to controlling these ever growing numbers is imagined, supernatural significance. In other words, gods. Of course, the most unique and distinguishing trait among our species is the ability to communicate— not only what mushrooms are safe to eat, the best way to snare a rabbit or how to make fire, but our innate skill at spinning a tale. Fiction. Humans have always existed in both the real world and the fictional. We love a good story. And we've been doing that sort of thing since we wondered what the flaming ball of light in the sky might be. When societies grew, the stories to control them grew also. Humans have always existed in both the real world and the fictional."

"There's always two," Rearden smiles. "You sound as if you don't believe."

The sparkle of snow rushing by the window pulls her attention. A trillion stars pass. "It is a myth," she says.

"Yes," Rearden agrees, "but there is more, isn't there, Professor Finnley?"Astrid returns her focus to the psychologist. "You've discovered something that has a ring of truth? Am I correct?"

Astrid is reluctant to speak with this man. Everything about him feels like a trap. She says, "Truth in that the stories contain power—so long as a population believes in them. Immense power. Religion, nations, currency, rights. . . therein are my interests." Astrid pats the manuscript in her lap. "An imagined reality and the power of belief can build monuments, cities, great pyramids. It can establish nations, racism, class structure, gender oppression, war, corporations—money. And like so many of antiquity's monuments, *Wyn Avuqua* fits in. Its culture had its share of gods and beliefs— and it was a real place."

"A real place, but its gods were not, as you say, real."

She does not answer.

"And what of the good that these *myths,* as you call them, have delivered to mankind? Kindness, hope, empathy?"

Astrid sighs. "As I've said, if humankind's imagined belief can build the pyramids it can certainly feed the hungry from time to time. Good works are a part of the insanity. Such altruistic character keeps society loving their imaginary gods."

"You sound rather cynical," Marcus says.

Astrid pauses before she speaks. "I am cynical. Knowing what I know, I too often see the lie in the center of the word belief."

"Ah," he smiles, "very good." The doctor looks down at his hands in his lap and asks, "And the *Wyn Avuquains*—the immortals—the, what did you call them, the Gafedetrion—" A slight smile pulls at the corners of his mouth.

"*Godrethion*," Astrid corrects. She studies Rearden's expression. She does not like this man. Her intuition tells her that he is withholding something. She wants to end the conversation. But more important, she does not want to agree with him, or entertain his speculations. She has discovered something in her research she can't explain. Something that doesn't match with her rational mind, and it is not time to share. And she'll be damned if she shares it with this man. Not yet, anyway. She takes a firm grip on the manuscript in her lap. Rearden notices her fingers squeezing the spine.

Rearden says, "Yes, *Godrethion*. So they didn't exist either, right? They are not, real?"

"Real only to your clients, perhaps," she quips.

Rearden smiles grimly. A stab of flame glints in his eyes. "I see. The gods are not real, but your ancient city is? So, tell me, won't you, Professor, why hasn't this grand city with its pillars of stone and its ancient temples been unearthed?" He glances at Molmer and then back to Astrid. "All of your research points to a place north of Priest Lake, Idaho. Have you any thoughts on how your droves of believers faithfully believe in something that hasn't been found and you, all the while, spin a tale about evidence—when you have none?"

Astrid slides her now glaring expression from Rearden to Molmer and back again. She wants to shake her head and protest, but to do so would show Rearden that he has scored a rhetorical point. But she feels heat rise to her cheeks. *The city is there somewhere,* her mind screams, *it must be—it has to be!*

"It's a good story," Rearden adds. "A story almost worth believing."

The Great Flood

November 11, this year
Terciera Island, Azores, Portugal
2:49pm AZOT

The weight of acceptance tips a balanced scale in Loche's mind. He watches his little boy mop up syrup with a piece of pancake on the tip of a fork. Under the table Edwin kicks at the legs of his chair. The fuel of afternoon breakfast is already firing the engine in his body. *This is my son*, Loche tells himself—*my Edwin*. But is it? There is nothing that would prove otherwise save a barely perceptible change in the boy's eyes. It is as if some trauma has left its mark there. Was it the fall? The estrangement of his parents? Or was there truly an eye he fell into? The same eye that Loche himself knows all too well? What ethereal, celestial character now hovers behind Edwin's gaze? The boy lifts a bite of egg to his lips.

Both father and son still smell like the sea. Even after the hot shower, Loche can taste salt in the air around them. Edwin looks up at Loche and smiles. Yellow yolk stains the corner of his mouth. "Where's mom?" he asks.

"She's downstairs," Loche answers with a smile. "How do you feel, Bug?"

"Good," Edwin says. His voice is bright.

The last cake bite is slathered in syrup and aimed not-so-accurately at the boy's mouth.

"Good?" Loche asks.

Edwin's answer is a grin. A speck of flashing glitter in his eyes. There is still something there Loche cannot describe.

"We're going to take another plane ride, Edwin."

The boy looks up.

"Do you want to take another plane ride?"

"Sure! Where?"

"We're going to visit a very old city called Cairo."

"Is Mom coming?"

"I don't know."

"I hope she does."

Loche places the silverware onto the empty plate, along with the napkin, and moves it to the side. "But before we leave we're going to talk to my friend George and a few others. They want to ask you some questions about what happened this morning, okay?"

Edwin's legs are still marching under the table. "Okay," he replies.

"Let's go."

They step outside into a narrow courtyard. The near sea blasts against the cliff face. They cross the villa's center and pass through the tall door of a long, high-peaked house. Loche follows Edwin into a sprawling wood floored hall. Monumental oil portraits line the room's perimeter. Sitting in high-backed velvet couches and leather arm chairs are George Eversman, Julia Iris, Corey Thomas, Athelstan, Helen and several others. Leonaie Echelle's eyes widen when Loche sees her. There are also several more men and women standing in and around the circle of furniture.

Loche notes a collective gasp when they enter—then a sudden attempt to suppress it. Feet shuffle. A few individuals reach to a wall or the back of a chair to steady themselves.

Helen waves and blows Edwin a kiss. There is a shadow of pain in her smile. She trembles. Loche acknowledges the huge man standing just behind her: Helen's new jailor, Talan Adamsman.

George gestures to a chair. Loche sits. Edwin climbs onto his lap.

"The *Rathinalya*, no?" George says to the gathering. His arms open and spread out, as does his grin.

"The boy is undoubtedly *thion*," Athelstan states.

"He is *Godrethion* if he is upon *Ae!*" Another shouts.

"Nay! He is beyond such a title," Corey says. Many nod and voice affirmation. "Much, much more. He is— he is. . ."

George looks at Helen. He says, "Edwin is beyond Nicolas Cythe, yes?"

Helen's answer is accompanied by a tear. "Yes," she says.

Outside, the ocean's voice thunders against the walls.

"He is *Thi,*" George whispers.

Edwin buries his face into Loche's chest to hide from the staring and attention.

"Menkaure," George says. "We take you to Menkaure pyramid."

Athelstan speaks, "*Anfogal*, of all places, despite augury, why Menkaure? That *omvide* has stolen too many of our people —"

"Silence," George says.

"What do you mean stolen?" Helen cries staring at her son.

No one stirs.

Corey Thomas answers, "Of all pyramids, Menkaure is least known to us. Those that have ventured there have not returned."

"And you're sending my son there?" Helen says.

George says, "Your son transcends the unknown." He then stands and crosses the short distance to the boy and his father. He kneels. "Little one," he says gently. Edwin clings tighter to his father.

"Edwin," Loche says to the boy, "George wants to ask you about your fall today. Will you let him?"

The child tilts his head slightly out of Loche's embrace. One eye peeks through.

"Little one," George says, "today, before you jumped into the water," he points in the direction of the cliff, "did you hear them calling?"

Edwin doesn't answer.

"Little one, like song. . . did you hear a voice calling your name?" George waits.

Edwin replies but his voice is muffled.

"I no hear you, little one," George says. "Did you hear a voice?"

Pulling away from Loche, Edwin says, "No. No. Not in my ears."

"No hear voice?" Loche asks.

"No."

"But someone call you to follow, yes?" says George.

Edwin nods. Someone in the gathering whispers, "*Elliqui.*" George glances at Loche and then back down to Edwin. "Little one, when you fall, you find who call you?"

Edwin releases his father and sits up quickly. He leans his face close to George's inquisitive stare and places his small hands on the immortal's cheeks. It is a strange sight. The small boy's expression is focused, calm and chillingly confident. George holds eye contact. Across from them, Helen rises to her feet. She is pale with terror. The others, too, are showing signs of discomfort—they fidget, murmur, flinch—as if each of the audience has suddenly come under the curling crest of a massive wave.

It is hard to breathe suddenly—movement slows and suspends as if submerged—the young boy and the immortal tethered, unmoving.

Panic invades George's face, but he does not look away. His right arm reaches to the inside of his tweed coat and he pulls out a long-bladed knife. When he aims the tip of the dagger at Edwin's temple, Loche lifts his foot from the floor, poises it to kick at George's throat. But the horror in George's face fades quickly. He lowers the dagger and his gaze to the floor.

Edwin recoils and sinks deep into Loche. George settles slowly back and sits.

"What was that?" Loche gasps.

George does not answer immediately. Instead he hides the knife and allows his lungs to drink in oxygen. He blinks. Disbelief and uncertainty crowd his face.

The others, too, appear to have been submerged and are now suddenly surfacing, breathing deeply. Helen remains on her feet, her hands cupped over her mouth. Beside her, Julia's arms are coiled around herself—glassy, squinting eyes. Loche holds his gaze to hers.

"Now I know," George whispers.

"What is happening?" Loche asks.

George takes another long look at the little boy. "The egg. It is true. Your son and *Thi* are one—" he begins to cough. "It is *Thi. It* is *Thi*."

"What are you saying?"

"The One. The All. Edwin brings with him the end. The great deluge of myth was water—this time not water, Heaven's legions will rain down upon mortal and *Itonalya*."

Loche gapes.

George struggles to his feet and turns toward the gathered immortals. "*Thi* has come," he says. "And with *It*," he twists and faces Edwin, "comes the flood." With a long look at Edwin he adds, "I have seen you before."

The Lie In Belief #2

November 11, this year
2 Newport Highway, Idaho
9:25am PST

The van rolls north. A gentle rain falls through the grey. The conversation moves to Professor Molmer as he runs through Astrid's research with Rearden. The main points: the uncovering of scrolls and written mythos, laws and pieces of historical record. And the *Toele*, the *Itonalya* tome. It contains the history of the so called immortals on Earth. He touches on the *Itonalya* language of *Elliqui* and how Astrid's team has managed to translate more than any other *Wyn Avuquain* expert.

Rearden listens with a genuine interest, his eyes often resting upon Astrid. It makes her uncomfortable. She lifts her phone and swipes to her text screen. The thought occurs to her that she has no one to tell where she's gone. No one waiting. She could send a note to her assistant, Marcel, to share with him the news. The text forms in her mind: *validation, new funding, there's more to do*. But she hesitates. She should learn more first. But other than Marcel—no one.

Her eyes tick up from her screen to Rearden as Molmer mentions the mysterious Albion Ravistelle. Rearden still watches her. Astrid ducks back to her phone and her thumb slides to Google. She taps in Dr. Marcus Rearden.

Jackpot. Criminal psychologist. Author. Celebrity. Photos of Rearden with politicians, lawyers, judges. Famous trials— mostly macabre and grisly murder cases. Quotes. The cover of his New York Times bestselling book, *Getting Away With Murder*.

She taps to images—the screen fills with photos of him. She scrolls. *Handsome in his own way*, Astrid thinks. *Especially as a young man.* She notes that in his latest pictures, he looks much older than he appears now. She stops herself from looking up to make the comparison. But it is obvious that some care or weight has lifted since these recent photos. The thought of Rearden going through with some sort of cosmetic surgery to maintain his vain celebrity almost lights a mocking smile.

She taps back a screen and sees the headline, *Dr. Marcus Rearden arrested for murder.* Again she resists the impulse to glance up at him. The article is one of many covering the same case. Suddenly it registers. Astrid recalls hearing about it on the local news. Rearden was arrested after confessing to the murder of a woman named Bethany Winship. A picture of Bethany appears in her scrolling. She is attractive, older and *altogether lovely,* Astrid thinks. But Astrid notes a strange hint of sadness in the woman's smile. She reads on. Rearden had strangled and drowned the woman in Sandpoint's Pend Oreille Lake—during his escape, he shot two police detectives. He also shot and injured a woman named Julia Iris just before capture in Coeur d'Alene (no photograph). This was less than two weeks ago, on Halloween. Her hand clenches the book in her lap. She can feel her heart rate increase.

The latest headline, not a week old, reads: *Undercover Rearden vindicated. Rearden's protégé, Psychologist Loche Newirth, is now wanted for murder.* She scans. The article tells of how Rearden was working toward bringing the young psychologist, Loche Newirth, to justice through some rather unorthodox methods. Several other links follow, connecting Newirth to a terrorist attack at the Uffizi in Florence, Italy.

Before she can read more, she hears Rearden say, "I have so many questions."

Astrid lowers the phone. She has her own questions regarding his recent past, but she refrains. Instead, she quickly asks, "Why are you so interested in my work, Dr. Rearden? Isn't your calling criminal psychology, that is, when you're not basking in the limelight as author and celebrity?"

Rearden blinks.

Something about this asshole, she thinks. She laughs lightly to give the impression that she is kidding with him.

Rearden chuckles. "So you recognize me?"

"Only because of the local news."

He nods. "I see. Yes. A sad story, I'm afraid."

"Sounds like it," she says.

Molmer interjects, "Marcus's part was helping the authorities capture Newirth."

"A rather long story that I'm not able to speak freely about," adds Rearden.

Astrid says, "I'm not interested in Mrs. Bethany Winship or this Newirth person—you didn't answer the question. What is your interest in my work?"

"Ah," Rearden sighs. "Truth is, the still-at-large Dr. Newirth will play a role eventually. But let's suffice it to say that my interest falls in line with his interest."

"His interest? You mean, Loche Newirth's interest?" she asks.

"Precisely. Believe it or not, like you, Newirth is. . ." Rearden pauses—searching for a word, "Loche is an authority on your particular subject of interest."

"An authority?" Astrid says dubiously.

"Indeed. He has insights that I believe would delight and shock you, Professor."

"You believe so, do you?"

"There's that word again," Rearden notes with a slight squint. "After Dr. Newirth murdered Mrs. Bethany Winship, he retreated to his lake cabin and surrounded himself with numerous texts on mythology, ancient history and the like."

Astrid says, "So you believe that by learning more about my work you can better understand Loche, and thereby find him?"

Rearden's face slides into a hard-to-read smile. Astrid feels her stomach tense. She feels fear.

"Yes," he answers. "There is truth enough in that. But right now, I can say no more."

Molmer points to the approaching gate. "We're here."

"Where?"

"The airfield."

"Airfield?" Astrid nearly shouts.

Molmer nods. "Yes. And Astrid, please know that I have your best interest in mind. In less than thirty minutes, you will be thanking me. And look, the sky is clearing. What happy chance. Have you ever been in a helicopter?"

Pocket Diary Entry # 2

November 11, this year
Terciera Island, Azores, Portugal
3:05pm AZOT
(Loche Newirth's pocket diary)

Nov 11- 3:05pm

—*I must find Basil. I must stop what I have begun.*
—*My son / my beautiful son is in danger. It is all my doing. He is with me, but he has changed. . .*
—*I can still see him, but IT is there, too.*

—*I cannot breathe.*

In the Laps of the Gods

November 11, this year
Terciera Island, Azores, Portugal
3:05pm AZOT

It is decided. They are to leave by nightfall.

George gives a speech about the sacred artifacts now in the care of the *Orathom Wis*: the Poet, the boy god, the writing contained in the pages of a red spiral notebook, the Leaves of Fire. "Holy elements," he calls them, "will deliver us. We will guard humankind. We will stay true to our mandate." Then he adds with gravity, "But the flood has come. Gods will fight in this war. Like long ago, they will fight to keep order."

Corey Thomas shares what he learned while in Albion Ravistelle's confidence. From out of his jacket he unveils a small leather pouch of leaves and holds them up.

"To William Greenhame, *hoy!*"

Every voice echoes: *"Hoy!"*

Corey explains how Albion's team, directed by Dr. Angelo Catena, has managed to take an ancient seedling from the plant, enhance it with the latest advances in genetic engineering, and grow a biological miracle. A pale fruit. Its juice as red as blood. The very tree marking the center of myth, of Eden. A true Tree of Life. Corey tells that three people have eaten of the fruit. He nods to the love of Samuel Eversman, Leonaie Eschelle. Loche's eyes move to the beautiful woman, her hair now more brown than grey. She meets his gaze, and for a moment he thinks she is trying to say something. A tear forms below her eye.

Leonaie stands and shares how her beloved Samuel had taken her to Venice for a treatment that would make her immortal. Many times during her recounting, her words are arrested by emotion. Others in the room openly weep when she tells of her first sight when she awoke as an immortal: the beheading of her love, Samuel. When she speaks the assassin's name, Emil Wishfeill, the very proper Leonaie spits on the floor. No one in her audience is shocked by the gesture. She hisses, "I will have him. I will have him for Samuel." Empathy and anger cross the gathering's collective countenance. Her voice lowers, "But I was made immortal, and I do not know what it means. . . I do not know how to go on without my Samuel."

Corey places a comforting hand upon Leonaie's shoulder. Watching her, his sorrow transforms to anger. He growls the name, "Nicolas Cythe is the second to have eaten of the fruit. The Devil now has the blood of our ancestors. The Devil is now immortal."

Corey pauses. "The third recipient is unknown to me. I am sure we will know in due time.

"Using the fruit of the leaves, Ravistelle will repopulate the earth with immortals—with the paintings he will aim the sickness of humanity heavenward, and with the death of Loche Newirth, his story will not be overwritten."

Helen is asked to tell what she knows. Listening to her speak, Loche wonders if she's telling the truth. There is a subtle kindness in her voice. It is foreign, but welcome. A levelness in her tone that doesn't appear strained or contrived. As she speaks to the gathering, her grey eyes do not stray from Edwin. Her hands are fists at her sides. She speaks slowly and carefully.

"It is true that Loche's assassination was planned," Helen agrees, "but there is a division in policy. Albion feels it is best to simply follow through with an assassination in order to keep Loche from writing something that would stop his war. Everyone on his council agreed except for two—Nicholas Cythe is one. *He* felt that killing the Poet was a mistake." Her eyes tick to Loche. "He said that the Poet could be trained. The Poet could be made to write whatever they wanted. With the right pressure—"

The weight of many stares fall upon Loche. "I, myself can't control the writing," he says, "how could they?"

Helen's eyes drift to Edwin, but she speaks to Loche, "He said that with the right pressure—he could preach to your subconscious—a way to push you and your muse into writing what they want."

"Preach to my subconscious? That should be an interesting experiment for the psychologist in me to witness."

Helen remains gentle but stoic. She looks at Loche, "They have ways to make you. Certainly, they can use those you love— or they can leverage innocent people, whole cities even. They can bring an entirely new meaning to terrorism, Loche. But they see such actions as barbaric. They won't stoop to human methods unless all else has failed. No, they will begin with a weapon—a weapon that seems made just for you." She glances toward Corey, avoiding eye contact. "The third to eat of the fruit—his name is Dr. Marcus Rearden. He is now *Itonalya*." She turns back to Loche. "Albion, Cythe and Rearden have become quite the trinity. Rearden knows how to find you in the dark. He knows you better than even I. It's Rearden that wants the chance to find a way into your mind. He has been given that chance. It is almost a race between them to find you. Rearden has access to everything in Albion's house. Everything—" she pauses. She starts again, "The paintings, Loche. He has spent some time in Basil's Center. He knows things. He knows things. . ."

A stone crushes Loche's abdomen at the thought of Rearden within the Center. His mind wrestles between the admiration he once had for his mentor, and the murderer that claimed the life of Bethany Winship. What other terrors lurk in Rearden's past? He nods. "Rearden knows me, it's true. But I still don't see how he, Albion or Cythe, for that matter, can manipulate my writing. It was the Priest Lake Journal that started all of this—and though I wrote it, something not-of-this-earth made it real. It seems to me they would have to persuade that entity to cooperate. Convincing a muse or a god seems a little beyond their reach."

Helen's eyes move to Edwin and they shine with sudden tears. "Is it?"

Concern darkens each of the gathered faces. Edwin is warm in his arms. Loche thinks of the little boy, just days ago, walking out of the back bedroom at the Priest Lake cabin, with one bare foot, the other wore a sock—his pajamas bedraggled. "Hungry," he had said. "Hungry, Daddy. Pancakes." How did he come to be there? Loche still wonders. The universe had tilted somehow. A portal between the pages of a book had warped history. Imagined lives winked into existence. Reality altered and augmented from a few short sentences. And the little boy stepped out of the dark and into the fire lit cabin as Loche's hand lifted from the last period on the page—from the puddled ink at the tip of his pen. This little boy, that has now fallen through the pupil of some seraphic specter and returned as both his son and god entwined, lies in Loche's lap, staring out the window of the great hall.

Suddenly, Helen's words are an inescapable avalanche. He no longer questions her intentions. He trusts her next sentiment implicitly. "If they capture you, Loche, you will wish I had taken your life when the chance came." She sits, "If they learn of what Edwin now bears and they take him, I will wish my own death."

Eyes and Ears

November 11, this year
Over North Idaho
11:10am PST

From the air Astrid scans the massive lake coiled around Sand Point, Idaho, its northern end disappearing into the grey. She notes how the lake's shape resembles a human ear. Even the name of the lake, Pend Oreille, French given, means *hangs from ears* or *earring*. The thought irks her. The indigenous tribes of the Northwest plateau were named Pend Oreilles because of the large ear jewelry they wore. Of all the amazing cultural attributes that the Pend Oreille tribes of Kalispel, Flathead and Kaniksu lived and practiced over the centuries, the Europeans named them *Hangs From Ears* or *Earrings*. Why not Un Avec La Terre (One With the Land), Âmes Douces (Gentle Souls), or Ami Des Immortels (Friend of Immortals)? Or better still, what the Immortals of *Wyn Avuqua* called them: *Aevas,* Earth's Heart. Somehow these powerful and accurate characteristics were, of course, missed by the European visitors from afar. Instead they chose the shiny thing—the earring.

The chopper takes a northwestern course over Schweitzer Ski Resort toward the lower portion of the Selkirk Mountain range.

"Why are we going to Priest Lake?" Astrid asks into her headset mic.

Molmer turns to her and smiles. "Of course you know the lay of the land, Professor. Yes, Priest Lake is our destination."

"But why?"

Molmer and Rearden exchange smiles—Molmer's is filled with delight, Rearden's is harder to translate. Molmer says, "I plead for your patience, yet again. Trust that the wait will be worth it."

Astrid folds her hands into her lap and looks at the slate-green wrinkle of hills and forest passing below. Logging roads and stream veins disappear under boughs. Her thoughts drift to a research trip in this area with her assistant, Marcel "Red Hawk" Hruska, two years ago. They were attempting to connect the indigenous tribes, the *Aevas*, with the ancient *Wyn Avuquain* Immortals.

She smiles at the thought of Marcel, and his enthusiasm on that trip. Nearly everything about Marcel is anomalous—but most of all, his appearance. Her twenty-eight-year-old assistant has Irish red hair and sea-blue irises. Combined with a galaxy of orange freckles, his skin is dark, as his dominating genetic traits are Native American. Thus, Red Hawk. At first glance, the word *exotic* comes to mind. His frame is wiry, strong and athletic. His passion for Astrid's work and the *Wyn Avuquain* myths transcends that of any of her former students.

To her amazement, her phone vibrates in her coat. *Service here?* she thinks. As she reaches to retrieve it she notices Rearden staring at her. She manages not to scowl at him but, instead, moves her attention to the illuminated screen. It is Marcel. *How very* Elliqui, she thinks.

Marcel: How did it go today?

And what to say? Validation? Funding? A future for our research? Then she is simply delighted that a familiar voice just entered her head, instant message or not. She glances down to get an idea of her location and then taps out:

Astrid: I was just thinking of you. Our Elliqui *must be getting better. You won't believe it but I'm currently flying somewhere between Atlasta Mountain and Mount Casey.*

Marcel: Either you mean you're figuratively delighted that things went well and you're "flying" or you're literally flying over the lower Selkirk. Which could it be, I wonder?

She grins.

Astrid: Both.

Marcel: What!?

Astrid: I'm on a helicopter with Molmer and a guy named Marcus Rearden. We're headed to Priest Lake. They are telling me a surprise is waiting for me.

Astrid: btw, Molmer says we're funded! No details yet.

Marcel: FANTASTIC! How in the hell did Molmer get you into a helicopter? :)

Astrid: I guess the need of a surprise beat my fear. That must be a good thing, right?

Marcel: I should say so.

Marcel: Um . . . You know who Rearden is, right?

Astrid: Google reminded me.

Marcel: Hmmm.

Marcel: Weird. The guy seems like a dick. Scary. I've been following the Winship case. Gal from Sandpoint. Friend of a friend.

Astrid's eyes lift from the screen to see that Rearden is watching her. She lowers her phone.

That does it, she thinks. "Dr. Rearden, can I help you with something? You seem to have the creepy stare thing down pat."

Marcus's face remains passive. He answers without hesitation—his voice hisses with static in her headphones. "I'm sorry. Apologies, truly. I'm afraid my newfound revelations over the last few days have distracted my wonted social propriety. You see, I am very much interested in you and your work, Professor. As I stare, I'm attempting to learn from you all that you know. An old psychologist habit."

"I'd appreciate it if you'd lose the attempt at mind reading, Doctor."

Rearden laughs, "You know a bit about that, do you not?"

"Not as much as a psychologist might. . . or should," she says.

"Ah, but we don't mind read. We simply help people to read their own mind."

"Well, I'm quite content with my mind, Doctor, so I'd appreciate it if you'd not stare—"

"But you do know a thing or two about mind reading, don't you? I mean, isn't that the fundamental basis of the *Itonalya's* language of *Elliqui.*"

Astrid waits.

"I would love to learn. It is a kind of telepathy, isn't it?"

Astrid watches him. Her first instinct is to deflect the question and change the subject—or remain silent and not answer at all. Instead, she starts speaking. She isn't sure why. "*Elliqui* is said to be the true communication between the divinities and the Earth, its inhabitants, its peoples. Telepathy is a word used to make some kind of sense of *Elliqui,* but it falls short of what *Elliqui* could communicate, according to my research. Telepathy from the Greek means *distant passion* or *distant experience, perception.* Of course, if the phenomenon was real, the Greek gives a good definition, that is, the key element to the word, *tele* or *distant.* According to *Itonalya* lore, *Elliqui,* as a form of communication, was ever-present—the Hindu's Third Eye might be a better descriptor."

"And now *Elliqui* is gone?"

"As the inhabitants of earth grew arrogant and rebellious, tension grew between gods and men, gods and immortals, and true *Elliqui* began to fade."

"Rebellious?" Rearden asks. "Yes. Yes, rebellious."

"It depends upon the myth, but the confusion of tongues was a trick to keep the inhabitants of Earth under the yoke of the celestial hand. You know the Genesis Tower of Babel story, right? Man builds a tower to challenge the greatness of God—God confuses the shit out of man by confounding his language so communication falls apart. If we can't communicate, we can't work together, right?" Astrid holds up her cell phone. "It even works for the human-gods controlling this damned thing. Boasted as the information age, the language these days is called information— but no one speaks it— or, at least, no one knows how to get at truth." She grins at the hand held device and adds, "Though it is crazy that I've got service right now. . ."

Rearden nods along. She tries to decide if he's humoring her or if he's genuinely interested.

"For the *Itonalya* myth, their confusion-of-the-tongues story influenced the Babel myth. Their myth was called, *Encris*— their particular fall from grace story. When the leaders of *Wyn Avuqua* no longer wanted to do the will of the One God, *Thi,* they rebelled. It is said that *Thi* then removed their language. *It* took away *Elliqui.*"

"The language is that old? How far back was Babel?"

Astrid shakes her head. "Well, we first have to believe that Babel was a real event. That's an entirely different conversation, but for now, let's say it did. When is a moving target. Some place the Tower somewhere around 2400 BCE. Some centuries earlier—others, later. Most, however, are using Bible math."

"Bible math?"

"Yes, the mathematic system created by the storytellers. Let's just say that in my research, their arithmetic is a little too faith based. They can stretch two and two and believe it will equal five. Using their Bible calculator, the Earth is only some six to ten thousand years old." She shakes her head. "Never mind that. I favor, along with other scholars, the Sumerian tower called Etemenanki and its back story, for there's some relatively credible scientific evidence placing the tower somewhere around, let's see, somewhere between the fourteenth and ninth century BCE. Some claim that the Sumerian Tower influenced the Babel myth— but *Itonalya* scholars have proof that *Wyn Avuqua* was the influence for both tales. There was no actual tower—but rather, the metaphorical tower that connected the Immortals to the Universe and *Thi*: the tower of *Elliqui,* if you will. Our research points to written *Elliqui* showing up around the tenth century BCE. That leads us to believe that the tower or Original Mode of *Elliqui* was toppled or destroyed around that time. And the mode did not disappear overnight. It fell slowly. Some *Elliqui* manuscripts say that it decayed like old age until it was finally silent. Thus came written *Elliqui.* Then the final destruction of *Wyn Avuqua* by the *Godrethion* happened sometime around the tenth century AD."

Molmer's voice crackles into her headphones. "*Elliqui* in its purest form was a kind of telepathic mode of speaking, yes. After it was stolen away, the immortals attempted to remake the language in written and spoken forms."

Astrid nods, "That's correct. It took centuries for the written and spoken forms to develop. And many of its early authors were slaughtered for creating and harboring it. But my team has managed to scrape together a few pieces and parts over the course of our project. Little jewels that ring inside the ear. *Elliqui's* combination of phonetics and intention provide a kind of higher connection when using the written or spoken *Elliqui*. That's the easiest explanation I can give over a headset in the din of a helicopter."

Molmer says, "It's getting foggy out there." The aircraft is now running the length of Priest Lake. Far ahead, she knows, is the mouth of the thoroughfare to the upper lake but it is not visible through the mist. "We're almost there."

Rearden is still staring at her. It is unnerving, but she refuses to look away. "Are you attempting to read my thoughts again, Doctor? If so, I would appreciate it if you'd divert your eyes." She is suddenly thankful for the backdrop of static in the headphones because she's sure that her last words would have sounded fearful otherwise. As Rearden processes her request she watches his gaze glide from her lips to the curve of her face to her forehead—then landing heavily on her eyes. He then turns away and searches the landscape below. She feels cold. Her jaw is clenched.

Rearden points down and to the left as the chopper starts up the winding thoroughfare. "Loche Newirth's cabin is just there." Both Molmer and Astrid see the tiny log cabin, but only for a moment as the chopper clatters by. "A dangerous man, Dr. Newirth," he adds. "Very dangerous."

Astrid shudders as the cell phone vibrates in her hand.

Marcel: Do keep me posted, okay? I've heard a lot of bad things about Rearden. Something has me feeling uneasy.

Astrid: Me, too.

Marcel: And. . . you okay? I know that every time you visit the lake you are reminded. . .

Astrid: Fine. Long time ago.

Montanha Do Pico

November 11, this year
Over the Azores, Portugal
3:35pm AZOT

Three choppers lift into the sky and vault southwest over the ocean. In the middle one Edwin Newirth holds his father's hand and watches the land slip away until all beneath is water. The helicopter headset is overlarge on him. Loche adjusts the microphone to the boy's lips and straightens the headband.

"Can you hear me?" he asks.

"Yes," Edwin answers. His little voice is a stab of midrange tone, punctuated by a quick crackle of white noise.

"Why won't mom fly with us?" he asks.

Loche squeezes the boy's hand gently, "I thought it would be fun for just you and me to fly together. You've never been in a helicopter before."

"No. It makes my tummy feel funny."

"Mine, too."

"There's mom!" Edwin says and waves.

Loche sees her face in the window of the chopper flying beside them—fingers spread wide against the glass. Even Helen had chosen to fly separated from Edwin, however reluctant. None of the others wanted to be near the child. At least, no immortal. The *Rathinalya* was too much.

"Are we going to Egypt now?"

"Yes," Loche says. "I expect we'll be landing at an airstrip to board a plane, soon."

"How far is Egypt?"

"I don't know exactly—but it is almost half way around the world from where we are."

"Is it as far as Spokane?" The boy is still watching his mother.

Loche smiles. "You mean from our house in Sagle, Idaho to Spokane?"

"Yes."

"A little longer than that drive, I expect."

They pass over another island and launch again out over the ocean.

"Why are we going to Egypt, Dad?"

Loche feels for his shoulder bag at his feet. He pulls the strap up and lays it over his knees. His umbrella is beside him on the seat.

"We're going to meet someone."

"Who?"

Loche squints. *My dead brother,* he thinks. "My brother," he says.

Then Loche hears his son say, *The Painter.*

He flinches at the sound of Edwin's voice—and then at the words he had said. The headset delivers a strangely clear and compressed sound into the ear, but these words of Edwin probed deeper, as if they appeared in Loche's mind. He scowls, trying to determine if it was indeed an aural sensation. Then, how could Edwin have used the word, *Painter*? Especially in the context of Loche's brother, Basil?

When he looks at Edwin, the little boy is staring up at him. A field of stars sparkles across the boy's face—

The headphones crackle, and Edwin says, "Who's your brother?"

Loche searches the boy's expression. The boy god is hiding there somewhere.

"Dad?"

"You haven't met him," Loche answers.

Loche recalls the Journal's description of his first meeting with Basil. He had written of him standing on the beach outside of the cabin at Priest Lake, Idaho. Loche went down to confront him— to ask him why he was loitering there. Shortly after, Helen and Edwin came down the path, and Loche introduced his family to Basil. In the journal, Edwin did meet Basil.

Loche says, "Maybe you have met him. Do you remember the man with the long hair and the brown jacket on the beach— at the cabin— a few weeks ago?"

"Yes." Edwin answers. "Yes, I remember."

It continues to amaze and frighten Loche—this twisted creation at the tip of his pen. He shakes his head. Dread and joy quarrel in his abdomen. As each day passes he has trouble dividing his written account and experiential memory. If he doesn't focus on the words, he can easily believe he met Basil there on the beach, the autumn chill, the reds and golds wreathing the still lake—Basil standing there, his hands in his pockets. Loche suppresses a smile when he thinks of Basil's first words. "The big, deep heavy," he had said. Loche can't help but to allow himself to grin, remembering Basil's next utterance, "Sorry if I've freaked you out—not my intention."

I've freaked myself out, Loche thinks.

Loche feels for the leather strap of his bag hanging over his knees. Within the bag is his small daily diary, a water bottle, protein bars, and most importantly, the Red Notebook—still unopened—still unread.

The next island is nearing—a floating garden plot on the wide blue. Rising from the center is a single mountain. It overshadows the small city at its foot. The high summit appears flat, save for a lonely pinnacle of rock. As the helicopters close distance, the strange peak begins to take the shape of a conical anomaly.

George's voice from the next chopper crackles in the speakers, "Mount Pico, Loche. You see?"

The rooftops and farmlands are left behind. Ahead, the land is pitching skyward. The forward windshield fills with the rocky colossus, and the three choppers take altitude, hurtling upward to the snow dusted apex.

The smaller pinnacle, massive in its own right, still puzzles Loche. "Where are we going, George?"

There is no response.

As the chopper rises to the top and hovers, Loche can see four large tents crowding the base of the pyramid shaped structure.

"What is that?" Loche asks. He marvels at the strange peak that dominates the northern section of the height.

George's laughter vibrates his eardrums. "That is our ride, Poet," he says.

Validation

November 11, this year
Upper Priest Lake, Idaho
11:50am PST

"Sweet Christ," says professor Astrid Finnley.

As the helicopter approaches the top end of Upper Priest Lake, the world around Astrid blurs save the one sight taking shape below. There, a little beyond the northern shoreline begins a formation of stone boundaries—walls—city walls—opening into a wide, almond shape—perhaps arcing four miles from point to point.

"Oh my God."

There, in excavated partitions of strata is what looks like an ancient city long buried and drowned under the upper marshlands of the lake. Its outer perimeter curves like the lids of a great eye, and in the center rises a crumbled and age worn acropolis.

"Son of a bitch!"

There, the high citadel is surrounded by its own outer wall, much of it destroyed and long fallen. A dozen excavation vehicles, support trailers and personnel are interspersed amid newer dig points. The chopper banks, tips and begins to circle. In the glass Astrid can now see the entire dig site at *Wyn Avuqua*, like a sculpted eye on the surface of the Earth. Upper Priest Lake shines silver and appears to drip like a tear from the city.

Astrid pants, unable to look away, "This is— this is—"

"Really happening?" Rearden offers. "Why yes. Yes it is, indeed."

"Look," Astrid points. Her hand is shaking. "There are the upper columns of the temple *Tiris Avu!* And the opening to the *Avu* stair!" The joy is overwhelming. She looks excitedly to Molmer and Rearden, but does not wait for acknowledgement before her focus rivets back to the site. Her cheeks suddenly begin to throb from smiling. "I knew it! I knew it!"

Not far from the eastern most gate is an encampment of some twenty wall-tents, a landing platform and a wide plot for support vehicles. The chopper descends, hovers and touches down. Astrid raises the strap of her bag up over her shoulder, pulls her cap onto her head, her gloves onto her hands and searches for the lever to open the door.

Molmer laughs, "A moment, Astrid, please. They will open the door for us." She sits back struggling to contain the surge of validation—the meaning. She's arrived at the city she has seen only in her mind's eye. "Are you glad that we kept it a surprise?"

She grins and wipes away a tear.

Pocket Diary Entry # 3

November 11, this year
Terciera Island, Azores, Portugal
3:57pm AZOT
(Loche Newirth's pocket diary)

Nov 11- 3:57pm

A pyramid. Never in my life. . . Is this my doing ?

High Tea

November 11, this year
Pico Island, Azores, Portugal
4pm AZOT

From the open tent door Loche can see an emerald grid of hedgerows and vineyards far below. The encircling blue of the Atlantic beyond is like an airy hangman's noose. His fear of the ocean. . . *ever present*, he thinks. A short distance away, across the flat summit, Edwin is searching the stone fissures and cracks for frogs. He is bundled up in a black stocking cap and coat. For some reason he believes frogs live at this height.

Loche touches Julia's hand. "Are you alright?" he asks.

"I don't know," Julia shrugs. "The *Rathinalya* is nearly unbearable. I've heard several others say they've never felt anything quite like it." She turns and watches Edwin for a moment. "Even Helen is forced to keep her distance. I suppose for me, it is a sensation I'll have to get used to."

"How are you able to manage it now?"

"I'm coming out of my skin, to tell you the truth." He sees her hand pinching the key beneath her blouse. "But I can manage."

He pulls her close. She is shaking.

"I won't be parted from you again," she says. "So I must figure out a way to bear this, this, whatever this is. I hope there is a way."

"Ribbit," Edwin says. His head down and his fingers scrabbling in the stones.

"I'll need breaks from him," she says. "I'll figure that out."

Half a dozen guards in all black walk the perimeter of the stony height. Loche thinks he can hear them whispering. Maybe they are questioning just how long they must endure the stinging *Rathinalya* emanating from the young god among them. Maybe they are lamenting the dark fate that seems inescapable.

"Poet?" George's voice calls from outside. "Join us, yes?"

Loche and Julia step out into the cold. Corey Thomas and George are standing a few meters from the tent, and both are craning their necks, scanning the pyramidal structure that looms above.

"How is the boy?" George asks.

"Looking for frogs," Loche answers.

George smiles.

"Why are we here?"

Corey interrupts, *"Angofal,* should we do this first?" He points to Loche's bag.

"Yes," George says.

"Loche, Julia, let us take your shoulder bags. We would like to provision them."

The two pass their bags to him. Corey hands them to another of the company.

"We are here because this," George says, pointing to the rising stones. "And tea."

"I don't understand," Loche says.

Corey laughs. "No—and why should you? Of course, your imagination may have catalyzed many strange and formidable powers, but you cannot be the sole creator. For from your creation come efficacies and artisans building upon your word. This, my dear fellow, is a pyramid."

"So I see."

"Ah, but do you? Mysterious structures, these. Millenniums old." He sighs and questions as if to some disembodied audience, "Tombs? Energy beacons? Extraterrestrial origin?" He shrugs and chuckles.

"This does not look quite symmetrically designed," Loche notes, "It looks more like a volcanic cone has pressed upward."

"Yes," Corey agrees. "And it is so. *Endale*, she too builds her own pyramids. The Earth, her art influences us all. Fascinating."

"Pyramids exist here in our lives," George says, "and they exist there, as well. In the *Orathom*. Or so says your brother, Basil, yes?"

Loche traces the triangular lines upward to the blue sky. Some fifty or so meters up, three of the *Orathom Wis* are steadily climbing. The summit is perhaps another twenty meters above. Given the rocky terrain, the climb does not appear to be difficult save for the steep incline.

"As a rule," Corey says, "Three at a time may use an *omvide*, that is, a pyramid."

"Use a pyramid?"

"Why yes, and after, there must be a period of waiting. Some thirty minutes." He says to George, "Enough time for tea."

"Yes," George agrees. "After tea, *omvide* is ready again."

Corey turns and calls, "Alice? Are they making tea yet?"

From inside another tent, Alice calls back, "Indeed, my Lord, Thomas." Alice appears with a tray of cups. Behind her, another of the company carries two silver pots. The flutes steam in the icy air.

Leonaie Echelle follows behind Alice, carrying a plate of yellow cakes. "Is this your first time?" she asks. Both Loche and Julia share a confused glance.

"So it seems. Though, I don't know what you mean," Loche answers.

Leonaie smiles. "Samuel took me to a pyramid in Mexico once. 1969, I think it was. We had tea and watched William and two other *Orathom Wis*. . ." she breaks off. She leans toward Loche and says quietly, "Dr. Newirth, I have something that I think you should have. . . But I don't know if. . . My Samuel would have wanted you to have it. . . " George's voice interrupts her, "See there," he says. Leonaie steps back and looks up the incline.

The three climbers have reached the top. At the summit (which is no larger than maybe five or so meters across, Loche figures), they turn and face the company below. One waves. George responds by raising his hand, as if signaling approval.

The three turn to the center of the summit, take two steps inward and vanish.

Loche scowls and rubs his eyes.

Julia says, "What the?"

"Now," George says, "we sip the tea."

Pyramids and Prophecies

November 11, this year
Upper Priest Lake, Idaho
12:05am PST

"*Lain*," the man says, his hand upon his heart, staring at Astrid.

Astrid replies without a moment's hesitation, "*Lain,*" and mirrors the man's gesture. *I'm home*, she thinks. Aside from her assistant Marcel and a couple of fellow *Itonalya* scholars, the opportunity to speak *Elliqui* with others is rare. And to speak it now, on the very soil upon which it was conceived, is delicious beyond description.

"Graham Cremo, senior staff archeologist," he says brightly. He is tall. Very tall. Thin, lanky and long limbed. *How does this man find clothes to fit?* she marvels. "I'm afraid my *Elliqui* is restricted to hellos, goodbyes, the usual restroom inquiry and, of course," he laughs, "where can I find wine?"

"*Thi twiv ressasht?*" Astrid grins.

He grins, "And I do have wine to share— or, let's see," he leans toward her and says trippingly, "*Thi twiv—jifoth.*" The last word lilts in question, as if he's unsure.

Astrid reassures him, "*Hoy.*"

"A thrill to meet you," Graham says, offering his hand. Astrid takes it. "I've read your latest work—Dr. Molmer sent it along. Your insight into this culture is uncanny." His smile is warm, framed by the shadow of a beard. He is nervous and doing his best to not show it—she likes that. "This must come as quite a shock, all of this."

"Yes."

"I expect you'd like to take a tour immediately."

"Yes."

Graham's smile widens as he asks, "Or would you prefer

a more *Itonalya* style introduction? Instead of wine, may I offer you tea?" A young woman, likely a college student intern, brings a tray of steaming cups.

Rearden receives his tea. "What does that mean, *Itonalya* style?"

"A sort of joke, for those in the know," Astrid answers. "It means there's no rush. This is the city of Immortals. *Itonalya* take their time with most everything they do—"

Molmer adds, "Those that cannot die have all the time in the world."

"And they do things right," Astrid adds.

Rearden nods thoughtfully. "Ah, yes. Of course."

"However," Astrid says, "I am very much human, and my time is precious—I was ready for the tour years ago. When do we start?"

"A vehicle is being brought around now and we're getting your clearance papers. It won't take long," Graham says.

"Clearance papers?" Rearden asks.

"It is frustrating. There has been some discrepancy over the land rights, apparently. Its not finders keepers here, after all. *Wyn Avuquain* treasure hunters have always been interested in Upper Priest Lake and the surrounding lands of course, but nothing of note has ever been found. The National Historic Preservation and the Archaeological Resources Protection Acts essentially control our doings, but a private land corporation has owned the property for over a century—well before the 1974 ruling. So, there's the rub."

Rearden listens without expression.

Graham turns to Astrid, "While we wait, can I answer any questions—"

"Only three hundred or so," Astrid laughs. "But your offer of tea makes me think of something specific."

"What might that be?" Graham asks, a faint grin blooming.

"The pyramid exists?" Astrid says. "The pyramid. . ."

Graham's answer is a fully lit smile.

An electric shock of excitement jolts through her.

Graham says, "There are two."

She grins excitedly. "Yes. Yes."

"Yes, you were right," Graham's hands wave excitedly. "The first, your *Omvide Mellithion* is mid lake—just where you thought it was. But it has been nearly destroyed and covered over by time. We've dug in from the eastern face about one hundred meters and found. . ."

"Crystal," Astrid finishes.

"Crystal," Graham echoes.

"And the other? You found *Omvide Dellithion?*"

"We have. We've uncovered about ten meters of the apex. It measures seven square meters across. We're guessing the thing goes down at least fifty or more meters. Radar pings perfect symmetry and alignment. You were right."

"I guessed, really," she grins.

"Pyramid?" Rearden asks, smiling. "Do tell."

Graham excitedly continues, "*Dellithion* is big. Almost too big to be believed for this part of the world, and it has been right under our noses. Well, not a kilometer north of where our noses are now, rather." He points to a large map tacked to a board. On it are a dozen hand scrawled notes, connecting lines and circles around dig points.

"No one believed me," Astrid whispers.

Simultaneously, and with a slight laugh, both Graham and Astrid say: "*Lonwayro.*"

"Pyramid." Rearden says again, his tone a little more controlled this time.

Graham says, "I can't begin to tell you the size of the job ahead. It'll take years to slough off the ages of vegetation and sediment. But just knowing that it is here nods to the *Itonalya's* supposed mode of travel."

"Excuse me," Rearden waves his bony hand between them. "Pyramid? Please, tell me about it."

Astrid lowers the white cardboard cup to her lap. Rearden is here for an education, she remembers—the reason Molmer wanted him to come along. But why? To capture the murderer, Loche Newirth? The excitement of where she is pushes the thought aside, and she answers, "Crazy, right? I've been on this lake countless times searching for clues to *Wyn Avuqua*, and I've never turned up anything. But a few years ago I discovered a document in Germany, purportedly written by the hand of an Immortal. She wrote in detail how pyramids were used and needed by the *Orathom Wis* to travel long distances to uphold their mandate. She wrote of *Wyn Avuqua's* pyramid."

Rearden smiles. "Yes," he says. "I have read that very document. But please, continue."

She levels her eyes at Rearden, "You see, the city of Immortals was to be kept secret from the rest of the world. The city was founded in the Americas, or at that time, a place over the edge of the flat earth. A place that didn't exist to any, other than the Immortals, and perhaps some of the indigenous tribes that inhabited the Northwest Plateau. Pyramids have long mystified us. There are more than a thousand scattered over the planet— some constructed by artisans, and some have been formed by forces of nature, strangely enough. Places like the Giza, Teotihuacan, even the anomalous structures in Bosnia continue to fascinate and befuddle historians, archeologists and scientists. Who built them, and how? Why are they here? What were they for? As with all big life questions, I'm afraid, I'm at a loss. But, according to the research I've done, and adding that to the shoulders of others, the *Itonalya* claim to have used the structures to move around the planet by simply crossing over the peak of a pyramid."

Rearden's head bobs slightly. "I see."

Astrid says as if to answer him, "I didn't say that I believed it. I've crossed over many pyramid caps—I didn't find myself anywhere other than where I climbed to—all I got were sore quads."

Graham's head tilts slightly, "You've never spoken the word *lonwayro* crossing the point? Even for fun?"

Astrid laughs and checks her voice for sarcasm, "That's funny. No. Not once."

Graham nods, "Come to think of it, nor have I."

A hard bound book appears before Astrid's face. It is held there by an attractive female intern. She nods for Astrid to take it. On the cover is Graham himself, his hands outstretched and spilling out below him are the pyramid stones of what Astrid recognizes as Khufu, the Great Pyramid. The title reads: *Mapping the Pyramids*. She reads the flap copy. She scans a review. She reads it aloud. *"Cremo brings the Pyramids back to the forefront of our imagination where they should endure. Sound research. Magnificent vision. History, for this reviewer, rewritten. Cremo is now the only expert on possibility." —The New York Times.*

She looks up. Graham is visibly nervous watching her read. "Expert. I love the sound of that."

At her praise, Graham smiles. His lower lip seems to lower and jut outward and his pupils comically misalign. Astrid then sees a near perfect Bill Murray impression from the film Caddyshack: "Cinderella story, out of nowhere, former greenskeeper, now about to become the Masters champion. It looks like a mirac- its in the hole! It's in the hole!"

Several people in the tent turn to watch and listen. Astrid laughs. Graham laughs.

"The New York Times was unusually kind," he says wrinkling his nose at the cover. "Sorry, I sometimes jump to movie quotes when I get nervous."

God damn it, he is cute. "I look forward to reading it." She sets it down upon the table. "I'm a little surprised I've missed the title."

"Oh," he chuckles, "there's a club on Amazon of seven million others that missed it, too."

"Hey," Astrid joins, "I have a similar book club."

"Well, down below there is so much more," Graham says pointing diagonally down and to his right. "Where I'm about to take you there are volumes on the many pyramids in the surviving texts. I've barely scratched the surface—I'm writing a follow up right now."

Rearden prods, "So, I understand that they used them as a kind of portal from pyramid to pyramid?"

Graham answers, "That is the myth. But obviously, they were really symbols of power for the Monarchy. They do, however, emit a kind of energy. This has long been known. There is science to support it. *Itonalya* lore claims that they used them as transportation from continent to continent, pyramid to pyramid." He laughs, "Of course such a vehicle before intercontinental sea voyages would have been handy, indeed. The world is covered with pyramids—on every continent. There's over one hundred and thirty in Egypt alone. From the *Wyn Avuquain* pyramids, the *Itonalya* could do their business of eliminating *Godrethion* virtually anywhere in the world and still have a home to return to. Here, on a continent untouched, or rather, untainted by humans—at the time, at least. Their own mythology depicted pyramids as travel portals—it's a great story." Graham raises his cup, "And as the ritual goes, when *Itonalya* would journey through an *omvide*, uh, excuse me Dr. Rearden, I mean pyramid, those left behind would drink tea."

Astrid smiles and raises her cup, too. "*Hoy,*" she says smiling at him.

"*Hoy,*" both Graham, Molmer and a couple of other field workers in the tent join in.

Rearden asks, "So, you don't really believe they are portals?"

Graham and Astrid stare at the psychologist for a moment. Astrid sighs. "Myth, Doctor. Just myth."

Astrid then says to Graham, "What I can't understand is how you've managed to uncover so much in such a short period. I was here six months ago—and the promise of finding evidence was still like probing for a clue to Atlantis. There was no excavation happening then."

Dr. Cremo looks at his hands. "I have done my share of exploring up here, too. And I can't explain it. It is strange, to be sure. It is almost as if one day it wasn't here, and the next it was. I've walked over this very spot several times—I've even shoveled into that soil before, just there several times," he points to a mound of earth from which a carved column is partially exposed. He sighs, "How I missed it then, I don't know."

"So it was you who made the first discovery?"

Graham's eyes move to Molmer and then back to Astrid. "Too kind, Dr. Finnelly, but it was you that made the first discovery."

"Say again?"

"Let me explain. As you know, Dr. Molmer has been monitoring your work—and he's kept me informed of your progress." Graham lifts a worn book from out of his field bag. Its pages are worn, wrinkled and water damaged. "Recognize this?"

"Of course," she says, "it's nice to know someone read one of my books. . ."

"It's genius," his face reddens with nervousness again. He looks down at the cover and says, "And, after all of your work and your sacrifices, I hope it is appropriate that I offer my sympathies—"

Astrid raises her hand, "Please, don't. It was a long time ago."

Graham raises his eyes to hers. He is kind. He is genuine. When he nods to her request, a flash of concern drifts through his expression—then it is gone. "My team and I used many of your findings to lead us to the first stones."

"Why wasn't I informed?" she asks.

Graham looks to Molmer.

Molmer answers, "I'm afraid, Professor, you've been too vocal about *Wyn Avuqua* in the public forum—a known spokesperson. This dig and what we've found must remain a secret for the time being. There are a number of reasons why, but for now suffice it to say that in order for us to carry on, everything you see and learn here must remain confidential."

Graham says, "Believe me, I—I mean we—that is, the team and I could have made faster work of it had you been involved from the start. We've been requesting your guidance since the beginning. But, I don't hold the keys to the kingdom, as it were."

"Who does?"

"That will be known in time," Molmer says.

"Then why am I allowed, now?" Astrid's voice is terse.

Graham's grin is cute, she thinks. "I thought you'd never ask— apologies, that's not very *Itonalya* of me, is it? Do I seem like I'm rushing— I'm sorry. You see, I'm a trained archeologist. I've got the chops and years of experience— and I know a thing or two about this culture, too— but not like you. We've arrived at a point that requires expert advice.

"Three days ago we discovered a chamber in the center citadel—"

"*Tiris Avu*," Astrid calls it.

"Yes," he nods. "We've uncovered a tomb—the enclosure's walls are covered in stone carved *Elliqui* runes. We found weapons, gold—" Astrid begins to sigh, "a veritable treasure trove of artifacts— all in stunningly beautiful condition. In the tomb itself we believe to be what remains of Queen Yafarra —"

"—the final ruler of the *Wyn Avuquains* on earth," Astrid completes his sentence. "Though, if the myth matches, her head will be missing."

"Yes, of course. But also, within her sarcophagus, should be," he pauses—his smile fades. Graham and Astrid stare silently at one another for a long moment.

"Of course," Astrid says finally. "Of course."

Graham takes a deep breath and continues, "If it is there, the discovery will change the way we understand our history."

"If *what* is there?" asks Rearden. "What?"

Graham's whisper is more to himself than to Rearden: "The Prophesy."

The two turn to Rearden. Astrid notices Rearden's hand trembling as he raises his tea to his lips. After a sip he says, "Prophecy?"

Astrid says, "According to *Itonalya* history, Queen Yafera made war upon *Thi*, the One God, and because of this, *Wyn Avuqua* was destroyed by *Thi's Godrethion*." She gestures to the ruin of the city surrounding them. Rearden looks out to another toppled stone pillar unearthed a few meters away. "The fighting was bitter—the tales tell. Nearly all of the inhabitants were slaughtered." Astrid points to the lake to the South. "It was said that one could walk across the water upon the floating heads of the slain."

Graham adds, "There's also the legend that the bottom of the lake is a graveyard of skulls." Astrid shudders at the thought.

"If this city is as great as you've claimed it to be, why would Yafarra risk its destruction by going to war with—" Rearden shakes his head as if he doesn't actually believe what he's about say—but then he catches himself. Astrid watches him wrestle with a thought, as if he is caught in some internal argument. He picks up, "By going to war with, *God?* I thought the Immortals were god killers—always at war with gods. Their purpose was to protect humankind from crossing spirits."

"Crossing spirits, yes, the *Godrethion.* But, in essence, the immortals of *Wyn Avuqua* were ultimately *Thi's* slaves," she answers. "And in all tales of slavery, eventually there's an uprising. And yes, you are correct, the *Itonalya's* mission was to keep the crossing spirits, or the *Godrethion,* or the *Oläthion*, that is, the great populace of Heaven, from interfering with the greatest of creations: *Endale* or *Ae*, or Earth. They were given this edict by the so called One God, *Thi*. The *Itonalya* claimed that the One God told the story of existence, and thus, existence came to be. When *Endale* was made, *Endale* ruled the One God's thought—it was the jewel of the night's sky and every god was drawn to it—and more important, drawn to the doings and dramas of its inhabitants. It's the *Itonalya* belief that the fate of the Earth determines the fate of the Universe."

Graham says, "Even the gods have their shiny thing."

Molmer adds, "As you're well aware, Doctor, all mythologies depict deities involving themselves in human affairs. After all, what would the wondrous Greek myths be without the gods playing their part? At some point, several millennia ago, the One God forbad intervention. They were causing the greatest of creations, the Earth, irreversible damage."

"And so," Astrid continues, "the *Itonalya* were placed at the door, here to destroy any god that managed to cross. The Immortals were slaves to the One God. *It* promised them an immortal life, but *It* did not grant life after death."

"*It?*" Rearden says. "Why do you say *It?* Doesn't *It* have a name or a gender?"

Astrid sighs. Should she have to explain such concepts to a psychologist? She checks her delivery and gentles her voice, "Gender classification for the One God usually makes it to the fairy tale history books depending upon who has the stronger arm at the time. Most human tales put a penis on the maker of all creation. In the last few thousand years, for reasons easily interpreted, stories have an overbalanced, masculine rule. Other, older tales provide the master of the Universe a vagina for a number of reasons. Whatever the reasons for giving God a sex has to do with imagined constructs.

"Immortals, on the other hand (or genital), didn't give fuck one about the gender of their Creator because they had centuries to discover the brilliant irrelevance of such a thought. Not to mention they celebrated the strong attributes that each sex brought to the feast instead of limiting them.

"A name? Human mythologies have many names for the character. Many you've heard, of course. Jehovah, Elohim, Yahweh, Odin, Zeus, Gaia, etcetera, etcetera. The *Itonalya* called *It, Thi*."

Astrid shakes her head, "But never mind all of that. Queen Yafarra was defeated, and she and her people paid for their hubris. The city was destroyed, the telepathic mode of *Elliqui* was finally extinguished, the lake was filled with *Itonalya* heads, and the rebellion was put down by *Thi's Godrethion.*

"But in the end, *Thi* took pity upon the surviving *Itonalya,* and as a kind of covenant *It* foretold of two brothers that would break the *Itonalya* bonds of slavery. Two artists. A Painter and a Poet who would somehow open a door between humankind and the deities. The *Godrethion* would no longer cross over and interfere. Instead, they would partake of the human condition through the art of the brothers." She shines out a genuine smile,

"Isn't that where the divine has truly lived, in art? If God or gods truly exist, art must be their home." A cloud covers the sun. She continues. "But until the Prophecy is fulfilled, *Thi* demands *Itonalya* loyalty and their service: to protect humankind by destroying crossing gods on earth."

"The prophesied brothers— with their coming—only then could the *Itonalya* cast off their long burden," Graham says.

"I've heard of this prophecy, as you call it." Rearden says.

Astrid answers, "Yes, there is ancient literature that discusses the prophecy. I've researched and written of it, and so have others, though we only have threads to the quilt, I'm afraid. In other words, what I've just told you is about all we know. But if we know anything about the mythological motif, for every mythology has prophecies, we might make some predictions of our own."

"Such as?" Rearden asks.

"Well, for the willing believer, prophecies come true. You know, predictions birth belief—and widespread belief makes it happen."

"You're referring to prophecy as self-fulfilling. Psychologically speaking, much like cognitive ease?"

"Cognitive ease?" Graham asks.

Rearden answers, "The idea that if something is repeated over and over, the mind will eventually believe that it is true."

"Like political propaganda?" Graham smiles.

"Like political propaganda," Rearden agrees.

Astrid nods, "Aren't such things the basis for a successful prophecy? Believe hard enough and it will happen? Hear the story enough—and it becomes true." She wonders at Rearden's controlled, almost too solemn expression. It is unsettling. "Or at least, perceived as true."

"True, Professor. Beyond your wildest dreams, true. Though, I much prefer the notion that augury comes to pass by the actions taken to defy it."

Astrid studies him a moment. "Yes, I agree with that, too."

"So do you believe in the *Itonalya* Prophecy?" Rearden asks.

She laughs. "I'm not the type," Astrid tells him. "Gods exist in stories, not in reality."

"Really? After all your studies, you don't believe the people of *Wyn Avuqua* were actually Immortal—that they were god killers— you don't believe in gods?"

Astrid says, "Haven't we covered this, Doctor? Come now, I'm an academic. We both know the power of ancient stories and myth. The *Itonalya* were a culture filled with metaphor and symbolism. Their war with the gods was a war within themselves and a war with ignorance. Their proclaimed immortality was a reach for a state of mind—an ideal—a harmony with their humanity and the universe. Perhaps the world's first visionary atheists. Killing gods is killing ignorance. Their city was destroyed by themselves when they allowed their gods to rule their society."

"So gods equal ignorance?"

"If you like," Astrid answers.

"The pyramidal portals and all that?"

"Megalithic monuments help the nonbelievers to believe. Come on, religions and belief systems have done stranger things."

"How very interesting," Rearden says. "And what of the death of the *Wyn Avuquain* innocent?"

Astrid studies the gaunt features and the strangely synthetic skin stretched across his face. *Who is this guy?* she wonders. *And how could he know that story?* She answers, "You mean the sacrifice that could have stopped the sacking of the city?"

"Yes," Rearden says. "Another crucifixion yarn no doubt?"

"Well," Astrid says, "the stories are in conflict. Some say it happened, others make no mention. Who knows. Maybe we'll find the answer to that question while we are here."

Rearden nods. "I do hope to learn the outcome of that mystery."

Blindside

November 11, this year
Upper Priest Lake, Idaho
4:20pm AZOT

Loche unscrews the cap of the aluminum water bottle and takes a sip. He then hands it to Edwin. The little boy takes a mouthful.

Looking down the pyramid's slope, Loche can see the congregation of immortals watching the climb. Helen is the nearest to the base. Her body is taut, nervous and prepared to vault up the jumbled rocks if Edwin stumbles or trips. The stones are smooth and piled stair-like enough. Edwin is doing well, so far. He doesn't look down. Instead, he takes another sip and then hands the bottle to his father. Loche wrestles between being proud of his young son, and fearing the god lingering in every word from the boy's lips—every glance—every gesture. He takes the bottle. Loche feels as if he has heard, *Thank you, Dad*, but Edwin did not speak. A sparkle of light glitters in the boy's eyes, and then it is gone. Edwin leans upward and climbs. Loche watches him a moment, then offers water to Julia, a few feet below him.

"I'm good," she says. "I just had a sip from mine."

Loche caps the bottle and drops it in his bag. Corey had stocked the bag with a half dozen more energy bars, a billfold of Egyptian pounds, Euros and American dollars, a flashlight, emergency blanket, a small first aid kit, his small olive colored diary and finally, a charged cell phone. Buried at the bottom is the Red Notebook. In an envelope tucked between the notebook's pages is a single leaf from William Greenhame's life-giving plant. George insisted that he take at least one. His umbrella is latched to the strap. He nudges the bag behind him and follows behind Edwin. He then pauses a moment and looks down. He finds Leonaie. After considering the contents of his bag, he recalls that she said something about wanting him to have. . .*what was it? Something that her Samuel would want him to have. . .*

"I've always wanted to see the Giza Plateau," Julia says.

Loche shakes off the thought and pushes himself upward, "Me, too."

"Of course I always counted on a long plane ride, some crazy traffic conditions and the very real possibility of dysentery."

"Ah," Loche smiles, "and who would have thought that kidnapping, murder, the fruit of life, and the war of gods versus immortals would happen instead. Just think of your travel companions: the prophesied Poet and a boy god."

Julia pushes herself higher and expires a laugh. "Dysentery is still possible."

"That it is," Loche agrees. "How is the *Rathinalya*?"

She doesn't answer at first. "Ugh. The climb is helping to keep my mind off of it."

Loche lifts Edwin up and over a particularly tall stone. He lurches himself up and then offers Julia his hand.

"But to think," she says lacing her fingers in his and rising beside him, "that in a few minutes we'll cross the summit of this pyramid, and in a blink we'll be atop a pyramid in Egypt—that's freaking me out."

"Beats Cairo traffic, I would think."

"I mean it. Unbelievable."

"Unbelievable?" Loche asks. "Still? Even after all that's happened?"

Julia shrugs, "I'm getting better with all of it, I must say. I'm harder to surprise." Her breath smokes in the air.

Loche thinks a moment as he watches Edwin take a few more strides ahead. He calculates the distance to the top. Maybe thirty more meters. The afternoon is pitching quickly to dusk. A light breeze whisks glittery snow. Not far now. But then what? The three *Orathom Wis* soldiers that went before are to clear the way in Cairo. Once Loche, Julia and Edwin arrive, they are to make their way to the Menkaure Pyramid, climb it and find Basil there. Find Basil there? Between the cryptic clues discovered by Julia in Basil's studio, and Loche's account of meeting Basil through the Center and their parting beside a massive pyramid, George and the others decided the best course of action was to pursue the signs. Follow the augury. Loche shakes his head. *Omens, signs, absurd*, he thinks. *Unbelievable.*

But George's worry at the mention of Menkaure is troubling. He refused to elaborate in detail about the pyramid and the *Itonalya* lost crossing its peak. Named after the 4th dynasty Egyptian pharaoh, it is the smallest of the three, and little was shared with Loche concerning its history. Though the name Menkaure is Egyptian in origin, George had informed Loche that the *Itonalya* have a word with the same pronunciation: *menkor* (mĕnkōr). George was reluctant to share the *Elliqui* meaning. It was the solemn Corey Thomas that whispered into Loche's ear, "It means *forgotten memory*. And don't ask me what I think it means. I've no idea."

Loche looks at Julia and says after a moment, "The unbelievability of it doesn't get old."

Then, a cracking sound. The air pops four or five times. Loche looks up at Edwin's slow but steady pace a few meters above. He turns to see Julia. She is looking down the slope. Below George and the others are now scattering. Around the perimeter of the summit bowl some ten or more figures have perched themselves in firing positions. There are more bursts of gunfire. Shrill whistles tear passed the climbers. Several shots miss and explode stones and dust into the air.

"Go!" Loche shouts. He lunges upward and places his body between the gunmen below and Edwin. "Go! Go! Go!" The air crackles.

Through the reports Loche hears George calling, "Gain the top, Loche! Hurry! Watch to the sides! Watch the blindsides!"

"Loche!" Now it is Julia's voice. "Behind you!"

Twisting, Loche sees two men appearing from over the side of the pyramid just below. One is leveling a pistol. In Loche's periphery, the blur of an object streaks. A stone from Julia's hand bounces off of the man's cheekbone. Blood mists. He falls back and tumbles down.

As the next man climbs over the slope edge toward him, Loche unsheathes his sword from his umbrella and charges. His legs welcome the horizontal movement and he feels as if he's flying across the distance. The man draws his gun and brings the barrel up as Loche's blade strikes it aside. The pistol fires into the air and falls, clatters and rolls. The man stumbles backward. He draws a short sword and angles it.

"Truly an honor, Poet," the man says. German accent. His voice is calm but his hand is shaking slightly. "I send word from Albion Ravistelle. Let go, says my *Angofal*, The Painter is gone, and so you should follow. Go willingly, Dr. Newirth. Save us all." Loche watches the man's trembling hand. The *Rathinalya*.

Then from some unknown place in Loche's mind, words form. They take shape with perfect confidence and power, and they rest for a moment in the back of his throat. He feels the resolve of what he is about to say and simultaneously is shocked that it feels right.

"Save you?" he says. "Save you? It was I that made you."

The man rushes and swings his sword to Loche's throat. Loche raises his blade, blocks the attack and takes a backward step up. The man presses and throws to Loche's legs. Loche again bats the advance away and moves horizontally taking a sidelong glance to see where his son and Julia are. They are still climbing, nearing the summit. More gunfire from below. Now *Orathom Wis* and soldiers of the *Endale Gen* are engaged with firearm and sword.

Diverting his attention has given his opponent equal footing. The two now are balanced on the steep incline with swords poised.

The soldier says, "Poet, you may have created me—all of us, but I will now keep you from you *unmaking* us." He thrusts forward, striking Loche's blade to the side. As he extends his arm with lighting speed, Loche feels the tip of the sword puncture his shoulder just below the left clavicle. He exhales. He tastes tin. His vision blurs to a burning red. His sword hand however, instinctually maneuvers low and swoops upward. It connects, piercing beneath the soldier's chin and up through the top of his head. The man's eyes darken and he collapses sidelong, rolling and tearing against the sharp stones.

Loche's pain is intense. He presses his hand to the wound and searches for Edwin. Edwin is nearing the summit. Julia is just behind him. Loche sheathes his sword and attempts to climb to his son, now far above him. The foggy shroud of shock is closing around his vision. He plots his next step, presses, leans forward and steadies himself with his hands. Blood rains on the rock.

When he looks up again Julia and Edwin are standing still, not three meters from the summit. Crowding around the pinnacle are five more *Endale Gen* soldiers armed with firearms and long blades.

"Stay where you are, Dr. Newirth," one of them says. "I send greetings from Albion Ravistelle—"

"Yes," Loche says. "I've heard that already."

The soldier raises his rifle and takes careful aim at Loche's head.

"No!" Julia shouts, lunging toward the gunman. Two soldiers quickly restrain her and force her body to the slope.

Edwin, swivels his little body and calls, "Dad?"

Loche lowers himself to his knees and watches the hand gently squeeze the trigger.

Is it possible?

Is it possible that he hears the snap of the hammer, the explosion of the firing cap—he thinks he can hear the ammunition ring its way through the barrel, its hiss as the cool of the evening air greets it, and the shrill whistle it makes as it launches toward his head. The sound of Edwin crying for him. Could it be possible that he hears the soldier's quiet exhale as the firearm kicks back? The sound of skittering stones to his left— quick footfalls? How could it be believable that he can hear the nauseating pop of punctured flesh, crushed bone.

And then she is there, in his arms. His wife, Helen. She has hurled herself from the pyramid edge to block the assassin's shot. The bullet has exploded her right cheek. Blood stains her white teeth. "Our son," she coughs. "Our son." Her eyes flatten and freeze on the sky.

"Helen!" Loche screams.

Can he hear the air leave her lungs? Even as he watches her consciousness shut down he thinks he hears the rush of a great river. A waterfall. The roar of an ancient defense within the immortal circulatory system. He registers the raging oceanic rush of wave and wind, a white foam collects where the bullet entered. It spreads.

Loche stares, witnessing the rejuvenating powers of his wife's blood seeking to restore her life. But the rising tidal wave of sound heightens. Its volume forces his hands to cover his ears.

As he does this he looks up the slope and realizes from where the sound is emanating. Edwin.

His little boy is standing near the summit's edge. Tears glass his sight. His arms reach helplessly toward his mother. His lips form the longing word, *momma,* over and over, but the only sound is the insidious rise of a towering sea scream, like a god's mighty voice before its raised hand strikes.

Loche's attention darts from his son, to Julia, now curled into a ball on the rocks, her mouth open and screaming—to the *Endale Gen* soldiers, dumbfounded, terror clawing their eyes—to those below, stopped in their fight, cowering together.

Then, silence save Edwin's little voice. He cries one word, "Momma!"

At his word, an explosion of wind and blue light blasts the five soldiers off of the summit like brushing dust from a table. They are pitched out and hurtle down the mountainside. Edwin's knees buckle and he sinks to the stones. The light fades. Julia crawls to him and cries, "Loche!"

Two shots are fired. George calls from below: "Run!" Rocks splinter and ricochet at Loche's feet.

He lowers his face to Helen and kisses her forehead. White foam is closing the grisly wound. He lays her body sloping uphill and grips her hand, "Thank you, wife."

"Loche!" Julia calls again. She is lifting Edwin up into her arms and moving. His shoulder pounds. He clambers. His fingertips bleed. More pops from below. A rattle of gunfire shatters around him.

As he gains the summit, Julia is crouched down holding Edwin. "Now what?" she cries.

Loche drops low and studies the small space. "We need only walk across and speak the *Elliqui* word, *lonwayro.*"

He takes her hand. She stands with Edwin cradled. The boy is weeping.

"Let's go," Loche says.

They take three steps.

Tiris Avu

November 11, this year
Upper Priest Lake, Idaho
12:48am PST

She sees it.

Wyn Avuqua.

Her heart sings the name. As the open Jeep sloshes and slides along muddied pathways, she imagines the polished white brick walls bursting up through the emerald forest veil, terraces draped with heavy ivy and flowering crimson amaranth, and the high silk banners coiling and stretching like green dragons in the air.

"We're passing through *Vifae* quadrant now," Graham tells Astrid. "Of course, you probably knew that." She notes that his voice sounds nervous.

The four Itonalya households, she thinks as her head shakes with marvel. *Vifaetiris*, or House of Wings, covers the western quadrant of the city. Northernmost is the House of Mind or *Keptiris*—east of the Citadel is *Vastiris* the House of Heart, and in the South is the House of Talons, *Shartiris*. *Wyn Avuqua* means: Heaven's Tear, and is thought to symbolize a tear of joy in the eye of *Thi*, the mingling of bliss and pain. The cities name represents the dynamic nature of the human condition—happiness and grief, love and hate, hope and fear—tears of joy. There are perhaps a few scholars, save the half dozen that have studied the *Itonalya,* that would admit *Wyn Avuqua* as the first inspiration to symbols such as the yin and yang or the Greek masks of comedy and tragedy. How will the world respond when they learn that the city exists? Will they believe it? Will they care?

She thinks of her Facebook news feed and how misinformation is mainlined to a meme-hungry population. Will there be an areal photograph of the site with the caption: *Columbus my ass*. Or, in this political climate: *Let's rethink immigration*. Will it matter to anyone that a culture existed here for millenniums? A people that managed to stay hidden? Could such a fantastic thing change the way people see the world. It is certain that this discovery will alter the story of humankind. The question is if anyone will give a shit. But to Astrid, right now, all that matters is she has not been chasing a ghost.

She grins. Partially excavated cobbled streets branch out from a crossing. She imagines the pathways back in the day, inlaid with smooth stones and outlined in moss. She sees herself wandering down into *Vifaetiris* to listen to the musicians and poets. The jeep jostles through a series of deep puddles. Mud spatters the windshield. Her face is misted with brown water. She wipes it away, still grinning.

But even as her attention is magnetized by the passing images of her waking dreams, her wide-eyed excitement is interspersed with looks to her driver, Graham Cremo. *My word he is tall.* She glances back to Molmer behind her. He smiles. Next to him, seated behind Graham, is Marcus Rearden. He appears to be uncomfortable due the lack of leg room. She smiles again, only this time because it is strangely satisfying to know that Rearden is uncomfortable.

The Jeep slithers down an embankment and pitches sideways. Graham easily corrects the direction as if he is driving on ice. He laughs. Astrid grips the door handle and her grin intensifies.

"Goddamn it!" Rearden spits from the back seat. Black, watery mud has splashed his upper body.

Astrid now stares at Graham.

"My apologies, Dr. Rearden," he says looking into the rearview mirror. "This is a messy business. We'll get you cleaned up when we arrive."

To Astrid he says, "Perhaps when we get there we could play a game of *Shtan*."

She smiles at him. "You've found a *Shtan* set?"

Graham laughs, "Many."

"*Shtan*?" Rearden questions. "You found. . ." he breaks off.

Graham glances into the rearview mirror and answers, "*Itonalya* chess, I guess you could say. It is believed that their game of *Shtan* influenced chess."

"Yes. Of course." Rearden says.

"Do you play chess, Doctor?" Graham asks.

Rearden turns his head to the landscape. He does not answer.

Graham turns north. The Jeep clambers over a weedy bank. He points to an obvious structure jutting out from the side of a low hill. "We're on the edge of *Keptiris* now. And there is *Tiris Avu*, House of Seeing." He points.

A chill needles along Astrid's neck. The citadel of *Wyn Avuqua*.

"I can't imagine your excitement right now," Graham says. "In some ways, I'm more excited for you to see this than I was when I uncovered it."

Astrid faces the approaching stronghold—the center piece of her long career—the very fortress that has held her heart through loneliness, divorce and years of what seemed to be meaningless searching. When she turns to Graham, he is smiling at her. She can't decide which dream has come true.

Pyramid G-1b

November 11, this year
Cairo, Egypt
7:45pm EET

A voice echoes in the black—a kind of foreboding narration accompanied by a dramatic music. *"Civilizations are like islands on the ocean of barbarism,"* the Vincent Price delivery resounds. *"Over this one, the Sphinx has gazed and watched for five thousand years. At the foot of such mountains of stone, everything becomes minute and insignificant. Man is an insect."*

Darkness. A sharp pain pulses beneath his punctured shoulder. The air is dry and warm. Edwin is sobbing quietly beside Julia. He is slumped over and cannot seem to raise his head. She stares at him, helplessly. Loche reaches and touches Edwin's hair. The boy's hand grips his father's arm. Loche looks around.

"It's okay. I've got you."

The child is warm.

"Momma. I saw Momma—" his voice is weak.

"I know. I know. She's okay. She's just fine. She just fell down. She told me to tell you that she can't wait to see you soon."

"She's not hurt?"

"No, not at all."

Edwin's breathing slows. "Those men—did I hurt them?"

"I don't know."

"I was scared. And then. . ."

Hollowed shadows well in the boy's eyes. His skin is pale in the dark. Loche lays his palm on the boy's forehead. It is damp with sweat. "Are you feeling okay?" Edwin doesn't answer. His color shifts suddenly to blue and then sickly pale again. Loche blinks.

"I'm so tired, Dad."

Tears burn and streak down. What had he just witnessed there upon Mount Pico? A blinding, blue wave of light and sound exploded from Edwin's forehead sending a shock-wave across the summit. Their attackers were pummeled from the height. The two closest to Edwin—their bodies were blown apart—mists of blood—scattering ripped flesh. Loche's abdomen lurches reliving it. He feels a rush of adrenaline and fear.

Loche gathers what he can from the surrounding sights.

It was just as George explained: *you'll take a step and it will be dark. You will be on pyramid G 1b. Or, on northernmost Queen Hetepheres' tomb, under Great Khufu. Find dark on horizon—north. You go south to Menkaure— maybe fifteen hundred meters south.* Loche's eyes begin to adjust. He rises up and peers out. He quickly finds north by finding the black portion of his three-hundred and sixty degree view: the empty Egyptian desert stretching to the Mediterranean Sea. Rotating right, the bright lights of Cairo spill out to the East. Circling south he can see the length of the Giza plateau. The megalithic stone pyramids of Khufu, Khafre and Menkaure, lit in electric blue, flaming red and shimmering gold, stand like god sentinels guarding the hidden stars behind the inky night. The thudding of his wound pauses. His breathing slows at the sight. His mouth opens, but no words come.

The strange voice on the air continues to speak: "*Their glory has defeated time. Three million blocks of stone, some of them weighing thirty tons. . .*"

Then, Loche understands. Thin streams of laser light flash and blink from a high modern building centered directly east of the Sphinx. It is a laser light show for tourists—the narration, the music, the dramatic lighting. His shoulder hurts again.

"I'm scared, Dad," Edwin murmurs.

Loche kisses his son.

"Are you almost finished with your book?" he asks suddenly.

"I—I'm still working on it. A few more pages to go."

"Are we still writing the good stories, Dad?

"That's all we can do," Loche answers.

"I can't see very good," Edwin says.

"It is dark up here."

"Dad, I think I did hurt those men, but I don't know how."

Loche searches desperately for some answer from the god curtained behind the face of his son. "Are you there? Answer me." Loche whispers.

As if in answer, like a deluge, images flood Loche's mind. A clear path ahead forms. He sees the capping blocks underfoot upon the Menkaure pyramid, the glitter of Cairo sprinkled across the desert, the empty expanse of dark to the West. For a moment he can feel the warm wind fluttering through his jacket from that high place. An overwhelming sense of urgency—*go now—go now.*

"We've got to move," Loche says suddenly. He was aware that the God had spoken, though not in words. Was this *Elliqui*? Loche now knows exactly where he needs to be. There is no question.

He stands. His shoulder burns and he groans.

"We've got to bind the wound," Julia says. Her hands are trembling.

"Can you manage, Julia? The *Rathinalya*—you're shaking."

"I must," she says. "If I stand apart from the two of you it is easier. Your wound. Let me—"

"No. We need to get to Menkaure, there." He points.

"Where are the three *Orathom Wis* that came before us?" Julia asks. Structures, low alleyways and deep pits strobe and flicker from the laser show between their position and the distant pyramid. "There's no sign of them."

"It doesn't matter. If they are out there, they'll have to find us. Let's go. Now!"

"Shouldn't we wait for George and Corey?"

"They know where we are going. We can't stay here. The attack can only mean the *Endale Gen* know where we are." Loche reaches down and lifts his son with his good arm. The child drapes on him like a heavy garment. "Let's go," he says.

Translation

November 11, this year
Upper Priest Lake, Idaho
12:55am PST

"For over a millennia, it was a hill," Graham answers. "Like a giant hand scooped soil and piled it over the higher structures. As I told you, I must have dug into this hill five or six times. But never mind, it's here now. Of course, nearly all the discovered towers have fallen, either during the city's final siege, or over the centuries. We're calling them *under-hill* towers." He points to three earth-moving machines. "Those things have enabled us to dig through time. And that," he points to the upper walls of the center of the ancient city, "that we believe is the center, *Tiris Avu.*"

Astrid stands in the shadow of a structure that had once only existed in her imagination. Despite the backhoe parked a few feet away she can almost place her self back in time. She inhales. The scent of soil and decaying leaves. The air is chilled and still. She scans the toppled stone artifacts here and there in the mud. Several researchers are working in various positions around the outer wall. Out on the periphery surrounding the site is another group entirely. The sight of them makes her uneasy. Then, angry.

"What's with the armed men?" she says pointing. "They look like some hired corporate security force. This is an archeological dig site, not a war zone."

She watches Graham take his own look around. When he returns to her his smile is dark. "The discrepancy of over who owns the site," he says quietly. "Let's not go into it now." Astrid nods and glances back to a black SUV.

Passing beneath the arched doorway she reads the *Elliqui* runes in the stone and translates three lines: *For the love of man / we are the guardians of the dream / we are the Moon children.* Then a phrase she's seen many times. *To defend the starlight life / defend the mortal.*

The courtyard of the house is circular and covers perhaps two acres. In the center rises the *Avu* tower itself, close to three stories. The higher walls are crumbled and uneven. Four staircases coil around the circumference, each leading up just beside an entrance to the tower and also descending underground. There are more carvings and stone decoration. Astrid is astonished at the incredible condition of nearly everything she sees. She reaches out and lets her fingers funnel into the smooth feathers of a sculpted wing. The rock is cool. Her other hand rises to caress a stone heart on the wall just beside it.

"Astrid," Graham says. He is standing at the staircase leading down. He steals a quick look toward the nearest security guard, then back to Astrid. "Of course there is much to see, but what's below is the priority. Let's be quick."

She steps down the ancient slabs of rock. Rearden and Molmer follow behind. They enter a wide tunnel with ribs of solid stone like ancient bones of a massive serpent. Electric bulbs are threaded along the ceiling and the foot path. Light from the entrance disappears. The air thickens. Moisture beads on the walls. Moving steadily down they pass three wide halls. Each are lit and contain several busy technicians.

"How deep does it go?" Astrid asks.

"My favorite question of all," he says. "We're not sure. But we've reason to believe that there's more below Queen Yafarra's tomb. Much more. We've just not gotten that far. We haven't found an entrance to the lower halls, yet. In fact, what you're about to see we found by accident?"

Around a final turn, they arrive at a dead end. Two armed security men stand beside a crack in a stone wall. It appears that the fissure has been chiseled and widened by the archeological team to allow better access. Seeing Graham, one of the security men extends a hand.

"Hello, Dr. Cremo," he says with a smile.

"Hi, Randy," Graham says shaking his hand. "I see they've replaced the lights on the fourth and fifth level."

"Yep," Randy replies with a laugh, "its nice now to see the slippery spots on the steps." He looks over Graham's shoulder.

Graham makes introductions, "Meet Doctors Molmer, Rearden and Finnley."

Randy examines each of their lanyards in turn, taking careful time to match the picture to the face. He does this with solemn professionalism. He studies Astrid a little longer than the others. "Dr. Astrid Finnley, cool. I got one of your books." Astrid smiles. He says to Graham, "Watch the subfloor at grid 3, behind the sarcophagus. They've covered it but there's still a risk of breaking your leg."

"Will do," Graham says and moves to pass inside.

Randy lays a hand on Graham's shoulder and says, "I'll have to call topside—give Eastman a heads up."

"I know."

Randy steps aside and nods to the other guard who is already speaking into the mic at his cheek. "Professor Finnelly has entered the Queen's Chamber, copy?"

"I'm sure *she'll* be right down," Randy adds.

"I'm sure she will," Graham says.

Astrid in the meantime is leaning her body to the right and left trying to get a glimpse of the glowing centerpiece in the chamber.

Graham extends his arm, welcoming Astrid to enter. "Welcome to the *Heron Atheneum*."

Cool air greets her as she moves across through the crack in the wall. The chamber is massive. Astrid rotates her body as she walks and takes in the images of her dreams: A vaulted ceiling filagreed with stone carved leaves glimmering gold. A portrait of the night sky—silver stars twinkle as a backdrop. Within a semicircle balustrade are two stone chairs and a single knee high platform upon which sit ancient stone carved *Shtan* game pieces. It appears that the game was abandoned while still in progress. There is perfectly preserved dark-wood furniture, long tables, hundreds of stacked boxes of various sizes and shapes, a gridded network of shelves that extend and branch into a vast matrix—and upon those shelves are books, books and more books. Some are crumbling, their covers flaking. Others appear untouched by the years.

Graham taps her shoulder. "Take these," he says. He offers her latex gloves. She pulls them on and reaches to one of the nearest volumes and gingerly sets it upon a table. The cover creaks as she opens it. Written in Old English with some scattered *Elliqui,* the author identifies herself as Cecily of the House of Wings. Astrid scans the text and learns that the volume is an account of Cecily's life—her immortal life. Her parentage, conquests, her role in *Itonalya* society, and the deities that she herself hunted and killed while she existed.

Astrid raises up from the page and stares at the seemingly endless shelves of books and scrolls just within reach. Her tears shine as she turns to see an open wood box on the floor nearby. It is filled with swords. The box itself had been wiped clean to expose its shiny, sap treated exterior. The interior is lined with an oiled leather. She had read of myriad *Wyn Avuquain* preservation methods, and she knows these boxes are called *tenesh,* meaning *safe hold.* She points at the weapons. Her mouth open—no words.

"Chamber Guard weapons?" he shrugs. "Many more have been found rotting in the mud up above and other places. These are virtually untouched by time. There is some damage, but the *Itonalya* had a way of extending their immortality to nearly everything they touched." He points to another stack of *tenesh.* "Those are full of royal keepsakes." Again, Astrid wipes at her tears then circles her gaze to the dominant artifact in the center of the chamber. A sarcophagus of frosted crystal quartz appears to glow. Its shape is perfectly rectangular. *Elliqui* runes decorate the outer edges of the lid, though it is difficult to see where the lid and the container join.

Astrid approaches with her arm outstretched. Before she touches it she suddenly pulls back and snaps the latex gloves off —removing the barrier between her and what she's sought for so long to touch. She lets her hand hover over the glowing stone for a moment. She closes her eyes. Then her fingers graze the cool surface and slide across the cut runes.

Of course the remains of the Queen of Immortals would be encased in quartz, she thinks. *Of course.* Somehow the thought had not occurred to her, but now as she stands with her hand resting upon the Queen's final bed, it makes sense. The mythological significance is obvious. Clear quartz was believed by the earliest cultures to be water that was turned to eternal ice by the gods. Both liquid and solid. It was also known as a sun stone that could capture light and emit a spectrum of otherworldly color. Even today, crystal is believed to have both healing and mystical qualities. Astrid opens her eyes and lets the subtle incandescence of the coffin instruct her in yet another aspect of this ancient culture: the remains of beloved Immortals were encased within eternal light, for only darkness is promised to them beyond. She shakes her head.

"So this is our savior, I take it?"

Startled, Astrid turns to see a woman, mid-fifties, glasses, short greying hair with long bangs swooped over her left eye. Her other eye is bright blue. She is long limbed and athletic—dressed in deep grey, similar to the security guards. Despite her smile, her face might look more comfortable with an angry scowl.

Graham starts, nervous, "Miss Eastman, may I introduce —"

Eastman interrupts, "Professor Finnley, nice to meet you, my name is Lynn Eastman, head operator here at this site for Coldwater Security. Graham tells us that you are the one that will save the day."

Astrid stares as if coming out of a dream. Eastman notices.

Three technicians enter the chamber. They wheel a cart of tools, cables and other archeological gear. Four more people enter. All wear lanyards and appear to have some kind of official air about them.

"Not to be irreverent, Dr. Finnley, for I'm sure this is a lifelong dream to be standing in this place, but we have all been waiting on needles and pins since your name drifted into our ears. According to Dr. Molmer and our very own Dr. Cremo, you are the one."

"I'm the one?"

"I haven't had the chance to share everything with her," Cremo says, moving beside Astrid and placing his fingers upon the carved runes. "I'd appreciate a few more minutes of orientation—"

"We've waited for you to assist us in opening the tomb," Eastman says. "And it is time to get on with it."

"You've waited for me?"

Eastman rattles off, "Expert advise. Translation. Your knowledge of this culture. We need as much information as you can give and as quickly as you—"

Graham interjects, "Archeology in some ways can be compared to a kind of crime scene. Every detail counts. Right now, this scene is undisturbed. Of all the uncovered artifacts, this one, as you're well aware, has been said to be the Holy Grail for the *Itonalya*. The tomb, once opened, should be a snapshot of the past unlike anything before it— and we are bound to do this right. You are the best *Elliquist* and *Itonalya* scholar in the world. Your perspective is paramount."

"Scholar. . ." Eastman says derisively. "Such a thing for this subject? I suppose now there is. How wonderful for you Dr. Finnelly. Tell me, what do you expect to find within the tomb? Dr. Cremo has given his estimation. We'd surely like an expert scholar's opinion."

The woman's tone is infuriating, but Astrid is used to such encounters, especially today. Pausing to consider if she should let the militaristic, self righteous nature of Eastman slide, she remembers her humiliating morning, the smug Grant Board, the culmination of her life's work stabbed and deflated by misinformed, administrative types kneeling at the alter of their Alumni sponsors and collective core underwriters. The vultures have lost the ability to reach toward truth. *Easy, easy, I'm just hungry and in no mood,* she thinks. Sweetness is the best approach. Sweetness is best, though she's not at all surprised when she hears herself speak (her tone very much sounding as if she were addressing a student), "Miss Eastman, why so haughty? It would make much more sense if you were asking questions in order to learn the answers."

Silence. The technicians stand still.

Astrid stares at Eastman. She's been here before. How many times has she needed to assert that the data is there—the books are real—the culture existed. The science doesn't lie. "Dr. Cremo," she says without looking away from the woman that she assumes runs five miles a day, drinks strange protein shakes and high maintenance coffee, "I'd like to hear what you think will be inside—then let's compare our expertise, shall we?" She narrows at Eastman, "Or, should we just keep our scholarly thoughts to ourselves and avoid the inconvenience of Miss Eastman having to think?"

Silence.

"Ah," Graham says. "Yes, I mean, no. . ." His inflection begs to ease the tension. "I—I believe we will find what remains of Queen Yafarra. Her skeletal remains—minus her skull. Likely her sword. No garments, of course—the slain Immortal has no need. And, it is rumored, Her Majesty is holding the *Itonalya's* written prophecy of deliverance. She will bear the scroll or book."

Astrid releases Eastman and turns. "The Holy Grail. The Prophecy, I concur. Though I think the document will be contained within *tenesh*."

Eastman waits. Graham points to the carved inscriptions and the embossed Household symbols down the center of the lid: a single eye, a bird's head, a heart, wings and clawing talons. Astrid feels the runes beneath her fingers. To herself, she reads the first line across the head of the tomb. Before she's able to voice her translation, Cremo points to the line.

"But I wonder," he stops her, "If you'll permit me—" his voice oddly enthusiastic, it eases the suspense a little, "to—to take a shot at reading the words? I can't translate them into meaning, but I'd love to try saying them. I've much to learn about *Elliqui*, of course. It would be an honor. I've been practicing."

He points to the first three word phrase, pronounces the words. He does well. She likes him. And he knows his stuff. That does it, she really likes him.

"*Sovereign and eternal sleep,*" Astrid translates. *"Here lies the death that we cannot have."*

Graham continues with half a dozen more lines. Astrid is impressed. The verses deal with the meaning of the Immortal monarchy—and how the tomb imitates mortality, almost yearns for mortal-like death.

"You're doing well," Astrid smiles.

Then Graham pauses, pointing to the last words. He says, "*Rav ea ag dre~shivcy.*"

Astrid is about to shake her head and correct him when Graham holds her eyes and says again, "Excuse me, no, it is indeed this: *Rav ea ag dre~shivcy zish.*"

He is way off. Astrid leans in and reads in silence, pauses, and then in her head, she translates Graham's attempt. A chill runs through her. What he is saying flashes red in her mind. The words mean: *Do not trust east man. We are in danger. Fear.*"

She freezes.

"At least, that's what I know—much still to learn." Then to Astrid, "Tell me if I'm wrong, but those lines mean, *we place our hope in the stars and what is to come.*"

Astrid glances at Molmer and Rearden. They are both curious and waiting for her to pass judgement. Eastman, too, with her arms crossed, waits.

She looks back at the words and nods. "*Lit.*"

Eastman, "*Lit?*"

"*Yes,*" Graham says, "*lit means, yes.*"

Menkaure

November 11, this year
Cairo, Egypt
7:55pm EET

Stairs for giants. The three travelers descend the tall pyramid blocks. Loche figures that it is about a half mile to Menkaure in a straight line, but the way will be blocked with tomb structures, cemetery partitions and walls. Julia suggests going around the dark side of the massive Khufu, but she then decides against it. "We should stay in the shadows, but not leave the light completely," she says. Loche agrees.

As they make their way down, Loche recounts again the reasons for coming here. There are two. First, the anomalous message Julia discovered in Basil's Venetian studio. She told of how Basil had splattered paint upon his walls, and the pattern resembled a constellation that Julia had memorized as a young girl. Below the rendering was a sketch of Elpis, the Greek mythological personification of hope. A spray of paint like a path led to a photograph of the Menkaure pyramid, and tacked underneath was an image of a woman with a pitcher upon her shoulder—Hebe, the goddess of youth. The equation, while rather cryptic and obscure to Corey, Julia found to be simple and completely obvious. She deduced that the accurate depiction of the star pattern was enough to believe that Basil was speaking to her, but with the addition of *hope* (her home was in Hope, Idaho), a picture of the goddess Hebe (the goddess of youth—Julia's name means, youth), all pointing to Menkaure—she felt that without a doubt, Basil was asking her to go to Giza. *Corey Thomas is likely still dubious,* Loche thinks. But Loche is not. Loche had studied the photo that Julia had taken of the studio wall, and there was no doubt that amid all of Basil's seeming chaos, the message was intended.

The second reason: Loche himself had experienced Basil within the painting at *Mel Tiris*. Before they were forced to part ways, the two were near a great pyramid. And now, as Loche's feet touch the sand at the foundation of these godlike megaliths, he is confident that they are moving toward something resembling a resolution. Will Basil be standing atop Menkaure smoking a cigarette and complaining about the pollution disaster that is Cairo? Will they be hurled into the void again only to find themselves at Stonehenge, Machu Picchu or Easter Island?

And maybe now, a third reason: the pyramid's name, Menkaure, and the *Elliqui* word *menkor* share the same pronunciation. Loche wonders if they share the same meaning. The meaning Corey Thomas had shared— *forgotten memory*. Perhaps there is something to remember in all of this. Or, perhaps, something best forgotten.

Drying blood sticks his shirt to the wound in his shoulder. The pain is searing. He can no longer carry Edwin. He sets the boy on his feet and takes his hand. Loche hisses through his teeth. Julia follows a few meters behind.

"Are you okay?" she asks.

"I'm fine," he lies. "It seems that now we're all three afflicted."

They thread through a narrow trench between Khufu on their right and the Queen's tombs on the left. They hear the dramatic narration droning on, but now the language is French.

A modern road is just ahead and then the causeway that connects the Sphinx to the middle pyramid of Khafre. Raising up, he can see to the East a portion of the tourist audience that have gathered for the light show.

"Let's get to the causeway, there," Loche whispers to Julia. "It's not far."

If they run, they might cross the distance unseen. Or at the very least, they will be dashing silhouettes—nothing more than passing shadows.

Julia points to where the land appears to drop. "Let's head there. It looks like a tunnel."

"Good," Loche agrees. "We'll follow you. Ready, Edwin?"

"I'm tired, Dad."

Loche kneels and touches the boy's cheek. "I know, Bug. So am I. But we need to try, okay? Once we stop, we'll have a treat and a rest. How does that sound?"

"I can try," Edwin says.

Julia starts. Loche takes Edwin's hand and the two hurry into the dark. Edwin tries to run. He stumbles and Loche drags him back up and carries him. They reach the road, scurry across and rush toward the sloping section near the causeway's midpoint. Once below the flashing lights they can see a small access tunnel leading through the stone embankment. Julia is already waiting for them, her back to the wall just to the right of the mouth.

Loche lowers Edwin down and sits beside her. She points into the tunnel. A body is lying along one side of the passage. The head is missing. Loche diverts Edwin's eyes.

"It is not *Orathom Wis*," he whispers.

"Dr. Newirth," a voice hisses in the tunnel. Then from out of a shadow one of the *Orathom Wis* soldiers appears and motions for them to join him. The three scuttle inside.

"I am Neil," he says. Green and purple lights flash from the tunnel's opening. "Ah, the netherworld is gathered in the glare. They know you're here. We've retired two of Ravistelle's people. We're not sure how many more have arrived." Neil stares at young Edwin and moves a little apart.

"How did they know?" Loche asks.

"The *omvide* at Mount Pico leads here. Though it is not likely, Ravistelle might not know which pyramid Pico is connected to, but he will know that you're in Egypt. Nearly all *omvide* lead here, for Egypt is a kind of hub to more remote locations in the world. There are over a hundred *omvide* scattered out there in the desert. George got word to us that you were attacked—so Ravistelle knows where you were. It is just a matter of time before the plateau and other pyramid sites will be swarming with *Endale Gen*."

"Where are the others?" Julia asks.

"Alexia is on the other side of the causeway. Gary is further afield, closer to Menkaure." He shakes his head and says to himself, "All the same, we take our chances, laughed at by time." He gestures to Edwin, "When this boy alone, so far from home, arrived here, we shuddered. We could feel his presence. Ravistelle's people, too. Remember, the *Itonalya* hunt gods not only because of our sacred charge, but also to extinguish the stings of *Rathinalya*." He looks at Julia, "How you've managed to stay near him, I cannot fathom. But then, you've not yet tasted the quenching relief of spilling a god's blood. Retiring *Godrethion* eases the chill." He gently touches Julia's forehead. "I pray you shall never have to kill—but if you do, know that the *Rathinalya* will be easier to bear." A sad smile drifts across his face. "Either way, it is the curse of our kind. *Ithic veli agtig.*" His hand moves from her forehead to her wrist. He gives it a friendly squeeze and then crawls a meter or two back to where they entered. He peers out, turns back and says, "But it is not just *Endale Gen* to watch for. The Giza Plateau has quite an efficient and impressive security force of its own. There are at least thirty or more armed men patrolling the site. We will need to move carefully." After a moment, Neil says. "Let's get you into the audience watching the light show. That will be the best way to hide you, and to move you to the southern section of the complex."

"We don't want to endanger innocent people," Loche says.

"Too late for that, I'm afraid. Innocence itself is at risk, good Doctor. But come. I will point you in the right direction."

He leads them east, following the stone wall of the causeway toward the Sphinx. Loche's shoulder burns. He pulls his coat up, hoping to hide the stains of blood.

Crossing the back of a high wall, Neil stops at a corner and nods toward a gathering of some two hundred people. He then gestures to the ancient lion-man towering above. "We marvel after those who sought the wonders of the world," Neil says to himself again. "Go to the gathering and blend in. You'll be safe enough there until we can clear the way forward." He points beyond to a huddle of low structures. "If we do not come, move steadily south and make your way to Menkaure. Stay in the crowd for a few minutes only."

Julia leads the way. The three enter the audience from the North. They step out of the darkness and into a festival environment. Loche takes Edwin's hand and leads him to the center of the commotion.

The program's narration has now shifted to Italian. The soundtrack is loud and distracting.

"Let's get closer to the edge of all of this," Loche says.

Julia nods.

After some polite maneuvering, the trio stand on the southern line of the audience plot. Three sickly trees separate them from the darkness beyond.

Laser light lines suggest the interior halls and chambers of the Great Pyramid in orange and green. Two dimensional hieroglyphic symbols dance like cartoon characters along the base. The music is cheesy.

Loche groans. "If Basil is here somewhere, I hope he can't see this."

"No, I don't think he'd approve," Julia adds.

When all three pyramids are lit from below, Loche tries to judge the distance to Menkaure, now just slightly southwest of their position. His vision blurs. Dizziness. A moment later he is on one knee. A wave of nausea rises and passes. Julia crouches down beside him.

"We should use the leaf," she says.

Loche shakes his head. "No. What if something happens to Edwin. I can manage. I can manage."

She opens his jacket. "You've lost a lot of blood."

"I can make it," Loche says. He pulls his coat tight around his throat when another overwhelming rush of anxiety forces him to his feet. He looks at his wristwatch. "We can't stay here. We've been here too long."

Julia looks around searching for help.

"See that man there," she says, "just outside of the lamplight."

Loche nods.

"He'll lead us," she says.

"What?"

"He's got to be looking for some kind of money making opportunity. Look around at all of these tourists. It wouldn't be the first time he's led tourists out there."

Loche doesn't answer. Behind his closed lids he sees sparks. Julia hands him her water bottle. "Here, drink this and rest a second. I'll be right back."

She approaches the man. Loche can see her talking with her hands and motioning out toward their destination. A moment later, she returns.

"He'll do it."

"What about Neil and the others."

Julia steadies Loche and leads him into the night. "They are out there. But I can't navigate us with you injured. This man will lead us around the Giza security at least."

"Did you get his name?"

"No time."

The moon is a crescent bowl. The four trudge through the cool desert arcing their course wide around tombs and tourist survey points. The pyramids, like planets, swing Loche into their gravitational pull. Everything becomes soundless save the shushing of his feet through the sand and the heaving of his breath. Menkaure is a spike of electric purple and blue beneath the white thorn of the moon. He blinks up at the sight and the pages of some mythological text at his cabin on Priest Lake open before his eyes. He sees his fingers tap at a photograph of the megaliths he is now hurtling toward. Can it be that he is truly here? Edwin is staggering along ahead of him. He can see Julia a few feet away and their mysterious guide—his stride confident and strong. None of this seems real.

As he stumbles and falls, his awareness blackening, he wonders if there are scorpions in the sand.

The Immortal's Deathbed

November 11, this year
Upper Priest Lake, Idaho
1:20pm PST

Steel cables dangle over the crystal. Four metal tongs vice-grip the thin sides of the top like fingers on the lid of a jar. The cables attach the tongs to a loop in the A-frame of the apparatus. An engineer with a goatee motions that he's ready to proceed.

Eastman circles the glass coffin. "Looks good," she says. "Graham?"

Graham is not listening. He inspects a tong connection point. "Mal," he says to the goateed engineer, "can we back this one off slightly and move it to the right maybe three centimeters? I'd hate to see a pressure crack in the crystal."

Mal levels his eyes to where Graham points. "Yes, I see it, too. It'll take a few." He pulls the tension pin and begins to reset.

Over the last half hour Astrid has wandered as far back into the vast library adjacent to the circular tomb as the lights allow. She's explored through aisles of bookshelves, nooks, touched the swords, stared at the ceiling, and has managed to keep from crying as well as ease the pain in her face muscles from grinning too much.

She had said to Graham, "I would love to explore a bit." His response was a near whisper, and another movie line from one of Astrid's top five favorites, *The Princess Bride*). Of course it was delivered just after a moment of electrical eye contact: "As you wish." Heat rose to her cheeks. Graham then added, "Please, don't get lost." But not in a way that sounded as if her getting lost would be inconvenient for him or the technicians. The way he said it sounded as if he would worry if she lost her way. As if he wanted her to stay nearby. Near to him. That is how she wanted to take it, anyway.

And one could get lost in the labyrinth of passages. There are only few florescent work lamps that she can see. The floor to ceiling shelves are packed with elegant leather bound volumes colored in earthen tones, scrolls in cylinder casings, and parchment boxes similar to the *tenesh* designs. Time has tumbled some entire rows. There are areas that have seen some water damage. But for the most part, the chamber is dry, and the mass of the collection is beyond her wildest dreams. She wishes her assistant Marcel could see this. She pulls her phone from her bag —no service. She types a note to him anyway:

Stop whatever you are doing and get up here right now. North of the marshes. Get a boat. Get an ATV. Get a chopper. Whatever you have to do! Use the credit card. When you get here, tell them you're my assistant. NOW! I am not kidding. NOW!

She presses send, drops the phone back into her bag and hopes a single bar might appear to hurl the message out to the nearest tower.

As she turns to find her way back she notes the long carved lines of *Elliqui* runes along the floor, and the image of a bird's talons embossed in the stone. It appears upon every fifth stone over what looks like an entire section. After some time wandering she notices the insignia changes to an embossed heart. It, too, appears upon every five path-stones, outlining what she believes is the near center of the library. The signs must represent the city's Four Household sections, and she assumes if she were to continue on she would find areas exhibiting a bird's wings and eventually, a head.

She reluctantly returns to the others for fear of missing something. She sits in one of the chairs within the *Shtan* game balustrade, watching the technicians check and double check their decisions. Rearden and Molmer are speaking together. From time to time, Astrid has caught Rearden seeking her out. She's now openly scowling back at him. It doesn't appear to phase him. Her feet are sore. She's hungry—forgot to eat. *Good,* she thinks, *that's good, maybe try the same thing tomorrow.*

"*Shtan,*" Rearden's voice says as he approaches the game table. His focus is riveted to the game pieces. "So I am to understand *shtan* influenced chess, yes?" He sits across from her.

"That is correct," Astrid replies. "Well, more accurately, the Chinese game Igo or go first, then chess—but yes."

His long, bony fingers lift a black pyramid from the board. "You know, Loche Newirth and I often played chess. We have had games in progress for over five years." He turns the game piece over in his hands. On the bottom of the pyramid is an engraved eye. "Ah," he says noting it, "Godsight. Am I right? The pyramids eventually became the pawns for Chess?"

"Yes," Astrid says. "But in Shtan, when the pyramid crosses the centerline on the board, they can move and kill in any direction."

"Like a king in chess. . ."

"Yes."

He holds up the pyramid between them. "Remarkable how the *Itonalya* used pyramids."

"Haven't we gone over this?" Astrid says with some irritation.

"Indeed," Rearden replies. "But I have been fascinated with the idea for some time now—well, in truth, over the last couple of weeks. I've done my share of research in order to learn everything I can about how I might bring Loche Newirth to justice. Call it knowing your opponent. What do you know about the pyramids at the Giza plateau?"

"I've been there," she answers.

"You must have read about Menkaure."

Astrid watches how the psychologist rotates the pyramid in his hand over the board as if he is considering a move during a game. Tiny blue veins bulge along his exposed wrist.

"Menkaure has its share of mystery to the *Itonalya*, it is said."

"Forgotten memory. . ." Rearden says. "That's what it means in *Elliqui*, does it not?

Astrid blinks hard. "That is correct," she tells him. "How did you know that?"

"As I've said, Professor, I've done some research myself. I've read that strange things have happened over the apex of that pyramid."

"So they say," Astrid responds blithely.

The sound of a machine winding up draws Astrid to her feet. She steps toward Graham Cremo as he glides his hand along a steel cable. He crouches down beside the tomb and studies the pressure points of the device. With his long legs bent and his torso taut, he looks like a frog. A cute frog, of course, about to leap. Cremo twists his head toward her and meets her eyes. He does not smile. *It is as if he's attempting true Elliqui,* Astrid thinks—*attempting to add more to his frightening translation. What danger? Why?* He points his focus back to the cable.

"I think that's it, Mal. What do you say?"

Mal nods. "I would think so." Mal looks for the wench operator's acknowledgement. He gives a thumbs up.

Cremo rises, moves back, and surveys with his hands on his hips and his head swiveling, pausing momentarily on each connection, cable and pulley.

"Professor Finnelly," Graham says turning.

Astrid joins him. His terrifying warning is gone from his face. All she sees now is hope.

"We're ready," he says. "Are you ready?"

Astrid casts a glance around. Her focus lingers a second longer on Eastman and Rearden, then back to Graham. She shakes her head, wanting to plead for a few moments alone with him—to find out the danger. But she knows it is impossible right now.

She wants to answer him with, *I've come this far—what will come, will come.* She squints. Too cryptic. "I'm ready, if you are." *That's better*, she thinks.

Graham nods at Mal. Mal and the wench tech start the machine. The two affix surgical masks. The gathered technicians and witnesses do the same. Molmer, Rearden and Astrid are quickly given masks. Astrid places hers over her face and moves nearer the coffin.

The cables tighten. Along the lid the steel tongs engage and squeeze. There is a slight crackle as the top of the tomb gently moves upward.

Graham lets out the perfectly delivered quote, "Open the pod bay doors, Hal."

Mal laughs with his eyes tracking from the cables to the machine's instruments. "Love that flick," he says. He quietly sings, "Daisy, Daisy, give me your answer do. I'm half crazy all for the love of you. . ."

Graham bends forward with his hands lying flat on the slab. "Good. Nice and easy. Nice and easy."

A rising pitch in the wench's motor suggests the weight is substantial. The cables are now fully taut and vibrate like a stringed instrument. Mal falls silent. The lid gently raises a centimeter.

"Here she comes. Keep it steady."

Two, three, four centimeters. A hiss of air pressure and a light, white vapor lingers from the fissure. Graham steps back. The scent is unmistakeable, even through the mask. It is similar to summer rain on rock. *Petrichor*, Astrid thinks. *How fittingly mythological*, she smiles knowing that petrichor's root meaning is stone fluid, or better, the blood of the gods.

The lid now clears the edges. Graham and Mal hoist the A-framed arm and rotate the suspended lid to the right exposing a rectangle of hazy vapor, like dry ice in water.

Graham stands motionless beside the open tomb and stares down into the white fume. Slowly it dissipates and mingles with the chamber air. Barely audible, Graham's voice is whispering, "Oh God. Oh God. Oh God." Astrid sees it, too. Unconsciously she reaches for Graham's hand.

In the mist is something that Astrid might have conceived of as possible, that is if her scholarly, academic mind would allow for such a reach. Of course the *Itonalya* were said to have been graced and cursed with the blood of the gods—a blood that sustains an immortal body—an immortal life. Astrid has tried in vain to empathize with the *Wyn Avuquain* metaphorical notion of long life, great joys, countless grief and anguish. Even the phrase *ithic veli agtig*, or *why does my death delay?* haunts her. Why one would want death to come, and yet, after so much time, it makes some sense how such a fate, an end, death could be lusted after— but this—this is the ultimate horror. Before her is a torture she can only blink at and search for meaning.

Encased within the tomb is a fair skinned, green eyed woman, a sword at her side, a crown upon her head and a *tenesh* at her feet. She is nude. Her hands are balled into fists, her eyes thrown open like lit windows at night. Golden hair is matted caked to her cheeks and shoulders. Her face is beautiful despite the terror and sorrow seated there. She has been encased there for over a thousand years.

Graham does not hesitate to touch the woman's brow.

"Oh God. . . she's warm. Jesus Christ, she's alive."

Menkaure #2

November 11, this year
Cairo, Egypt
7:15pm EET

"I've got you. Stay! Stay! Stay! Loche!" It is Julia's voice.

A blurry speck of light sharpens into a thorn of white in the Egyptian sky. Edwin's face is crowned with stars. He feels pressure on his shoulder, but no pain. To his left, Julia has both palms bearing down upon him.

"What—what are you doing?"

"You fainted," she says.

"Yjb 'an nasrae," a voice says.

"Who's there? Where—where are we?"

"That's our guide, just ahead," she replies. "I think he wants us to hurry."

Memories, like heavy stones, tumble into his mind: *Giza, desert sand, pyramids, must escape, Menkaure. . .*

"Are you alright, Edwin?"

The child does not answer.

Julia says, "He's very tired." She slowly lets her hands ease the pressure, "How's your shoulder?"

There is no sensation save a slight tingling. He moves to touch the puncture but finds nothing there but dried, flaking blood.

"I had no choice—I used the leaf, Loche. I used your father's leaf to heal you."

The pain is gone. "So it is true? The leaves can heal."

"Yes," she says. "It was—it was amazing. Just ama—"

"Yjb 'an nasrae," the guide hisses. "Yjb 'an nasrae!"

"Can you walk?" Julia asks. "We've got to go."

Loche sits up from the sand. Energy surges through his limbs. He blinks. Hopeful. Powerful. "I can," he says.

Julia starts to repack the strewn contents of Loche's bag. The Red Notebook, water bottle and other items she gathers out of the sand and secures them inside. She places the strap back over Loche's head and motions to the guide who is crouching a few meters away in the dark. "After you."

On the verge of sleep, Edwin staggers. Loche lifts him onto his back for a piggyback ride. "Not long now, Bug."

The guide ducks low and runs. Julia, Loche and Edwin follow. The cold desert air tastes sweet. Jutting out and circling, the lights of Cairo and the laser light show fade. With each footfall forward the stars above seem to pierce and rend the black sky deeper.

"Look," says Julia through running gasps.

"I see it." Above Menkaure, like a splashed mist of silver paint, the trail of Julia's constellation hovers over the apex. The lucida appears to blink—but only when it is positioned in one's periphery.

He can hear Julia singing, breathy and quiet. "Just find that single star and watch it blink. . ."

Their guide takes a sharper turn now, his course circling back toward the dark side of the approaching pyramid. "No guard," he says. "No guard here. Come."

And no sign of Neil, Alexia and Gary. Loche searches the thick dark but can see nothing but a black horizon, and a blacker, approaching triangular colossus.

At the base the stones are waist-high. The climb will be tough. And long. The peak disappears into the cosmos. Stepping between Loche and the pyramid, the guide motions to the rising stairway to the stars. He points to his open palm. It is difficult to see the man's facial expression in the dark, but after a moment, Loche understands.

"Of course," Loche says, "payment." Loche sets Edwin on the pyramid edge and rummages in his bag for the wallet that Corey gave him. His fingers brush over the Red Notebook, the energy bars and other items, but no wallet. "It's not here," he says.

"I hope it made it back into the bag," Julia says. "It may be in the sand where you fell—"

The absurd notion of money at this moment wrinkles along Loche's forehead. Finding nothing, he pulls his hands from the bag, unbuckles his wristwatch, passes it to the guide and shrugs. "It's all we have," he says.

The guide takes the watch, holds it close to his face and examines it. After a few moments he whispers, "Marr." With a glance to the apex, to Loche's face and then to the timepiece again, he says, "So be it. Shukraan." Then he waves and points upward, "Eajil. Tslq. Tasalluq Alan."

Loche turns and lifts Edwin atop the first block. He and Julia climb up beside him. Looking back, their guide is gone.

"I guess the watch was enough."

"Hopefully," Julia says. "Hopefully it didn't insult him and he's off to find security."

"Let's not wait to find out."

Julia scrutinizes the steep rise. "Here we go again."

Edwin begins to cry after they manage clambering over some thirty blocks. "I'm tired, Dad. I want to sleep. I want to sleep."

Loche holds him and kisses his forehead—it tastes like dust and salt. "It won't be long now. Let's have a snack and see how we feel, okay?"

Julia is already handing Loche an opened energy bar and her water bottle. "Chocolate, peanut butter," she tells Edwin. The boy takes the bar and bites into it. His tears subside as he eats.

Loche feels Julia's hand caress his back.

"You okay?" she says.

"I feel strangely alert. It must be the properties of the leaf." As he speaks he scans below. Nothing. A welcome breeze flutters into his open coat.

"Well, like Edwin, I could use some sleep, too."

"It's been a long day," Loche says. "We're at the halfway point by the look of it."

"Then what?" Julia asks. "Somehow I don't think we're going to find Basil sitting up there."

"I think you're right," Loche agrees. "But then, stranger things have happened."

"And I know we shouldn't celebrate just yet, but there's been no sign of Albion's people—no security either."

From below, Loche hears a whisper, "Dr. Newirth?" It is a woman's voice.

As Loche whirls toward the sound. His sword rings from the umbrella sheath.

"Fear me not, Dr. Newirth. I am Alexia Lerxt, *Orathom Wis*."

Relieved, Loche raises his hand and waves. He's unsure if the shrouded voice waves back.

"Gary and Neil are scaling the opposite faces. It is safe above. Proceed at will. But do hurry. We have eliminated three *Endale Gen*. Gary has spied seven more approaching from the North. We must hold the way. You must cross the apex before us. We will follow, if we are able, after tea."

Turning, his little boy is staring up toward the apex tracing the cluster of crowning stars. Loche says, "Are you ready?"

The boy god in his mind:

—*A thousand poems with each step.*

The words come, soundlessly. Loche has trouble distinguishing if he indeed heard something or if he simply understood—a bridge between words and simple knowing.

—*That is why we come. That is why we die.*

Edwin's little face is now tranquil. Loche wonders at him.

—*You remember me, do you not?*

His son's visage transforms into the deity at the Center of Basil's painting. Loche's mouth begins to reply but feels the answer lift out of a thought:

—*I do. What of my son, Edwin?*

—*We are here.*

—*Leave my son! Leave him be!*

—*Your son, like all sons, like all daughters, children, are heaven on Earth. I exist with them.*

—*Leave him with me!*

—*Not yet. We must end what you have begun. When it is done, we shall part.*

—*When what is done?*

—*Cross the omvide.*

Edwin begins to cry again. "I want to sleep, Dad."

—*Cross the omvide,* the thought forms.

"Come on," he says lifting Edwin and lunging higher.

"Are you alright?" Julia asks.

Loche does not answer.

Fifteen minutes later Loche, Julia and Edwin stand a stone below the Menkaure *omvide* summit.

"Of all the pyramids, this is the one with no recorded destination, and a lengthy missing person's list," Julia says. "And Basil wanted us to come here."

"The big, deep heavy," Loche offers.

She smiles and looks skyward to her constellation. "At least the stars are familiar." Their light is so clear, so close, Loche thinks that if he reached up he might pluck one from the night. With Edwin between them, the three hold hands, step to the top and start across.

"*Lonwayro.*"

The air sweetens.

God Save the Queen

November 11, this year
Upper Priest Lake, Idaho
1:50 pm PST

Marcus Rearden's words are like a fracture. "So much for your metaphorical immortality, Dr. Finnelly." There is a trace of mocking laughter in his voice.

Astrid cannot understand. She's forgotten to breathe, and realizing the fact, she gasps. Her hand covers over the mask—over her open mouth.

"Get a medic in here, now!" someone says.

A white-coated tech lifts a radio and makes the call.

Graham's fingers search for further signs of life. The Queen of the Immortals lies silent, stoic and wide-eyed within a coffin of crystal. Alive.

"Mal, let's get the *tenesh* and the sword out of the way." Two technicians approach. Mal moves to Graham's left and pauses a moment. The wooden sap covered *tenesh* measures roughly a single square foot, maybe six inches deep. A metal handle is bolted to its top, the cruciform sword is unsheathed, and there are darkened patches of oxidation along the fuller. Lacey veins of blue and green patina stretch the length of the blade while the cross guard and pommel are both blackened steel. Engraved into the heavy cylinder of the pommel is a solitary eye. "Careful," Graham says, "it's still quite sharp."

A leather skin still clings to the hilt. Mal's gloved hands hover over it. "Why do I sense that I shouldn't touch this?"

"I was thinking the same thing," Graham agrees.

Astrid searches the sarcophagus for more signs, more runes—perhaps a warning. "Wait," she cries. Mal's hands jerk away, suddenly.

"There," she points.

Queen Yafarra's right hand is lying just below the sword's black cross guard, against the razored edge. *Is it moving?* Graham thinks as he lowers down to inspect it. Her hand is still. However, a small, carmine wound is sliced into her skin. Tiny red beads are forming at the wound's center, along with strange, whitish rings surrounding them.

"Mal," Graham says, "let's take the sword. Nice and easy."

Reluctantly, Mal lowers his hands again and nudges his fingers beneath the hilt.

Lynn Eastman's voice is heard, "Assist him," she says. One of her security officers positions himself beside Mal and reaches to the blade. The moment his fingers touch the steel, several things happen at once.

Yafarra screams. Her fisted left arm catapults out of the quartz and smashes into Mal's chest. Her leg rises, kneeing the security officer in the chin. There is a nauseating crack as his head ratchets too far to one side. Both men fall away. Graham presses both of her shoulders back into the coffin, as he advises, "Easy! Easy!"

Astrid rushes to the coffin. She rips her mask off and cries, "*Ag shivcy. Ag shivcy. Fenor. Fenor.*"

Yafarra's impossibly green eyes latch on Astrid for a moment, but a moment only. With a vicious nod her forehead knocks against Graham's cheek. The blow sends him back a pace. Yafarra's knees rise. She kicks toward the ceiling and her body vaults forward and out of the coffin— her sword whistles into her grip. Her other hand grips the metal handle of the *tenesh*. As her feet touch the stone floor, she wobbles and stumbles.

"*Ulk! Valso!*" the Queen of Immortals says. She raises the blade in defense. "*Ulk! Valso!*" rattles from her throat, like pebbles in a box. She searches the faces surrounding her.

Astrid says, "*Song, fenor.*"

Tears appear in Yafarra's eyes. When her circling scan lands on Marcus Rearden, she cries out, "*Ag nesh! Ag nesh!*"

Rearden pales.

Yafarra reaches one hand toward the psychologist, "*Diloy veli. Rathche, chalfea shawis.*"

He freezes. "I—I don't know what she wants."

Astrid moves between them facing the Queen. "*Fenor,*" she says gently. "*Fenor.*" She lowers her eyes and stares at Yafarra's feet. "*Fenor,*" she repeats. "Peace, peace, peace."

"What did she say?" Rearden begs.

Without turning Astrid answers, "She is speaking to you. She said, '*It is not safe here. Come to me, family. Protect the crown and Queen.*'"

Rearden gasps, "Why me?"

"I don't know," Astrid replies calmly—her eyes averted.

Frantic, Yafarra's face twists with panic, "*Thi gzate,* Iteav! *Ne!* Iteav!"

"Astrid?" Graham asks, "What now?"

"Her son," she translates. "Her son, Iteav. She wants her son."

"Aethur! Aethur! *Ne. Ne.*"

"She now calls for someone called Aethur. *Find Aethur,* she says.

"Tell her to stand down!" Eastman says.

Astrid replies, "We might deflate this situation if we all take a knee and show her there is no threat. We are in the presence of a Queen, don't forget. We're in her city."

Holding a hand to his bruised cheek, Graham removes his mask, joins Astrid and lowers himself to his knees. Astrid follows.

"Everyone! Now!" he says.

"*Fenor,*" Astrid breathes out as she bows down.

One by one they lower themselves and wait.

Only a few remain standing—Lynn Eastman and her Coldwater security team.

"Eastman," Graham growls, "now is not a time to flex your—"

"You do your job, I'll do mine," she interrupts with gentle precision. "She may have been a Queen once—but now she threatens the safety of all within this chamber. I am tasked with protecting not only you, Professor, but everyone here. Tell her to drop the sword and the *tenesh*." Astrid watches Eastman's hand move to her holstered pistol.

"Miss Eastman, please. Yafarra's culture is civilized beyond—"

"Professor, do as I ask."

The calm in Eastman's voice is maddening.

Twenty heart beats pulse in Astrid's ears.

"Tell her to drop her sword, or I will make her drop it."

Yafarra is listening and watching as the two converse, skeptical of the group still standing. Particularly the woman.

"I will try, but I don't think—"

"She will drop it one way or another," Eastman states.

Astrid raises her face to Yafarra. "*Lain, O chalfea, Yafarra. Thi Astrid Finnley. Fenor. Ag zish. Tengnen lifoth. Uta nesh. Uta nesh tengnen.*"

"What did you say?" Eastman demands.

"I said polite things," Astrid answers.

"What did you say?"

"I introduced myself. Offered greetings to her Majesty. Assured her there is nothing to fear. I then asked her to offer her sword and the *tenesh*."

Astrid's gaze drifts to the floor, stunned that she has just introduced herself to *the* Queen Yafarra of *Wyn Avuqua*. Never in her wildest dreams had such a thought crossed her mind. And if the notion had occurred to her, it certainly did not include kneeling before Yafarra in a sacrificial, beheading position. *Sweet Christ,* she thinks, *I've just asked a royal daughter of immortal blood, after being buried alive for over a thousand years, to give up her sword while she is surrounded by a host of strangers with masks— and she's naked. Oh Christ.*

Astrid says quickly, "*Menoth usag ag arch.*" She bows lower.

"What was that last piece?" Eastman snorts.

Astrid replies, "Forgive the idiots still standing."

Imaginings

Place and time unknown

Loche Newirth remembers the first time he saw Julia Iris. It was at the Floating Hope restaurant while he waited for Basil to join him. He was seated at the counter. She was serving. It was just days ago.

Of course, the experience was imagined.

It is strange to think of the traits that attract one person to another, especially now while peering into a colorless mist of impenetrable fog atop what he assumes is another pyramid far from Menkaure. He looks to his right and sees Julia crouched down beside him. Edwin is dozing, leaning against her. She meets his gaze. He remembers again the moment she turned and said her first word to him, "Coffee?" Certainly, her beauty arrested his breath. Her smile shot a volt of electricity through his senses. The rawest form of attraction. But there was something more. A familiarity. A trust. As if he'd known her for his entire life. Perhaps somehow, he did.

Of course, the experience was imagined.

She moved with confidence. Thinking back, Loche pictures her gliding from table to table—professional attire with a hint of sensual grace, elegant poise and a way of bringing comfort to everyone in the room. It made sense when she revealed that she owned the boat. The memory is a delight.

Of course, the experience was imagined.

Julia represents a number of firsts for Loche Newirth. She was the first to make the world around him disappear. Even now, her nearness can eclipse the horrors encircling their every move. He thought he had felt love for his wife, Helen, but upon meeting Julia, love had been totally redefined. *Quite likely,* he thinks. The first time he'd felt it. Never before had he experienced anyone or anything to cause him to question his marriage. Julia was the first.

Of course, the experience was imagined.

But how could the taste of her skin linger? The joy in her voice still lilt in his ears? The depth and breadth of her past life be as real as his own? He introduced her on paper in a few short sentences—that was all. There was no mention of her upbringing, or how her own choices through the years forged the woman she had become. Julia had her own memories. Her own light. A thousand untold stories she'll never tell a soul.

Loche may have imagined her—wished her to life, but that was all. Julia's life was hers.

"Julia?" Loche says. "Are you there?"

She is staring at him. "Of course," she answers. "I'm right here."

He kisses her.

"Can you imagine," he asks, "when this is all over, what it will be like for you and me to wake up together in, say. . . a bed? Maybe it will be midmorning and raining outside."

"I would love that," she says. "Maybe it will be foggy."

Loche searches the nebulous white around them for some landmark. "Let's start down and find a place to rest."

Somewhere out there in the fog, they are being hunted.

As soon as he secures Edwin in his arms, the little boy falls asleep. They descend slowly. The pyramid steps are steep and smaller than the Egyptian blocks.

This experience is not imagined.

Julia is beside him. He knows her. Not everything, but he knows her. They move together. Down and down. Step by step.

"Do you feel it?" Julia says. "It feels like—

"Like home?"

"Weird," she says.

A slight breeze unveils the tops of evergreens.

A section of flat stones juts out and away from the slant of the pyramid and they walk along the smooth path for another few meters. The air is cool. More spikes of cedar and bull pine appear. After a few more strides, a drop off to a blurry haze stops them at an edge. They look for another route when, like lace blown from a window, the veil peels back revealing a crystal blue lake. Slanted light angles and sits on the shoulders of southwestern hills. Loche follows the line of surrounding mountains and ridges. He scans the shape of the shoreline. He inhales the sweet decay of maple leaves, and the moisture rising from sun on moss in the cracks of rock at his feet.

His heart nearly bursts. Another kind of love. *This is—it must be—home.*

He looks to Julia. She is searching the sky and the shores.

"I'm not seeing things, am I?" Julia questions. "This is the upper lake, right?"

Upper Priest Lake.

Imagined or not, Loche knows this place. Julia knows this place. Imagined or not, they feel for the first time they have an advantage over their pursuers.

But before Loche can puzzle out an answer to her question, he surveys their exact position. Directly across the lake is a nook he's stared at for years. He traces a line back to his feet and stares down for a moment—the sheer cliff face—a drop of some fifty or more feet.

"This is where I fell," he says almost inaudibly. He shudders. "This is the cliff I fell from, but something is—something is different." His joy at being home darkens as he turns and looks back.

A massive, perfectly symmetrical pyramid rises from out of the hillside. The stones are a frosted white—a kind of quartz. They are standing on a kind of foot bridge from the pyramid center.

"Where are we?" Julia gasps, taking in the anomalous structure rooted beside an Idaho lake.

Loche feels his head crook to one side.

"Not where are we?" he says, "Maybe we should be asking, when are we?"

The Risen Past

November 11, this year
Upper Priest Lake, Idaho
2:07 pm PST

Yafarra's eyes lock on Eastman. As Astrid counts the thud of heart beats in her ears, the Queen seems to grow in stature. Washes of pink have now risen to her cheeks. Vigor and strength ridge-line her biceps—her stance is balanced and poised to attack. Moment by moment, she regains vitality. Noble defiance defines her face. She glares across the bowed gathering to Coldwater's head of security.

"I don't think she's going to lower her sword," Astrid says still bowing, her voice calm and low. "Eastman, you must understand, force is not the answer here. Try to understand the difference between your job and paycheck versus the mindset of an undying, ruling monarch of armies that destroy gods."

Eastman draws her pistol. "That was then, this is now. Last chance, Professor."

Astrid, with as much humility as she can pack into the tone of her voice, "*Lifoth tengnen.*"

Yafarra remains poised and focused on Eastman.

In Astrid's periphery, two security men come into view and move steadily toward Yafarra. One carries a police baton, the other produces a taser. Yafarra's eyes snap to their approach, to their weapons, to Astrid, to Rearden and back to Eastman's pistol. Astrid senses more security officers moving into positions behind her and Graham.

"Eastman," Astrid pleads, "your men are in danger."

"I don't think so," Eastman says. Again, her calm demeanor is infuriating. "Never bring a knife to a gun fi—"

Before Eastman finishes, before the officers behind Astrid find their positions, before the two nearest security men reach Yafarra, the man holding the taser is screaming. Still gripping the taser, his severed hands clop to the floor followed by a splash of blood. Yafarra's sword, in a continuing whirl, flips around and gyres upward, slicing into the baton in the other officer's hand. It dislodges and twirls into the air. The Queen takes a step and kicks the stunned man's forward knee. There is a gruesome snap as he topples over, and the clatter of a pistol hitting the floor and skittering away. His scream joins the chorus. With one hand gripping both the sword hilt and the *tenesh* handle, she catches the baton with her other hand, spins to the left and hurls it at Eastman's pistol. Eastman manages to discharge the weapon before it is knocked from her grip.

A bullet tears through Yafarra's chest just above her right breast. A spray of crimson jettisons from her back and splatters the wall behind her. She falters but keeps her balance. Her free hand slaps to the wound and presses, the other grips the sword and the *tenesh*. Without a pause, her body vaults—blurs. Yafarra's voice is heard calling "Astrid, *avu! Avu!*" as she disappears in the shadows between the bookshelves.

Pocket Diary Entry # 4

Unknown
(Loche Newirth's pocket diary)

Here's a first.
I do not know the time.
I do not know the date.
I do not know the time of day.
But strangely, I think I know where we are. Edwin, Julia and I-we are at Priest Lake. The ridge lines and my gut tell me. Even the scent of the air brings a memory of home. But knowing where we are does not help me to decide where to go.

I am not sure why I am making an attempt at putting words down. Habit, likely. So much has happened I can't seem to make sense of any of it. We're healthy and alive.
> *The stars are bright—*
> *EDWIN.*
I cannot control what is happening. The pithy phrase, "Do not worry about what you cannot control," comes to mind. Who was the first to tell me that? Rearden? Ironic? But knowing that our current state has come from my "story"—a story that I thought was in my control. . . and now I'm a character. What now?
> *Maybe it means that a character in a novel should attempt to control the story.*
> *Isn't that what should happen—to make a good story?*
> *Trouble is, this is no fucking novel.*

A Far Country

Date unknown
The Realm of Wyn Avuqua

The wash of the Milky Way cascades across the center of night. In spite of Loche's fear of the ocean, the idea of mariners steering by the stars has always fascinated him—that patterns of glitter suspended in the dark could direct a lonely traveler's course—that connect the dot gods pointed the way home, or to fortune, or to doom. Loche looks up from his pocket diary and wishes he had studied the sky more often. There is a calendar up there, for those who can read it. A compass. A trillion eyes. Infinite words. The stars have always told stories—pointed the way.

Beneath a sprawling cedar tree, Edwin sleeps in Loche's lap. His breathing is abnormal. Julia attempts to cuddle next to the child, sharing the shiny chrome emergency blanket. She is fidgeting. "The *Rathinalya* is easier to handle when he sleeps." she says. There has been no more communication from the god hiding behind Edwin's face.

A small wood fire hisses and crackles at their feet. Loche holds a half eaten energy bar. Blueberry, by the smell of it. Edwin managed a few bites before his eyes fell shut again. He packs it back into his satchel. He feels the ringed spiral of the Red Notebook buried at the bottom.

He shivers. "Must be fall," Loche says, his voice hushed. Every sound seems to disturb the deep quiet of the woods. "But I can't say for sure what month—or year. Judging from what I know of this place, my guess is late October or November. There are still leaves clinging to branches." His breath steams, "Winter is coming."

"I'm not a fan, please don't say that," Julia says. She shivers and points. "I've only been on Upper Priest twice, and both times I imagined a pyramid could have stood there, long ago." She points to the place where they arrived, now a half a mile south, across a shallow bay. The thing is set like a jewel. "But we're in Idaho— a pyramid, here? Who would have thought of such a thing?"

"Well," Loche replies, "I've thought such things. I've written such things." He senses Julia turning her face to him. "I gave Upper Priest a fictional past. In the Journal I wrote of *Wyn Avuqua*— not in great detail, but I thought long and hard about the city. I saw it in my mind's eye. I even sketched it a few times." He nods to the surreal site across the bay, "My imagination put a pyramid there. And there is another one a little farther north. I'm glad to hear you thought that the hill had a pyramidal quality—glad I wasn't the first to imagine such things." He thinks a moment. "It is just as I envisioned you, Julia —I only conceived pieces and parts. *You* made up the whole— filled in the reality. It appears that my version of *Wyn Avuqua* and the culture therein has done the same thing.

"I'm beginning to recall a lot of things that I couldn't before. *Elliqui,* for example. I had much of the foundation for the language in some of my notebooks from years ago. The day I realized its rightful place was when I wrote the Journal. It made sense somehow. The ways of the *Itonalya* haunt me. I'm fascinated with the way they view the world. Life."

Julia laughs lightly, "Your imagined culture with an imagined past that you created—and you were fascinated with them before they were real. And now it's all. . ." She shakes her head, "I don't think I have the right comeback for you."

"I don't think there is a proper comeback," Loche sadly smiles.

"What made you want to create them?"

Loche feels a sudden dread. He answers, "Ultimately, I wrote the Journal to fool Marcus Rearden. I wrote it all to fool him into believing I was either crazy or enlightened. I wrote it to capture him. I used my old writings and imaginings as background. It appears that the power of well aimed delusion and fiction can fool and capture even the most brazen of intellectuals," he laughs sadly. "Validation, I suppose, for any worthy, up and coming mythological prophet.

"However, the *Itonalya* were inspired mostly by talking with a client of mine, William Greenhame. At the time, before my near drowning incident, William was mentally ill. I had diagnosed him with several disorders—I worried about him—but most of all, I enjoyed listening to him. Despite his wild claims of immortality and what I believed to be a made up British background, much of his philosophy made sense."

"How so?"

"Not to sound naive or reductive, but William would say things like, *'Take love, dear Doctor. Imagine love that lasted not a mere lifetime, but for an age of the earth. Imagine if we loved without the fear of death.'* He believes that eventually the world would spread love to all. It is proper evolution, he would say. By removing death and fear, the world would learn that love is all. Then he had this little rhyme, *'Love each other, love the land, the sky and the sea, love the differences we have.'*"

"That doesn't sound crazy," Julia says. "It sounds like a John Lennon song."

Loche laughs again. "William told me he knew John Lennon."

"Really?" Julia says.

"Really." Loche smiles again. "I didn't believe him then, of course." He adds, "William said that Lennon's story is better than Lennon himself. I suppose that's not an unusual thing.

A few seconds of silence pass.

"Albion knows Jimmy page," Julia says.

"Really?" Loche asks absently.

"Yes."

"Cool."

The fire snaps. With his free hand, Loche throws more dead branches on the blaze.

"William's claim of immortality was outlandish to me— And though idealistic, his logic seemed plausible. That is, if we did not die, and our bodies carried us through the centuries physically healthy, it raises the questions: would we carry on with the way things are now if we could escape old age—death? Would money still be the great motivator? Would we make war? Would we allow some parts of the world to starve while allowing others to destroy ecosystems? Eventually, as William emphasized, 'Love is real—everything else is a dream.'"

"But isn't that Albion Ravistelle's utopian vision?"

Loche nods mournfully. "Well, it's the vision I gave him. In the Journal, Albion was simply a misguided villain. But then, I began to agree with him—his desire to heal the world. He promised me my own impossible dream."

"What is that?"

"To heal the condition of being human. To end suffering. In the Journal I even made a sort of blood brother pact with him. It wasn't until I realized that Albion's role was that of a catalyst, a psychically violent one, that I stopped what I had begun."

Julia shivers. "Maybe you were the catalyst."

Could it be? Loche wonders. His fiction has changed everything. It wasn't Albion, William, Nicolas Cythe or Julia, or his characters that brought him to this moment. He was the prime mover. He wrote the story.

"I suppose I was," Loche agrees. "But now I feel like I'm a character."

Julia shivers and nuzzles closer to Loche. "Me, too," she says. Her fingers squeeze the dangling key around her neck.

They fall silent. Julia sleeps. Woodsmoke dangles in the splayed hands of the cedar. Far off a squirrel cries. The flames are warm on Loche's face. Eyelids are heavy. They droop shut. Orange blurs to black and back again. He sleeps.

The drowse is thick and weighs on his every limb. He dreams of vibrating coils of light like silk ribbons in the wind, tracing across a vast expanse of green woodland. Above him is Julia's constellation, the single star blinking—watching. Basil waits beside a high stone. He is afraid.

A slight chill brings him back. A quick peek. The fire is low. Slender flames struggle to dance in the chill. Pale morning perches in the trees. A pair of high leather boots are planted just inside the circle of the firelight.

A moment later, the anomaly registers and Loche snaps awake.

Standing before him is an extraordinary looking man. His coat of ringed mail glints brighter than the fading flames. A long coat of orange cloth is draped over his shoulders and belted at the waist. A black, metal cross on a cord hangs flat upon his chest. Under his arm is a leather satchel and a sheathed broadsword. His face, bearded and framed in draping dark hair, is turned to the three figures huddled at the base of the tree.

Loche's hand moves to his umbrella and grasps the hilt. Julia, feeling him move, flinches awake and sits up.

A flurry of words is hurled at them. The man's expression and tone are incredulous, and the language is difficult to catch. Old English? Anglo Saxon perhaps? Loche is astonished that he remembers the sound of the words—sounds he's not heard since boarding school in Canterbury.

"Aér gé fyr heonan, léasscéaweras, on land *Itonalya*."

Loche does not draw his sword. Instead, he shakes his head and raises his hands, indicating he does not understand.

"Ne seah ic wídan feorh under heofones hwealf, sceaðona ic nát hwylc." A confused glare surveys Loche from head to toe. "Sé moncynnes." He cocks his head and scrutinizes Julia. His tone darkens, "Godes andsacan þé þú hér tó lócast. Godes féond, *Orathom Wis!*"

The anger in the man's voice is threatening. Loche can sense Julia bristling. "Let's move," she whispers. "I can't stand the chills—"

He then bows slightly and his words gentle. "Á mæg god wyrcan wunder æfter wundre. Weoroda raéswan, Géata léode, umborwesende, winedrihten." He stares at Edwin. His gaze is both adoring and fearful.

"We do not understand you," Loche says. "We are from far away." He feels Julia grip his arm.

"Ah," the man replies after a few seconds. With incredible speed he unsheathes his broadsword. It flashes in the morning air. He raises the blade and points it to the stars above the pyramid. "Sægde sé þe cúþe, frumsceaft Gode, swutol sang scopes feorran reccan."

Loche and Julia turn to each other. The two then lower their faces to Edwin. The little boy is now sitting up. He climbs out of the chrome emergency blanket. His sneakers crackle on the pine needles as he stands. He looks into Loche's eyes.

When Edwin begins to speak, Loche cannot believe what he hears. Stranger still, he cannot fathom how he translates the boy's words to meaning. From his son's mouth comes Anglo Saxon, carefully articulated. His tiny voice is gentle. As he speaks, Loche discerns—hears—somehow understands what is said.

Edwin says, "You know me, do you not?"

The man's face pales with sudden acknowledgement. With pained reverence he lowers himself to one knee. He answers. Loche hears his words. They, too, are Anglo Saxon, and Loche understands their meaning.

"I do, Lord," The man says, "you are *Thi*. You are the Creator of all. You are my Maker. I am your servant, Etheldred— Our Summoner's High Captain."

Edwin's child voice replies in a calm, wholesome timbre as he turns away from his father to the stranger.

"Yes, I am *Thi*." He raises his arm and gestures to Loche now rising behind him. "Behold, for this is my father. My Maker."

Assembly

November 11, this year
Upper Priest Lake, Idaho
2:15pm PST

"Holy shit!" the medic cries out as he enters the room. Her mouth drops open at the sight of the severed hands clutching the blinking taser casing. "Holy shit!" The room is moaning in pain. The three injured security officers are being attended to by their comrades. Rearden is kneeling beside the man with the broken leg and cradling his head. The medic says, "What the hell happened?"

What the hell happened? What the hell is happening? Astrid feels vertigo as her mind seeks reason. She rises from her knees along with the rest of the gathering. She feels Graham's hand on her arm assisting her. She is lightheaded.

Lynn Eastman stoops and finds her pistol. Raising it, she aims at the library entrance. Her other hand taps a transmitter in her ear. "I need two teams in Citadel Tomb. Now! Code Red, I repeat, Code Red. We have a Foamer." She calls out for Davis and four of the other security officers and orders them to gear up. To the rest of the group she says, "All of you should exit the chamber and proceed to the briefing tent. Coldwater teams will secure the area."

"Eastman," Graham says, "you should not corner her. Let us see what communication can do."

"I have every intention of communicating with her," Eastman says, "You and the professor will assist us in the search." She says to Astrid, "She called your name, Professor— followed by *avu. Avu. . . Avu* means eye, correct?"

"Correct."

"What do you think she means?"

"I don't know."

"Well if anything happens to cross your mind, you'll share it with me."

Astrid does not answer.

As they move toward the exit, Astrid notices Rearden rising from beside the man with the broken leg. He adjusts his suit coat.

"I believe I should come along as well," he says to Eastman.

"Why is that, Doctor?"

Rearden looks at Astrid. "For some reason she looked to me for help. Perhaps that is something we can use."

Eastman weighs the request. "Perhaps you're right," she agrees.

Just as Astrid is about to protest, stretchers arrive with the second and third security team. The man with the broken leg searches the stone floor around him. "My weapon," he says. "Where's my weapon?"

The Army of God

Date unknown
The Realm of Wyn Avuqua

Trunks of trees along the forest path bear strange marks—
rough hewn slashes as if riders had dragged their swords across
the bark as they passed, like a child might clack a stick down the
ribs of a picket fence. A reek of smoke and something else—
something abhorrent and sour hovers in the air. Loche watches
Julia stagger along the trail ahead of him. Two armored soldiers
roughly shove her forward. Several more men lead the march
eastward, up and through dense trees. Edwin is draped upon
Loche's back, his arms wound around his father's neck. He is
silent. *Thi* is silent, too.

Behind, Etheldred follows close. Another group of some
twenty or more soldiers complete the train. There is no sound
save the dull thud of footfalls upon the forest floor.

His forehead has stopped bleeding. When they were
forced to move from their small fire, two men laid hold of Julia
and held her down. Another tore at her clothing. Loche kicked
two teeth out of one man's head. A moment later, Loche was
blinded by his own blood spilling into his eyes. Etheldred put a
stop to his men's interest in Julia and ordered all to march.

"Forgive them," he told Loche. "You harbor an immortal
—our enemy. They know only to torture and kill them."

The company of soldiers move efficiently and with
deliberate focus. They follow the orders of Etheldred without
question. They are lean faced and keen eyed. But their
similarities end there. Loche notes different armor types and
styles. Some wear light leather tunics, others wear varying
versions of metal plate, some more, some less. Their weapons
appear to have the signatures of not one culture, but many. Loche
has heard the words of at least four different languages; through
some miracle, he was able to understand all of them. A select

group wear Etheldred's orange surcoat and bear dangling crosses. Yet, marching just beside is a huge man wearing furs and a leather breast plate that Loche imagines could be Viking in origin, but he cannot be certain. And next to him, a dark skinned, dark eyed soldier whose curved scimitar and filigreed armor reflects a Middle Eastern influence.

Julia moans. Her hands are visibly shaking. From time to time she flinches and swings at some invisible threat, or raises her arms and cowers. When she loses balance, one of her captors slaps her arm, or punches at her legs to keep her moving. They jeer at her. They tell her that over the hill is a line of men waiting for her. They say she smells like flowers.

Etheldred calls for the company to halt just as they are about to crest the hill. He motions for Loche and Julia to follow him to the top.

As Loche gains summit and looks down, air leaves his lungs. The stench and smoke now make sense. Stretching the length of a wide valley is a crouching army of thousands—tents and pavilions, troop formations, fires, siege engines, wave upon wave of horses, men and arms. A word, as if from a dream, whispers from between his lips, "*Godrethion.*"

Julia falls to her knees and cries. Setting Edwin on his feet, Loche drops to her side and pulls her close.

Etheldred watches the three with curiosity. He then places himself between the massive host and Edwin.

"My Lord," he says to the little boy, "your army has come. The Army of God." He bows low.

The Shadows Between the Bookshelves

November 11, this year
Upper Priest Lake, Idaho
2:17pm PST

"For those of you just joining us, the target has escaped into the Citadel Tomb Atheneum, North. She is a naked woman, blond, green eyes, about six-one, physically fit, armed with an ancient broadsword— and now, from what I gather, she's got a nine millimeter Ruger firearm." Eastman levels her focus at the newly arrived security teams, "I know that sounds like a pumping wet dream to some of you, but let me be clear, this bitch will cut your goddamn heads off."

Graham interjects, "I can't imagine she picked the gun up —she wouldn't have any idea what it is, much less, how to use it —"

Inclining her head toward Astrid, Eastman responds, "And according to your expert professor here, there was to be a skull-less skeleton in the tomb. I'm not taking any chances with this woman's fortitude or adaptability. She's survived over a thousand years in a box. Learning how to use a gun shouldn't be a challenge.

"The dark aisles—" she continues, "watch the corners. You are authorized to use whatever force necessary. This one is a Foamer, so do what you need to do. Bring her down."

Graham asks, "Foamer? Why do you call her that?"

"A term of endearment." Eastman smiles at the archeologist. Astrid is suddenly stunned by the perfect angles of Eastman's face. Her crystal blue eyes are like a cool June morning. *So beautiful it's unsettling,* Astrid thinks.

"Endearment? You mean you've encountered an immortal before? I don't understand—" Graham says.

"You don't have to understand, Graham. You're here to do a job, and you don't want to know mine."

"You must allow us to communicate with her before using force," Astrid pleads. "Her intelligence is light years beyond—"

"She's right. Force is not the answer here, Eastman," Graham says. "If you want to keep us all safe you'll let us attempt communication." His voice transforms into a comical and angry impression of Billy Crystal from *The Princess Bride*, "Or have fun storming the castle."

"Professor, certainly," Eastman says. "But in the end, I will have her down. Davis, get these two some earpieces so we can all stay in contact."

"Will do," Davis answers.

An ear bud is handed to Astrid and Graham. She places it in her ear. "Don't lose it," he tells her. "It also sends out a tracking signal. Don't want anyone falling down a shaft somewhere. . ."

Astrid shudders.

Eastman says, "Once inside we'll split into two teams. Astrid and Rearden go with Davis here. Davis, you lead your team along East Wing. Stay in contact. Graham, you'll come with me."

Astrid looks at Graham. He taps at his ear, "Can you hear me?" Astrid nods. "See you in a few minutes, okay?" She tries to smile and steadies herself. "Not quite what you expected?"

"It never is," she replies. She watches as he joins Eastman's group. They disappear into the rows.

The seven man team with Astrid and Rearden enter into the shadowed labyrinth. Sound is muffled. A cascade of dust particles meteor through the light of a florescent work lamp as they pass. A solitary piece of parchment flutters to the floor. The team whisper in strategic tactic talk. "Clear left—clear right—

hold," and so on. After a few minutes Astrid tunes out the military-speak and allows the images of embossed *Elliqui* runes upon leather book spines to enchant and transport her. *Could this be a dream*, she wonders.

A musty decay is heavy in places, though Astrid finds it strangely pleasant. *The smell of books*, she thinks. *Really old books*. Her mind somersaults considering the stories calling to her from surrounding shelves. She smiles, *This must be heaven.*

Questions storm through her mind. *How could Yafarra have survived? This is myth—how could all of this remain hidden for so many centuries? How could this library keep from being destroyed by time? Or destroyed when the city was sacked? What's in these books? What fills their pages?* A thousand more questions in the time it takes to walk ten steps into the twisting stacks.

Her mind flashes to the young security officers who were injured. She shakes her head. "That didn't have to happen," she says quietly.

"Professor," Eastman's voice fires through the ear bud. "If you have something to say, please make it worthwhile. Otherwise, cut the chatter."

She bites her lip then mouths the words, "Fuck off."

Graham puzzles, "*Avu. Avu.* Why *Avu?* Astrid?"

"I'm working on it," she replies.

Aisles are curving inward now. Some cyclone up to the vaulted ceiling, three, maybe four stories above. They pass carved, hissing serpents that coil around yellowing stone columns. Faces of demons and heroes burst from walls, from terraces, from cornerstones. A grey mouse darts across the path. A spider scurries into a silken corner. The air, the dark, the winding halls feel far older than her imagination can reach. The stone tiles on the floor continued to be marked with talons.

"How deep does this go?" she whispers.

"So far we've explored only a fifty meter sized maze, roughly. But there's more. Much more beyond," Graham answers. "There are only a few aisles that are straight. Rows twist and curve in all directions it seems. We still have to figure out the pattern."

Astrid looks back and sees Rearden a few paces behind. Then she strains to see the light from the tomb chamber. It's gone. She quickly counts how many turns they've made.

"You mean the labyrinth has not yet been sorted out?" she says checking the panic in her voice.

There's silence for a few steps. Graham slightly apologetic, says, "Not yet. We only opened the chamber a few days ago."

Astrid's feet stop. She looks down. Carved into the tile at her feet is an embossed heart the size of her two hands together.

"Keep up," Davis's voice darts into her ear. "Keep moving."

"Wait," Astrid says. "The Queen will know her way through this. Pursuing her is a mistake. She'll know every turn."

At that moment, a piercing scream stabs into her inner ear from the tiny speaker. There is the report of gunfire far off to the right. Three cracks. "Man down! Man down!" Eastman's voice shouts.

Davis raises his fist up, turns and motions for his company to halt.

"God damn!" Another security guard's voice transmits, "She came right out of the fucking books—Ripley is down. I repeat, Ripley is down."

Astrid stares into the sculptured hurricane of shelves trying to determine just where Eastman's team is. Her abdomen aches and her hands are clustered into fists. Terror claws, tearing at the cage of her ribs. She suddenly crouches, opens her palm and presses it into the embossed heart in the stone floor. It is cool. Bone dry.

A moment later, Eastman says, "Stab wound to the upper leg. Pretty bad. I'm getting him out with two to escort."

Graham fires off another movie quote, "Eastman, you're going to need a bigger boat."

"She could have taken his head off," one of Eastman's team says. "Why didn't she?"

Astrid replies, "She won't kill a human unless she must. She's alive to protect humans, or so the tales tell. But we should take this as a clear sign she doesn't want us following her—"

"We got a couple of shots off," Eastman interrupts, "but she managed to disappear. She's moving eastward."

Graham crackles in, his tone is frustrated, "How can you know that? Rows turn in on themselves. For all we know she might be circling back."

Eastman's reply ignores the archeologist, "Davis, report."

Astrid raises her face to see her team leader's head swiveling at a kind of crossroad—three connecting aisles like the base of a trident. His tone is nervous, "We're working our way inward. No sign of target."

"Graham is right," Eastman says, "it's tough to know directions in here. But I think she may be moving to you."

"This library is no Dewy decimal, gridded floor plan," Davis mutters mournfully.

Again, Astrid tries to feel the turns she's made, draw out the progress through the maze as if she were penciling a shape. Behind her, talons were pressed into the rock— now hearts are beneath her. Ahead Davis is struggling to choose the next direction.

"Graham," she says tapping her ear. Revelation blooms in her mind, "Look down. What do you see pressed into the floor?"

A moment passes. Astrid moves to Davis and stands beside him. They both trace along through the shadowed paths.

"Wings," Graham answers.

Wyn Avuquain heraldry. Four Households, each making up the body of a heron: talons, heart, wings and head. Faded depictions of the bird on ancient parchment lights in her memory. She's seen the shape a thousand times. A profile view of a heron facing east. The library is in the shape of the bird. It suddenly makes sense. They entered at the talons and rose upward to the main body—the stones then depicted hearts. Eastman and Graham took a western route. Their tiles depict wings.

Avu, Astrid thinks. *Avu* means eye. And then it is simple. If they keep moving north, the stones will show a bird's head. In the center of that section, as in every artistic rendition she's seen, is an eye.

Yafarra is moving to the eye. Avu—eye.

She opens her mouth to speak but stops short. She may have solved the riddle, but sharing it with Eastman is another thing. Graham's *Elliqui* warning before they opened the tomb tingles along her shoulders. She cannot lead the Coldwater teams to Yafarra. But Graham must know. She searches the shelves, the floor, the carved serpents strangling the alabaster columns. A line of *Elliqui* runes carved into an archway catches her attention.

It clearly states in icy cut symbols the sad saying, *Ithic veli agtig. Why does my death delay?* She points to it, knowing full well that her team leader, Davis, will have no clue as to what it means.

"Graham," she says, "I'm seeing an etching in the stone over here."

"Yes? What does it say?" he responds.

She takes a deep breath, and lies. *"Othayer rav ea ~ Yafarra gal avu iqua kep~Avu iqua~Gal yuth~Yuth."*

Eastman's voice is quick to respond. "Translate, Professor."

To Graham she had said, *Escape Eastman. Yafarra goes to the bird head's eye. Bird's eye. Go north. North.*

"It means," She replies to Eastman, *"We are the Guardians of the Dream. We hold the doors."*

"So what?" Eastman says.

"We study this stuff, Eastman," Astrid says. "Let us geek-out, okay?"

"Graham?" Eastman asks.

A moment passes. "I'll be there to see it with you," the archeologist says. "We'll geek out together." His voice is confident as if her meaning is clear. Astrid smiles. He continues, "The *Itonalya* protect us— we should protect them. There's so much to explore, Astrid. For now all we have is a bird's eye view. More to come."

Astrid nods. She turns to see Rearden staring at her. He says nothing.

Davis reports, "No movement from our position."

"Okay," Eastman crackles in the earpiece, "Keep moving."

Davis and his team take the corridor to the right, leading into yet another section of coiling shelves. It is getting darker.

If there is a time, it is now, Astrid thinks. She moves slowly along with the others and, when she is able, she steps to the side, just beyond the sight of the two security officers near to her. She stops, waits a moment as they pass—pivots slowly and rushes through the nearest opening in the network of shelves. She stops. Waits. Then, strides back toward the crossroad and bounds up the center aisle.

Her heart booms in her chest. Her eyes adjust to the dark. The last thing she hears before she tears the transmitter out of her ear and crushes it underfoot is team leader Davis, "Where is professor Finnley?"

The Sport of Angels

Date unknown
The Realm of Wyn Avuqua

Messengers were sent to tell the host that *Thi* had come. *Thi*, ruler of the *Olathion* sky—maker of life, light and darkness. *Thi*, Lord of all gods. "Our Lord has come," The Summoner's High Captain, Etheldred bade them tell.

Even before Captain Etheldred's company had reached the army's perimeter, horses, carts and heralds were sent to meet them. Mounted knights arrayed in similar fashion to Etheldred rode up bearing high banners and escorted them to a large horse drawn cart.

Loche now watches the green land pass and the massive host of gods draw ever nearer. Loche holds Julia's hand. She grips him desperately. She is pale and having difficulty staying conscious. She has not spoken or made a sound since she beheld the sprawling army. *Rathinalya.* Edwin sits on his lap—but there is no sign of his young son in the boy's face. Instead, a foreign, calm curiosity is seated there. He appears fascinated and thoughtful. Etheldred sits beside him on the wagon.

"We have arrived," The Anglo Saxon captain says in his own tongue, but Loche can still somehow understand him. "Our brothers and sisters from across the great waters. We come from every homestead, hamlet and distant desert. Over endless seas, to destroy the City of Immortals. From armies along the coastlands from deep within the mountains, we are called. We are *Thi's* army. We have come to do Its will. We are God."

He slaps Loche's shoulder, "The joy! That with the sunrise on a single, fateful day, you awaken as a god. One of a legion of angels." He motions to the armed city ahead, "All of us woke with the same memory. The knowledge! The power! We can speak beyond our own languages—our stories are shared—

we feel *Thi's* creation as a man, yet for the first time in our mortal lives, we know what we are somewhere deep within us— we are gods and men together." He bows his head to Edwin. "And *Thi* has called upon us to destroy *Wyn Avuqua*." He looks darkly upon Julia, "Destroy those that rebel against *Thi's* will. And lay in ruin *Wyn Avuqua* and her people, we shall."

He spits. "The *Itonalya!* Murderers. Now we know who they are. *Thi* has shown us. Now is the time for our revenge. Murderers, killers— god killers. Look," Loche sees the perimeter gate opening for their entry. Horns blast. Cheers resonate from behind the timber barriers. "This army knows the horrors they've committed. We shall not allow a single Immortal to survive."

As the cart clatters within the wooden battlements, Loche feels the weight of many eyes upon him. The clamor of shouting voices and cheers rises as they enter. Underneath the noise, Loche hears a woeful baying—a horrible cry of pain.

Etheldred says, "I will now take you to our Summoner and General. She comes from my island over the sea. She is great beyond my ability to tell. Of the lore of gods and our new awakening, she is the teacher. She knows the path between life here and the Hereafter. Unlike any of this host, she has been here before."

"Dad?" Edwin says.

When Loche turns he discovers the source of the writhing scream. At first he is not able to discern what he is seeing but he instinctively reaches to his son, covering his eyes and pulls him into his embrace.

Surrounded by a large number of jeering soldiers is an elevated platform upon which, lying flat and restrained, is a naked man. Leather straps secure a small, black iron cage to his abdomen. Just beside the platform, an ebony robed soldier is stoking a bright fire. A bellows pushes out walls of heat. A thick metal rod is pulled from the red coals. It glows pink in the cool, grey morning. The robed man lifts the rod and rests its incandescent end atop the iron cage. The ring of soldiers let out a frenzy of shouts and cheers.

The restrained man's mournful cry rises above the din.

Loche squints when he thinks he sees movement within the black cage. As he focuses, two dark shapes are scurrying and scrabbling against the iron bars. A moment later he notes pools of blood streaming to the edges of the platform.

Loche feels a hand slap upon his turned shoulder. When he turns, Etheldred is grinning.

"Oh, worry not, Julia, *immortal*," He says to her. "This is not that poor *Itonalya's* first time. He cannot die in this manner. But we shall place him beneath the rodents again before midday. His suffering is joy to us. Perhaps you will provide us with such pleasure, if my master wills it."

Another scream. Loche holds both Julia and Edwin tighter to him. Swiveling back, he sees within the iron cage two slate grey, frenetic rats struggling to escape the glowing metal rod just above them. The heat forces the ravenous creatures to claw and burrow down through the man's abdomen. A white foam clumps and piles beside his wriggling form. His screams turn to moans.

"Make it stop!" Julia cries suddenly.

Helpless, Loche lets his eyes flit from the torture, to Julia, to his son and halt upon Etheldred. He studies the madness spreading across the man's face. He sees a semblance of humankind, but a missing aspect that he cannot pinpoint, as if the man is devoid of life force—or the knowledge of love. It is as if Etheldred lacks the conditions that light a human from within. Loche feels a sudden shock as he considers the notion that Etheldred lacks what he can only name a soul.

The wagon stops beside three large pavilions.

"And now," Etheldred says, standing. "Now we shall have counsel with my Lord."

At that moment, two men seize Julia from beside the cart's railing. They yank her down by one arm and a handful of her hair to the muddied path. From behind, two men pull Edwin away from Loche. As he feels his son's hands let go, he turns. Etheldred's gloved fist lands three vicious blows to the side of his head. Loche falls back. "You befriend an immortal, you are our enemy," Etheldred growls. Julia begins to cry out. Edwin is now high up on the guard's shoulders and steadily moving away deeper into the massive encampment. A train of soldiers gather and follow cheering and calling out to the little boy. Loche reaches toward his son. Edwin looks back. Another crippling blow blurs Loche's eyesight.

"Edwin!" he coughs.

Amid the fury of sound, Loche hears the tortured immortal cry out again.

"This sound on the wind," Etheldred is almost singing as he leans down to Loche's slumped body, "will be the sound of all of *Wyn Avuqua* in the coming days. Slaying the enemies of God is the sport of angels. Our Lord has commanded, and we shall obey."

Heart

November 11, this year
Upper Priest Lake, Idaho
2:45pm PST

Hearts. Still, only hearts under her running feet. Every few minutes she halts, stoops and lets her fingers trace the outline of the symbol embossed in the rock. Of course there is the chance she could be running in a circle, but her gut tells her that she has managed to keep a steady course northward without too many backtrack moments. The imprint of a bird's head should appear soon—it must.

She's heard her name called out. Several orders to return or to stop where she is. Eastman had yelled: "It's more dangerous in there than you're ready for, Professor. Stop!" When the muffled calls started, including Professor Cremo's name, she felt her decisiveness was not completely foolish. *He's slipped away, too,* she thinks.

Life-sized sculptures of *Itonalya* warriors, royalty, and other characters out of the city's own mythologies frighten her to a halt at a corner. The first image she sees in the dim light is a magnificent stone effigy of a maiden holding a long spear—a flowing marble cape draped over her shoulders. Upon her shield is the Eye of *Thi*. Astrid stares at this masterpiece of ancient sculpture for what feels like a full minute without breathing before she decides the maiden is not Yafarra.

At another stop, a massive work of carved marble depicts the first Guardian of Earth, *Mellithion* with his sword raised to the heavens and the beautiful *Endale* in his embrace. The massive bulk of the god *Chalshaf* and his wounded, bleeding eye tower over them both. The drama of it elicits a tear. She stands at the scene dumbfounded—almost forgetting the danger surrounding her. Reluctantly, she looks to the floor again and follows the hearts.

She is within a story. She is a part of her dreams.

Passing beneath an archway she discovers what she had been waiting for. She stoops low to make sure. She pulls her cell phone from her pocket and touches the screen—risking its light to insure her guess is correct. The stone tile imprint now depicts a heron's head. She feels the embossed shape. In the center is a raised bump. An eye. Glancing at the cell phone she sees that a message from her assistant Marcel has somehow made its way to her: *I'm on my way! Save some discoveries for me.* She feels a sudden but fleeting relief. She tucks the phone back into her pocket.

Just north of the archway is a half circle of entrance rows —five separate pathways. She pauses and searches for any sign that might provide a signpost toward the *Avu*.

When she hears voices not far behind her, she bolts straight ahead into the center aisle. The shelves seem to welcome her.

There are new light sources. Above, the vaulted ceiling is pale green. Stepping out into a round room, like a clearing in a forest, she looks up. She supposes the illumination is reflected sunlight from hidden surface openings in the upper architecture. It is not bright, but it is enough to navigate by.

A half hour? A full hour? A full day? She wonders how long she's been alone threading the labyrinth. Thoughts scatter from the danger, to another standing sculpture, to the stacks of books, to the joy of being here— here and now.

After another series of direction choices, she stops at the end of a long, narrow path. Beneath the greenish glow is a hemisphere of stone rising from the tiled floor, perhaps eight feet high. It glows like the frosted quartz of Yafarra's tomb. Astrid can see a host of sculpted figures, *Itonalya* sentinels, positioned in a semicircle around the dome. She crouches. She watches the room for movement. Looking down, she slides her foot to the side. There is a stone carved head. *The eye must be near. She's made it. But now what?*

Several thoughts now crowd for attention. *Should she simply call to Yafarra? Should she ask for permission to enter the chamber? What about clothes? Should she remove her coat and offer it to the naked Queen?*

"Is that you?" a voice whispers from the shadows just a few feet from her.

"Graham?" Astrid whispers back. She scans for him.

He coughs. She sees his lanky shape dim against one of the sculptures. A welcome surge of relief eases the muscles in her shoulders. She takes a step into the chamber and then freezes when Graham cries, "Wait. Stop."

A sculpture has one hand clamped upon his shoulder, the other aims a sword into his cervical spine from behind. The sculpture is not a sculpture; it is Yafarra.

"*Ag shivcy,*" Astrid says. She raises her hands.

"Astrid?" Queen Yafarra asks.

"*Lit,*" Astrid says.

Astrid is too far away and it is too dim for her to see the Queen's expression. A moment passes. Down some impossible pathway behind, she can hear security team chatter. Eastman is near.

Astrid lets out a flurry of *Elliqui.* She tells Yafarra that Graham is a friend, that the enemy is coming, and if there is a way to escape, they must do so now.

Yafarra's response carries a trace of fear. She asks how long she's been entombed.

There are sounds of boots on stone.

The answer, "Over a thousand years," evokes a pained inhale from Yafarra.

She releases Graham and lowers her weapon. Graham takes a step away and turns slowly. Yafarra stumbles toward the ancient sentinels. In the gloom, her bullet wound and the streaks of blood down her body are black. And there's something else— some kind of white liquid or foam. Astrid and Graham watch her free hand gently touch the faces of the sculptures as she passes them. Even in the faint light, her tears glitter. She mutters a stream of phrases, most of which Astrid cannot translate. But two names she repeats over and over.

"Aethur," she mourns. "Iteav. Aethur, Iteav."

After she slides her hand along the brow of the last sculptured sentinel, there is a faint cracking sound. The quartz dome trembles, arcs back and opens, revealing a stairway into the deep.

"*Veli*," Yafarra gestures for Graham and Astrid to descend. She lifts the wood *tenesh* from the floor beside the widening fissure.

She calls out—her eyes pointed over Astrid's shoulder, "*Itonalya! Veli! Veli!*"

Marcus Rearden appears beside Astrid. Adrenaline pumps through her body. Her breath leaves her.

"I followed you," he says passing her.

"*Veli!*" Yafarra hisses.

"They aren't far behind," he adds.

Astrid counts the beats of her heart, watching Rearden join Graham and Yafarra at the next yawning rabbit hole. She cannot yet determine the threat Rearden poses, and the shock of his being a stride behind her in the dark is like a nail dragged along her spine. But what choice now?

A moment later she is standing beside Graham. He takes her hand.

"After you, Rearden," Astrid whispers.

Marcus descends.

"*Gal*," Yafarra says.

The crystal dome closes over them. Astrid Finnley enters into the bird's eye of the *Tiris Avu* library holding the hand of Graham Cremo.

Still, she thinks, *following hearts*.

Insulting the Sun God

Date unknown
The Realm of Wyn Avuqua

Loche buttons Edwin's coat. The boy's eyes track snowflakes descending to the grey grass. "How many are there, Dad?" he asks. Loche smiles. He snugs the collar a little tighter and scrunches the stocking cap on the boy's head.

"Too many to count," Loche answers.

"More than a hundred?"

"Yes."

"More than fifty hundred?"

"Yes."

Edwin's feet begin to dance a bit. "Hurry, Dad."

"Okay," Loche says, "half a second. You need to bundle up before you go— it's cold out there."

"I will count them all," Edwin says.

Loche looks out the window.

He feels his eyes widen.

There is falling snow. But now each snowflake slows and stops. They hover as if attached to gentle strands of silk dangling from the grey-black afternoon sky. Fear injects adrenaline into his bloodstream.

Edwin begins to laugh. "Now they will be easier to count." The little boy's laughter intensifies.

It is the laughter that wakes him. Or it could also be the stunning pulses of pain from his left ear. His vision blurs and then sharpens to see two lightly armored guards clicking the flashlight from his bag on and off again. Each time it illuminates, there is a sigh of wonder and then they laugh in suppressed hysterics. After a few seconds studying the two men, Loche struggles to return to where he left off.

His last memory was watching Julia and Edwin being wrestled away from him while the air filled with cheers of adulation, and cries of agony and pain.

Throbs of pressure keep a kind of sickening beat to the chuckling guards. In the torchlight Loche sees his bag upon a low table, its leather strap hanging down and touching the dirt floor. There is little else in the enclosure. Three knee-high stumps surround what looks to be a small ring of stones for a fire where a dull smolder of coals glows. Cold starlight flickers through an opening in the high peak of the canvas above. Loche's arm is outstretched on the moist soil. He can feel some kind of fabric beneath his body, and below that, he guesses, is a bed-shaped pile of pine needles and leaves. His feet, legs and chest are chilled and prickling as if a fever is kindling in him. There is no sign of Edwin or Julia. Tears rise. But then to his great surprise, his fear lessens when he sees his umbrella handle jutting out from beside his bag.

He wonders why his possessions were not confiscated when Edwin and Julia were taken. Perhaps the bag was overlooked due to the excitement of the One God's presence among them. That weighty reality might very well be enough to miss other things.

The guard snapping the light on and off hands the mysterious item to his companion, and then reaches to the long, black object. He raises it and examines the fine, soft material of the closed umbrella. Tipping it upward he studies the handle. The other guard leans in and eyes the thing with interest. He clicks the flashlight and aims the beam to get a better look.

Loche lifts up on one elbow and rises as quietly as he can. Once to his knees he lays his palms on his face feeling for the cuts that need stitching. He's relieved to feel nothing too bad. A hardened gash is scabbed over above his left eye. When he moves his hand to his ear he feels a wound that is still wet to the touch. The sting of it forces a wincing hiss from his lips.

The two guards spin around at the sound.

The Anglo Saxon sounds again, yet meaning forms easily in Loche's head, "Ah, alive and awake," one of them says.

"Where is the boy and the woman?" Loche demands.

The guards do not answer. They regard Loche's condition with a kind of piteous scorn and turn back to the strange fabric stick.

"The boy and woman?" he repeats. They ignore him.

Loche assesses the room once again. To gain the exit he must pass the guards. They stand between him and the wood framed door. He scans the lower hem of the tent. It is bordered by heavy logs. There is no lifting the canvas wall and rolling out. He must go through the door. The guards take no notice when he raises one knee and sets a foot on the ground.

As he lifts himself to his feet, one of the soldiers turns and says, "Sit. And stay sitting."

The man is holding the umbrella by the metal tipped end. The other pushes his hand beneath the ribbed fabric and tries to push up to open it. It doesn't budge.

"You're doing that wrong," Loche offers, nodding to the umbrella.

The two look at each other, the mysterious object and then Loche. "It is an umbrella," Loche tells them. "An umbrella."

"Umbrella?" one repeats.

"Yes," Loche says. "May I show you?" Loche holds his hand out.

The two exchange glances again.

"It keeps you dry in the rain— and it keeps the sun—"

"We know that, you fool!" the one holding it says. "How does it open?"

"There is a hidden latch," Loche says, gesturing for them to hand it over.

With another survey of his condition, and apparently assessing Loche could do no harm, the guard hands the umbrella over. Loche's thumb finds the release button and is about to press it when he pauses.

"We should not open an umbrella inside," Loche says, his focus ticking from the guards to the door.

"Why?" one asks.

Loche answers, "It is bad luck."

One guard laughs. The other says, "It will be bad luck for you to delay. Open it."

"Very well," Loche says.

There is a slight click and the spring loaded shade opens out with a puff of air. From behind the umbrella, Loche cannot see their faces, nor can they see him— but he can hear their laughter.

"Again," one says.

Loche pulls the halter ring down and the umbrella closes. He thumbs the release and it wafts open again. The guards laugh. Loche closes it saying, "One should only open an umbrella outside—this is bad luck."

"Again," they say in unison this time.

This time there are two clicks. The first releases the hinge pin for the shade to open. The fabric widens and flutters taught. Loche hears them laugh again as they disappear from view. The next click comes from the twisting of the handle. A quick singing of metal rings as Loche draws the razor sharp rapier blade from the umbrella pole. With one whirling movement, the umbrella shade pulls away to the left while the outstretched sword follows in its wake. The blade slices through each of their throats in succession. They drop soundlessly to the ground.

Bird's Eye

November 11, this year
Upper Priest Lake, Idaho
3:20pm PST

The Queen's luminous skin, a mere blur in the dark, is all Astrid can see ahead. She's lost count of the number of steps. Over a hundred. Maybe two hundred. The passageway has been a consistent slope downward with no turns. She can feel the smooth rock walls if she stretches her arms out wide. So far, there's been no openings or doors. Graham is close behind. Rearden is somewhere back there, too. She can hear him whisper to himself every few paces. She thinks she hears him repeating the name *Loche*, and someone called *Nicholas*—but mostly the sound of his voice reminds her of a snake's hiss. She feels her feet shuffle a little quicker. The pale light of Yafarra feels safer than the slithering of Rearden at her heels.

The weight of the earth above and the stifling still air is maddening. She tries a couple of deep breaths—her lungs greedy for oxygen. Graham's comforting hand is suddenly on her shoulder.

She imagines Eastman and the security teams arriving at the Crystal Dome above. What is she thinking? Has Eastman worked out that the dome is a secret passage? Is she wandering among the sculpted sentinels—following the barefooted prints of Yafarra on the dusted stone floor? Is she ordering the steel wench to be brought in so she might pry her way in?

Keep moving.

Keep breathing.

After another deep inhale, Graham whispers to her, as if to cheer her, "Bird's eye—that's where we are."

"Bird's eye," Astrid repeats. She feels herself smile.

Her entire career has been spent following the blur of a ghost. And now, within arms reach, is an impossible truth. She is following the Queen of the *Itonalya* beneath the Crystal Dome of the *Tiris Avu* Library. She is under the Bird's Eye. *Too much to be believed*, she thinks.

When the walls at either side disappear, there is a change in the air as if they have entered into a large chamber. Astrid inhales the wider atmosphere and raises her face, searching for anything but black. There is nothing. Lowering her gaze, she cannot locate the dim glow of the Queen.

"*O Chalfea*? Yafarra?"

There is a slight scraping sound, then a flash—a spark to her left. She turns toward it. After three more dazzling strobes, a flame kindles and she can see Yafarra holding a small torch beside a shoulder high stone trough. The trough resembles a flower box one might see below a house's picture window, though its length wraps around the entire room. Yafarra drops the torch into it. Immediately a faint fume of oil rises, and a perimeter rectangle of flame ignites illuminating the chamber.

The veil of shadow pulled away, Astrid inhales with shock yet again. Virtually untouched by time, a dry stone room surrounds her. A bed chamber. Colorful woven tapestries soften the walls. Wardrobes, cabinets, a wide desk, chairs, a rack of swords, bookshelves, all artfully made with gold filagree and carved adornments. Facing the opposite door is a large bed. The orange flames flicker and dance in the sword blades and glass beads dangling from the ceiling.

Yafarra, trancelike, walks to a corner shadow where a suit of armor stands. The armature is her exact height and it is menacing to behold. It looks like a tall, *Itonalya* warrior fully girded—nearly indestructible. The silver helm and breast plate glint in the firelight. Every article has red-black stains of smeared blood. The white and gold cloak is also bespeckled with the spray of battle. Yafarra stares at her armor and reaches toward it. Her fingers touch the side of the helm, the gorget, the breastplate. She whispers words in Elliqui. Astrid translates, *"The Heron is dead. The Heron kept silent. The Heron saved us all."*

"Do you think that when the city was sacked," Astrid conjectures, "the defenses of the lower halls held?"

Graham answers, "Maybe. But I believe when the *Godrethion* stormed the keep, they never discovered the lower library or the crystal tomb. The entrance could be closed—and when it was closed, it looked like a rock wall. As I said, the only way we found it was through technology."

She is wonderstruck at the condition of the artifacts. Certainly time has left its mark here, but the builders took great care against moisture. The air, the stone, the walls are all bone dry. Astrid turns her body in circles, scanning.

A burst of fright shudders through her when she thinks she sees a face peering at them from one wall. But as her eyes adjust to the orange firelight, she sees the face is an elegantly made mask of wood or leather, much like the masquerade masks that are the trademarks of Venice. It is a handsome shape, almond eyes, death pale with a single red teardrop upon its cheek. A moment later Astrid feels her stomach suddenly cramp when she recalls the meaning behind the mask itself. It is an *Ithicsazj*—the sacrificial death mask used to calm a captured god before the eventual beheading. The inner leather surface was said to have been coated with sedating oils and herbs meant to relax and alleviate fear. Astrid stares at the face for a moment and wonders how many eyes have closed behind it.

She then turns to Yafarra, who has lowered herself to the floor. The *tenesh* and sword lie a few feet away. Her naked torso is spattered and streaked with blood. Astrid rushes to her and holds her hands out in a gesture of care. Yafarra meets Astrid's eyes and nods. The bullet wound is covered over with a white foam. Yafarra moans in pain. Her expression remains sturdy. She presses her fingers to the injury and waits, staring at Astrid.

Professor Astrid Finnelly watches as the gruesome hole diminishes and fades from pink to a slight blemish upon Yafarra's pale skin.

All of her scholarly, academic interpretations of the *Itonalya's* mythic meaning are dashed. What she once deemed to be metaphor, is now revealed to be fact. The inhabitants of this city were truly, immortal.

She shakes her head.

Her thoughts jumble.

Graham appears at the Queen's side with the white and gold cloak from the armor stand. The heavy fabric is soft and remarkably well preserved. He pulls it around her shoulders and covers her body as best he can. Yafarra studies him for a moment, curious and thoughtful.

"Iteav?" the Queen asks. "Aethur?" Her eyes glittering with sudden tears. She searches Graham's face, then she turns to Astrid. Astrid responds with an expression of helplessness.

Yafarra's arms rise from out of the heavy cloak and she places her palms gently upon Astrid's cheeks. Her hazel-gold eyes seem to speak, to invite Astrid into a shared gaze. The Queen holds her face and stares intently.

Blinking, Astrid thinks she hears her speak, though there is no sound. Then all at once, it registers. A knowing, an imprinted thought, but not her own, forms in her mind. A rush of heat rises to her cheeks. *Elliqui*, she thinks. *Elliqui* in its Original Mode. She had read about its telepathic character—but never truly believed it possible. Yafarra's simple utterance drifts easily into her mind and waits there.

Astrid concludes there is nothing more powerful in all of existence than this connection, this communion—thoughts that can reach across a field of light and mingle like stars on the surface of dark water.

—*We are one,* the Queen's thought aligns. This thought is heralded with a single thread of golden light vibrating somewhere behind Astrid's eyes. For an instant, Astrid tries to focus on the beam, but when she does this, the glowing string darts into her periphery.

Astrid raises her fingers and lays them upon Yafarra's cradling hands. Tears burn in her eyes. The intensity of her smile almost hurts.

—*I, I see you,* she tries. As this thought leaves Astrid's mind, she senses a pale green line of illuminated thread leave her eyes and reach to Yafarra. The woven, silky light lingers out and pulses in the dim room.

—*And I see you.* The deep green of illuminated morning leaves, Astrid thinks. The light of Yafarra's reply is like fragile vines branching across her thought.

Astrid's hands begin to tremble as Yafarra's next utterance threads its way in. This time the transcending ray turns to a pale blue, serpentine noose. It is a torturous, suffocating sensation. Her lungs arrest, and she begins gasping, gulping for oxygen. Graham's hand grips her shoulder.

—*A thousand years deprived of breath,* Yafarra's suffering overwhelms Astrid's mind. *A thousand years frozen in stone. In blackness. Ever and anon, dying. Tell me that I am free.*

The strangling horror recedes and Astrid can feel her body relax. The snake of light recoils and is replaced by another golden tendril.

—*Tell me that I am free,* the thought persists.

—*You are free,* Astrid sends. She's fascinated that her reply flings a rope of white, like a line to one that has fallen overboard.

—*Iteav. Where is my Iteav? Tell me that he lives.*

"Astrid?" she hears Graham say. The slender wires of light dim slightly. "Are you alright? What is happening?"

"We're speaking together—in thought," she tells him. "It is—it is *Elliqui.* True *Elliqui.*"

Yafarra's expression is trapped in disbelief. She shakes her head and lowers her hands from Astrid's face. She leans to the side and reaches across the stone floor to her sword and *tenesh.* Graham turns toward the items and assists pulling them into her possession. She sets the sword next to her long legs. The *tenesh* she pulls onto her lap and begins to unclasp the knotted metal latch. She fires a thin ray of lit silk into Astrid's vision.

—*Where is my son, Iteav? Where is The Poet, Aethur?*

Astrid shakes her head.

—*The Poet can see beyond all others. He can see from on high. He weaves the paths upon which we wander. We named him Aethur. But he is in pain. He is tortured.*

"What is she saying?" Graham asks.

Her thoughts still entwined with Yafarra, Astrid answers, "She wants to know where the Poet is. His name is Aethur."

Rearden speaks suddenly. "The Poet? Here?" Something in the psychologist's voice raises a field of goose flesh along her shoulders and arms. "Here?" he repeats.

"Yes," Astrid answers.

"She calls him Aethur?" Rearden asks.

"Yes."

At the naming of Aethur, Yafarra's eyes blink away from Astrid. The Queen looks up at Rearden.

"Why does she call him, Aethur?" says Rearden. His tone slightly incredulous.

"What do you mean?" Astrid says.

"That's not—" he breaks off as if weighing his words. He then finishes without hesitation, "That's not his name. That is not the Poet's name."

Astrid scowls. "What the hell do you mean, Rearden?" she blurts out. "What do you know about any of this? How would you know the name of the prophesied Poet?"

Rearden doesn't answer.

He is gaunt. His skin is almost translucent in this flame lit room. How old is this man? His black suit fits him well. He looks relatively healthy, but there's something strangely synthetic about his appearance as if he were wearing makeup, or perhaps he's had plastic surgery. *He's unnervingly calm,* Astrid thinks. *Why is he here?* she wonders yet again. *Professor Molmer invited him. But why?* A million electrical impulses trigger in her mind attempting to unravel the question. She doesn't trust him. A barrage of images tick behind her eyes—pictures of him online with his high powered connections, his awards and stories about his illustrious past in criminal psychology, his recent murder case in Sandpoint, Idaho.

"Aethur?" the Queen says aloud. Her fingers are now clicking back the latch on the lid of the *tenesh.* Rearden leans in closer, his eyes trained on the wooden box upon Yafarra's thighs.

"Aethur?"

Aethur. When the name filters through the translation center of Astrid's brain, her body jolts. She stands. She steps back a pace. Her heart pleading with her coursing blood to deliver more oxygen.

"What's the matter?" Graham says standing, his arm out in a gesture to steady her.

"*Elliqui*," she whispers. "Aethur. Aethur. Of course!" She looks down to Yafarra and then back to Marcus Rearden. Marcus' raised hands are shaking as he watches Yafarra begin to crack the lid to the *tenesh*.

"What's wrong?" Graham asks, reading her panic.

"Aethur," she responds haltingly. "The word—the name means. . . new earth."

Yafarra opens the *tenesh*. The lid hinge creaks. From out of the oiled leather sheathing, she gingerly presents an anomaly: an eight and a half by eleven, red notebook. Its binding is a spiraled coil of wire. Printed on the cover is the name of the manufacturing company: MEAD.

"Aethur," Yafarra repeats again. "Loche."

Rearden smiles. "New earth? Newirth. Excellent."

"Loche," the Queen says. "Loche Newirth. *Lit,* Aethur. He is in pain. . ."

Water Rights

Date unknown
The Realm of Wyn Avuqua

Loche Newirth takes another look around him before he leaves the pavilion. He has covered the bodies with the dirty swathe of bed fabric. In the dim light it would be difficult to see the blood stains in the dirt amongst the many other blackened patches of sour earth within this tent. He touches the strap of his unspoiled bag and umbrella, slung beneath the guard's foul smelling orange surcoat he has draped over his own clothes. With the cumbersome broadsword hanging at his side and leather helm he figures the costume is enough to pass among the throng unnoticed. With one last steadying breath he steps into the gloom.

But what now? How to find Edwin? Julia? And how long had he been unconscious? He glances at the sky. It is still black and moonless. Icy stars glitter through the woodsmoke rising from innumerable fires down the grid-like roads. *Godrethion* ranks, low tents, huddled soldiers around low burning flames, and lines of torchlight stand between him and what he believes should be his destination. In what looks to be the center of the *Godrethion* encampment, a high walled fortification of cut timber juts up above all else. At each corner rise archer towers. From his position Loche can discern guards on the battlements.

Where in God's name is Basil?

Without hesitation, he marches with purpose. His stride is bold, though his lowered eyes are alert to each potential threat. Two approaching soldiers nod to him as they pass by. Loche returns the gesture.

His head hurts. The cold of the air bites the wounds on his brow and left ear. His abdomen is wrenched and aching.

A gathered group of orange coated men around a fire call to him. Loche acknowledges with a raising of his hand pointing to the fort, still far ahead. As he does this his right foot tangles into a scrubby tussock sending him faltering forward and down into the mud. This sends laughter into the air. Loche quickly stands, wipes the freezing mud from his chest and face. Without turning to the group, he splashes onward. The laughter fades.

His hands tremble. He is sweating despite the cold. Dizzy. After a few more paces he finds a shadowed crossing of pathways. A cluster of low, gnarled trees clings to the edge of a gentle slope. The turf has been tramped down by marching feet. A few meters away the land drops into a shallow dell. Some kind of structure has been erected down there, but it is too dim to see it clearly. Loche reaches into his bag and produces an energy bar. He gnaws mechanically, scanning for his next few moves toward the fort. A moment later he is chewing the last bite and rummaging for his water bottle. He forces two long gulps and plugs the bottle with the cap knowing he must eat or pass out.

Somewhere below him, down the slope, a voice moans, "Water. Water." Though his mind translates the utterance, the word is clearly not Anglo Saxon, but it is not English either. He takes a reluctant step toward the voice, trying to catch a glimpse of the speaker. His eyes adjust to the dark and he discerns a gridded structure of poles and ropes resembling a kind of jungle gym one might see in a park or playground only, given the circumstances, Loche is certain that its purpose is sinister beyond words. Confirmation comes when he perceives the vague outline of a kneeling man with his arms tied high above his head. He is naked. Suddenly, Loche realizes that there are several men and women bound up in the apparatus.

"Water," the voice breathes out. Loche wonders at the language. It is not until he is able to see the man's features that he understands. Before him is a dark skinned, powerfully featured face. The dark eyes are framed with matted black hair. If Loche were to have seen this man in his own time he would have noted him as a Native American. A grisly cut has been dragged across his chest. The right side of his face is swollen as if his cheekbone has been shattered.

Loche raises his bottle and attempts to pour a little water into his mouth. The man coughs most of it out. The sound is painful.

None of the other captives stir or make a sound. Helpless, Loche lays his hand upon the man's brow.

"I am sorry," he whispers, his anger rising.

The man stares. The whites of his eyes send a chill through Loche.

Anglo Saxon words from his left: "Trying to keep him breathing longer? More sport, eh? I thought they were all dead. Still stirring, is he?" Lying upon the ground nearby are two guards. One is asleep, the other raised slightly on his elbows and watching Loche. He is wrapped in a blanket. Loche nods. "Amazing. These savages are stout, I'll give them that—but not as enjoyable as the Foamers, of course." Loche turns back to the Native American man. The guard continues, laying his head back and stretching his legs out, "Only a matter of time before all these lands are ours—we, the gods, will it. You can finish him if you like. If not, the cold will take him."

The Native American's eyes remain fixed on Loche. Then, a subtle flicker in his pupils, and whatever life was left within the man departs. No struggle left, no cries for mercy, no pleading for the suffering to end. It is as if the man's final need was simply kindness before his spirit left his body. Loche lowers the bottle without looking away from the man's widened eyes. William

Greenhame's image of a sculpture's gaze—that faraway place beyond sight, enters his mind. But this is no sculpture, Loche thinks. This is not art.

Dropping the bottle into his bag he pushes to his feet and backs away from the macabre scene.

"There will be more tied here in the morning," the guard calls as Loche strides again toward the fort.

His feet are aching cold. Every step jars his injuries, and his worry over Edwin and Julia has his stomach in knots. No alarm has been sounded, yet. *It won't be long before they find the bodies*, he thinks. But his powerful stride shows none of his fear.

After threading his way through company after company, he stands just meters from the fortification's first gate. Torches illuminate the pathway into the ward. Two pikemen hold positions on either side. They appear unconcerned with the traffic that passes between them. Several soldiers, a group of priests and a cart of supplies gain unhindered access.

Just as Loche is about to step onto the path and march through, the pikemen stop a single hooded figure under the escort of two stout soldiers. His colorless cloak is caked with dark stains of mud and possibly blood. The man sways and staggers. After a short exchange, the man stumbles backward and falls heavily upon the stones lining the path. One of the escorts lands a vicious kick to the ribs while the other lays hold of the cloak attempting to yank him upward. The two guards stare at the violence a moment and then lean over to assist in standing the prisoner on his feet.

"Ah yes," one of the guards says, "This will suit. Just what she asked for. He's had his wine by the look of him."

"That he has," another replies.

Their banter prompts Loche forward, hoping that he will pass unnoticed. He hears the cloaked man try to speak, but his words are nonsensical and slurred.

"Yes," the other pikeman says, "drunk. He'll be perfect. Send him to the stage." He gives the drunkard a shove as three soldiers grab his cloak and march him roughly up the road.

Loche moves steadily closer to the gate. After five determined paces, his body freezes. Now approaching the entry are eight soldiers and a group of four hooded monks robed in white. The soldiers' livery is the same light mail and orange coat as his own. Four appear to be escorts. The other four bear a kind of decorative stretcher upon which lies a small motionless body.

A moment later, Loche is following two steps behind the small parade and the gilded bier—just out of reach of his unconscious son.

My Heart

November 11, this year
Upper Priest Lake, Idaho
4 pm PST

In one long day's time, Astrid's world has reshaped. Beginning with Molmer's invitation to validate her life's work, she thought the morning just might become a worthwhile story to tell her assistant Marcel. If anything else, the entertaining of Molmer's claims would be a distraction from the Grant Board's humiliating reception of her research. Then, of course, two hours later, as she gaped at the eye-shaped, recently unearthed *Wyn Avuqua* from the air, how, indeed, could the day get stranger, or better?

Never Mind the impossibility of meeting an adorable archeologist (that speaks a little *Elliqui* and seems to be enthralled with her every word) just a short time before entering into the ancient citadel of *Tiris Avu.* Perhaps the old, pithy saying *follow your heart* has some merit. She's followed her academic heart, and that led her to not only *Wyn Avuqua,* but also to Graham Cremo. And further, what of the astonishingly preserved *Itonalya* scrolls, manuscripts, artifacts, textiles and sculptures lying in wait for her to study? And crossing the threshold into Queen Yafarra's tomb—seeing the crystal coffin? Career validation—meeting the love of her life. . . What more could one ask for?

Have I died and gone to Heaven?
And if so, what dreams may come?

Being a realist, it seemed to Astrid upon seeing the crystal tomb, the frequency of surprises must at some point begin to recede. She figured her proverbial Holy Grail moment would be when the ancient scroll within the sarcophagus was spread out on a table before her, and her latex-gloved fingertips traced the *Elliqui* runes of the long sought after Prophecy—the tale of the Two Brothers to come, the Painter and the Poet—their works that would end the mythic war between the immortals and the gods— that would be the moment—the last surprise. The Prophecy would be the cherry on top of what she would report to Marcel (and likely everyone she knew—and everyone she would ever meet) as the best and most thrilling day of her life.

Then, things shifted, again.

How could she ever explain or fully understand the reality of being witness to a living, breathing immortal woman buried alive for over a thousand years? For her entire career in academia Astrid has held fast to her subject's tenet of metaphorical immortality. Certainly there are *Itonalya* scholars with literal interpretations of the culture's immortal claims, much like creationists thinking the earth is six thousand years old. What mythic denomination doesn't have its literalists? Even with some of the scientific delving into the plausibility of *Itonalya* genetic cell regeneration, Astrid had remained immovable in her stance: immortality for the *Wyn Avuquains* was the society's reach toward a higher level of thought—a psychological revolution. End of conversation. Next.

Well, almost correct.

Having watched a mortal wound heal beneath a halo of white foam has forced Astrid to widen her perspective. Perhaps now, the missing puzzle pieces to her research will be easier to assemble. Perhaps. *Unbelievable* echoed in her head as she threaded her way through the shadowed library labyrinth. The true weight of *awesome,* too, seemed to resonate. Her inner thesaurus couldn't seem to land on just the right way to describe pursuing a nude immortal, freshly risen from a thousand year slumber. *Phantasmagorical? Inconceivable (like Vizzini from The Princess Bride)? Fucking nuts?*

Fucking nuts.

But what to make of this recent turn has Astrid blinking repeatedly and staring without a single syllable. Yafarra is clutching what looks like a middle schooler's faded red spiral notebook to her chest. A notebook that does not fit into the category of ancient artifact—does not align itself with any rational notion of right place, right time. The book simply doesn't belong.

Fucking nuts.

"It must have been planted there? Placed into the tomb recently, yes?" Astrid says to herself. After a beat she says, "But, Newirth. Loche Newirth. . . How could she know who Loche Newirth is?"

Yafarra watches her speak.

"Couldn't have been placed there. No way." Graham says. "The lower halls were only found by sheer accident."

"What do you mean?"

"You've seen for yourself the incredible condition of the halls—the treasures. We can only assume that when the city was sacked, these lower levels were never discovered. Otherwise, they would have been plundered and destroyed just as everything above. We found a tiny fissure in the tomb wall and pinged the radar across the lower foundation. Needless to say, we were astonished with the results. When we pried our way in—which took considerable force." He takes a look around. Yafarra stares at him intensely. "And there's more—so much more to discover. We're the first to visit the lower halls in over a thousand years."

The two look at each other and share a brief expression of wonder and gratitude—to be together here at the rainbow's end. Or the beginning.

Then simultaneously, they puzzle further. Astrid nods, grasping for another plausible explanation for the notebook. She turns to Marcus. "Rearden, you told me that Newirth would play a role eventually? That he was an authority on the subject of *Wyn Avuqua?*" She glances at the notebook. Yafarra is wide-eyed, listening and watching her. Astrid demands, "Time for some answers, Dr. Rearden. You are obviously interested in that notebook. Why don't you enlighten us. Why are you here?"

Rearden doesn't seem to hear her. Instead, his eyes remain fixed on the document held to Yafarra's breast.

"Hello?" Astrid mocks. "Anybody there?"

Slowly, he says, "Oh, I'm here. And so was he."

"Well?"

"What a question. Why am I here? Indeed, my dear, what a question. . ."

How a black revolver appeared in his hand, Astrid does not know. Another sudden item in the stone chamber that did not belong. What other turns of fate are to come? Will the waves of shock eventually slow? The firelight sparkles in Rearden's eyes and gleams on the barrel of the gun.

Astrid blinks. Images flash in her mind of Gonzaga's hallways with its thousands of black and white photographs. Alumni displayed within glass cases lining the cold corridors. Then the memory of a view from her Venice hotel room: a sable gondola crossing a Venetian canal—her husband on the phone— he says he is leaving. Then, her ex husband's note, waving like a hand from the refrigerator door: *If I could change what happened, I would. Beginning again is all I can do—make a new story. I wish it was with you.* Then, her disheveled desk covered with notes, research books on myth, several coffee cups—most of them half empty. It has always been this way. She has always been lonely. Suddenly, the shock of loneliness is a physical pain. She blinks again and sees Graham Cremo's smiling face at the helicopter pad just hours ago. He had extended his long arm and squeezed her hand. He greeted her with *Elliqui: "Lain."* His light had pierced through every shadow she hid within. His light had threaded through her soul.

When the firearm discharges, a bullet rips through Graham Cremo. He teeters for a moment, his eyes wide with confusion. One hand rises to the wound and his fingers search, as if for a pen inside his coat. Then his gaze pleads with Astrid. He says, "Astrid, my heart. Oh my heart."

A shadow covers Astrid's sight.

Moirai

Date unknown
The Realm of Wyn Avuqua

Within the inner ward are several small, stout buildings surrounding a great hall made of timber and canvas. The contingent strode directly through the gate toward a peaked pavilion connected to the east entrance of the great hall. Edwin's bier rested on a stand of crossed logs.

Now the four white-robed priests have formed a semicircle around the boy. They are kneeling, their heads are bowed. Loche watches their lips move. If it were quiet, he would hear the hiss of their whispering prayers. Instead, the enclosure is filled with the sound of a raucous celebration just through the entrance to the larger structure.

Loche stands beside his son and chances a long look. The boy is covered in white fur—a blanket made of rabbit pelts. His face is pale and his breathing is low. Without thinking, Loche reaches his hand out and touches his boy's forehead. There is no fever.

"I pray thee," one of the hooded priests says, "remove thy hand."

Loche pulls away, reluctantly.

"So we are all celestial," The monk says (Loche wonders if the man's language is a form of Greek—he is still astonished he can understand the words—and astonished his words can be understood). Rising and standing beside him the monk says, "but *It*, the One—most ancient, most radiant—how could we not desire the touch of Its presence here—here within Its greatest of creations? And here before us is *Thi—Thi* as a young master. A young boy. What perfection. What beauty." He offers Loche a kindly smile, "You are forgiven. I am Erinyes." There is a feminine quality in the voice. "Ah," he says with an empathetic sigh while appraising Loche's face, "what fear you have! And that is beautiful, too." The priest looks back down at the sleeping boy. "Do not be afraid. *Thi* sleeps. Only sleeps. Herbs the Fates hath given will keep him sleeping until middle night." The robed figure gestures to the three priests still deep in prayer.

"What herbs?" Loche asks.

"Roots and leaves from the Lakewoman," Erinyes says with an airy, circular hand-wave westward. "She hath given them to us to place our Lord *Thi* to sleep. To sleep while our people prepare to do *Thi's* bidding."

The monk's shadowed eyes drift from Edwin back to Loche. "Do not be afraid. Do you not see the thread that connects him to all things?" Erinyes points a finger and waves it over Edwin's chest as one might through a candle flame. "These strings of silk shining in the light of mighty *Thi* Itself. And the Fates," Erinyes's finger now points to the three kneeling monks, "they decide which threads to let dangle, and those to cut. Even the mighty *Thi* is subject to their will. But you know this already, do you not?"

The monk looks up at Loche. For the first time, Loche discerns features in the deep of the hood, but he is still unclear if he is conversing with a man or a woman.

"This day," Erinyes says, "I am but a mouthpiece to the three whose scales weigh the destiny of All."

Loche stares at his son. He flinches when the reveling company next-door lets out a collective cheer.

"Ah," the monk says. "She comes."

Loche raises his face to the hall. He sees a reddish glow of torchlight and moving shadows. The smell of roasted meat, lamp oil and sweat wafts from the opening.

"Come, shall we listen to our Summoner? She that has rallied stars to this forsaken wasteland?" says the monk to Loche and the other escorts. He slaps Loche's shoulder, "So far from our homes? So far. . ."

The monk takes Loche by the elbow and gently leads him a few steps away from Edwin into the great hall. Loche positions himself so he can still see his son. Turning his attention inside, the great hall is filled with armed soldiers, priests, and others that Loche cannot classify. In the reddish glow it is difficult to see faces, but after a few moments he can distinguish that the overall mood of the room is celebratory. The heady fume of wine fills the air. Mouths full of meat, wine and bread are laughing and spitting out stories of war and conquest—drums and lutes and pipes accompany the chatter and shouting of voices. Large dogs gnaw bones beneath low tables. A quarrel breaks out between three men in a far corner. One is stabbed and cries out. Just a few feet from the dying man, several shapes writhe together in silhouetted copulation. Near the west doors, a group has begun to dance in whirling circles. In the center of the hall, two high peaked fires illuminate a raised staging area. It is enclosed with waist-high timber railings.

Despite the chaos, and the thudding pain at his ear, a steadying calm settles over Loche. He turns and takes another look at his sleeping son. The praying monks still hold vigil. The exit to the adjacent pavilion is a mere fifteen steps. Ten at a dead run. He scans for any sign of Julia.

A high-pitched whine pulls Loche's attention back to the stage where a man carries what looks to be a kind of bagpipe. The riotous clamor lessens and slowly quiets. The piper then blasts a melody bringing voices to a halt. Its intensity rivets every eye to the stage. Loche wonders if the song is an anthem of sorts. He, himself, feels the haunting pull of it.

When the last notes die only the breathing torches fluttering in the gloom and the crackling fires are heard. The piper turns and steps down. Several soldiers, all wearing varied regal attire, surround the stage and face outward. Etheldred is among them, still garbed in his orange coat and glinting mail, but now wearing a high helm with plumes of white feathers. Slumped down beside Etheldred, Loche recognizes the drunk and muddied priest from the gate. He recalls the pikemen saying the cloaked man was perfect. *Perfect for what?* he wonders. The man is hunched down leaning against the timber stage supports at Etheldred's boots. His face still shadowed within his hood.

Then from the darkness between the two bright fires, a woman appears. Her gold and silver robe is like a stab of sunlight. She is slender, tall and moves with a commanding confidence. Her leg breaches the gown as she strides to the center of the stage. There Loche can see that she is wearing plate armor greaves. A long sword, swathed in a scabbard of leather and white fur, rests on her thigh.

"All hail!" a foreboding command resounds. "Our Summoner, Cynthia, goddess and deliverer of the Lord God, Almighty *Thi*."

The silence explodes into a fury of battle cries.

Loche sees the woman's eyes swirl like green glitter in a jar. A familiar chill scrapes along his spine. Erinyes, beside him, says, "Serpent."

Loche sees the Devil.

The Exchange

November 11, this year
Upper Priest Lake, Idaho
4:15 pm PST

Somewhere above and behind, a resounding boom thunders through the chamber.

The thought suddenly occurs to Astrid that she has spent her life studying the dead—dead cultures, dead languages, dead stories, the dead past. A student of history, she has delved into the effects of war, famine and plague. Ancient tombs and mass graves in some strange way have, over the years, become home. But she has never imagined that death could look like this.

Another rumble reverberates through stone.

Astrid cradles Graham's head. Her sight has telescoped to a single, narrow circle. In its center is the lifeless face of Graham Cremo. She searches frantically for the connecting line of light they shared. Instead she feels tears on her face.

Words do not form when she tries to speak. Only a breathy, moaning cry. She does not immediately feel the cold of the firearm's barrel against her temple. She does not immediately register Rearden's voice demanding, "The Prophecy, Professor. Yafarra will hand the Prophecy to me." She does not immediately realize that her sobbing is mixed with the word "No," over and over again, or that her emotional surrender is an outpouring of bottled up loneliness. She holds Graham's head as if she had known him for a lifetime—as if she has done this before.

The bitter irony hammers through her. She found a candle burning in the dark of her heart, in this lonely life, and it has been snuffed out. She has discovered that the past she's pursued is not dead, but more alive than she could have dreamed. The flash of a loss in her past takes her breath, but she cannot fully see the incident. Everything blurs as if she were submerged in water. She crimps her eyes shut and wrestles with the thought. Finally words come.

"What have you done?" She hears herself scream at Rearden. She's shocked at her ferocity and sharp articulation.

"What I am about to do to you if you do not relay to Her Majesty that the Prophecy. . .that Red Notebook should be handed to me." Rearden's manner and tone is eerily calm and steady.

"You've killed— you've murdered—"

"I know what I've done, Professor. It cannot be undone." After a pause he shifts his tone, as if he were speaking to himself, "At least, not as long as the Poet lives— and the Prophecy remains unread. . ."

Astrid seeks out Yafarra. The Queen's expression is a storm of anger and sadness.

"What are you talking about?" Astrid says.

"The Prophecy," Rearden demands, ignoring her question and extending his hand to receive it.

"She will not let it go," Astrid says.

Far back through the preceding tunnel, a booming shudders and crackles through the walls. A fine dust sifts down through the orange light. *They've breeched the Eye*, Astrid thinks.

"Oh, I believe she will hand it over," Rearden insists. "She is *Itonalya*. Ancient *Orathom Wis*. It is in her blood to protect humankind. Can't you see her struggling?"

Yafarra's face is twisted with confusion and wrath. She clutches the Notebook tighter as her focus tacks from the gun against Astrid's head, to Graham, to Rearden.

"She's weighing her position. She's trying to work out a solution. She'll eventually choose your life as the most important part of this equation. . . just watch."

Astrid nearly spits, "Or she might be reliving a thousand years trapped in a coffin, you sadistic fuck."

"Tell her to give me the Prophecy," Rearden dismisses Astrid's response. "Tell her now."

"If I don't?"

Rearden's thumb clicks the pistol's hammer back. "Please, Professor Finnley, I'd prefer not to kill further. But if I am refused, you both die. You from a gunshot, Yafarra, I'll shoot and dismember." He waits. "Tell her."

Astrid and Rearden lock eyes. Glassy tears magnify the gun, the Red Notebook, the body of Graham. A tornado of responses blow through her mind. *Fuck you, do it, you won't get out of here alive without us. And good luck taking Yafarra's life, you idiot. Dying here is the best I could ever ask for.*

Rearden sighs. "Should I count to three?"

"Fuck you." She diverts to Graham's seemingly sleeping face.

Rearden sighs again, only this time with an air of pity mixed with impatience. "If only you knew the depth of this document. You could be of some use to me." He shakes his head. "One. . ."

Fear jolts through her nervous system. Her body trembles. Graham's skin is cooling. She laces her fingers in his. Bitter gun smoke lingers in the air.

"Two. . . Don't be a fool, Astrid. All your life you've sought this moment. To know the contents of the Prophecy. Do not throw your life away. Not now."

She closes her eyes and braces herself. She feels the strength of her arms pull tight and her shoulders straighten.

"What resolve," Rearden's voice is tinged with marvel. "Pity," he adds. "Three. . ."

As if in answer to Rearden, Yafarra's voice says, "*Nit! Ag!*" When Astrid opens her eyes she sees the Queen extending the Red Notebook with her long arm.

Rearden reaches out and takes hold of it. For a moment the two remain gripping it between them.

From Yafarra's lips comes a hissing string of words. It takes a moment for Astrid to register that the words are English. Broken, halting and laced with a haunting, indeterminable accent, but English, nonetheless. "You will fall, Marcus Rearden. Aethur will find you. He will cast you into the abyss."

She pierces Rearden's gaping expression with a calm, knowing smile.

A thread tugs at the corner of Rearden's confidence. "So you can speak—" Rearden starts.

"Abyss," she says, striking his words from the air. "You desire the writing of the Poet, but you do not yet know the power of his words. You do not know the power of your own words. You will fall. You will fall."

Rearden studies her for a few moments before his incredulity passes. As he takes the notebook he growls, "My good Queen, I know much more than you give me credit for. If I am not mistaken, no one has read what is in that notebook. And doing so could potentially change everything. You, this place," he pauses, "and maybe me. . ."

Yafarra does not respond.

Rearden tucks the Red Notebook into his coat. "Well, we shall soon see."

"Not yet," Yafarra says.

A kind of smile spreads across Rearden's face. The expression bears no connection to happiness or fulfillment. Instead Rearden's face looks as if some torture behind his eyes is forcing him to smile. He then raises his hand to his ear and taps his transmitter. The gun is still leveled to kill. "Eastman," he says, "I have the Prophecy."

Yafarra crawls to Astrid. The two sit together, staring at Dr. Marcus Rearden in the flaring light. Graham's forehead is chilled. The clatter of boots can be heard running toward them from the black tunnel when Astrid feels Graham's hand squeeze hers.

The Garden of Evil

Date unknown
The Realm of Wyn Avuqua

"Hold your breath. Breathe not. Do not speak a word. I know your story, for it is mine also. . ."

Cynthia speaks slowly with crystalline elegance, each syllable sharp and cutting, each word weighted with its full meaning.

"We the Banished. And now we are returned." There is a longing in her timbre—a cello-bowed fullness and want in her pace.

"I am the Summoner, but it was not I who called you to this distant land. It was the voice of *Thi*." Her long hair glimmers in the flickering light. She stands motionless and waits as if to allow the roaring fires a moment to speak. "It was not I who made you. It was the word of *Thi*," Again the fire hisses and crackles in answer. Her glittering eyes track from uplifted face to face, but it seems to Loche that she is staring at him alone. "It was not I who filled your hearts with vengeance and a thirst for blood. It was the tale of *Thi* that kindled you, that lit you, that burns in you now."

Her arms open outward and spread, "And behold, we have each awakened. Each of us gods! Your blindness is healed, and you find yourselves within the paradise you have pined for. Though it was not made for you. A fleeting moment within the glory and joy of *Thi's* work. Though we have been starved of it and long ago banished from its shores. *Thi* has granted you entry to Its most prized garden—Its beloved jewel—Its masterwork. Though only to perform a single, bloody task. You are gods! You walk upon *Thi's* Earth, among his children. And for this brief season, *Thi* grants our will in this place. All for the price of obedience."

She raises her hand in a gesture of warning, "And what does our Lord command? For It did not open Its gates idly. He has given us a purpose, has He not? A valiant and noble task, yes? He has bred within us a fury toward his disobedient subjects: the guardians of this coveted place in existence—the rebellious, treacherous, Immortal race. They who have hunted and slain our kind since the beginning." Her long arm gestures to the northwest—a finger pointing like the tip of a blade, "The *Itonalya's* city of *Wyn Avuqua* will be destroyed. We shall grind its walls to dust! We shall put to flame its houses, its temples, its words! We will fill the lake waters with heads and build a bridge across *Thi's* sight!"

The roar of furious approval rattles Loche's ribcage as if his heart is raging against the bars of a cell. Cynthia watches and listens for a moment and then raises her hand against the din. The voices quiet. The fires crackle.

"It was not I who summoned you hither to kill. It was *Thi*." The woman lowers her arm and appears to consider a sudden thought.

Her sparkling green eyes widen and an overdramatic expression of round-mouthed wonder appears on her face. "But something eludes me, my dear brothers and sisters. Something so very confounding. Tell me, if you can, why does the mighty Lord God, *Thi* call upon. . . us? Have we not been banished from this place? Am I the only one here that is confused by this? Has He no other way to shepherd and punish His flock of undying guardians than to call upon. . . us? And now, after refusing to share paradise, to capture it back for himself, he uses us?" Her incredulity recedes and a look of grace and thoughtful piety forms. "Shall I show you how I feel about this hypocrisy? This injustice?"

The fires snap and breathe. The throng is silent. Loche turns his head to learn if their faces are answering her question. Those he can make out seem pained and empathetic, as if they are being injured by some hidden weapon and then asked to worship both the weapon and the hand that wields it.

"Shall I show you my pain? For I know it is yours also."

A collective agreement begins with nods, quiet mutters of, "Aye," and the stamping of feet.

"Very well." The armored woman smiles and turns her face in Loche's direction. Loche flinches as her focus pierces through the shadows and brooding atmosphere of the host— through to his very soul. A violent chill slides down his back and he feels his disguise has been compromised. His hand raises to steady himself in the doorway.

Cynthia points, "I shall also share our pain of exile with our Maker, our Lord God! Behold, Soldiers of the Void, the mighty *Thi* has come to us! And I shall place Him before you!"

Loche turns to see Edwin's bier now being hoisted just behind him. The hooded priests lead the procession bearing tall poles with suspended oil lamps. The throng obediently provides a narrow aisle as they pass into the enclosure.

Loche falls in and takes a position following just behind Edwin's sleeping face. His boy is an arm's reach away.

Expressions

November 11, this year
Upper Priest Lake, Idaho
5:15 pm PST

It is impossible for Astrid to read Yafarra's expression as they emerge into the cold gloaming. High work lights prick the dusk. Yafarra squints looking up. She searches the sky, then to the perimeter lamps, to a passing mud splattered utility truck, to a toppled stone column half uncovered from centuries of sediment and the world's turning soil. Sorrow marks her eyes. Wonder glitters in her tears. Anger is stretched across her trembling cheeks and lips. Her wrists are bound by a zip tie. Astrid can only guess at the fury, confusion and focus Yafarra must be balancing with every step out of her newly departed grave.

Astrid senses the look on her own face now. Her wrists are also bound, and she feels tears as she scans for Graham's body.

As soon as Eastman and her teams stormed the Queen's chamber, Astrid screamed for them to help. "He's still alive!" She kept shouting. With a nod, Eastman singled out three of her people to lift his body and evacuate him. That was a half hour ago. Yafarra and Astrid were then bound and forced to kneel beside an ancient, chest-like cabinet. A preliminary search of the chamber was conducted. Eastman did not speak a word. Dr. Marcus Rearden stood beside her, expressionless, his unnerving, creepy peeks straying to Astrid from time to time.

The November air diffuses in Astrid's lungs, and clarity, hope and needed energy pumps through her circulatory system.

Eastman leads the small procession of guards, Marcus Rearden, and the two women into what Astrid guesses is the site's security area, which is nothing more than a huge wall tent with a perimeter fence. Several security-styled vehicles crowd a muddied lot a stone's throw away. Just beyond the lamps is the dark tree-line and the edge of the dig-site itself. Inside the tent are a computer bay, a few desks, munitions and a small break area.

Another burst of oxygenated blood explodes through Astrid upon seeing Graham's body on a stretcher at the far end of the enclosure. He has been bandaged. Intravenous fluid drips from a hanging bottle through a catheter in his arm. A clear mask fogs over his nose and mouth. It looks to Astrid as if the bullet hit him just below his left shoulder—a red blotch in the white dressing, dangerously close to his heart.

"He'll live," Eastman says quietly, "maybe. For your sake, I hope he does. At least for now. It's pretty bad." From a shelf, she takes a small document case and opens it. The black rectangular case is metal and fitted with a complex locking apparatus.

"Dr. Rearden," Eastman says, "please place the Red Notebook within." Astrid notes that this is the first time Eastman has addressed Rearden since her team broke their way into the Queen's chamber. "The contents are not to be perused until the Board decides."

"Understood," Rearden agrees.

Eastman watches Rearden place the book inside. She shuts the lid and presses the latch closed. A dim, red light appears on a black square beneath the leather handle.

"Travel arrangements have been made. Arrangements I think you'll find preferable to a transcontinental flight. You'll be in Venice faster than you can imagine."

Rearden laughs. It is the first seemingly genuine sound Rearden has made. "Oh. I can imagine." Then he whispers to himself, "Forgotten memories. Forgotten memories."

"We have sent word to The Board and Mr. Ravistelle," Eastman says. Rearden nods.

Astrid recalls Ravistelle's face projected onto the screen earlier that morning. An image from nineteenth century London, and another from this century.

"Shame about Graham." Eastman sighs without raising her eyes from the locked case. "He is important to the operation. We still have some need of him, for now. . ."

Astrid feels the wind knocked out of her when her voice cries, "This son of a bitch shot him!"

"You'll have to carry him across," Eastman continues as if she did not hear Astrid, "You'll have assistance when you arrive." Eastman leans toward Rearden. Her voice hushes, "Ravistelle and the Board want all of this kept quiet, as I'm sure you're fully aware." She pauses and glances over at Graham's body. "Obviously, given your actions."

Rearden's face remains stoic.

"All potential leaks are to be silenced. No loose ends." She nods toward Astrid. "But let's get the necessary information we need from them before we—"

Rearden suddenly raises his hand. The gesture is easily understood and Eastman changes the subject away from business best left private. With a subtle smirk, Eastman says, "Take Dr. Finnley to the vehicle. Secure her inside and return for orders."

Rearden turns, and again Astrid grasps for some way to read a facial expression. A slight smile, or is it a deep regret seeking to be hidden beneath a smile? Is that insanity she sees, or a hardened resolve? Is there a caring, a sympathy in the way his head is slightly tilted, or is he pitying her ignorance? Is his face young or old?

Then a cold terror takes her breath. Down some black abyss within her abdomen, she translates his countenance. For an instant, it is completely unbelievable. But the exquisite duplicity, the elegant meaning, the flickering fire behind that masked half-smile are unmistakable. Her mind wriggles for a way out. If Graham could, he would likely say something about a gangster movie at this point. That indiscernible gesture from the Godfather that condones and orders a death. Almost *Elliqui*-like, Astrid sees Rearden's meaning and intention as if Michael Corleone himself was sending the traitor, Carlo, to the death car.

Astrid locks eyes with Yafarra. "Graham *shawis*," she cries to the Queen. "Graham *shawis!*" The Queen's response comes as a barely perceptible narrowing of her eyes. And as two black-coated security guards shove Astrid roughly into the cold, she thinks she heard the word, or felt, "*Courage. Courage, Astrid.*"

A white van idles and its back windowless doors open to receive her.

Hold Your Breath

Date unknown
The Realm of Wyn Avuqua

Loche attends the procession to the stage, keeping his eyes forward. He senses a slight nudge of vertigo when the shadowed audience surrounding him bows and kneels. For a brief moment it feels as if he himself, the bearers of his son and the Fates with the bright lamps held aloft have all risen into the air and now glide a short distance above the ground. Loche chances a quick look to the side at what he can only describe as a religious rite: the riotous throng bowing in reverent submission as God passes through. God. However, there is something much more frightening and profound weighing in his senses. Not an agreed upon ritual or construct, but instead, it is as if each individual body in the enclosure cowers beneath an invisible axe angled just above them.

Loche keeps his head down as he passes Etheldred at the forefront of the aisle. The intoxicated monk is still comatose and splayed on the ground.

The procession steps onto the platform. The Fates set the lighted poles at each corner and kneel at the bases. Edwin's bier is laid upon a timbered x-shaped halter that suspends his sleeping body at the back of the stage. The guards with Loche descend from the stage and stand just beside the stair. Loche stands with them—Edwin on the far side—too far away.

Cynthia pronounces, "He hath come to us. Behold, our Lord God, *Thi*."

Loche notes a reluctance and a mocking smirk as the woman turns her back to the audience and takes a knee before Edwin. She waits a few moments, stands and says to the congregation, "Rise."

They obey. Bodies lean and heads tilt to get a glimpse of their Maker. Some begin to weep openly. Others tremble.

"Let *Thi* see the pain He hath caused." Cynthia shouts. "Bring forth one of His guardians. Bring her!"

From between the fires, Julia Iris appears. Two large captors throw her to Cynthia's feet. Loche takes an unconscious step toward her—the handle of his umbrella suddenly in his grip. He freezes. Waiting. Watching. His eyes flitting from his son to Julia.

"This one," Cynthia points, her tone mocking, "is an innocent. Innocent *Itonalya*. Is there such a thing? But I have learned that this one has never killed—has not yet sought to ease the crawling in her skin that we—we holy people, cause her to feel. Can't you see?" Cynthia picks at Julia's jacket with curiosity. She lets her hand graze over the waterproof parka. She pauses at the touch of it, then her hand gathers a handful of Julia's hair. She says, "Look how calm. Look how docile."

Julia raises her face. There is no trace of fear. Her dark eyes squint slightly at the towering, armored woman but do not waiver. It appears to Loche that she is attempting to work out how to escape. But she cannot hide the effect of the *Rathinalya*. Her right hand clutches the key necklace under her shirt and her right leg trembles beneath her kneeling body. The series of Julia's trials cascade across Loche's memory. From Rearden's gunshot wound to Helen's vicious cruelty, Julia's newly found immortality has brought little joy. *But now what?* Loche wonders. *What more will she be forced to endure? Can I stop it?*

"The pain of exile," Cynthia pronounces, "is something we have all shared in words together—told our tales to one another, have we not?" She drops a venomous scowl to Julia, and then turns to the sleeping boy, "But mighty *Thi*, my Lord and Maker, I think it infinitely more powerful to show you the torment and misery you have wrought within us through banishment."

The two guards grab Julia's shoulders and arms as she involuntarily flails her body to escape. Both of Cynthia's hands seize Julia's face. One clamps over her mouth, the other pinches her nostril's shut. Cynthia wrenches her captive's head and crushes it against her armored abdomen.

"Does it not feel like this, brothers and sisters?" Cynthia hisses between her teeth. "Banishment from *Thi's* creation? To endure perpetual epochs away from *Thi's* masterwork? Does it not feel like this?" The throng is silent, but Loche senses an overwhelming wave of empathetic pain and longing. Tears form in the eyes of some watching— as if Julia's desperate need of air is a sensation well known among them—but only a metaphoric hint at the real torment they have been forced to endure as they suffered the torture of banishment.

Julia writhes and thrashes, thirsting for oxygen. The white ovals of her eyes are wide in terror.

"This is what we suffer! We, deathless gods through time unfathomable, beholding that which we cannot have!" Julia's body jerks violently. "And if by some miracle we break *Thi's* ancient law, and we arrive here, we cross over, and we taste the salt of the sea, touch the lips of a lover, hear the voice of a laughing child, scent the spilling blood of our enemies—"

The woman's merciless grip tightens, tearing deeper into her victim's skin. Julia slowly loses strength. Her resistance convulses and recedes. The two guards let go as her arms drop limply to her sides. Cynthia throws Julia's head forward and down—her right cheek smashes into the wood slatted stage. Her nose is bleeding. She coughs, spraying blood out in bright red beads.

The struggle between rushing to her aid and remaining hidden starts a hammer-like pressure beating within Loche's inner ear. He shakes his head attempting to rouse his senses to some kind of order.

"And behold, the suffering of the Immortal!" Julia's eyes flip open as she heaves in gulps of air. "Our treacherous enemy that, for eons, has starved our lungs from life's breath—we do not forget! We cannot." She speaks to Julia, "The sight of your pain is to us like the delicious oxygen you drink in now, *Orathom Wis* cur!"

Cynthia crouches down beside Julia. "But for this short season," her tone softening, "we are not banished. For this brief moment in eternity, we will breathe, and we shall taste, and touch. We shall listen to the screams of our enemies, and we shall watch them bleed."

She appeals to the throng, "Shall we make her bleed?"

The chorus of ecstasy and anger is like a dagger stabbed into Loche's ear.

Julia struggles to gain her composure. A light white foam envelops the cuts along her nose. Her right eye is swollen shut.

Cynthia raises her hand and the clamor dies again.

"Or shall we make all of our enemies bleed?" she asks simply. She rises from Julia and strides to Edwin's raised body. "For we are but surrounded by enemies, it seems." She positions herself behind the sleeping child and stares out to the assembly.

"Some of our enemies we must seek out. We will know them by sight." She looks at Edwin, "But, as the Fates would have it, enemies are delivered into our keeping without understanding. So often our piteous senses seek outward for adversaries, when in truth, the real demon lurks within."

The gathering issues sounds of revelation and fear. Loche's adrenaline surges and his focus narrows on the distance between his son and himself.

A man nearby utters a whispered, "No."

Others sound out affirmation. "Our Creator is our torture," one shouts.

A few begin to chant, "*Thi* is pain!"

A gleaming long-bladed dagger flashes like a spark thrown from between the framing fires. Cynthia raises it with both hands above her head and aims its point downward at Edwin's chest. She holds the pose and watches the audience. Gasps of shock rush in the air like the sound of sea spray in a storm.

Many things happen simultaneously.

Seeing the suspended knife, Loche's hand flies to his sword hilt. Just as his body commits to a lunge forward, a hand on his shoulder yanks him back. The heat of a hissing whisper tears into his left ear. "Do you believe in the Devil?" the voice says. "For there she is. Behold the Nicolas Cythe to come." Instantaneously, Loche notes that the words are spoken in perfect modern English. His head swivels to see another robed man. Within the shadowed hood are the familiar deep brown eyes of Corey Thomas. His breath smells of scotch. "You have friends here. You are not alone. Do not attack yet. Be still. Trust me. . ."

At the sight of the dagger, a maniacal tremor of both debate and epiphany sweeps through the crowd. One shouts, "It must be done! God hath taken our lives, let us take His! Kill the boy god!"

Another cries, "Stay your hand, O Cynthia! Vengeance will be *Thi's* in the end!"

"If He is truly *Thi*, He will save himself!"

"Kill him!"

For Loche Newirth, reason and hope fade. Periphery blurs. The single instinct to hurl himself to the space between the dagger and his son ignites every muscle. Unable to process Corey's words, his legs press toward his son. Corey's grip intensifies and sends flashes of searing white light through

Loche's vision. His limbs paralyze. His mind overloads with helpless fury.

"Do not move, Loche. Not yet. She will not strike. Wait."

Cynthia holds the sacrificial dagger high and surveys the riotous storm before her.

She cries out, "Hold your breath, brothers and sisters. Hold your breath. . ."

When the Doors Shut

November 11, this year
Upper Priest Lake, Idaho
5:45 pm PST

When the doors shut, there is no light. She cannot see her hand before her eyes. She questions if her eyes are indeed open. She questions if she will ever see light again.

When one sense is removed, the others become more acute. Her feet can feel the gentle vibration of the running engine. She can hear its low hum. The scent in the stifling compartment is similar to most new vehicles. A kind of manufacture's perfume: new oiled parts, sweet polished leather. She would reach to find a door handle if she could. The plastic zip tie holding her arms behind her back cuts into her wrists. She stoop-stands, turns and lets her fingers search for a latch. There is nothing but smooth, cold metal.

Her mind is seething. Thoughts crowd for space like strobing pictures on a screen. Rearden's face behind a pistol. Yafarra encased in crystal. A red spiral notebook. Graham Cremo's pale face. The mystery of Aethur or Loche Newirth. . . The blackness sucks oxygen from her lungs. Her chest concusses as if a stone bangs against her rib cage. *An anxiety attack is coming,* she thinks. She suddenly becomes aware that she has been screaming and crying out, "Let me go! Let me go!" She holds her breath. Perhaps for the first time in her life all she can do is weep. The darkness somehow makes it easier. No one can see her crying.

Courage, Astrid.

The thought drapes over her, *They are going to kill me—They are going to kill Graham.*

As if in answer, she imagines Graham beside her saying, *But they need us still. They have questions about the site and*

Yafarra, and I'm sure, the Itonalya. Things that only we can answer. But we've seen too much— and they won't let us go knowing what we know.

Astrid inhales slowly, and for a moment believes he is with her. *I'm sorry I couldn't get you out earlier,* her mind lets him say. *I'm afraid we were both trapped by what we love.*

Astrid lets the thought sink in. Graham's warning at the crystal tomb did not deter her. In fact, it spurred her on. She saw a door. A door to her dreams. A door she has longed to open and, come Heaven or Hell, she would open it. She finds it ironic suddenly that the door upon which she gazed when Graham issued his warning in *Elliqui,* was the lid of a coffin.

The vehicle gently dips as if a driver has climbed in. Instead of the a door slamming, it closes with a quiet, yanking click. It drops into gear. Then, movement. It begins to roll. Menacingly slow.

Again, Astrid wishes that this imagined Graham in her head would quote a movie—but she is afraid he would bring up some vision of a car crossing into the Las Vegas desert with Joe Pesci at the wheel and a body in the trunk. Or fat Peter Clemenza telling his henchman to, *leave the gun. take the cannoli.* Instead, her Graham is silent. She feels his hand tighten on hers.

The compartment wobbles over uneven roads, and thuds into ruts and holes. The vehicle is still rolling slowly.

Just as Astrid is about to pose the question, *why so slow?* The van accelerates and the engine pitch winds up in bursts. She is thrown to the side and her body crashes to the floor. She braces her feet and presses back against the wall. The vertigo of speed, breaking, the pressing of hard turns, and the rattle and pounding of the wheels forces every sinew and muscle to anchor. Below is the scrape of gravel and skidding tires. Another turn and the van throttles up. The road smoothes as if they have skidded onto pavement. She notes the transmission gearing up to an even cruising speed. Gut wrenching, blind curves follow. Her temples ache from squeezing her eyes shut. Stomach acid burns the back of her throat. She imagines a view through the windshield and attempts to predict each wind in the road and the double yellow lines snaking just out of the reach of the headlights.

The van brakes hard and she vaults forward to the front of the compartment while the rest of her pulls back for balance. Then a sharp turn to the right. Astrid guesses they have left the pavement and are now hurtling down a dirt road.

"What's the rush?" she cries.

When her imagined Graham does not answer, she pictures another of those packed-with-meaning, blank expressions from Eastman's face—one eye hidden by a swoop of grey hair, the other eye winking to the driver, *Get rid of her fast. No loose ends.*

A faint taste of dust rises. The turns, the whirling motion and rattle of the wheels—what dark clearing is the driver heading for? Will she be able to see the lake before the end? The sky? She did not tell Graham that she felt. . . something. . . something electric. . . when they met. . . she did not tell him that for the first time in her life, the door to her heart could open.

The van lurches hard to the left, slows and halts. The engine dies. Silence. The Graham in her heart whispers, *we'll find a way out of this.* His fingers find her cheek. *Ag shivcy. Linna avusht.* She tries to believe him.

The driver's door opens. Shoes crackle on the ground. Footsteps circle around to the back of the vehicle. Keys chime. A key slides into the lock, the latch clicks and indigo light pours through the widening doors.

The driver peers into the dark compartment. His eyes are concerned, curious and familiar. So, too, is the tuft of red hair sprouting from his head, the carved and elegant face, the glowing blue eyes. "Professor Finnley?" he says, straining to see.

"Marcel? Marcel! Oh God, Marcel!"

Framed in the door with the glittering night behind him is Astrid's assistant, Marcel "Red Hawk" Hruska.

"I stole a van," he says. "And a professor."

The Old Law

Date unknown
The Realm of Wyn Avuqua

Shadows bend and waver. To massive pillars of fire bookend the stage. Between their high flames, a knife is held aloft by the hand of the Devil. Below its point is young Edwin, asleep. Julia Iris tries to crawl away, teetering on the edge of consciousness.

"Wait," Corey hisses again into Loche's ear, "it is not his fate to die—not yet." The chaos of debate rages through the enclosure.

Cynthia lowers the knife and steps back from Edwin's sleeping body. She circles around the bier and positions herself in the center of the stage. Cold air whistles in from an open door. The blazing flames brighten, devouring the new oxygen. Cynthia neither motions or gestures but the monk at the far corner of the stage, Erinyes, rises as if summoned.

"Remember," Corey's voice whispers, "we must take care in our actions. We must not alter what is to come. Beware of all you do."

With both hands, Erinyes pushes his hood back. Loche is again confounded by the features of the face now fully visible in the firelight. Is it a woman? A man? In the expression there is the weight and surety of a male's dominating nature, yet, somehow, as the robed figure raises open palms high above the long locks of black hair, as if to embrace the assembly, the face takes on the comfort and care of a woman's grace. Erinyes's focus is unmoving. The irises are alarmingly black—profoundly dilated. Posed and staring across a sea of silent gods, Erinyes's otherworldly visage reminds Loche of the shuddering terrors within Basil Fenn's Center—the blurred streaks of light, the smears at the edge of vision. *Erinyes belongs across the gulf*, he thinks.

Cynthia pronounces, "The Old Laws we must obey. Even our Maker, our Lord and Light, *Thi* is bound to the Law. The Fates will decide. . ."

Erinyes shouts for all to hear, "As with all that bear a thread of light to our prison, our exile, fate shall decide. *Thi* has broken His own command and has interfered with His beloved creation. So it is just that His thread be cut." A murmur of approval rustles through the crowd. Erinyes turns to the still kneeling Fates and says, "*Thi's* destiny shall be determined in the old ways—His path shall be dictated by blood. Only through a contest of arms shall the Fates be appeased and the Old Law upheld." To Cynthia, Erinyes says, "A lesser god must win the right to cut our Maker's light. Chance commands. . ."

Cynthia replies, "I will obey,"

Erinyes calls out to the witnesses, "Cynthia seeks the right to kill *Thi*, our Maker, our Creator. But *Thi* must have a champion. Bring one of *Thi's* immortals—bring one of His Guardians!"

The challenge incites jeering shouts from the host. Two soldiers wrestle the cloaked drunk at Etheldred's feet forward and stand him up. It is suddenly clear to Loche that the drunkard's presence and condition was planned. Immediately, the man falters, tips and tumbles back. But before the guards need to catch him from falling, his legs straighten and flinch, and he catches himself. Laughter erupts from those at the front of the assembly. Gaining his balance, the cloaked man is escorted to the stair with slaps and shoves, and he is thrown upward onto the wood planks. The cheering and mockery continue.

"A Guardian! *Thi's* guardian. An *Orathom Wis!* A *Wyn Avuquain* soldier is before you! Shall this be *Thi's* Champion?" Erinyes asks.

Riotous applause and approval.

The man laboriously crawls toward Julia near the edge of the stage. Her wounds are now ebbing a white foam. She brushes at her left eye as if struggling to see. The drunkard gets to his feet after some unsteady wobbling, his cloaked head angling down as if studying her—as one immortal might show concern for another. Julia, too dazed and injured to notice him, rolls onto her side and presses her hands over her eyes.

A sword clangs onto the wood platform at the man's feet. The hood swivels to it. After a swaying pause, he bends to pick it up. Rising, he nearly totters over. His legs stumble to a clumsy balance. More laughter explodes from the crowd.

Erinyes calls, "Bring wine!"

Someone in the assembly jeers, "The *Itonalya* has had his share!"

Loche watches Cynthia, who is stoic, still. She has already drawn her sword and she rests her gauntleted hand upon the pommel, the blade tip is tacked to the stage.

A wooden tray is brought to Erinyes with two goblets of wine. Erinyes presents the tray. Cynthia takes a goblet. The tray is then brought to the man. His gloved hand reaches to receive the wine but misses the cup's thick stem. He tries again to take hold of the goblet. He staggers, sways and then holds his palm out. His hood shakes from side to side as a gesture of *no*.

Insults and mocking cries are thrown. "He's had too much!" some cry out. "Can't hold his wine!" others laugh.

Cynthia lifts her goblet high and proclaims, "For the right of vengeance! To the death of *Thi*. To our freedom." Her army cheers. She tips the wine into her mouth and drinks, then tosses the goblet out to the assembly.

The drunkard, his body still lolling to and fro as if he were standing on the deck of a boat at sea, lifts his hand again, signaling both Erinyes and Cynthia to wait.

He leans over and fumbles the long cloak to the side exposing his forward leg and high leather boots. He crams his hand down inside the cuff above the knee. After a moment of struggling, his body attempts to raise back up, pulling against something tucked down against his calf.

It is at this moment Loche hears Corey speak into his ear suddenly, "When it is time, get Edwin out of the fort. Go through the east door. Once you're out, follow the others. But now, wait. You'll know the time. Remember to take care in all you do. We cannot alter what is to come."

The man frees from his boot what looks to be a bottle—a glass bottle. Loche squints to make out the contents. Even in the orange firelight and the man's fumbling, Loche recognizes the liquid and its container immediately. It is a nearly full fifth of The Macallan single malt scotch.

The cork squeaks out.

Then the man's clear voice rings. The sound of it sends an electric jolt through Loche's heart. "To the Old Law," he proclaims in modern English, delivered as if it were a line in a play. "And to this beautiful boy—my dear grandson!"

He lifts the bottle to his lips and tips it back. The hood falls away and drapes his shoulders, exposing an angular face and long dark hair. Standing now between the two raging pillars of fire, pulling a mouthful of scotch, is William Hubert Greenhame.

Loche's breathing halts. Tears rush and blur his vision. Disbelief and joy collide in his mind.

Doubling Back

November 11, this year
Upper Priest Lake, Idaho
6:01 pm PST

When Marcel cuts the zip-tie, Astrid whirls around and throws her arms around him. She cannot let go. Marcel holds her. She has never hugged him and does not immediately note his awkward embrace.

He says, "I take it that stealing the van with you in it was the right choice?" Astrid squeezes harder. "I didn't like the look of those men. And when I saw your hands were tied—well, what else was there to do?" Astrid squeezes again. "And, I mean, what did they expect? You don't just leave a nice van like that running without anyone to watch it—this is a bad neighborhood." Astrid feels a smile. "There are ruffians about." She releases him, rests her forehead at the center of his chest for a moment and then looks up at him.

A spray of orange freckles almost seem to glow on his pale skin. Clear pinpricks of stars crown his shoulder-length red hair. His twenty-something eyes are troubled, confident and frightened all at once.

"Professor," he says lowering his arms, "what's going on?"

How to answer? Astrid wonders. Her life's work vindicated? The glory of *Wyn Avuqua's* unearthing? The reality of a living, breathing Immortal Queen? The anomaly of a 1970s spiral notebook found in a millennia-old coffin? Of all the ways to begin, she cannot shake the horror of the dark ride to what she thought would be her end.

Opening her mouth to answer him, she has no words. He watches her. "Professor, what is going on?"

"Graham Cremo. . ." she says, finally.

"Graham Cremo?" Marcel repeats. "Graham Cremo. Who is Graham Cremo?"

The fear subsides.

Tonight she will not be strangled, or shot in the head here in the woods beside Priest Lake—buried in a shallow grave. Silenced. Tonight she has escaped assassination through sheer luck. Fate. Because her assistant Marcel Hruska just happened to find her—just in time. Luck. . .

Graham, however, is so far, not so lucky.

"We have to go back," she tells him.

"Who is Graham Cremo?" Marcel says.

"They are going to kill him. They were going to kill me," she hears herself say. She hears her own panic. She steadies herself.

"Okay. Okay," Marcel says. "Slow down."

"Graham is the head archeologist on the dig. He was hurt. He was shot. Now they are going to kill him. We have to go back."

"Prof," Marcel says, his palms out like a calming pair of leaves, "Don't sweat it. Look." He steps to the side.

Marcel parked just within the trees, high up on a steep hill overlooking the entire excavation site. If Astrid were to throw a stone it might very well land just inside the fence line along the northwestern wall.

"It felt as if you drove much farther," Astrid says without looking away from ancient *Wyn Avuqua*.

"I parked my ATV over there," he says pointing to a particularly shadowed niche just a little northeast of their position. "I decided to visit *Wyn Avuqua* from across country. When I saw the western fence and the Coldwater Security guys, for some reason I opted to climb over instead of go through one of their gates. As usual, I trusted my spirit guide. I headed toward the *Avu*, and you were just coming out. But you didn't look happy

— and your hands were tied. I followed you and that tall woman to their security headquarters tent. I listened from outside—heard that Rearden dude—and some other things I didn't quite understand. Then they put you into a van. You were screaming." Worry flashes across his face. "They left you in a running van. A chance came when no one was nearby—so I got in and slowly drove you out of there.

"So yeah, I drove for a little bit. Once I left their service path, I raced down to that old logging road we know, I circled back and took the wide portage trail. That rounded me back and up here—and here we are. I'm pretty sure there's no finding us for a short time, at least. I don't think they would guess that we would return. . ." He casts a dubious glance at the van. "Do you think they can track this thing?"

"Probably," Astrid says.

"Well, that said, if there's a time to go and see if we can help your friend, Graham, it's now. Let's roll. The game trail down is right over there," he points and takes a step in the direction.

"No," Astrid feels the sudden rush of clarity. "No, I have a feeling they've moved him."

He turns to her. "Where?"

"Want to see *Dellithion Omvide?*" she says.

Marcel's white teeth catch the cold glimmer of the sky. His smile is huge. "They found the fucking pyramid?"

The Impossibility of William Greenhame
1010 A.D.
The Realm of Wyn Avuqua

Two long pulls of scotch, a slight wavering of balance, a subdued cough (or chuckle), the cork planted back into the throat of the bottle. William of Leaves says in slightly slurred Anglo Saxon to Cynthia, "I know what you're thinking. You've seen me before, yes? Or perhaps not. We drift in circles. Such wide, whirling, magnificent circles." He leans and sets the bottle on the stage beside his right foot. "Nothing?" he says rising and pointing to his own face, "This visage doesn't ring a bell? Ring-a-ding-a-dildo?"

Cynthia stares blankly.

William stares back. A moment passes.

"You know, ring a bell." After another beat he says, "Ah! Of course. A little early for you to understand Dr. Pavlov's bells. Let me see, that would be an early twentieth century idiom. You see, Dr. Pavlov offered, or rather, will offer much to the fields of physiology and neurological science. His experiments were the foundation of classical conditioning. It is really very simple. Each time he fed his dog, he rang a bell. After a time, the dog became conditioned to expect that when the bell was rung, food would follow. Much like if you and your brood, here," he motions to the crowd, "hears the suffering of an *Itonalya* or a human being—and at the sound, each of you toss yourselves in a twitterpated orgasm and lose all sense of your godlike potential. So, when I ask if my face rings a bell, I'm really asking if you're truly ready to have your head handed to you, by me, for by now, you should know what happens when we meet."

Cynthia's green eyes study William from head to foot while he speaks. She does not appear to be listening, but Loche imagines that by some twisting or folding of the void between

Cynthia's divinity and her human form, some essence of William Greenhame lingers within her memory—even if they have not met yet. *We cannot alter what is to come.* Corey's whispered statement settles over Loche's thought like a net.

"There is something about you that is odd," Cynthia says stepping closer, her course circling around behind. "Something odd, indeed."

"Understatement," William clarifies, his index finger raised between them.

"Will you champion for the Old Law?"

"You're a tool, Cynthia. But yes. And be warned, it is my turn to win— despite my pain in the neck."

"Your turn? What might that mean?"

"Oh come now, Cy," William says. "May I call you *Cy*? You don't recall my magic trick? The bit with those precious leaves? The trick that has yet to be played upon you? Well, let us recollect together. To do this we should take a short look back on one of your many popular biographical moments: you, slithering about in the limbs of the aptly named Tree of Life. Let it not be said that you've never had an interest in botany. Goodness, you have, without a doubt. Especially the forbidden kind—the kind of plants and fruits that some claim created Hell and damnation. At least that is what Eve might say, and has she got a bone to pick with you over the whole affair! And so it goes that you've not given up on that nefarious little hobby of yours—wanting to taste a little of that magic plant—wanting a piece of what was forbidden—so you persevered.

"Thanks to my loving mother, I've an in with the aforementioned tree, or at least a distant seedling relative—and when last you and I met, I pulled my full strength abracadabra bit upon you and your rather unsavory crew, and managed to prevent you from getting your dirty mitts on it. Tell me you remember," William burps. "Perhaps I shouldn't go into too much detail.

There exists a very real possibility of damaging not only the future, but more important, the magician's creed: never share the illusion's secret—or, if you prefer, keep safe the prestige. I can see this has you frustrated. Don't be too troubled. In time, you'll remember, though I dare say, by then, it will be too late. Or it will be the other way around."

He bends, seizes the bottle, rises, chirps the cork from the throat, pulls, packs the cork back, bends, and returns it to the wood slat beside his right foot.

He blurts out, "My, my, how wonderfully befuddling to speak of a shared experience as both memory and predestination. There should be a word for such a puzzling quagmire. Oh, let's gather and surmise, shall we? Let me think."

William lays a finger along his chin and considers. Cynthia continues to circle her prey. She has given no response, nor has any expression appeared on her face save that of complete control. But Loche senses a mask hiding a profound and seething contempt.

"The word must encompass a paradoxical truth, yes?" Greenhame deadpans. "Promises to be tricky." He brightens with mock enlightenment, "How about, impossible? Yes, Impossible. What we are yearning to define is, I suppose, for the most part, impossible. One of those rare words lacking vicissitude, for it rests firmly in that dreaded absolute category. I'm not one who appreciate absolutes, of course, save in matters of love, perhaps. I will always love love, you see. Always." A tender smile spreads, "As George would say, Stupid crazy." He nods determinedly, "I say that this vexing conundrum betwixt you and me should be called, impossible. And yet, I dare say, it may not be that in truth. Ah, here we are, Cy, you and I, twisting together on the wheel of time. How we circle back. . . "

Cynthia, still pacing a gentle gyre, says, "You know nothing of impossible."

"I'll grant you that," William says, his attention straying to the scotch bottle, then to the crowd, "especially given present company." He addresses the audience, "You know, impossible?" and then rattles off the word impossible in several different languages, Greek, Chinese, French, Arabic, and others. Loche hears them each articulated, though in his mind, the maddening meaning of impossible, impossible, impossible pounds against his reason.

"And speaking of impossible," Greenhame segues with a lilt, "do you truly believe that killing this boy will set any of you free?" He faces Cynthia. "Free. . .whatever that may mean? This is, of course, the year of your lordlings, 1010, and while I must accept that cleverness and simple intelligence for you and your hooligan host is challenged at best, you cannot tell me that by simply ending *Thi's* mortal life here, such an act will eliminate *Thi* from the continuum of existence. If so, I must suggest that we spend some time discussing the definition of impossible."

Cynthia replies, "As I've said, *Itonalya*, you know nothing of impossible. And clearly, you know nothing of the Old Law—"

"Come, come," Greenhame says, waving her off with his left hand and raising his sword with his right. "Let's not bandy words— ah, you likely have never played the game of bandy. No. Not yet. A game a few centuries from now that will involve batting a ball back and forth. Much later it will be called tennis. To bandy words means. . . Oh never mind." Greenhame shakes his head with a kind of humored frustration.

"But you speak true. I am *Itonalya*. The Earth's chosen guard. I am *Melgia*. I am no crossing deity. I am no trespassing god come to leech upon *Thi's* masterwork. I am no seraph sent to deviate humankind from their intended course—beauty and truth. I am no fucking Devil, *Cymachena*, like you, you misguided bitch, a killer of innocence in the name of your Old Law. I'm the

New Law. As one of my sons might have said, 'Fuck that shit, I'm the big, deep heavy!'"

Corey's voice from behind hisses, "Now! Get Edwin out through the east door!"

Where It Leads

November 11, this year
Upper Priest Lake, Idaho
7:21 pm PST

Astrid reaches for Marcel's hand. His fright tingles in the air around her, and she can almost hear his synapses crackling and arching their electrical charges between reason and utter disbelief. From under the cover of the dark tree-line, Marcel and Astrid have just witnessed three people disappear into thin air, Dr. Marcus Rearden, Dr. Graham Cremo and Queen Yafarra. It is certain that neither witness could readily process the sight without a mental wrestling match.

With her other hand, Astrid lifts the cell phone she had miraculously kept from being confiscated. She lowers it down to hide the illuminated screen and notes the time: 7:21pm. "A half hour or so and we can follow," she whispers. She then smiles sadly, looking back up to the anomalous structure, "but no tea. . ."

Surrounding the fifteen meter high pyramid are a half dozen armed security personnel along with their supervising officer, Lynn Eastman. Her hands are on her hips.

Just before the three travelers crossed the top Astrid heard Eastman tell them, "Walk slowly, and carefully." Then, as they vanished, both Astrid and Eastman muttered, almost simultaneously, "I'll be damned."

Graham was not conscious when the trio crossed. He had been hoisted to the height on a stretcher by two burly security guards. At the top, they balanced him in between Rearden and Yafarra and stepped down. The three vanished a moment later.

And at that moment, Marcel asked a poignant question, "What the fuck?"

"Precisely," Astrid had answered.

Marcel's question was repeated several times while they hiked up to the clearing upon which they now stand. Along the way, Astrid told him everything— from the Grant Board meeting earlier that morning, to Yafarra, to Rearden, to the Red Notebook, to Graham, to her potential murder. Between her gasps for breath along the uphill game trail, she could hear him whispering over and over, "What the fuck." And as if her tale wasn't enough—as if *Wyn Avuqua* unearthed wasn't sufficient, the fifteen meter high apex the of the whispered pyramid of the Sun or *Dellithion omvide* is a stone's throw away, and three figures just vanished as they crossed its top.

Two large earth-moving machines are silhouetted against the sky like sleeping dinosaurs. A single wall tent and a few work lamps illuminate the newly discovered dig site. Along the opposite border of the clearing are three security vehicles.

Marcel asks, "So, that was Rearden, your Graham, and. . ."

"Yafarra."

Marcel nods. "Yafarra."

"Yafarra," Astrid says again.

"The Queen Yafarra, daughter of Althemis Falruthia of *Vastiris*. That Yafarra?" Marcel asks.

"The one and only," Astrid agrees.

"What the fuck?"

Lynn Eastman is still standing at the base with her hands on her hips watching. "I'll be damned," Astrid hears her say. She then turns toward the tent and calls out to her team, "Let's get back to it."

Astrid scans through the blurry light. The guards disperse and walk back to the two vans parked beside a temporary path cutting through the glade. From what Astrid can see, the path looks treacherous and tricky to navigate. Eastman lingers a little longer and takes an appraising glance around the clearing. When her gaze returns to the pyramid she starts walking slowly to the vehicles. A few minutes later, the vans start down through the narrow fissure. Their red tail lights blink and fade in the trees.

The night is moonless. Faint starlight blues the newly exposed stones of the pyramid. Astrid's body is frozen at the sight. A breath of wind combs the upper treetops.

Marcel says, "Can we just stare at this for a few hours? It is just as the Elders said. The spirits are with us. But I can't figure out how we missed it. How? How did we miss this?"

Astrid puzzles. "I don't know," she says after a pause. "We were just here, Professor."

"Yes."

"How could we have missed. . ." Marcel's voice trails off. A moment later he asks, "Where do you think that *omvide* leads?"

Astrid purses her lips and squints at the peak. *Where? To the mystery of Albion Ravistelle? To Albion's home—Italy? Venice? To the Red Notebook? The unequivocal proof to her life's work? To a deeper labyrinth? To their death?*

But Astrid feels a truer answer. It comes in the form of a quickening pulse, a change in her breathing, and a surge of adrenaline. She translates the answer to words, "It leads to Graham."

Othayr

1010 A.D.
The Realm of Wyn Avuqua

When Cynthia's thrusting sword blurs and is parried by William, the collective roar of the host lances painfully into Loche's injured ear. He vaults forward, pushed by both his own volition and the shoving crowd jostling for a better view. The contingent of regal guards surrounding the stage, Etheldred among them, have now turned to the fray and are crying for blood. Colliding with the chest-high platform, Loche attempts to thread his body downward between the shoving weight of the bodies behind him and the rough timbered edge of the stage. With some effort he drops and rolls underneath. Squinting through the slats of light, he sees that the space is just high enough to crawl on all fours, and he scuttles across the distance. He halts just below his son's bier and peers up through the boards. Edwin is there; one of his little arms dangling. Surrounding Loche on all sides is a wall of stomping heavy boots and armored lower legs. After a moment's consideration as just how he might pry his way out of the maddening throng he is suddenly astonished at a random, fleeting memory. A memory from his younger days, college perhaps—an experience that Basil Fenn would surely appreciate, when, at a riotous rock concert in Spokane, Washington, seeing a band blaring out an aggressive mixture of infectious rock hooks punctuated with dual drummers and a wicked horn section—a group called Black Happy—he recalls his body being pressed against the front row rail while the rapturous audience behind knocked him down. All he could see was feet jockeying for position. Certain that he would not escape being trampled to death, or at least, being injured badly, Loche concluded that the only way to rise up was to become one with the crowd and mosh. Moshing, was the frenzied, primatial dance of the period, the mid to late 1990s. To Loche, and to most, the ritual resembled more of a gang fight than a dance.

There is no sneaking a way up and out—inspired by his memory, Loche decides to mosh his way through. With all of his might Loche kicks his legs into the first set of shins before him. They immediately shuffle to the side and back. This movement starts a chain reaction. A moment later, the pushing and shoving spreads in both directions around the platform perimeter. At the first opportunity of an opening, Loche shoulders out, pressing like a lineman, and tunnels an opening. Once on his feet and straightening, he presses again. As he does this he is surprised to see, despite the wake his shoving had begun, not a single eye in the audience has strayed away from the duel unfolding upon the stage. Erinyes and the fates remain kneeling in their respective corners with their heads bowed. They take no notice of the riotous throng.

William's eyes flit from Cynthia to Loche. His acknowledgement is a subtle, instantaneous hint at a smile. Then his attention snaps back to his opponent. With a sweep of his right leg, he kicks the scotch bottle over on its side and it rolls to Julia. She grabs hold of it and glances up at William—her wounds rapidly healing now. William allows a full grin to bloom across his entire face. He jumps away from the stage. It takes a moment for Loche to understand how William manages ten, maybe fifteen paces, and how he comes to an en-guard position upon a long feasting table. Loche blinks. *He walked on their heads*, Loche realizes.

In pursuit, Cynthia simply steps off of the stage and into the supporting arms of her followers. They move her across the space as if in flight, and she steps gracefully onto the table. Swords engage again ringing amid the enthralled cries of the company.

With the duel's change of location, the horde flow toward it as if a drain had opened on the opposite side of the enclosure.

Loche's focus rivets on his son. He rolls onto the stage, stands and pulls Edwin into his embrace. A yell from his left, "Hold! Hold!" Soldiers are drawing weapons. "Release the boy!"

Before the guards reach the stairs they are assailed from behind. A long knife flashes from out of Corey's cloak and he stealthily dispatches two of them. Loche suddenly notices more cloaked shadows garroting the others. A cowl is thrown back and Loche recognizes the *Orathom Wis* from the Giza Plateau, Neil. Catching Loche in acknowledgement, he cries out over the distracted throng, "The sign of eth is rising!"

Loche squeezes Edwin to his chest and whirls toward Julia. She is on her feet. A pair of gauntleted hands grip one of her ankles. Another of the horde gains the stage and restrains her shoulders. With movements Loche can only describe as poetic, Julia breaks the arm grasping her ankle with a sweeping kick from her other foot. Simultaneously, she uses the round base of the scotch bottle to collapse the windpipe of the second foe by jabbing it like a heavy spear. Her adversaries fall away. She rushes across the stage to Loche.

Below, Neil shoves forward, presses open a space for the two on the ground. He points to a breach that his companions are opening toward the east passage.

"Follow Alexia, there!" Corey points.

Alexia has carved a path to the east door with the aid of several others. In the tumult and confusion, the collective attention of the assembly has not yet detected their presence. Only the few gods near enough to see in the dim enclosure have noted something unusual—and they were subsequently cut down. By the time Alexia leads Loche, Edwin and Julia out into the cold starlight, the howling throng is still too engrossed in the unfolding duel to raise an alarm. Loche turns as he passes through the door and sees William Greenhame's glance straying from his opponent to his son and grandson's exit.

"Do not tarry," Corey shouts, "he'll be along in time. Go!"

"He is alone. We cannot leave him!" Loche says resisting Corey's pull.

"Nonsense! He is far from alone." Corey's reply is almost a laugh. "And do not think the old fellow doesn't have a plan. . . and a canister of tear gas among other things! Move, Poet! Go!"

As they exit a peculiar explosive pop resounds.

Outside, Corey stops, "Loche, remove the orange coat. Hurry."

Loche passes the sleeping child to Julia. He drops his disguise at his feet. His bag is still slung diagonally across his chest with the umbrella clipped to the strap. He reaches to take Edwin again, checks his hold on him and nods to Corey.

"Off we go then!" Corey says.

Loche guesses the rescue party numbers eight or so as they pick up a steady run toward the inner ward's gate. Just ahead, Loche sees Alexia reach into her bag. She tosses two small objects to her right and one to her left. Rummaging again she produces another mysterious object, and she holds it in her right hand—a kind of remote control. An instant later there is a series of blinding flashes, followed by ear-shattering, concussive blasts that echo into the night. The gate guards and pikemen are dumbfounded, shocked and terrified. They take no notice of the fleeing band.

Loche feels the throbbing of his blood against his injured ear. Surrounding them on all sides now is an astonished and curious encamped army, rising to its feet in alarm.

Just ahead of Loche is Neil. His hand drops more incendiary devices as they run. A few moments and a good number of yards later he detonates the charges in their wake.

Strobing lightening-blinks flash across the landscape. Then, the oppressive pounding of several percussive explosions. To Loche it is as if a club smashes into his spine between his shoulder blades. For an instant he loses balance and stumbles. Correcting himself, with the aid of Julia, he focuses as best he can on the approaching wall, his eyes straying to the torture grounds to his left and the dead Native American hanging there.

Alexia, the first to arrive at the encampment's gate, surprises the keepers. Horns sound the alarm as the first two guards fall. More guards descend the towers and upper bulwarks to assist. In moments Alexia is surrounded.

Looking up, Loche can see melees have begun on the towers beside the gate. The brief engagements end with orange surcoated men being hurled over the wall. Thereafter, the mechanism of weights and pulleys that control the doors activate.

An opening in the wall gapes. Arrows whistle in from the dark. Alexia remains standing while several of her assailants drop away, many screaming from bolts piercing arms, legs, torsos and throats. The few that remain standing are met by the remainder of Corey's company as they rush the gate.

Loche is marshaled with Julia before him, "Do not pause! Run through. We will clear the path!" Corey shouts.

Another series of charges blast from far behind. The white light flashes just as Loche passes beneath the timbered arch and out into the narrow field before the pines. In the flickering he sees a cluster of some twenty archers positioned just beyond the reach of the tower's torchlight. His pace slows but he is shoved forward.

"Keep going! They're with us!" Corey shouts.

Loche's legs are rubber. His lungs feel as if they've been sliced with razors. A thundering wash of blood beats and courses through his hearing. His right foot catches upon a hidden stone and he tumbles forward. Two arms catch him and stand him back up. It is the foremost archer. His face is dark, elegant and elongated. Carved as if from stone, the features are angular and powerful. Again, Loche immediately thinks: Native American.

A moment later, another set of hands seize him, and with gentle precision guide him and the cradled Edwin through the dark and into the trees. "We are here to help. Come, quickly," Loche can only see the white ovals of the man's eyes in the gloom. The two are lifted up onto the back of a rather large horse.

"Who are—" Loche starts.

"I am Vincale," the man says quickly, "no more questions now."

Horn blasts scream from the encampment.

Vincale presses leather reins into Loche's right hand. "Hold the boy to your chest and let the horse—"

"I don't know how to ride!" Loche says.

"Do not fear. These horses are of *Wyn Avuqua*. They will bear you safely."

Corey assists Julia onto a saddle. He then climbs onto another along with the rest of his company.

"Where is William?" Loche asks. "We cannot leave him."

"We will not leave him," Corey says, "but we cannot wait for him here."

The small band of Native Americans have now retreated under the cover of the trees and climb onto horses without saddles. Many let fly arrows back toward the gate.

Vincale explains, "We will ride out together. Once we are within the trees we'll divide our company to throw off pursuit."

"*Othayr!*" Vincale calls. "*Gal!*"

The horse beneath Loche flexes and its muscular body lurches into the thick dark ahead. They pass through the trees like water through a fissure. The pace is swift and nearly silent. He feels the gentle puffs of his son's breath on his neck. With one arm Loche squeezes him tighter to his chest. His other hand grips the leather rein. An unexpected smile forms. Cedar, crisp pine and the musk of damp soil mix in the air. Each step of the horse cracks open the forest floor. He inhales the aroma of moss, wet root, decaying leaves. For a brief moment he forgets the searing pain of his bleeding ear—the weight of his position in existence —the gravity of his writing—the oncoming army just over the ridge—the city of his imagination awaiting the hand of God to gouge it from the face of the Earth. In this moment, trees appear to lure him and his son into their embrace. An occasional glinting star pierces and searches beneath the dark canopy. Right now, they pass like shadows unseen.

The forward company crosses a stream. Vincale halts and waves them north. He then turns and leads Corey, Julia and Loche along the stream into the inky black of the forest.

A Dissertation:
We Will Not Find Supernatural Trickery

November 11, this year
Upper Priest Lake, Idaho
8:01 pm PST

It takes thirty or so minutes for Astrid and Marcel to cross the dark grass between the trees and the rising pyramid cap. As they approach, a memory floods Astrid's mind. She can hear one of her professors, Dr. Geoff Herzog. He compliments her.

"Concrete, Astrid. Concrete work." Astrid stares at the cover sheet to her dissertation lying on his desk. "You've based your study on reality and history and used the motifs as they should be used—myths should instruct and entertain. I particularly like the way you treat literal interpretation of miracles and supernatural claims. If only humanity as a collective would stop for a moment, take a good look at the stories and compare them to the world as we know it. Did God create it all? I mean, really?" He points to a newspaper clipping tacked to a bulletin board behind him. "Gallup survey—fifteen per cent of Americans believe we evolved through natural selection alone. Fifteen per cent? Fifteen. Sweet baby Jesus!"

Astrid listens. Nods. Fully aware of those still caught in the snare of ancient belief. "Evolution steals our souls," she says quietly. "No one wants that."

"Darwin, the soul killer," the professor shakes his head, "the God killer." His fingers tap the cover sheet. "Another piece I enjoyed was your use of the apple. How it served as a symbol of knowledge for both Adam and Eve, and for Newton, as well."

"Yes," Astrid smiles. "Only the affect of Newton's apple is provable. And far more useful."

"Well, whatever the case," he laughs, rising to walk Astrid to the door, "I suppose we should be thankful that we no longer blame God for lightening strikes as our ancestors once surely did. It is just a matter of time before all the superstitious nonsense is weeded out. Your work, Astrid, is bridging the old and the new. You're showing us that the belief in Thor's hammer and his lightening was the first step to finding lightning's true origin."

"We're evolving," Astrid agrees. "Maybe in a few years that Gallup survey will hit 50 per cent."

"Good afternoon, Miss Finnley."

"Good afternoon, Doctor."

Outside the door Astrid lowers her face and reads the cover sheet to her dissertation:

The Need For
A New Human Narrative

---

presented to
The Faculty of the Department of Mythology and
Religious Studies at Gonzaga University

In partial fulfillment
Of the requirements for the degree
PhD of Mythology and Psychology

---

by
Astrid Finnley
August 2007

Clive Wadden, PhD., Chair
Geoff Herzog, PhD.
Sharon Butterworth, PhD.

Keywords: Greek, Sumerian, Egyptian, Jewish,
Christian, Celtic, Itonalya, Native American:
Mythologies, Civic Religion, Mystery
Religion, World Civic Cults, Demeter, Dionysus,
Yafarra, Orpheus, Wyn Avuqua.

ABSTRACT

Given humankind's internal struggle against its existential demise, no time in history has witnessed the collateral damage of the conflict as acutely as the present. Diagnosed depression, anxiety and mental illness cases have reached epidemic proportions. Recent recorded suicides, nearly one million per year, point to a soul sickness within society and suggest that the old narratives humans have used to provide some meaning or hope that existence in some way matters no longer possess the power they once did. With the failing of these old narratives (ancient myths, religion, and economic and political structures), and facing the rapid evolution of technological advancement, humanity now stands at a crossroad between the old gods promising pearly gates and everlasting life versus the cold, scientific scalpel that cuts belief from reality — cuts the soul from existence itself. Somewhere in between, humanity is in need of a narrative that marries the power of the gods of lore with the evidential basis of the universe as we come to understand it. What can we discover about the supernatural, fantastical fictions of myth? How does the power and magic of ancient narrative affect us to this day? Can they be used to provide some insight into present day's concrete, silicon reality. It was said that death would come to a mortal if he were to behold Zeus in his full glory. This dissertation proposes that we are now staring into Zeus' eyes. Into the eye of Thi. What we see there is perhaps too much for some. But if we hold the gaze of the god king, we will not find supernatural trickery, no dead rising from the grave, immortality, no serpent tempting Eve, the Red Sea parting or the transportation from one pyramid to another. If we stare long enough we will understand that the bloody and ugly millennia from the burning bush to the Hubble telescope merely constitute the birthday of humanity's new narrative. This new narrative will show god and its magical hand within the universe we discover around us; how

stories of the fantastic have allowed us to reach
for the stars — and to touch them. The magic is in
the stories, alone.

"Ready?" Marcel asks, turning and offering his hand to
Astrid as she climbs the last stone to the apex.

"Do you want me to say it, or do you want to say it?"

"I think you should say it." His red hair shines dully in the
starlight. "You never have. You never believed. We walk across
the top and you say it. Okay? You say it."

Astrid extends her hand to him. He takes it. She squeezes.
"Remember what Eastman said? She told Rearden to walk slow
and with caution."

"Yes. Okay."

All along her arms and legs rise goosebumps—as if she is
staring down into frigid lake water and being encouraged to dive.

"Say it like you mean it, Prof. You've got to mean the
word. *Elliqui*. Mean it."

She takes her first step.

She waits for the shock of cold.

After she speaks the word *Lonwayro,* a dull but sudden
light illuminates the low clouds. *The face of Zeus*, she thinks. *The
face of Zeus.*

We will not find supernatural trickery.

The air is somehow thick. Distant engines drone. Some
obstacle bars the movement of her forward leg. She tastes the sea.

They are no longer in Idaho.

Your Plan, Your Gift
(A Dream)

Date unknown
The Realm of Wyn Avuqua

Loche Newirth is dreaming.

"Are we still the storytellers, Dad? Are we still writing the good stories?"

"Yes Edwin, we are still writing the good stories."

Each heartbeat floods Loche's left ear with the rush of an ocean spindrift, and every few minutes a sharp pain jabs inward.

A suffocating sleep.

Dreamscape.

Muted colors like underdeveloped film.

Edwin grins. He twists out of Loche's embrace and runs to the opposite end of the tower office and pauses beside a bookshelf. Some of the titles glow from the spines of hammered gold leaf. A candle flickers on a nearby shelf. The door is open and the stairway down to the living room below is dark. Helen's portrait catches Loche's eye. A photograph taken shortly after Edwin was born—her eyes sparkle from behind the glass and her smile is adoring.

Loche sharpens a pencil and points his attention toward a journal entry. It reads:

"Was this your plan, Loche? Is this your gift?"

The gun laid heavy on the stage floor. I cowered and crawled backwards. I had killed my father's son. I stood and backed away, crying, loathing the sight of these men huddled on the stage—blood stained swords upon the planks, a man cradling

his dead son, his friend weeping beside him—all beneath a
glaring spotlight.

"Dad?" Edwin calls from across the room. Loche raises
his head from the page and cannot see his son. The room has
suddenly transformed into the timbered walls of his log cabin at
Priest Lake. Flat grey light dusts the air. The hearth is black and
cold. All around him is a chain of yellow Post It notes—and
scattered books—and half finished plates of food. A pen is jutting
out from the cluster of his fist. Rushing surf deafens his left ear.
Red smears and splashes on the window catch his eye. Edwin
appears outside looking in through the pane. His little face and
wide brown eyes stare at him below the slashes of a painted
word: MURDER.

"Dad?" Edwin's voice again. "Was this your plan? Is this
your gift?" The little boy rotates away and runs. Loche rushes to
the glass. Outside Edwin speeds across a wide lawn, hand in hand
with a gaunt, spindly limbed man. The man cranes his head back.
A smile cut across his face. It is Marcus Rearden.

"Was this your plan? Is this your gift?"

Fireside Stories

1010 A.D.
The Realm of Wyn Avuqua

Loche wakes. He is lying on his side, spooned around his sleeping son. A small fire hisses and snaps a few feet away. He raises himself onto an elbow.

He had fallen asleep not long after arriving at what Vincale called, "A safe place." Blinking heavily, he tries to scan the jagged stone walls of a cave. The fire is warm, his son's face is peaceful and they are no longer under the cold, icy stars.

Through the cave's mouth the silhouettes of two figures stand at the edge of the stream. Their voices are low in conversation. Julia is asleep on the opposite side of the fire.

"Was this your plan, Loche?" a voice asks. "Is this your gift?"

The words echo and resound in his mind. They are words he had written. And the voice speaking them is unmistakable.

William Greenhame sits with his hands folded in his lap. He is leaning now into Loche's view signaling his whereabouts to his son. "I'm right here."

"W-William. . ." Loche breaths out. A sudden rush of tears. Loche painfully sits up and extends both of his hands and William receives them.

"I ask you again, did you plan any of this?"

"William—I—"

"Your gift—it seems to keep on giving. . . or we just continue to unwrap it and discover new surprises as we go. For example, here we sit beside a fire in the year 1010, as far as I can tell, not far from the city of Immortals, *Wyn Avuqua*. The One God, *Thi*, the creator of the omnitude of existence, or insert any other whole ball of wax synonym here, has passed *Its* life force into your sleeping son—making Edwin the most powerful entity to—that—" he shakes his head and lets go of Loche's hands, "words fall short, I'm afraid. And as such, Edwin's new found position has certainly raised my station as perhaps the most proud grandfather to ever exist." A frown develops as he studies the little boy, "Proud, and terrified, I must admit. And if these plot points are not enough to bludgeon your better judgment into whimpering submission as to what's believable and what is not," William dramatically spreads his arms wide, "behold, I am here —as far as I can tell. I am alive. You thought me dead, I know," William says quietly with a quick glance to Julia. "And you would have been right to believe it."

Loche can find no words.

William takes Loche's hands again, raises them and presses the palms together. He then encases his hands over Loche's for a long moment. Color in his face pales.

"*Ithic veli agtig*," he says, a grim smile tangling in his expression. "I know now, without doubt, nothing waits for me," his hands pull away and gesture to a faraway ether, "nothing waits for us lingerers—we *Melgia*—we guardians of the dream."

"What happened, William?"

He touches his throat thoughtfully. "I told you did I not, that I would return my grandson and your beloved Julia?"

Julia is awake now, still lying bundled in a blanket. She is listening. Firelight glitters in her eyes as she watches the reunion. William smiles at her, "I'm sorry to wake you again, my dear." She nods.

William's fingers graze the scarf around his neck. He says to Loche, "My head, dear boy, was in a bag. My head was in the bag. *Gavress*, we call it. All that is me was cast into the sea. *Linnasisg*, the ending of the light." He waits a beat and adds, "But you know of *Gavress Linnasisg*, yes? Of course you do, for you wrote of such a ritual in the Journal, though you failed to name it then. Poor Felix Wishfeill falls to Samuel's sword in

Venice. You remember. And in one of our favorite little restaurants—not far from Lord Byron's home. You were listening to Joni Mitchell. Do you recall? Who can forget Samuel's line, 'How about I double bag these, what say you?' Of course I do not believe that when you wrote about our lovely barmaid Maria bringing Samuel two plastic garbage bags that you intended for your imaginative head-disposal imagery to pullulate into a rite among those plagued with life ad nauseam. Alas, poor Samuel."

"William, I—"

"Surely you could have no idea of how something as simple as a severed head and a sack could influence idioms and the time continuum."

"William—"

"Etymologically speaking, the phrase head in a bag has joined with many such bag-centric phrases, you know. And since my head has been bag enveloped, if you will, I must admit, I've not been myself. I find myself talking more than is—"

"William," Loche's voice is raised slightly. His father jumps at the sound. "How did you survive— how did you—"

William chants, looking into the fire,

"There's a head in the bag.
There's a head in the bag.
The head is my head.
It is my head in the bag."

The flames crackle. He then says, "Few would understand the historical meaning of such a stanza. Few would want to know the truth of it. Where the utterance came from or why the words bring a horrifying chill to those that perpetuated the phrase into an idiom is certainly not common knowledge.

"There are many phrases like it. Phrases that mention *a bag,* for example. Like *a mixed bag.* It was strange to think of that then, for I did, when my head was in the bag. Pointless, really. But I wondered. I wondered about it. Then the saying, *It's in the bag*, crossed my mind. I tried to smile, but could not. Smiling stung like a cut spreading open. I recalled something about the New York Giants in 1915. Or 1916. I could not remember exactly—but the Giants were on a winning streak one of those years—anyway, when the bag of replacement baseballs was removed from the field, the New York crowd believed that the game would again be won by their beloved team. Thus, the game was *in the bag*. Today, *in the bag* has come to mean eminent success is near.

"At the time I was recalling this I did not think the phrase applied to my head.

"Then I thought, *What of the cat is out of the bag?* I had seen a market farmer attempt this trick once sometime around the middle of the nineteenth century. When selling hares, a wicked merchant might exchange a cat in the bag for the rabbit. The swindle would be discovered later by the duped customer. *The cat is out of the bag* has come to mean truth shall be brought forth."

William shivers. After a moment, he continues.

"There's a head in the bag.
There's a head in the bag.
The head is my head.
It is my head in the bag.

"The verse is long known among the *Itonalya*. It dates back to the founding stones of *Wyn Avuqua*. Countless years lost in the mist."

William clears his throat.

"It was black inside the bag. Then I could sense a rustling, a slight breeze maybe against the plastic. Movement, certainly.

Jostling. Then vertigo, oddly." He winces. "Then sudden light. Stunningly clear. Painful. Of course my eyes were frozen open, impossible to shut. Above, a breach in the sack widened. A grip of fingers clawed through my hair, then I was lifted up and out."

"A flashing of images, sounds and smells followed: sea air, crying gulls, a far off shore, crests slapping against the boat side, spraying mist. The time had come. I knew. After all of this time, I knew, finally, the truth. The end was near. The ocean.

"But who has a fist full of my hair? I wondered. Before my existence was winked out, I wanted to know. *Who will cast me to the nothingness that waits*?"

William looks down at his hands.

"As if in answer, a voice spoke, almost chanting, 'And at last,' the voice said, 'and not without great reverence and pity, I banish you, William Greenhame, William of Leaves, William, son of Radulphus. I grant you your wish—*our* wish. Your death is no longer delayed. No dream, no waking—the water has no memory. Nor shall you. *Gallina.'* The hand gripped tighter. Then Albion Ravistelle's face appeared before my failing eyes. Albion Ravistelle. 'My old friend,' he said, 'How I wish I could make this journey with you—to know finally if there is anything beyond for our kind. Fear not, young William, I shall avenge the fallen *Itonalya*. The gods will be torn from their thrones on high. Heaven shall be here. If only you could have seen clearer.' Albion paused and stared deeply into my immovable eyes. 'Why do I feel you hear me, Greenhame? Even now, so far from me—from this life? Can you hear me?' I could see the shape of his tears. They dropped heavily and were swept away from his face by the ocean wind. Albion turned as if tracking the tears out to sea. He smiled watching them mix with the splashing mists spraying across the prow of the boat. 'Go with my tears,' he said. 'William, go with my sorrow. I will never forget you.' Albion then spoke the words of *Gavress Linnasisg*, in its entirety to honor my passing."

William pushes a stick into the fire. He stares in silence for a few moments.

"With a sudden jolt, I felt a rounding arc—forceful and fast. The burning pain at my scalp eased suddenly as the world spun, sky over sea, bright blue tumbling to grey—somersaulting out above the whitecaps. Then sound muddled, deadened—vision blurred. I could sense the chill of water and the stinging bite of salt. I thought, *this is how we end. The sea eats the life of the immortal. This is how it has always been.*

"I bobbed to the surface, face upward, lolling on a wave. There was a drone of engines and the smell of petrol. Albion's boat tore away back to the shore. Shrieking gulls circle above ——the water has teeth—thought drowned—I gave up.

"There is no knowing how long I floated on the surface of the Adriatic when light appeared again." William laughs suddenly. "Light. I recalled the phrase *let there be light*. A good one, I thought. A fine line. A group of words that I wish I had come up with to begin one of my own books. But, alas, it has been commandeered by one of the better known tomes in the history of the earth. Nevertheless, my mind thought, *what is this clear, unending light? A light beyond anything known. Perfection beyond its capacity to understand. Beauty and refuge and starlight. Is this Orathom?*"

William raises his face to his listeners. Tears are in his eyes.

"Light. The brightest light I will ever know. And her voice —her sweet voice. She said, 'My sweet William. My dear, sweet William. I've got you. I've got you. Come back to me, William!' It was my Lady. Oh, the sight of her. She was light framed in the pink afterglow of the sunset. 'It is me, my sweet husband. It is your Diana. I've got you now. I've got you now. Go no further. Stay. Stay. Stay!'"

A warm smile spreads on his lips.

"Your mother saved me—she always has saved me. Beloved Diana. She plucked my darkening thoughts from out of the deep, deep sea. The biting salt. The stinging fangs. She lifted my face to *Dellithion,* and showed me her radiant, shining face. Ah, my sweet. How many labyrinths have you led me out of, wife?" More tears suddenly overflow and tumble downward. He waits for the sudden squall to pass. When it does he attempts a thin smile.

"Our gifted dear Dr. Angelo Catena played savior as well. Though I cannot fully explain just how he reunited my head with my body nor would I want to. I was told in the simplest of terms that the process might resemble something like the grafting of stems and roots wet with rain and warmed with sunlight. Yet, truly, what I recall are sights, sounds and sensations best left unspoken. But here I am before you! Or at least, most of me. Always will the memory of pain seethe from where Nicolas Cythe's blade did its worst," he pulls at his scarf and reveals a raw, red scar encircling his throat. "And then Albion performed the rite and cast my mind to the Adriatic. *Gavress Linnasisg.* Had I floated much longer on the waves, I would have been beyond hope, or so sayeth the good Dr. Catena." He shivers. "And I know now the horrors of how long the mind carries on after our end. Oft we have wondered and oft we have dreaded an answer. Alas that I now know." He tightens the fabric of his scarf. "And I am also aware of the oblivion that follows. I am afraid of it, Loche, quite afraid."

"Where is Diana—Mother?"

"I would think she is at home sleeping late, dearest woman. She sleeps more and more these days. How I wish I could be lying beside her." William's focus softens and his gaze falls into the fire. Loche watches as his father's expression drifts from halcyon to uncertain to afraid like sunlight through ragged stone hued clouds on a spring day. "She bade me tell you to finish what you've started and come home. And, as is my wont, I am here to help you."

Loche looks at Julia and says, "Home."

"And what a charge your mother has laid upon us, yes?" William nods to the two figures conversing just outside of the cave.

"But how did you find us? Here of all places—of all times?"

"Ah, that was easy," he answers. "I called George."

"You *called* George?"

"I telephoned him when I was feeling better."

The pressure in Loche's ear throbs.

"George shared with me the events I had missed while I was in pieces. In pieces, dear me. . ." He shakes himself and picks up, "Clever that Basil left a message for you, Julia. Cryptic and wonderfully ripe with mystery. Just the sort of thing I enjoy. I learned you were to cross inscrutable Menkaure. And as the Middle Earth wizard, Gandalf, would say, 'When I arrived there, I found you, but lately gone.' Of course I did find some of Albion's charge slouching about, these *Endale Gen*. Nothing more than treacherous, oath breaking *Orathom Wis*. They were little trouble."

Loche says, "So George and the others are alright?"

"To my knowledge, yes. Though, we spoke not long after you three had crossed from the Azores to Egypt—and shortly after they had repelled Albion's attack at the Omvide. Since then, I'm afraid, I've been rather busy tracking you across both the world and through time. Miraculous, is it not?" He chuckles as he pats the slung bag hanging at his side, "I'd simply call him again, but I'm afraid my mobile is quite void of bars.

"There are five of us. The three that preceded you to Giza, Alexia, Neil and Gary. Ever faithful Corey and I met at Giza and crossed some hours after you. It is good to have some of our own along, is it not? We also have the *Wyn Avuquains*—of which, Vincale is one. They will aid us. And, let us not forget, we have an army of people that were born here. Yes, those you're likely calling Native Americans." William shakes his head, "A wretched name if you ask me—grouping an entire continent's population together with a name that describes nothing and was derived from someone who in no way discovered this continent. Barbaric. Idiots. No, these people simply don't call themselves anything other than what they are: human beings, or people. They do offer distinguishing traits in terms of regions, however. Our new friends claim to be from the flat land above the lake, or so Vincale tells me. Not unlike how the Franks, or the French denote the place where they are from: Western Europe." William puzzles a moment as if trying to recall something. His index finger searching beneath his scarf, "Though, if I'm not mistaken, the word French may come from the Germanic word for javelin. Nevertheless, even the name English, or Angles, another word originally rooted in the Germanic tradition—again points to a location. Angles means narrows or narrow waters—likely referring to the Sclei estuary along the Baltic Sea."

Loche watches and listens to William pontificate. What was it, two, three weeks ago that he discovered William posed like a statue upon his office desk? Loche's paperwork, coffee cup and family portrait swept to the floor. The manic depressive man was dressed like an eighteenth century nobleman, held a kind of ballet dancer pose, and out of the corner of his mouth requested coffee with cream and sugar. As William continues to elaborate on the etymology of the word Indian, Loche's mind becomes saturated in wonder at the thought.

"—of course sail-happy, Columbus arriving in the Caribbean thought he had landed somewhere near India, so he labeled each and every soul without proper knickers Indian. Complete ignoramus, Columbus was. Not stupid, mind you, he just lacked progressive intention and the benefits of a well chosen think tank. And being low on the mental food chain he and his fellows, raped, pillaged and enslaved the populations they encountered—spread small pox and a number of other particularly nasty bugs. The villainy! Ignoramus, I say again." William sighs. "Notwithstanding, there is another school that believes the word Indian truly stemmed from the Spanish words en dios—in god— or more accurately, the people of god. Such a claim might cause a time traveler (one quite frazzled from over thinking the egg, chicken, egg riddle) to think that maybe our En Dios friends will have a hand in naming themselves when eventually they share these events with the droves of future colonialists. Events in which we are now playing a role—gods and immortals at war upon these flat lands above the lake. For they are wrapped up in gods, no? It is obvious they do not regard the *Godrethion* army we just escaped from as gods—for those bastards, I sense they harbor a rather profound contempt. No, I suspect they witness godlike traits in those that dwell within the walls of a city not far from here. The city of our *Itonalya* ancestors, *Wyn Avuqua*."

William reaches out and tilts Loche's head slightly. He examines the dried blood caked below the injured ear. "So, do not be too troubled, my boy. We have friends—and that, too, is a gift." He frowns. "I do wish I had a leaf to press upon your injury."

"You escaped the encampment." Loche says

"Why of course! A few well placed explosives is enough to baffle even the most sophisticated modern warrior, never mind a Northumbrian grunt that still considers fire to be a pretty neat idea. Scared the absolute shit out of them, to be exact. It is unfortunate we did not bring more— but then, as Corey quite providently warns, 'We must not alter what is to come.'"

"What of their leader—their summoner, Cynthia?"

"She lives. Alas." William answers frowning. "And it took much for me to flee and leave her breathing! But again, we must not alter what is to come, though it grieves me beyond words that *Wyn Avuqua* must fall. Cynthia will play a large role in the city's demise. Had I slain her—such an act would cause a ripple in time larger than we should allow."

"And explosives in the middle ages won't cause a ripple?" Loche asks rubbing his injured ear.

"Oh, come now. What's a few thunderous booms and some flashing light to a host of gods? Never you mind! They are gods, after all—though many of them are still coming to grips with the full reality." He lets out a laugh, "And I cannot completely fathom what we are going through. . ." William allows the fire an opportunity to add to the discourse. It hisses and snaps.

"And what are we doing here? I wonder. Oh yes, we have come in search of your brother Basil—the Painter. We have followed signs that have brought us back in time—to a place where the story has been seeded, you might say. We've come with the belief that Basil will show us how to stop the invasion of heaven. That he can somehow stop the thousand natural shocks from becoming the infinite natural shocks echoing in eternity."

William shakes his head slowly, "But you will not find Basil here. You do realize that?" A line of discomfort tugs at his expression. "Loche, you gave your brother a gun. . . and the two of you thought his death was the answer. It was not. It was not." Anguish wets his eyes. He masters it quickly but cannot help his voice from quavering, "It never is." Again, his fingertips search the hidden wound beneath his scarf, and he offers a sad smile of acceptance. His head shakes from side to side, "Basil is dead. But whatever the cause, and whatever the effect, we are slaves to our fate only if we choose."

The poet in Loche reflects over William's last sentence. Whatever the paradox tangled between free will and predestination might look like to William, Loche's image is suddenly clear. From out of his bag, Loche produces the Red Notebook and holds it up in the firelight.

Julia slowly raises up and sits. William reaches to the spiraled book and touches the cover.

"And there it is," he whispers. "So it is true. You have again written."

Loche lowers the book to his lap.

"And you do not know what is written within its pages?"

Loche shakes his head.

For a long time, William does not speak. His focus drifts from the shimmering flames to the red cardboard cover of the notebook and back again.

Edwin's right arm twitches. Loche caresses the boy's forehead. Another spike of pain lances his inner ear. He winces. Julia is suddenly beside him, her arm drapes over his shoulder.

"No one has read its pages?" William asks.

"That is correct," Loche answers.

"Indeed, a gift! It is a gift that you have, Loche Newirth. When shall we unwrap this one, I wonder?"

The Planter

November 12, this year
Venice, Italy
5:13 am CEST

"Maria Vergine!"

Astrid notes immediately the Italian expression as it reaches her ears. It is a whispered cry of shock. A series of rapid breaths follow, and then, "Madonna! Oh, Santo Cielo!" But at the moment she hears the voice, she is stumbling forward. In mid stride she trips on an obstacle at her thigh. Marcel's hand grips her shoulder. There is the sound of a frightened hiss. Another, "Maria Vergine!" She lunges for balance, but cannot recover. She tumbles forward. Marcel falls with her.

Cold, hard stone and something like a ledge or a short stair meets her falling body. Thankfully, Marcel's grip slows the descent and the two drop in a kind of controlled tumble.

Above is a square frame of sky. A spray of starlight is scattered across it. The air tastes of morning. She is lying face up in a kind of courtyard. White marble pillars and Roman arches line her periphery. Sitting up she turns to see the reason she fell. It appears that the *Dellithion omvide* in Idaho dropped her and Marcel on the top of a— she studies it a moment, searching her vocabulary for the right word to describe the large stone basin in the direct center of the courtyard. *Yes,* she thinks, *it is a big— planter. A planter.* Maybe six feet in diameter, the stone bowl sprouts a kind of ivy and is crowned with a half circle of thin, rusted metal for the tendrils to climb.

All the sensations and sights collide again with a fearful Italian whisper in the air.

"Da dove sei venuto?"

Astrid climbs to her feet and whirls around.

With a broom handle outstretched like a spear, an elderly man wearing a dark green jumpsuit stands just inside the courtyard. He is short, with keen, piercing eyes. Salt and pepper hair. His body is poised to fight. In his face is both fear and wonder.

"Da dove sei venuto?" he repeats sotto voce.

Astrid's quickly translates: "Where did you come from?" She blinks at how easy the words make sense—at how long it has been since she had spoken Italian.

But, regardless of the vernacular, the answer would not be simple. To the old man, likely a custodian, (the embroidered white rectangle at his breast pocket reads: Fausto), Astrid raises both palms and says, "Stai calmo." Stay calm. She grimaces. What will assist this poor fellow who just witnessed two people trip out of thin air? She tells him in Italian that it will be all right, that she and Marcel will not harm him, and that she can explain though she knows her claim is impossible.

Marcel's Italian chimes in beside her. Mirroring Astrid's palms out gesture he tells the man that it will be okay—please be calm.

Fausto's wide eyes snap back and forth between the two strangers. He asks again, "Da dove sei venuto?"

Astrid and Marcel look at each other. For some unknown reason, perhaps because no other explanation could suffice, Astrid turns, looks at the planter, points and answers Fausto, "There. We came from there."

The butt-end of the broom is still angled in defense. The old man's attention is latched to the stone basin.

"There?" he asks. His tone oddly curious.

"Yes," Astrid replies.

"You came from there?"

"Yes."

Fausto's face lowers. Astrid's focus follows. They are standing on a stone floor. A symmetric grid of white bricks lines out a square within a square. From corner to opposite corner, white bricks cut diagonally across the courtyard, crossing at the center—at the planter.

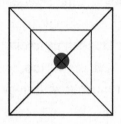

"There?" Fausto's tone is still hushed, but no longer alarmed. He lowers the broom and sets its bristles down on the floor. "I do not know what to say."

Marcel and Astrid lower their palms almost simultaneously.

"I mean," Fausto continues in Italian, "for a moment I thought you had broken into the museum."

"Museum?" Astrid says.

Fausto nods. "Yes, Pinacoteca Manfrediniana. This is the museum at Santa Maria Della Sallute."

The courtyard registers. She and Marcel had both visited here. She, in fact, has been here at least five times on research trips. As she scans through the half-light, she recognizes the square, the balconies, inner ward—even the hum of boat traffic wafting over the walls from the Grand Canal a stone's throw north. She knows this place. It was just this morning, or *yestermorn*, that she projected images of the basilica's two high spires before the Washington Grant Board. She showed images of the Elliqui runes carved into the building's foundation. They read: *For the love of Man, we await the Poet, we await the Painter, Until then we shall destroy the plague of gods among us.*

Below the words were embossed symbols of the Eye of *Thi* and the four households of *Wyn Avuqua*, the Talons, Mind, Heart and Wings. The memory of her hand slipping into the bowled stone heart on the *Avu* Library floor sends a tingle through her fingers.

What else could be waiting below the bricks they now stand upon? Glancing down at her feet and tracing the white grid of the square court, Astrid is struck by a sudden revelation. The painted lines resemble a graphed pyramid.

Marcel says, "Yes. I see it, too." He is studying the lines and the planter apex. "It must be still underground, except for the cap."

"Under our very noses," Astrid agrees.

Fausto watches them. His head tilts looking at Astrid. "I don't believe it," he says finally. "But I have always wanted to—wanted to believe. Sweet virgin Mary. . ."

The ancient tales of the *omvide* passages—portals—the doorways the *Itonalya* used to step from continent to continent, country to country, exist. Astrid turns to the planter. She imagines the buried stones of a pyramid below her feet. Somewhere in her mind she still thinks it cannot be true. Even now. Even after crossing the ocean with three or four steps.

Fausto's appraisal of her continues. A slight smile grows on his face. To Astrid, his expression is akin to someone that has suddenly come to understand the answer to a difficult problem. Fausto then says, "The *omvide* is true. And you're. . . you're Professor Astrid Finnley. Something tells me that we should get you out of here!"

Ruler With the Spear

1010 A.D.
The Realm of Wyn Avuqua

"She is here," Corey says as he enters the cave and lowers himself to his knees.

William's attention is still fixed on the Red Notebook. "A visitor?" he says.

Corey nods. "A visitor, indeed." Loche notes a peculiar tone in Corey's voice. It carries a sentiment he cannot quite place.

"And who might it be?" William asks turning toward the entrance. Outside, the silhouette of Vincale has been joined by a cloaked figure carrying a high, straight staff. "I sense from the chill in my skin that it is a *Godrethion.*" Curiosity floods his face as he shifts his body a little further to the side to get a better look. "Though, there is something. . ."

"A bridger, true," Corey answers. "Yet she is somehow separated from the unwholesome *Godrethion* brood we just left. That sort call her Lakewoman. Vincale tells me the *Wyn Avuquain's* call her," he pauses, "they call her *Lornensha,*" Corey waits another moment watching William closely. "It was she that grew the herbs that have provided young Edwin such a sound sleep."

William nods thoughtfully, "Lornensha, you say? An *Elliqui* name meaning *ruler with the spear.*"

Corey studies William's face. "That is correct."

Loche asks, "Has she come to wake Edwin?"

"No," Corey answers. "Edwin should wake any time now. And he will be quite all right and well rested. She has come at Vincale's request. She has come to aid in your healing, Loche." Corey gestures to Loche's left ear and the various wounds he received from the *Godrethion* guards.

"A healer?" William says. "A healer and a god? A rare thing. I've known only a few through these long years."

Corey turns to William with another expression that is difficult for Loche to read. He opens his mouth to speak but says nothing.

William says, "One woman in particular—"

"My friend, I—" Corey's interruption dies. He stares at William for a few moments and says nothing more.

Blinking, Loche sees text. A hundred or so lines stack behind closed lids. He sees his hand scribbling the name Corey Thomas. Sentences describe Corey's long four-hundred plus year history, and many detail his enduring friendship with William Greenhame. Though Loche never wrote of how the two immortals met, he had outlined many adventures they shared prior to the events depicted in the Priest Lake Journal. These writings, likely in the hands of Albion Ravistelle at present, were scrawled into notebooks when Loche found time to write in his office tower in Sagle, Idaho.

While watching the two maintain eye contact for a few seconds, Loche is reminded of their close bond—or at least the close bond he recalls crafting into their relationship with his words. Infused in their brief exchange are centuries of heartache, victories and losses, kinship and memories—memories well beyond the planting of Loche Newirth's story seedlings. Though Loche may have written it—they lived it. Centuries. It occurs to Loche, *What haven't these two seen? What have they not experienced?*

"You must listen carefully, my friend," Corey says to William, gently. "Though you've heard me say it already—and you, too, are quite cognizant of our actions in this place and time, but we must not alter—"

"—alter what is to come, indeed." William finishes.

Corey reaches out and rests his hand upon William's shoulder. William's grin disappears.

Another blink and Loche sees the text of a story he wrote involving Corey and William in New York City at the apex of prohibition, 1927. The two went in search of a man named Frank Valennte, a Cosa Nostra soldier under Salvatore Maranzano whose operation ran booze from the Canadian border into the city. As for Corey and William, such law breaking was just fine by them. However, Frank's other activities included murder, extortion, prostitution and a list of atrocities he had perpetrated during World War I. Even those occupations, though despicable, were of no import to Corey and William. The real concern, of course: Frank Valennte was a bridging god on Earth. A particularly evil *Godrethion* at that. All told, to an *Orathom Wis Itonalya*, Frank's business and his seraphic trespass sadly canceled out the glory of delivering spirits to New York's speakeasies. Valennte's sordid past also provided a certain job satisfaction to the assassins within both Corey and William: the darker the god, the greater pleasure in sending it back across the gulf.

But the crux of Loche's recollection of this story is not Frank Valennte, nor is it the bridger's eventual death at William's hand—instead, it had everything to do with the short part of the tale when William and Corey, at a speakeasy, had each finished their fourth Vesper Martini, and were ordering their fifth. Blurry and drunk, William shared with Corey his earliest memories of childhood; of his parents, Geraldine and Radulphus. He told of how his mother was murdered by the Bishop of London and his sentinel monk Cyrus, how William learned that he himself was an *Itonalya*, and of the meeting of Albion Ravistelle and the death of his father, Radulfus. William told the story brimming with tears, and Corey listened to his friend intently. The martinis intensified his empathy and compassion. When two yellow ribbons of lemon peel lay in the bottom of their empty conical glasses, the two cried together. A pair of drunk friends lamenting the circling seasons, the missing of loved ones, and the passing of joy to tragedy and back again. William had just ordered more drinks, when Frank Valennte entered the dimly lit speakeasy. The gangster was then not-so-cleverly dispatched by an incredibly drunk and emotional William Greenhame.

And now, over a century later (or, given their current position in time, several centuries before—Loche shakes his head at the thought), the two immortals exchange a look filled with much more than Loche can read, or write. But he knows the real depth of their friendship. *What haven't they seen together?* Loche considers again. *What haven't they encountered?*

With his hand still on William's shoulder, Corey watches the visitor at the cave entrance. "This is something rather unexpected. When was the last time you heard me say that, William?" His forehead scrunches as if struggling to understand something. "I think you'll agree this is a tricky one, but you must heed our mandate. We cannot alter—"

William raises his hand and silences him. "The suspense is killing me. Won't you end it?"

"Very well." Corey then stands and gestures to Vincale to enter. Vincale, in turn, bows to Lornensha. She quickly steps inside and into the ring of firelight. Her staff is in fact a tall spear with a leaf shaped head of tarnished, sharpened steel. Its tip glints in the orange light. When she throws back her cowl, woven coils of hair drop down, framing her pale, caring gaze. Loche is immediately struck by a sudden, puzzling familiarity: her elegant high cheekbones, deep brown irises and luminous expression of both curiosity and concern force Loche's focus to slide from her to William and back again. Then he notices that William's eyes are thrown open like lit windows.

Lornensha does not speak, nor does she offer any gesture of greeting. Instead she sets her spear beside the fire and brings her face close to Loche's. With a gentle touch, she nudges his chin to the side, inspecting his injured cheek and ear. Strangely, Loche does not feel uncomfortable with her proximity. She smells of pine and some sweet herb that Loche can only guess at.

He hears William speak her name. "Lornensha." But his inflection does not sound as if he is calling to her or asking for her to acknowledge him. His intonement denotes a kind of wonder, as if he is again considering the name's origin to himself. "Lornensha," he says again. Both Loche and the Lakewoman turn to him.

William's eyes are spilling long streams of tears as they flit, searching every feature upon the woman's face. His mouth is slightly open. She stares back at him—a sad question shadowing her expression. "Lornensha," he says, but this time his muttering quavers and ends with a whisper. His hand raises as if to caress the woman's cheek, but he stops himself and withdraws it.

Corey is suddenly kneeling beside William. "My friend. . ."

William stands abruptly, strides quickly out of the cave and disappears into the dark.

Corey bows his head. Lornensha watches William exit and then immediately returns to Loche's wounds. A moment later she rummages in her satchel and produces a flagon and a pewter cup. Into it she pours what looks to be clear water. She places it on a stone adjacent to the glowing coals of the fire. Her hand reaches back into the green sackcloth satchel searching for something more.

"What happened?" Julia asks.

"I don't understand, Corey," Loche adds.

"Nor do I. Nor could we ever understand such a thing," he says quietly. "How we drift in circles. . ."

"Was it something about her name?" Julia asks.

"Her name, yes. And her face," Corey answers without raising his head.

"Lornensha is an *Elliqui* name, right?" Julia asks.

"It is." He pauses and looks into the fire for a few moments. "In a couple of centuries a Germanic tribe will have a different name with the same meaning—for the same person. For this person. . ."

Lifting his gaze from the flames he tells them, "That name will be Geraldine."

From her satchel Geraldine of Leaves raises a dried leaf of deep green. She crushes it to pieces and then stirs the flakes into the steaming cup of water.

The Mask Maker

November 12, this year
Venice, Italy
5:21 am CEST

The metal gridded door locks behind them and Fausto drops his keys into the front pocket of his dark green jumpsuit. All above is glowing like tarnished steel. Their breath steams in the cold.

"Come, come, Astrid Finnley," Fausto beckons. He starts down the pavement walkway, the high walls of the Salute on one side, the waters of the Adriatic on the other. "I have your books," he chatters on in Italian. "I have seen you here before. I know about your work. Come, come!"

They follow behind him. He keeps talking. Astrid feels her stomach cramping. She tries to remember the last time she had eaten. She watches Fausto's strange gait. His short legs waddle more than walk. In his wake, Astrid thinks she smells leather, saw dust and perhaps oil based paint. His excited prattling continues, "I have been the janitor at the museum for almost twenty years. . . only three mornings a week. . . part-time. I have another, much more important job. . ."

Her heart is still banging in her chest. The sights of Venice send her reeling into memories. She has spent months in this city. Most of that time was spent between the pages of books, peering into stone fissures, or seeking some new piece of evidence she could add to the massing puzzle of her research. Anything that could prove. . . make sense. . .provide some meaning. The last time she visited she received a phone call from her husband. His voice was sad. He said very little. He offered a list of bills, cancelations, meetings to be attended when she returned—and then ended with, "I'm moving out." Astrid remembers listening to him as she watched a black gondola cross the canal below her hotel window. It was early morning, like now. It was overcast, like now. She remembers nodding to his requests and his decision to leave without feeling a single emotional flutter. Nothing. After she hung up the phone she stood watching the gondola as it disappeared around the corner of a building. A moment later she had imagined the small boat sinking. She had heard her voice saying, "The bow was empty. I turned and the bow was empty!" The sound of her voice had sent a shock of fear through her—then a face had appeared in the reflection of the window as if a stranger was standing in the room behind her. When she realized it was her own face, she had studied it, fascinated at how she did not quite recognize herself.

Fausto leads them along the paved walkway, passed a football field to their right and moored luxury yachts to their left. "I remember when you and your team visited. . ." Graffiti stains the concrete perimeter walls. Astrid cannot read any of the fading, stylized words. They cross a bridge. A road opens to their left and Fausto turns into it, keeping his brisk pace, continuing to chatter. "And what chance that it is you that suddenly appears," he says. Astrid and Marcel exchange a glance that is both amazed and slightly confused. Ahead, a maze of medieval structures rise around them. It is not long before Astrid feels lost as Fausto navigates them through a convergence of alleyways, across two more bridges and into a courtyard between two high towers. He talks all the way. But he talks so fast that neither Astrid nor Marcel can fully catch everything. However, two things are apparent: he knows about Astrid's published works and is a fan— he has a conspiratorial interest in the mythic *Itonalya*.

What chance, Astrid thinks.

They pass jewelry shops, art galleries and wine grottos. They are the only ones awake, seemingly. "It is all connected. . . I knew it . . . I will show you. . ." There are no other walkers. Windows and doors are dark.

When Fausto's voice stops, his legs stop, too. His thick fingers dig into his front pocket and he produces a fistful of jangling keys. He picks through them, searching. "Here," he whispers as he slides a key into the lock of a heavy wooden door. "Here is where I work. Where I live. Come, come."

He opens the door and steps aside for Astrid to pass. He then gestures for Marcel to follow.

The room's light is amber and warm. She is standing within a cavernous workshop. Like Fausto, it smells of leather, wood and paint. Benches of silver tools, hammers, stumps and brushes crisscross the wood floors. From the walls stare a thousand faces with black, empty eye sockets. Some have elongated noses, while others have crowns, or horns, or wings, or checkerboard cheeks. Cats and jesters hide in the corners. Regal, austere faces don the sun over one eye, the moon over the other —sable teardrops stain cheeks, tiny jewels cluster around eyes, monsters and deities, plague doctors and ivory skinned goddesses —grinning comedians, grimacing tragedians.

"I am Fausto Boldrin," he says. He opens his arms wide as if gesturing to the audience of faces. "I am The Mask Maker."

Fire Tending

1010 A.D.
The Realm of Wyn Avuqua

"Dad?"

A fingernail grazes along Loche's forehead. With a swinging pull of vertigo, Loche's consciousness surfaces from a deep sleep to see the face of Edwin. Joy gushes through his senses and he grabs the little boy and pulls him down hugging him tight. Edwin giggles and hugs his father back.

"How do you feel?" Loche asks.

"I'm hungry."

"I bet you are." Loche studies the boy. He searches for the God hiding somewhere behind Edwin's eyes. For the moment he senses nothing save the wide awake and curious face of his son.

"Dad," his little voice whispers as if in secret, "where do we go when we die?"

"We go. . ." Loche starts, "we go to another place. Some call it Heaven." There is a lilt in his answer—as if it were a question.

"Will you be at Heaven when I go there?" Edwin asks.

"Yes," Loche says, "Yes, I will find you there."

"How do you know? How do you know you'll find me?"

"Because I am your Dad. I will always find you."

"I don't want to go, Dad. I want to stay with you. With you and Mom."

"I know, Bug."

"If I go, will you come and find me?"

"I will always come to find you." Edwin's questions roll stones into his stomach. A sudden fear drags like a nail down his back. "I won't let anything happen to you, Bug. I've got you."

Loche sits up and looks around. A flat ashen light is seeping through the mouth of the cave. The fire has been cared for and it crackles, sending up long yellow flames. Outside, William, Vincale and Corey prepare the horses. The trees are indigo. The stream whispers. Julia and Lornensha are kneeling a few feet away, preparing what looks to be a much needed feast of dried meat, cheese and a cracker-like bread.

Julia twists to Loche and says brightly, "How do you feel?" She hands Edwin an energy bar. Gratefully, he gnaws into it.

There is no pain stabbing in Loche's ear. His fingers search for the dried blood but they find only a ridge of a cut that is dry and already healing. The concoction Lornensha had him drink must have done its work in the night. He remembers little after he took a few sips.

"I'm—" he starts, double checking, "I'm good, I think."

"Where are we, Dad?" Edwin asks.

He looks at Edwin's deep brown eyes and says, "I don't know if I can really tell you for sure. We're—"

William's voice sings out, "The realm of *Wyn Avuqua,* young Edwin! You have come to the land of Immortals with your father, your grandfather and—" he casts a quick look to Lornensha, pauses a beat as a desire to say more crosses his face, then adds, "and with very good friends." Edwin leaps up and runs to William. As he holds the boy he says, "And with you, also, young master, I sense you bring behind your awareness something well beyond my ability to describe. *The One* accompanies you, it is true." Edwin's head raises up with a slightly confused expression while his jaw works a dense and juicy bite of a blueberry energy bar. The immortal levels his eyes with Edwin's, just as George had at the *Orathom Wis* council in the Azores on the other side of the world, seemingly months ago. After a few seconds, William sighs and his broad grin breaks open. "But never mind that now. Are you quite ready for your sword lesson?"

"Yes!" Edwin cries.

"Breakfast first," Julia says. Lornensha sets food on a plate woven from cedar boughs beside the fire. Edwin runs to it, sits and begins to carefully inspect the offering. He tastes the cheese. He thinks deeply about the flavors. His stare is ensconced in the fire. Julia sits beside Loche and offers similar fare.

The meat is surprisingly tender, but salty. Gamey, too. The cheese is sharp, but light as a cloud. Loche tastes brine, citrus and cream. There is an instantaneous surge of energy as the food arrives in his belly. He hears himself quietly moan with pleasure. Lifting another chunk to his lips, he watches Lornensha. He traces the shape of her face. He then looks to William. The resemblance is uncanny. Even Edwin, now in a food trance staring at the snapping fire, carries similar facial architecture: thoughtful ovals, shapely lips, proud and high forehead. Loche attempts to recall his own visage—does he share the same nose, chin, smile?

Lornensha eats in silence. She does not appear to notice the lingering stares from William, Julia and Loche.

"We will indeed speak of this," William says to Loche. "And by this, I mean the stunning reality of being in the presence of—" he nods to Lornensha. Lornensha takes no notice. "I dare say, such a discussion may require your expert psychological counsel."

The thrill of a laugh emanates somewhere deep in Loche's abdomen, but he quells it and remains silent. His psychological expertise? A long-ago college lecture queues up in his head—a professor enters the classroom with the words, "Let's talk about your mother. . ." and then he ticks down the evolutionary psychological chain from Freud's Oedipus Complex to Harlow's monkeys to the thousands of self-help bookshelf crowders exploring the relationship between mother and son. How, psychologically speaking, can any sense be made of William's 600 years of life and the connection or disconnection to his mother, the effects of her death upon him and the supernatural torrent storming around them? There is nothing in Loche's academic or experiential past that he can conjure to assist, assuage, understand. Another laugh gurgles somewhere deep, only this one has the character of lunacy and madness—for after all, add the staggering reality of meeting your mother three hundred years before you were born.

It is not a laugh, it is a cry.

As if by some divine mercy, Julia's eyes draw Loche's attention and suddenly the impossible is simple. She holds him for a few moments. All light, matter, a coil of cosmos spiral into a single, inescapable knowing as he falls into her fire-lit pupils. She gives a subtle nod to his little boy. Edwin is looking at his father. Loche looks at William. William studies Geraldine of Leaves as she tends the fire. The great grandmother presses a long branch into the flames and a thousand stars burst and sparkle heavenward.

Across the Canal

November 12, this year
Venice, Italy
6:00 am CEST

Fausto leads them through the workshop and into a high ceilinged room, its wood floors aglow with an amber sheen, its walls an aged parchment yellow. Oil portrait paintings, framed photographs of family. "My beautiful daughter," he points to a picture of a lovely dark haired woman holding a baby. Fausto stands beside her with glistening eyes. His beard is white. Shelves packed with a lifetime of trinkets, tools and the occasional spying mask surround them. At one end is a comfortable kitchen next to a living room. Beyond that in the shadows is what looks to be an office-like space with a desk, a wall dedicated to books and collage of papers and notes tacked to the wall.

Fausto gestures to comfortable dining stools. He fills his kitchen countertop with a block of cheese, a plate of biscuits, a jar of Nutella and a container of yogurt. He makes coffee in a glass press. He shakes his head every few seconds and sighs, "Unbelievable." He pours the coffee. He gestures at the food and says, "Eat, eat."

Astrid obeys. The biscuits are sweet and crunchy. The coffee is bitter and strong. She hears herself sigh. The caffeine rises to her senses and carves away the fog. While she momentarily allows herself to forget the danger, the freakish reality unfolding before her, their host begins again to prattle in excited Italian about bits and pieces of Astrid's research and his own summations in comparison. He speaks fast, and though Astrid can follow a good portion of his chatter, the food has captured her primary focus.

She also notes a collection of his hand made masks mounted on the wall, overlooking the dining area. Fausto's artistry is unparalleled. In the center of the observing faces is a piece that lifts a chill from the base of her spine to the top of her head. She recognizes its shape, and its frightening purpose. The last time she saw this particular mask was on Yafarra's bedchamber wall at *Wyn Avuqua*. Its elegant styling and unforgettable beauty make her think it could have been smuggled from the *Avu* Atheneum itself. It is Fausto's attempt at an *Ithicsazj,* the death mask of *Wyn Avuqua.* A damn good attempt.

When Fausto says, "It was then that Dr. Loche Newirth and Basil Fenn came to Venice that I started to make a connection," that Astrid feels the crumb of a biscuit lodge in her throat and the trance of breakfast disappear. She coughs and presses her palm to the table. Recovering, she says, "What?"

He says, "Dr. Loche Newirth and Basil Fenn. Basil Fenn the painter."

"Connection? What do you mean, connection?"

"Did you not hear me?" Fausto asks, a little perturbed.

"I'm sorry," Astrid says, "My Italian is not what it once was."

The old man smiles, "It is okay. I have been told I speak a little too fast—and too much." He leans in, "I've never met Dr. Newirth, but I have seen him. Twice. Once here in Venice. Once in Florence. At the Uffizi. That awful—horrible night. . ." Fausto looks down at his hands. A shadow tugging at him. "Basil Fenn shot himself that night, you know."

"You were there?" Marcel asks. "We heard about the terrorist attack, but what has that to do with Loche Newirth?" He looks at Astrid, "He is from our part of the country. He was wanted for murder."

Fausto nods. "Yes. I've read that." He points to the dark end of the room where his desk sits. "But he is wanted for much more than that."

Astrid feels her forehead scrunch. "What do you mean?"

Fausto again drops his gaze. His face seems to transform, as if he had quickly raised one of his masks to hide his fear. "I mean," he says after a moment, "that Dr. Newirth is not simply a psychologist from the United States."

Marcel asks, "You said that you saw him in Florence, and then a second time—here in Venice. Where was that?"

"Oh, just across the canal. . . two weeks ago, maybe."

"Across the canal?"

"Yes," Fausto says brightening, "he was a guest of my friend Albion Ravistelle."

"Albion Ravistelle, is your friend?" Astrid and Marcel say in chorus.

"Yes. I have known him since I was quite young." He pauses, seemingly weighing his guest's current view of the matters at hand, "You do know, Mr. Ravistelle cannot age. He lives on and on. He is what you have written of extensively, Dr. Finnley: an *Itonalya*." He shrugs—or shivers, Astrid cannot tell which, "Some have all the luck. I grew old, he stayed the same. Through all of your scholarly work, you must have met him. Yes?"

Astrid shakes her head. *In my dreams,* she thinks. He has been simply a face in two time-stained photographs—one at the turn of the nineteenth century, one shot likely from an iPhone. "No," she replies. "We have not met."

"He is. . ." A finger drags along his mustache and down his short beard, "he is very powerful. He is one to be treated with respect."

"I see," Astrid says.

"And," the mask maker says, "you are in luck. He is coming here at midday. He is coming for a mask."

Astrid feels her jaw drop. Dumbfounded she asks, "Why, Fausto, is he coming for a mask?"

"Why, he's hosting a masquerade ball, of course."

I Don't Know

1010 A.D.
The Realm of Wyn Avuqua

There are moments when it is difficult to tell if the sun has indeed risen. Grey, blurry light smears the world to a worn black and white photograph. Far away, lightening spears through the shoulders of slate grained clouds. A single crow caws from a hidden perch in the cedars. Vincale leads the company north, keeping their movement tucked into the trees. Every so often they cross into the open and follow a shallow tributary for a short distance and then climb back along the tree line. Hiding.

If one speaks, the voice is instinctively hushed to a whisper. Every sound is like an alarm: the slosh and clop of the horses, the rush of water over stones, gentle gusts weaving through the comb of the evergreens.

"Loche, do you know where you are?" William asks from a few feet behind.

"We're on the eastern slope above Upper Priest. We should be approaching the marshes, right?"

"That is what it looks like to me," Greenhame agrees, "though, I do not think that the marshes have become marshy yet. Perhaps in another two to three hundred years."

Loche had lost count of how many times he has hiked around his beloved Upper Priest Lake. Even now, a thousand years before his time, he is able to discern familiar sights: the ridge lines of hills and mountains to the South, the steep cliff faces across the valley, and even some massive boulders that were likely deposited here by some primeval glacier scraping its way from Montana to the Palouse three hundred miles westward. The northernmost shore of the upper lake, in Loche's time, is a gateway to a quagmire of marshland and muddied pools of womb-like nutrients. Loche had once paddled his kayak into the metabolic labyrinth and followed a vein as far as he could until he became tangled in the walls of thick vines and decaying foliage. Later that evening he had written a short burst of verse trying to capture the essence of that fertile, embryonic network that feeds the lower lake:

> The ovum skim that drools down the stream vein
> Where the lake's green glistening sac had burst,
> Like tears at birth it clings to everything at first.
> How heat has flayed its delicate underbelly
> And purged the yolk-spine legs to dangle free
> Down they glide, spreading wide like limbs in the breeze.

A sudden blink and he can see the handwritten lines behind his closed lids. So long ago— and yet it has not yet been written. Or has it? He tries to trace the circle back to find the beginning. The lake's birthplace—the seed of an idea for writing —his own beginning, or ending.

As Vincale turns his horse into another clearing, steering the company quickly across, Loche notes that William is correct: the land underfoot is solid. The marshy floods have not yet drowned the land here.

Loche has let Edwin hold the reins of their horse for most of the morning ride. Beside rides Julia. She has not spoken since they left the cave. Ahead, just behind Vincale, is Lornensha. William and Corey follow at the rear.

"Are you all right, Julia?" Loche asks.

After a moment, Julia purses her lips. She answers, "I don't know. I don't know."

Loche says, "Wait." He takes hold of the leather rein and pulls the horse to a stop. Surprise surges through him. He tries to maintain a composed expression, for what is about to happen next is something either out of character to his conservative nature, or simply beyond his ability to imagine himself doing—or both. He is self conscious but earnest and he feels his lips try to restrain a smile. He lowers himself from his horse, lifts Edwin and carries the boy back to William. William happily takes the boy, settles him in the saddle before him and hands the reins over. Only a shadow of the *Rathinalya* can be seen wrestling in the corners of William's expression as he watches Loche curiously. Loche returns to his horse, ties it to a loop upon Julia's saddle and then stands beside her and looks up. After a moment he asks in a whisper, "May I ride with you?"

Julia smiles.

He whispers again, "I think the chance of riding on horseback with you in the year 1010 on the medieval shores of Upper Priest Lake is an opportunity, exquisitely rare."

Julia's smile widens. He hears a good natured chuckle from Corey.

"I mean," Loche says, "I know it may seem to be a little outside of my heroic reach, but I would. . ."

"Get up here," Julia orders, sliding forward to make room. Loche pulls himself up and straddles the horse behind her. She leans back into him as he coils one arm around her waist and pulls her close. He can smell salt on her skin. With his other hand he threads back her long hair exposing her neck and he touches his cheek to hers. He gently nudges the horse forward and the company again falls in behind Vincale.

They do not speak. Loche closes his eyes and feels the heat of her skin. She wraps an arm over his and squeezes. A moment later, Loche turns and touches his lips to the slope of her cheek, to her ear, to the corner of her eye. He inhales her. Her fingernails gently dig into the back of his hand.

"I don't know. I don't know. I don't know," she whispers.

"Nor do I," Loche whispers back. He rests his forehead upon her shoulder. Exhaustion, fear and terrible confusion wrestle. "I am sorry, Julia. Sorry for everything."

Their bodies sway as the horse climbs onto higher ground.

"Where is Basil?" she asks quietly. "And why did he want me to come here?" Loche does not answer. "If we find him, I'm going to punch him in the gut." Loche wants to offer a pained laugh. But he cannot. Instead he focuses on the next set of coming heartbeats—the next breath. "I don't know how much more I can handle. . ."

"I wish I knew how to answer you," Loche whispers finally. "I can only assume that his message to you and our encounter within the portrait are linked." He sighs deeply and gestures to the indigo green surrounding them, "There is something here that will stop what's begun. He knows that we need his help. That much I shared with him."

"Loche," her hushed voice barely audible, "do you think he wanted us to come here to change the past? Change the past to make an alternate future?"

Of course the thought had occurred to Loche. How could it not? Even as Corey has so thoughtfully put forth—We cannot alter what is to come—Loche's mind has rehearsed and chased down through a few of the potential rabbit holes to where such altering might lead. But he's found little to ease him. Whether it is the violent and dark conditions of his current place in existence, the brief periods he has had to puzzle over it, or the simple fact that his human brain cannot fathom infinity, his meanderings through cause and effect and the thorny way of fate and self determination have all arrived at yet another opening in the earth where rabbits disappear. A feedback loop. A snake eating its tail. What if, begins each attempt. He then arrives again at what if. He feels certain, however, that he and his companions could change the future. But what is mind-boggling are the varied repercussions of which nothing could be authored or controlled.

Or could it?

Blood throbs achingly against his temples. *Too much,* he thinks, *too much. Chicken or the egg?* Did Basil want Loche to come here to seed a future that will prevent The Journal? To remove Loche, the seeming author of all, out of his own story? Or is there some other force at work?

He filters through the time travel stories he knows, books and movies: *The Time Machine, Somewhere In Time, Back To The Future, Slaughterhouse-Five*—this list goes on. None of them offer any comfort or help. Though their time travel storytelling conventions seem plausible, his gut tells him, as does the cold medieval air, the bloodlust of their enemies seeking to capture and torture, and the terror of not being able to protect his son against any of it, this story is not that simple. This is not a movie. This is not a book.

What if he dies here? Will he be born again nearly a millennia later, or disappear from existence? What if he somehow manages to save the city of *Wyn Avuqua* from its prophesied destruction? Will the immortals carry on and keep the balance of this Old Law, as it's called? If he is to share what he knows with the *Wyn Avuquains* about what Albion Ravistelle will do in the future, will they pursue him, cleave his head from his body to stop the invasion of heaven? Will they succeed in the assassination attempt of Basil Fenn and Loche Newirth? Will they kill Loche's father William Greenhame as a boy? Will they kill William's mother Geraldine of Leaves or Lornensha to nip the bud even closer—quicker?

Or will nothing stop the masterwork of *Thi's* story? Will what is to happen, happen? Will this little blue world whirl on its spindle in the dark just as it did the moment it was hurled into its gyre—the burning stars looking on? Nothing to stop it arcing along its circle? Nothing to alter its ending where it started? What if there is nothing to stop it from feeding upon its own tail?

What if. What if. What if. . .

Julia says, "You all right, Loche?"

He turns to catch a glimpse of Edwin. The little boy is leaning back into William. His face stares up into the stony sky.

"I don't know," Loche answers.

Fausto's Web

November 12, this year
Venice, Italy
6:15 am CEST

Astrid's author photograph is tacked up high on Fausto's wall, just below a torn page from a newspaper—its headline reads, *What Really Happened At Ravistelle's Uffizi Art Showing.* Magazine articles, Post-It notes, lines of yarn connecting photos, places, dates and lists of questions create a webbed wall matrix of conjecture. Many of the faces in the photos are not familiar. There are a few, however, that scrape chills along her shoulders and arms: Albion Ravistelle, Basil Fenn, Marcus Rearden, and Professor Molmer. And a drawn square without a picture has a handwritten caption, Loche Newirth or Aethur?

"What the fuck?" Marcel says.

"As I said, I never met him," Fausto tells them. "But over the last few weeks I've had the pleasure of meeting and getting to know an American with a rather close connection to Dr. Newirth — and to all of this."

"Who might that be?" Astrid asks, her eyes still tracing the pattern of Fausto's conspiratorial collage.

"Basil Fenn's stepfather, Howard Fenn." Fausto's index finger points to a picture of a kind-faced man in his late sixties, early seventies. He is seated in a wheelchair. "After the horrible Uffizi event, Howard Fenn has remained here in Venice. He is now enfolded into Albion's household. His knowledge has assisted in all of this," he gestures to the web on his wall.

"Albion hasn't shared—"

"No!" Fausto raises his hands. "No, Albion will not answer any of my questions. He tells me not to meddle in things beyond my *mortal facility*. He knows nothing of my private investigation." He then begins to wring his hands, "I shiver to think of what he would do if he knew how much I've meddled."

After a long pause, Fausto says, "I was there. Albion did not know I was there, but I was there. At the Uffizi. It was no terrorist attack! Nothing of the sort. What happened was beyond rational explanation. Young Mr. Fenn. . . Mr. Fenn shot himself in the head—just before he told everyone his paintings were not of this world. He said the paintings were dangerous. When he raised the gun, I could not bear to watch. I looked away. Then something. . . something happened. Nearly everyone in the gallery was struck by some kind of trance— a strange light—like smoke—like string—like a spider's web reached to them from the stage. I was afraid to look." Fausto points to three sketches he has drawn of his experience. "Then Basil's paintings, all of them covered by black shrouds, were being stolen. Men and women with swords appeared—they fought over the paintings." Fausto shudders. "I have never seen such things save in movies." He points to a photograph of Albion Ravistelle, "Albion appeared with sword in hand. . . my friend, Albion. And he was face to face with a young man with an umbrella. It was Dr. Loche Newirth. The two dueled— Dr. Newirth killed two men himself, escaped to the stage and then disappeared as the melee ended." The mask maker fixes Astrid with a pleading look, "After all you've studied, you must know, by now, Dr. Loche Newirth is the Poet. And his brother, Basil Fenn, is the Painter. The Prophesy—the Prophesy."

Yafarra's voice calling for Aethur enters Astrid's ears. Then Dr. Rearden's words through the headphones on the helicopter, "Dr. Newirth is an authority on *Wyn Avuqua*." A battered spiral red notebook encased within an ancient tomb flashes in the torchlight beneath the stones of *Tiris Avu*. And now, of course, the connection to the artist Basil Fenn. . .

"Of course," Marcel says. "Of course! Or, at least, the fucking craziness seems to align with more fucking craziness."

Astrid asks, "Why were the paintings hidden? You said they were covered."

Fausto shrugs. "All I know is that Mr. Fenn said they were dangerous."

"Where are the paintings now?" Astrid asks.

The old man points to the North. "Albion Ravistelle has them."

Astrid tries to remember when she first heard or read about the reports of a terrorist attack at the Uffizi in Florence. The stories were filled with the usual cast of characters, weapons and senseless violence. The gallery showing was attended by celebrities, politicians and world leaders. There was little, if anything, reported about the actual art. Though there was the peculiar rumor that young Basil Fenn's art had never been seen before. There was no mention of his death except in articles similar to the ones tacked to Fausto's wall—articles written by fringe journalists. What truly happened there appears to have been covered up. But why?

As if in answer to Astrid's question, Fausto says, "Albion had plans to show the paintings to all of those important people. Instead, the audience watched a suicide. . . and something else. . . The attention and story in the media wasn't something Albion wanted, that is why he and his people spun the news to say it was some terrorist thing. But this next event is private. At his own residence."

"Private?" Marcel asks.

"Yes. To accomplish what he failed to accomplish at the Uffizi. This time with much more security and control. Even the attendees will leave their identities at home."

"How do you know this?" Astrid asks.

"I am the Mask Maker. In the last few days I have been asked to make many masks for many important people. They are all attending this private ball. They are attending as masked revelers. In secret." He shivers, "Something sinister disguised as something festive. A mask upon a mask. . ."

"What do you think Albion means to accomplish, Fausto?" Astrid asks.

The old face grays. He whispers, "I do not know. I do not know—but the paintings are dangerous. Very dangerous."

"Dangerous?" Marcel says.

"Howard Fenn has explained that Basil's paintings—the Painter's work will change everything—life, death, Heaven, Hell, the place beyond. . ." His whisper trails off into a series of fearful gasps for air.

"And Mr. Ravistelle plans to share these paintings at this masquerade ball he's hosting?"

Fausto nods.

Astrid turns to a nearby easy chair and lowers herself onto it. A gloomy rain taps at the window. A wave of exhaustion covers over her like a heavy blanket. The weight of myth, belief, art, murder, prophecy. Somehow, Graham Cremo's tall, lanky shape enters her thoughts. *Is he recovering? Is he okay? What would he have to say about all of this?* she thinks.

Fausto's voice shakes her out of a stupor. "Professor Astrid Finnley— I have questions, too. Tell me, if you will—how did you get wrapped up in all of this? How did you find an *omvide* to bring you here? Why have you come? Do you realize the danger you are in?"

The old man's concerned face is smiling. His eyes are curved like half moons. His hair shines white in the dim light from the window. She hears the questions but cannot find the right words.

"*Wyn Avuqua* has been discovered," Marcel tells the old man—answering for Astrid's blank expression. He then recounts their day, carefully braiding both of their timelines together. His Italian is strained but effective. Fausto's expression twists from shock to anger, joy to disappointment, wonder to fear. Astrid's attention strays from the conversation to the droplets of water streaming down the window. Thick clouds of confusion crowd her thoughts. *Wyn Avuqua,* she thinks, *means, tear from Heaven. Aethur means, new earth. Thi thia means, I love you.*

Graham. Graham Cremo.

"So it is as I expected," Fausto says after Marcel's story ends. "You are in danger and pursued. You are here seeking what I seek. The answers we all seek. Has the time come for the mask of myth to be removed and the truth to be revealed?"

Fausto kneels down beside Astrid.

"You must be grateful and excited to know that all of your work will soon be exalted, venerated and established as fact. After all the criticism, all the hardship you've endured to bring these things to light."

The mythology professor from Whitworth College feels tears begin to burn. She only hears his Italian words—too weary to translate further.

Kindly, Fausto says, "O' chiu' bello d' 'a vita e' 'o durmi." It means the best thing about life is sleeping.

She swoons. *Shtan means godsight. Shivcy means, fear.* Thi thia *means, I love you.*

"Enough for now," the mask maker says, his hand gently squeezes her upper arm, "rest now. I will wake you well before Albion visits. Rest now. You are safe."

Sicuro means, safe. Nesh means, safe.

Astrid's body leans back into the chair. Before she falls asleep she feels a soft and heavy blanket cover over her, like a pall—like a shroud over a painting.

The Shape of Rain

1010 A.D.
The Realm of Wyn Avuqua

Loche remembers Julia's words, awestruck and crushed into a monotone muttering, "Is this what your eyes saw?"

She said it just after the company had navigated through a seemingly impenetrable wall of trees and they threaded out into the open air. She said it when massive blocks of ivory hued stone rose from out of the green turf before them—the battlements, the high, coiling green and gold pennants of *Wyn Avuqua's* outer walls. She said it just the western gate opened and a small company on horseback, their helms and spear tips gleaming like grey sparks, exploded out to meet them. Now, longing horn notes wind in the gloaming.

Vincale turns his mount to Loche and the others and announces, "Behold, *Wyn Avuqua*, City of the *Itonalya!*" His gaze halts upon Edwin, "We are the Guardians of the Dream."

In Loche's periphery, Corey rides forward and stops. William, with Edwin before him, does the same. The two immortals do not speak. They are still. *Sculptures,* Loche thinks. Both appear to breathe the sight, or perhaps their gazes are questioning whether what they are seeing is truly there.

As if in answer to the ringing horn note on the wind, Corey's voice sounds out a quiet, sorrowful melody:

> *A Wyn Avuqua*
> > *Endale che*
> > *Thi col orathom*
> > *Tiris liflarin thi avusht*
> > *Lithion nuk te lirych*

The sound of the *Elliqui* words braid meaning in Loche's head:

Oh, *Wyn Avuqua*
> The pearl of Earth
> Our only paradise
> I see your towers in flame
> The hand of God bears the torch

As the melody lilts and awaits a resolve, William's voice joins in and the two complete the melody:

> *Orathom thi geth*
> *Fethe thi geth*

The words crash through Loche's heart. Their spell has flooded into each of the company as well. Julia lowers her head. Vincale's hand rises and rests upon his breast. Lornensha's eyes close and she raises her face slightly as if the evening's mist of sky is kissing her brow.

An ocean rises and wells as the words wash over Loche. A missing, a longing, a need that can only be defined by the shape of rain, the weight of tears, the measure between love and endings.

> *Orathom thi geth*
> *Fethe thi geth*
>
> We want only rest.
> We want to go home.

Masks On the Counter

November 12, this year
Venice, Italy
11:16 am CEST

Astrid is dreaming.

She sits in a cold classroom. It is late February. Ice clusters in the corners of a huge plate window. She shivers. Professor Clive Wadden's lectures. His baritone vibrates the air— the walls—the sheet of note paper beneath her fingers.

"It is as easy as A is for Apple. A is an A. We need not make it complex. Tell me, how is the apple of the Ancients and the apple of the modern era dissimilar? How are the Egyptian pharaohs or Christ, and the Fab Four, dissimilar? All are stories. All are brands. All are icons. They are the characters of narrative despite their organic reality. An apple grows on a tree. We make a pie. Now, an apple from the Tree of Life is a different matter, of course. A taste of that apple will open your eyes to sin. Today's apple connected to the internet will open your eyes to the modern information age—or cat memes. Pharaohs and gods preach peace and love just as the Beatles sermonized, All you need is love."

Hands go up. Wadden says, "Sylvia?"

"Pharaohs were gods, the Beatles were a pop group."

Wadden stares at her. Waits. He then replies, "I could as easily say that the Pharaohs were a pop group and the Beatles were gods."

Sylvia shakes her head, "Well, no. The Pharaohs as gods managed to build pyramids—they were worshiped—"

"And the Beatles weren't worshiped? Come now. Beatlemania? I think both Christ and Mohammed would have been slightly jealous— John Lennon was absolutely correct on every level when he stated during an interview that the Beatles were more popular than Christ. The problem was, the Christ fearing American public had no idea of what a god looked like when they saw one. They were, and perhaps still are, expecting white-bearded ghostly fathers, galloping horses from the clouds, or rays of phantasmic light from Heaven. It is a new day. Humanism has begun to blur the supernatural branding. We're getting too smart. Elvis, Madonna, Steve Jobs, The Beatles are emissaries sent to teach us about how we believe in stories.

"And as far as building pyramids? Well, perhaps The Beatles did not build pyramids, but they were certainly involved in constructing something far more enduring than a megalithic structure of stones. They and their contemporaries gave us a completely new foundation to thinking—a new perspective on humanism. They helped us all to think for ourselves. To question the old tales—the old mythologies. War is out, love is in. Blind ignorance is out, searching and thought are in. They gave us the keys to our own minds—that due to thousands of years of superstition, fear, and the ignorance of bondage, were locked away in the churches and temples. They gave us the weapon that would kill god. Our minds." He laughs. "And because we know better, we don't regard John Lennon as a lightning throwing, all seeing, ruling from on high god. At one time, a walrus, maybe. But his brand, his symbol, his message, his place in the cosmic drama is fixed. His story, like every deity, is the same."

Astrid's hand goes up.

"Miss Finnley?"

She says, "Is not the greatness of this deed too great for us? Must we ourselves not become gods simply to appear worthy of it?"

Professor Wadden smiles. "Ah, Nietzsche. He was the fifth Beatle, you know."

"Astrid. Astrid. Wake up." It is Marcel. He is whispering. "Ravistelle is early. He is here. Astrid. . ."

She sits up quickly. "What?"

"Ravistelle is in the storefront," he points to a place she has not yet seen.

"How long have I been asleep?" Outside the day is brighter, but not by much. The silver sky leaks out an even sheen while clusters of slate clouds knuckle their way in from the ocean. She rubs the drowse from her eyes. Fausto's desk, his web collage, his books and his new friends from the United States are hidden—curtained off from the rest of his living space. The adrenaline rushing into her bloodstream is becoming an expectation.

Marcel stands, crosses to the curtain and peeks. "Just through the door there is Fausto's storefront. He sent me to wake you as soon as he saw Ravistelle turn the corner."

"How long has he been here?"

"Not a minute."

"Did you see him?"

"No."

Astrid stands. "Is there a way we can see him?"

"Probably," Marcel says facing her. "But Fausto said we should stay in here."

The adrenaline converts to confidence. "I did not cross the planet to hide in a back office while Albion Ravistelle is in the house." She slips through the curtain and moves quietly in the direction of voices.

"Aren't these the people that wanted you dead?" Marcel whispers, following her closely.

She does not respond. She rushes silently to the opposite door, leans her head through and listens. She hears voices. Some laughter, someone says, "Oh, look at this one." Astrid descends three stairs, and enters into a room of high shelves—a maze of rows. Upon the selves, lit up bright with a spectrum of color, and displayed for sale are hundreds of empty-eyed masquerade masks. Tiny white price tags dangle on strings and whirl in the warm furnace breeze. Through the rows she sees shoppers. A couple of Americans, "Honey, look at this one. . ." An elderly woman with her hands behind her back peruses in the far corner of the shop. Fausto is speaking quietly to a man at the front counter. The man wears a suit of deep grey. A long coat is folded over his arm. His back is to Marcel and Astrid.

Rounding a row, careful to remain behind Ravistelle, the two position themselves within hearing. As they cross the aisle, Fausto and Astrid catch eyes. His expression is unmoved.

"What beauty, my friend," Albion says. He leans down to inspect the mask maker's work. One hand hovers over the piece sitting upon the counter as if he were placing a blessing upon it. "I have never seen anything like it. Fausto, my friend, you have yet again outdone yourself."

Fausto appears relieved and delighted with the compliment. What might be thirty-seconds tick by when the front door opens and a quaint shop bell rings. November's chill rushes in as the American couple and the elderly woman exit.

"Buongiorno," Fausto waves.

Ravistelle continues to admire the mask. He issues a satisfied sigh every few moments. Fausto remains still, his pupils flitting to the shelves seeking for the fugitives he is hiding.

"How is my bride's mask coming along?"

Fausto nods, looking tense now. Albion's attention is still immersed in the treasure upon the counter. "It is nearly finished. It will be the perfect counterpart to your mask here, though it is beyond anything I have made before. It will be my masterwork."

Albion breathes out another sigh of satisfaction. "As it should be for my beloved."

THE SHAPE OF RAIN

"And how is Helen?" Fausto asks. His tone is simple and neighborly.

"She is well. She is traveling, currently, but she will return in time to join the festivities."

"And your daughter, Crystal. She is well I hope."

"She is," Albion replies. "She, too, is abroad with family." He raises up and stands straight. "You will have the masks delivered to my house?"

"I will," Fausto says, placing a soft cut of velvet over the mask. "Perhaps tomorrow."

Astrid can now see Albion Ravistelle's profile through the shelves— a face that has haunted her dreams. His eyes are dark and complex. His posture is elegant, reverent and noble. The tone of his voice demands attention and something near worship. "I thank you," he says.

Then there is a shift. An expression barely perceptible in his face, the way the quality of sunlight changes as a single high altitude cloud casts a distant shadow. "There was no need for her to run, Fausto." The mask maker does not raise his focus from the delicate process of wrapping his work. Albion says, "She must have been terrified. I know she is here."

Astrid is suddenly aware that she has been holding her breath. And now, her lungs thirst for oxygen. She closes her eyes and allows her lungs to drink in the air, slowly—silently.

"I know Astrid Finnley is here, and I know you are hiding her." Albion's voice is quiet with both a quality of sadness and something else—something cruel, pitiless.

The Mother of God

1010 A.D.
The Realm of Wyn Avuqua

The *Wyn Avuquain* vanguard lead the company through pastures and recently harvested farmland to the gate. They are slow. Banners emblazoned with the Eye of *Thi* whorl in high breezes above the gates. Watchers from the tower, sentinels and archers cast skeptical, vigilant faces. Torches punctuate the platforms down the wall-line eastward. Glancing up Loche thinks he can see bent bows in the narrow arrow slits.

He and Julia ride alongside Vincale.

"Why is it that you aid us?" Loche asks.

"You travel with immortals, do you not?" the Captain of *Wyn Avuqua* replies. "We know that you come from a time out of our reckoning—of that, we do not fully understand. It does not frighten us. Our kind have lived through ages of the Earth, and there is very little in life that we fear. Time we do not fear. You and yours that travel upon it, we do not fear."

"You have met others like us?"

"Travelers from distant centuries? Yes, there have been a few. Some have sworn to the City and the Queen, and have joined us. They have cast off their former lives of future memory. Many have found a home here in this place, in this time—a home and sanctuary closer to their living souls than any on *Endale*. *Wyn Avuqua* is a homecoming to the *itonel*." He gestures to Corey and William as an example. Both are silent and captured within a trancelike joy. Even Julia, her back pressed against him, seems airy and elevated somehow. Loche wonders if she is finally feeling some relief from the consistent *Rathinalya* she has been forced to endure since Edwin's fall into the sea. Vincale smiles, "And those that become one with the City—they take up their holy burden and guard the doors against the *Godrethion*." His tone darkens, "Others have been slain. *Gavress*," he whispers and places his hand over his chest. "Three that I can name have retired to faraway islands away from man. So yes, there are others. Yet you are human. . ."

Vincale twists in his saddle and casts a long look at Edwin. He says, "And I daresay, there have been none like. . .like this boy." Edwin's cheeks shine with a smile, and a sudden, single flash of glitter in his oval sockets. Vincale shudders looking ahead at the approaching gate. "None like he. . .*ag, ag*. Nay, I know not what this means. The Templar must know—the Queen will bring the truth of this frightening turn. . ."

Templar, Queen, truth, Loche grapples. "Templar?" Loche puzzles. He turns to William. "Knights Templar?"

"Not a whit," William says. "The Order you are referring to is still a century or more away from forming. No, Vincale is not speaking of that Templar. The word you're hearing is accurate enough, however, to describe the ministers of the four *Wyn Avuquain* households. They indeed occupy and work in the temple, *Tiris Avu*. The *Elliqui* word is *Tircan*. It means temple minister. I dare say that it may one day inspire the medieval Latin templaris."

As they near the bridge to the gate Loche asks Vincale, "How did you know to come to us—to rescue us?"

"William Greenhame sent his summons with the *Aevas*. William Greenhame then entered the *Godrethion* horde to find you."

"The *Aevas*?"

"The people of Earth's heart," Vincale replies. "This is their homeland, too. They have been here for centuries beyond count, and they are our friends, and our hosts." As the gates open to receive them, the captain says. "But we knew of your peril before William Greenhame's message arrived."

Standing just behind the threshold of the opening iron doors, a formation of men and women wait to receive the visitors. Their garments are made with heavy woven cloth of ivory white and brown. Well-fitting and shapely, the lines are cut to resemble ivy vines and leaves with elegant curves at the sleeves and mantles of green. Some wear long broad swords at their sides. But the three figures dressed in black, standing at the center of the gathering, are as anomalous to the surrounding environment as Loche himself feels. One extraordinarily large man with dark eyes and an angular face stands behind two women.

Vincale says, "These travelers are like you, I expect. They arrived at our gates just before William Greenhame's message. With their word and William's summons, the Queen sent me to your aid. All three are *Itonalya*. . ." Loche feels his lungs suddenly starving for air upon seeing the trio. "One boasts a claim never before heard in any known memory of our people."

"What claim?" Loche asks.

As the horses enter into the City, Vincale halts the company and nods to the receiving contingent, and then he gestures to one of the women in black.

"She claims to be the mother of God."

A moment later, Edwin is crying out, "Mommy! Mommy!" William lowers him to the cobbled road and the little boy bursts toward a kneeling, arms wide, Helen Newirth.

Covenant

November 12, this year
Venice, Italy
11:36 am CEST

"Our friendship has been long," Albion says, turning his hard gaze from Fausto and stepping to a nearby shelf of masks. His fingers run along his chin. He examines the faces. "And I know, you have had questions. Questions. Oh, so many questions. And as I've said to you, all these years, answers for you— answers for you are dangerous. So very dangerous."

The tiny bell above the door chimes. Two large men wearing long dark grey coats enter. One turns to the window and flips the open sign to closed while the other drops the blinds.

Light blue branches of veins appear along Fausto's forehead. His skin pales. He glances at the shelves toward Astrid and Marcel in the shadows, and then to the two men now standing on either side of the doorway. Their faces are stern, almost angry.

"I've entrusted you with my secret. And other secrets," Ravistelle continues, "for we have known each other since you were a child, after all. And I have been with you all along. But as you might expect, I'm disappointed that you would keep secrets from me, my dear, Fausto. All that I've shared with you, and now you hide things from me." His shoes tap the wood floor as he moves to inspect several framed pictures on the wall. "Perhaps it is unfair of me to expect you to carry my secrets. Unfair of me to place the weight of my secrets upon you," he pauses, tilting his head toward Fausto, "upon you and your family."

Fausto quakes. "Albion—" he starts. He wets his lips. His eyes plead.

Ravistelle raises his hand. "If I wanted to take Astrid Finnley now, I could. I know she is here somewhere." He returns to the counter and places his palms gently upon Fausto's hands. "Do not fear. I am willing to forgive you for hiding her from me. How could you not be filled with even more questions after watching her appear out of thin air? How could you not be filled with a desire to know more about your friend Albion Ravistelle and his long, long, long life?" He pats the back of Fausto's hands. "I know. I know.

"Fausto, I have something I want you to do for me."

Fausto opens his mouth but can only nod affirmation.

"Good. I know Professor Finnley is afraid. Tell her that she need not fear. She was invited, after all. Our treatment of her at the dig site was ill-managed. It is not our intention to harm her. It is our intention to include her. Now, this may be difficult for her to believe, given what she's seen and heard. So I will now grant her that grace. As I've said, I could take her now, but I would rather she come to me freely."

Ravistelle gestures to the larger of the two men behind him. The man steps forward and produces a wooden box the size of a laptop computer. Ravistelle receives it, studies the dark mahogany grain, the subtle relief work of ivy leaves around the lid, and then sets it upon the counter. He slides it beneath Fausto's fingers.

"Please place this into the hands of Professor Astrid Finnley and her assistant, Marcel Red Hawk Hruska." He drops his gaze to the box with a reverential bow, "Within is my peace offering to her—and my covenant. Once she has examined it, please ask her to join me at my house, tomorrow evening—where we shall dine and speak more of these things. You may accompany her and bring the beautiful masks you have made."

Ravistelle unfolds his coat. Whirls it over his shoulders and smiles. "Thank you," he says. "Perhaps, my friend, it is time that I shared more of my life with you."

He turns toward Astrid hiding in the shelves. He seems to stare directly into her eyes. "Tell her, Fausto. Tell her not to fear me. Answers await her at my house."

The bell rings. The three men exit.

The clock ticks beside the register. Fausto does not move save for the slight involuntary quaking of his shoulders.

Astrid rounds the shelving row with Marcel.

Marcel says, "Fausto? Are you alright?"

"I have never been so afraid," he replies. His voice is as coarse as sandpaper.

Astrid carefully lifts Fausto's fingers, sets them aside and slides the box toward her. She finds the lip of the lid and lifts it away. Inside she discovers a worn, brown leather bound journal. She stares at it for a moment. She looks up to both Marcel and Fausto with a question staining her expression. She digs the book out and flips open to the first page. Scribbled in bubbly, feminine letters is:

To my husband, Loche—for your words.
I love you,
Helen

"Jesus Christ," Astrid whispers.

"What? What is it?" Marcel asks.

Astrid flips the page. The handwriting is different. It reads:

October 26th, Priest Lake.

What is real and what is make-believe? Have I become what I have longed to cure? Have I finally gone crazy?

"What is it, Professor?"

She raises her face to them. "We have the Poet's journal."

The Trust of Helen Newirth

1010 A.D.
The Realm of Wyn Avuqua

Helen Newirth enfolds Edwin in her arms. Towering over her with the *Rathinalya* tugging at his jaw, her jailor, the formidable Talan Adamsman, watches the reunion closely. Wide-eyed, with her hands clustered into fists at her sides and smiling at the mother and son reunion is the newest to the *Orathom Wis* ranks, Leonaie Eschelle.

Edwin turns to Loche while being smothered in his mother's kisses and tears. His little grinning face fades into a translucent mask then back to smiles—the sight sends a nail dragging down Loche's spine. The boy god from Basil's painting appears from behind Edwin's skin. Shadows pool in *Its* eye sockets and two tiny pin-pricks of light, both horrifyingly reminiscent of the yawning Center, glimmer like distant stars. The two faces crossfade back and forth at a pace that matches Loche's breathing.

The psychologist shakes his head and squeezes his eyes shut to make it stop.

Julia says, "Loche?"

An instinct from some impossible to understand neurological firing struggles for mastery in Loche's mind. Its directive is to scream to the entwined entities of God and Son, *Hide yourself! Not here! They will. . . they will kill you. . .this is no place for a god!* But all that comes from Loche's mouth is the vapor of his breath in the cool, autumn dusk.

"Loche?" Julia asks again. He feels William's hand on his shoulder.

It is the massive Talan Adamsman that breaks the phantasmic stranglehold on Loche when he says, "George believes that Helen still has a role to play—so he allowed us passage to find you."

Corey says, "But I see, Talan, that you are still her chaperone."

"I am," Talan says. He bows as William dismounts and stands beside Corey. "William Greenhame. William. When word came of your fall, I laughed. William Greenhame, I told them, even limbed and thrown to the sea with the fishes, William will live. *Gal Ashto!* Good to see you, my friend."

William bows in return, "*Lain,* Talan."

Talan motions to Leonaie Echelle. She is pretty. Her hair even more brown than the last time Loche saw her in the Azores —age shuffling off its coils from her face and her frame. But behind her *youthing*, there is nothing that can hide the grief she carries—the death of her beloved, Samuel Lifeson. Each time Loche has seen Leonaie he has noticed tears weighing below her eyes. This meeting is no different.

Talan says, "Miss Leonaie Echelle has come at her own request. George approved of her coming. Her errand is unknown to me."

Leonaie's smile, though sad, is still piercing and bright. "I am here to speak with Dr. Newirth. I will need to speak to him in private as soon as we are able."

Helen lets out a breathy snicker, "Yes. Place me on the private convo waiting list, too, won't you?"

The massive Italian man scowls at Helen—his thick eyebrows angle angrily. "As for Helen—George does not trust her. . . nor do I. Nor do any of you, I expect. But I believe her youthful urges are finally finding the right road." He faces Loche, "After all, you are alive, Dr. Newirth. If Helen had not escaped my supervision at the Azores *Omvide*, the bullet meant for you may have met its target. I am thankful for my failure and letting her slip from my grasp. One can never order fate completely."

Helen's detached and myopic tone sounds out, "Husband, I saved your life. And please, don't be so shocked to see me. After all, because of this little fellow, we'll always be a family." Her voice has its familiar, unsettling quality.

Edwin's cheeks glow crimson.

This is no place for a god. Loche thinks again, but a strange relief unwinds the muscles along his shoulders. Perhaps the grafted boy and God heard his frightened plea. George Everman's voice drifts through—as does the sound of a sizzling omelet, "Trouble for Edwin is that we, *Orathom Wis,* eat the gods." The *Itonalya* already know, of course. The *Rathinalya* is enough to place the boy on the plate. But if the god shows itself, its swirling, glittery eyes, Loche believes a ravenous, immortal mob might devour them all. At least Helen will be there to protect Edwin if things go terribly wrong.

And what exactly has gone right? he thinks.

"Always a family," Helen continues, "And you're stuck with me."

Corey speaks, "We, Helen, may be stuck with you—but it does not mean that you have earned our trust."

"You speak of trust, Corey Thomas?" Helen sighs, sarcastic. Her words border on laughter. "You? Which trust, I wonder? Albion's? George's? Really, Corey, I've learned much from you over the years—but you're not the only one that can pull off double agent. But never mind—time will tell."

She kisses Edwin on the forehead and stands. Her head swivels and her eyes take in the entry court of the West Gate of the City. "And, Corey, here we are in *Wyn Avuqua,* as told in the *Toele.* Can you believe it? You do remember our first bottle of wine together, don't you? Beside the canal in Venice? What was I, 19? We spoke of this place—the true home of our kind. Do you remember?"

Corey listens but remains stoic and impassive.

"And we talked about what we were all waiting on. . . how did we say it? Waiting on this omen thing from this place?" Her fingers comb through Edwin's hair. "And didn't you instruct me, all those years ago, to consider the dictum: the less you care, the longer you last? Well, I *do* care, Corey Thomas." She gently places her hands on either side of Edwin's face. She then says to Loche, "And I've lasted long enough to know whose side I'm on."

"And whose side is that, Helen?" Corey asks.

She answers the question with her grey eyes studying Loche's face. "Loche knows. . ."

"And what of trust?" comes the deep baritone voice of Vincale. "I can see now the only trust one should keep is that anything is possible. I can trust that divisions between the *Itonalya* will indeed widen, for I see between you, great chasms. Even now in the City, cracks are forming between us. I shudder to think of what is to come for our people. Never would I have thought that one *Itonalya* could not trust another."

William says, "You can trust there is nothing sacred— even we. Time will crumble the very mountains of this world."

Vincale shadows. "Come," he says. "I am to bring Loche and his son to *Tiris Avu*. The Queen waits. She above all will want to learn how the moon's children will one day break faith."

The Big Deep Heavy

November 12, this year
Venice, Italy
10:10 pm CEST

Astrid hands the Journal she has just finished reading to Fausto and asks in English, "Can you read this?"

"Si."

"If you have trouble, Marcel will help you. Capiche?"

"Si," Fausto says, his hands trembling as he takes the Journal. He stares at her. "What," he asks haltingly in English, "what does it say?"

Astrid shakes her head. "For the moment, I don't know how to answer you." She reaches to the book and touches the back cover. "There is an envelope—a letter—at the end of the book. The letter is written by Albion Ravistelle. He tells of the events that follow where Loche leaves off, and the way his story —" her words bang into a wall, "the way his story—" she scowls. "Changes— changes—" She gives up. She whispers, "Changes everything." After a moment she smiles lamely, "I don't know if it will help you in your research, or if it will cause more confusion. But you should read it. You deserve to read it."

The Mask Maker wonders at her. Glassy eyes blink. He backs away with the leather book and closes himself inside his bedroom. Astrid turns toward the small kitchen, passes Marcel, asleep on the couch, and sits at the table beside the window where she has been all day and into the evening, reading. She folds her hands, places her elbows on the table and rests her head upon her knuckles.

"Fuck," she whispers.

Strewn all over the table are notes. Most of the scribbled lines ending with question marks. Many have deep cut underlines and ballpoint circles.

Is Loche, God?
Does the Devil really exist?
If Heaven is to fall, what does that mean? Is it happening now?

A wine bottle without a label atop the small refrigerator catches her attention. She does not hesitate. She rises, grabs it and finds an opener in the first drawer she tries. She pulls the cork. The collar of the bottle plinks the rim of a glass as she pours. In the dim light the wine appears black. Bringing it to her lips she gulps until it is gone. She refills and takes another long pull. The wine is sweet—fragrant, like bruised flowers. Thick, like blood.

"Fuck."

Did Loche change the past?
Did Loche kill the Painter, Basil?
Did Basil ever exist, save in narrative, save in memory?
Did he create Helen? Albion?

"Fuck."

She continues to scan the notes. Some lines are hers, others are copied from Albion's letter.

Did Loche create the Itonalya?
Can he do it again?
Wyn Avuqua?
Why could we not find the city, and then suddenly, it's there?!!!
Marcus Rearden? Bethany Winship?

How can a story meant to capture a murderer, change
existence?
—same way a story about crucifying a the Son of God
can change existence?

A chill claws through her. Aloud she says, "Dr. Marcus
Rearden. . . What are you trying to do now?"
Astrid puzzles still looking at the sheet of notes.

What of Basil's paintings in Albion's possession?
Albion plans to show them!

Tears rise. She poses a question to the empty kitchen, the
gods that may or may not be listening, the scribbled journal in the
next room, her students on the other side of the planet, her ex-
husband's note waving in the furnace heat at home, and the man
that has somehow captured her heart, Graham Cremo:
"What about me? Did Loche Newirth create me?"

Like the Book

1010 A.D.
The Realm of Wyn Avuqua

Edwin waves at the gatekeeper in his stone house beside the gigantic cog and wheel machines. The keeper waves back. Slacked heavy chains bow to the high parapets, to the massive doors and back down into funneled wheels beside the entry. Ahead, a mossy green cobblestone road starts a gentle climb into a dozen or so cedar trees. It feels to Loche that he is not entering a city, but rather another forest, a forest glittering with tiny torches.

"Tomorrow," Vincale says, "if the Lady allows, you shall wander the City under the light of day. But even as *Dellithion* visits *Endale* elsewhere, you are blessed to enter *Wyn Avuqua* at night. For in darkness her embrace can be evermore alluring. . ."

A gentle rain begins as the last of the grey light fails. A rushing stream somewhere distant threads through the pines. They pass high gabled buildings and networks of pathways that lead into clusters of distant houses. They pass other travelers on horseback, people on foot and an occasional wagon with glowing yellow lanterns. They are greeted with smiles, and *galinna* and *adnyet*. But the greetings are quickly stifled by the realization that a god travels within the party. Their smiles fade to dark wonderment.

Vincale's warm voice from ahead keeps the train heartened. "All is well," he says. "Follow and do not be troubled."

Every so often they cross below pinnacled stone arches. Icons are embossed at each apex. Loche squints, trying to make out the image.

"The talons of a heron, Loche Newirth," Vincale assists. "We are now passing through *Shartiris*."

Corey to his old friend, "*Shartiris*. William Hubert Greenhame. . . we are riding through *Shartiris*." Then whispering to himself in disbelief, "We are riding through *Shartiris*."

"A wonder!" William replies. To Leonaie he says, "Those of the House of Talons are the warriors of the City, though, I dare say, all are trained in the art."

"That is indeed so," Vincale says.

William, his voice lighthearted and at ease, "See there. . . Leonaie, these must be the spires and chimneys of the lower Armory"

"Right again, William Greenhame," Vincale replies.

Leonaie's looks to the passing sights and to where William points, but Loche notices her focus often returning to him. She wears an expression he cannot yet read. Back at the gate Leonaie had leaned into his ear and whispered, "We must speak privately—as soon as it can be managed."

High above the tree-line jut three brick chimneys. Orange sparks and feathery plumes of smoke rise from their tops like freshly extinguished candles. The structure below appears to be conical. Through the thick dark an overlarge open door hurls an incandescent heat into the night. On the air is the tink, tink, tink of many hammers, and the breathing of bellows as if within the forge a dragon sleeps.

Blinking, Loche sees the black and white grid of text behind his lids. William is suddenly at his side. He asks quietly, "Is it anything like you imagined? Is this what you saw when you wrote of it?"

Loche tries to recall. He thinks of the key hanging around Julia's neck. The key that will open the door to his circular office tower— the key to the cabinets containing his journals, notes and poetry. There, outside his round office window, he would watch the trees fill with purple dusk, and the forest glade just down the hill from his driveway would suddenly reveal a stone cabin, or a circular citadel with five spear-like towers, or a tavern smelling of yeast, crisp woodsmoke and spilled ale— bright candles in the windows, and yes, a conical armory would sometimes appear with three high chimneys and he could almost hear the ring of hammers pinging on anvils. Yet, those images and sounds and flavors were fleeting. Just as they would form in the architecture of his imagination—just as he would enter, explore and struggle to explain his discoveries onto paper, his visions could very easily vanish—crumble—die. His imagined ocular citadel, *Tiris Avu*, its monumental foundation rivaling that of the Pantheon, or the weighty core of the Pyramids of Giza, or the sure, modern footing of the Empire State Building, was no match for the destructive force of reality: a bothersome phone call, Helen's voice from the kitchen below beckoning for some mindless chore, his worry over a hurting client, the occasional tussle with existential dread. And so, too, the delight of his six-year-old son knocking on the office door with two wooden swords and a challenge—or the little boy's thudding footfalls across the floor into Loche's lap with a thousand questions about stars, bees, donuts, video games and how to build jet boots could, and often did, nudge aside the best laid megalithic plans. During those moments he felt like the metal between the hammer and the anvil. He was at the pressure point between fiction and reality. A casualty from the collision of colossal forces. Loche can hear Edwin's voice, *When is your book done, Dad? Are we still writing the good stories?*

Loche gazes up to another series of arches and notes two more icons carved into the stone signage: a heart and a set of wings. The company enters into a lantern-lit maze of bridges and canals. Just beyond, *Wyn Avuqua's* center fortress, its circular ward and five towers, *Tiris Avu,* rises out of the landscape. It is familiar and terrifying all at once, like a dream coming true. Had he seen it from here before? Did he know this was going to happen?

Had he conceived of the gatekeeper? The warrior class of *Shartiris?* The way the City's lamplight flickers across the valley like moonlit water? The eye-shaped kingdom of immortals with its towers, high battlements, armories, libraries, temples, music houses, sculptures and simple homes—fires in their hearths, bread on their boards?

Yes. Yes it was like what he had seen in his mind's eye. It was what he had written. It was the dreamscape of his poetry.

"Son," William asks again, "is it as you wrote it?"

"No," Loche answers. A sharp chill searches beneath his jacket. "It is now real and I can do nothing to control it."

"I do not agree with you, Son," William says. There is a quiet terror in his words. "But I fear that when you learn to control it, and control it you will, Death will be your teacher."

Newirtheism

November 13, this year
Venice, Italy
10:21 am CEST

"So what we have here is what I'm going to coin as Newirtheism." Astrid's hangover is not as intense as she was expecting. She can still taste the wine in her mouth. Her head throbs a little. She feels about how she might feel during the start of any Monday morning lecture. But better. Probably because the bottle of wine was exquisite—no sulfites—no preservatives—and more than likely bottled by a family owned winery just walking distance away. She scans the kitchen to see if there is another bottle hiding somewhere.

"Newirtheism?" Marcel repeats.

"Yes," Astrid says, rising, opening the small white cube of a refrigerator. *Voila—wine.* She seizes the bottle, sets it on the counter and jabs the corkscrew into the throat. "My only chance of not losing my mind is using what I know in order to process all that we are involved in. The Journal and Albion's notes are beyond anything I or anyone involved can fully understand—including Dr. Newirth himself. But laying what I know of myth and history over what we have just learned, I think we can at least find a place to stand within it."

"Gods exist. . . afterlife exists. . ." Marcel says seemingly to himself.

Astrid purses her lips and thinks. "Maybe."

"Maybe? How can you say that? Maybe? After all we've seen already. After what you've seen?"

"That's just it, Marcel," she says. "Rearden. . ." A chill skitters down her neck. She shakes her head. "Rearden will take some thought—do you recall Rearden's words in the Journal—it was a repeated motif throughout the work. He said, many times: there are always two."

Marcel says, "Yes—Always two."

"Correct. But perhaps Rearden's, or rather, Loche Newirth's words *for* Rearden were not entirely accurate—or complete. Loche kept referring to words and pictures. Always two. Two ways of perceiving."

"Yes, and Loche wrote of William saying similar things, too."

"Yes." Astrid thinks a moment. "Instead of two, maybe the line should have been, there are always three. . ."

"Okay. What's the third?"

"Well, stories can be shared with words and pictures—but what if they could be shared through experiences. In other words, I can tell you—I can show you— but what if I could attend you."

"Attend?"

"Yes. Say for example you taste wine from an unlabeled bottle," Astrid pours two glasses. She hands one to him. He sips. "And you tell me about its flavor, texture, its deep crimson color —almost blood-like. You describe how the spirit gets you slightly buzzed and giggle-drunk. You go on and on with your story. You even snap a picture of it for me to see. Or in this case, you raise the glass and show me. I'm quite inclined to believe everything you say. I got the words—I got the pictures. But to fully believe, or rather, to know, I must experience it for myself, yes? I must attend it." She tips the glass up and drinks the contents in four deep pulls.

Marcel watches her. "Professor?"

She sets the glass on the counter. "And I agree. And I believe you. It is true. Good fucking wine." She returns to the table and lifts up the Journal between them. "Now let's say you see a ghost—or better yet, you experience one of your tribe's elder spirits, like you've claimed so many times. You tell me that you swear on your Elders, and your Elder's Elders that you experienced it—even after I suggest you may have had low blood sugar at the time, or you were stoned at the time, or maybe depressed, or tired, or some physical, organic biorhythm was squirting an overload of this or that kind of hormone or a random electrical synapse firing across your frontal lobe—you're still telling me that you fucking saw one of your spirit guides. Okay. Fine. Then you show me a picture. And it's a good one. Say, from your cell phone. I may be inclined to believe you— but I wouldn't."

"You would have to attend me," Marcel says, nodding.

"I would have to attend you," Astrid agrees. "Myths and belief systems are made from two things—words and pictures—very seldom from attendance in the grand scheme. We know that myths were created to establish moral values, to control masses and the like. But this. . ." she sets the Journal down on the table. "This is something entirely new. And with the lenses I've looked through all of my career, it is fucking terrifying."

Marcel waits, his mouth slightly open.

"Let me put it to you this way," she says, pressing her palms together. "We know now, in the twenty-first century that gods have never existed. We made them up. Humanism, history and time has taught us that."

"Some attend such a notion," Marcel says—a nervous smile on his lips, "But I believe gods have always existed."

"Yes," Astrid agrees. "I know." She fills her glass to the rim. "And you're not the only one, of course. But, you see, Newirtheism has just replaced belief with knowing. Belief with fact. If the twentieth century killed God and advertised it for all to see on its philosophical billboards: God Is Dead, then Newirtheism, in my mind, has just brought to life what was never really alive in the first place."

Marcel shakes his head, "But Professor, God, or gods live within us—they—" His words fall away as he watches Astrid empty another full glass of wine into her mouth.

She slurs, "There is something missing. Something I can't quite put my finger on."

"Professor, after reading—I couldn't help but wonder about my personal past. I mean—" Marcel shakes his head and he raises his hands as if he is trying to grab an imaginary idea from the air. "I mean, if I'm reading Loche's writing correctly, and deciphering Albion's notes—life, as we know it now, is only weeks old. I mean, everything was different before Loche fell into the Eye." His face scrunches. "I mean, take *Wyn Avuqua*, for example. I've been fascinated with the folk tales and controversy of *Wyn Avuqua* since I was a kid. Since I was a kid! But if Albion's notes are correct, it would mean that *Wyn Avuqua* has only truly existed for a couple of weeks—since Loche fell into the Eye and wrote it into existence. His writing changed the past? My past, too?"

Astrid feels a heavy stone drop into her stomach. "Yes," she says. Her tone is dark. "I've been thinking that he created a past. And when I think hard about it, I feel this strange ache. It is difficult to describe. Like I've forgotten something."

"I feel it, too. A worry, almost. A worry. . ."

Astrid nods. "Can you recall the first time you learned of *Wyn Avuqua*?"

Marcel looks out the window. His eyes shut. He takes a deep breath. "Well, yes. Of course. My grandmother told the tales of the ancient city. I must have been four or five, I guess. We lived on the Rez at the time. But—"

"But, what?" Astrid leans toward him.

"But the harder I think about it—search out details—the ache gets worse. That worry—that worry almost becomes, well, dread." His face pales even more than his usual pale. After a moment he asks, "What does that mean, Prof?"

Astrid's eyes stray to the wine bottle. The alcohol in her blood is now cushioning her own ache. *It is impossible to work out*, she thinks. *Just like trying to make sense of a believer's blind faith, or the insanity of placing an afterlife ahead of the life you're living, or placing all of your hopes, dreams and identity upon a story—a myth.*

"It seems to me that this will be a topic of discussion with Albion Ravistelle. I'm guessing he's feeling the same kind of ache we are. But like the Journal says, it can all be true. Seams now exist in both our stories and in reality. This might cause our little arrogant self-important perspectives some distress, I think. I wonder what other godlike entity we'll try to make up when our canonized characters of myth start doing things we would never expect. This may be the first time in human history that the entire race will attend the reality of myth and afterlife." She considers another glass of wine. "They are real! Newirtheism. It is really happening."

"What about Rearden, Professor?" Astrid sees the gun in Rearden's hand. "What do you think his role in all of this is?" She hears Graham's desperate gasp for breath.

"It is because of him, Marcel, this entire story began. He is a murderer. And he's after something."

"The Red Notebook?

"He got his hands on that already. But I think he's got a score to settle with Loche."

"What do you think is written in the Red Notebook, Professor?"

Astrid reaches for the bottle, "Life."

"Life? What do you mean?"
"I don't know yet."

Pocket Diary Entry # 5

Unknown
(Loche Newirth's pocket diary)

?

I've been here before. In my office tower at home-I've visited this place. The sensation is beyond my ability to-

WHAT I'VE WRITTEN IS LIKE MEMORY—

Templar and the Queen

1010 A.D.
The Realm of Wyn Avuqua

The time travelers take seats in a high balcony above a large auditorium within *Tiris Avu*. Loche tucks his pocket diary away after only scribbling a line or two and places Edwin upon his lap. William and Julia bookend father and son. Helen and her chaperone are set apart from the others by four, tall sentinels with silver armor beneath deep green cloaks. Helen's eyes seldom stray from her son.

"Sit and be silent," Vincale whispers. "The Order hears news of the storm that gathers in the East."

Below is a circular, marble chamber with rising ringlet rows of perhaps two or three hundred seats, most of which are vacant. The audience seating surrounds a large crescent shaped table gilded in heraldry and symbols. Loche recognizes the icons as the four Households of the City: talons, a heart, a set of wings and the head of a long-beaked bird. At the table are four regents (or Templar as Vincale called them), two men and two women. Each wears the vestments of their house. Within the crescent's curve is a high round dais adorned in gold filigreed vines and leaves. The emblem of *Thi's* eye is carved into it. And upon the carving is a throne. Upon the throne is a woman. She is clothed in simple white. Her hair is gold and woven into a thick braid. It drapes heavily over one shoulder.

Between the Queen's dias and the crescent table stand two men. One is unsteady and staggers as he speaks, as if he had recently been injured. Facing the Templar he waves his hands. Fear rises in his voice. His companion is rigid, still and stoic. Both wear livery similar to the green and silver sentinels, but their cloaks are stained and weathered, and their armor is dinted and blurred with mud. Loche's mind flashes to the gathering of the *Orathom Wis* to repel Albion's attack at *Mel Tiris* just a few days ago. The ceremony with the drums, the prayer, the green surcoated pikemen, the strange familiarity of it all—William had said that day, "You should know—you made all of this."

Loche's looks at the key hanging at Julia's throat. And it was true. Between the covers of several notebooks, once protected behind locked cabinets at his Sagle, Idaho, tower office were sketches and elaborate descriptions of the massive hall he is now sitting within: the circular fortress surrounding the hall; the city surrounding the fortress; the immortals and humans that made up its citizenry.

He studies the massive banners hanging from the high ceiling, the bright torches illuminating the circle of the chamber, and the proud sentinel pikemen at each arched door. Upon another stage positioned near the back of the chamber are four figures enclosed in a ring of different sized drums. They stand motionless and reverent. The memory of the drums at *Mel Tiris* sends a jolt of adrenaline through him. Against the wall to their right is a massive, semicircular hearth. A fire roars within it. In his mind, he has been here before.

Then the shouting of the wounded sentinel—angry and frightened—yanks Loche's focus back to the Templar and Queen below.

"Ten thousand or more!" he shouts. "Do you not hear me? Ten thousand *Godrethion*! More arrive every day! Our southern sortie was ambushed. Some were cut to pieces. Others, along with our *Aevas* guides were captured. And we—" his words crack into pleading, "we were set free to tell of their fury. They are coming! Will you not listen to me? *Thi* hath come to punish us!" He bows his head and weeps.

The Templar of the House of Heart asks, "Your wound, Sentinel. Show us." She extends her long arm. Her skin is dark and her wide eyes are filled with concern.

The wounded *Itonalya* soldier throws his cloak to the side to reveal a bloodied, bound knee. But jutting from the knotted cloth where his lower leg should be is a length of a stout tree branch. "They took my leg, Lady Roblam," he answers simply.

"Come, come!" The House of Talons stands. He is large, bald and muscular. His shadow stretches out across the marble floor. He casts an uneasy glance into the balcony, at Loche, the boy god on his lap and Lornensha. For an instant, the bald man's head jitters and he quickly masters himself. Ignoring the *Rathinalya*, Talons says, "We knew this day would come. We have prepared for it. We shall follow through with our design."

"There was no agreed upon plan," The House of Mind says. His voice quavering, edging toward rage. "This division between us has now been drawn to the point of destruction. *Thi* has awakened an army and has brought them across the sea. A shore, thus far, beyond the reach of men. *Thi* has set them to rage at our seeming rebellion." He, too, searches the balcony with a darting scowl and then shakes it off.

"Seeming?" Talons mocks. "Seeming? You are the head of our body. You despise slavery beyond all of us! Come now, you know of the new awakening of our kind. You know of the changes to come. . ."

Mind stares at the huge man, and the long sword dangling at his side. "It is true," he agrees, his voice controlled. "Slavery is abominable. But, as I have maintained, our freedom awaits us not through rebellion but through our loyalty to *Thi's* creation—*Thi's* mortal children the *Ithea*, like *Mellithion* to *Endale* herself. Do you not recall the great deluge? Was that not enough warning? Was it not warning enough when *Elliqui*—" Mind steadies his voice, "when *Elliqui* was taken from us. Was that enough to slow our disobedient hearts?"

The House of Wings answers, "Our sages found words to remake *Elliqui*, and thus words have been placed onto our tongues and into our tomes—"

"Counterfeit, Bannuelo!" he shouts at the Wings Minister. "A mere mask to what was once pure and without strain." There are many quiet gasps from those in the surrounding audience. As if in response, Mind stares out into the ringed rows. "Some of you are too young to remember true *Elliqui!* Some of you will never understand how connection to *Endale*, and sky, and *Thi*, and how the quiet whispers of stars entered *Itonalya* thought all at once. When some of you decided to throw off your duty to your Maker, the Mighty *Thi*, our first injury was the falling of that high beacon of speech. Yes, our sages worked to replace it through years of bloody, blasphemous trials. What cost? Too many of us have turned away from protecting *Endale* and the *Ithea* from the stars. Too many of us want more than our promised, undying bodies. Too many of us have allowed the terrors of gods among *Ithea*—the plagues the *Godrethion* bring, the wars, the horrors. Oh *Mellithion! Mellithion* hides his face."

"Maghren, Minister of the House of Mind, please harken to me," says Bannuelo of the House of Wings. She rises and steps into the crescent between the Queen and Templar. She places her hand upon the shoulder of the injured sentinel. "How many hundreds of years have we debated this question? And through our countless debates, realizations, and compromises, as with all determinations, a verdict must be acted upon in a single moment. The moment has come. With caution have we rejected our sacred mandate. Treasonous it might one day be said. Treasonous to her Majesty's will," she lamely gestures to the Queen, "and most certainly to *Thi* above. But the spirit of our people calls for liberation from the old ways, the Old Law. Each *Itonalya* must make their own choice. Your House, Maghren, has continued to keep *Thi's* will. Blessed be the faithful. And there are numbers within the other Households that still hold with you. Many still fulfill their duty to *Thi*—journey to distant lands and eliminate bridging gods from *Endale*, protect the *Ithea*, walk in the footsteps of *Mellithion*," she pauses—her face sours, "and embrace their bondage, just as *Mellithion* always has. But as my brother, Yanreg of the House of Talons has pronounced, we, the majority that have entreated freedom and have forsworn allegiance to *Thi*—we have long prepared for this day. Now, right now, *Thi's* army gathers at our gate. Our will must prevail over the Old Law."

The House of Mind shouts, "The Old Law promises our freedom. The Prophecy! The Painter and Poet will herald our freedom. *Thi* has promised. The time is not now! Our work for humankind is not done. Not yet."

Yanreg's bellowing voice shouts louder, cavernous and menacing, "You speak of ancient myth, folk tales and rubbish! Whispers of the Silent Author! Whispers of madmen and long gone sages! No more children's stories of our deliverance—the wolves of god are at the gate and you speak of prophecy." A steely glare, quick as a flash of light, stabs out from the Yanreg, from the floor to the balcony—to Loche and his boy. Edwin shudders and turns his face into his father's shoulder. "Dad," he says. "Dad. . ." Loche holds the boy.

Maghren's face pales. His fingers touch his forehead as he turns to the Queen frustrated and incredulous. The Queen shows no expression. The House of Mind says, "And so you, Yanreg, reject our Lord's promise. You and those that follow you choose the path of madness. You propose a parlay with the *Godrethion*? You will pledge peace between Immortal and god on Earth, you will allow them to do what they will on *Thi's* creation, and in return for our protection we will help to shape a new world?"

Yanreg of Talons laughs, "So you have been paying attention all these years to our recommendations, Minister of

Mind. Yes. Remember, the *Godrethion* horde has wants just as we. They, too, are slaves to *Thi*. And their mortality here can be managed by us. We shall grant them leave, life, fortune, power—all the horrors and delights that their borrowed fleshly shells can take, and over time, we shall create the world around them and make our own Heaven, here. *Thi* shall no longer reign over us." Another sudden tremor shakes through his shoulders. He refrains from looking into the high seats.

Now Maghren laughs. Tears shape above his cheeks. "Peace? You of the House of Talons, the leader of our warring body? Peace? Do you believe what you say? Truly? You believe that *Thi* will not bring calamity and a fate worse than abomination?"

Yanreg's large body looms in the torchlight. Seconds pass. Loche sees a smile ooze onto the man's face. "You know my mind, Maghren," he hisses.

"And you know mine," The House of Mind growls.

Roblam of the House of Heart rises from her chair. Her dark skin is luminous in the firelight. She says, "And we now balance upon the blade—yet again between freedom and chains. The long years of debate must now be ended. Outside, a storm gathers. The army of *Thi* has come with wrath to chide and chasten our rightful plea. Do we ride to meet the horde and rend them from *Endale*, and uphold the Old Law? Show *Thi* that we are again servants to the will of old? Pray for forgiveness?

"Or, as the Templar Yanreg of the House of Talons has so wisely advised, do we forsake *Thi*, renounce our ancient summons and protect gods on earth, strike a peace, and together, god and immortal, rise against our Maker? Rule, order and create our own paradise upon these shores? It is a choice between slavery and freedom." The House of Heart waits. Her gaze circles the chamber. When her line of sight crosses Edwin and Lornensha, Loche sees a subtle tug of worry flinch through her.

The woman faces the raised dias. "I prithee, Sovereign Queen Yafarra, what is your will?"

When Queen Yafarra rises, the Templar stand up from their seats and then bow to a knee. Yanreg of the House of Talons is deliberately slow in this ritual. His face is a smear of smiling resentment. The Queen rests her gaze upon him until it forces Yanreg to lower his eyes to the stone floor.

The torches breathe. The hearth fire crackles. Loche squeezes his son to his chest.

"Heron, Templar, you know my will." Queen Yafarra says. Her green eyes find Edwin and Loche in the balcony. "I am the Old Law. I will not allow our body to turn from our sacred mandate." Her voice is quiet—haunting. There is a breathy depth behind her melodic, thoughtful timbre. "But with all of my heart, I desire freedom. I am Queen Yafarra, daughter of Althemis Falruthia of *Vastiris*, the Sovereign Monarch of the *Orathom Wis* of *Wyn Avuqua*. I wield the Red Scepter. I am the Heron. But on this day, I kneel before my Maker, and my will is nothing." There is a collective gasp as Yafarra bends to her knees and bows her head.

Edwin swivels into Loche's chest and hides his face.

Yafarra says, "I shall speak to God. And if it pleases Him, He shall advise me."

Black Boat on the Water

November 15, this year
Venice, Italy
3:24 pm CEST

On the way to the canal they follow a young couple holding hands. Astrid watches how the boy gives the girl's hand a gentle squeeze every few steps, and how he leans his head toward her when he speaks. After passing a dozen or so buildings, the girl drags him to a small alleyway and throws her arms around him. As Astrid, Marcel and Fausto pass, the two lovers are lost in a deep kiss. Marcel says nothing. Fausto sighs and smiles. Astrid stares. A moment later she shakes her head and tries to understand why she feels like crying, why the knot in her stomach has suddenly tightened, why she wishes Graham's hand was in hers.

Marcel says something about Fausto's delicious lunch. The antipasti of fried sweet peppers with vinegar and olive oil (a deeply yearning olive oil, if olive oil can yearn), smoked prosciutto, and moist mozzarella on crunchy bread. Astrid can still taste the oil and the salty cream of the cheese. Fausto laughs and thanks Marcel for the compliment. His laugh seems forced. He sounds nervous.

Each of them carries a medium-sized suit case. Within are the masks that Albion had ordered, all save one: the mask Fausto had promised for Albion's bride, his beloved Helen. "I will tell him that I need a little more time," Fausto had said to Astrid nervously. "It will be done in time for the ball." Astrid carries the Journal of Loche Newirth in her shoulder bag. She thinks it feels heavier than it looks. *Maybe,* she thinks, *its heavy because I'm hung over.* She quickly feels the bag to make sure she packed another bottle of Fausto's wine. Her hand feels it. She sighs.

"It's Marcus Rearden that terrifies me," she says suddenly. Neither of the men respond. "What in the hell is he up to?" Again, the men are silent. "My gut tells me to believe Loche's journaling. There is something there that just feels like the truth. And the truth is: Rearden is a murderer." She listens to the sound of her footsteps on the pavement. "It is strange to think that all of this—all of this—Loche, prophecy, *Wyn Avuqua*, Basil Fenn—all of this happened because of the murder of Beth Winship—because Marcus Rearden murdered an innocent person." She hears a sigh come out of Marcel. A flustered, can't-get-my-head-around-it sigh. "Rearden is not the type, I think, to forgive and forget. He is not through with Loche Newirth."

Astrid stops talking, but her mind chatters on. She turns the problem that is Marcus Rearden over and over.

When they arrive at the canal, they walk for a minute or two south. Turning the corner around a high weather beaten building, Fausto waves at a gondolier near the water's edge. The gondolier waves to Fausto.

"Ah," Fausto calls to him, "very good. Very good."

A few moments later the three are seated in the center of a long black boat. The lanky pilot oars them out.

"Buon Pomeriggio," the boatman says as the trio settle themselves.

"Ciao, Alessandro," Fausto says. "When did you get back — you've been gone a long while."

"Si," Alessandro says. "Gone long, yes. You've been well, yes?

Fausto's focus drops to Astrid's shoulder bag as if he can see the leather cover of the book inside. "Yes," Fausto says.

"Who are your friends?" Alessandro asks. A weird smile expands across his face.

The Mask Maker introduces them. "Astrid Finnley and Marcel Hruska, meet my friend Alessandro," he says without hesitation. "Alessandro has been a gondolier for many years here in Venice." He smiles up at the orange haired man, "You've been taking some time away for yourself. That is good."

"Yes," Alessandro says.

Astrid and Alessandro nod to one another. She turns to the afternoon sky and the short crossing to Albion's house.

Alessandro says, "You make masks for Ravistelle's ball?"

Fausto's face pales slightly. "Yes. You know about the ball?"

That weird grin stretches out again.

"Well, it is supposed to be a private affair," Fausto replies. "But I expect you know everything that's going on, as usual."

Alessandro's eyes smile, "Boat drivers always hear— always know. Crazy."

"Of course," Fausto says. He then leans delicately toward Alessandro and his voice falls to a near whisper—almost as if he and Alessandro have had secret dealings. "It is to be a very important gathering. A lot of important people. Tomorrow night." His eyes dart to Astrid and then back to Alessandro, "I believe they will be showing—paintings. . ."

The gondolier is silent. After three or four pulls on the oar he tells Fausto, "Careful with that Albion, my friend. Careful what you do there." He lifts the oar out of the water and crouches down on the back of the boat. "Fausto, Astrid and Marcel—do be careful. Remember, too, that I am a friend. I am your friend." He then stands, dips the oar back into the canal and pulls against the water. Astrid watches his elongated shape sway with the current.

"Albion," he mutters to himself, "stupid crazy man."

Alessandro delivers the trio to the pier outside of Albion's house. They step onto the dock and the boat quickly makes its way back out into the canal. "See you soon, Fausto, my friend," the boat driver calls.

The Mask Maker waves.

Into the *Avu*

1010 A.D.
The Realm of Wyn Avuqua

Down into the center of *Tiris Avu.*

Somehow, Loche knows the way.

Down, into the earth. Down spiral staircases into a round room. Massive. An open crystal tomb in the center. Its lid is laid aside. Into a labyrinth of bookshelves. Warm light bathes the spines of leather tomes, scrolls and sculptures. Huddled over desks are scholars, and scribes and the occasional child, reading or writing. The vaulted ceiling is ribbed in gold. The floor tiles depict talons and hearts and wings.

When they arrive at what Vincale calls, The *Avu,* he lays a hand along the cheekbone of a sculptured sentinel. Loche watches him and knows that a hidden mechanism will clatter below. It does, and the hemispheric dome rolls gently, silently back. Beneath is a staircase into an amber light. The captain leads them down. They enter a wide chamber. Loche has seen this place in his mind's eye. Troughs of fire line each wall. There is a beautiful bed with high carved posts, story-filled tapestries, finely made furniture, an oak desk with quill, ink, scrolls and what looks to be a globe of the earth—its formations are astonishingly accurate. The figure of a warrior looms in a corner of the room. A tall armature clad in the Queen's armor stands like a solemn guardian.

Vincale asks them to sit. They obey. A moment later attendants enter with trays of breads, cheeses, fruits, and goblets filled with a drink named *Anqua*. William, Corey and Helen take the cups gladly, almost greedily. William drinks deeply. He notices the younger immortals, Julia and Leonaie watching him. "Oh my dears," he says motioning for them to take a goblet for themselves. "The *Wyn Avuquains* call it *Anqua*: god water. But it will not have the name we know it by for some years. We time-hoppers call it Scotch. It will ease the *Rathinalya* my grandson has been cutting you with. . . drink and take comfort. *Anqua* is the best medicine when you're in need of squelching the gods among us." He taps his high boot, "That is why I brought my own bottle." He laughs. The cork of The Macallan is visible in the cuff.

The eager hands of Julia and Leonaie almost collide as they reach to the tray. They tilt the cups into their mouths and drink.

Edwin notices an open trunk a few feet from his father's chair and points. Lying in and around it are what looks to be a collection of a child's toys. Small carved soldiers, a pair of wooden swords and a stuffed leather dragon. Loche nods and Edwin darts across the floor and sits. Lornensha rises from her chair and joins the boy. The two inspect the beautifully made figures. From the trunk she lifts out a leather pouch. Pulling apart the drawstring she produces four wooden horses, one green, one black, one grey and one blue. When William sees the horses, he coughs a mouthful of scotch back into his goblet. "Oh my sweet word," he cries, and looks at Loche.

"What is it?" Loche asks.

William does not answer. Instead, with a bewildered grin he shakes his head and stares intently at Edwin. Edwin makes clip-clop, clip-clop sounds as he trots the blue horse along the floor. Lornensha studies the leather pouch.

"Circles," William whispers.

Queen Yafarra enters the chamber holding the hand of a boy who looks of an age with Edwin. In their wake follow four women dressed in long light green gowns with dark purple mantles. Two of them light candles, the others set a small table with plates and fill two goblets with water.

Yafarra pauses just inside the entrance. She is clothed in a long coat of soft woven fabric of spring green. It hugs her shapely, long torso. She rests a long gaze upon each of her visitors in turn.

Vincale, William and Corey stand as she enters and they lower their eyes reverentially. The others rise and mirror the gesture.

The young boy lets go of Yafarra's hand and walks over to Edwin and Lornensha. The two boys size each other up for a moment. Edwin raises the green horse and hands it to the boy. In return, the boy smiles.

"Welcome, Loche Newirth. Poet." Yafarra says. "It has been foretold that you would come." She looks at Edwin. "And you bring with you, your son. Your son, God. *Thi.*" Her head tilts at the sight of the boys. "Behold, *Thi* and my son now play with toys upon my bedchamber floor." Wonder lights in her face.

"Welcome, William Greenhame of the *Orathom Wis.* Father of *Thi's* Poet. Your courage to bring your family out of the grip of the *Godrethion* horde shall be sung for centuries to come.

"Welcome, Corey Thomas and Talan Adamsman. Welcome to our younger *Itonalya* sisters, Julia Iris and Leonaie Eschelle. May you find here at *Wyn Avuqua* the beauty and light that hides within the burden of life perpetual. May your time here bring wisdom.

"Welcome Helen Newirth." A barely perceptible glint of light shimmers in Yafarra's eyes. "Wife of the Poet. Mother of God. What trials you have borne, I do not know. What allegiance you hold, I do not know. No one in your company trusts you— save, of course, your son—our God. Therefore, let his trust be mine. If you betray me, you betray your son."

"Lornensha," the Queen smiles. "Welcome."

"Your Majesty," Lornensha replies. She is still kneeling upon the floor with the children.

Yafarra says to her visitors, "Lornensha I have known for many, many years. As you have already learned, she is a god among us. Her gentle spirit we have allowed to live upon *Endale* for she brings light and healing to humankind. She has taught us much about the cultivation of herbs and roots—of love and care —of gentleness."

Yafarra moves to a chair. After she lowers herself onto the cushion, Loche and the others take their seats. "Edwin Newirth," she says. Edwin does not hear her. He and the young boy continue to gallop horses through toy soldier troop formations. "Edwin?" she says again. Edwin turns to her. "May I see you?" The boy looks to his father, to Helen then back to the Queen. Yafarra holds a hand out, "Come, Edwin." Her smile is motherly and warm. "And you, too, Iteav. Let me see you both."

The boys rise, each still holding a wooden horse. They walk to the Queen. As they stand before her, she brushes the long hair away from young Iteav's eyes. His hair is the color of rust and orange. She focuses on Edwin.

Loche cannot see his son's face, but he can easily tell what appears there by Yafarra's struggle for composure. The glittery swirl of blue in Edwin's irises, descending into a pool of impossible black, unfathomable depth, the craze and fortitude of the godhead. Yafarra's hands clamp upon her knees. Loche thinks of how George responded when he looked into his son's eyes and saw the infinite power lurking there. George had groped for his dagger, the muscles along his jaw taut and bulging—but he then mastered the overwhelming *Rathinalya*. Yafarra does not reach for a weapon. But her gaping expression is strangely similar to George's. Loche wonders what his own face must have looked like when he fell from the cliff into the Eye. Julia takes a long, shaky pull from her goblet. William and the other immortals follow suit. The sound of a wave curling high and towering roars in his ears. But before he takes a step to intervene, the Queen flinches, and pushes her eyes up and out of the void before her. She lays her hands along either side of Edwin's face and kisses his forehead. Iteav watches his mother and Edwin with a face brimming with fear.

"I know now," the Queen says finally. "You are the One. The All. It is true. You are the flood."

She touches her son's cheek, "Iteav, bring Edwin Newirth to see your other things." She points to an adjacent room. Iteav takes hold of Edwin's hand and pulls him along. The two boys exit the chamber and rush to another open trunk along a far, opposite wall.

Yafarra looks at her hands, folded in her lap. Her posture is straight and elegant.

"So Loche Newirth, Poet, you have brought your son and God into a city filled with godkillers—into the eye of a storm. As you have witnessed in the Great Hall, a pestilence has poisoned *Wyn Avuqua*—the rebellion against the Old Law and *Thi* has finally overwhelmed even the Templar. And outside there waits the Hand of *Thi* ready with His ten thousand spears to discipline his disloyal immortal flock by blood. There is little a Monarch may do when faced with such calamities. There is no sunlight in these dark days.

"I do not yet know your power, Poet. Nor do I understand fully the power of the Painter. It has been prophesied that with your coming, the *Itonalya* will finally be freed from our duty to *Thi*. Am I to believe the time has finally come?" She pauses. Her eyebrows angle inward as she says, "But my heart tells me that you have come on another errand." Yafarra waits. Loche feels the urge to reply, but he refrains. He is certain Yafarra will ask for him to speak when she is ready.

"You and yours are not the only travelers from centuries afar to have visited my court. And I can see in you a desire to portend some news of great import. I have been alive and have served *Thi* for nearly two thousand years. And though I am trapped in a body of flesh and blood, my mind, like those of my kind, has achieved a kind of time-travel itself. I can in some capacity see eventualities ahead by looking back from whence I came. But so, too, I have learned that knowing what is to come is much like changing how I remember the past, neither will bring an unchallenged truth to the present.

"And so, now, Poet Loche Newirth, why are you here? What do you seek? I shall now listen to your full tale. But you must take care in what knowledge you share, for as the wise have whispered: When meddling in the affairs of time, the Fates always have their say in the end, even if stories have a way of writing themselves."

Each face in Yafarra's chamber turns to Loche. He feels compelled to stand. Into what might be a nightmare or a far off memory, Loche reaches for the right words to begin telling the story he is living—the story in which he has become a character. Through the far door he can see his son. As if in answer, the boy turns to him—but it is not Edwin. A widening pupil-black circle swallows the flickering firelight in the chamber around the boy. . .

"A man named Marcus Rearden murdered an innocent woman." He stops. He breathes. "And to capture him, I have risked everything. Everything. . .and everyone."

Can the Past Change?

November 14, this year
Venice, Italy
5:07 pm CEST

"I want to see Graham Cremo," are Astrid's first words to Albion Ravistelle as they enter into the wide lobby of his house. She then rattles off several weighty questions. Albion politely listens. "But let's start with Graham. I want to see him."

"In due time," Albion Ravistelle says. "I will gladly answer all of your questions, Professor Finnley. To address your most pressing need, Graham Cremo has undergone surgery. Though he is in critical condition, the arts of good Dr. Catena will rekindle his health."

"Critical?" Astrid's worry eclipses all else.

Albion nods. "We are very hopeful and confident, Professor." She searches for truth between his words. Albion then shuffles to answering her other questions as a way of changing the subject. "Queen Yafarra, daughter of Althemis has been rather difficult to communicate with. She is unwilling to cooperate. She is reticent to answer our questions and inexorable beyond any immortal I have known or heard tell of. We are holding her— comfortably, I should add, in quarters above.

"What are you doing in all of this?" Astrid asks.

"By all means, a good question. I am attempting to remake the disaster that is the human race—grant them immortality—erase the heavens and the gods above, and start over here on this potential paradise called Earth. Such an endeavor does not come without some discomfort, I admit. But I assure you, violence is my least desired tool. Most of the heavy lifting has been done through art—words and pictures. The paintings of Basil Fenn will eliminate God. The words of Loche Newirth will enable all else.

"But Loche's work is troubling, I must admit." Albion opens his palm and holds it out to Astrid. The gesture is obvious. She glances to Fausto and Marcel, then she reaches into her bag, lifts out the Journal and places it in their host's hand. Albion studies if for a brief moment and then walks to a dark oak bureau. He lays the Journal down beside the Red Notebook. A burst of adrenaline rushes through her when she sees the Prophecy. "You three have read the Journal—so your eyes tell me. For how could your eyes ever be the same after reading such a thing? And now knowing what you know, like me, you must be filled with wonder and want of more. I know the look on your faces.

"And behold," he says laying his fingers on the cover of the spiral notebook. "Our author's—or should I say, Aethur's latest collection of scribbles. A sequel? The end of the tale?" Albion pulls his fingers away suddenly as if the cover were a hot, searing grill. Astrid judges the gesture to be overdramatic. The immortal says, "Aethur, we are learning, can change the very roads we plan for ourselves, the roads we've trodden and the paths that stretch out far beyond our sight." He scowls. "To be completely transparent, Dr. Finnley and young Marcel, we are afraid of the book. We are not willing to risk all that we have endeavored to build just to be reordered, manipulated or completely effaced. We believe if it is read, change will follow— change we cannot control."

An attendant enters the long dining room with a tray of long stemmed wine glasses. Astrid is the first to reach for one. She takes a long drink, her gaze locked to the face of Albion Ravistelle. She is still in disbelief, still in shock—and still slightly hung over.

The immortal raises his glass. "A toast, and a wish." Fausto raises his. "Here is to our long years of study—and a hope that what we've learned will help us to determine our next step." He drinks. Astrid and Marcel do not.

"What step, Mr. Ravistelle?"

"Come now, Dr. Finnley, drink. After all, you were invited. You were invited to help me, for I believe there is no one else in the world like you—no one knows what you know of our ancient roots—knows how the intersection of the past and history and myth, and now, so it seems, the simply unbelievable."

All four drink. The sweetness of the wine, lacy and elegant, makes Astrid want to cry.

Albion swirls his wine and stares into its funnel. He then looks to her and asks, "Dr. Finnley, what do you think is written in Aethur's Red Notebook? How do you think it came to be found with Yafarra? With all you've uncovered in your *Wyn Avuquain* research, what can you tell me about how Yafarra came to be entombed, how the city finally fell, the—"

Astrid shakes her head and empties her glass, tilting back without looking away from Albion. The movement silences him.

He chuckles. "I see. More wine then?"

She tries to smile, but cannot find the shape in her mind. "I don't know how to answer any of those questions, Mr. Ravistelle. With all due respect, you're the immortal—the one that would have had centuries and centuries to uncover, study and research. . . Christ, you are the culture. You must know more that I know."

Albion nods thoughtfully. "Yes," he agrees. "Yes. A thousand times, yes. You are correct. Why would I not know the complete history of my kind? How could I not know that the prophecy was a Red *spiral* Notebook, and that it would be entombed with Queen Yafarra? Of course, I should. How could such a tragic event during the cataclysm that was *Wyn Avuqua's* end be overlooked by historians?" He frowns into the whirlpool of his cabernet. "Vexing. So very vexing. You see, this is again why you are such an important voice to us—and to those I represent.

"Perhaps we should begin with this: tell me your thoughts on just why *Wyn Avuqua* was one day a legend—an impossible to find jewel—and the next, it is uncovered, massive and seemingly impossible to overlook."

A headache begins to pound. "I don't know, Mr. Ravistelle." She pivots to Marcel's pleading look. She's sure it matches her own. "The two of us made research trips there just weeks before Professor Molmer took me to the dig site." She squints and then joggles it off. "But I—but I feel—"

Albion moves a step closer to her and leans down, attentive and curious, "Precisely," he breathes, "you feel. What do you feel?"

"I feel as if something is wrong—or I feel a dread when I try to remember certain things. I feel like some of my memories are. . .they are. . . well, new. . . or somehow broken. I don't know how to say it. And when I try to understand it, the feeling intensifies—it is like worry—like worrying about something you can't control." Marcel nods beside her. Albion's carved countenance, handsome and thoughtful, watches her. There is nothing more for her to say. She feels a wave of nausea, and if she were to continue, she is certain that she would vomit.

Her next words slip out in slurs. "I can't help but place this all into a mythical context. I mean, when I try to recall my first memories of learning about *Wyn Avuqua*—it's like—it's like —like my failed marriage. I remember it being something very different than what it was—now I remember new things about it all the time."

Albion watches her mouth as she speaks.

The nausea fades. Her focus sharpens. "I don't know, Mr. Ravistelle. If Loche is the prophesied Poet, wouldn't he pack his work with more than a plot and characters? He would indeed lace themes and metaphors into the narrative. Like, well like that quote from Herzog, 'How might one love a story for what it is not about?' Newirth's work is myth. Myths have a lot of different ends, and one not to be overlooked is how we interpret our past by rewriting it to make sense of our present." Astrid feels the wine massage her headache and ease its pressing. For the first time she holds Albion Ravistelle's gaze with confidence. "Maybe," she says, her voice shifting into her wonted lecture cadence, "maybe we missed the wreck and majesty of *Wyn Avuqua* because we never really understood it—and when we tried, we made excuses, filled in the holes with conjecture and guessing—like something in our heart of hearts felt the city was only imagined, and never truly real. Maybe I missed it because I didn't know the difference." She places her empty wine glass down between the Journal and the Red Notebook. "One thing is for certain," she says to herself, "if Loche Newirth can write a city from out of nothing and into the consciousness of all of us, I for damn sure can accept that everything changes—even the past."

A Day In Wyn Avuqua

1010 A.D.
The Realm of Wyn Avuqua

A rare sight: sunlight. It is golden. It reaches into the chamber from a high portal in the stone wall. Julia lies on Loche's chest. His open hand rests upon her back. He can feel the bones of her spine between her shoulder blades, the gentle thud of her heartbeat and the warmth of her body stretched along his. She has slept. Deeply. This sleep has been perhaps her first relief from the torture of the *Rathinalya* since Edwin's fall.

"Awake?" Loche whispers. She does not stir. He combs his fingers through her hair.

The fire in the hearth has faded to orange coals. The table beside is still arrayed with meats, cheeses and fruit from the night before. Loche lets his eyes drink in the ray of distant sunlight. He cannot recall the last time he has seen the sun. He cannot remember the last time he felt comfort. Julia's soft breathing, the scent of her in the air, the soft weight of her hair lying across his skin—he had forgotten this feeling—he realizes how much he has missed the touch of a loved one.

And today, he muses, *is a day off.* A half scowl, half smile forms at the absurdity of the thought. There is no escape from the nightmare—no turning away from the circumstance he has founded. But the Queen commands.

Last night's memory returns. Loche Newirth, the Poet, told his story to the Queen while Edwin and Iteav played with toys in an adjacent room. William took up the story once or twice, as did Julia and Corey. Leonaie Echelle spoke of how she came to be immortal through the efforts of her lover, Samuel Lifeson. She then recounted his tragic death at the hand of the assassin Emil Wishfeill. Helen remained silent. When the Queen asked her if she had words to add Helen replied quietly, "Not yet."

When Loche found no more to say, the Queen called for Iteav and the healer, Lornensha, to accompany her while she thought more on these things. She then bade Loche and his companions to take food and to rest. "Helen Newirth, you and your young son, along with William Greenhame and Talan Adamsman, will stay in this Tower. A mother should have time with her son. Like your companions, I feel you are to be trusted only in that your motherhood is true. If there is more to discover, time will show. Be with your son." Helen's face flushed with gratitude. The expression seemed odd seated there. "Leonaie Echelle and Corey Thomas—on the morrow, I will have questions. Please enjoy what hospitality *Tiris Avu* has to offer, but be prepared for my summons.

"Loche Newirth, Poet," Loche can almost see the Queen's green eyes studying his face. "Tomorrow you and Julia Iris will visit *Wyn Avuqua*, the city you have seen only in your mind's eye —you will explore the tear that fell from Heaven. Listen to our poets and our musicians. See our homes and our works. Maybe then, Poet, you will find a way to deliver its beauty, and its people from doom.

"I shall now name you in the tongue of the *Itonalya*—I shall name you for the new world you herald by your coming here. I name you Aethur, son of William, Poet, and father of God."

"The sun is shining," Julia says. "I'd forgotten what that looks like."

"That's what I was thinking," Loche says.

Julia's arms squeeze. "Are you ready to see the city?"

"Not just yet. I'd like to hold you for a while longer."

"Good," she whispers. "Good."

A loud knock upon the chamber door startles them both. "My Lord, Aethur?" From the stone hall shouts an enthusiastic and friendly voice, "I have come to show you my home, *Wyn Avuqua*. A bright day has come and our time is short. The Queen has sent me as your servant."

Loche rises. The air is brittle and freezing. He pulls a robe over his shoulders and opens the door to a dark eyed, dark skinned man. He wears the deep grey surcoat and green mantle like those of the Queen's house, *Tiris Avu*. Upon his chest, embroidered in silver thread is the full body of a Heron. Circled around the symbol are many runes. The man is slightly shorter than Loche, but stout and seemingly immovable in both stature and his expression.

"I bid you, good morning," he grins. "I am Teunwa. Let us take *Dellithion's* light as a sign that the storm on our borders is but a passing breeze. And while His light shines, we may feel the delights that my home has to give."

The Message In The Stars

November 14, this year
Venice, Italy
5:42 pm CEST

"Tell me what you see," Albion asks. He opens the door and allows her to enter.

Stepping through, Professor Finnley gapes. The walls, the floor and the ceiling are splattered with a spectrum of paint like a psychedelic sky of stars. Tacked upon the starry fields are hundreds of images, ranging from quick pencil sketches to torn out magazine pages and photos, to famous portraits done by master painters. There are canvases upon easels with incomplete images, scattered scribbled notes in a twig-like hand, an unmade bed, two long shelves of LP records and a turn table. Near the center of the room is a round dining table. Upon it is a half full bottle of The Macallan and three empty glasses.

Astrid feels her breathing quicken. She glances at Fausto and Marcel. Both are awestruck and fascinated. "This is Basil's studio," she says to herself. "Loche Newirth wrote of it in the Journal."

"It is as he left it," Albion says. "We have analyzed his process. We have studied his half-finished work. We have tried to understand why he chose to surround himself with certain photos, images and, if you will, inspirations. In truth, we have come away more confused."

"What are you looking for?" Astrid asks.

"I think you know already. Do you not?" Albion smiles. "Loche Newirth."

Astrid feels her face frown, "You and the rest of the world, it seems."

"We know that Loche, Julia Iris and his son Edwin crossed over the Menkaure *omvide*." Albion crosses to a section of wall and points. "What do you make of these?" Below a flurry of paint spatters are three images. One is a sketch of a woman carrying flowers. Underneath is a magazine photo of the pyramids of Giza. A line of paint points to Menkaure pyramid. Finally, there is an image of a woman carrying a pitcher.

Astrid looks at Albion. "Elpis, Menkaure and Hebe. You should know that."

"Of course. Though, I must admit, we somehow missed its meaning."

She looks again and tries to understand. Elpis, the Greek goddess of hope. Hebe the Greek goddess of youth. Menkaure pyramid. "I don't get it," she says.

"Nor did we. But now, I believe we do—cryptic though it is. It is a message to Julia Iris." He waits. He watches Astrid puzzle. He says, "Hebe goddess of youth. Julia. . . Julia in Latin means youth. And Elpis goddess of hope—"

Astrid smiles and fills in the blank, "Julia was from Hope. Hope, Idaho."

"Yes," Albion says.

"So, Basil wanted Julia, and presumedly Loche, to go to Menkaure."

"That's what we believe."

A knot clusters tight in her head. She says, "Why?"

Albion shakes his head.

"So, let me see if I'm following you. You believe that Basil left a message for Julia so that she would take Loche with her across the most mysterious *omvide* known—an *omvide* in which no one has ever reportedly returned from?"

"That's what we believe."

Astrid watches the immortal's face. She notes the carved jawline, the peppery eyebrows and the unshakeable focus. Within the countenance, however subtle, is a crease of doubt—a worry. For a moment she thinks she is simply imagining a weakness. But her gut could not be more sure.

"You want to kill Loche Newirth. That is why you are searching for him."

"The thought had crossed my mind," Albion replies. "I have vacillated over eliminating him, yes. Though, now, I must admit, I simply want to speak with him again."

Astrid looks at Marcel and Fausto for a burst of courage. Then to Albion she says, "Talk, huh? You want to make sure he won't write you out of existence."

Albion looks into his wine. "That would be a preferable course for all involved, my dear. You included."

Astrid wonders a moment. The addition of *you included* rattles in her mind.

"Well, if he's crossed Menkaure, good luck with that."

"Yes," Albion agrees. "It is troubling. Have you thoughts on Menkaure?"

She shakes her head, "Not much. But there's someone here that does." Albion waits. "Graham Cremo is the expert."

"Yes," Albion says. "Certainly part of the reason he is here."

"There is one thing that strikes me," Astrid says after a beat. "From what I know of Basil Fenn, from the Journal, at least, he doesn't seem the ancient history type."

"You would have been delightfully surprised at Basil's knowledge," Albion offers.

"I'm sure," Astrid agrees. "But if I'm not mistaken and my math is all wrong, wasn't Basil dead before a single *omvide* formed in history? If I'm able to put together this labyrinth of Loche Newirth's reweaving of time, Basil, before his death, had no knowledge of the power of pyramidal travel. I mean, just like

Wyn Avuqua materialized between the time of Rearden's capture and now."

Albion nods slowly. "I see. And?"

"Well, wouldn't that mean that someone else left that message?"

Pocket Diary Entry # 6

November 14, 1010 A.D.
The Realm of Wyn Avuqua
Two hours after sundown (4:30?)

Our city guide, the ebullient Teunwa, has finally solved the mystery of the date.

November 14th, 1010 AD

4:30pm (I'm guessing.)

—

I am reminded of lines from the movie, Gladiator—

> *Marcus Aurelius: And what is Rome, Maximus ?*
>
> *Maximus: I've seen much of the rest of the world. It is brutal and cruel and dark, Rome is the light.*

Since my arrival here in this time, I have seen cruelty and brutal darkness. I have witnessed the human condition crushed beneath the weight of ignorance and violence. Though I've not ventured into this world as the character Maximus, I have read my share about life in this time in history—and I can now say, remarkably, I have lived within in it—albeit, if only for a few days.

This is a time when surviving birth is truly a blessing. And living passed the age of seven is considered lucky. Mothers often die of infection. Winters and starvation kill entire villages. When pestilence and disease come, it is the wrath of some malevolent deity or some ontological retribution for sins. Medical remedies are ruled by the planets, spices and herbs, and the careful balance of bile, phlegm and blood. Nights are lightless and cold. Beyond the rivers, or the hills, or the walls that surround your home, there are demons and barbarians and monsters. Journeys are perilous. Water is poisonous. The ocean, if it is real, has an edge that drops off into the stars. War, murder and justice are somehow all related. And to speak out against the way of the world is to risk your life and your soul to eternal damnation, for the will of Almighty God is perfect, predetermined and beyond contestation. And though love exists, and the promise of hope, this is a dismal time in human history. It is brutal and dark and cruel.

It is astonishing to recognize how belief in a supernatural god had kept these horrors alive for so many centuries. How thoughts and prayers were thought to contain a strength beyond education and personal action; how the baby steps to science were blasphemous; how women were subjugated and dehumanized; how the rich could wage war under the banner of God and the poor would die for it. Think of it.

It is unsettling to think that in my own time many of these issues still cloud humanity's growth. It is certain that we have made great strides against plague, war and famine. Science, individual thought and human rights have become cornerstones to the architecture of our technological age. But have things changed that much? In the twenty-first entury are we still haunted by our medieval ghosts?

I would argue that we are haunted. Women are still striving to attain equal footing with their male counterparts. The upper classes and the elite still hold the reins of war. Plague and disease are now under the firm hand of science (save a few holistic holdouts from the organic, old world), yet instead of ubiquitous and universal health for all, illness is monetized. The racial and religious wars from the ancient world are still under the spell of vengeful, historical vendettas. Instead of famine, our foods are processed, sugar infused and addictive. Though we are educated well beyond a medieval royal, for example, we are blinded by an age where information is so available and ever-present, it has become nearly impossible to discern fact from fiction. The educated have become mistrusted and ignorance is celebrated. So like our Medieval ancestors, a unified knowledge, and faith in that collective cannon is still out of reach.

But then there is Wyn Avuqua. If Rome was the light, Wyn Avuqua must be the sun.

Now the moon rests on the ridge line above the western gate. As I write this, Julia lies on a cushion in what we are calling our Avu Tower apartment. Her eyes are closed. Her cloak is pulled across her body like a blanket. The fire is warm, and its light flutters into the corners and along the ceiling.

And what a day it was. Our lively guide, Teunwa, had clothing for us to wear so that our visit through the city would not draw too much attention. For Julia he brought an insulating chemise, smooth and soft, and over that, a long woven evergreen frock with a high neck—simple, beautiful and functional. The sleeves were long and its hem rested just above her feet. He suggested that she wear her own boots for he did not anticipate anyone would notice. From a box he lifted a belt of linked metal flowers crafted to look like the heads of white and yellow daisies or deliavu as he called them. Hanging from the belt was a leather pouch. Perfect purse sized, Julia had said. To finish the ensemble Teunwa provided a body length cloak with a deep hood. Its dark green hue nearly black.

I was given a similar cloak, a warm undershirt of some soft cotton-like material, a green billowy-sleeved long waisted tunic with wooden leaf buttons, and a muted yellow-gold waistcoat. The pants earthen-toned made of some mixture of wool and cotton. I was also given a thick belt with a leaf shaped buckle and a leather pouch. "Man-purse sized," I said to Julia.

As I pulled the clothes on and noted their artistry and careful making, I couldn't help but think of William Greenhame and his fastidious and eccentric mode of dress. Between my receptionist Carol and myself, we looked forward to seeing what William would wear at each visit to my office. I remember calling him an antique shopper. I remember diagnosing him with Schizotypal Personality Disorder along with obvious Narcissistic Defenses. Now I see him quite differently. Now, he is simply an immortal man over six-hundred-years-old (recently beheaded and healed) with a knack for fashion and doing the best he can with all of it. Now, he is my father.

Once we were dressed we joined Teunwa in the great hall for an Itonalya breakfast, which consisted of a moist flat bread, a sharp cheese and sweet huckleberries. The tea was dark—robust— almost like coffee.

He then led us through Tiris Avu's main gate and out beneath a frozen blue sky.

Every few moments I would feel fear rise—the danger that surrounded us. I would fear for Edwin. Several times during the day I turned my attention back to the Avu wanting to return—to check on him—to make sure he was okay. Teunwa, sensing my dismay, would place a hand on my shoulder, "Your son is with his mother and your father, William Greenhame. Do not fear. The Queen commands, come. . ." Teunwa's confident and enthusiastic tone served as a kind of balm—just enough for me to shove aside the menacing peril lurking beyond the walls. And the deeper we ventured into the City of Immortals, it seemed those periods of *fear lessened. For the utopia that is Wyn Avuqua has a power I cannot fully comprehend, and an enchantment beyond my ability to describe.*

—Teunwa seats us behind him on a single horse drawn wagon.

—Fountains. So many fountains. Basins of marble and grey stone.

—High misty plumes of water. Waterfalls cascade from rising hill tops-from towering clusters of slate and granite.

—Grey-blue sculptures of herons perch on arches, hunt in wide green pools, nest in column niches and along lines of carved runes.

—Solemn marble Itonalya Sentinels hold posts at crossings.

—Yellow-gold leaves whorl on the breeze like schools of tiny fish.

—There is a trace of chill in the sunshine.

—Canal traffic—oared boats made of redwood.

—Roads are of smooth stones edged in mossy green.

—Carts roll past drawn by stout horses.

—We pass village squares. Clean, quaint. The smell of bread, woodsmoke and autumn leaves.

—An unseen single voice sings a happy melody.

—Teunwa drives our cart through Shartiris in the South.

—The pinging hammers of the armory. Inside, the bellows dragon breathes and wafts its heat out to the road as we roll by.

—We see long stone buildings, and training grounds, and markets with weapons, armor and banners of grey upon which are embroidered clawing talons.

—Rising out of the earth is the Shar Temple obelisk. It shines in the morning light like a silver blade.

—Lines of armored figures pass us bearing pikes and long swords march toward the outer walls. Stern faces both female and male.

—We cross beneath another marble arch into Vifeatiris, the House of Wings—the western quadrant.

—Banners of deep blue with a pair of white, wide-feathered wings slap at the high wind.

—Architecture shifts from angular to lyrical.

—We circle around a massive tree. The tips of its branches still fluttering yellow-gold leaves. They seem to glow against the sky. It is the largest tree I have ever seen.

"Behold," Our guide said, "Aldyar. The Hope Tree." He looked up and sighed at it. "A wonder, is it not? It is believed a god fell from the sky and was caught by this tree."

Julia said, "A god fell here? Into the city of Immortals? Into the city of godkillers? Bad luck."

Teunwa laughed, "Yes, so the story goes. Bad luck one might think, but Mellithion let him live. The god was Ressca. Ressca taught us how to hope, how to feel both sorrow and joy to its fullest." He stared at the high limbs for a long time. Finally he said, "A story for another time. Come."

We followed.

—Each dwelling has the sinuous quality of a middle eastern temple or a European cathedral. Even the pathways curl and coil almost without order—and yet, the way is easily navigable.

—There are more voices on the air raised in song.

—Teunwa tells stories—fills in gaps—speaks incessantly. He is delighted to share.

"These are our houses of worship," he told us. "This is where we learn how to breathe through each day, each year, each century." He speaks of meditation, of loving action, of unity, of harmony with the earth. "We will not die," he tells us, "so we will nurture the earth, the people, and the places we live toward beauty and longevity. Some of us believe that your mortal kind will one day learn how to live the lives you have as opposed to your wonted desire to live for an afterlife. This teaching is not an easy task."

I noticed elderly men and women in the shops, upon balconies, walking along the paths. Children, too.

"Mortals live here, Teunwa?" I asked.

"Of course," he said. "We teach them how to see beyond their curse, they teach us how to see beyond ours."

I saw people of all races—the world gathered. Some mortal, some immortal.

—We cross into the northern quadrant of Keptiris, the House of Mind. Again, the heraldry changes to a long beaked heron head on a field of emerald green.

—More fountains surge in gardens. They spill into canals.

—Teunwa stops the cart at a high steepled long house.

We were greeted by a tall, hazel-eyed Itonalya man and his wife. His wife appears much older, obviously mortal. Years tug at the wrinkles beside her eyes. The two are friends of Teunwa and we were invited to take food and drink.

I watched Julia study the couple. It is easy to see that she was trying to empathize with the tragedy of love between a mortal and an Itonalya. She held my hand tighter while we listened to their stories. She tried to hide her teary eyes.

They offered us salted meats, and warm bread and butter. Our cups were filled with a honey mead, but its sweetness was muted and replaced with a delicious hoppy finish. The flavor sensuous. After a few sips the alcohol tingled into my limbs. I was reminded of the Itonalya scotch.

They told us about the deep libraries of Keptiris—the scribes and the scholars and the schools. They spoke of some of the most learned mortal minds that have left their homes to study here at Wyn Avuqua.

—More soldiers cross beneath distant stone arches toward the northern gate. A faraway bell clangs.

"They go to the watches," the immortal man said. He then asked Teunwa. *"What news from Tiris Avu? They say the Godrethion army has grown yet again. There is rumor that a truce is to be made."*

Teunwa shook his head. *"I do not know enough to tell,"* he said to his friend.

"We must not allow them to live," the man's face frowned angrily. *"It is against all that we are. Why have we not ridden to meet them?"*

"The Queen will bring the will of Thi. She will be faithful to the old ways."

The man's wife said, *"What if they breach the walls. What if they. . ."* Terror arrests her voice.

"Do not fear, wife," her husband said with surety, though when he looked to Teunwa, Loche thought he detected a shared shadow of doubt between them. *"The Wyn Avuquain walls will shield us."*

—Pale grey clouds throw their shadows over the western peaks. In the afternoon, we enter into the final quadrant, Vastiris, the House of Heart—banners of black with a centered white heart.

—Here live the artists, poets, writers and musicians.

—Here stands a coliseum, perhaps the brother to the structure in Pompeii.

—There are workshops, storefronts, sculptures, more fountains, ale houses, tall stone turrets that Teunwa calls readeries, (structures designed specifically for writers to read their works to audiences).

"This is where I live," our guide told us. He points to a hill and a cluster of low timber houses—their colors match the autumn reds and golds of the season.

For thousands of years Wyn Avuqua has prospered and remained relatively undetected by the outside world. They have dwelled in peace with both the landscape and the indigenous tribes of the region since its first stones were stacked by the First Born tribe—in a time too far back for me to grasp. As we return to the gate at Tiris Avu, Teunwa told us that members of every race, people of every age, and the Itonalya have lived and learned together here. "The only footprint of our existence here should be seen in the preservation of love, knowledge and beauty. There is no higher aim. The footprint of our city is indeed no footprint at all—it is an eye that searches eternity for our place in it."

I could spend the rest of my life here.

But—

To know the doom that awaits—the horror crouching just outside the walls. We travelers from the future know the outcome. My hand shakes as I write.

This is one story's ending I know. . .

Where is Basil? What are we doing here?

I hear someone coming—

The Sun Room

November 14, this year
Venice, Italy
6:22 pm CEST

"I thought we were going to see Graham," Astrid says. Her hands tremble. She recognizes the symbol on the control panel's metal casing—or at least, she read about it in Loche's Journal. Above a single lit button is an embossed crescent moon opening over a ladder. She points at it.

Albion nods and places his hand on her shoulder. "We will visit Mr. Cremo in due time." He notices her shaking hands. "Professor, do not be afraid. Your intuition and memory serve you. Behind this door are the works of Basil Pirrip Fenn. Behind this door is the answer you've longed to know your entire life: Is there a Hereafter?" He smiles. "I suppose you may be growing weary of revelation after revelation— but the answer is yes." The smile fades, "At least for now. At least while Loche's word remains. . ."

"I—" Astrid starts. A sudden fear grips her. She imagines how Loche described the effects of Basil's work—The Silk—infinity—madness. "I don't want to—"

"Please, Professor, Fausto, young Marcel, do not be afraid. You will not look upon the full face of God this evening. But you may, if you choose, peek through a parted curtain to see a blade of grass upon the fields of Elysium."

Astrid stares.

"We have found a way to show Basil's art through a kind of filter. Each painting contains what the artist called a Center. After many failed trials, we have found a way to unveil Heaven without destroying the mind of the viewer."

Albion presses the button three times. The elevator descends.

"Of course, the experience is unforgettable. Disturbing for some, for others thrilling beyond measure—but without doubt, different for all. For our plight, as Loche has so aptly described, your eyes will bleed human imperfection into Paradise. However, what once caused a crippling mental break, now brings wisdom —or something near to it."

"My friend," Fausto's voice quavers, "I do not want to see what my heart tells me I should not."

Albion's laugh is light, "As I have said, Fausto, do not fear. You do not have to look. You may if you wish. I bring you to the Sun Room to simply show you the truth. It is your choice to see it or to look away."

The elevator halts. The doors slide open. A blinding white light forces all but Albion to squint. He gestures for them to enter, "Behold, the Sun room."

It is just as Loche described. A round room of indeterminate size. Massive. Pillars, Roman numerals embossed into the marble floor, and around the perimeter are what looks like a thousand curtained windows. Astrid feels her skin tingle into gooseflesh. Behind each curtain is one of Basil's paintings.

"Over the last few days we have had a great many people viewing the Painter's work. Those that were sick in heart and mind have found comfort and health. Others have found madness and pain. But now we have found a way to shield the viewer from any permanent harm—and we can share the truth with those who will help to reshape our dying world."

"The masquerade ball?" Astrid asks.

"The masquerade ball, yes." Albion agrees. "Our attempt at the Uffizi to share the work was shortsighted. This time we hope to elude the press as best we can, conceal the participants through an age old device: a mask. In the Grand Ballroom on the main floor we will present fifty of Basil's works. Then we shall lead the revelers down to the Sun Room to see the wealth of the Hereafter that we have taken as our own. Our guests are the most powerful people in the world. With the aid of these political and economic leaders, we will start the motor of the world. The gathering will be the beginning to a new consciousness. A New Earth."

"What of the *Orathom Wis*?" Marcel asks. "You must expect their resistance."

Albion waves his hand, "The *Orathom Wis* were the first on the invitation list. What is left of them, that is. Their resistance? It is possible, though I am of the mind they will understand our kinship is now more important than our differences. We shall come together. It is inevitable."

Astrid's eyes are now adjusted to the glaring white of the space. She turns her body in a circle as she walks into the room's center scanning the curtains covering eternity. Her body freezes when she sees one of the niche's curtained shields parted. At a distance she sees a painting upon an easel. She quickly averts her eyes.

"Ah," Albion says. "The only work in the Sun Room that does not require a shroud, though, I dare say, it should. Also, the only work here that is not of Basil Fenn's hand."

Astrid begins walking toward the piece. The others follow. As the black and red swirl of it sharpens, she sees the content. Upon the canvas is the depiction of a murder. Astrid easily reads who is who. The victim is Bethany Winship. The killer is Rearden. Astrid tries to look away, only to swivel back to the thing's leering, bleeding, vicious embrace. She feels as if she's seen the painting before, if only in her mind. Loche's description scrolls in her memory: Twisting in hues of red and black—a monstrous, lurid smile, lips of thin blood like scars mingled with gargantuan, murderous eyes bearing down upon another face, a pale, sleeping form. Bethany Winship. Around her throat are gripping, claw-like fingers. A wounded, bleeding sunset fills the background glowering down and mirroring itself upon a still body of water. Reflecting in the water are the two figures, but instead of the foreground's strangling embrace, the figures are intertwined and intimate—delicate and pure. The right corner of the work holds a signature—L. Newirth. And below that, the title— Marcus Rearden, Murderer.

Astrid shakes her head and turns away.

Albion stops beside her and continues to examine the work. "Magnificent, is it not?"

"It is not," Astrid says quietly.

"Love and death intermingling. Power and weakness. The innocent and the killer." He shakes his head and sighs appreciatively, "Perfectly Rearden."

"Fuck Rearden," she spits thinking of the last time she saw him. "He shot Graham in cold blood."

Albion turns to her. "As I have already said, my apologies for his behavior. Inexcusable. But The Board and my associates have given the good doctor carte blanche in the matter of Loche Newirth. He and he alone knows Loche's nature. Rearden is our best chance at either silencing the Poet or bringing him to heel."

"Death or submission. Aren't those the very things you and yours are fighting against, Mr. Ravistelle?"

"Why, yes, Professor. But more so against the one that created it."

Two attendants approach. One hands Albion a clipboard. As Albion turns to them and scans the attached document he says, "There can be no success for any endeavor while the power of creation exists in the hands of one. If Loche can create gods he can destroy the world. If he can wink characters to life from his imagination, he can remove them. What he has done thus far, I am uncertain if I would offer my blessing—save that I am still alive—I am still here—and I have found a way to survive the blunder of his failed plot. While he lives, he threatens existence."

"So you will force him to create what you want him to create, is that it?"

Albion thinks a moment, staring at her. "Yes." He signs the document on the board and hands it back to the attendant. "Or I will kill him. It is very simple. And, my dear Professor, Loche Newirth is fully aware of my intentions."

"If that is so, aren't you concerned that he is already working out how to write—"

"—write me and all of us out of the story?" he interrupts. "Indeed, a potential complication. Though," he glances back up at the painting, "we have an influential force at work on the problem as we speak."

"Rearden?" Astrid nearly laughs.

"Rearden," Albion says.

"You trust that asshole?"

"Professor Finnley—I have been alive for over a thousand years. Whether I trust Rearden or not is beside the point. He will perform his allotted function, and he will answer to me—that is all I require of any person."

"And if he betrays you?"

Albion waits. He grins. "Time will tell."

Astrid mirrors the grin and returns it mockingly. "Time will tell indeed, Mr. Ravistelle."

Words From the East

November 14th, 1010 A.D.
The Realm of Wyn Avuqua
(evening)

High above in the dome of the tower is an oculus. Its circle of sky is pinpricked with stars.

This time they are not led into the *Tiris Avu* Auditorium—this time, Loche feels as if they are being ushered. This time they are not given seats in the high balcony, but instead they are marshaled onto the main floor to positions on the perimeter of the crescent moon table and the Queen's dias.

The Templar are seated. The Queen's green eyes glitter watching Loche enter into the chamber. The Queen's son, Iteav, sits upon her lap. Lornensha stands just to the side of the Queen's riser, elbows bent and fingers interlaced at her waist.

"Dad!" Edwin's voice laughs, and from out of the shadows the little boy bounds across the Templar circle. Both Loche and Julia kneel down to meet him. Now, in the surrounding torchlight, Loche can see his company of time travelers, William, Corey, Leonaie, Talan and Helen. They do not speak. William moves across to join his son and grandson. He sets a hand upon Loche's shoulder.

Vincale steps beneath the high oculus and says, "Emissaries from the *Godrethion* horde have come with terms. You are all summoned to bear witness and to listen." He bows before the Queen.

"Bring them before the Heron," Yafarra commands.

Two sentinels pull open the heavy chamber doors and a *Godrethion* contingent is escorted down the aisle to the dias. There are four. Loche can see the two in front. One wears a hood and cloak, the other wears the orange surcoat over chain mail. As they come into the light, Loche recognizes them both. The hooded figure is the monk, Erinyes, the ghoulish Fate that had drugged Edwin—the monk whose face was an amalgam of both feminine and male traits. Striding alongside the monk is the *Godrethion* captain under Cynthia the Summoner, Etheldred.

Loche feels Julia's hand squeeze his wrist. Anger boils up within him suddenly.

The other two figures are not familiar. Loche's notices their clothing is modern military, black tactical attire. The uniforms are similar to those of Albion's *Endale Gen* soldiers he and Julia encountered on the Montanha Do Pico *omvide* at the Azores. He searches their faces but he cannot remember meeting, or seeing them before. Yet, there is something familiar in the face of one of the men. He looks to William and Corey to learn if they show any signs of recognition. But both of their immortal manners are solemn, stoic and calm, but there is a gleam in their eyes—a slight narrowing of sightline—a hidden glare. When he sees Leonaie Echelle's expression he is certain she shares a past connection with the soldiers. Her face is pale. A tear wells. Her hands cluster into stones at her sides.

William leans to Loche and whispers, "Behold, Albion's assassins. One I do not know. The other is the son of Felix Wishfeill. His name is Emil. He killed Samuel Lifeson." At the man's naming, William's whisper transforms to a vicious hiss. "Leonaie will want words, I expect. As will I. . ."

Loche stares at Emil. The man is fully aware of his enemies surrounding him, but his glare is set upon Loche and Edwin. A subtle smile flickers on his lips.

Vincale's proud baritone interrupts Loche's thought, "You are come to the Heron Templar and to our Sovereign Queen Yafarra daughter of Althemis. *Gal Ashto*, you will kneel in greeting."

Etheldred smiles. "We do not bow to faithless murderers."

A breathy hiss from one of the Templar slices the air.

Yafarra's expression is unaffected. Vincale's sword rings out, flashing in the firelight, and he lunges toward Etheldred. The blade swings in an elegant circle, aimed for the man's throat. A fraction of an instant before the blade is to cut the head from the body, Yafarra's hand rises and she says, "*Ag,* Vincale." The blade halts as if striking a wall, the razor sharp steel resting against the exposed skin just above Etheldred's gorget. A gentle line of red appears. Tiny beads of blood form. Vincale holds the blade there, frozen. Loche thinks he can see the *Wyn Avuquain* captain struggling with his Queen's order—the blade pressed against the skin—sliding a millimeter or two—just to nick—just to cut. Reluctantly, he pulls the sword back and down.

Yafarra says, "We have murdered, it is true. And there are some here that are faithless, it is true. But you are not our judge, Etheldred."

"Am I not, Yafarra?" Etheldred says. "Am I not? We have not crossed the deadly seas to break bread with you, *Itonalya* Queen. *Thi* has brought us here," He raises his long chain mail wrapped arm and points at Edwin in Loche's embrace. "There is your judge, O mighty Queen."

Edwin's face buries between Loche's neck and shoulder. Tears wet his skin.

Vincale says, seething, "Why have you come? State your terms."

Etheldred waits. He casts a long appraising study of each of his audience. His gaze rests upon Loche and Edwin the longest. Finally, he faces the Queen. "Yafarra, we propose a peace. A peace that will save your city," he gestures to the Templar Yanreg of the House of Talons, "and an opportunity for our warring tribes to be delivered from bondage."

Templar Yanreg rises, bolstered by these words. "As I have said. Peace can be made. . .we can rule *Endale.*"

Now the monk Erinyes steps forward, throwing back the deep hood. Black hair falls framing massive black pupils, like twin pools of ink. "Yes," the androgynous monk says to Yanreg. "Yes, together we will rule this world, and peace can be found, and none of us will live beneath the yoke of slavery, and your jewel of a city—this tear from Heaven, *Wyn Avuqua,* will be spared. The answer is simple. The ending is easy to see, is it not? There is but one task to perform before our lives will be our own to govern, and the world is ours to rule. . ."

"Why have you asked for parlay?" Subtle threads of Yafarra's patience fray, but do not break. Her voice rises slightly, "What are your terms?"

Erinyes' slender wrist protrudes from his draping sleeve and he points at six-year-old Edwin Newirth. The boy's arms grip as his face tucks deeper into the nape of his father's neck.

"The godchild must die," Erinyes hisses.

The surrounding faces of the assembly snap to Loche. He tastes stomach acid. Every muscle tenses. His feet involuntarily take two steps back.

Erinyes continues, "*Thi* has broken the Old Law. His Law. If we vanquish Him here, *Thi* will be no more. And we shall be free."

At this statement, chaos erupts.

Maghren of the House of Mind roars angrily into the tumult, "You know not what you speak! *Thi* is beyond His own will and does not know death—"

Yanreg of the House of Talons shouts simultaneously, "My brothers and sisters, freedom awaits us!"

William Greenhame bellows in his raised stage voice, "The only deaths today shall be you and your kind! One by one, we shall remove you from the consciousness of this world! We are the *Itonalya!* And Emil Wishfeill, assassin, soon—your end shall be soon."

Etheldred sneers, "It is the only way you will save your people. We shall float the heads of your women and children on the waters of the lake! We shall make a bridge to Hell."

Helen, in tears, steps in front of her son, "No!"

Loche loses track of the opposing voices—the heat and fury of fear rising. All he can feel now is his son's clinging arms. He scans for the nearest exit. When he takes a step backward in an attempt to disappear while the outburst is at its height, a large sentinel blocks the way. A firm hand grips Loche's shoulder and shoves him into the light of the high oculus before the Queen.

Yafarra watches the outburst of the assembly without emotion. She does not seem to hear any single expressed opinion or plea. Instead, her lancing, emerald eyes remain steadily aimed at Loche. She raises her hand. Seeing the gesture, Vincale shouts, "Silence, all!"

Julia is at Loche's side. He can hear her whisper to him, "Where is Basil? Where the hell is Basil?"

Erinyes seizes on the quiet. "The only choice before you is this: either the godchild is given to Cynthia, Summoner of the gods on Earth—she shall take His life." The black pupils of his eyes seem to pool wider. "Or, before the gates of *Wyn Avuqua,* before the eyes of the *Godrethion* army, the hand of the mighty Queen Yafarra shall cut the boy's head from the body, the boy's legs from the body, the boy's arms from the body. And when we see that *Thi* is dead, we shall withdraw. When *Thi* is dead, we shall have our peace. When *Thi* is dead, we shall all be free. If you refuse, you will all die. And so shall *Thi.* Choose."

Again, fury and pandemonium. Edwin's arms coil tighter at the explosion of sudden anger. Loche scans a for route out but sees only defeat. Too many sentinels, too far to run, and too many eyes upon him and his son. Most notably, the eyes of Queen

Yafarra. But there is nothing troubled in her countenance. The gentle slope of her cheek tilts slightly at Loche. She is riveted to him.

This time, Yafarra speaks the word, "Silence." It is not a shout, but its weight of command and power brings the cacophony of debate to heel.

Erinyes' dilated pupils dart from one enraged face to the other. Obviously, the monk's presented choice has hit its mark. Erinyes smiles then bows before the Queen—the gesture now contemptuous.

But Yafarra does not take notice or offense. She continues looking at Dr. Loche Newirth and the boy cradled in his arms.

Yanreg of the House of Talons says, "Gracious Queen, you must see the wisdom in this. Our survival, our freedom, our hope for the future of our kind—"

"No more words," Yafarra cuts in. "No more words." She lifts her own little boy, Iteav, from her lap and places him on his feet. She kisses his forehead. She rises. Her white and silver dress presses the darkness back. "Edwin Newirth," she says gently. "Edwin Newirth. Lord and Maker, *Thi*. Will you come to me?"

Loche feeling Edwin's arms loosen, lowers his son to the floor. His mind wrestling with the action. Every fiber in his being struggling to resist, but he releases the boy anyway. His vision floods with stinging tears. He hears himself say, "Edwin, no. Edwin—"

Edwin's feet touch the tiled floor and he runs to the Queen's dias and clambers up with a lifting pull from Iteav. The Queen holds their hands. She still stares at Loche.

Glitter swirls in Edwin's irises.

"Guards of the *Avu*," she says. The sound of twenty spears rap once upon the stone floor. Loche flinches. Her voice almost a whisper, "Our visitors from another time, remove them." From behind, William, Corey, Leonaie, Helen and Talan are restrained by the Queen's sentinels. William manages to wrestle free and land a cracking punch. Corey, too, presses against his assailant, but the resistance is short-lived. More sentinels close in and bend their limbs to nearly impossible angles strangling movement.

"And Loche Newirth," she says. "Take him to the high tower overlooking the East gate. There he shall remain." Hands seize upon Loche. His body presses away but is immediately met with a heavy fist to his midsection. The blow sucks the air out of his body.

"Tell your Summoner, Cynthia, Master of the gods on Earth that I, Queen Yafarra will free us all. I will deliver us from our ancient chains of bondage. Midday, on the morrow, before the eyes of gods, men and immortals, I will kill the child."

Loche looks to William. To Helen. To Lornensha standing close beside the Queen's throne. Then, electrical signals fire in his brain. These bursts of neuro-sparks ignite every reflex in his body, and he convulses. For an instant he breaks free and is able to take two steps toward Edwin. An instant later, another bright electric shock flashes through his brain as some hard object knocks against his skull. White light blinks. As his cheek smashes against the floor tile, and what he guesses is a knee crushes downward between his shoulder blades, he feels his umbrella being pulled away from beneath his cloak, his bag torn from his side. He sees Yafarra turn and descend from her dias. She holds the hands of the children, leading them away into the torchlight.

The Artwork of Basil Fenn

November 14, this year
Venice, Italy
6:40 pm CEST

Silence.

Flash.

Gone.

The three word refrain of Loche's writing echoes like a maddening song that she cannot stop. Loche described what Basil's work could do. He warned of its horror—its permanence —its stranglehold. *The Silk.*

Albion and the others have already turned away and are walking to the elevator. Albion's offer to look was denied by all. Astrid included.

But she lingers in front of one curtain. She stands upon the embossed Roman numeral X in the marble. She stares at the closed curtain.

Silence.

Flash.

Gone.

The chance to look upon the celestial realm of the gods— the abodes only imagined and described in the mythological tomes of men—the chance is before her.

"Wait," she says. Her eyes trained on curtain X. "I will look."

A moment later Albion is beside her. Marcel, too, joins and touches her upper arm with a supportive squeeze. She glances toward the exit and sees Fausto cowering back facing away.

"X marks the spot, my dear?" Albion says quietly.

"The number ten has never let me down," Astrid replies.

"I am delighted that you have changed your mind."

"I'm not so sure I am," she tells him. She is finding it hard to swallow. "Marcel," she says, "maybe I should be the only one to look this time. I trust you'll take care of me—you'll take care of how I come out of this thing?"

His hand again grips her arm in affirmation. "I'll watch you."

"You need not be afraid," Albion consoles. "As I have said, we have found a way to see through without harm—that is, unless you regard illumination as harm."

Astrid nods. She wrestles with her intellectual protocol—her habitual disbelief of the fantastical. And yet, just beyond the curtain is the seeing that will demand believing.

"Let's do this," she says.

Albion's hand raises in her periphery. An attendant says, "Apri dieci."

The crimson curtain splits and widens. An easel cradles a large canvas—maybe six feet by eight feet. Its background is smeared in eggplant purples, deep reds and lit with streaks of yellow ochre. The face of a woman is offset to the right in the frame and she is staring up as if into the sky. Her hair is deep walnut with two swathes of blond coiling down beside each of her cheeks. Her eyes are attractive and amber like summer iced tea.

Astrid feels her eyes flit from point to point, feature to feature searching for the Center as Loche had described. A few seconds pass. The portrait is beautiful, nearly ineffable. The woman's expression is yearning, sad and reaching. The emotion of the face brings to mind a beloved Welsh word that she remembers reading about years ago: *hiraeth.* Its multilayered meaning gathers homesickness, longing, and nostalgia, a yearning for a home that you cannot return to, no longer exists, or maybe never was. *In the woman's eyes is a quiet hiraeth,* Astrid thinks.

She blinks.

She considers that the feeling is perfectly aligned with her own need and yearning. Perhaps the face upon the canvas is a mirror to her own pain.

She blinks again.

She searches.

"It is beautiful," She says finally. "Basil is truly gifted. But is there more than this?"

Turning to Albion, she sees him scrutinizing the piece closely. A faint crease of frustration in his forehead. A subtle doubt in his composure.

"Is something wrong?" Astrid asks. "I was expecting the *silence, flash, gone* thing. Am I doing this wrong? What about the Center—isn't that a part—"

"Silence," Albion hisses.

Their host scans the portrait. Marcel faces the painting. "Wow," he says scanning the work. "This Basil is good."

"Mr. Ravistelle?" Astrid says.

Albion does not respond. Another few seconds pass. Finally he says, "Chiudi dieci." The curtain closes.

Something has gone wrong, Astrid cannot help but think. Albion abruptly turns on his heel and starts toward the elevators. "Come," he commands. "We will return to viewing Basil's work tomorrow evening."

Astrid follows. "Is there a reason I could not see—"

"It is possible our precautions have abated the work's potency. I will say no more until we look into the matter further."

Locked

November 14th, 1010 A.D.
The Realm of Wyn Avuqua
(late evening or early morning)

Close your eyes
Have no fear
The monster's gone
He's on the run and your daddy's here
Beautiful, beautiful, beautiful
Beautiful boy
Beautiful, beautiful, beautiful
Beautiful boy

The song wakes him.

He hears his voice murmuring the words.

There is a deep indigo glow from two shoulder high openings in the circular parapet. From where he is lying, Loche sees stains on the heavy wooden door, and remembers why his fingers burn and sting. He can see where he has scrabbled with his fingernails into the wood beside the hinges; where he has torn the pads of his fingers to bloody shreds trying to claw his way free. Splinters. Cuts. Black smears and splatters on the wall, on the door, on the floor beside his face.

There is a similar pain in his throat, too. As if he has somehow swallowed a mouthful of sand. When he mumbles John Lennon's lullaby melody, the flavor of blood and a searing pain rises. He knows it is because he has been screaming. Crying. Pleading. His voice finally broke. His body finally fell.

And yet, the door remains locked.

Before you go to sleep
Say a little prayer
Every day in every way, it's getting better and better
Beautiful, beautiful, beautiful
Beautiful boy

Julia's father had a song for his daughter. A lovely lullaby
to help her fall to sleep. *A single star*, Loche remembers. And his
own father, William, had a lullaby for his sons. The melody
hauntingly similar to the one now vibrating in Loche's throat. But
William's lyrics were different. Right now, Loche cannot catch
those words. He wishes he could ask his father to sing to him
now. He wishes his father could sing to Edwin.

Edwin's face flashes into his mind and an electric jolt
sears through him. He screams. He reaches for the door to dig
into the hinges again. But just as his arms rise, they drop and thud
to the cold stone.

And yet, the door remains locked.

Beautiful, beautiful, beautiful
Beautiful boy
Beautiful, beautiful, beautiful
Beautiful boy

And then, Vincale is there. A single torch flame flutters.
Shadows jitter. The immortal is crouching before him, his free
hand gently touching Loche's cheek.

"Aethur?" he says. "Poet?"

Loche sees him. He puzzles how the figure entered the
small chamber without notice. He hears his own voice like stones
in a paper sack.

Beautiful, beautiful, beautiful
Beautiful boy.

Vincale speaks, but Loche is not entirely sure he hears the
words. He is not entirely sure Vincale is really before him. To test
his perception, Loche throws a bloodied hand toward Vincale's
face. The Captain of the Guard catches the hand with his own.
Concern crowds around the immortal's eyes. Slowly he frees
Loche's bleeding fingers.

"Aethur?" he says again. "Harken to me. If there can be any comfort in this hellish time, may I offer it? I come on two errands. First, I bring tidings from the Queen. She bade me tell you that at midday tomorrow, you will witness the death of your son from this tower, and *Wyn Avuqua* and the *Godrethion* Army shall witness both Edwin's death and your anguish. There is no other way. It is both our mandate, *Thi's* fate and our only hope of survival. This sacrifice will save our race from oblivion."

A sound of fury gurgles from Loche's mouth, but it is distant and weak. Paralysis. Torture. Hatred. His hand rises toward the voice. A pathetic attempt to strike. Vincale catches the bloody fist and holds it.

He says as if to himself, "The only comfort I can offer you is this: the boy will have no knowledge of what is to come. He will not feel pain. He will not feel fear. He shall wear the Death Mask—the *Ithicsazj*—the inside of which is coated with oils and herbs to calm, to ease, to free. . ." Vincale leans his face to Loche's. "I swear to you, Aethur, Edwin will feel nothing. He will only feel light and hope."

Loche cannot move his legs. He is sobbing. Saliva strings from his lips. Needles of wood are scattered below the hinges where his fingers have dug into the door.

Still, the door remains locked.

Out on the ocean
Sailing away
I can hardly wait
To see you come of age
But I guess we'll both just have to be patient.

Vincale takes his eyes from Loche and lowers them to the floor. "With all of my heart—with all of my light—my soul bleeds for you, Poet. You have my pity."

After a moment, he gently lowers Loche's hand and lets it go. He then reaches into his cloak.

"Before we part, Aethur, I bring a gift from one of your companions. A gift from Leonaie Echelle. The Queen herself has agreed that you should have this, for I am told, Leonaie Echelle has carried it with her since her lover, the immortal *Orathom Wis* Samuel Lifeson was killed. I do not know the full tale, but I am told that Leonaie Echelle used this as a weapon to defend him against his assassins. I am commanded that only you are to see it."

Vincale lays a black velvet bag beside Loche. It is just slightly larger than a thin paperback novel. Loche tilts his head at it. Dread rises from out of his gut. Adrenaline stabs light into his optic nerves. He imagines fine strings of silk coiling up from the object.

"Leonaie Echelle says it was made by your brother, the Painter. The Queen believes that it may aid you in the darkness ahead—that it may in some way assuage the sacrifices that you have authored. *Galinna. Galinna,* Aethur."

Vincale rises. The door opens. Vincale exits without turning. The door shuts out the torchlight. Keys rattle securing the lock.

Before you cross the street
Take my hand
Life is what happens to you
While you're busy making other plans.
Beautiful, beautiful, beautiful
Beautiful boy

The black rectangle weighs almost nothing. The weight of air, perhaps. The weight of Heaven. Inside is a painting by Basil Pirrip Fenn of Sandpoint, Idaho. A curious artist. A dedicated artist. A dead artist. Inside the black bag is a door. Behind that door, Basil will be waiting.

Loche stares at the covered painting and mumbles. "Julia, I found him. He was here after all. Here in this locked cell. Here where I am no more."

He reaches into the bag, pulls the rectangular painting out, and turns it over like a key in a lock.

A Bed and a Book

November 14, this year
Venice, Italy
7:21 pm CEST

Albion leads Astrid, Marcel and Fausto up a dark stairwell, across a long oak paneled room to another stair. He holds a lit candlestick.

"Graham Cremo?" Astrid says. Her tone is frustrated.

"No," Albion replies. "He is resting currently. Dr. Catena believes that your reunion with Graham Cremo should wait until morning. We shall obey the good doctor."

Astrid protests, "Mr. Ravistelle—"

Albion stops halfway up the stair forcing his guests to halt behind him. Astrid falls silent. He does not turn. "My dear Professor Finnley," he says calmly, forebodingly, "I clearly heard my voice. Did you not hear me? No. In the morning we shall consider bringing you together with Graham Cremo." His tone reminds Astrid of how she might respond to a haughty student: calm, firm, and nearly ready to explode. She was not prepared for the effect of the scolding. She felt like the haughty student.

He remains still for several seconds. The candle flame whispers. Finally, he begins to ascend the stairs again.

Albion opens a door to a warm, amber lit suite overlooking the canal. The spires of the basilica are framed in the window. Upon a table in the living room is an overlarge book. Its cover is aged and flaking.

"Tonight you shall sleep in my house, Professor." He gestures to the book, "And more reading for you. As a lover of books, I believe this one will interest you greatly."

Astrid moves to it. "It is the *Toele*," her voice quaking.

"It is one of two surviving—though, given what we are learning from the dig site at *Wyn Avuqua,* this volume may have lost some of its value. Nevertheless, I believe it will hold your interest."

Albion turns to Marcel, "You shall sleep in the next room. I have a few items there that will interest you, as well."

Marcel nods.

Astrid stares at the book. Her temples ache. Her body is exhausted.

"And Fausto," Albion starts, "I understand that you must return to your shop."

Fausto nods meekly, "Yes. I have finishing touches to make to Helen's mask so that it will be ready for tomorrow's revelry." He bows. "My other responsibility, too. I work tonight at the museum."

"Of course," Albion says. "One must do one's job." He motions for Fausto and Marcel to leave the room. "Goodnight, Astrid. Tomorrow we shall speak to Graham about what he knows of Menkaure—and where he thinks good Dr. Loche Newirth has disappeared to. Goodnight."

When the door closes Astrid's attention drifts from the book to the view out the window, then back to the book. She removes her long coat and lays it on the chair. She sits and leans back. She starts to cry for reasons she cannot quite put a finger on.

Moments later, she is asleep. Basil Fenn's portrait of the homesick and lonely woman hangs in the architecture of her dreams. The body of Graham Cremo lies before her stretched out on a hospital bed. He is unconscious. His face as pale as an *Ithicsazj*.

Silence. Flash. Goodbye.

1010 A.D.
The Realm of Wyn Avuqua

—I'm right here, he hears his brother's voice say.

The walls of his cell are still rough and slate gray. The floor is ice cold. Through the ports the sky is now a coat of nighttime sable. Nothing has changed. He saw the Silk. He felt the vertigo of the painting vaulting him through the Center. But his prison has not altered.

—Loche. . .The voice again. He turns, and sitting beside him is Basil Pirrip Fenn. You look like shit.

—Are you. . .Loche starts, are you really there?

—Ah, good one. Are you fucking with me? You've been saying that since the day we met— or the day you wrote me.

—Have I crossed over? Are we in the Orathom*?*

—I am, Basil answers. But you appear to be a little different than before. Tell me, what do you see?

Loche's gaze circles.

—Stone blocks. High openings like windows. A high tower prison.

Basil nods.

—Fuck. Bummer. Not me. I am sitting just were we left off. I am watching lights from the sky strike down like lightning in the center of your old city—Wyn Avuqua. I'm still on the side of a pyramid.

—I don't understand.

—Don't get me started.

Basil touches Loche's shoulder. A fountain of gentle sparks crackle along his arms to his wrists and across his back.

For a moment, the floor and walls become transparent as if they were made of clear crystal. He can now see what Basil is seeing. It is the fall of the City of Immortals. It is the sight he recalls from their last meeting.

    —My son, Edwin. . . Loche cries.

    —What's happened? Basil asks.

    —My story— my art—it is taking his life.

    Basil looks away.

    —They are going to kill him, Basil. They are going to kill him. It is because of me. Because of what I've done. Because of my story.

    Uncontrollable sobs heave from Loche's heart.

    Basil nods. Worry, frustration and anger battle for places in his expression.

    —Of course. Of course that's happening, he says after a moment. Every sacrifice for one's art—in life and death. Even here—suffering has made it through the Center. If you want to know what the afterlife is facing—it is the terror you're feeling now. Fear. There is no escaping it, yet.

    —I cannot stop it, Basil. They have me locked away. Even if I could escape, I am just one man.

    Purple and yellow bands of light, like coiled ribbons on the wind, surge from the sky to the city.

    —There must be some reason you wanted us here, Basil. Your message for Julia—the message you left for her to find in your studio. . .

    —What message?

    Loche stares at his brother.

    —You didn't leave a message for Julia to come to this place? She said she found a message that was for her and her only. . . In your studio in Venice. Basil?

    —Not me.

    —But she. . . she was certain.

Basil continues to stare down the pyramid. Violet spears of light thrust down into the southern quadrant of Shartiris. Flames and smoke rise.

—I am sorry, Brother. It was not me. If I had to guess, I'd say somebody else wanted you to come here. For what, I don't know. But there's a reason for everything. I know that sounds fucking stupid, but there's truth in it. You were meant to be here.

He stands and offers Loche a hand up. What should feel like sloped footing is actually the solid stone floor of his prison beneath his feet. But his sight shows him the angled line of pyramid blocks.

—And Edwin? Man, I wish I knew. All I can say is this is your story, you get to say when its over. You get to choose the ending—even if you choose for it not to end—it's your call. From where I am, I can see how we bounce around in time and place searching for beginnings and endings, the hows and whys—but there's no way to see the end until we are making it.

A sad smile drifts onto his lips,

—And I suggest never making an end. . .if you can manage it. Whatever happens, Loche, you need to own it. Get free. Find a way to remake it. You are where you are supposed to be. Edwin is where he is supposed to be.

Basil turns his face to Loche.

—I have found a way to close the Center. I found a way.

He smiles. Long dark curls frame his face.

—You were right, he continues. And I am where I am supposed to be. I can find my art from here—and only I can close the doors. Hopefully soon, I'll have them all shut forever.

He pauses and watches a massive battering ram breech the east gate of the city.

—What that means for the afterlife, I don't know. Maybe it means there will be no difference between where you are and where I am. I wonder if that will change things?

Loche closes his eyes. He tries to find an image of Edwin smiling.

—We are the last great mythic story, Loche. We are characters in the final myth to end all myths. Maybe after us, humankind might consider a different way of living. Who knows, with Heaven gone, maybe the idea of ending suffering might be truly worth considering. Imagine it. A new earth. A mythology for a new earth.

He touches Loche again. Again a trillion sparks tingle through his chest.

—You may say I'm a dreamer, Basil says. But I'm not the only one.

—Own it, Brother. Get free. You make the ending you want. Try to figure out why your story exists in the first place. I don't know if we'll ever see each other again. If we do, it will be here in this strange place between a painting and the eye. Or between the pages of a book. I guess that's where we can always meet. It's where we always have. . . I'll be right here.

Light winks out. The cold chamber is dark again save for a pale moon glow. In his hands is a rectangular canvas frame.

The image on the canvas is a self-portrait of Basil. In the dimness it is difficult to see color, but the brush strokes are fluid and painterly, almost sketched. Loche stares at the rendering and is reminded of the first time he met Basil beside Priest Lake. He stood on the beach with his hands stuffed into the pockets of a brown corduroy jacket smelling of cigarettes and patchouli. On his head was a green stocking hat. His breath steamed in the cold air. *The big deep heavy.*

Scribbled in the corner of the work is Basil's signature. Loche then scans for the pinhole of light that bridges this life and the next. A stab of panic rises when he realizes that it is not there. The door had been closed. The Center on this painting is no more.

The Art that Changes Us

November 15, this year
Venice, Italy
9:35 pm CEST

Tap, tap, tap.

Astrid is startled out of a deep sleep. It takes her a few moments to recall where she is. The gothic arch of the window, the lit spires of the cathedral across the canal, the ancient book on the floor beside her chair—she shakes her head and says to herself, "In the house of Albion Ravistelle."

Tap, tap, tap.

She rises. Her back aches. She crosses the room to the door. "Yes?" she says. "Who is it?"

"Professor?" a quiet voice whispers from the hall, "Professor Finnley? Please forgive the interruption, may we speak? My name is Howard Fenn. I am Basil Fenn's Stepfather."

Astrid opens the door to discover an elderly man seated in a wheelchair. A red and gold blanket is draped over his knees. A document bag hangs by its leather strap from the chair's handles. His eyes are friendly and tired. "Please forgive my sudden visit—but I feel that our time to speak privately before tomorrow's event will be somewhat limited—and things change so fast. . ." He takes a quick look from side to side. "May we speak together?" Whispering he adds, "We may not have much time."

Drowse still fogs Astrid's periphery, but she steps back and nods to Howard. "Of course. Please come in."

The old man wheels into her chamber and positions himself across from two leather armchairs. Astrid closes the door and joins him.

"May I offer you—"

"Please, nothing for me," Howard interrupts. "As I've said, it is likely we won't have much time. There's little that goes unseen under this roof—and I'm quite sure that my visit is perhaps not completely secret. Whether anyone will mind our speaking together, I do not know. Nevertheless, I felt I should take the chance."

Astrid attempts to focus by blinking her eyes. She waits.

"What I'm about to share is between you and me. As far as I know, no one has yet discovered—" he breaks off. His heavy lids blink three times. He starts again. "You have found yourself in the whirlpool—in the Center. I would imagine you're feeling the vertigo?"

Astrid nods and appreciates his simple tone and genuine demeanor. She intuitively feels at ease with this new acquaintance. "I've spent my life studying and searching for the stuff of myth—and I—I found it. The past couple of days are beyond rational explanation."

"And shall continue to be," Howard smiles. "Yes. Yes. I've had a similar shock—many years ago, of course. It landed me in this chair." He grips the sides of the wheels and glances at his motionless legs. "I looked at a piece of art not meant for me— or anyone—then everything was different. So very different."

Astrid looks at her hands in her lap. "Everything was different," she echoes. "I've done something similar—I've looked at Loche's Journal. Another art piece that has changed—"

"Yes," Howard nods, "I've read the Journal, too. Which brings me to why I've come." He stares at her for a moment. "I've read your books." She is about to reply with her usual, Oh, *those* things, but she holds her breath instead. "I've read your books. . . and they are wonderful, if you ask me," he says. "Professor, I've come to speak with you about your books. Since my accident with Basil's painting and the condition it has left me in, I've spent all of my time exploring and fact-finding to learn about my son Basil, his gift, his place in this world and his relation to the mythic audience that surround us all. Loche's depiction of my research and findings in the Journal is accurate to a point. Accurate as far as his story can tell. Yet, for all of his divine talent, the story he has made is making itself."

The pit of Astrid's stomach clenches. Worry and fear pour into her bloodstream. The feeling she has tried to explain to Albion and Marcel when she thinks about how the past shifts— how new memories form from out of a void of nothingness.

"Your books," Howard says, "I read some time ago." He pauses and looks away. His expression reads as if he is deciding if he should jump into a cold lake or simply turn and walk away. "Your books I read a few years ago—but your books have only just appeared in my memory. Today! When I heard you were here, Professor Finnley. If I concentrate I can track other changes in my memory's timeline. I don't know why I'm able to do this and others are not—notably Albion Ravistelle and others. Maybe it's because of my experience within the Center that left me crippled. Maybe because Loche wanted me to see. I don't know."

Astrid reaches her hand out and rests it on the man's knee. "I can somehow feel the same things. As if the past is changing— and when it does there is a brief time when the change can be seen or felt. A profound sadness or worry—"

Emphatic nods from Howard. "Yes," he agrees.

"—like something incredibly important you failed to see, or forgot or were unable to understand— then suddenly—it's clearly before you. *Wyn Avuqua* was like that. Discovering it."

More enthusiastic acknowledgment. "Your books. . ."

"My books?" Astrid says, "You keep saying."

"Your books have changed, too." With a wave of his hand gesturing to the ancient book upon the table, he says, "And I would expect the *Toele* has amended as well."

"What do you mean?"

"For me, this knowing lasts for a brief time before it slips into memory and the feelings of worry we've described. I've even written journal entries of my own only to find them slightly changed days later." He stops, scratches his head and puzzles for a few seconds. "Or, goddamit, at least I think they've changed. Clarity is dependent upon reference frames. . .reference frames, some relativity and a goddamn stiff drink!"

"What about the changes in the texts?"

"Professor?" he asks. "Do you recall writing about the death of an innocent at *Wyn Avuqua* before the city fell?"

"What are you talking about?"

"The killing of the One God, *Thi* before the gates of the city?"

Confusion squeezes Astrid's forehead. "No. In all of my research I've never—" An avalanche of fear crashes into her abdomen. "I don't remember the. . ." But she does remember.

The boy god. The Queen of the city dismembers the innocent boy to buy peace with the *Godrethion* horde, only to be betrayed.

Howard watches her. His face seems to mirror the shock of her own revelation—her own discovery.

"Hold on to it," Howard offers, "it can slowly slip into memory—as if it has been there since the moment Loche's timeline placed it."

She inhales the cool atmosphere of the chamber—the scented candle wax, the smell of the old tapestries, the taste of anxiety. Howard digs into his document bag, produces one of Astrid's books and holds it up. Astrid raises her hand and lets the pads of her fingers touch the cover. She traces the shape of the pyramid below her name. She remembers the section about the boy god, the killing, the bloody aftermath. Like a déjà vu—like a fading dream after waking—like a forgotten thought pressed back into the subconscious, she teeters on a line between memory and discovery.

"Oh God," she whispers.

"Precisely," Howard replies grimly.

"The boy god." She lowers her hand. "The boy god is Aethur's son. *Thi* is Loche Newirth's son."

The Death Mask: Ithicsazj

1010 A.D.
The Realm of Wyn Avuqua

He is dragged from his cell. He is wrestled and shoved along a high battlement. When he resists, he is struck. When he falls he is kicked until he stands. He is pulled and pushed up a coiling stair, shoved through a door and out onto a high parapet overlooking the eastern field. Guards chain his ankle to a brick pillar to keep him from jumping to his own death. They leave him there alone. He hears the gears of the door lock bolt.

A freezing rain falls, turning to snow. He does not raise his hood.

Below, between the city wall and the distant tree-line, a small stage has been constructed. It is blanketed with snow. Upon it is a long, butcher block of a table, and three men in sable cloaks, each holding different weapons. Beyond, issuing from out of the trees like blood from a wound flows a *Godrethion* throng of some five hundred soldiers. Their banners hang lifeless in the cold. They form a line a stone's throw from the sacrificial dais. Cynthia is at their center upon a high wagon. Beside her is Erinyes and Etheldred.

From out of the gates of the city to meet them rides Vincale, leading a force of *Itonalya* on horseback. They position themselves in a formation on the opposite side of the stage leaving an aisle open to the gate behind them.

Loche's hands shake uncontrollably. He tries to see Edwin's face in his mind. He struggles to hear his voice.

"Are you almost finished with your book, Dad? Are we still writing the good stories?"

"Yes, Edwin. We are still writing the good stories."

"Will you be at Heaven when I go there?"

"Yes, I will find you there."

"How do you know? How do you know you'll find me?"

"Because I am your Dad. I will always find you."

"I don't want to go, Dad. I want to stay with you. With you and Mom."

"I know, Bug."

"If I go, will you come and find me?"

"I will always come to find you."

Far to his right he can see another high parapet and two figures waving to him. It is difficult to see through the weather, but it is apparent that it is William Greenhame and Julia Iris. He does not wave back.

A horn sounds. A fully armored Queen Yafarra exits the city and starts down the narrow aisle toward the stage, holding the hand of a tiny figure—a boy—a child—Edwin Newirth. The boy's stride seems unbalanced and confused. Loche notes a slight stagger. Behind them trails Lornensha. She is carrying a basket of what looks like plants and herbs.

Loche feels his hands gripping his own head. His finger tips digging into his scalp. Cold rain and snow blow into his wide, horrified eyes. His mouth forming the word "No," over and over but without voice.

The three climb the short stair to the stage. The boy turns in circles, taking in the massive audience. Loche can see the *Ithicsazj* mask glowing pale like a dead face in the winter gloom. He remembers Vincale describing the sedative qualities of the mask.

Yafarra leans down to the boy as if to speak. She then points in the direction of Loche's parapet, and the boy waves. Loche's hand rises. He cannot breathe.

"Oh sweet mercy," his lips move, but no sound.

"No. No. No."

The Queen lifts the child onto the table and turns to receive a long handled axe.

"Stop. Stop. Stop." Loche can hear his whispering mouth now. "Please, God. Stop."

For a long moment Yafarra stares at the sacrificial innocent upon the table. Her white and gold cloak glowing in the gloom. With one last turn to face the father, she whirls and the axe arcs overhead. The head of the small boy is cut from the body and it drops into a basket. An instant later, the crack of the cleaving blade through the spine to the thick table reaches Loche's ears. Clop.

What follows is deafness. Loche can feel a tearing, seething pain in his throat. He is screaming. His chest cavity convulses as every living cell within him struggles to understand what he has seen. When he collapses and his mind gives way he rolls over onto his back. His lungs slowly, reluctantly suck at the grey November air. All above is a blur of silver streaks. He tries to trace single drops of rain from their highest slipping point in Heaven until the sockets of his open eyes are filled like pools—as if he were a drowning god peeking up toward home from beneath the clear waters of a lake.

The Map To Heaven

November 15, this year
Venice, Italy
10:10 pm CEST

Tears flood Howard's eyes. "What? How can that be?"

The sequence of happenings ticks through Astrid's mind. "You have heard that *Wyn Avuqua* has been found?"

"I have. Albion told me."

"There is an archeologist. Tall. Thin. His name is Graham —"

"Graham Cremo," Howard says. "Yes, he is here, too."

"Is he alright? He was shot—"

"By that bastard Rearden. . ." Howard says. "I don't know Mr. Cremo's condition, Astrid. I'm sorry. But I do know he is under the care of Dr. Catena."

Her own rush of tears begins. She shakes it off.

"I have read of Dr. Catena," she says.

"Yes." His voice drops to a near whisper. "A talent beyond talents, if you ask me. He has developed a path to cure illness. All illness. I don't know enough—but I understand that in his laboratory he has taken an ancient root or plant and has cultivated it into—well—the Tree of Life. They are calling it The Melgia Gene."

Astrid's jaw slowly drops.

Howard continues, "A truly remarkable thing, if you ask me. With more research, Albion and Catena will be able to give the gift that was once reserved only for the gods. The gift of immortality."

"Thus," Astrid says, "Albion's Heaven on Earth."

"So it would seem," Howard says. "Somehow I don't think it will be that simple. But with immortals, they tend to find solutions where mortals leave problems for their children—and on and on. . ."

Astrid lines up what she knows and tries to order it into understanding. She does the arithmetic. She feels her eyebrows scrunch together.

"Have you heard the Prophecy has been found?"

"Yes."

"Have you seen it, yet?"

Howard shakes his head. "No."

"Do you know that Queen Yafarra is here in Albion's House?"

"I have heard that, yes. But I don't understand how—" Howard stops speaking as he watches Astrid try to weave a lifeline to throw out to him.

"I was there when Yafarra was discovered—inside the sarcophagus. There is no record of how or why she was put there. . ."

"No record, yet. . ." Howard says. His tone is dark.

"Yes," Astrid says, reluctant to fully agree. "But within the tomb, just as we were expecting, was the Prophecy."

"And. . ." Howard says glancing at his watch.

"The preserved book is a red spiral notebook like one a middle school student would use—the Red Notebook, it's called."

Howard gapes.

"Aethur is Loche Newirth. He was there— or he is still there. And his son was the innocent—the Red Notebook must speak of these things. . ."

"And to fill in a blank or two: Albion and the others will not allow anyone to read—"

"That's correct," Astrid finishes. "There is a fear it will again twist the story further."

"As if we need more of that," the old man says to himself. "Professor Finnley, our conversation must come to a close. Time is short— and I'm sure it is already known throughout the house that we are together." Concern rises in Astrid's expression— Howard eases it with a kind touch to her upper arm. "Ah, don't worry. When you live in a house with immortals it takes a little time to learn that their fears and senses of urgency are quite different than ours. They do not see change as we do. They are more apt to allow you to do what you want so they might slowly craft a future to house it. It is said that the only way they change is because we do. We cause the waves, they command the tides."

"And who rules the oceans, I wonder?"

Howard grins. "Loche Newirth, it would seem."

He twists in his chair and digs into his document bag again. "But being under this roof doesn't mean you should not be careful. Simply be as true as you can. Truth outlasts everything— or so they say. Before I go, take these." He hands her a rolled piece of parchment and a light rectangular object swathed in a black velvet bag. "Inside the bag—you can guess. It is one of Basil's paintings. There is rumor that something is changing within his art. The Centers are closing. Of course there are a great many paintings—and many are still devastatingly powerful. This one's window is fully open." He touches her arm again. "You will not lose your mind looking upon it," he smiles. "This one Basil made for me years ago. It will take you there and return you—but what you'll see, I cannot say for sure." He points to the scroll. "And this—this is a map of Albion's House. I believe he himself drew it. You can find your way around—"

"I get the feeling Albion would not want me wandering his halls," she says setting both of the items down on the table between them.

"You're probably right. But as I said, what you do he will watch and react to—and he's likely already planning what you'll do before you've even thought of it. The fellow is over one-thousand-years-old. He has a knack for forethought. And he's not afraid of anything." Howard shrugs, "Not afraid of anything that I'm aware of anyway."

"Why are you giving these to me?" Astrid asks.

A light glints in the old man's eyes. "So you can continue your search—so you can continue searching for what has haunted you your entire life."

Howard turns his chair abruptly to the door and rolls toward it. She follows him.

"Will I see you again tomorrow? I have more questions. . ."

He looks up at her. "You'll see everything tomorrow—and nothing. Tomorrow is the Masque. Tomorrow the wheels will be set in motion for a new world, or what Albion calls his New Earth. All will don masks." He frowns looking at the door. Astrid opens it and he wheels out into the hall. His chair spins and he faces her. "Good night, Professor. May your search continue. What will you find, I wonder?"

Astrid closes the door.

She returns to her chair and stares at the black velvet bag containing the answer to every question she has ever had; beside it, an aged piece of rolled parchment—a map—a map of Albion's House.

She grasps the rolled paper and unknots the leather tie. Dropping to her knees she spreads the map out on the wood floor. She scans the staircases, the connecting corridors, the lobbies and chambers both secret and open. There are rooms hidden within rooms, parlors deep below the Sun Room and tunnels leading out of the House beneath the canals to the West and East. When her eyes find Dr. Catena's laboratories, her index finger begins to draw a path back to her room. She plots her course to Graham Cremo. She stands, grabs her bag and steps out into the dark hallway. Looking back she notices the black bag with all the answers inside of it still sitting on the table. The door latch clicks shut as she turns toward the first staircase—toward Graham—toward what has haunted her her entire life.

The Seige of Wyn Avuqua

1010 A.D.
The Realm of Wyn Avuqua

"I've got you!" a woman's voice keeps saying over and over. "I've got you!" Her face is familiar. Loche has been staring at her for some time now, maybe five or ten minutes. She was the first through the parapet door after he heard the tumblers turn. Behind followed a rather tall man, mid to late thirties, though, something about him seemed far older. His hair is dark and shoulder length. A weighted worry shadowing his face. The two kneel beside him. She cradles his head. The man stares. He is crying, but strangely in control.

"I've got you," she keeps saying.

Loche pushes them back and begins to frantically search the parapet again. His eyes downward, scanning through the gloaming for something he has lost. He knows why he is searching. He has read about it many times. He has even watched a grieving parent in his office during therapy exhibit the behavior. The poor man could not stop pacing, looking out the door, beside the desk, out the window. Some psychologists call it search mode.

"He was just right here?" Loche hears himself say. "Did you see him?"

The two observe Loche, tears shaping below their eyes.

Loche knows his behavior. He knows why he is frantic. He looks down onto the field. Did he miss something?

Now the stage where Edwin was killed is overrun. The snow has deepened. The base of the mountains has vomited the *Godrethion* horde onto the white plain. They have begun to lay siege to the city. He thinks he can hear the light tick of snow touching down.

"Edwin. Edwin was right here," he repeats. When he whirls around to the couple now climbing to their feet, a line from one of his text books rolls into his memory: The most frequent immediate response following death, regardless of whether or not the loss was anticipated, is shock, numbness, and a sense of disbelief.

Loche laughs at the maddening accuracy of the sentence. "Did he go out the open door?" He begs.

"Son. . ." Loche hears the word—an aching word—the wrong word for this moment— "Son," the man says. "You must come with us. We must leave this high place."

"Not without my son," Loche says. *There's that word again,* he thinks.

The woman seizes Loche's upper arms and presses her face into his, "Loche! It's Julia. Don't you know me? Loche!"

Three arrows whistle and snick against the stones to their right. Julia pulls Loche nearer to the door. "Loche, we have to go now. You have to come with us."

The man bends to Loche's chained ankle and inserts a release pin. The casing splits. He casts the chain aside. The ring of the metal spins Loche's thought toward the outer edge of the parapet so that he might check to see if Edwin is hiding there. Two strong hands grab hold of his shoulders and rotate him around.

"Boy!" An open hand slaps a wincing sting across his face. "Loche!"

Loche sees William Greenhame. His eyes are swollen from rage and tears. Beside him is Julia Iris.

Before he can exhibit cognition, William shoves him through the door to the landing of the spiral stair. Like he was ushered up, he is now ushered down. He stumbles and falls twice. Each time he is hauled roughly back to his feet by both William and Julia. At the base of the stairs wait Adam Talansman, Corey

Thomas and Leonaie Eschelle. They face the lower tunnel in defense positions.

Corey embraces Loche and says slowly, *"Liva hoy gosht. Thi thia, Aethur. A thia gos ning."* Releasing him, he pulls from under his cloak Loche's umbrella and shoulder bag. "Take these again, my friend. But I am afraid the Red Notebook is no longer ours."

Loche stares at the items. Leonaie rushes up and assists in fitting the bag over his shoulder and then clips the umbrella onto its buckle. "Dr. Newirth," she says. But when Loche meets her eyes her voice falters. He can see her struggling for words. She shakes her head mournfully. Then both she and Julia bookend him and slide their arms around his middle.

"Any sign of Vincale?" William says joining Talan beside the opposite passageway.

"Not yet," Talan answers.

"When he released you, did he tell you where Helen was?"

"He did not," Talan replies. "The second time I have failed in minding Helen Newirth."

Corey says, "We can't stay here, William. *Godrethion* have taken the Eastern Gate."

At that moment a clatter of boots echoes down the passage. Orange torchlight illuminates the corners and the shadowed hall. A moment later a voice calls, "William!"

"Vincale!" William shouts back.

The Captain of *Wyn Avuqua* rushes into the small lobby with four sentinels of the city. He stops before Loche and bows his head. "If the Queen had words for this moment, she did not share them with me, Aethur. My heart breaks for you. . ."

Slumping forward lazily, Loche says, "Edwin. Where is my son Edwin? I just saw him a moment ago," he turns and points up the stairs, "just there."

Vincale waits. He surmises Loche's lolling expression—his fractured awareness. As he lingers there he realizes Loche's breaking point has been reached.

"You must escape the city, Aethur. You and your companions must escape. If you remain there will be no dawn for our kind—you have meddled too long in the affairs of fate and time."

"Captain," William says, "Where is the Prophecy? The Red Notebook."

"*Tiris Avu* is now under siege," Vincale says. "They are inside the walls. Two towers have fallen."

"The Prophecy, Vincale! We cannot leave the Prophecy behind!" William shouts.

"That is not all!" Vincale says, his voice raising. "The Templar under Yanreg, have rebelled—all save Maghren, Minister of *Keptiris*. He is faithful, still. The treachery of Yanreg is deep. When I left the Queen, she and Maghren were defended within the *Avu*—but now I cannot say. They were besieged by not only *Godrethion*, but the Templar and their loyal sentinels. It grieved me to part with her," he turns to Loche, "but she bade me to bring you out of the city and out of this time."

"And that was all?" William asked.

"That was all there was time for, William."

"The Prophecy! What of the Prophecy?"

"It is in the hands of fate, or it is in the hands of the Queen."

"Is she mad?" William shouts again. "She has killed my grandson, and now she is to toy with the existence of the *Itonalya* on Earth? What madness is this?"

"I cannot speak for her choices in this dark time, for I was taken aback when her axe fell. But do not judge the wisdom of Queen Yafarra until—"

William's eyes glitter. Fury lights within him. "I watched her murder my—"

Corey reaches to his friend, "Not now, William. We must move."

William demands of Vincale, "Where is Lornensha? Where is my—my mother?"

Vincale does not answer immediately. He then replies, "She tends to the fallen."

The company rushes out of the wall-lined passages and into the late afternoon gloom. A host of *Itonalya* still fight just inside the East Gate and are managing to plug the flow of *Godrethion* entry. Enemy soldiers can still pass in and around the defense. Buildings are aflame. Above, on the battlements, *Wyn Avuquain* sentinels are overwhelmed with too many high ladders. *Godrethion* rise up against the walls like a crashing wave.

"There!" Vincale points. "We must get to the dike at *Keptiris*. Along the northern wall are the Book Houses. The North Gate is just beyond." He points. Ahead, perhaps a mile, Loche sees a snowcapped, single grey wall and beyond that a line of high peaked, three story houses. At the apex of each is a proud, sculpted Heron. He feels his body spin to search again for Edwin.

Corey shouts, "Is the North not besieged?"

Vincale yells over his shoulder as he starts toward the dike, "Every wall is besieged. We are surrounded."

"We do not have the numbers to fight our way out, Vincale!" Corey says.

"We shall go beneath them."

"Beneath? What do you mean?" William asks.

"In the lower basement of the Book Houses is a tunnel that will lead us directly to *Dellithion Omvide*."

William groans. He looks at Loche. "Another tunnel."

The Maze Of You and Me

November 15, this year
Venice, Italy
10:45 pm CEST

The great Daedalus of Greek myth was said to have built a labyrinth to imprison a monster. Daedalus' crafted maze was so meticulous and clever that he himself narrowly escaped his own art with his life.

Astrid studies the map as she descends a third staircase. Though she has a well plotted course to Dr. Catena's laboratories, she cannot help but be turned around and befuddled by the turns and elegant twists veining through Albion's house. She waits at corners and listens. She hurries down long wood paneled corridors. She scans ballrooms and lobbies for watching eyes. So far she has encountered no one, but every so often she glances up to corners in the ceiling where small hemispheres of smoked glass monitor her quick pace through the maze. It occurs to her when she arrives at yet another staircase that perhaps the monster's eyes follow her. The monster may just be waiting for her below.

Another corner. Another hallway. Another rush to the next turn. Two men appear from out of a door just feet away. Astrid slows her pace, smiles and says, "Good evening." She is astonished when the greeting is returned in kind. The two men, both elegantly dressed in suit and tie, continue their quiet conversation and walk toward the elevators.

Another stair, another hall, another lobby—then, she arrives—or at least she guesses. There is no sign or placard, but instead, she peers through an automatic sliding glass door. Within are laboratory furnishings and implements. As if it were a hospital ward, several doors encircle a reception-like desk. Against the walls are carts. Astrid sees hanging tubes, stacked boxes of latex gloves, glass cylinders full of cotton swabs, locked drawers, metal trays with sharp stainless instruments— a big plastic bottle with white letters: ALCOHOL. She wishes for wine. On rolling stands are a couple of monitors. They flash lines and numbers. In the dim light there is no color save the baby blue of bed sheets and taupe hued walls.

To the right of the door a hallway slants downward. At the bottom, maybe twenty feet or so, is another glass door. The room behind it emits an inviting green light. An armed guard stands at the entrance. Seeing the guard, Astrid's face ducks to the map. She sees Catena's Laboratory clearly marked in Howard's scribbly handwriting, but the lower hall is not depicted. She cannot help but think of Catena's Tree of Life lab experiments. The Melgia Gene.

"Posso essere di aiuto, Signorina?" the guard says, not-so-friendly.

"No assistance, thank you," Astrid replies in Italian. "I am visiting a friend here." She walks through the sliding glass door telling herself not to run.

Two women rise up from their computers from behind a reception desk. Astrid braces for resistance—for expulsion—for an ear breaking alarm. Instead, the taller of the two nurses smiles and says, "Hello, Professor Finnley. I expect you are here to see Graham Cremo?"

Astrid feels her hands rolling the map back into a scroll. "I am," she says. She braces her feet, thinking that at any moment white-coated, Italian orderlies will appear at her sides and wrestle her to the linoleum.

The woman makes a quick notation on a clipboard and points to the right. "He is asleep right now, Professor. But you may visit. We would prefer that you allow him to wake on his own. As you can imagine, he needs all the rest he can get."

"Of course," Astrid says. Her breathing slows slightly. "How is he?"

The nurses exchange a glance.

"He is still in critical condition. The gunshot wound has shattered his clavicle and he has suffered blood loss—but don't worry, he is in the care of Dr. Catena," her lips stretch into a wider grin, "Dr. Catena is his best hope." She points to the left. "Just four doors down. Room 10."

Astrid moves. She rushes. Inside her chest a heavy pendulum swings and batters against the cage of her ribs. Above the door she notes another security camera. She raises her middle finger at it. She is not sure why. Maybe because of Albion's all-too-composed demeanor. Or his command of Basil's existence-altering art that he seems not quite qualified to command. Or maybe because the watching eyes remind her of the rankling all-seeing deities of her chosen field of study—and right now, they should not get to witness her face when she sees Graham. They are none of the monster's business—these matters of the heart.

She turns the handle, enters and presses her back against the door to close it. The room is dark save the neon glow of a patient monitor and a small, candle-like lamp. On the bed lies Graham Cremo. He is sleeping. His tall body is longer than the bed. Astrid feels a smile arc as she notices his big feet jutting out from the blankets.

Slowly she moves to him. She attempts to read the blinking monitor and make sense of his condition. Her fingers touch his arm and her focus drops to his face. *Beautiful*, she thinks.

When she begins to whisper, she is both hopeful he might, or might not hear her.

"If I could change what happened, I would. Beginning again is all I can do—make a new story. I want my new story to be with you."

To Dellithion Omvide

1010 A.D.
The Realm of Wyn Avuqua

Far to the South, smoke rises from *Shartiris,* adding a darker bruise to an already wounded sky. The nearer *Tiris Avu* burns like fallen torches in the grass. Loche stares at the higher center tower that still stands and wonders if Queen Yafarra and her son Iteav are hidden somewhere within listening to the boom of beaten doors, marching boots in the halls and the screams of fallen immortals funneling up through the cylinder tower. He wonders if Edwin is with them.

They have come the mile to the dike. He sits with his back against the rock wall. Julia and Leonaie are still at his sides. They are breathing heavy from the last sprint. One of Vincale's sentinels fell just minutes ago as a sortie of some ten *Godrethion* spied the company crossing a road. William, Corey and the sentinel turned and gave battle as the rest continued north. Only William and Corey returned.

"Come," Vincale says, lowering himself down from the wall. "We will enter into *Keptiris* through the arch. I can see the Book Houses from here. We've enemies to pass, but their main strength is still outside and pressing the wall. I think they are finding that we are not easy to kill. Come."

The captain moves through a low fissure in the stone.

They pass the *Keptiris* fountains that just a day before were filled with light and the music of water. Now, haunting every fountain are at least two or three severed heads. The spray of the water is a ghostly pink in the dim afternoon. The mist smells of tin.

Loche is dizzy with every step. Soon the wall behind them is just a black line drawn across the horizon. Beads of ice sift down between the raindrops and crackle on his hood. There is no sign of Edwin. They cross into another huddle of low houses, and Loche is struck with the feeling that he has been here before. Rounding a hedge, he understands the feeling. A muffled cry from Julia confirms his fear. The highest of the log houses is on fire. The very house where he and Julia had visited the day before —where they had gathered beside a warm hearth, where they dined and sipped wine. Laughed. It is the house of Teunwa's friends. The couple's bodies are heaped upon the long porch. Both are headless. Blood is spattered across the snow. Julia squeezes her arm tighter around Loche as they trudge forward. He watches the white vapor of his breath gust in rhythm with Julia and Leonaie.

Itonalya resistance is all around them. Groups of *Shartiris* press an enemy host back through a dike arch just yards away. To their left, houses are being routed by a large force of *Godrethion*. The god-soldiers mutilate unarmed women and children. A sudden volley of arrows sings from out of the dark sky. The expertly aimed bolts fell nearly twenty enemy soldiers. The surviving raiders run for cover.

Thus far, Loche has not needed to draw his sword, for the artistry of Vincale and his sentinels, along with Corey, Talan and William, have effectively carved out their path with little effort. But at any moment, it seems, a larger *Godrethion* host could take notice of their flight and smother their escape. Vincale is careful to keep the company in alleyways and beneath the boughs of trees.

Loche scans the roadside and the path ahead. He cranes around to see if Edwin is running up behind them. Blood sloshes in his brain like oil in a bottle. He feels he is peering into pages and pages of text—line upon line of inky words imprinted upon the sky, upon the vapor of his breath, upon the stonework road beneath his feet—like a swarm of insects. His hands come up and he tries to bat them aside.

"Not long now," Vincale says between heaves. He gestures ahead. "They have not yet gained the center Book House. Hurry!"

Loche feels Leonaie and Julia yank him forward. He tries to read the words drifting in the rising smoke over *Vifaetiris,* but either the words or his eyes cannot stay still long enough. They descend into a narrow lane between high poplars and drop into a round courtyard. Five massive cedar trees reach overhead and shelter them from the falling sleet and snow. They stop. They wait. Vincale scans the entries and exits to the courtyard. From somewhere to the West comes the concussive pounding of heavy stones against the walls. Following after each chalky crack is a roar of frenzied soldiers.

Far to the North comes the unmistakable cracking of an automatic weapon. Four bursts. William looks at Corey. Corey says, "Neil? Alexia?"

William looks at Leonaie, "My guess is Emil Wishfeill has not yet departed. . ."

Leonaie's arm flexes slightly behind Loche's back.

"Now," Vincale whispers, "follow," and he rushes to the opposite side of the wide clearing. The company stays with him in a tight cluster. He leads them up through another lane of high trees to the face of a dark house with three steep gables. The captain does not linger but rushes straight to the heavy doors and enters.

Inside, Loche can see nothing but fading-to-black stairs down, and passages to his right and left. "Torches," comes Vincale's voice from the dense dark. The two sentinels reach to the sconces and pull down the unlit torches. Vincale produces flint. Before he can strike the steel across the stone, Loche hears a familiar click and ring behind him and he turns. William's face strobes twice in spark-light, and then illuminates by the flame of a Zippo lighter. "Basil's lighter. . ." he says with a grim smile. "I did not like him smoking cigarettes."

The torches hiss to life.

Vincale leads down the stairs. At the bottom they rush through a pillared room. Open books upon tables and overturned chairs appear to have been quickly abandoned. Shadows unsnarl from the blackness and shift as the torchlight passes. Through another door, along another corridor, into another maze of pillars and bookshelves. Finally, Vincale halts at the top of yet another descending staircase. Far below an orange light flickers along the floor.

Vincale says, "Below is the tunnel to *Omvide Dellithion*." He motions to the staircase. "By the time we enter, it is likely we will be trapped in between by the Enemy on both sides. We will not exit without a fight."

William's says half mockingly, "Why am I not surprised by this?"

"Let us hope by the grace of *Thi* our strength can match what we meet at the end."

"Your Queen has killed *Thi*, Captain," William growls. "Whatever we meet, our own grace will deliver us." Vincale does not answer but starts down the stairs and into the tunnel. William's eyes narrow following their guide. "And into Hell we go. . ."

Don't Die

November 15, this year
Venice, Italy
11:01 pm CEST

"Don't die," Astrid says to the sleeping archeologist, Graham Cremo. "Please, don't die. I have spent my life chasing the past—the dead—the gods, stories, ghosts, entire cultures—all dust—all gone. I chased after them because I was running from my own past. I don't want to chase the dead anymore. But if you die—Graham Cremo—I will keep chasing. I will not stop. I will find you. And I will follow you. Because you have made me feel alive for the first time in my life. Don't die."

Astrid squeezes his hand. His skin is cool. Another ancient myth enters her mind, this time from the *Itonalya* tomes. The love story of the moon and the earth—when they finally touch. A single, enduring line from the tale slips from her lips, "I came for thee, for I heard you calling." *He would know that story,* she thinks. *He would, absolutely.* She stares. "I don't even know you. We shared just a few words—a short few hours together." She shakes her head. "I don't understand what is happening to me. But I heard you. I heard you."

She raises up to the blinking patient monitor and squints at the readout. His oxygen level, his blood pressure, and his pulse all translated into numbers and electrical symbols. It says nothing about what he dreams. There is no measure for his character, his needs or desires. It cannot show his joy or sadness.

Graham's expression is calm, almost blissful. She lets her fingertips touch his chin. She then moves to his lips. Before she knows what she is doing, she feels herself slowly bending to kiss him. She halts halfway between and memorizes his face. "You wouldn't believe it, I think, if you knew how I feel. Is it *Elliqui* that connected us? Why can't I stop thinking about you? Why are you eclipsing everything I've experienced over the last few days? I've sought after these revelations my whole life, and now, there's only you.

"And I need your help, Graham. I can't do this alone. I don't understand why history is shifting. It seems as if everyone senses something— but I can actually watch it happening." She begins to cry. "And even my own past is—is. . ." she breaks off, stands straight and looks to the monitor again. Graham's heart rate has accelerated slightly. She wipes her eyes. "I've been alone for so long. I vowed I would never do this again. Not after what happened. Not after. . .the accident." Again, she stops herself. "I said I would never do this again.

"Who are you? Why you? Why now? Why in the middle of all of this?" she motions to the enormity of Albion's house, and to the discovery of *Wyn Avuqua*, the torture of Queen Yafarra, the writings of Loche Newirth, and the impending masquerade ball that will continue the storming of Heaven. "All of this." Her arms lower to her sides. She sniffles.

"Jesus Christ, Graham. Don't die. Don't die because I love you—and I don't care why or how. I just love you."

The monitor shows his heart rate has increased again. Her eyes train to it. As she tries to work out the change, she hears Graham's voice.

"You had me at don't die." He is smiling. His eyes are still closed.

The Space Between

1010 A.D.
The Realm of Wyn Avuqua

"I don't think I can run all the way—" Leonaie cries—on the verge of hyperventilation. For the last five or ten minutes the company has been jogging. Her voice interrupts the sound of rattling armor, buckles against leather and clumsy footfalls. Loche staggers and stumbles. His eyes are half-lidded and he feels a thin line of saliva dangling from his lips. Awareness tips and sloshes between the long, poorly lit tunnel, and flashes of his son's little severed head plopping down from a roughhewn table to a basket on the floor. *Why didn't Thi within Edwin blast the enemy with the oceanic power like on the omvide in the Azores?* Loche wonders.

"Let's walk now," Vincale says. "We're nearing the exit." Far ahead a single indigo dot has appeared. With each step it grows.

Julia whispers, "Loche?"

Loche hears her, but he is in the middle of an impossible riddle—somewhere between what he knows about the will of God and the will of right and wrong. His head tilts. His eyebrows scrunch together.

"Loche, can you hear me?"

He glances at her and wonders briefly if he should ask her how they got there? And more important, if she knows where Edwin is.

Vincale stops abruptly. "Quiet," he hisses. He ventures a few paces forward and listens. He kneels down, assessing the dark hole ahead. "They wait for us."

William joins him. "That they do. . ." he agrees. He swivels to Corey at the rear. "Have we pursuers?"

"None that I can hear or see," Corey answers. "If they come it will take them at least ten minutes to cross the distance."

William says, "The tunnel is narrow enough for only two to fight side by side. We have a chance if we stay within the mouth."

"Let us all draw our weapons and proceed," Vincale says.

"If I am not mistaken, they are expecting us," William adds, his sword flashing into the firelight. "My son, the Poet specifically." Loche sees William's eyes glitter. "Loche," he says gently. "We will need your steel. Draw. Let us return to where we belong."

Julia unsheathes Loche's rapier and presses it into his grip. Tiny, tear-shaped flames reflect in the mirror-like steel. Down the long blade he can see hairline dints, and nicks in the razored edge. *A measure of the blade's life*, he thinks. *A measure of the defense of love.*

"Let us go," Vincale says.

Slowly, the company starts toward the exit and the pyramid beyond. The free air wafts in. Though it is cold, it is welcome. Both Julia and Leonaie remove their supporting arms from Loche's waist and draw weapons.

Just outside, but within the dim light of the tunnel, are what looks like three posts driven into the ground. Atop the posts are gruesome heads. As they draw nearer, William is the first to speak, "The sign of eth is rising. O my broken heart. Willowdale shall grieve."

Loche squints and immediately recognizes the tortured faces upon the poles—the three *Orathom Wis* escorts from the Giza plateau: Neil, Alexia and Gary.

As if in answer to William, a woman's voice enters the tunnel, "Come out travelers from afar. Do not be afraid."

Without hesitation, William passes Vincale and steps into the snowy night. The company follows.

"Ah. . ." William bellows, his arms stretched out as if to embrace the encircling horde of *Godrethion*. At their center stand Etheldred and Erinyes the Fate. "Behold, the Netherworld gathered in the glare," William pronounces.

Torches burn. Maybe fifty points of flame wiggle in the still cold. Just beyond are the first blocks to the rising Pyramid of the Sun, *Dellithion Omvide*. Turning his eyes to Erinyes, Loche notices the two men from the *Avu* auditorium, almost shadows themselves in their black modern attire standing beside. One is the assassin, Emil Wishfeill.

"Where is your Summoner Cynthia?" William shouts. "Certainly she would like to bid us farewell."

Erinyes replies, "She sees to Queen Yafarra's torture."

William smiles. Loche sees it. He knows the smile.

Vincale whispers to William, "Beware what you do here. Time will not forgive an act against it. . ."

William says simply, "God is dead, so why should any of us care, my lord?"

William then announces, "May I present Mr. Corey Thomas. . ."

To Loche, the speed of time overlaps.

Overhead, Loche thinks he sees four or five objects fly like flung stones. A second later, each of the objects emit a pupil piercing flash followed by a series of concussive explosions. Loche, Julia and Leonaie are hurled onto their backs by the shock wave. *Godrethion* bodies scatter into fragments. Some are thrown nearly twenty blocks up onto the pyramid behind them. William then tosses three more grenades to the astonished horde. Again, the night blinks white three times and the entire right flank of *Godrethion* bursts into grisly parts. The white landscape is splattered with red. In the center, Etheldred and Erinyes are now struggling to stand back up amid the massacre. The *Godrethion* at the rear turn eastward, drop their weapons and flee. Vincale and his sentinels rush into those that remain before the *omvide* and strike them down.

Loche's ears ring. Julia and Leonaie assist him to his feet.

Etheldred and Erinyes draw weapons.

"Come again," Etheldred hisses at William. "Let us finish what we have begun."

William sheaths his sword. "Lay down your sword, knave," he says quietly.

Etheldred closes the distance to William in a blink. The quickness is uncanny. He raises his sword as Adam Talansman, steps between and extends his arm. The tip of the immortal's sword finds an open slot below the High Captain's gorget and it slides through the soft flesh of his throat. As he falls back and Adam pulls the blade free, Then Vincale, without expression or anger, begins a slow trot toward Erinyes. The trot becomes a full run. His opponent raises his blade in defense as Vincale leaps into the air. With his left hand he throws his palm downward to the rising sword tip. The blade punctures his hand. When Vincale lands upon his feet, he clamps his hand into a fist and maneuvers his arm to force the trapped blade down. He then pivots, whirls his sword and cleaves through the top half of Erinyes' head.

Fate falls.

But just as the cut hemisphere splashes to the snow and mud, an automatic weapon opens fire. Vincale's torso erupts a dotted line of bloody holes. From the ground, concealed by two dead bodies, Emil Wishfeill empties the clip into the captain. He then rolls to his side and raises a pistol.

Time, again, flips forward onto itself with ferocious speed. Loche feels his eyes bat five times.

One.

Emil squeezes the trigger four times. Two shots for each of the *Wyn Avuquain* sentinels. They drop. Simultaneously, Emil's companion rolls from out of the carnage beside him and with his handgun fires into both of Adam Talansman's knees.

Two.

Adam tips to his right and buckles. Three more shots report before William manages to lunge toward him, sword out.

Three.

Just as the extended blade punctures through the assassin's skull, a final shot explodes through William's chest. The immortal falters and lowers himself onto his side cursing and spitting blood.

Four.

Loche hears Talan growling obscenities. Behind, Corey is struggling to stand, but he cannot. Turning to find Julia, he finds her crumpled like a rag in the dirty snow beside him. He crouches and reaches for her. "Julia," he says. The sound in his voice is strangely clear, "Julia?"

Her head rotates toward him. Blood splashes from her abdomen. A white halo of foam is already rising from the wound. "I'm alright," she whispers. "I can't move." His eyes search for Corey and Leonaie. Both are down. Corey is struggling to move. Leonaie is motionless. Her left shoulder is a blister of blackish red.

"Loche," Corey's weak voice calls, "run! You must run!"

Five.

The icy ring of the pistol barrel presses against Loche's temple. "Just you and me now, Poet. And no time to waste. Across the pyramid we go. Move!"

Loche stands. His feet anchor. Emil slaps the side of the gun against the back of Loche's head. The blow flashes a band of electricity across his vision. "Move. Now."

Loche starts toward the white pyramid blocks. He passes through the moaning of mangled *Godrethion*, severed arms and legs, dropped weapons—the dead.

From the ground, William calls, "We will find you, Son. Stay alive."

"Hurry," Emil's voice says. "Before long this area will be filled with both *Godrethion* and *Itonalya*, and I have no more patience for either. I've done my job, Poet. Now it's time to finish it."

Loche considers the man's words as he climbs the first four stones. "What do you want with me?" Loche asks.

The waist-high stones are smooth. Snow still falls.

"Me? Nothing. I couldn't care less about you Dr. Newirth. However, I can't help but feel some satisfaction from the—if you'll permit me—from the poetic justice."

"Poetic justice?"

"Oh come, come," Emil says. His breathing is now heavier. "You were there. Venice. Remember? In a way, you were the cause of my father's death."

Loche lowers his head and glances back. The firearm is pointed at his back. Emil pauses in his climb. "Eyes forward," he says, "and do hurry."

Looking up and ahead Loche guesses they are nearly halfway up. He does remember. Samuel Lifeson killed Felix Wishfeill in order to protect Loche. "I was there," he admits. "I'm sorry for your father's death."

Emil laughs. "*I'm sorry for your father's death*," he repeats mockingly. "Always the psychologist. . . What a perfect, empathetic answer. So kind. So void of responsibility." His laugh intensifies. "One would think by now," he coughs, breathes, and laughs again, "that the wise, wise Poet of the events that are now unfolding before us might somehow understand the idea of revenge. Even at this very moment you are still so. . ." he coughs again, "so—even. So psychologically correct. What, Doctor? Are you waiting for me to grow a conscience? Are you waiting for those unhealthy minds, the greedy, the murderous, the ambitious to find your version of well-being?"

Another stone block higher—and then another. Loche's heart batters against the bones of his rib cage. He feels confused. He glances around suddenly to find his little boy.

"Samuel Lifeson may have killed my father—but it was due to you, your work and your presence—therefore, I've taken great pleasure in my appointed task."

In monotone, Loche says, "I am sorry for you—sorry that you're taking pleasure in the pain of others."

Emil laughs again. "Do you not have a single trigger, Doctor? You behave as if you're wanting to guide me to some version of health. Your version." His tone slides into thoughtful revelation, "Or maybe you're missing the entire purpose. You're no good to anyone mentally stable, Poet."

"What is that supposed to mean, exactly?" Loche asks between gasps.

"Well, from my limited point of view, if a poet isn't tortured, what is his work worth? And my appointed task is your torture. You are feeling the bite of torture—are you not, Dr. Newirth."

Numbness. Bleakness. Helplessness. Loche freezes. He slowly rotates and looks down upon Emil and the still aimed firearm. Distant *Wyn Avuqua* burns white and orange. Loche imagines streaks of light bombarding the city from the nothingness of sky.

He is numb. No tears. No quavering. No emotion. He says, "I have watched my six-year-old son hacked apart before my eyes. My baby son. My beautiful boy—murdered. I do not know this word torture. There is no word—there are no words—"

A faint smile dangles on the edges of Emil's lips. "I know."

"Have you come to kill me?" Loche asks—begs.

"Oh, no," Emil answers. "Too easy."

"Then why have you come?"

"You still don't know? I was sent to kill your son—and to force you to watch. Something that has become my particular calling card. Of course, I don't think I will ever match the experience of two armies witnessing a father fall to pieces while his son is sacrificed. Quite messianic. Quite biblical, if you ask me." He takes a breath. "That was the first task. Now it is complete, and I am to return you to Venice—if such a thing is possible."

Loche's eyes glass.

"Who sent you to do this?" Loche's fists ball at his side. "Who would want such a thing?"

Emil's smile and triumph fades. "You still have no idea?" He waits. "Why, Dr. Newirth, your old friend Marcus Rearden has authored this. Despite his professional ethics, I believe he would call the act retribution." He laughs, "Revenge, Loche. It is Rearden's vengeance for the death of his wife. For what you have done. For what your hand has written."

From out of the shadows, a gleaming broadsword blade appears. "For what *your* hand has written, motherfucker!" Catching the light of the burning city, the silver blade flickers like a tongue of fire, and slices through the air, and through the wrist of Emil's outstretched hand. The gun rattles to the stone, followed by a wail of agony. He drops to his knees and hugs the mangled limb to his abdomen.

"My beloved Samuel warned your father! Warned him not to tangle in the affair." Leonaie hisses, stepping before the cowering assassin. "Your father did not listen. Your father was a fool!" Her shoulder is wet with blood and white foam. The sword is heavy in her hands, and clearly she has little or no experience in wielding such a thing. But strangely, with uncanny grace, she whirls the blade away from Emil and punches the pommel into his lower jaw. Teeth crackle. Emil slumps onto his side and curls into a ball. "This is going to hurt," she tells him. "A lot." She stoops over, searches the flat stone for a moment and then lifts Emil's severed hand. "Look here, motherfucker," she says calmly. "Look here. Remember how you made me watch?" Crimping the fingers of the hand closed, she molds it into a fist. "Watch this. Look here," she says, this time to herself. Nudging her thumb beneath the middle finger of the hand, she flips the dead finger up and dangles it before Emil's pleading face, "Long bone, motherfucker. Samuel Lifeson says hello." She then says over her shoulder, "Loche, a bag! A bag!"

Loche jumps down a block to Leonaie and touches her shoulder. She is vibrating. Heat radiates through her coat.

"I am here, Leonaie," he says.

Suddenly, as if by a miracle he has returned to himself. He is back.

The woman lifts the mangled hand and smashes it into Emil's head. Once. Twice. Emil's eyes roll back.

"Wait," Loche says.

Leonaie pauses. Her breathing steams.

"Emil?" Loche says. "Dr. Marcus Rearden sent you to kill my son?"

The man is crying. Even in the dark Loche can see the purple balloons of bruises swelling around his eyes and nose.

"A job," he manages to slur. "Just a job."

"Rearden? Rearden sent you—and then you were to take me to Venice?"

"Yes," Emil replies. His face is pale. Blood splashes now from the stump of his arm and squirts into the snow. He cradles it, presses it— "Help me. . ." he pleads.

"Why kill my son?"

Emil cries, "Help me."

"Why?" Loche yells.

"He wants to hurt you—and erase everything you've created. Everything you are. He wants to make the myth real. . ."

Loche stands. He feels his eyes narrow. A subtle nod to Leonaie tells her he is finished speaking. At the gesture, Leonaie again pounds the severed hand against the side of Emil's face over and over again. The bones of the fingers snap. She continues to strike. The tissue of the hand liquifies. She continues to strike. Two bones in her own hand break. She continues to strike.

When she stops, the hand of Emil is unrecognizable. She lets the pulverized flesh slip from her grip onto the slushy stone —a nauseating, squishy sound as it smacks down.

Emil is dead. His eyes are completely swollen shut, and masked in blood and welts.

"Your line is ended, Wishfeill," Leonaie says. She looks up to Loche. Her expression is one Loche has never seen before. Something between bliss and terror—between contentment and grieving.

Loche kneels down and lifts her chin. "Leonaie, I must go. I must find Rearden. I know now what I must do." Through her tears, Leonaie smiles. She nods. "Please tell the others. Please tell Julia that I must do this alone."

With a quick glance to her now mending shoulder, Leonaie says, "They will be just fine, Loche. We will all be fine. Go. For your son, go."

Loche kisses her on the forehead, stands and rushes up the last few blocks to the apex of the pyramid.

At the top, he gazes at the fall of *Wyn Avuqua*. A tower in the citadel topples and crashes into flame. A host of *Godrethion* pour into the west gate like a flood of black blood. The almond shape of the city breaks. The shape of a tear beads below the eye. Loche turns, steps, speaks the word, *Lonwayro*, and vanishes.

Dedication

November 15, this year
Venice, Italy
11:15 pm CEST

Graham Cremo's arm rises up and his finger-tips graze Astrid's cheek. His touch sends a jolt of electricity down to her abdomen. He then weaves his hand into her hair and gently pulls her down. But instead of a kiss, Graham connects her forehead to his and holds her there. His eyes stare into hers.

"*Lain*," he whispers.

"*Lain*," she replies.

"I heard the whole thing."

Astrid smiles. Tears wet her cheeks. "Everything?"

"Everything." His voice is easy and light. "I would have never thought you'd feel like I do."

"You do?"

"I do."

"You do what?"

"Like you do."

They both laugh.

"So I'm not completely crazy?" Astrid asks.

"I didn't say that. But it sounds as if *crazy* is happening all around us."

Then, from a shadowed corner of the room, Marcus Rearden's voice says, "Crazy is happening all around us indeed."

Astrid's body jerks up straight and she spins toward the sound. Marcus is sitting with his legs crossed in a simple folding chair just far enough out of the light to be hidden. His presence is menacing.

Astrid stammers in both horror and anger, "You b-b-bastard. Get the hell out! G-g-get out!" Graham's hand clamps down on hers as if to calm her—to steady her.

Marcus leans forward into the neon monitor light. Astrid can only make out the dark sockets of his eyes and the gleam of his wet teeth. He appears almost blurry, ghoulish. "I'm finding it difficult to separate you two. Must I shoot you both to accomplish this?" He raises into the light a hardcover book. It is Graham Cremo's *Mapping the Pyramids*. "But I'd like for Mr. Cremo to sign his book first. A lovely read. My favorite chapter is 'The Menkaure Hypothesis.'" From his lap he produces another book. Astrid recognizes it immediately. "And, Professor, maybe you can autograph your book, too. Perhaps we can talk about the chapter, The Fall of Wyn Avuqua.'"

"What in the hell do you want with us, Rearden?" Astrid growls.

"I think I just told you," he answers. "Your autograph and some discussion of your chosen topics." He waits. His teeth shine again in the greenish glow. "Graham, your hypothesis that Menkaure pyramid could punch a needle through time is fascinating beyond measure. Deific. Poetic." He tilts the black shadows of his eyes to the cover of Graham's book, "And, now it is no longer hypothesis." He tosses it to the floor and then lifts Astrid's title. "I knew, of course, when I saw the Red Notebook appear with Yafarra. I couldn't have hoped for better evidence. But now, it appears the past is changing." His index finger taps the cover. "Now a young boy is said to have been sacrificed before the gates of the ancient city." He sits back into his chair and blurs into a black silhouette. "Your book has changed. Your words have shifted. How does it feel to have the hand of Fate as an editor?"

She shivers as if the legs of spiders tap the skin of her back, along her spine, down the length of her arms.

"What dazzles me to the point of giggling is trying to work out just how your written efforts inspired my aim—inspired the story I wanted to insure would be written."

Astrid hears her voice say, "Julia's message."

"Very good. Mr Cremo, your books and early essays on the possibilities of time travel—*The Menkaure Hypothesis* in particular was an excellent read. And Professor Finnley, your work on the ancient *Itonalya* inspired a messianic sacrifice. The death of God, if you will. To think it was me that sent Loche and his son back to make it happen." There is a slight sparkle of his teeth in the dark. "It seems only right and proper that a psychologist should be the one to spell the end of God, don't you think? Come now, I can see you trying to figure out how I connected the dots. Let's just say that along with a goodly amount of time with Albion Ravistelle, access to nearly his entire library, and a look into a couple of Basil's paintings— experiences I won't soon forget—I learned a little more than I already know about Loche Newirth— and his son Edwin. And, because of my efforts, the history books are changing."

For Astrid, it clicks. It was right before her eyes. It was written in the stars for her to read.

Rearden rises to his feet. His pale, skull-like features peel away like a mask removed when he enters the neon from the monitor screen. "But never mind all of that." He joins her at Graham's bedside. "Albion has shared with me that you have read Dr. Newirth's Journal. Is that true?" Astrid's breathing arrests. "Yes, I see," Rearden says. "Ah, all of these books. All of these stories. What a wonder these stories are."

Astrid gasps, "What do you want?"

Rearden's right hand slides slowly through the air and hovers over Graham's shoulder. He lowers it and lets it rest upon the wound.

"There is another story that needs to be read. And it is time for it to be read," he says. "And you—you are the one to read it. You are the only one, knowing all that you know of these matters."

The Red Notebook flashes into her mind. She can see Yafarra pulling it from the *tenesh*. She flinches, reliving Rearden firing a bullet into Graham—Rearden stuffing the document into his coat. "W—what are you saying?" she asks.

"Astrid, tomorrow I will bring the Red Notebook to you, and you will read it. You will then tell me what it says."

She shakes her head. "No. You can't want that. If it is read it will shift—it will change—Albion fears that it will—he will never allow you to—"

His quiet laugh interrupts her, "Albion. Bless his immortal mind. For one so old—he is not so wise. Albion has sent me to find and bring Loche Newirth to this house. Albion believes that I am a mere tool. A tool that will bring the Poet to Albion's feet. Alas, Albion. While I have his allegiance, I also have access to his knowledge, his house and the devastating paintings of Basil Fenn. Mr. Ravistelle has given me every resource to accomplish the task. But I have given little in return." Rearden sighs. "You see, Professor, I, too, believe that when the Red Notebook is perused, Loche's words will change the world as we know it. But not just anyone can read his words and produce such uncanny permutation. No. Not just anyone."

Astrid stares at the psychologist. Branches of blue veins grapple upward along his temples. Where there should be wrinkles in his seventy something skin, there is a stretched, almost translucent film. She then looks at Graham. His gaze is fixed upon her. Concern clouds his eyes. She wishes he knew what she knew. Then, Rearden's riddle makes perfect sense. She remembers the last words of Loche's journal—and how the author taunted Rearden. The chilling lines: "Marcus, searching for the hands that move us will bring your kingdom to its knees. Like me, you crave to defeat the disease, and like me you will find written across your heart—a forgery. Something that will lose you the game. You will become what you've struggled to cure." Astrid sees that Loche was right. Craze lurks around Rearden's eyes. He has gone insane. He has gone mad.

Then the memory of her conversation with Marcel drifts through: "What about Rearden, Professor? What do you think his role in all of this is?" She had replied:"It is because of him, Marcel, this entire story began. He is a murderer. And he's after something."

Astrid struggles to keep her voice even. "The Journal was written for you. Everything changed because you read it."

Marcus smiles. "Very good, Professor. It was dedicated to me. And if I read the Red Notebook, we can expect even more changes. You see, not just anyone—only I. Only me. Loche is counting on me reading it. And it will be my undoing if I do."

"And you want me to read it for you—to tell you what's written there?"

"Again, my dear. Very good."

She looks down again to Graham for courage. "Find someone else. Have Albion do it."

"My dear, I am not Albion's friend. I am not Albion's helper—and he is not mine. I no more support his cause than I support the efforts of the *Orathom Wis*. I have my own interests."

"Revenge, Rearden? You can't be serious. . ."

A sparkle of teeth, "There is a bit of retribution, certainly. But it is not my sole aim. No, I feel that Loche's education is not yet done. I have taught him nearly everything he knows. But there is one last lesson to complete before I must face my next decision concerning Loche Newirth."

"I won't do it, you crazy fuck—"

The patient monitor sounds an alarm—and Graham winces and cries out in pain. Rearden's fingers jab down into the wound. He presses and holds there for a few seconds. "I think," he says as he lifts two bloody fingers, "you'll do as I ask. Tomorrow. At the Masque. I will find you."

The Planter #2

November 16, this year
Venice, Italy
5:10 am CEST

Loche Newirth sits down beside a sad looking bush and dangles his legs over the edge of a circular brick basin. He smells the fume of petrol mixed with cold ocean. A consistent hum of distant motors reverberates within the square courtyard he has found himself within. Above is yet another grey sky. The shape of the light has the look of very early morning, but he cannot be sure.

He looks down to his black, *Wyn Avuquain* cloak. His boots are caked with mud and snow. Around him, white marble pillars and Roman arches line the perimeter of the enclosure—as do electric light fixtures. There is some comfort in knowing that he has arrived in a time that has light fixtures. *But what time?* he wonders.

Thirst, hunger and fatigue wrestle for his attention. He closes his eyes and lowers his face.

"Maria Vergine," a voice says to his right, followed by, "Madonna! Oh, Santo Cielo. Ancora?" In the tone, Loche catches surprise, shock and wonder—but he also detects a kind of calm acceptance.

Twisting, Loche sees an old man in a dark green work suit. The patch on his pocket says, *Fausto.* Both of his hands lightly grip a broom handle. The brush of the broom has swept a small pile of debris and dust.

Before Loche can get a word out, the custodian says, "You. . .you. . ." He shakes his head. "You Loche Newirth. C'è una ragione per cui sono venuto a lavorare stamattina. Sei a Venezia!" He pauses. Wrinkles scrunch across his forehead as he searches for words. "You in Venice," he says. "Vieni con me—come with me, Loche Newirth. Come with me."

The Walls We Place Behind Us

November 16, this year
Venice, Italy
5:15 am CEST

Rearden had walked behind her all the way back to her room within Albion's house. He said nothing. As Astrid fumbled with the key to her door, he said, "Tomorrow. Tomorrow at the Masque. Until then, I'll keep an eye on Graham." She did not turn. She did not speak. She entered and shut the door, leaving him in the hallway. Half a minute later she could hear his footsteps receding toward the stairs.

That was hours ago. She is fairly sure it was hours ago.

The black velvet bag containing Basil's painting was still on the table. The ancient tome, the *Toele*, sat beside it. She found her own book in her shoulder bag—the one Rearden wanted her to sign. She flipped it open to the chapter, "The Fall of Wyn Avuqua." She lowered herself to the sofa as she read. She did not recognize many of the sentences. She did not remember writing them. Worry punched into her stomach. Rearden was telling the truth. An entirely new element was included in the story of the city's fall: the sacrifice of a young boy—the One God, *Thi*. She dropped the book.

That was hours ago. She is fairly sure it was hours ago.

Her hands found the *Toele*. It did not immediately occur to her that the pages were centuries old. The elaborate and delicate illumination did not capture her attention. When the *Elliqui* runes suddenly shifted and changed upon the page, she rubbed her eyes. She slammed the cover shut and sat back.

That was hours ago. She is fairly sure it was hours ago.

"Hold on to it," she could hear Howard Fenn say. "It's like a vivid dream that disappears as soon as you wake! Hold on to it!" And so it was. She had never heard tell, or herself written of the death of *Thi*—but her own book now shares a version of the myth. Tension pressed against her temples—this seemingly endless headache—she shut her eyes—the image of Queen Yafarra beheading a small boy with an axe. An innocent boy.

That was hours ago. She is fairly sure it was hours ago.

How the black velvet bag came into her hands she cannot recall. Unknotting the clasp and slipping the piece out was easy. She flipped it over and saw the rendering of a young boy standing beside a lake. A tiny fleck of light in the water's reflection drew her pupils. Her feet sought the floor, but there was no floor now below her.

Silence.
Flash.
Gone.

That was hours ago. She is fairly sure it was hours ago.

The headache is gone. The blurry clock face reads 5:15 am. Her sinuses are plugged. She has been crying.

"Hold on to it!" she hears herself say. It is like a dream—a dream receding like shadows behind walls. Only this time, it is not a dream. It is a memory. And it has nothing to do with ancient cities, immortals or the vengeful acts of a deranged psychologist.

Vestiges of years ago vault through her mind in reverse: a note fluttering on the refrigerator door from her ex husband. It reads: If I could change what happened, I would. Beginning again is all I can do—make a new story. I wish it was with you. The divorce. The yellow file folder labeled DONE. The screaming. Her husband pleading, "Baby, don't do this—we still have us! We still have us! Please come home."

A funeral.

A boating trip to Upper Priest Lake—Professor Astrid Finnley and her little girl; she and her daughter—then an accident —her little girl was on the bow—then she was not—she was on the bow—then she was not.

She is floating. She is floating face down. My baby is floating face down.

Astrid raises her hands and holds her head. The memory returns. Something forgotten returns. It is still there, hidden by a wall she placed behind her. She lies back and lets the cresting wave of sleep pull her under.

The Next Sentence

November 16, this year
Venice, Italy
6:15 am CEST

From the high window above Fausto's workshop, Loche can see over sienna rooftops and the canal to Albion Ravistelle's home just a mile west. A cold rain falls.

For the last hour he has been sitting beside the water streaked window. In his hands is the *Ithicsazj* of Fausto's making. When he saw the mask hanging on the wall, he pulled it down, and has not yet let the thing out of his grasp. Every few minutes he lowers his gaze to the empty sockets and searches for Edwin there. The red, beaded tear upon the cheek and the pale, bluish finish—a snapshot of the last time he saw his son's face.

When they first arrived at the shop, the enthusiastic Fausto had placed Loche before the web of research. Pictures of each character of the drama were tacked up and connected by yellow yarn, described with Post-It notes and arrayed much like Loche remembers his cabin walls not two weeks ago. Fausto spoke excitedly and waved his arms—occasionally saying, "You see? You see?" Loche managed to learn much despite the limited English of his new Italian friend: Albion Ravistelle is to hold a masquerade ball this evening; the paintings of Basil Fenn will be displayed to a host of high profile, important guests; a Professor from America has discovered the ruins of *Wyn Avuqua*, and she is here, in Venice. But the information that brought Fausto's chattering to a halt was when he shared that psychologist Marcus Rearden was currently across the water at Albion's house. Loche cannot be sure why Fausto fell silent at the mention of Rearden, his old mentor, but he can imagine that the expression on his face was conjured by the name.

Loche was given coffee, bread, cheese and fruit, and then shown upstairs to a bedroom. Not long after he had seated himself beside the window looking into the dreary day, Fausto knocked on the door and called, "Dr. Newirth, tu hai un visitatore."

The door opened and standing there, tall, lanky, wearing an overcoat coat of green with grey lapels, and a weird, thin-lipped grin was George Eversman.

Loche did not rise. George did not speak. The immortal entered, nodded to Fausto to leave them alone, closed the door and moved to an easy chair across from Loche.

The two have not yet spoken.

A clock keeps its steady cadence just beneath the prattle of raindrops bursting on the roof. The mask seems to pull Loche's eyes to it again.

"They. . ." Loche tries. "They killed Edwin, George." Anguish and grief floods over him. Blind with tears, Loche weeps. His fingers trace the mask's chin, mouth and cheeks.

George does not interfere but simply watches Loche. Concern haunts his eyes. A few minutes pass. Finally George says softly, "Loche, have a good cry."

A good cry.

And amid the chaos, the fantastic circumstances and the horror of losing his son, with his tears comes his professional point of view. A voice somewhere inside his head whispers, *A good cry. Crying is good. Emotional tears contain stress hormones that get excreted from the body through crying. It produces endorphins. Crying is a path to health—a clearing of grief—enables the heart and mind to re calibrate. You have shifted from a sympathetic to a parasympathetic state—Let go. . .let go. A good cry.*

The sorrow comes in heaves and waves. Between each his chest tries to control the pulsing tempo of sobbing. He squints to see through his veiled sight.

Bethany Winship, his client, Rearden's late mistress, enters into the office of his memory. She is both crying and laughing. "Oh my word," she says, her eyes glinting and wet, "I know that I get up and I get down, but this is ridiculous." Her face is pale blue. Upon her cheek is a red painted tear. Her throat is welted and bruised—pink shadows of gripping fingers stain her skin.

The wonder of it. The horror.

Loche's mind then shifts to a beloved quote from Washington Irving. "There is sacredness in tears. They are not the mark of weakness, but of power. They speak more eloquently than ten thousand tongues. They are messengers of overwhelming grief, of deep contrition, and of unspeakable love."

The tips of Loche's fingers hover over the solemn countenance of the mask. Through his blurry vision he again searches for Edwin.

"He not there," George says finally. "Your boy not there. Won't find him there."

"They. . .they killed him. . ."

"I know," George says, piteously.

Loche raises his focus to George. His eyes flash clear, "How do you know?"

"Not figured it out yet?"

"Figured out what?"

"No. Not yet, eh?" George shakes his head slowly. "What is my name?"

"Your name?"

"Yes."

"George."

"True, dat. What other name?"

"George Eversman."

"Yes." The immortal waits.

"What?" Loche asks wiping his nose.

"My given *Elliqui* name means same as Eversman."

Loche nods, "So?"

"Loche, I am Iteav. I am the only son of Yafarra, Queen of *Wyn Avuqua*."

A billion electrical impulses spark and burn within the chassis of Loche's skull. His eyelids slip shut. There in the firelight of his memory he sees the young boy Iteav sitting upon his mother's lap. He sees Iteav and Edwin playing in a far room. He sees the immortal little boy lifting up a toy horse and handing it to his son.

"You were there? You saw it?" Loche says.

"No," George replies. "I was not. I did not see Edwin die."

"You knew I was there, in *Wyn Avuqua* all along?"

George thinks a moment. "Foggy, Loche. But yes, maybe."

"Do you remember *Wyn Avuqua*?"

"No," George says again. "Or, little. What I know most is from stories—the tracing of my lineage. I do not remember my life there."

"You do not remember playing with toys—you and Edwin?"

George looks away to the grey light outside. He searches, then answers, "Maybe. I somehow know your son. But I don't know how. Long ago, Loche. A thousand years and more ago, Loche." He explains further. He tells of dreams—of high towers —of a woman's face, green eyes, gold hair—of a horrible *Rathinalya* caused by thousands of gods. There is little else he can share from his childhood. He shifts to the shores of the Agean

Sea and his parents—growing up in near Rome—discovering his immortality in his late teens.

"You do not remember your mother?" Loche asks.

"Only stories. Only tales. Maybe I see her face in dreams. She calls me in dreams. She tells me she is sorry. She cries over me."

"How long have you known? Known you are Yafarra's son?"

"Long, long time," he answers. "I am *Angofal* for that reason. I am *Chal*. I am King."

"Why are you telling me this?"

"Because you and me have lost dear ones. Because across the water, in Albion's house is the one that put to death my mother: Nicholas Cythe. And across the water, too, is the one that put your son to death: Marcus Rearden. Across the water, we have work to do."

"Yafarra was killed then?" Loche asks. Remembering the dull clop of her axe causes his body to flinch. *It was she that dealt Rearden's blow,* he thinks. In a dark chamber of his heart she has been paid. "How was she killed?"

George shakes his head, "No one knows truth. . . But tales tell that Devil took her life—Summoner of *Godrethion*, Cynthia. Cynthia now Nicholas Cythe." He frowns, pointing west across the canal. "I missed my chance at Uffizi when we last meet. When we meet next, Cythe will be no more. Tonight. Tonight at the masquerade ball." The immortal shifts in his chair. His fingers lace over his lips. He asks, "You were there? You were in the great city. Menkaure took you to *Wyn Avuqua*?"

Loche nods.

"You see my mother?"

"Yes."

"You see how she die?"

"No." Loche feels a stab of anger. He can still see her escorting young George and Edwin out of the Templar chamber from his place on the stone floor. The paralyzing stab of betrayal is still fresh. He wishes he knew how she was killed. He wishes he could have seen it. He shakes his head to master his fury. "No, I did not see her die. I crossed over as the city was falling."

"Basil? Find Basil there?"

Again Loche nods. "Yes, within a painting. He found a way to close the doors. He is closing them one by one. Soon all of his paintings will be without Centers. But he fears that the damage his work has done cannot be mended."

George's head tilts as he listens.

"Julia and William and the others," Loche says. "Will they make it across?"

"Do not fear for them. I believe you will all meet again before this day is over.

"Why was I taken back to *Wyn Avuqua*, George? I don't understand. I could have found my brother by looking into Leonaie's painting here in this time, to learn what I needed to learn. Help me to understand."

A smile widens on George's lips like a stretching rubber band. "Why does it rain right now? Why do we learn what we learn when we learn it? I think answer is clear. Certain. Real. You made myth. Myth made you. You have now lived the story—no longer just words—pictures. You were there. I do not think Basil called you across Menkaure. Another force called you. Another took you there. Now all is real."

"Another?"

George shrugs. "The world is full of angels and devils and undying travelers. None of us know how the next few pages will spell out our fates—none of us know what the next sentence will bring. We simply go forth. We go to learn. We go to see." The rubbery smile pulls tighter. "And you, Aethur, Poet, you of all, made it all. The answer will come."

George's gaze lowers to the artifact in Loche's hands. "And the mask that you have chosen, you shall wear." Loche looks down at the *Ithicsazj*. "I give Fausto that mask, you know. It from *Wyn Avuqua*—so I was told."

"This? This is the. . ."

George blinks his heavy lids. "Yes. Very old. I did not know its history until a few years ago. But I have had it since I was a boy. It come with me to Europe when I was young."

George stands. He extends an envelope filagreed with gold leaves and vines to Loche. "You and me have official invitations." He grins, "We still have *Orathom Wis* inside Albion's house. But two is all we got. Julia and William will come in through back door. But you and me enter in like all the others. We will wear masks, we shall drink, and we shall avenge our fallen dear ones with steel." The immortal's voice shouts, "Come, Aethur! We go to the next page!"

Champagne Breakfast

November 16, this year
Venice, Italy
6:15 am CEST

"What I'd give for some champagne," Astrid says. Marcel watches Astrid's index finger as she directs his attention to the delicate pages of Albion Ravistelle's *Toele*. "You're seeing that, right? I'm not losing my mind?"

The two stare at a kind of optical illusion—or bona fide supernatural occurrence. The *Elliqui* characters in several places on the page change—entire lines reorder and shift—stories alter —unbeknown additions appear. The anomalous editing is slow and ghostlike.

Marcel looks at Astrid, "What the hell happened while I was asleep?"

Astrid shrugs. "Much, apparently."

"Are these changes happening in your book?" he asks.

"No—or maybe. I'm not sure yet. These changes here tell of Yafarra's last stand in the *Avu*."

"How she was entombed?"

"So it seems."

Marcel lifts and opens Astrid's book and flips to the chapter, "The Fall of Wyn Avuqua". He mutters to himself, "So I guess history is no longer written by the winners but something else altogether." Astrid can see that he has found the section on the killing of the innocent.

"So, Marcel?" She says latching her eyes to his. "You know the tale of the *Wyn Avuquain* innocent, right?"

Incredulity rises into Marcel's expression. "You want me to answer that question, seriously?" He sees that she is indeed serious. "Um, yeah. Of course I know. It is one of the oldest—" He breaks off. He scratches his head. "I mean, you discovered documents about it years ago. . ." His red eyebrows furrow. "Why does my stomach hurt suddenly? I have this weird feeling we talked about this before—like, yesterday. But. . ." He lowers the book and stares at his teacher. "What the fuck? We've always known that story."

"We have?" She asks. Astrid studies him and tries to connect some kind of cypher to the impossibility. Her stomach growls.

"Yeah. Right?"

"You slept last night?"

Marcel nods. "Yes. But what does that have to do with anything?"

Astrid shrugs. "I'm not sure. It's all I can figure. Maybe these shifts in history insert into our memories after we distance ourselves a bit. Maybe sleep."

"Haven't you slept?"

"Barely." The weight of fatigue is heavy, but somehow easily ignored. *Breakfast would be good*, she thinks. *And champagne.* She gestures to her book, "Tell me, is there anything in there about Yafarra's last stand?"

Marcel scans. Pages flip. A few moments pass. He thumbs to the index and searches. "Well," he says standing, "I'm not too sure how to answer you. What's written here—the tale I know— is the same as it ever was."

"And what tale is that?"

"The story you pieced together from several sources—"

"Yes—and?"

"That Yafarra was slain—her head was taken—and she was entombed by Templar—with the prophecy, and hidden." He reads from the book: "—the author of this German account leaves no clues to Yafarra's remains save this: Her Majesty shall always remain within the Heron's talon."

She turns back to the *Toele*. "There is perhaps one other surviving *Itonalya* tome like this— it is only rumored, of course. And now with *Wyn Avuqua* discovered, I'm sure there are hundreds. But Albion's *Toele* is now—right now—changing."

"What does that mean? Like, lines of history run side by side—and the change is happening right now—in real time?" Marcel's excitement and wonder makes her smile. But the smile is laced with more pain than joy.

"Real time? No damn idea what that might mean."

Marcel shrugs, "Me either, at this point."

"What has me disturbed is who or what is holding the pen."

Marcel recoils. "Ugh. Brain hurts."

"Noted," Astrid agrees. A warble from her stomach seems to agree.

"What is the author saying."

The pads of her fingers touch the parchment. They slide gently across the runes, over the words, through veils of meaning. She reads in silence.

"I don't know how to answer you. I could pour over this book for months—years. One page seems to contain more than I've been able to gather in my entire career." She sighs. "It would take too much time to locate anything on Yafarra's last stand. If my book hasn't changed on that subject, maybe this one won't either."

"Seems to me that Yafarra's entombment was meant to be a secret. How, after all, could anyone tell of it?"

"You're right," she nods. "It is said that what few *Itonalya* escaped were not aware of the inner dealings of Yafarra's court. Therefore, like us, their accounts are a matter of conjecture."

Astrid closes the *Toele*. "Another time, my love," she says to it as she rubs her hand over the cover. "Another time."

She tells Marcel about her evening. Everything from her visit with Howard Fenn to her encounter with Graham and Rearden to the surreal experience within Basil Fenn's artwork.

"Busy as usual," Marcel says when she finishes. "So you're the lucky one that gets the first read of the Red Notebook. Swell. After the Journal, I don't think it wise to keep up on Newirth's work. Have we decided yet that these things are above our pay grade and its time to get out of here?"

"You read my mind—but I'm not leaving without Graham."

Marcel narrows his eyes, "Sounds like Rearden has you stuck. What? Did he say, 'You read this and tell me what it says and then I'll let you go'?"

"Not exactly."

"What did he say?"

"It's what he didn't say that troubles me."

Marcel says, "What do you mean?"

Astrid thinks for a second. "If Rearden succeeds with either bringing Loche to some kind of murderous state and gets him to write—the outcome could be catastrophic. If he fails with that he'll figure a way to kill the man. Jesus, he's designed the death of Loche's son already." A sharp stab of pain presses into her temple at the thought. "The Red Notebook is his last wild card—his remaining unknown. It will either benefit him, destroy him or do nothing at all. One thing is for sure, though—no matter what it says, I will know. I will have read the secret. And it's damn certain he won't let me live knowing it."

Marcel's chest puffs up. "Then we won't let that happen. He can't just kill you openly."

"No. But there's a reason he wants me to read it at a Masque. Tomorrow's event, despite its high-class crowd, will be dangerous. I've been through Albion's House. There are a lot of shadowy nooks—a lot of places where a killing could take place." She shivers. Pages from Edgar Allan Poe's *The Masque of the Red Death* flutter in from eighth grade—the colored rooms, the chiming clock, the pursuit of Death into the last black chamber.

"I won't let it happen. I'll shadow you everywhere you go. I'll get some kind of weapon." His sentiment seems outlandish, yet his ferocity provides some comfort.

"Whatever happens," she says, "He can't know what it says—and he can't be allowed to possess it."

"Maybe Fausto can help," Marcel says.

"Maybe. But I think we may need Albion and his sort in the end." Astrid puts her hand on his shoulder, "If you lose me, I'll find you. Don't go risking your skin to find me. These people are dangerous. If you lose me, find us a way to escape."

"Speaking of Fausto, I've already had some ideas about that," he says with a mischievous grin.

There is a knock on Astrid's door.

"Professor Finnley?" a voice says from outside. "Delivery."

Astrid opens to see two smartly dressed attendants with two carts. "Albion Ravistelle sends his compliments to both you and Marcel Hruska." His open palm directs their attention to the hanging garments and boxes stacked on the higher of the two carts. "I bring a wide range of attire—gowns and doublets, cloaks and cowls." He bows his head. "And from Fausto Boldrin—masks. The most beautiful masks in all the world." The attendant behind with the other, lower cart then announces, "And I bring breakfast and champagne."

Wine Before a Duel

November 16, this year
Venice, Italy
6:15 pm CEST

He can almost hear the Joni Mitchell song. Loche imagines Samuel Lifeson sitting at the bar smoking, drinking and singing along with Joni's haunting refrain. He can see Felix Wishfeill's head bulging in a plastic bag—a doubled plastic bag.

George sips his wine. Maria sets the bottle in front of Loche.

"You were here before?" George asks.

"I was."

George nods. "Stupid crazy, yes?"

Loche smiles sadly. "Rearden used to have a saying about crazy."

"Rearden is crazy," George says.

"Yes," Loche agrees. "He used to say that every psychologist faces three fears at some point in their career. He called them his Three Heavy What Ifs: *What if I can't help them? What if I can't handle it? What if I go in with them?*"

"Okay. . ." George says questioningly.

Loche stares into his glass. "I'm going in with them. . ."

"Good," George says. "So I go with you." He raises his glass. "Here's to crazy."

"Stupid crazy," Loche adds.

They drink.

"I love a sip of wine before a duel," George says. "It makes me think of joys we protect."

Sweet Sixteen

November 16, this year
Venice, Italy
7:10 pm CEST

The female vocalist's voice she knows, without a doubt, but she struggles to place her. Astrid Finnley stands near the bandstand beside the high, gothic-arched entry watching and listening to a quartet of musicians as they perform a version of Led Zeppelin's "Rain Song." Even with the mask, she knows the guitarist is Jimmy Page. His movements are as familiar as his guitar stylings. Sharing the stage with him is a percussionist behind a small glittery gold trap kit, a thick-fingered bassist playing an old and weathered upright, and a short, voluptuous siren with long dark hair and a voice like a rock goddess.

For the last hour Astrid has alternated her position between the gothic doors and the balustrade overlooking the canal, watching masked guests present their invitations at the dock and again at the stairwell. Out on the water flash a hundred or more media cameras. The flickering lights remind Astrid of distant lightening.

Marcel is cloaked all in purple and gold. His mask is deep green. His red hair is tucked back into his hood. A few curls straggle out and hang to his shoulders. He does not take his eyes off her, and when she moves, he moves, staying just apart enough to appear as if they are not together. Having him near and watchful eases her anxiety.

But it is the woman's voice that comforts her the most. Or perhaps it is the mere distraction of trying to figure out how she knows the voice. Its timbre resounds from out of her youth—her teenage years.

"What a show," she hears someone say as they pass. Their companion replies, "Oh just wait—Ravistelle will deliver."

How could one not get caught up in the thrill of this moment? Astrid looks down at her gown that spills across her shape like a burgundy gloss. A cloak with a long, airy cape is tied at her throat. Her hair is up, coiled and woven into the shape of a flower—and her mask is a deep brown encrusted with red rubies like droplets of wine. Men notice her standing alone. Their white teeth smile under their masks. Their eyes scan her body. She exchanges her empty champagne flute for a full one as a waiter passes.

Art, music, wine and song in Venice—elegance, glamor and danger. She is high. She is terrified.

The song ends. The vocalist thanks the audience for their applause—and it is when she speaks that Astrid recognizes her. She says to herself, "Ann Wilson. It's Ann Wilson from Heart." Immediately the opening riff of "Crazy On You" explodes into her internal playlist. But only for a moment.

Ann Wilson announces, "Ladies and Gentlemen, please join us in welcoming our host, Mr. Albion Ravistelle. . ."

Lights swing to another stage at the back of the hall. Applause begins as Albion appears from a dark corner. He wears a simple tuxedo. A cape is clasped at his throat and thrown back over his shoulders. His mask is the one Fausto had labored over. It is magnificent, simple and exuding decadence with its white jewels, gold highlights and solemn countenance.

"And here we go," a woman nearby says to her friend. "This is going to be great." She lifts her phone and frames the immortal in the screen.

Albion steps to the microphone. "It appears that my identity is now known, for I stand before you as Albion Ravistelle." He bows. There is friendly applause. Albion's lips smile below his mask. "I recognize no one and I know you all. How wonderful and exciting that we are gathered here. Welcome to Venice. Welcome to my house. Welcome to the beginning of a

New Earth." He reaches into his suit coat and produces an envelope. From it he unfolds a handwritten letter. "Before we begin, a word from my sixteen-year-old daughter, Crystal. I received her letter this morning and I feel compelled to share it with you." He lowers the letter to his side as if he is struck with a sudden thought. "To think," he lilts, "what the world will be like for my daughter—for my daughter—your daughters and your sons—all of our children—and our children's children—when they inherit the work we have gathered here to begin." He pauses. His thoughtful tone then picks up, "When I was Crystal's age, what a time it was. A very different time indeed." He shakes his head. "It seems like centuries ago." He raises the letter, "And still we live in a world ruled by constructs that deplete our delicate and finite home. Tonight, esteemed guests, we will rewrite history so we might create a future free from our repeated mistakes."

"'Papa,' she writes." Albion grins into the paper. "'In the days since I left you, Dr. Bonin and I have traveled through parts of the Eastern Europe, the Middle East and Africa. So much pain. So much suffering. What would happen if we loved others like we loved our own children? Why can't that happen.'" Albion raises his face to the audience. His mask covers what Astrid imagines is an expression that likely mirrors hers: a kind of patient humoring of a naive notion. "'You've told me that things like tribalism and nationalism blind the world to love's potential —but the children know nothing about those things. You've said many times that the world economy, in order to survive, must always be growing—and that growth does not support love. In order for it to grow there must be want—there must be scarcity. But the children know nothing about those things. We have seen war-torn cities and villages. We have heard stories of genocide and killing—all in the name of God, country and money. Papa, what do the children know of these things? What lessons are the right lessons, Papa? I have so many more questions—I cannot wait to talk with you when I come home. I miss you. Your loving daughter, Crystal.'"

As Albion folds the letter and slips it into the envelope, he says, "You may say I'm a dreamer." Albion speaks the words, yet Astrid imagines she hears John Lennon's melody. "But I'm not the only one. I hope someday you will join us. And the world will be as one." He lightly chuckles.

"Ah, to be sixteen again. How is it that we," he gestures to the room of leaders, politicians, CEOs and dignitaries, "have not yet looked back into history and made judgements on our choices—what was backward, naive, corrupt, wrong? War? Famine? Illness? Last year, suicide claimed more lives than war and crime-related deaths combined. And those three figures together are just slightly less than the people killed by sugar diabetes. Many of your constituents prefer economic growth over ecological or social health. Much of the world's population cannot envision a world without the mortared constructs that have been nurtured by power hungry governing bodies." He laughs cheerfully, "It is a wonder we've come this far."

"But, my dear ladies and gentlemen, by some miracle, we have come far. Though war, illness and famine still exist, they are becoming unprofitable and obsolete. For the first time in the history of humankind, a light is shinning at the end of a long, dark tunnel. All of us can see it. That light—that pinprick in the black, like a single star, is guiding us to the next few baby steps in our evolution. We trundle toward a New Earth. We leave behind a past once full of meaning. Those gods and religions, messiahs and dollars, countries and anthems—those old fears will fall into the history books as the humanchild's bad choices.

"What did we seek when we were sixteen?" His eyes scan out from his mask. "What did we believe? My lovely daughter believes she is immortal. She believes in love. And she believes that if she could get everyone to see as she does, we will all become gods. Is that not the definition of youth?

"But then we come along, we the dignified, the powerful, the respected. We teach history. We teach the limitations of love. We teach war, pain, political economy, racism, sexism, fear— need I go on?

"Ah to be sixteen again. Close your eyes and think of it— Put aside the idealism or pure intentions of the mind—but think of the body. The body, for a limited time, immortal. Think of the power, the energy, the youth of that long gone sixteen-year-old body of yours. I know many of you still feel as if you're sixteen —but the flesh has sloughed that former coil off. Remember its vitality? Its ability to move? Your prime self?" Albion opens his arms and spreads them wide, "Your prime self can return. Death is no longer a mystery. It is a poor part of human design. It is simply something to correct. A problem with a solution.

"But first, the mind must rekindle its true calling, its compassion, its empathy, its belief in love paramount. And this is why we gather here tonight, ladies and gentlemen, to look upon the paintings of Basil Pirrip Fenn.

"Surrounding us in this hall, now shrouded in their own masks, are works that will once and for all illuminate you to your place in existence. By your will and your witness, you will assist in taking control over what has always been beyond the reach of humankind—true free will. Our eyes are our weapons. The afterlife of myth, whatever gods that rule beyond—we are no longer their servants, their entertainment nor their concern. Tonight we will take the communion that will establish a New Earth, and by doing so, we shall abolish the old powers and engineer Paradise, here. On behalf of The Board, and myself, join us."

There is delighted applause. The lights dim deeper. Beaming spotlights slash through the darkness and point the revelers to the shrouded easels. From the performance stage an entrancing orchestral tone bleeds from Jimmy Page's guitar, both ominous and inviting. The spider web of cables vibrates as each shroud begins to rise into the air like a sable phantom. Astrid overhears a woman say to her group, "What drama. . ." Another replies, "I love it. What a presentation."

Astrid watches Albion descend from his riser. He is joined by three attendants and they escort him toward an exit at the rear of the hall. Before he reaches the door, the lights in the room shift. It is suddenly a little brighter. All of the spotlights go out. The shrouds freeze, their hems resting just above the bottom edges of the framed paintings. Albion stops and turns.

A single spot light slashes to the center of the audience. It illuminates what at first appears to be another shrouded painting. But the covered frame has legs. Legs and high boots. Beside the frame, a stout woman with thick curls of red hair bursting out from either side of her mask shouts out, "My Lord, Albion. Please, stay."

Some of the crowd applaud at this theatrical turn. Smiles shine below masked eyes. Giggles can be heard. The woman beside Astrid says, "You see. I told you they wouldn't easily let us see the artist's work."

"My Lord," the woman's spirited voice shouts. "Come, come. Before we present the work of Mr. Basil Fenn, I have for you a gift. A gift that this time you will not lose."

Albion quickly steps back up to his riser. Another spotlight flashes onto him. The heads of the crowd swivel to Albion as if perfectly choreographed.

Despite his mask, Albion does not appear surprised. "Why, Olivia Langley," he says. He waits. He watches her. "I did not think you would accept my invitation."

"I booked my flight as soon as I read it. I was so excited! I am so excited!" The crowd gives a chuckle to her so excited delivery. Olivia's joy is contagious.

"Well," Albion says, almost as if he had rehearsed, "I, too, am excited you have come—for I have made a great many arrangements for you and those that have joined you."

"Oh, my dear Albion, how very thoughtful of you." Olivia moves around the man holding the frame covered by a shroud, her blue eyes never leaving Albion. With one hand she leisurely gestures for the onlookers to form a wide circle. "Before we get to our receiving committee, won't you permit me to offer you a gift."

Albion lays the palms of his hands upon the podium. "Of course, my dear."

"Behold, the prices we pay for paradise!" Olivia takes hold of the shroud and snaps it to the side and down. People jockey for a view of the work. Astrid, too, moves to the side and forward to see the work.

It is a portrait in oil of a man with shoulder length brown hair, an attractive face, hazel eyes and an expression that is both questioning and sure at the same time. After a moment of studying the work, Astrid looks back to Albion. His expression, even with a mask, appears sorrowful and troubled.

"Know you this man, my Lord?" Olivia asks.

Albion stares at the portrait. He does not answer.

"My Lord, know you this fellow?"

"*Gavress*," Albion replies. "*Gavress*, Olivia."

"Rest in peace?" Olivia says. "No such thing for us, my Lord. Do I sense some remorse? Longing? Regret?"

"You would be a fool to believe otherwise, Olivia."

"Well then," she says turning to the painting, "this gift shall in some way assuage those awful burdens."

Olivia places both hands on either side of the large painting, lowers it to the floor and moves it to the side. The man holding the work is now visible. His face is covered by a mask of leaves and branches molded out of leather. Around his throat is a woven wool scarf dangling down well below his knees. The hood of his cloak is thrown back revealing long locks of brown hair. He removes his mask. It is the man in the painting.

"*Ithic veli agtig*, my friend," he says.

The eyelets in Albion's mask fill with two full irises.

A firm hand grips Astrid's upper arm. Her head jerks to see a figure wearing a black tuxedo and cloak, but his mask is white and droops down over his cheeks. Rearden's hiss is unmistakable. "Your expertise is now required, Professor. A reading, I beg." As he pulls her back into the dark and toward a far door, she can still see Marcel. He is transfixed by the drama unfolding beneath the spotlights.

What Is Written there?

November 16, this year
Venice, Italy
7:21 pm CEST

Astrid is shoved along the corridor. If she does not walk fast enough he grips the back of her upper arm and push-pulls her along. She does not cooperate with the pace. Her heels do not cooperate with the pace. "Take it easy! Where are you taking me?" Rearden is silent. She recognizes the last few turns and the final staircase. Through an archway the doors to the infirmary and Dr. Catena's laboratory appear. She shivers at the thought of Graham being hurt again—tortured.

Silhouetted down the hallway to the right are two security guards. The body of a third guard is on the floor. Astrid can smell tin and bitter smoke. At her feet are empty ammunition casings.

The guards turn to Rearden. Rearden says, "It has begun?"

The guard replies, "Yes."

"Good," Rearden says.

He shoves Astrid through the door. The ward is abandoned. As they pass room 10, Graham's room, Astrid sees the door is ajar. Within, the bed is empty. Rearden does not notice. At the furthest door from the nurses station, room 17, Rearden twists the knob, and pushes her inside. Before she is shut in, she cranes back hoping to see Marcel haunting their steps. He is not there.

The patient monitor lights the space in neon, save for a single lamp near the bathroom. Along the far wall is a bed and upon it, asleep or drugged, is Yafarra. Her hair is draped back and arranged above her head like a fountain of gold. In a chair beside her is a figure in black. He wears a hood and cloak. There is another visitor's chair at the end of the bed. Rearden lets go of Astrid's arm and points to it, "Sit."

She glares at him. "Sit," he says again.

She obeys.

Rearden reaches beneath his cloak and produces the Red Notebook. He sets it onto Astrid's lap. "Read," he commands.

Her face drops to the worn cover. "Fuck you," Astrid says. *God*, she pleads in her mind, *where is Marcel?*

"Read," he says again. His voice struggling against rage.

"Rearden, no. You have no idea what you're toying with."

The figure sitting beside the bed slips a long bladed knife out from under his cape.

"*Ag*, Astrid. *Ag!*" The sound of Yafarra's voice snaps Astrid's attention to the bed. Yafarra's eyes are horror wide. "*Ag!*"

Rearden sighs. "The only word she's said since her arrival here. No. No. No. I'm weary of no."

Yafarra looks to the hooded man beside her, to the knife and then back to Astrid. "*Ag!*"

"It was my hope that Yafarra had read the work—after all, it has been in her possession for some time. But she is reticent to my demands. When I introduced my colleague here, Mr. Nicholas Cythe, Her Majesty became downright combative. But no has remained her chosen theme and fixed response." Rearden's teeth glow green in the electronic light. "Nicolas and Yafarra go way back. Way, way back."

Nicholas turns his face to her. Two swirling pools of green glitter coil in the sockets of his eyes. He tilts his face slightly. Astrid feels cold. Her skin crawls.

"*Cymachkena. Cymachkena*," Yafarra whispers through her teeth at Cythe.

Evil dragon, Astrid translates. She feels her eyes widen and the pace of her heart arrest—Devil, Yafarra calls him. Devil. Evil dragon. Could it be? Could such an entity truly exist?

"We have brought the two of you together to insure the words are read and Loche's meaning is shared. What is written there, I will know of it. Astrid? Read."

Yafarra tries to sit up, but she cannot. Restraints are belted one her ankles and across her chest and abdomen. "*Ag*, Astrid!"

Rearden's hand slashes through the air and cracks against Astrid's masked face. "Read." He slaps her again, hard. And again. Blood dribbles from her lower lip. The mask drops down around her neck. The sting is maddening.

Yafarra cries out. Nicholas' blade stabs into the woman's right arm. Blood shoots onto the white sheets. *"Ag!"* she shouts. She spits at him again, *"Cymachkena!"* Nicholas then stands and begins bashing his fist against the side of her head and into her chest with his full weight. There is a grisly snap of rib bones. Yafarra coughs blood.

"Stop!" Astrid screams. "Stop," she pleads. Her hands find the wire spirals and she lifts the notebook.

"*Ag*, Astrid!" Yafarra tries through pained breath—through saliva—through already foaming pink blood. "Do not! Do not." Her body stills. Her muscles let go.

Nicholas observes her for a few seconds, then stabs the blade into her right thigh and lets it stay there. He then calmly turns to his chair and seats himself.

Astrid opens the cover. Rearden averts his eyes slightly. "What is written there?"

The Move on the Board

November 16, this year
Venice, Italy
7:21 pm CEST

Loche Newirth is relieved when he hears his father's familiar voice, *"Ithic veli agtig."* He is also amused when William Greenhame draws a sword, stretches himself into his wonted, painfully unusual ballet pose and adds, "I'm not dead yet."

Silence. Albion Ravistelle tears his mask from his face as if to remove any possible hinderance to his vision. He squints into the sheer light. He stands mute, but his expression demands, *Is it really you?*

William savors the quiescence—the wonderstruck shock —the image of wheels turning in his old friend's mind. William waits. And waits a little longer. Finally William says, "Mark me. I am thy former friend's spirit."

The audience chortles at the line and their heads twist to Albion for a rebuttal. He blinks. "William? You were—you were gone—"

William bows lower. "How I love my wife. It was she that drew me home from the sea."

Marvel and confusion battle for control over Albion's face. His mouth curves into a smile and his eyes glitter with seeming gratitude and suspicion both. After a deep breath, presumably signifying the acceptance of Fate's toying hands, Albion asks, "So you've come again to prevent our inevitable evolution? You've come to stop us from entering a New Earth?"

William says, "I've come to tell you a number of things, but for now, I'll limit myself to two items."

Albion waits. William waits.

Albion asks, "And the items are?"

"The first item is to tell you that you are a nutter. Completely mad. A lunatic. Gifted, yes. Brilliant, pretty good speaker, but for the most part, a looney." William gestures with his eyes to the wide, dark periphery of the chamber. Albion looks around. Just outside the circle of Basil's paintings—just beyond the reach of the spotlights, a large group of men armed with both handguns and lightweight swords have surrounded the revelers. Loche feels for the handle of his rapier. He notes the men are masked and wear the same tactical attire as Emil Wishfeill.

Greenhame says, "Second, know that I am not here to stop you. Instead, I am here to help you."

Albion casts a slightly confused glare at each corner of the room. "Help me? And just how will you do that?"

"Albion. Albion Ravistelle. They will not allow you to continue. You are not their leader. A single mind cannot rule the human collective. They will not allow your intervention, nor our intervention any longer—we *Itonalya*. The age-old *Godrethion* have hunted us, they have slain our ancestors—they have killed —killed," Greenhame's voice breaks. His next words are a struggle to bury sorrow, "Killed—my grandson. Killed my Edwin." He halts. A slight shake of his head and he resets his tone, "And now our beloved *Alyaeth*." He opens his embrace to the surrounding faces, "These mortals we have spent lifetimes protecting—now they have no need of us. The New Earth Albion, will not be of our making—it will be theirs. It was always theirs."

The encircling group slowly encroaches.

Albion turns to his nearest assistants. Loche locates them retreating behind the advancing men. Their eyes still on their former master.

William says, "You have been replaced, Albion. The Board is making its move."

Albion takes a nervous step back from the podium. For the first time, Loche sees fear tugging at his seemingly unshakable demeanor. But it is but a passing shadow.

"Well then," he grins at William Greenhame. "Treachery! Seek it out!" His cloak waves up and over his shoulder and a bright blade sings into the air.

Sigourney's Line

November 16, this year
Venice, Italy
7:37 pm CEST

The Devil watches.

Marcus Rearden watches.

Astrid cannot remove her eyes from the page. She attempts to command the muscles of her face to refrain from wrenching into horror—into joy—into haste. Every impulse yearns toward tears. She checks her breathing. She concentrates on staying calm—without expression. Marcus Rearden's keen ability to read faces is unparalleled. One wrong move and its over.

Cythe slowly rises and reaches for the knife embedded in Yafarra's thigh. He yanks it out. Yafarra groans.

"What does it say?" Rearden hisses.

Composure. Her heart pounds rapid, ghostly pink blemishes into her vision. She reads the page again.

Rearden's palm cracks across her face. "Tell me!" he demands.

Her eyes meet Yafarra's. She could not help it. The two connect. Seeing the exchange, Rearden shouts, "Last time I will ask!" The sting of his hand sends a flash of white through her head.

Then there is a sickening thud with a simultaneous low ringing tone. Nicholas Cythe falls forward. His forehead bashes into the patient monitor. An instant later he is on the floor unconscious. Blood squirts. A gruesome divot is gouged into the back of his skull.

Astrid swivels to see Graham Cremo holding aloft a large red fire extinguisher. Rearden turns just as Graham growls, "Get away from her, you bitch!" The impact ratchets Rearden's chin down. There is a muffled crack as the spine fractures. His body collapses into a heap beside Nicholas Cythe.

Graham wobbles as he lowers the heavy canister to the floor. He is shaking. He is wearing a light sweat suit. "It was a toss up. . ." he breathes heavily, looking down at his handiwork, "tough choice between Sigourney's line or 'No one puts baby in a corner.'"

Astrid rises and throws her arms around him. "I thought they had taken you—I thought you were—" She holds him tight.

"I'm okay—a little unbalanced, but okay." He lets her go and moves to see her face, "Are you okay?"

She stares at him as if trying to connect silky lines of *Elliqui*. When he smiles, she smiles.

From the floor, Cythe's hand twitches. White bubbles have formed within the cleft of the wound. Rearden issues a moan.

She shoves the Red Notebook into her bag. "We need to get out of here."

The Move on the Board #2

November 16, this year
Venice, Italy
7:40 pm CEST

Loche stands still. There is no sign of Marcus Rearden. He watches three figures repel down to the floor from the light tresses on the ceiling. Their feet hit the floor and they draw swords. Fifteen or twenty revelers break from the crowd and move to the center of the hall. They, too, draw blades from out of their cloaks.

"Any that still hold with me, come," Albion cries to the gathering, his back to William Greenhame. "Any that still hold true to the Old Law, and any that can imagine the New Earth. We have been betrayed."

Half of the audience is smiling, their disbelief still suspended by the champagne, the glamour and the magic of a Venetian masquerade. The other half appears to sense that something has shifted. The masked, modern security force with their naked, machete-like weapons and military formation is blatantly out of character for the event's aesthetic. A few revelers begin to back their way out toward the exits. Some cower together in clusters.

Loche Newirth watches with calm ambivalence. His eyes scan the room for a sign of Marcus Rearden. His forefinger and thumb gently pluck at the pommel of his sheathed sword.

A woman's voice over the PA system, "Mr. Albion Ravistelle? May I have your attention, Mr. Ravistelle?"

Behind the podium now stands a tall, short-haired woman. One eye is visible. The other is hidden behind a curtain of light grey bangs.

"I hear you, Lynn Eastman," Albion says without looking at her. "What may I do for you?"

"For me, you may avoid bloodshed. Drop your weapon. There is no reason for violence. By order of The New Earth Board, I am tasked with removing you from your Chair and your responsibilities."

Albion laughs, "I'm afraid I will not comply. My design will not be compromised."

Eastman remains without emotion. "Mr. Ravistelle, your design has nothing to do with you any longer. The Board has elected a new leader, and he has ordered your arrest."

"Let me guess. . ." Albion growls.

Marcus Rearden, Loche's mind screams.

"Dr. Marcus Rearden has developed a future path that will insure the survival of the human element in this evolutionary pursuit." Her single blue eye scans the audience. "After all, Mr. Ravistelle. You are, and always have been, outnumbered."

A warm hand reaches into Loche's cloak and covers over his hand. At the touch of her skin, Loche knows her. "Julia. . ." he says.

Her dress is purple velvet. A thin strap lies over one naked shoulder. A silk cape cascades over the other. Her mask is obviously made by Fausto. An elegant plume of violet and green feathers rises gently above her head like wisps of summer cloud.

Loche throws open his cloak and draws her inside. She smells of lavender and lilac. He pulls her close. Her arm wraps around behind him and squeezes."

"I am with you." She whispers. "Where is he? Where is Rearden?"

The Stairs

November 16, this year
Venice, Italy
7:49 pm CEST

Bruises throb beneath Astrid's mask as she moves. Rearden's long cloak is tied around Yafarra's throat and it drapes over her hospital gown. She wears his white mask. Graham is covered in Cythe's masquerade garb. They leave both Marcus Rearden and Nicholas Cythe on the floor and start back toward the glass doors to exit the ward. Graham stumbles. Both Yafarra and Astrid clasp an arm around him and walk as quickly as his legs will allow.

"You read it? You read the Notebook?" Graham asks.

She hesitates. "We shouldn't talk of it. Not here. Not now."

Graham agrees, "Understood." They limp a few steps. "What now? I'm not up to my usual combat potential, you know, so I may have to sit the next round out."

"I wish I knew. If we get back to the ball we might be able to blend in and think a moment."

"A party," Graham says, "I could use a drink."

"Me, too."

As they arrive at the glass door, Astrid stops. "There are guards down the hall to the left. We'll be seen."

Graham peers through the glass to the narrow staircase leading up. "If you can make it to the stairs, I'll sit my ass down."

"You'll sit your ass down?"

"That's right. They are not after me, Astrid. They want you, the Red Notebook and Loche Newirth. Those stairs are not wide enough for two to climb side by side. You and Yafarra go and I'll block. They won't hurt me. They've kept me alive this long—"

"I'm not leaving you. It's you and me, together."

He grins at her. She expects a line from a movie. He shakes his head. "Yes. You and me. But not yet. We each have our own part to play in this story. Mine is to block. I can't run. Not yet. If we stay together now, you'll be caught—the Notebook —Loche—"

"Professor Finnley!" The voice of Rearden rounding the ward corner forces the decision. Graham says, "Go."

The panel of glass slides to the side and the three rush across the hall. Just past the corner a guard shouts, "Stop!" Graham buckles and drags his left foot. Both Yafarra and Astrid lend their strength and haul him forward. At the base of the stair, Astrid vaults up. Yafarra follows, with Graham managing to stay just behind her for the first ten steps.

Astrid looks back to see the guards starting upward with Cythe following close. At the mid point, Graham stops, turns and waits. Cythe slows his pace and begins to climb slowly.

At the base of the stairs, Rearden pauses and watches. He shakes his head as if pitying their feeble attempt to escape. Two more guards appear. One leans toward the psychologist and speaks.

From below comes the hated voice of Rearden, "Nicholas, tell me that you have this all in hand."

Cythe does not answer.

Rearden looks up, "It has begun. The Ballroom requires my presence," he says to Cythe, "You may have Yafarra, if you must. But I would prefer Professor Finnley and Graham Cremo be left alive to assist me in the days to come."

"As you wish," Cythe hisses.

"The Red Notebook will be delivered to me immediately."

"As you wish," Cythe says again.

Rearden disappears down a hall to the left toward the elevators.

"Go!" Graham shouts at Astrid as she pauses looking back. Graham puffs up. The first advancing guard missteps, and Graham kicks at the man's knees. The guard loses his balance, and with a single push he falls over the railing onto a marble floor. Close behind is the next guard. With a baton he lands two vicious blows to Graham's upper arm. Graham does not budge. The next swing of the baton is blocked by Yafarra now descending to assist Graham. The third swing smashes into Graham's head. The full weight of his unconscious body drops onto the security guard, pinning him down.

Astrid halts. She reaches into her bag and grabs the only thing she can find that is sharp: a pen. She leaps down the ten or more steps to assist. She freezes when she sees Cythe leap up and over the barrier Graham had made, and claw into Yafarra's hair. He winds her to him until his fist controls her head. He bashes her face into the railing. "Yafarra!" He hisses. "Queen of Immortals. Queen of nothing. I told you I would find you!" His knife flashes into the light. Three thrusts of the blade pound into her abdomen. Yafarra smashes her left fist into Cythe's right eye. He reels for an instant only. "Your city I have razed and ground to dust, your people I have slaughtered one by one—and now, you are the last of that House—the crowning piece to the realm of old."

The blow to Yafarra's face hurls her up onto Astrid. Astrid's arms embrace her as their bodies tumble back onto the stairs behind. Cythe reaches to his side and pulls a sword from a sheath. "Now, I'll have your head, your arms, your legs—I'll dress you as you dressed *Thi*— and you can join him in oblivion!"

Astrid and Yafarra look into each other.

Quantum entanglement moves faster than light.

The speed of thought.

Astrid remembers these lines. Perhaps it was from a former Prof of hers that had said those words, or maybe it was she herself that scribbled the idea when trying to come to some scientific explanation to support her *Elliqui* research. The speed of a single thought can come and go as quickly like the throwing of a switch.

Yafarra's head lies upon her shoulder. Astrid turns to her. They have connected before. Astrid has seen The Silk. She sees it now.

Astrid is witness to a memory.

Quantum entanglement moves faster than light.

Astrid is standing in a round stone chamber. She recognizes it to be the very chamber below Tiris Avu at Wyn Avuqua—yet the torch flames are bright, the floor shines, the tapestries shine in bold yellows and golds.

Yafarra is there. Blood stains her steel breastplate and her cloak. Kneeling before her are four armored figures. Astrid recognizes their individual heraldry as the Wyn Avuquain Templar. The Heron.

Dust sifts down into the torchlit enclosure. The sounds of distant screams, the thunder of beating doors and marching feet echo against the stone walls.

The Fall of Wyn Avuqua.

Yafarra closes something into a box—into a tenesh. Something rectangular. Something red. Turning, she lowers the tenesh into a single crystal tomb behind her.

One of her Templar, House of Heart, says, "This cannot be."

The House of Talon's says, "They will not find this place. They will come to the door and find only a wall of stone in the dark. They will find nothing. . ."

"Where is Iteav?" The Queen asks.

House of Mind says, "The Lakewoman has taken him away."

Yafarra's face is a storm of fury and tears. "And Aethur? Is he away."

"He is, Lady," bows House of Wings.

"Then it is time to defend the House, my friends. Within the tomb the Prophecy shall be placed." She stares at the yawning sarcophagus and adds, "And so, too, shall I be placed."

The Templar cry out in opposition.

House of Mind protests, "My Queen, if we fail at the doors and the Library is not discovered, you will be trapped for eternity. There is no worse outcome—"

"And thus my punishment shall equal my sin," She tells them.

"What sin?" The House of Heart demands. "We were betrayed!"

"Nay!" House of Wings shouts above the others, "Nay, you cannot commit this. This is madness."

Yafarra listens and watches the Heron. She leans her sword against the tomb. She removes her greaves, her cloak and breastplate. After a few moments the Templar voices fall silent. They watch her slowly unclasp the gorget from her white throat. When she unties her gambeson and lets it fall to her feet, she raises her face.

When Astrid looks up there is no vaulted stone cathedral. All above are eyes. Tiny pinpricks of stars. Yafarra commands the Heron, "After you enclose me within, take my armor to the Avu. Then return, bid me farewell— and if the Heron survives this storm, come for me. But do not let them in. Do not tell the secret. I will defend the answer through eternity. The Prophecy leads to life—we cannot allow our children to bear our sins. We must save them. Gallina."

Heart and Wings arrange the bed. Mind and Talons raise her up and lay her down. Her sword they rest upon her breast. Each in turn touch their fingertips to her forehead.

Gallina.

Quantum entanglement moves faster than light.

"*Afa?*"

Cythe's sword rises from out of the scabbard. A short sword. Its sharp edge cuts the air. Heavy. Made to hack limbs from the body. A weapon made to send *Itonalya* to oblivion. Astrid's study of the weapon rises to the creature's eyes. Pupils like two green, whirling vortexes made to devour light. To end it.

"*Afa?* Mama?"

Yafarra's body tenses and her head raises up at the sound of the words on the air, "*Afa? Mama?*" She stretches, turning her face upward.

"Mama? Mama mia?"

The yearning and pained call pulls Astrid's attention to see a man standing at the top of the stairs. He says again, "*Afa?* Mama, mama mia?" in such a way that pierces Astrid's heart. He looks familiar to her suddenly. He is tall. Lanky. Orange, unruly hair. A face that is strangely structured. His lips are long and thin as if they were made of string. The shape of tears streak down his cheeks. Alessandro, she remembers. Alessandro the gondolier. Fausto's friend. He draws a rapier.

Cythe says, "George. George Eversman. What fortune. Today I not only take the mother—I shall also take the son."

"Mama?" George says heedless to the Devil's taunting.

"Iteav *gzate a thebre! a thebre!*" Yafarra cries. "Iteav! Iteav! Iteav!"

The Poet and His Immortals

November 16, this year
Venice, Italy
7:53 pm CEST

Loche takes Julia's hand. He turns his hooded face to her, "It's time," he says. "It is time to make an end of all of this." He leads her from the rear of the crowd into the circle of paintings and joins the armed immortals under the lights. In passing Loche notices the hazel eyes of Leonaie, the caring brown eyes of Corey Thomas, Athelstan's peculiar stance, Alice of Bath's round shape, and Adam Talansman's towering frame. And others he seems to recognize, too, despite their masks. He comes to a halt beside his father, William Greenhame. Facing the podium, Loche pulls back his hood. The *Itonalya* react almost simultaneously with fearful exhales of wonder seeing his choice of disguise: the *Ithicsazj*. The purplish-blue pallor of the face and the blood tear running along the cheek almost forces the immortals to take a step away from the Poet as if he were generating a spine tearing *Rathinalya*.

William pronounces to Lynn Eastman, "May I present the Poet, Aethur. My dear son, Loche Newirth. The Poet has come!"

Albion turns to Loche. His masked face cannot hide a sudden humility and willing obedience. "Mr. Newirth," he says bowing his head. "Ever have you ruled the pages upon which we appear. Make for us now an end to be told over and over again, until the world believes it was we that made it new."

Loche says, "Protect my brother's art. Protect the innocent. Protect each other. I have come to defend all you have done, all you will do and all they will say of you." Loche's sword slides from out of its umbrella casing. "Where is Marcus Rearden?"

From behind Eastman comes a familiar voice. "Good evening, Loche," Dr. Marcus Rearden says. "I think you may have lost control of your story."

The Bane of Immortality

November 16, this year
Venice, Italy
7:53 pm CEST

George Eversman's wiry frame snaps from the top of the stairs to Cythe like a flung rubber band. Yafarra wriggles forward onto her belly and reaches for the steps above her. Astrid rolls to one side to protect her, and tries to pull her upward. At the same time she reaches a hand down to Graham. His eyes are open. The guard he had tackled is now standing and hurling his baton at George Eversman. The guard misses his target. Graham grabs the man's ankle and trips him over the railing.

George falls upon the Devil and they cluster into an embrace. A moment later they tumble down to the base of the stairs. George pounds his fists into Cythe's chest and face, sending mists of blood into the air. Security guards join the fray to assist Cythe in restraining George's seemingly mindless ferocity. They wedge the two apart.

"The *Angofal* is mine," Cythe shouts climbing to his feet, "The *Chal* is mine and mine alone." The two guards let them free and cower back as if from the lashing of a whip.

George whirls away and stands. He glances up the stairs at his mother, then back to Nicholas. His expression is something Astrid cannot quite place. It is partly blank, partly halcyon. As Cythe raises his sword and dagger in preparation for George to attack, George stands with his arms at his side, his blade point down, and his head slightly tilted. He studies his opponent with thoughtful curiosity. One moment it seems as if he is indifferent and aloof, the next, he appears to be having a kind of revelation —a quickening. The brown pools of his eyes brighten.

"Come, Iteav," The Devil says. "The sea calls for your head. The sea hungers for the head of your mother. Let us feed it."

"Tell me, Cy," George says. "What happens after? What is there for us when we, the *Itonalya,* fall? When the sea takes us?"

A peculiar gleam flashes in Cythe's gyring irises as if the revelation of George had crossed between them. A tugging, troubling question.

"What will existence be without you, I wonder?" smiles George. Nicholas Cythe's mouth opens to respond but George cuts him off. "Oh, I know." George waits. He again traces from Cythe's feet to the top of his head. "I know, no more fear."

Astrid sees George move between two blinks. The speed is uncanny. He lunges forward on one leg, his body stretched out. She is certain she sees his sword swing from right to left in an elegant circle. But now, he is standing just as he was before: his arms at his sides, and his sword tip down. She blinks again.

Cythe's eyes are closed. The ghoulish green of his eyes is hidden. His head slips to the side and falls to his feet. His body follows.

George looks to the security guards. They back away and flee. One of them shouts into his radio, "Mr. Cythe is down. We need back up!" As they disappear down the hall, George grabs a handful of Cythe's hair, lifts his head and rushes up the stairs.

When he arrives at his mother's feet, he kneels and stares into her face. Astrid watches the reunion. She imagines wispy lines of spring green and ivory threads of light weaving and lacing together their memories, their sorrows, their years of pining for one another. The Silk, as Loche called it.

Yafarra sits forward and throws her arms around his neck. "Mama," George says. She cries and tells him: *My baby boy is alive. Forgive me. Forgive me.*

Astrid's eyes stream and blur watching. Graham's hand touches her knee. "When all of this is done, we must find some time to talk."

"You call it. I'm there," she says.

Graham leans toward her and touches his forehead to hers. He says, "I came for thee, for I heard you calling." He squeezes her tighter.

Yafarra continues to speak to her son in both Elliqui and English. She tells George, "You have killed the Devil—let us hope I have saved God."

A clamor of boots rushing toward them from the hall below silences the Queen. She looks up to Astrid and touches the Red Notebook. She says in perfect English, "Astrid—you must go. Go now. Run. Find Aethur! You must find Aethur." The landing below fills with ten or more security guards.

"Go, Astrid Finnley," George says. "Do as she says. Find The Poet."

Graham says, "We got this. Find Loche!"

Astrid kisses Graham's lips, rises, vaults up the stairs and rushes to the next staircase leading to the masquerade ball.

The Battle of the Masques

November 16, this year
Venice, Italy
8:01 pm CEST

"Gentlemen, gentle ladies," Marcus Rearden says to the twenty or more sword bearing immortals in the center of the ballroom. "You are frightening our witnesses." He speaks to the audience of revelers—many are still uncertain as to the drama unfolding before them, others are clustering and huddling together in fear. "Please, there is no reason to panic. The Board has assumed control. Many of you are quite cognizant of some of the fantastical elements to the endeavor before us, and some of you may still be nonbelievers. Nevertheless, I assure you, The Board and myself—the Human contingent—and, my dear peoples, you and your governments and companies will control Basil Fenn's work from this day forward, and we will also control," he points a finger, "Dr. Loche Newirth, Poet extraordinaire—the author of the play before you. What you are about to witness is the denouement—which I have taken great pains in crafting.

"There in the spotlight with swords in hand are the effigies of a bygone epoch no longer needed by us. The gods of old are dead, now, so too should the guardians of that Old Law, pass away. You are here to witness, for all of Humanity, the end of the ancient immortals."

To The Board soldiers Rearden says, "Bring me Newirth."

Loche reaches for Julia's hand. "I love you," he says.

She watches her fingers interlace with his. "I love you," she tells him.

Three handguns report to Loche's left. Three immortals drop.

"Close distance," William commands. "Take their firearms."

Like a spreading firework, the *Itonalya* explode outward and cut their way into the Board's ranks. Loche and Julia find each other's eyes just before their swords connect with their enemies. More gunfire echoes in the hall. Several pistols clatter to the wood floor. Many hands are still attached to them.

To Loche's right, William disarms two soldiers. Another Board soldier behind him fires a bullet through his chest. Albion, extends a steadying hand to William and thrusts his blade through the forearm of the shooter. He then kicks forward with his right leg and breaks the man's knee. William presses his hand to his wound and laughs companionably to Albion, "How I loathe firearms."

Two men roughly grasp Loche's shoulders. He feels another set of arms seize his throat. With a sidestep, Loche stabs one soldier. Julia's sword hacks across the face of the second. Loche twists his body and punches into the abdomen of the third. He breaks free. Julia is then pushed away, and the battle flows between them. She looks back. He reaches for her.

William is suddenly at his side. Pain is in his voice, but joy, too. "Son, we will win this battle." He points to another group of *Itonalya* entering the chamber from the eastern door. "But I believe the war shall be theirs. We are outnumbered." A stray sword juts toward his face but misses. He bats it away and dispatches its owner. "An escape has been planned—we can move many of Basil's works, but not all. After tonight, we will be forced to make a peace, or we shall forever be hunted."

Loche faces his father.

William nods over his son's shoulder. "Cut the head from the snake. For Edwin. For all of us. Show no mercy."

Turning, Loche can see Marcus Rearden on the other side of the paintings, maybe ten yards away across a storm of steel.

His old mentor's eyes are red with fury and he is trained on Loche. He carries a broadsword.

Loche pushes toward him.

But Rearden's ardent fixation is suddenly interrupted. Loche watches the man turn away from him and affix to something near the west exit. Standing alone beside the gothic arches leading to the canal is a woman wearing a disheveled burgundy gown. Her mask is dangling from its leather strap around her neck. Purple and black bruises crowd around her terrified eyes. She is staring at Rearden. In her hand is the Red Notebook.

She turns to the door, pulls it open and rushes out into the cold.

When Loche swivels back to Rearden, he sees the man bashing his way to the perimeter of the battle, running toward the exit in pursuit of the woman.

Loche finds Julia. She has already been watching him. "Go, Loche. End this!"

The Bridges

November 16, this year
Venice, Italy
8:19 pm CEST

Get some distance, she thinks. *Distance between you and that fucking bastard. Distance between the moments. Distance for some time to think. Find a place to hide. Hide out and make a plan. But where to run?*

Names rattle through her mind. Friends she had made in Venice over the years. If she could find a safe spot for an hour—a single precious hour—she could figure out what to do next. She could call Anthony—her painter friend she met on her last trip here. What about Fausto? Fausto would take her in. Can she remember the way?

She lost her high heels a long time ago. Her bare feet are numb. Each step causes the contusions on her face to throb. Yet, the icy November night is some comfort to the pain. The brisk air invigorates. It presses her onward.

Rearden saw her. She's certain of it. He will come after her. Without doubt. She runs through a gauntlet of low buildings until she reaches what looks to be a bridge. Pausing beside it she can see that it runs across the canal and connects to the Santa Maria Della Salute.

Her breath billows in heaves. *Think.*

Then she sees him. Rearden is sprinting up the causeway. His confident stride bounds toward her as if he knows exactly where she is.

Astrid bolts onto the bridge. She takes a handful of the fabric of her skirt and balls it into her fist so her legs might wheel without hinderance. Her lungs burn.

She hears him, "Astrid! Stop! I only want to talk with you!"

Astrid ignores him.

"Professor! Stop."

When she reaches the end of the bridge, she hazards a look back. Rearden is gaining.

She drops down off of the ramp and runs along the walkway around the southern end of the Salute. At her first opportunity she turns right. A few yards further she finds a door ajar. She bashes through it and slams it shut.

"There you are!" a familiar voice says.

Spinning around she sees Marcel Hruska.

"Jesus!" she exhales.

"Not the Messiah, no. Just me."

"Rearden—Rearden is—" she points—out of breath. "We've got to—got to—"

He holds up a key ring. "I lifted these from Fausto— getaway insurance. Come on. Out through the in door—let's go across the pyramid."

The metal door bangs open. Rearden rushes in and growls, "The Notebook, bitch!"

Marcel pounces and lands a fist to Rearden's chin. He throws another punch connecting with his stomach. Rearden bends forward with the blow and drops to his knees.

"Run, Professor. I've got this motherfucker!"

Astrid whirls her body toward the museum court and cuts through the archway toward the planter. Climbing, she looks back through the lamplight hoping to see Marcel. He does not come. A cry of pain screeches into the night.

The hated sound of Rearden's voice comes next. It echoes against the stone. "Astrid. . . Astrid. . . I will find you. I will find you. . ."

She hugs the Red Notebook to her chest and takes a step across the planter. She speaks the word, *lonwayro*.

Astrid Finnley leaves Venice.

The Planter #3

November 16, this year
Venice, Italy
8:37 pm CEST

As Loche runs down the ramp on the southern end of the bridge, he catches sight of Rearden just before he disappears to the right. He hears the distinct clang of a metal door slamming shut. He hurries toward it, but carefully, keeping his eyes on the several nooks and inlets in the high stone wall beside him.

Still some distance from where Rearden vanished, he hears a scream. His heart feels a jolt of electricity. He grips the handle of his sword tighter and advances. After another twenty yards, Loche finds a door. It is shut. A black, metal security grate is latched over its top. He places his hand on the latch and lifts it silently. The grate swings without a creak. He then turns the door nob and nudges the door open so he can peer inside.

He sees a body huddled on the cement, cradling what looks to be an injured arm. Loche pushes inside with his sword outstretched. The injured figure recoils. Loche notices a cloak and mask. But most notably, fire red hair.

"Who are you?" Loche demands.

The man tears his mask down to his throat. His eyes are a bright blue. "You're—you're wearing the death mask," he says.

"Who are you?" Loche says again.

"I'm Marcel Hruska," he answers. Loche shakes his head. The name does not register. "You're wearing the *Ithicsazj*— wait. . ." Marcel says wincing and pulling his arm tighter to his chest. "You're Loche Newirth. Dr. Loche Newirth."

"Your arm," Loche says, "are you alright?"

"It's broken—Rearden broke my arm."

"Rearden? Where is he?"

"You need to stop him, Dr. Newirth. He's after Professor Finnley. He's going to kill her. Please stop him," Marcel pleads.

"Where is he?"

Marcel's eyes point toward the museum courtyard. "The *omvide*! Please stop him."

Loche runs to the archway and crosses into the line of roman pillars that mark the perimeter of the ancient underground pyramid. The court is empty.

A second later, Loche is on top of the planter.

A second later he is squinting under a gravel-gray sky. His eyes sting beneath the flat daylight. Far down the ridge-line he can see a ruined city. Mud and vines claw over the half uncovered forms as if the earth was unwilling to let the sky see it. Excavation vehicles are parked near to the site. Loche knows the shape of the surrounding hills—he was just here—but that was a thousand years ago. From this very place he watched *Wyn Avuqua* burn in the distance. He watched the high towers fall. Now he sees the city of his imagination has been found.

There are no workers or archeologists. There are no people, save two. One is a woman in a burgundy dress carrying a red notebook about a half mile away. She runs along a carved path to the dig site. Not far behind her is Marcus Rearden. He carries a broadsword.

The Shadows Between the Bookshelves #2

November 16, this year
Upper Priest Lake, ID
11:54 am PST

"Have you any idea how long I can wait, Astrid? Any inkling at all? There is no other way out of the library. We both know that." Rearden walks to the stone, *Shtan* game table at the library entrance and sits. His fingers lift the black Heron head. He scrutinizes its heft and its elegant shape. "I won't be pursuing you into the shelves, my dear. I think it best that you join me here for some polite conversation. . ."

Astrid peers out from four, maybe five rows deep in the shelves. Work lights still illuminate the crystal tomb and the surrounding chamber. The tomb's cap is still clamped in the grip of the lifting machine. It hangs over the casket. Behind her, a few lamps light distant alcoves. But the rest of the library is dark. She has the advantage in here. She knows the labyrinth. She could lose him if he would only come in after her.

"What was her name, Astrid? Sofia, was it? Your daughter's name? What a shame to lose a child. And in such a way. . . a drowning. A drowning when mommy was not paying attention. When mommy was searching for something else.

"The official report was she was thrown from the bow of the boat—and you noticed too late. What a nightmare. What a horrible thing to carry. It must be maddening not having a place to put that grief, that anger. No one to blame. No one to blame but yourself."

"Fuck you!" Astrid screams through a storm of tears, "you evil fuck!"

"Tell me what is written in the Red Notebook," Rearden says, scanning the shelves and putting the *Shtan* piece down.

Astrid turns away and peers into the gloom behind her—seeking an escape—anything to stop the memories.

"You don't seem to understand what we might do, Professor Finnley. Loche Newirth may be the Poet, but we can author, too. We have seen it happen. We have witnessed time travel. We have witnessed history change. Think of it, Professor. Why could we not turn the hands of time back to change the unfortunate events of our past? Why can we not use Newirth to rewrite our past to make sense of our present place—to assuage our guilt—our transgressions? Reverse useless, pointless tragedy?"

She hears his feet move on the stone. Peering through the shelving she cannot locate him. She finds another viewing point. He is standing facing the shelves. His hands are out as if he were inviting her into his embrace.

"Astrid," he says, "you have chased the dead since the death of your daughter." He turns in a circle and gestures to the magnificent chamber and library of knowledge surrounding them. "I dare say, you have found death. Death all around us. The immortals will soon be no more—and the notions of gods, afterlife and their disastrous and dangerous tomes—their misguided systems of belief will be driven from the minds and hearts of all.

"We will write our own destinies. We will correct our wrongdoings. We may even bring our missing loved ones home.

"So tell me, Professor Astrid Finnley. What has Loche written in the Red Notebook?"

Far down one of the curving rows Astrid knows there is a heart embossed into the cold stone. She imagines placing her hand down into the tear shape. Her daughter Sofia would have loved to see the hearts.

Glass shatters. A thud of two heavy things colliding sends an involuntary jolt through Astrid. She peeks. Rearden has fallen face down and is not moving. Standing over him is a phantasmic, ghoulish horror. It wears the corpse blue death mask of *Wyn Avuqua*. The blood tear on its cheek is in the shape of rain.

Going In With Them

November 16, this year
Upper Priest Lake, ID
12:00 pm PST

Loche Newirth wants to pretend that what has happened is not real. He wishes he had seen it coming. He recalls his mentor, friend and fellow psychologist Marcus Rearden, telling him once: "When a client of yours takes his own life, you'll want to take your own. You'll believe that it was your fault. And I assure you, after that, there's no going back."

Loche lifts the stoneware urn from beside the entrance to the tomb chamber.

"Damn you, Marcus," he says quietly. "Damn you."

There are three fears that every psychologist will face at some point—*What if I can't help, handle, or I go in with them?*

Undeniable pleasure shoots up through Loche's legs into his stomach, into his entire circulatory system as the stone urn explodes against Marcus Rearden's cranium. The body falls like a wet rag.

Loche stops suddenly—squeezes his eyes shut—he breathes. He imagines a distant boat engine drone and fade away toward the thoroughfare—a cluster of birds scatter from the treetops above him—the water laps the shore. He can almost smell the winter breathing through the pines.

Loche cannot help his old friend Marcus Rearden. Loche cannot handle the grief—his baby boy Edwin—his baby boy Edwin. He cannot handle the fury. Loche will go in. Loche succumbs to madness.

He turns Rearden onto his back. He straddles his chest. His fists bash the head back and forth. It is wonderful. Almost beautiful.

The woman in the burgundy dress has appeared and is standing near.

She is watching.

She is speaking.

Loche cannot hear her.

He stops striking the face. He climbs to his feet, takes a grip of Rearden's ankles and begins dragging him to the center of the chamber.

Rearden moans. Loche laughs lightly.

Are you almost done with your book, Dad? Edwin's voice says.

"Almost there, Bug," Loche says. He kneels down beside the murderer of his son and watches the scars bubble and foam. Rearden's eyes open.

Dad, where do we go when we die?

"We go. . ." Loche starts, "we go to another place. Some call it Heaven."

Will you be at Heaven when I go there?

"Yes," Loche says, "Yes, I will find you there."

How do you know? How do you know you'll find me?

"Because I am The Poet. I will always find you."

Loche draws his sword. He lifts Rearden's right arm as if it were a fallen tree branch and extends it up. He then hacks the sword through the elbow and pulls the forearm away. Rearden's face appears to scream. Loche does not hear him. He tosses the grisly limb into the crystal casket. He glances up to find the woman in the burgundy dress. When he finds her, he stares. She has fallen to her knees. She is mouthing words and crying. She is waving a Red Notebook.

Loche stomps his foot down upon Rearden's rib cage four or five times. Lightening forks of pleasure stab through his senses. He positions one of Rearden's legs so he can remove a foot. With a roundhouse, baseball swing, Rearden's right foot separates from the ankle and flops to the floor a yard away. Loche retrieves it and tosses it into the crystal tomb.

The weight of Rearden's body minus an arm and a foot is surprisingly heavy. Stooping, Loche lifts the writhing flesh and bashes him down into the sarcophagus.

Little black dots of fatigue haunt Loche's periphery. He takes a breath. And that is when he sees an unexpected image.

Dangling before his eyes, there on a leather lace is an antique key. He studies it for a second. It confuses him. He touches his cheek and feels the hard surface of the *Ithicsazj*. He tears the mask off his face. He watches the key and lays his fingers upon his cheek again. The wet of Rearden's blood from his finger tips rouses him slightly. Sound unplugs and a menacing ringing forces his eyes shut.

When he can see again, the key is still hanging there. Behind the key is the face of Julia Iris. She is speaking.

"Loche," she cries. "No more. No more. It's over. Come back to me. I am with you. I will always be with you."

Loche turns and can now see the woman in the Burgundy dress—*what did Marcel say her name was? Astrid? Astrid Finnley?* Kneeling beside her is William Greenhame, and another man he does not recognize. He is very pale—and extremely long-limbed. One of his arms is wrapped around Astrid. His shoulder is bandaged.

"How long have you been here?" Loche asks Julia. Anger seething within him, "Rearden!" he hisses. He points at the mangled body. The white foam is working to bring him back.

Julia pulls Loche's chin to face her. Her eyes glisten. "Loche," she says, "Loche, read this." She lifts the Red Notebook.

Loche lowers his eyes to the open page. He reads what is written there.

The Hand of Yafarra

November 16, this year
Upper Priest Lake, ID
12:21 pm PST

Lowering the notebook, Loche Newirth crawls to Astrid. His face is smeared with Rearden's blood. Stained with the horror of vengeance. But beneath the scars of his fading madness, Astrid sees a man grasping for impossible answers—for a way to thank an indifferent universe for reversing its cruelty. Loche places his hand upon Astrid's cheek.

She says, "I'm Astrid Finnley," through gentle sobs.

"I am Loche Newirth. I am Aethur." he says. He hands the Red Notebook back to her.

The Poet stands and grasps the hand of his muse—Julia—and rushes out of the Queen's chamber.

Rearden moans. He spits Loche's name.

William Greenhame and Graham Cremo assist Astrid to her feet.

Peering over the edge and into the sarcophagus she can see Rearden working out his next move. He has maneuvered his severed limb into a position to rejoin. His leg is wriggling in search of the detached foot.

He sees Astrid's face hovering over him, notices that she is not alone and recognizes William Greenhame and Graham. Fear glazes his eyes.

Astrid flips the Red Notebook open and holds it over Rearden's face. She says, "Loche didn't write a word of this. . ." she tells him. "It is in the hand of a woman that saved God and rewrote history."

Confusion bleeds into Rearden's face.

"Read it. Read it and know that you failed."
She forces the book into his face like a weapon.

Aethur—
I will exchange my child for yours.
I will sacrifice my Iteav to save the life of Thi,
        the life of your son, Edwin.
He is alive, Aethur. Your son lives.
He is with his mother where your ink bled us all to life.
Go with light, Poet.
Go with light.

Astrid drops the notebook onto Rearden's face and nods to the massive stone cap dangling on its steel cables above the tomb. She says to William and Graham, "Let's put a lid on it."

Where the Ink Bled

November 16, this year
Upper Priest Lake, ID
1:10 pm PST

Loche Newirth and Julia Iris crash through the brush along the lakeshore. Loche stumbles and falls. Julia pulls him up and steadies him. This happens several times. Loche has thrown off his *Wyn Avuquain* cloak. He feels various injuries pounding through his body as he runs. He does not feel the gashes on his knees, but he sees the blood. Sharp slashing branches scratch his face. A few more steps—another crash upon the stones.

They ford the cold water of the thoroughfare at a shallow point. They run the trail leading toward the dike.

The cabin comes into view, smoke rising from the chimney. The two stop and stare.

"You go," Julia says. "You go. I'll be right here. This is—this is—" she kisses his lips. "This is really happening."

Loche smiles.

A moment later he is on the landing. He turns the handle and enters.

Books are scattered, on the table, on the bed, stacked on the kitchen counters—most of them mythological texts: Irish, Egyptian, Sumerian, Greek. Many are open with curious notes scrawled in the margins. Pages are ripped out and are tacked to the log walls. A huge map of northern Italy is laid out on the kitchen floor with more messy scribbles. There are long rows of yellow Post-it notes stuck on the wall. They stretch around the room from corner to corner, many times over. On them are names, dates, and events—all written in his hand. He tugs one down. It reads:

Lie to reveal. Lie to reveal the truth.

Another:

Basil Fenn. Artist—keeps his paintings secret. Refuses to show them. The few that have seen his paintings, have been hurt. Wounded. Killed. Gods look through them to see us. Gods look through.

Loche shakes his head. The room whirls suddenly and he pushes his palm to the wall to steady himself. His focus anchors to another note:

What is made up is real. What is real is made up.

He looks out the picture window. The glass is streaked with thin red paint strokes. He catches his reflection in the glass. The cuts on his face and forehead suddenly become more painful. Mud is smeared across his cheek and chin. But the face in the reflection is his: carved angles, grey, thoughtful eyes and short, light brown hair.

The bedroom door opens. Edwin Newirth rushes out, "Daddy," he sings.

Loche drops to his knees and the two latch together. Helen appears in the shadow of the bedroom. "Where have you been? What took you so long?"

The scent of his little boy's sleepy skin—his freshly shampooed hair—his little feet—the sound of his voice.

"Pancakes," he says. "Pancakes."

Loche lifts him into his arms and carries him outside onto the deck. The grey shoulders of the sky are breaking. A clear hole has opened like a flood of blue water.

"Julia?" he calls. He peers into the trees searching for his muse. He feels a smile forming on his lips. "Pancakes?"

Epilogue

(Summer, a year and a half later)

"Friends, what have we learned from the story we have just been told? Is it true? Did it really happen? Does it mean a Hereafter exists? Is there a race of Immortals living among you, quietly guiding the world toward another evolutionary step? Look around. We stand within the Queen's Chamber at *Tiris Avu, Wyn Avuqua. Wyn Avuqua.* The city that was once a fiction, its architecture a string of words and imaginings scribbled into an ancient tome or a whispered tale to children before they drifted off to sleep and dreams has now clawed its way out of the mud and the past. It now rises around us. Its walls, doors and gateways, its sculptures, its banners caught in the evening breeze, its secret passages, great halls and libraries—its ghosts. Can you hear them?"

William Greenhame lifts his open hand and dramatically cups it behind his ear in a gesture of listening. He leans toward the audience as if to hear a secret. The room is silent. William is posed atop the sealed crystal tomb in the massive round chamber beneath the citadel. He wears a white billowy sleeved Elizabethan poet's shirt. His knee high boots are brown. A swept hilt rapier hangs at his side. He is addressing roughly seventy VIPs—the first to experience the *Wyn Avuquain* Complex and Museum before its official grand opening tomorrow. They have spent the day exploring and visiting each attraction. The last stop is the lower Heron Atheneum which William is about to unveil.

"Shhh," William hushes gently. "I can hear the voices say, 'The past changes behind us just as the future will change the present. They both move. They both breathe.'" William's presentation is compelling and delightfully entertaining. Some in the audience actually tilt their heads as if straining to hear a ghost sharing its heart.

"He's good," Astrid Finnley whispers, smiling.

"I think he's found his calling," Loche agrees. "He'll get

the job, I hope."

Astrid chuckles quietly. "Are you kidding? He asked if he could sign a hundred year contract."

William's loud and sonorous stage voice startles the audience out of their enchanted state. "Behold!" he pronounces. At that moment, dazzling theatrical lighting illuminates two towering wooden doors behind William. They are closed. Their long hinges are gold and they coil across the door like filigreed vines.

"Behind these doors, friends, are the truths we have been longing to know, alternatives to the old narratives—new beliefs to believe."

William raises an old iron key. His eyes lower down to his grandson a few paces away, standing in front of his father. The boy holds a wooden sword souvenir from the museum. On the blade *Wyn Avuqua* is embossed in elegant calligraphy. "Edwin Newirth, will you help me? Take this key and place it into the lock? Will you unlock the new Earth?"

Edwin steps forward then looks to his dad. Loche nods and smiles. William presses the key into the boy's little hand. "Take this key and place it into the lock." He moves to the door, inserts the key and twists the gears. The latch mechanism clicks. He grasps the iron handle and pulls. Light floods out of the doorway into the circular chamber. The crystal coffin glows white.

The audience lets out a collective gasp. The ancient bookshelves wind and curve back into the warmly lit library.

"Come," William says leaping down from the tomb, taking hold of Edwin's hand and leading the way. "Come, my friends. Within are more Good Books than you can imagine."

The astonished audience follows after him. Before William and Edwin turn into the first curve in the Talons section, they look back and catch Loche's eyes. Edwin raises his wooden sword. William waves, smiles, then turns his attention back to his guests and says, "What a wonder stories are. It is all we are."

Loche feels Julia squeeze his hand. He turns and kisses

her cheek.

Astrid watches the couple for a moment. Across the room she can see Graham speaking with his friend Mal and Marcel Hruska.

As the last of the VIPs enter into the Atheneum, Astrid says, "Do you two have a moment?"

"Of course," Loche says.

Astrid leads them to the stone *Shtan* table. They sit.

"Can you believe it has been a year?"

Loche shakes his head. "Time plays tricks."

Astrid nods. "We've done it."

"You've done it," Julia says. "The park is amazing, Astrid. It will change the world."

"Thanks," she says modestly. "I hope it makes a difference."

"Are you sad to miss the grand opening tomorrow?" Julia asks.

"Today's soft opening is enough for me. But Venice calls. Exciting stuff on the horizon. I meet with Helen and Albion on Thursday morning," Astrid says.

"What time is your flight?" Julia asks.

"Early. Way too early."

Julia says, "It's a shame you can't cross the *omvide*."

Astrid nods. "Yes. I'm grateful that I at least got the chance to experience it when they functioned."

"Venice," Julia sighs. "I wish we were going with you."

"We'll be working for most of our time there, I'm afraid." She gestures to Graham, "We're hoping that afterward we might visit Monterosso for a few days and drink wine. George Eversman invited us."

Loche feels a tug at his heart. He can almost smell George's homemade pesto.

Astrid looks down at the table and pauses. She lifts the wings *Shtan* piece. "It's like you said it would be, Loche," she says.

"What's that?" Loche asks.

"They've done it."

Loche nods, "Yes. Incredible. How long before the trials start?"

"They have a group of one hundred people ready to receive the treatment. It is truly amazing. Graham, myself and Leonaie Echelle are meeting with Albion and The Board to discuss their new goal set and the education the recipients are to receive. Immortal Education 101," she chuckles.

"They aren't going to call it that, are they?" Julia asks.

Astrid smiles, "No. But Leonaie is lobbying to title the courses, Lifeson Studies. The treatment for the recipients has a name now. They are calling it the Lornensha Treatment."

"Interesting," Loche says.

"The story about how Lornensha saved the life of Iteav— George—and her leaves that brought us the *Melgia* Gene. Good reasons for the title they thought. Lornensha, the healer."

Loche nods.

"I think it's perfect," Julia says.

"Yes," Astrid says. "To think that immortality will be ubiquitous. We have conquered death." She then turns slightly toward the centerpiece of the chamber—the coffin. "We must change to accept it," she adds quietly. "If only we could make the Earth immortal."

Loche's attention strays to the crystal coffin. He imagines a faint shadow wriggling within. A moving stain in the ice.

Astrid, too, stares darkly at the sarcophagus. She asks hesitantly, "Do you agree with George about freeing Rearden when the time is right?" Loche does not answer. She shakes her head and sets the wings *Shtan* piece back onto the board. "Yafarra says that Rearden will face his demons in there, and when he comes out, if he comes out, he'll be changed."

Loche is not so sure. His heartbeat accelerates. The memory of blood—the sound of Rearden's screams—the horror in his mentor's face as Loche cut him limb from limb. *What is this story?* Loche rises abruptly. He walks across the chamber and stares into the icy glass. He says quietly, "Can you hear me,

Marcus? The cure, Marcus. How do I heal? How do we heal?"

Julia is suddenly at his side. Her fingertips graze along his neck. He feels her warmth. She says nothing. Reaching for his hand she interlaces her fingers with his and pulls him toward the stair leading out into the sunlight.

The End

AFTERWORD

LATE WINTER
Tying Things Up

Boy, there are a lot of things to tie up.

In a corner of this empty living room I have peeled back the carpet to reveal another layer of carpet. Getting my fingernails beneath it, I pull and discover yet another layer—a spectacular circa 1973 olive green and orange over white crotchet pattern. I can feel my eyes widen. I like the look of it. I don't know why Farah Fawcett, The Fonz and my mom's date bars come to mind (likely Sunday evenings when I was a kid, lying on the basement floor watching TV with my brother). The memories are dashed, for as I pull now on this bottom layer I quickly learn it has been glued down. Taking a firm grip of the triangle of carpet layers, I pull and my legs push. Staples snap, the backing rips and the wall trim splinters. A thick tar-like residue remains adhered to the floor like a black foamy sticker. And cat. Oh yes, cat—you know the stench. The house hears my first string of heated profanity—something about wanting to meet the bastard that thought gluing was a good idea—I suggested plagues upon him—upon his own house—et cetera. A few minutes later I am scraping the tar. I find the floor. Douglas fir, aged wood floors. Scarred, stained—perfect. But this is going to take some time.

The carpet's stains, the cat piss, the furniture crop circles read like a diary of the house. How many memories, footsteps, wine spills, nervous, hundred-turn paces happened on this floor? How many pitter-patter sprints to the Christmas tree? How many wrestling matches?

I lay back, stare at the ceiling and whimper, "Boy, there are a lot of things to tie up."

It is another story altogether to explain why I am lying here on three layers of carpet in a house that was built in 1910. A house my son and I have just purchased. Another story entirely to explore the shocking and unexpected turns of matrimony and how it breaks. Another tale for another time to discuss the better part of the dark three years that have knocked me down on this overly cushioned, mattress-like floor. And, I think, if I stay down here, where its dark, I'll stay here—so I sit up, I climb to my feet, I put my hands on my hips and I say to the house, "Alright, my darling, be that way. I'll have your coverings. There are new memories to make. Out with the old—in with the new. Let's get on with it. Boy, there are a lot of things to tie up."

Why do I keep saying that? *Boy, there are a lot of things to tie up.* Probably because during all the monumental shifts in my world over the last few years, I've been in the process of writing the third and final book of a rather involved trilogy. The story was seeded sometime around 1996 and has since crowded my daily thoughts, my journals, countless conversations and, I'm thrilled to include now, it has inserted itself into a relatively notable number of readers. And it has been remarked by many that the Newirth Mythology is, thankfully, not spoon-fed fiction, but rather, "Thoughtfully complex and meticulous with plenty of unexpected pathos." (I didn't write that, someone else did.) Aside from the story's penchant for a cliffhanger or two—or three, there's the occasional unresolved philosophical meandering (for instance the heavyweight "why am I here" puzzlers), and never mind the time jumps from a witches pyre in the 14th Century, to an evening with Led Zeppelin's Jimmy Page, to a psychologist's journey across an ocean of death to what some may name the place where artistic inspiration is birthed and others, the Afterlife. Bearing all of this in mind, my publisher, Andreas, Dad, my friend Scott, my editor, Allison, the very nice gal at Safeway, nearly every fan I've met at signings, almost every person that knows I'm working on the last book of a trilogy has, in one way or another, expressed, in no uncertain terms, a kind of proclamation or unchallengeable edict from deep within the collective knowledge of spun yarns, for don't we all know a story or two ourselves—and by God, we all know that stories should end a certain way. They have all said regarding my not yet released, third and final installment: "No pressure. But, boy, there are a lot of things to tie up."

Other reader comments include—this one is my personal favorite, "How does it end?" That's a toughie to answer. Second place is, "Do you know how it will end?" I typically shake my head gesturing no while I say, "Yes, of course." And coming in third, but not necessarily last, "What's it like putting a book together? Because, hell, there must be a lot of things to tie up." Sometimes I think I just might have the right energy and vocabulary to effectively answer. Certainly I've been doing this long enough to at least offer my particular method and process when it comes to creating a long piece of fiction. For example, I might talk about how most of the story develops out of simply doing the work, staying at the desk and writing it. I might discuss themes and plot and character development, et cetera. But in the end, endings and knowing how to put together a book has mostly to do with, well, you've likely guessed: tying a lot of things up. Into a neat little package— with a bow, no less.

Meanwhile, I make lists for the house: paint (hobbit colors: burnt umber, yellow ochre, autumn leaf crimson), brushes and scrapers, electrical tape, masking tape, work gloves. Call on new furnace. Call a flooring company. Make a dump run. Fix the ceiling fan, the back door hinge, the leak in the kitchen, the broken railing, the rotted porch steps. Create a room to sleep in. A room for Michael my son to sleep in. Make a home.

I crimp my eyes shut after a few hours of demoing a water damaged bathroom floor and keep reminding myself: the house is scarred, stained and perfect. I take a break from hacking out the bathroom floor and survey the rest of the house to determine the right position for a temporary writing desk. It isn't long before I fully understand that I can only do one thing at a time. One foot and then the next.

Daylight slips into evening. I pour a scotch. Dusty and tired I sit on the porch and watch a violet sky fade into purple.

In the morning I wrestle a desk into a corner, open my laptop to the where-I-left-off-place and turn to the kitchen to brew coffee. The wreckage of my life crowds around me—boxes and boxes of books, LPs, a turntable, two drum kits in cases and art supplies. A bag of tools sits beside a massive pile of old, stinking carpet.

I think of the trilogy's main character, psychologist and writer, Loche Newirth, and his horrible plight. How the stories he has written—his works of fiction have become real, and they are destroying not just the lives of those surrounding him, but worse, eliminating the promise or chance of life after death. I recall thinking early on about worst case scenarios for my story, and how I wanted to do something I'd never seen done before. Typically, the worst case scenario for one's characters is, well, death. Imagine it: the gun is held to the captive's head, the bad guy says, "Don't take another step or else" So, now we've got some tension, right? Death and its permanence—and we all agree to define that as bad. Well, for the Newirth Mythology, I wanted death to be a scenario, but certainly not the worst case. Instead, I put into harm's way the hope of an Afterlife. The destruction of what some might call Heaven. It took some doing. First, you need to provide some plausibility that an Afterlife truly exists outside of mythology, outside of the hearsay, "I saw the light" stories, and the old, "There's an afterlife because, well, it would be stupid if there weren't." Then you need to surround the Afterlife with potential killers, put a gun to Heaven's head and say, "Take one more step and the Afterlife gets it," and so on. Needless to say, Loche is in a bad way. And so is everyone else. You too, I expect, if you happen to be hoping there is a place waiting for you beyond this life

SPRING
Supernatural Trickery

"Let me make this perfectly, abundantly (add more adverbs here), clear— I do not believe in the supernatural.

I do not believe in ghosts, hauntings, or what the Immortals in my story would call Bridging Spirits or Bridgers, or *Godrethion.*

I do not believe in gods, prophets or messiahs.

I do not believe in planet position personality predictions, augury lifted from out of palm wrinkles, nor foretelling from flipping a few cards.

Neither do I hold faith in McKenna mystic psychonauts, meditation, shamanism, yoga, crystals, essential oils, new age manifestation, Hicks existential high vibrational gonna-get-it-done-now-to-find-fucking-meaning spiritualism."

I share these personal laws aloud one late, rainy afternoon in May as I witness my new bedroom door close entirely by itself, accompanied by a Stokerian hinge creak—a groaning, longing, spine scraping, torture chamber creak— the kind the vampires of Transylvania pay high dollar (or lay) to have installed. I stare at the door in mid stride with a bucket of paint hanging from one hand, and in the other, a raised hammer. I wait for the gooseflesh to smooth out—my breathing to slow—my eyes to find the reasonable answer.

I tick through logic. Wind? No, there's no wind inside. The heat is off. I bumped it when I passed? No, I am on the other side of the house—and have not been to the bedroom in hours. My heavy footfalls perhaps? I say aloud, "It must be. . ." and I drop off. I try again—my inflection rising questioningly, "The explanation is easy Scoob—the door opened because— the weight— of the— tri layered— carpet—being gone—has allowed the foundation— to settle— a little ——bit."

I open the door, press it to the wall and place a doorstop at its base.

After this, I begin talking to the house in earnest.

I place a book or two upon a shelf. I say, "Hello, House. I'm placing a book up here." The last piles of cruddy carpet I heft into a dump pile outside. I say, "House, I'm cleaning up your floor. Making room for new memories." All the baseboard trim has been removed for the painters coming tomorrow. "House," I smile, "new clothes tomorrow." I startle at another sound. Hail clatters on the porch and the metal roof. I listen carefully to make sure it is not a chain being dragged from room to room upstairs. After some time with my head tilted ceiling-ward, I'm still unsure.

Later, at my desk, I try cleaning up a few paragraphs from the day before. I stack words into new sentences. Tools and dust and bent nails and sandpaper, clutter the corners of the room around me. Ignoring the chaos, I secretly wish the bedroom door, there on the other side of the dark living room would yawn and creak closed again. Loche Newirth would love for that to happen. But then, I think, with all he's been through now, Loche might likely use a scary groaning door as a sleep aid.

Part Three, The Shape of Rain has its share of supernatural bumps in the night, or to be more accurate, bumps in the mind. If *Part One, The Invasion of Heaven* dealt with the power of stories and the transforming influence of myth upon beliefs and behaviors, *Part Two* tells of the repercussions of said beliefs—murder, assassinations, the descent into the maelstrom of madness. These stories tell of supernatural lovers. Betrayals. Of trespassing gods upon the Earth and an Order of guardian Immortals sworn to send them back across the threshold of death —and all of this, created and penned by the main character, a conservative psychologist and non-theist, Loche Newirth, whose writing has altered the course of history, and his catalogue of created characters are all now living and plotting to interfere with our mythical beliefs of afterlife, our notions of gods, and the hope that our lives in some way, matter—*Part Three, The Shape of Rain*, wrestles with it all. Each day I have errands within the narrative. Lines to follow. Plans to see through. Each day there is seemingly something new. I move my characters through the paranormal while they struggle to see through their new lenses of reality.

SUMMER
The Burrow

My son and I have given the house a name. We call it The Burrow after JK Rowling's description of Ron Weasley's house in the Harry Potter series. A house, she wrote, "that looked like it was held up by magic." In the center of our Burrow is a staircase that coils its way up to four small, almost hobbit-sized bedrooms, each meeting at the stair landing. It feels like a fort, as Michael describes it, "Like Ron Weasley's fort. . ." Thus, we call it the Burrow.

But long before the name The Burrow caught on, I wanted the interior of the house to match what I imagined Bilbo Baggins's home, Bag End, would look like. Now the walls are painted a parchment yellow. The old-world wood trim around the doors I have stained to a rich mahogany. And the floors? Did I mention the floors? After cleaning, sanding, a few repairs, and swathing an oil color stain somewhere between burnt sienna and chocolate, the hardwood patina turned out better than I could have imagined. These are Bilbo's floors. This is the floor of an Irish pub (only slightly cleaner). And now when I rise in the mornings, the entire house glows amber and gold. There's hand made crockery in the kitchen, and swords in the hall, and medieval maps on the walls, and candles. Quill and ink on the desk, and old books on the shelves. And tucked away in a room near the back is a desk lit with a single lamp. Four coffee cups, two empty, two half full, stand guard around an open lap top.

It seems the more I find the proper places for things, I find more places that need filling. A lonely corner of the living room is without a lamp. The empty walls up the staircase need framed pictures of Sheree, Auntie Jo, Auntie Mel, Uncle Stan, Shakespeare, Buttercup and the Man in Black, Jeff Spicoli, a picture of my band mates Cris and Cary, Scott and Mark.

Then, at the same time, I feel as if I have too many things, (or better stated, too much shit). The pack-rat genetic trait has been firmly lodged in my DNA. My father's voice, "You never know when you'll need—" insert peculiar metal rod that's been leaning in the corner for twenty years, or bag of old coat hangers or the weird tool that does that thing that you found with the stuff that you got from that guy that time when you needed that thing. . . you know, that thing. Why do I continue to haul around this Barry Manilow record? Why do I keep T-shirts that are over thirty years old when I don't wear them? And while these questions deserve consideration, all I can think of is, where in the hell do I place the T-shirts, the Barry Manilow record, the coat hangers and that thing I got from the guy with the stuff that time. For some reason, all of it needs to stay.

Head scratcher. . . head scratcher, indeed.

Michael has left a wooden sword leaning just beside my desk. It is in my best interest to pick it up when I rise to refill my coffee cup, lest I am defenseless against an imminent attack. Outside, the backyard is shaded beneath the canopy of a walnut tree. Moving patterns of electric blue sky wink between the leaves. It is hot. Michael and I should be at the beach, but there's a book that needs to get written. There is so much to do. So much to tie up.

The messy baggage of the roommates of my mind. . . these characters of mine. I have shared the very small place that is my head with Loche, and Basil, and William Greenhame, and Albion, and Julia, and Helen for over twenty years now. Their stuff is scattered everywhere. I have Loche's earliest thoughts, Basil's first paintings, William's history drawn from countless sources. There are so many pieces and parts that I have decided to include an appendices at the end of this final installment, *The Shape of Rain.* Call it excessive. Call it Tolkienesque. Call it what you want. All I know is—these things need a place. They need to stay.

In order to begin telling Loche's story it was necessary for me to complete the back history of the *Wyn Avuquain* Immortal race, their belief systems and their heritage. At the same time it enabled me to offer the Pacific Inland Northwest of the United States a mythology of its own. Included in the appendices are maps, character lists, historical timelines, treatises on Immortal culture, charts outlining the *Itonalya* influence upon astrology as we know it, rules for the game of *Shtan*, and various definitions and footnotes.

Also, I've made room for a few of the earliest *Itonalya* folk tales—for example the Lay of *Melithion* and *Endale* which tells of the love story between the Earth and her guardian, the Moon.

The final section of the appendices is dedicated to the *Itonalya* language, *Elliqui*. Included are usage rules, grammar, pronunciation tables, letter and tone charts along with both English to *Elliqui* and *Elliqui* to English dictionaries. The effort is a culmination of work that I began, I think I can safely say, when I was fourteen. Since then, the language has grown considerably in both its depth and sophistication. But in the last decade the lexicon has taken on a life of its own. Words have begun to link larger meanings—metaphorical if not etymological.

FALL
Scarred, Stained and Perfect

The sun's light slants and adds a little extra shadow to everything. Trees along the street explode into reds and golds. Mornings are brisk. Frost on my windshield.

Days roll together as I face the final few chapters not yet written. I rise before Michael to make his lunch. I brew coffee. I wake the boy and we wrestle into clothes, brush hair and teeth, and on the way to school discuss the finer points of swordplay, dragon culture, why leaves turn colors. When I return, I notice how the house looks more like a home. I've managed to pull together some furniture. There's art on the walls. There are coats hung on pegs, clothes in the closets and things placed where things should be placed. At least for now.

Truth is, I don't have any idea how to do this whole house/home thing. I don't really understand how my furnace works, or how to fix a sink or if the sofa is really in the right place. And this thought occurs to me: there will always be loose ends. Each year, the leaves will pile up and they will need to be raked. The washer and dryer will break down. We'll change the paintings on the walls and swap out the pictures on the shelves.

There's no end to what we'll do here. Things will always be a little scarred, stained— and perfect.

I settle in behind my desk, scan emails, put fires out, then I fill the screens with the book. I read, edit, work a few sentences. I stand and pace. The coffee is bitter. I try a thread, pull it through the fabric of the story. It tangles an hour later—I pull it out—cut it—try another. Sometimes I move the story forward: Astrid Finnley to Venice—Loche through the gates of *Wyn Avuqua* in the year 1010AD. Fausto's shop. Hours pass.

Truth is, I don't have any idea how this book will end— not until I arrive there. Rain taps at the roof. In the back of the house I think I hear the bedroom door creak ever so slightly. The thought occurs to me that I've been listening to that recording voices saying, "Boy, there's a lot of things to tie up," over and over since I began *Part Three*, and now I suddenly question if this vein of logic is true. Do all stories have to end neat and tidy, wrapped with a bow? How tidy is a life after all? And how beautiful is the ragged hem that is our story? A rage and defiance rises up within me. Embrace the unexpected, and what is natural. Don't over think. Let go and accept the chaos—take the non novel path—as in life, so too it is in fiction. "Yes!" I tell the Burrow. "Yes!" I shout at the lines of text on the screen. Maybe it is not about tying it all together, but rather, unraveling it—to find what is inside. Pull back layers. Find the floor.

When Michael bounds up to my desk with sword in hand, "Are you done yet, Dad? How does it end?" now for the first time since I began, I truly believe I have an answer for him. "Dad, how does it end?"

I tell him, "It ends scarred, stained and perfect."

APPENDICES

With the recent discovery of historic *Wyn Avuqua* and its vast underground libraries of lore and history, the following collected material for this appendices, in comparison, will likely one day be seen as trivial, if not erroneous. However, until scholars deliver their findings from the Heron Atheneums, this material is meant to provide readers of *The Newirth Mythology* access to some of the available background and foundations of *Itonalya* culture in order to fill in and enrich Loche's story. All the following information has been mined from three sources: the writings of Loche Newirth, the research of Dr. Astrid Finnley, and the *Toele* from Albion Ravistelle's collection.

The enigmatic, supernatural writing of Loche Newirth and its effect on existence is questionably a problematic and delicate subject: a riddle not for the faint of heart (nor the impatient thinker). In an attempt to solve the riddle of Loche Newirth's work, I have tried to learn as much as possible about his life and his art. Like his brother Basil Fenn, Loche kept his art secret. However, prior to writing *Part One, The Invasion of Heaven*, I was granted access to his collected notebooks and journals, most of which were recovered from Albion Ravistelle's Venetian compound—and others that were still secure, deftly hidden by Loche himself within his modern castle in Sagle, Idaho. Numbering in the hundreds, some novel length, some only a few pages of scrawled notes and sketches, the books contain much concerning *Itonalya* history, linguistics and life stories of individual immortals living in different time periods and places all over the globe. There are several notebooks dedicated solely to Loche's poems, while others were filled with maps, *Wyn Avuquain* heraldry and cultural mores. Even the *Itonalya* game of *Shtan* was contained within its own set of booklets. The Newirth canon was, of course, captured by Albion Ravistelle (a character he created—certainly one of many freakish happenings—see the first sentence of this paragraph). The work was purportedly studied by Albion, Dr. Marcus Rearden, and a few others in the course of events told in *The Newirth Mythology*. The Newirth canon, however, must be distinguished from the supernatural volume he produced known as *The Journal* or *The Priest Lake Journal*.

Photo courtesy of Allison Bogart from *The Newirth Artifacts*[1], ©2017
The Journal of Loche Newirth (The Priest Lake Journal)
From the Albion Ravistelle Collection, Venezia, Italy.

By having access to this powerful work along with the rest of the Newirth canon, I managed to thread together a humble string of novels (*The Newirth Mythology*) to share Dr. Newirth's tale, or, more accurately, to tell what was most important to him: a story about stories. But to this day, the effect of his words and how they have shaped reality is still perplexing—the lie awake at night kind of perplexing (again, see the first sentence to this paragraph).

After months of pouring over Loche's poetry, histories and early *Elliqui* linguistics, all written prior to *The Journal*, I

---

[1]   Allison Bogart. (2017). *The Newirth Artifacts*. New York: Italic Semicolon Publishing.

realized that I was searching for a kind of cypher—some key to the mystery that is Loche Newirth. It wasn't until I finished *Part Three, The Shape of Rain* that the cypher appeared: Professor Astrid Finnley.

For a brief time it was believed that Loche's canon and *The Journal* were the sole sources for *Itonalya* history—but soon after Dr. Marcus Rearden (to whom the work was dedicated) read *The Journal,* books on the subjects of *Wyn Avuqua*, lost immortal civilizations and *Elliqui* suddenly appeared in the market place. Stranger still, these subjects seemed to insert themselves into the consciousness and memory of a vast human (and immortal) collective—as if some vague knowledge of *Wyn Avuqua* has always been there—like Atlantis or Delphi. Largely regarded as pseudo-history, *Itonalya* myth found a group of impassioned voices. Over time enthusiasts began to uncover evidence and artifacts. Findings led to reports, reports to books, websites, et cetera. The search for the lost city of *Wyn Avuqua* captured the fascination of fringe writers as well as conspiracy theorists.

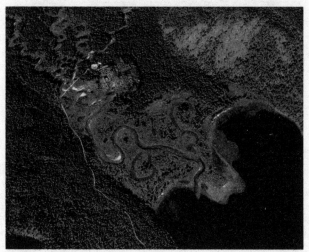

Photo courtesy of Jones, Johnston and Fryless (JJF) Helicopter Service, LTD. Dig site at *Wyn Avuqua*, 2018. Upper Priest Lake, Idaho. USA.

It also attracted the talent of serious academics like Professor Astrid Finnley. Her early work has been published in over thirty countries and translated into twenty-five languages. Nearly all of her work has been centered on ancient myth (Greek, Roman, Sumerian, Celtic) and how those historic narratives still inform our current technological age. Dr. Finnley claims that she first learned about the *Wyn Avuquain* immortals when she was a girl and she did not take any of the stories seriously until she uncovered an *Elliqui* scroll during an archeological dig in Germany in 1992. Since then she has written three books on *Itonalya* culture.[2] A portion of this appendices is drawn from Dr. Finnley's thoughtful work.

Finally, the *Toele* (ancient story) has become known as the holy grail of *Itonalya* literature. Of course, that distinction has since been undercut by the incredible wealth of *Itonalya* lore recently uncovered within the Heron Atheneum at Priest Lake, Idaho.

Photo courtesy of Allison Bogart from *The Newirth Artifacts,* ©2017
Itonalya Toele #2
From the William H. Greenhame collection. The Burrow Museum, Cd'A, ID.

Nevertheless, for centuries it was rumored there were only two

[2] Professor Finnley's works:
Finnley, Astrid. (1994). *The Tear of Heaven:Lost Cities of the World and Why We Lost Them.* Seattle: Will Dreamly Arts Publishing.
Finnley, Astrid. (2002). *The Twin Toele: Immortals Among Us. Spokane.* Kite House Publishing.
Finnley, Astrid. (2008). Elliqui: *The Silent Foundation of God.* Seattle. The RUB Publishers.

surviving texts from the fallen city. Albion Ravistelle's coveted *Toele* came into his possession when he lived in London around 1300. Albion claims Eloise Smith (Alice of Bath) came upon the book during her overseas pilgrimages. According to Albion, Eloise would not divulge where or how she attained the book. The other *Toele* and its whereabouts have been unknown until now. After the entombment of Dr. Marcus Rearden, and the reconciliation between the *Orathom Wis* and Albion Ravistelle, the second *Toele* was revealed to be in the possession of William Greenhame. William claims that the book was willed to him in 1531 by his dear friend, the Immortal, Redairic Cedars. The story in brief: because Redairic failed to host a long-awaited and promised celebration, three disgruntled (rightfully so) and insidious revelers from the North brought their deadly grievance and challenge to Redairic's house. Redairic and all of his followers were killed in the quarrel. Ironically, a year later, Redairic's *Toele* was bequeathed to William at the party Redairic was meant to host.

The information contained in the *Toele* is extensive. I have included here mere seedlings that are pertinent and most hopefully, entertaining.

Since *Part One* and *Part Two* of *The Newirth Mythology* were published, there have been many requests for more information about *Itonalya* culture, both early, late and times in between; questions about Loche Newirth, his euprophecy[3], his enigmatic place in existence, and most notably, the language of *Elliqui*. These appendices are meant to fulfill those requests. It is also my goal to provide a preview to the wealth of *Itonalya* knowledge now being unearthed at the ruins of *Wyn Avuqua*, and

---

[3] *Euprophecy* is a portmanteau word to define the anomalous phenomenon that is Loche Newirth's writing. If the definition of *prophecy* is the foretelling or prediction of what is to come, usually declared by a prophet, very often divinely inspired, *euprophecy* acts as its reciprocal. For example, a definition of *euprophecy* might be a retelling of history declared by an ordinary man or woman using the human imagination. This act, through a non-summoned supernatural force, changes the past and redefines reality. Another definition might reside somewhere within the idea of how we believe the past was and how that belief changes to define our ever evolving perception.

many other places around the globe. In the coming years I anticipate an explosion of new works on the ancient belief systems, culture and influence of immortal thought and perspective from the *Wyn Avuquain* Heron Atheneum. I look forward to delving deeper and learning more from all doing research on these topics.

Michael B. Koep
January, 2018

APPENDICES

Contents

APPENDIX I.
CHARACTERS
OF THE
NEWIRTH MYTHOLOGY

Alphabetical

What follows is a complete list of characters in *The Newirth Mythology* along with brief character descriptions. By accessing the list, readers risk spoilers. To avoid spoilers, please take note and proceed with caution when seeing this spoiler identifier: Δ.

Δ : spoiler ahead
i : The Invasion of Heaven
ii : Leaves of Fire
iii : The Shape of Rain
Ithea : mortal
Itonalya : immortal

Aethur • Δ *iii, Ithea*. The *Elliqui* name given to Loche Newirth by Queen Yafarra of *Wyn Avuqua*. The name means, *new earth*. *(see Loche Newirth.)*

Adamsman, Talan • *iii, Itonalya. Orathom Wis*. Born in Sicily sometime around 1900. His father was a merchant fisherman from Favignana. George Eversman found him when he heard the tale of a stout young Italian boy that survived a fishing accident. At twelve, Talan was yanked off the back of the boat by a tangled line. He was underwater for nearly an hour while his father and two other fishermen struggled to save him. The boy awoke completely unharmed from the incident minutes after he was laid on the deck. George Eversman trained him as *Orathom Wis* and he became widely known among the *Itonalya* as the Talan the Fisher King, who used fishing wire to garrote *Godrethion*. He was given the task of watching over Helen Newirth while in the custody of the *Orathom Wis* during the New Earth War. Adam killed Etheldred the High Captain under Cynthia the *Godrethion* Summoner before the omvide Dellithion in 1010 AD.

Alin, Bishop, Walter • *i, Ithea.* Born 1949 in Minneapolis, Minnesota, educated in California, student at California State University, Los Angeles and Immaculate Heart College. Ordained to the priesthood in may of 1972, he was appointed (by Pope John Paul II) Titular Bishop of Cell Ausaille and Auxiliary Bishop of the Archdiocese of Los Angeles in 1989. Bishop Alin had heard of the supernatural paintings of young artist Basil Pirrip Fenn through Catholic Priest, John Whitely. Bishop Alin, after (purportedly) seeing the work for himself, contacted Albion Ravistelle.

Athelstan • *ii, iii, Itonalya, Orathom Wis.* Born 1491 in Ireland, County Cork. Athelstan's immortality was discovered by his elder brother, Perkin, who witnessed eight year old Athelstan's arm break from falling out of a tree, and then miraculously heal minutes later; the elder brother believed Athelstan to be a sorcerer. Perkin helped to conceal the secret and assist his brother until he died in 1531. Athelstan, devastated by his brother's passing moved to Germany where he met Albion Ravistelle. Ravistelle brought him into the *Orathom Wis* in 1539. A t h e l s t a n was Loche Newirth's door warden during the battle of *Mel Tiris* in the New Earth War. He also fought against The Board during the battle of Masques.

Bannuelo of the House of Wings • *iii, Itonalya, Orathom Wis.* Born sometime around 1528 BCE. It is written in the *Toele* that Bannuelo of the House of W i n g s w a s t h e oldest *Itonalya* known when *Wyn Avuqua* fell. There is some mention of Bannuelo being a direct descendent of one of the earliest creators of the written and oral language *Elliqui*, the Silent Author. She became Wings Minister in the year 357 BCE and served both King Althemis Falruthia and his daughter, Queen Yafarra. Bannuelo was loyal to the Old Law, but she was also a proponent for change knowing of the augured brothers. She was slain in the year 1010 AD at *Tiris Avu* defending Queen Yafarra and the lower halls.

Alice of Bath • *ii, iii, Itonalya, Orathom Wis. (see Eloise Smith.)*

Bonin, Yorick, Dr. • ii, *Ithea*. Born 1943 in Milan. College professor. Close friend to Albion Ravistelle. Helen Craven's teacher during her stay in Venice between 1975-1987.

Bytor, Gary • Δ *iii, Itonalya, Orathom Wis.* Born 1221 in the village of Willowdale, Essex. Gary's immortality was discovered when bystanders observed a simple cut heal itself over the course of a few seconds. He was then told by his mother that he was one of the *Old People from over the sea.* Willowdale, it has been documented, produced several immortals over the centuries. Instead of fearing the mysterious condition, the families of Willowdale embraced it and supported immortals and the *Orathom Wis* plight through the centuries. Gary Bytor was slain in the year 1010 AD after crossing *omvide* Menkaure to assist Loche Newirth during the New Earth War.

Catena, Angelo, Dr. • Δ *i, ii, iii, Ithea*. Born 1955 in Cortellazzo, Italy. Graduated 1970, *magna cum laude* from Oxford University with degrees in biochemistry, psychology and neuroscience. Has worked closely with Albion Ravistelle in Venice, Italy since 1977. He was the first to make major breakthroughs in DNA research and was a co-developer for the *Melgia* Gene derived from the plant fond by young William Greenhame in the fourteenth century. Dr. Catena has also conducted experiments using the psychological and divinized art of Painter, Basil Pirrip Fenn.

Chatfield, Alan • *i, Ithea.* Loche Newirth's attorney in Idaho.

Cole, Richard • *ii, Ithea.* Road Manager for the rock group Led Zeppelin. Richard was one direct connection that brought Helen Storm (Newirth) to the attention of Albion Ravistelle.

Craven, Helen • *ii, Itonalya, Endale Gen.* Helen Craven is the birth name of Helen Newirth. *(see Helen Newirth.)*

Cremo, Graham • *iii, Ithea.* Born 1968. Graduated from UC Berkeley with degrees in history and archeology. Graham acted as the lead archeologist and chief researcher at the archeological dig site at *Wyn Avuqua,* Priest Lake, Idaho.

Father Cyrus • *ii, Godrethion.* Birth details unknown. Father Cyrus was a leader of a Sentinel Monastic Order under the Bishop of London, Stephen Gravesend (d.1338). Monks of this Sentinel Order practiced monastic silence and were also trained as soldiers. Father Cyrus was the primary motivator behind Gravesend's short lived and little known inquisition across England during the years 1335-38. The Sentinel Monastic Order, along with Bishop Gravesend, burned well over one hundred men, women and children claiming all were heretics, witches and sorcerers. Father Δ Cyrus was the reincarnated bridging spirit *Cymachkena* (*Elliqui:* dark dragon), or in other mythological texts, the Devil, Satan, Lucifer, Iblis, Set, Pluto, et cetera. Cyrus was slain by Albion Ravistelle near Strotford Manor, England in 1338. *(See Nicolas Cythe, and Cynthia Summoner of the Godrethion.)*

Cynthia Summoner of the *Godrethion* • Δ *iii, Godrethion.* Born in Wessex, 981. Cynthia is the reincarnated bridging spirit *Cymachkena* (*Elliqui*: dark dragon), or in other mythological texts, the Devil, Satan, Lucifer, Iblis, Set, Pluto, et cetera. Over the years 991-1010, she summoned, gathered and organized the massive *Godrethion* host to cross into unexplored North America to lay siege to the city of Immortals, *Wyn Avuqua.* She was slain by Vincale at Tiris Avu, 1010. *(See Father Cyrus, Nicholas Cythe.)*

Cythe, Nicholas • Δ *i, ii, iii, Godrethion.* Born 1977. Very little is known about Nicholas Cythe save that he was an extremely successful European businessman who owned vineyards in Italy and Spain. It was said that much of his fortune was built by his family, but there is no evidence to support the claim. Nicholas Cythe is the reincarnated bridging spirit *Cymachkena* (*Elliqui*: dark dragon), or in other mythological texts, the Devil, Satan, Lucifer, Iblis, Set, Pluto, et cetera. During the New Earth War, Nicholas was closely associated with Albion Ravistelle, the *Endale Gen and* The Board. He was the first recipient of the *Melgia* Gene developed by Ravistelle and Dr. Angelo Catena—the first *Godrethion* to become immortal on Earth. During the Battle of Masques, he was slain by George Eversman. It is said that his death was the end of the dreaded *Cymachkena Shivtiris*, as slain immortals are denied a Hereafter and doomed to oblivion.

Eastman, Lynn • Δ *iii, Ithea.* Born 1970 in Michigan, Illinois. Educated at New York Military Academy. In 1995 she was recruited by the private security company, Coldwater, owned by an international conglomerate known as *The Board. The Board's* mission was to assist in the progression of the *Melgia* Gene and the evolutionary acceleration the human species. Lynn Eastman served as the Lead Operator at the *Wyn Avuqua* dig site, Priest Lake, Idaho. She led The Board forces against the remaining *Itonalya* at the Battle of Masques.

Echelle, Charles • *ii, Ithea.* Born 1941. Husband to Leonaie Echelle.

Echelle, Leonaie • *ii,iii, Ithea-Itonalya.* Born 1923 in Paris, France. Leonaie and her parents immigrated to the United States before World War II. Leonaie met the immortal, Samuel Lifeson in 1963 when she was visiting family in France, and the two fell deeply in love. Their relationship continued until Leonaie realized that Samuel could not grow old with her. She married Charles Echelle in 1989, but she never stopped loving Samuel. In 2015, Leonaie began suffering from the early stages of Alzheimer's disease and she was admitted to Greenhaven's Retirement community in Coeur d'Alene, ID. Leonaie was one of the first recipients to be given immortality through Albion Ravistelle's and Dr. Angelo Cantena's genetic breakthroughs with the Melgia Gene. Leonaie now sits on The Board and writes curriculum for new Immortals.

Erinyes • Δ *iii, Godrethion.* Very little is known about Erinyes. The *Godrethion* host that destroyed *Wyn Avuqua* told stories that the Monk, Erinyes, was a Fate (a story likely derived from the Greek Moirai: Clotho, Lachesis or Atropos). Erinyes' sex was mysterious, though most deemed the Fate to be female. It is also believed that Erinyes' teaching was the foundation for the violent Monastic Order of Sentinels that emerged in England sometime around 1250. *(See Father Cyrus.)* During the Fall of *Wyn Avuqua*, Erinyes was counselor, herald and soldier under the command of the *Godrethion* Summoner,

Cynthia. Erinyes was killed by Vincale before the *omvide Dellithion* in 1010 AD.

Etheldred • *iii, Godrethion.* Birth year unknown. Etheldred was a Field Marshal in Wessex before he was summoned as a *Godrethion.* Cynthia of Wessex appointed Etheldred Earl Constable during the planning stages of the *Wyn Avuquain* campaign. Just north of the *omvide Mellithion,* Etheldred's sortie captured Loche Newirth, Julia Iris and young Edwin Newirth prior to the siege of *Wyn Avuqua.* Realizing that mighty *Thi* had crossed over within Edwin, Etheldred marshaled his captives to Cynthia. During the siege, Etheldred was killed by Adam Talansman before the *omvide Dellithion* in the year 1010 AD.

Eversman, George • Δ *i, ii, iii, Itonalya, Orathom Wis.* Born 1002 in the City of *Wyn Avuqua.* George's birth name was Iteav and he was the only son of Queen Yafarra. Eight-year-old Iteav was beheaded, drawn and quartered before the gates of *Wyn Avuqua* by his own mother to enable the bridging *Godrethion, Thi* (Edwin Newirth), to escape the city. Iteav was restored by the healer *Godrethion,* Lornensha, and brought secretly to Italy where he spent most of his life. Over the centuries, Eversman drew together the remaining *Itonalya* and founded the modern *Orathom Wis* which would continue to follow the Old Law of eliminating bridging deities on Earth. During the The Battle of Masques, George Eversman killed and cast into oblivion the *Cymachkena,* the Devil.

Fenn, Basil Pirrip • Δ *i, ii, iii, Ithea.* Born Basil Godell, 1975, in Canterbury, England to Diana Godell and Bill Hagenemer. Later he was sent with his brother Loche Newirth to live with Diana's twin sister Rebecca and her husband Jules Pirrip in the United States. After an assassination attempt that killed the surrogate parents, the brothers were separated and hidden. Basil was sent to live with Elizabeth and Howard Fenn, who changed his name to Basil Pirrp Fenn. Basil is the augured Poet foretold in *Itonalya* lore. His paintings were believed to contain doorways or portholes between this life and the next. This porthole allowed deities to look upon the human condition and feel its beauty and power without interfering in human affairs. However, his paintings, if looked upon by human eyes, would draw the imperfections of mortals into the sphere of the gods, thus invading and destroying the fabric of the supernal realm. It was also believed that he and his brother, the Poet Loche Newirth, would end the long slavery of the Immortals to the One God, *Thi,* and rid the world of divine intervention forever. Basil took his own life at the Uffizi in Florence, Italy, in October of this year.

Fenn, Elizabeth • *i, Ithea.* Born 1953 in Lacey, Washington. Step mother to Basil Pirrip Fenn.

Fenn, Howard • *i, iii, Ithea.* Born 1951 in Olympia, Washington. Step father to Basil Pirrip Fenn. Howard met with a terrible accident while raising his step son, Basil. Howard beheld an early work of Basil's that nearly claimed his life. The experience placed Howard into a coma for several days. When he revived, doctors were uncertain if he would ever speak or walk again. Basil, wracked with guilt, painted a portrait with the intention of healing Howard. With John Whitely, Basil visited his stepfather and showed the painting. It brought Howard back to mental health, but he would never regain the use of his legs. After the Battle of the Uffizi, Howard remained with Albion Ravistelle in Venice to study *Itonalya* History.

Finnley, Astrid, Dr. • Δ iii, *Ithea.* Born 1970 in Coeur d'Alene, Idaho. Graduated *cum laude* from the University of Idaho in 1994, and finished her doctoral degree in Mythology and World Religion at Gonzaga University, 1999. She is currently a Professor of Mythology and History at Whitworth University in Spokane, Washington. Most of Astrid's work has been in linguistics, but her obsession was the controversial subject of the *Itonalya* and their ancient city known as *Wyn Avuqua.* She self-published three books on *Wyn Avuquain* lore, language, historical evidence and cultural relevance. Most of her work has been regarded as pseudo history and speculative fiction by scholars, and her insistence on the subject has damaged her credibility as a historian and educator. In 2015 she received a grant to research the connection of Sumerian, Celtic and Egyptian languages, but she instead used the funds to complete her research to prove, once and for all, the existence of *Wyn Avuqua.*

Fryless, Mallory (Mal) • iii, *Ithea.* Born 1971 in Coeur d'Alene, Idaho. Studied history and world religion at the University of Idaho before dropping out. Started his own business with Graham Cremo doing research excavation. He was a site dig site manager at *Wyn Avuqua*, Priest Lake, Idaho.

Geraldine of Ascott (of Leaves) • ii, *Godrethion.* (See Lornensha)

Godell, Alexander • i, *Ithea.* Loche Newirth's birth name, given by his father William Greenhame and mother, Diana Godell. After the Moses Lake assassination attempt his name was changed to Loche Newirth. *(See Loche Newirth.)*

Godell, Diana • Δ i, iii, *Ithea.* Born 1944 in Canterbury, England. Diana gave birth to Alexander (Loche Newirth) and Basil Godell (Basil Pirrip Fenn), the augured Poet and Painter of ancient *Itonalya* myth. Discovering their divine purpose, Diana and Bill Hagenemer (William Greenhame) sent the boys to the United States to live with Diana's twin sister, Rebecca and her husband Jules Pirrip. After an assassination attempt in Moses Lake, Washington, that killed both Jules and Rebecca, the surviving boys were split up. Basil was sent to live with foster parents Howard and Elizabeth Fenn. Alexander was sent back to Diana in Europe and the two went into hiding. During that time she changed Alexander's name to Loche Newirth. When Loche decided to attend college in the United States, Diana remained sequestered. In 2010, it was William Greenhame, not Albion Ravistelle, who assisted in the faking of Diana's death. The elaborate scheme was designed to throw off pursuit for fear of her capture and torture. Unfortunately, she was found and taken by the *Endale Gen*, and used as a hostage against the brothers. Following the Battle of the Uffizi, Diana was rescued by William Greenhame. Her aging body prevented her from fighting in the New Earth War, but she was a powerful support to her husband William and her sons. At William's request, she stayed far from the front. When she learned of her husband's beheading, she returned to Venice and was fortunate to retrieve William's head from the surface of the Adriatic. She then arranged for Dr. Angelo Catena to restore her husband.

Gravesend, Steven, Bishop • Δ *ii, Ithea*. Gravesend was elected in 1318 and consecrated in 1319. As a suspected *Godrethion* (a rather powerful and murderous one), the *Orathom Wis* had sent Albion Ravistelle to eliminate him. Gravesend was, in fact, not a bridging spirit, but very often in the company of the *Godrethion*, Father Cyrus whose spirit emitted a profoundly dark *Rathinalya*. During the attempt on the Bishop's life at Strotford Manor in 1338, William of Leaves had intended to poison the ailing Bishop, but at the last minute changed his mind and decided to pour the tainted wine on the floor. But before the boy could tip the rim, Gravesend seized the cup and poured the drink into his own mouth. As breath left his body, he confessed that he had condoned and ordered the death of hundreds due to the powerful influence of Father Cyrus.

Greenhame, William Heubert • Δ *i, ii, iii, Itonalya, Orathom Wis*. Born in 1332 to Father Radulfus Grenehamer and Geraldine of Leaves near the village of Ascott, England. His parents were both *Godrethion*. In 1338, attempting to save his mother from the being taken by a witch hunting mob led by Bishop of London, Stephen Gravesend, William's throat was cut by the Sentinel Monk, Cyrus. To the great shock and delight of his father, The wound miraculously healed. Albion Ravistelle, who was hunting *Godrethion* (suspecting the Bishop of London to be a bridging spirit), discovered the young immortal and took him under his protection. During the New Earth War, William was   beheaded by Nicholas Cythe. *Gavress* was performed by Albion Ravistelle on the Adriatic Sea just off the coast of Venice. But before William's demise, his head was recovered from the water by Diana Godell. His body, too, was retrieved by assistants to Dr. Angelo Catena. Dr. Catena restored William to health through the use of the newly developed *Melgia* Gene and the ancient, magical leaves of William's mother, Geraldine. William then followed after his son Loche across Menkaure. During the Battle of Masques William managed to bring Albion Ravistelle back to the Old Law.

Grenehamer, Father Radulfus • Δ *ii, Godrethion.* Birth year unknown. Husband to Geraldine of Ascott. Father to William Greenhame. Was presented with the post of Vicar at St. Mary the Virgin, Ascott, 1331. Married in secret to Geraldine in 1332. Albion Ravistelle was aware that Radulfus was a *Godrethion,* but decided to allow him to live given the Priest's wholesome works. He was killed at Strotford Manor, England by Father Cyrus while protecting his son William in the year 1338.

Haganemer, Bill • *i, Itonalya, Orathom Wis.* One of many names William Greenhame has used through the centuries. *(See William Greenhame.)*

Hartman, Andi • *iii, Ithea.* Born 1970 in London, England. Graduated *magna cum laude* from Oxford University with degrees in criminology and psychology. Joined the Secret Intelligence Service (MI6) counter terrorism unit in 2007 She was accepted onto The Board in 2009.

Hannazil, Chet, Senator • *iii, Ithea.* Born 1943 in Salt Lake City, Utah. American attorney and Republican politician. Graduated Brigham Young University in 1967. Received his J.D. degree from Florida State University, College of Law in 1971. Elected to the US Senate 1988. The Board appointed him Chair in 1999. He was stabbed to death with a ball point pen by Albion Ravistelle at The Board's final meeting of this year.

Herzog, Geoff • *iii, Ithea.* Author, educator and historian. One of Astrid Finnley's professors from Gonzaga University in Spokane, Washington.

Hruska, Marcel "Red Hawk" • *iii, Ithea.* Born 1991 on the Coeur d'Alene Reservation in Idaho. Studied history at the University of Idaho. Currently working on his masters at Whitworth University in Spokane, Washington. Marcel Hruska has assisted Professor Astrid Finnley in her work concerning the Indigenous Tribes and their connection to the *Itonalya* of *Wyn Avuqua.*

Iris, Julia • Δ *i, ii, iii, Itonalya.* Born 1980 in Coeur d'Alene, Idaho. Graduated *cum laude* from Gonzaga University in Spokane, Washington, 2004. Julia raised the capitol to design and build a restaurant in Hope, Idaho called The Floating Hope. In October of this year, Julia received a mortal gunshot wound to the stomach from Dr. Marcus Rearden. She woke hours later in complete health with Loche Newirth at her side. Following this life altering discovery, Julia struggled to come to terms with not only her newly found immortality, but also her personal identity and place in existence. She was abducted by Helen Newirth and used as ransom for Helen's son, Edwin. While a captive, her education as an immortal began under the tutelage of Albion Ravistelle. She was rescued by William Greenhame. As Julia accepted her new life she embraced both mercy and compassion as moral guides, and these meditations allowed her to serve as a kind of moral compass to Loche Newirth. During the New Earth War, Julia fought alongside Loche Newirth and the *Orathom Wis.* She lives with Loche and Edwin Newirth in North Idaho.

Iteav • Δ *iii, Itonalya.* Born 1002, Iteav is the only child of Queen Yafarra of *Wyn Avuqua.* This is the birth name of the *Orathom Wis Angofal*, George Eversman. *(See George Eversman.)*

Jakes • *ii.* An English soldier under the rule of Edward III.

John • *ii.* An English soldier under the rule of Edward III.

Langley, Olivia • *ii, Itonalya, Orathom Wis.* Born 1907 in Cork, Ireland. Olivia was presumed dead after a wall in her family's stone house collapsed and crushed her five year old body. Her parents frantically dug her out from the rubble. When she was pulled free they wept over the unmoving, deformed body. Not long into their lament, Olivia's legs began to twitch, and suddenly snapped back into their normal, healthy shape. Then Olivia sat up and asked why they were crying. Her father was elated beyond words, but her mother was fearful of something more sinister and claimed that the Devil was at work. This fear drove a fissure between the family. The division was so acute that Olivia and her father were forced to leave Ireland. The two immigrated to the United States in 1914. It was ·in New York, at a Manhattan speak easy that William Greenhame, Corey Thomas and Samuel Lifeson met Olivia and her husband (a bandstand singer and jazz guitarist, Angus Windiman) for the first time, by pure chance, in 1927. Without knowing why, Olivia simply walked up to the trio and offered them each a piece of chewing gum. Learning of the terrible accident, William brought her into the *Orathom Wis* a year later. Olivia eventually became part owner in one of William's franchises, Greenhaven Retirement Communities, where she helped to assist families and their elderly loved ones. There she met and cared for Leonaie Echelle. During the New Earth War, Olivia fought in the Battle of Masques.

Lifeson, Samuel • Δ *i, ii, iii, Itonalya, Orathom Wis.* Born 1395 in Ireland. Samuel managed to keep his immortality secret from his family and his community until his mid-forties when talk circulated that his physical body did not seem to age. By the time he was fifty, many of his friends felt as if he was concealing some dark secret. Samuel, uncertain how to explain his immortal body, decided to leave his family and friends without a word and begin a new life. Samuel would do this three more times over the next century. When he met William Greenhame, Samuel found meaning for the first time. He joined the *Orathom Wis* in 1528. In the early 1960's Samuel met the love of his life, Leonaie Echelle. Determined to stay with her, he planned in secret to make her immortal through the Leaves of William Greenhame, and the science of Albion Ravistelle and Dr. Angelo Catena. During the New Earth War, Samuel fought at the Battle of the Uffizi. He was beheaded by the assassin Emil Wishfeill in Venice of this year.

Lerxt, Alexia • *iii, Itonalya, Orathom Wis.* Born 1921 in Fernie, British Columbia. How Alexia's immortality was discovered is unknown, but sometime around 1930 Alexia's family relocated to the village of Willowdale, England. Willowdale, it has been documented, produced several immortals over the centuries. Instead of fearing the mysterious condition, the families of Willowdale embraced it and supported immortals and the *Orathom Wis* plight through the centuries. Alexia Lerxt was slain in the year 1010 AD after crossing *omvide* Menkaure to assist Loche Newirth during the New Earth War.

Lornensha • ∆ *iii, Godrethion.* Birth year unknown. Also known as the Lakewoman. According the *Wyn Avuquain* accounts, Lornensha was a healer that had dwelt just south of the *omvide Mellithion* along the shores of lake *Fethequa* (home water) for fifty or more years before the fall of the city. How and why she had come to make a home there is not known. During that time Lornensha built relations with both the *Aevas* and the *Itonalya* through her herb lore and her art of healing. She was often called to court to hold counsel with Queen Yafarra. Lornensha was not immortal, yet through her arts she managed to grow a plant that provided her a kind of ever-youth. After the fall of *Wyn Avuqua* in *1010*, and the entombment of Yafarra, Lornensha was tasked with restoring the beheaded and torn Iteav. Though she was successful, Iteav would struggle with language and speech for the rest of his long, long life. Lornensha brought Iteav to a small village outside of Rome where he was adopted by a family of farmers. Lornensha then journeyed north to the Germania in the mid 13th Century, and changing her name to Geraldine along the way. A hundred years later she would journey to England and meet Radulfus Grenemer, marry and give birth to William of Leaves. *(see Geraldine of Leaves.)*

Maghren of the House of Mind • *iii, Itonalya, Orathom Wis.* Birth year unknown. He became the Templar *Angofal* and Minister of *Keptiris* in the year 101 AD. As the Minister of the House of Mind, Maghren, like his predecessors, served as High Councilor to the reigning monarch. Maghren was known as both a legalist and a staunch supporter of the Old Law. Maghren was a loyalist to Yafarra's Crown. In the year 721 AD, during an Itonalya campaign to sustain the Wessex monarch, King Ine, Maghren was sent to put down a rising power (and *Godrethion*) within the Wessex royal line named Cynewulf. Cynewulf gathered an army and marched on Ine's Castle claiming that he would take the head of any man that dealt with Immortals. Ine was outnumbered and caught by surprise. Fearing that Cynewulf was *Cymachkena Godrethion*, Maghren sent runners to the *omvide* just south of Bath in hopes that Yafarra could send a contingent of *Itonalya* to save what would be a certain slaughter. Yafarra herself crossed into Wessex and led eight other *Orathom Wis* against Cynewulf's army. Their arrival was just in time. Ine had been captured, and Maghren was slowly being cut apart. Yafarra's wrath and retribution was horrifying. She and her *Orathom Wis* decimated Cynewulf's followers until Cynewulf stood alone before Ine. Yafarra then placed the future of Wessex into the hands of Ine and allowed the two to duel for the crown. Ine was victorious. Maghren never forgot Yafarra's aid and he defended Yafarra's policies through the centuries. Maghren was killed in 1010 defending Queen Yafarra and the lower halls of *Tiris Avu* during the Seige of *Wyn Avuqua*. His body was never found.

Molmer, Dr. Chad • *iii, Ithea.* Born in 1949 in Portland, Oregon. Graduated from Washington State University in 1970. Completed his doctoral decree in History at Harvard University, 1977. Dr. Molmer was the chair of the GU Grant Board that funded the research of Dr. Astrid Finnley. Molmer, a believer in Dr. Finnley's work, secretly knew she was using the funds to research the controversial *Itonalya*.

Newirth, Edwin • Δ *i, ii, iii, Ithea.* Born 2011 in Sandpoint, Idaho to Loche and Helen Newirth. In November of this year, young Edwin fell from a height into what Loche Newirth described as "The Eye of *Thi*," an incident that crossed the spirit of the One God into Edwin's physical body. Thus, Edwin became of great interest to both the *Godrethion* horde and the *Wyn Avuquain* Templar. It was believed that if the boy, *Thi,* was killed, the One God would be cast into oblivion freeing *Godrethion* and *Itonalya* alike from their age-long bondage. It was decided that Edwin was to be sacrificed by the *Wyn Avuquains* to buy peace. Before the sacrifice, Queen Yafarra secretly exchanged Edwin with her own son Iteav. Edwin escaped the city with his mother, Helen Newirth and the two crossed back into their own time. They took refuge at Loche's cabin.

Newirth, Helen • Δ *i, ii, iii, Itonalya, Orathom Wis / Endale Gen.* Born 1958 in Los Angeles, California. Helen's immortality was discovered when she fell from a Hollywood Hotel in the mid seventies and lived. Guitarist Jimmy Page, who witnessed this event, introduced Helen to Albion Ravistelle with whom Helen fell in love with, spending the next few decades striving to impress him. She learned her place as an immortal and *Orathom Wis* assassin. As a final test to prove her love to Albion she agreed to pursue and become the muse to both Basil Fenn and Loche Newirth. Her attempts with Basil failed, but with Loche she succeeded. She married Loche in 2001 and gave birth to their son Edwin Newirth in 2011. When the life of her son came into question, Helen did everything in her power to protect him, including distancing herself from Albion.

Newirth, Loche • Δ *i, ii, iii, Ithea.* Birth name: Alexander Godell, born 1978 in Canterbury, England to Diana Godell and Bill Hagenemer (William Greenhame). After the assassination attempt that claimed the lives of his surrogate parents, Loche was sent back to England to live with his mother. He moved to back to the United States in 1988 to attend college. Graduated from the University of Washington in 1994, and finished his doctoral work at the University of California, Berkeley in 2000 with degrees in behavioral and child psychology. During his time at Berkeley, Loche attended courses taught by Dr. Marcus Rearden. Loche met Helen Craven just after graduation. The two relocated to North Idaho in 1998. In 2001 the couple married. Loche began his own practice in Sandpoint, Idaho in 2004. Their son, Edwin Newirth, was born in 2011. When Loche learned that his mentor, Marcus Rearden had murdered Bethany Winship, Loche crafted a far-fetched, mythological tale in order to bring Rearden to justice. The attempt narrowly succeeded, but the story contained some inexplicable supernatural element that brought Loche's characters and fictional history to life. Loche now lives in North Idaho with his son and Julia Iris.

Page, Jimmy • *ii, iii, Ithea.* Born 1944 in London, England. English rock musician, guitarist, songwriter and producer best known for his work with Led Zeppelin. Jimmy Page's interest in the supernatural and the occult brought him into contact with Albion Ravistelle sometime around 1970. They became close friends. Δ When on tour in the United States, two years later, Jimmy witnessed a groupie fall from a high rise hotel balcony— and live. The groupie was Helen Storm (Helen Newirth). The impossibility of her recovery prompted him to contact Albion sometime around 1970.

Peterson, Robert • *ii, Ithea.* Born c. 1287-88 in London. Robert Peterson practiced as Bishop Steven Gravesend's physician at Strotford Manor. In 1338, Father Cyrus was revealed as the instigator for the deaths of hundreds of innocents, as well as the source of illness (both mental and physical) in Bishop Gravesend, Robert Peterson was the first to attack the Sentinel monks, allowing young William of Leaves to escape into the tunnels. In 1350, Robert Peterson's family was infected with the plague. William Greenhame heard the news and brought his mother's leaves to heal the family. Robert spent the next five years completely immune to the virus and used what knowledge and skill he had to ease the sick and dying. He passed away in 1355 in his sleep.

Pierce, Justinian (The Mountain) • *ii, Itonalya, Orathom Wis.* Born 1799 in Magpie, Victoria, Australia. Justinian survived being pierced with fifteen arrows during a raid on his village when he was a boy. His father, fearing the village would suspect the boy to be possessed by some evil spirit, took him to England. At the wedding for a mutual friend, Justinian met William Greenhame and Samuel Lifeson. Soon thereafter, Justinian joined the *Orathom Wis* and became known as their greatest archer. Justinian fought at Battle of the Uffizi. He was slain at Seige of *Mel Tiris,* this year.

Pirrip, Jules • *i, Ithea.* Born 1946 in Seattle, Washington. Husband to Rebecca Pirrip and was briefly a surrogate parent to young Basil and Loche in the early 1980s.

Pirrip, Rebecca • *i, Ithea.* Born 1944 in Canterbury, England. Rebecca Godell (maiden name) is the twin sister to Diana Godell. Rebecca and her husband Jules Pirrip became surrogate parents to young Basil and Loche in the early Eighties. The couple was killed in an assassination attempt meant to take the lives of the boys in 1981.

Pratt, Neil • *i, Itonalya, Orathom Wis.* Born 1596, just north of the village of Willowdale, England. Neil's immortal condition was discovered in his mid twenties. Neil was mortally injured fighting to preserve the forests surrounding his home from Royal logging practices. Willowdale, it has been documented, produced several immortals over the centuries. Instead of fearing the mysterious condition, the families of Willowdale embraced it and supported immortals and the *Orathom Wis* plight through the centuries. Δ Neil Pratt was slain in the year 1010 AD after crossing *omvide* Menkaure to assist Loche Newirth during the New Earth War. Neil was known among the *Orathom Wis* as their Poet Laureate. Neil has produced eighteen books of poetry. In his book,

Caress of Steel, Neil tells of his search for meaning as an *Itonalya.*

Rearden, Elanor Maylen • *i, Ithea.* Born in 1948 Kennewick, Washington. Graduated from the University of Idaho in 1970 with a teaching degree. Married Marcus Rearden in 1975. Elanor suffered a fatal heart attack at her home in October of this year. Her husband claims the heart attack was caused by her shock at seeing a painting that depicted him murdering a woman, Bethany Winship. The painting was made by Loche Newirth. Consequently, Marcus holds Loche responsible for the murder of his wife.

Rearden, Marcus, Dr. • Δ *i, ii, iii, Ithea.* Born in 1948 Lewiston, Idaho. Graduated from Washington State University in 1970, and finished his doctoral work at the University of Minnesota, Twin Cities Minneapolis in 1974 with degrees in behavioral and criminal psychology. Married Elanor Malen in 1975. They relocated to Los Angeles California in 1978, where he worked closely with the LAPD homicide division. His psychological expertise helped to capture and convict over thirty dangerous murderers as well as develop an entirely new protocol for interviewing suspects and witnesses. His work brought fame. He released several books, all of which have become bestsellers. The novel, *How To Get Away With Murder,* won several book awards and is now used in university criminology classes across the United States. Rearden taught for a brief time at the University of California, Berkeley. During that time, Rearden met Loche Newirth. Marcus became a mentor to Loche Newirth early in the Twenty-first Century and taught the young psychologist much about the practice. In early October this year, Marcus Rearden murdered his mistress Bethany Winship. The act prompted Loche Newirth to find a way to bring his old mentor to justice. *The Journal* was written to trap Marcus within his own lunacy. It succeeded. Marcus was arrested on the 31st of October of this year. However, through some freak, supernatural occurrence, The fantastic concepts and characters in *The Journal* became real. On November 3rd, Albion Ravistelle freed Rearden from his Idaho jail cell and brought the psychologist back to Venice. Albion then spent the following days learning as much as he could about The Poet, Loche Newirth from Rearden. Rearden, in turn, researched, too, plotting his own authorship of Loche's torture and demise. With Access to Basil Fenn's paintings, Albion Ravistelle's *Toele*, *The Journal* and Loche's canon, Rearden designed the elaborate torture and murder of Loche's son, Edwin. His purpose was not based solely in revenge—Rearden pressed for a psychological enslavement of Newirth—a mastery over Newirth so that he might author his own will using the author's gift. Also, during his time at Albion's House, Rearden managed to over throw Ravistelle's command over The Board. During the Battle of Masques, Rearden implemented his coup, but his position as leader was short-lived. Loche Newirth captured Rearden at the ruins of *Wyn Avuqua*. Mad with the loss of his son, Loche nearly killed Rearden. Julia interceded, pleading for Loche's better nature and mercy. Loche left Marcus alive. However, Dr. Marcus Rearden has never been found. It is whispered that Rearden is entombed in the crystal sarcophagus in the Atheneum chamber at *Wyn Avuqua*.

Rapasardi, Giovanni • *i, iii, Ithea.* Born in 1971 in Padua, Italy. Giovanni still serves as one of the primary sword instructors for the *Orathom Wis* in Europe. According to

Samuel Lifeson, *"Rapsardi's expertise matched with his humanity is the perfect balance for the Itonalya Guardian. On the one hand, he teaches a fluidity of defense—the defense of one's life, as only a mortal could, but simultaneously the aggression and ferocity of fighting to live; that which the Deathless often lack."* During the New Earth War, Loche Newirth received his first lesson in swordplay from Giovanni. Giovanni also fought alongside the *Orathom Wis* at the Battle of Masques.

Rapasardi, Maria • *i, iii, Ithea.* Born in 1966 in Padua, Italy. The elder sister to Giovanni Rapasardi. Maria moved to Venice in the early 1980s and opened her own bistro and wine bar. She is still there to this day. It was in Maria's bistro that Loche Newirth met Samuel Lifeson—and where Samuel killed the assassin, Felix Wishfeill. An accomplished fencer herself, Maria learned swordplay from her brother, Giovanni Rapasardi.

Ravistelle, Albion • Δ *i, ii, iii, Itonalya, Orathom Wis / Endale Gen / The Board Chair.* Born 811 AD. Albion's birth name was Rexmurum (King's wall) and was born in Rome during the reign of Charlemagne. He was born into slavery. When he was five he stabbed the master of the house while trying to defend his mother from a beating. While he delivered a mortal wound, the master returned in kind and broke the boy's neck. When Albion awoke, his mother jubilated. The two fled Rome to Greece where his mother found sanctuary with family. She taught him how to conceal his immortality. When she died some thirty years later, Albion left Greece and began learning as much as he could about agriculture and farming. For over two hundred years Albion bought and sold various farms across what is now Tuscany. He was not discovered by another immortal until 1221 when George Eversman visited purely by chance to inquire about some of Albion's medicinal herb gardens. Upon learning Albion's immortal condition, George began to educate him about the past and future of his kind. Albion never forgot about his early life as a slave, and though he was an influential and loyal *Orathom Wis* for many centuries, the memories of his bondage, his pride and his ambition led to his rebellion against the Old Law.

Roblam of the House of Heart • *iii, Alyeth, Orathom Wis.* According to the *Toele*, Roblam was the youngest Templar in *Wyn Avuquain* history. Born in 990 AD, Roblam was granted the *Angofal* and Heart Minister title when she was eight-teen-years-old. Traditionally, the House of Heart Minister was reserved for a mortal in order to balance the immortal state of mind with the mortal's thirst for joy and gratitude for what time they have upon Endale. But never had the Templar seen a woman so young with such zeal, passion and foresight as Roblam. When her predecessor Vorwen of the Green, passed, Roblam brought her full heart and compassion to the office and served Yafarra with steadfast loyalty. She was descended from the *Aveas* tribes that dwelt in the lands surrounding *Wyn Avuqua*. Despite her passion, she was known for having the last word after her fellow Templar would debate overlong. In the end, Roblam would often pronounce the best solutions and synthesize matters into simple terms. Roblam was killed in the year 1010 AD in *Tiris Avu* defending Queen Yafarra during the Seige of *Wyn Avuqua*.

Smith, Eloise • *ii, iii, Itonalya, Orathom Wis.* Born 1231. Also known as Alice of Bath. Alice's entire village and family perished during the famine of 1235. Albion Ravistelle found and rescued her when he heard tell of the single surviving child from the village. He brought her under his tutelage when she was three. Alice eschewed violence and chose the role of servant to those of her kind. For centuries Alice kept Albion's house in London and assisted him in his practice as an apothecary. Alice was an avid traveler. She would often take year-long holidays. She wrote extensive travel journals and was a collector of books. Alice was the first to discover a complete *Toele* from *Wyn Avuqua*. She gifted the book to Albion, but never divulged how or where she found it. Sometime around 1930 she left her station with Albion claiming that he had become selfish and was denying the Old Law. During the New Earth War Alice served the *Orathom Wis*.

Stell, Aloysius • *i, ii, iii, Itonalya, Orathom Wis / Endale Gen.* Aloysius Stell is one Albion Ravistelle's names. *(see Albion Ravistelle.)*

Stiddam, Darrel, Detective • *i, iii, Ithea.* Detective for the Coeur d'Alene Police department. Officer Stiddam was the first on the scene at the Cd'A city graveyard on October 31 of this year. He took Dr. Marcus Rearden under arrest.

Storm, Helen • *ii, Itonalya.* Helen Storm is the name Helen Craven was given when she was living on the Sunset Strip in Los Angeles, California. *(See Helen Newirth.)*

Tenuwa • *iii, Itonalya, Orathom Wis.* Tenuwa was a herald to Queen Yafarra. He was cheerful, dark skinned, dark eyed and very fond of exposing strangers to the wonders of *Itonalya* life, art and culture.

Thomas, Corey • Δ *i, ii, iii, Itonalya, Orathom Wis.* Born 1545 in Florence, Italy. Corey's father taught him how to use a sword from a very young age. By his eighth year, Corey had developed into a dangerous opponent to most adult men. During that year, Corey's father was challenged to a duel over a family debt. His father was slain. Young

Corey vowed vengeance. His father's killer thought it would be best to dispatch the boy in order to prevent a future vendetta. Corey, drew up his father's sword to the laughter of all. Moments later, the money lender was dead. The lender's followers then surrounded and stabbed the little boy to death. His body they took outside of Florence and left it beside the road. An hour later, Corey woke alive and well. Bloodied and bedraggled, the boy was picked up by a passing wine maker on his way to his vineyards north of the city. There, Corey learned how to make wine, and continues to manage his vineyards to this day. His new family concealed his immortal condition. Corey met Albion Ravistelle s around 1800 and joined the *Orathom Wis* sometime after. During the New Earth War, Corey Thomas acted as a spy for the *Orathom Wis* for he was deep within Albion's confidence. Corey fought at the Battle of the Uffizi, the Seige of *Mel Tiris* and the Battle of Masques.

Vincale, Captain of *Wyn Avuqua* • Δ *iii, Itonalya, Orathom Wis.* Born 221 AD in *Wyn Avuqua.* Son of Leafseed. Vincale held high ranks in the houses of *Keptiris* and *Shartiris* prior to his advancement to *Tiris Avu* under Queen Yafarra. Vincale aided in the escape of Loche and Edwin Newirth during the Siege of *Wyn Avuqua.* Vincale returned to *Tiris Avu* after his task was done to defend the Queen. When he arrived the lower halls were already sealed off and all but one of the Templar had been slain. He then came upon Yanreg of the House of Talons just as he was begging for a parlay with Cynthia, the *Godrethion* Summoner. Cynthia demanded the whereabouts of Yafarra. Yanreg promised to provide the information in exchange for his safe passage. Cynthia agreed. But before Yanreg could speak, Vincale shot him with arrows (later beheaded him). In a futile attempt Vincale's sortie then attacked the massive *Godrethion* host. Vincale killed Cynthia but was later overwhelmed by her host and slain. This last stand at *Tiris Avu* is told in full in the *Toele*. Vincale is a hero of *Itonalya* literature. William Greenhame once remarked that if he and Diana were to ever have another son, he would name him Vincale.

Whitely, John • *i, Ithea.* Born 1969. High school friend of both Basil Pirrip Fenn and Helen Craven. After graduation, John attended St. John's Seminary in Camarillo, California, and was ordained to the priesthood by Bishop Walter Alin in 1999. John was witness to the powerful nature of Basil Fenn's paintings, and how Basil used a painting to heal Howard Fenn's psychological malady. The disturbing nature of the art impelled John to share the experience with Bishop Alin. Bishop Alin then contacted his old friend in Italy, Albion Ravistelle.

Wishfeill, Carol • *i, Ithea.* Born 1964 in Raffadali, Sicily. Immigrated to the United States when she was four with her mother. Carol was the first spy for Albion Ravistelle when she became Loche Newirth's receptionist. She was the younger sibling of the *Endale Gen* assassin, Felix Wishfeill.

Wishfeill, Emil • Δ *ii, iii, Ithea.* Born 1974 in Raffadali, Sicily. Son of *Endale Gen* assassin, Felix Wishfeill. Emil followed closely in the footsteps of his father and became the most ruthless and surgical assassin under the command of the Ravistelle organization in Venice. During the New Earth War, Emil was responsible for the slaying of nearly twenty-seven *Itonalya Orathom Wis*. One of which was Samuel Lifeson. During the Battle of Masques, Emil was killed by Samuel Lifeson's love, Leonaie Eschelle.

Wishfeill, Felix • Δ *i, Itonalya, Endale Gen.* Born 1901 in Raffidali, Sicily. Felix's father was an assassin for a local Mafia chief named Cuffaro. On a rainy winter night in 1911, Felix followed his father and two other men to a barn in the neighboring village. Through the slats in the walls, he watched his father execute a rival Mafia member. When Felix cried out and his father discovered that he had seen the murder, the other two men shot both father and son. Felix, after having been shot four times, woke an hour later and returned to his home. His mother, a believer in black magic and the supernatural, hid the boy. A year later, Felix avenged his father by killing both men, their wives and children by setting both houses on fire and gunning down any that tried to escape. He did this in one night. He did this when he was ten years old. Not long after, the story reached the ears of Albion Ravistelle. Felix Wishfeill in pursuit of Loche Newirth was killed in a sword fight in a Venetian bistro by Samuel Lifeson in October of this year.

Williamson, Tracy • *ii, Ithea.* Born 1958 in Orange County. Tracy Williamson was Helen Craven's best friend. In the early 1970s the two were avid music fans and were fixtures on the Sunset Strip.

Winship, Bethany • Δ *i, Ithea.* Born 1950 in Kansas City, Kansas. Maiden name, Bethany Denise Owens. She relocated with her parents to Sandpoint, Idaho in 1968. She married Roger Winship in 1975. The couple had two children. Bethany began to suffer from anxiety and depression sometime around her fiftieth year. She met psychologist Marcus Rearden in 2004 and began therapy. A passionate and unhealthy love affair began between them. After many attempts to remove herself from the relationship, she sought council elsewhere. Little did she know her newly chosen therapist, Loche Newirth, was once Rearden's student and protégé. In October of this year, in the heat of passion and fearful of exposure, Dr. Marcus Rearden drowned Bethany Winship on the shore of Lake Pend Oreille, just south of Hope, Idaho. Her tragic murder set into motion the events that are told in *The Newirth Mythology.*

Yafarra, Queen • Δ iii, *Itonalya, Orathom Wis.* Born sometime during the fifth century BCE. When her father, King Althemis Falruthia of *Vastiris* was slain during the Sibling War, Yafarra, heir to the *Wyn Avuquain* throne, was faced with a broken nation. Yafarra, like her father, supported the written and oral forms of *Elliqui* that were created to help assuage the dying Original Mode of the language (see *Elliqui*: On Translation, Pronunciation and Use). The creation of this new *Elliqui* form was met with opposition—opposition led to conflict, conflict led to the Sibling War. Shortly after the death of her father, Yafarra put down the last resistance to the acceptance of new *Elliqui* and brought the *Itonalya* together again. The written and oral forms of *Elliqui* then took a central role in Old Law doctrine. Yafarra was the last monarch to reign in *Wyn Avuqua.* In the winter of 1010 AD, one of the prophesied brothers Loche Newirth, came to *Wyn Avuqua.* With him came his son Edwin—crossed into Edwin's spirit was the bridging God, *Thi.* At the same time, *Wyn Avuqua* was surrounded by a massive *Godrethion* army that had come to sack the city. *Godrethion* emissaries were sent to the Queen with terms: if Yafarra kills *Thi, Wyn Avuqua* would be left in peace. Yafarra agreed. However, at the last minute she sent Edwin with his mother Helen to escape across an *omvide.* She then appeared on the sacrificial alter with her own son, Iteav.

There she cut him apart before the *Godrethion* horde. Though the ruse worked, it did not stop the Godrethion from sacking the city. Yafarra was pressed back into *Tiris Avu* and deep into the Heron Atheneum where she commanded Templar to entomb her in order to protect the written prophecy (The Red Notebook). She was liberated from the crystal sarcophagus a thousand years later by Graham Cremo and Astrid Finnely. She later fought at the Battle of Masques against Marcus Rearden's take over of the *Endale Gen* and The Board.

Yanreg of the House of Talons • *iii, Itonalya, Orathom Wis.* Yanreg's birth year is unknown. He became the Templar *Angofal* of *Shartiris* in the year 622 and was at first a talented and thoughtful military strategist, who had led successful *Itonalya* campaigns in both the Byzantine Empire and through what is now northern Europe against armies driven by *Godrethion* rulers. By the Tenth Century he had become hubristic and combative to both the *Itonalya* Crown and his fellow Templar. In 1010, Yanreg was the first to begin communications with the *Godrethion* Horde's Summoner Cynthia and her lead envoy, Erinyes. Many believed that Yanreg was deceived by the Enemy into believing that if he were to assist in delivering the City, he would be crowned King, despite Kingship and monarchy being things he publicly denounced as the primary sickness to the realm. None withstanding, it was whispered by Templar and his closest advisors that Yanreg secretly sought the power to rule. His connection to Cynthia the Summoner inevitably led to his support in the sacrificing of the boy God, *Thi* (Edwin Newirth) in order to buy peace. When the *Godrethion* did not honor their word and attacked the city after the sacrifice, Yanreg fought bravely in defense of his people.

In the end, however, Yanreg begged Cynthia for parlay promising to tell of Yafarra's location in return for his safe passage. Before he could divulge Yafarra's whereabouts, Captain of the Guard, Vincale, shot him with arrows. Later, Vincale beheaded Yanreg. No *Gavress* was given.

APPENDIX II.
ITONALYA MYTH:

As far back as the second millennium BCE, terrestrial events and the movement of celestial bodies have played dominant roles in humankind's attempt to understand itself, its calendars, its gods and its position in the universe. Astrology began with the Indian, Chinese and Mayan cultures, evolved through the Babylonians, Alexander the Great, Ancient Greece, to Rome, appeared in the plays and poetry of Chaucer and Shakespeare, and it still thrives today as a horoscopic art maintaining its roots in omens, prediction and guidance. While humans have worshiped, studied and relied on the stars, so, too, have the *Itonalya*.

Professor Astrid Finnley's research of the *Toele* allows us a glimpse into the distant past and the first creation tales from the *Itonalya* dating back to the third millennium BCE.

In *Itonalya* lore, the allegorical significance of the sun, moon and earth is representative of God, Immortal and Human. The sun god, the immortal guard, the moon, and the delicate, dramatic and coveted beauty of earth were the primary components, the holy trinity, if you will, of *Itonalya* society. The mighty creator, *Thi*, is the foundation for all else. Lastly, but no less enigmatic, is the appearance of a godlike bird, a Blue Heron called *Teniqua*, as it is named in many places in the *Toele*. The Blue Heron would have been an important totem to the *Wyn Avuquain* landscape then, just as the bird is today.

With regard to limited space I have chosen to include only three tales here for readers interested in *Itonalya* myth. Of the hundreds of translated stories, what follows can be linked back to events recorded in *The Shape of Rain*, *Leaves of Fire* and *The Invasion of Heaven*.

The tales are from the *Toele's* epic poem, the *Lay of*

Melea, or the love story of the Earth and the Moon—*Endale* and *Mellithion*. The first, *Of the Court of Thi and the Making of Dellithion and Endale*, tells how the *Thi* made the sun and the planets of our solar system, and most importantly, *Endale* and *Mellithion*. For the *Itonalya*, this tale depicts their fundamental curse and mission through the character of *Mellithion*, the first immortal guardian to the coveted *Endale*. The second and third tales, *Of Mighty Chalshaf First Born*, and *Of Ashto the Teacher of Time*, tell of the beginnings of *Endale's* education among her celestial siblings. In these stories, both *Chalshaf* (Jupiter) and *Ashto* (Saturn) visit the earth with their godlike powers and wisdom. Their teachings nearly destroy *Endale*. However, *Mellithion* prevails in defending her from these greater gods and he casts them back into the darkness. But the damage of their *bridging* could not be reversed.

The tales of *Chalshaf* and *Ashto* are highly abridged translations. Following after are summaries to the eight other gods of the Lay of *Melea* and their dealings with *Endale* and *Mellithion*. It is hoped that these stories (however cut down) will provide those with an interest in the *Itonalya* a glimpse into their ancient beliefs and fascinating culture. We look forward to complete versions of the *Toele* and the Lay of *Melea*, among many other *Itonalya* works in the years to come.

Photo courtesy of Graham Cremo, ©2018
Avu, Tales of Sky. Heron Atheneum One

OF THE COURT OF THI AND THE MAKING OF DELLITHION AND ENDALE

Each glittering point of light in the night's sky is an eye. They are what we, the *Itonalya,* call *Oläthion* and they are the thoughts in the mind of *Thi*, The One, whose sight sees all, knows all and has created what is.

Thi bade the *Oläthion* to sing their tales and their histories through sparkling streams of light. Their voices cry out and ride upon flames, cutting through time's black depths and fathomless gulfs until, each by each, their minds touch, their eyes see through their siblings' eyes, their stories become known, and they do not feel alone. Through light they share. *Elliqui* is the light. The voice of *Thi*.

Tales beyond number, beyond imagination, flash across heaven. Stories. Luminous stories of clustered, searing suns tearing the sky and spilling new stars out into the black. Sparks telling of tiny worlds with swirling clouds of poisoned smoke and seas of boiling blood. Dramas of colliding, bejeweled cities made of fire, and radiant frozen spheres—joyous cascades of molten rock and skies scarred by lighting; all gleaming from eye to eye amid the Order of Creation, *Oläthion*. And *Thi* was pleased.

We began as a lonely pale light flickering in the mind of *Thi*. A yellow fleck on the edge of Its imagination. This small sun harkened to the countless tales woven in the surrounding starlight. It saw far into the depths of Its siblings and their stories, and knew that it was holy among the thoughts of *Thi*. Then, from out of the distant dark, a glowing charge gave it blessings of welcome, and it knew that it would now forever be named *Dellithion*.[4]

For an age, the young *Dellithion* drifted among Its siblings perceiving the stories of its kin.

---

[4] The *Itonalya* often regard *Dellithion* (the sun) and *Thi* (the One creator that is all) as the same entity.

Many say that time began for the *Itonalya* when *Dellithion* shone out Its own tale into the night. The celestial audience turned to perceive and they saw *Dellithion* shimmer with gold tendrils of flame, and from Its surface eight spheres of mist and stone and fire were hurled out from Its embrace. Each was adorned in starlike garments, bright in the ebony gulf. Orbs of swirling crimson and ice blue, solemn globes ringed with jewels, gold, and tiny pale stones hastening out toward the end of *Dellithion's* story.

The stars watched and let the drama glow within them. And they were glad. And so it was that *Dellithion* entered into the great family of *Thi* and became one of the mighty *Oläthion*.

But then, *Dellithion's* story ending, the void darkened and the *Oläthion* eyes turned away to other tales. *Dellithion* flashed out to gather their attention but the audience gazed far off for they now sought stories of greater power and depth. *Dellithion* watched as Its creations drifted into the quiet dark and It felt alone and afraid.

But *Dellithion* still had more to make, and though Its place within *Thi's* Court was to most a meager and insignificant trifle, the small star trembled for an age yearning to bring its master work to shine.

It is said that *Dellithion's* coveted jewel, *Endale*, the treasure of every eye amid the Court of *Thi,* the envy of every story sent on streams of starlight, shaped from Dellithion's desire to reflect the power of its siblings back to them; to reflect the love of the light that connected them all; to reflect *Thi*.

Said to be formed from teardrops of sun and oceans of flame, the delicate blue green world took its place among the Court of *Dellithion*. Her beauty was unlike any tale known among the Great. The *Oläthion* could not look away.[5]

So beautiful was *Endale* that *Dellithion* Itself stared in

---

[5] The *Itonalya* employ the poetic notion that Endale's (Earth's) beauty is so great among the stars is proven by every night's sky full of stars. No eye of heaven can look away.

hopeless wonder and love, neglecting the others of Its Court. Over time the Court of *Dellithion* cried out for their maker to mark them, heed them, to look upon them. With great effort, *Dellithion* pulled his gaze from his precious *Endale* and turned to Its other children, but not before placing a guardian to protect Its beloved *Endale* in Its absence.

From the highest peak upon *Endale, Dellithion* tore a root of stone. A mountain. Raising it to the void, before Its eye, It bore spears of flame into the shaping rock. *Mellithion,* the Sun named it. A tiny sphere to protect the King's treasure. Smooth *Mellithion* became and white as naked light. As he cooled, his skin shimmered to pure gold. *Dellithion* flung the guardian to *Endale* and the two entwined into a dance amid the stars.

Such was the curse of the Moon, for he was given the strength of the *Oläthion,* but not the gift of tales. Instead, he was a servant, forever cursed to behold the beauty of *Endale*, unable to look away. To hear her. To follow her. To protect. And never to know freedom. *Mellithion's* curse also bore an unquenchable love and a devotion beyond any tales known among the Siblings or the *Itonalya.*

i
OF MIGHTY CHALSHAF, FIRST BORN

So beautiful was *Endale* against night's shroud that she attracted the eyes of the infinite celestial audience, the *Oläthion.* The ancient Order marveled and stared deeply into her, pining to know her story and her future. Her nearer kin, The smaller Court of *Dellithion,* also found it impossible to draw their attention from her beauty. And as the great *Dellithion* removed Its gaze from *Endale,* secure with *Mellithion's* vigilant eye, It went to each of Its children, each in turn, to insure their obedience and assure them of Its love.

When It had turned away, the Sun's first born, *Chalshaf,* mightiest of the Court, drifted across the black distance to behold

Endale. He was vast. A swirling ball of impenetrable cloud and vapor. Immense and powerful.

At his approach *Endale's* surface quaked, mountains crumbled and her great oceans rose up as if reaching out to touch the giant.

Chalshaf's face was a rolling vapor of orange and white. In the center of his bulk, red and menacing, was a deep chasm whirling like a storm of blood. It was a gaping wound.

He spoke to her. "You are coveted and loved, *Endale,* by our Maker, *Dellithion. Dellithion* cares more, it seems, for you than the others of His Court. More than even I, the mighty *Chalshaf,* first born, Ruler among the siblings of *Dellithion's* thought. But you are weak. You are delicate. How is it that our Maker hath placed you higher than I? How can this be?"

Chalshaf waited and watched, and as he did so his jealousy was overthrown by *Endale's* beauty, for he understood she had no knowledge of such adoration. *Chalshaf* saw innocence and a glimmer of the great wisdom that would grow within her.

"Now I see," he said, "For you seek not power or justice. You want only peace and a view of the *Oläthion* sky." *Chalshaf* turned his gaze to the stars and said, "But a time will come when the powers of heaven will fall upon you. They will take from you that which is purest, your story. They will make you pine for the strength to rule—the desire for power. You cannot allow it, *Endale. Dellithion* will not allow it. Even now, as you behold my strength, I sense your covetousness, your desire."

Endale replied, "I am afraid. I do not feel envy."

"Not yet, perhaps. One day you will long for power, for power will lessen your fear."

"I have *Mellithion* to protect me in my Lord's absence," *Endale* said.

"You do. But if you are truly to become one of our Court, you must learn to rule what you make, and rule your yourself. I will not harm you, *Endale.* I bring warnings. Beware of power. I shall show you the pain it brings. Perhaps with the taste of this wisdom you will remain as you are, the jewel of purity we long to

582 THE SHAPE OF RAIN

know—the peace we long to feel.

"Behold the hurt my Maker, *Dellithion*, hath given me." Chalshaf glowered down into Endale's light and the wound upon his face coiled like a hissing snake. "For long ago, I alone sought power over *Dellithion's* will. I have paid a heavy price. But, in the end, *Dellithion's* payment has been more in wisdom than in pain. Thus, I will teach you, *Endale*, to challenge all before you. Even those closest to you. Receive the hurts that come so that you may find strength.

"Look, you, *Endale*. See the hurricane. Harken to the tumult of thunder, the power of chaos. Behold how my face churns in storm and fury. Take from me this lesson." *Chalshaf* brought his lips to hers and a tempest spread across her body. Lesions of swirling rain and snow and howling winds tore great ragged fissures into her surface. Water and stones funneled into her skies and blotted out the distant light of *Dellithion* now far away.

Endale cried out in both joy and pain. Joy for the power brought forth a new strength. Pain because she could not control it.

"Do you see, *Endale*? The chaos that is yours to command? Use it to defend yourself."

"Stop!" *Endale* screamed. "I am not the lord of this gift. It rages beyond me."

Chalshaf, now overwhelmed with desire pressed her further.

When *Mellithion* rose from the sea and beheld the terror of *Chalshaf* brooding over his lover, he shone like *Dellithion* Itself in wrath. It is said *Mellithion* was the first to forge a sword and to wield it against the Gods, for as he tore across the horizon, a sharp streak of flame gathered in his wake. Long and gleaming, the blade rung out as a knife scraping on a stone. The moon wedged himself between *Chalshaf* and his beloved, and he swung the sword around from behind. The weapon dragged across the sky, sparked into flame and smote the giant's mighty helm. *Chalshaf* rolled back, his face filled with storm and confusion.

Mellithion stabbed the point of the sword into *Chalshaf's* menacing eye, and the giant fell away, shrieking in pain.

"Fly! Be gone, *Chalshaf!* Be gone!" *Mellithion* commanded. "I am the guardian of she that was made pure. She who is not destined to be one of you. She is *Endale*. She is beyond the starlight."

Chalshaf whirled and rose up. His bulk blotted out the light of the distant sun. *Endale* cowered and wept while the Moon stood firm, eclipsed in the giant's deepening shadow. But before *Chalshaf* attacked, *Mellithion's* fury abated. He stared at the raging giant with sudden pity and awe. How the wound upon *Chalshaf* glared—how the giant himself would never allow it heal—how the pain drove his anger. The moon could see how *Chalshaf* ruled: with the memory of storm, ire and violence.

Mellithion felt pity for the god.

It is said that *Mellithion* was the first to offer the hilt of his sword to an adversary. He did this without fear.

Chalshaf laid hold of the weapon and struck Mellithion with vicious, deadly blows. The stabbing pits into the once smooth face of the Moon. Great fissures and deep chasms were lanced into him. Flakes of his gold skin fluttered and floated into the void. *Chalshaf* roared, "No servant, no guardian, no simple imitation of a god shall command me! It is I that rule this court." The giant struck him again. More gold tore away. "Do you see, *Mellithion*, your disguise breaks and exposes your true self— *Dellithion* may have made you in his image, but beneath, you are stone and dust."

Endale watched the cruel giant strike again scarring the silent and still Moon. She cried, "Stop, mighty *Chalshaf!* Mercy, I beg!" *Chalshaf* heeded the melody of *Endale's* weeping voice and stayed his hand.

Gently, with a slight quaver, for his pain was great, *Mellithion* said, "*Chalshaf*, what weapon will kill the anger within you? I hath given you my sword— and it has done nothing save injure us both. My visage shall bear your violence for eternity— and you shall live on, and your wound of anger will finally consume you. Can you not see that I am not your enemy? I am a humble guardian. I was made to protect a strength beyond all powers. It is she, *Endale*. Fair in the empty darkness. Pure beyond measure. If only I could become as she. If only we sparks across heaven could become as she. For truly, I am mere stone and dust, arraigned in the armor my lord hath given me. And though our armor and injuries are akin, they exist only because of the love we long for, though we fail to know it. But behold, *Endale*. Let us allow her to show us peace. Let us allow her to bring us hope."

Chalshaf's anger lessened, and the words of the tiny moon brought a rush of admiration. He beheld the now broken and injured guard as a giant among the *Oläthion*. Slowly, *Chalshaf* bowed. His great bleeding eye closed as if in prayer.

Chalshaf said, "Never shall I come to *Endale* in this way again. But I cannot look away. The story within her is beyond my strength to resist. She will lure all light to her cheek as the ages pass. You know this. A time will come when a door will open to her favors—a door you will have no power to close. And though your intentions are to save her, as are mine, we will both fail. Therefore, take from me your sword." *Chalshaf* turned the hilt of the moon's sword to him. *Mellithion* took it. "I will make this covenant with you— where you find me seeking the light of *Endale*, smite me and send me hither. Know that I will obey, know also that I will return again and again, for there is no peace outside *Endale's* light. She is the very light in the eye of *Thi*. Protect her, *Mellithion*, for the love of *Thi*. Protect her from me. From the sky."

With that, *Chalshaf* backed away into the darkness, his eye ever trained on the churning blue green face of *Endale*.

ii

OF ASHTO, TEACHER OF TIME

The early scholars of *Keptiris* were said to worship *Ashto*

(Saturn, later the Greek's Kronos), though by the time of the last *Wyn Avuquain* monarchs, *Ashto* had become less of a god and more of a curse word. The precise reason for this is unknown. However, because the archetype was representative of the passage of time and the cyclical patterns that govern the universe, it would not be too far beyond the pale to assume that the younger *Itonalya* (just over two centuries old) would have a profound sense of frustration at the beguiling monotony of the *Ashtonian* message. The message is rooted in the circular seasons as well as the birth, youth, age and death cycles that dictate the nature of life as we know it. Apart from this stands the *Itonalya* curse of an ageless body without the divine capacity to fully transcend human empathy, or in the words of William Greenhame, "The burden of lifetimes of thought without rest." Thus, like the *Itonalya* phrase *ithic veli agtig* uttered as a kind of lamentation, the words *gal Ashto* might be akin to our expletive, *goddamn it.*

However, *Ashtonian* philosophy was held in high reverence to most due to the god's central purpose: teaching. The *Itonalya* believed the passing of wisdom and the pursuit of knowledge was among the highest aims. *Ashto* as teacher was paramount in early agriculture, the healing arts for mortals, along with the study of history and time. Structure, guidelines and the firm nature of reality, like a good teacher, make up Ashto's thematic elements. Sources also place the god of *Ashto* into the love story of *Endale* and *Mellithion* which I have included here. Of the myriad tales and proverbs where this influential character is core, this story is one found in the *Toele* and is often quoted by *Elliquists* throughout the canon. I find it also relevant for readers interested in the *Itonalya's* devotion and duty of protecting the children of *Endale*.

OF ASHTO THE TEACHER

"What is forever?" *Endale* asked.

Mellithion did not reply.

"Will you not speak? Will you not see me."

The moon saw her. He could not look away save only to protect her. But his thoughts remained silent. He drifted along the horizon and hungered for her. She swirled and turned in drifting blues and glowing whites. He was shade and grey. A mere stone at her feet.

"Please, what is forever?" she asked again. "I long to know the secrets to the sky, to the shining eyes, the chambers of light beyond. How distant? Show me. Please show me. Take me hither."

Mellithion wondered about the mysteries that lay hidden behind the curtain of night, and he, too, wanted to know. But just as the desire came to lead her out to the marvels that *Thi* had forbidden, he fell deep into the mystery of her beauty, and he was content.

"Please, *Mellithion*. What is forever? Do you not want to see the where the lights come from?"

Mellithion spoke, and she was surprised by his sudden presence in her thoughts. "Forever is you and me," he whispered.

Endale looked upon the moon and she knew that he loved her.

It was then another voice entered their thoughts.

"There is no forever," the voice said. "All will pass away. But time is long, so be content."

There, rising above *Endale's* deep blue oceans was a great sphere of gold and white. It wore wide, thin rings of ice and dust. *Mellithion* drew his sword and pressed himself between *Endale* and the intruder.

"Be gone!" *Mellithion* commanded. "We seek no audience with thee."

The voice replied, "I dare say, you do not."

Mellithion sensed no malice, but instead, a calm, fatherly demeanor. "I mean no harm, valiant guardian, guard to the jewel of the *Oläthion.*"

"Who are you?" *Mellithion* asked.

"I am *Ashto*. *Ashto* the Keeper of Time. I am the Teacher."
Mellithion stared.

Endale also marveled at the rings of gold and the bright bans of light turning in his eye. "My dear," *Ashto* said to her, "Forever is where we begin and end. The arcing circles by which we travel—the rings that connect us—the wheeling paths that teach order." The mighty sphere paused as he beheld her. "When I look upon you, I am struck with a feeling wholly new and impossible to escape. I understand now the whisperings of the *Oläthion*. Your beauty is beyond understanding."

Ashto looked upon the piteous moon and sighed. "You too, I expect, sense the same feeling? For you are wise beyond your light, *Mellithion*. You are correct, there is no forever, though I wonder now if love is not the answer to your question, *Endale*."

"Why have you come?" *Endale* asked.

"Perhaps, I myself have come to learn," *Ashto* said, "for I sense a deep wisdom in your guardian. One day, he may be a teacher. But I have come to teach you the ways of the *Dellithion* Court—the path that will lead you closer to forever."

Mellithion rose up, "The Lord *Dellithion* forbids all audience with *Endale*—"

Ashto interrupted, "The Lord *Dellithion* is far away, and I am certain It would agree with my counsel. *Endale* must learn control, must study the nature of the *Oläthion* sky, the boundaries separating her from certain oblivion—her meaning and how to share it in story, in light.

Ashto's crowning rings sparkled against the night as he began to sing an ancient melody.[6] The song enchanted both the earth and moon and they fell into a deep sleep.

When they woke, the starlight was whirling and streaking

---

[6] Which song *Ashto* sang to the Earth and Moon is still hotly debated. There are three recurring songs that appear in varying texts. In the earliest version of this tale, *Ashto's* song tempts *Endale* to seek knowledge for herself by embarking upon a great journey. This of course was not the will of *Thi* and would have been regarded as an act of disobedience. Centuries later another song of *Ashto's* was inserted into the tale. Still a song of temptation, it promised *Endale* and *Mellithion* both that they would themselves become gods if they followed the teaching of *Ashto*.

in long lines. They could see *Dellithion* beaming far out in the void as they vaulted out and around It— winding in a speeding circle.

Ashto's song continued, "Look how she breeds. Her oceans teem—her trees bear fruit. Walkers have appeared on her shores. What lessons we learn from our children. What horrors come from their doings if we do not guide them."

"Children?" *Endale* asked.

"Yes. Do you not know them?"

And behold, the children of *Endale* gazed up into the night's sky, crawlers and swimmers, beast and bird, and *Endale* felt them upon her breast and she wept. She made her tears into the shape of *Thi*, into the image of all seeing *Thi*, countless eyes so she could see her children whether under the soil, beneath the seas or upon the wide lands.

She could feel her children tremble as she hurtled through the inky void. And when she beheld them, she could see that they too were trapped within *Ashto's* teachings and the ring of his questions.

Time broke upon the face of *Endale*. Time. Springs and summers burst forth new life. Autumns brought decay and age-worn fear. Harsh winters buried the dead. And it was not only upon her body, but it was also within her children. Seasons passed. Her children suckled, and they gained from her body nourishment to sustain them. They were born. They grew and they died and folded back into her flesh. She felt the joy of their joy, the gratitude that is life, and the fleeting brevity of their existence. She felt the pain of their need and want, and when they bit into her, she gave freely, for they only ate that which would sustain them.

Mellithion marveled at this new wisdom, but he strained against it for it was his burden to do the will of *Thi*. He cried out for her to take care and slow her pace. He pushed against her, held her, and was then forced to let go for her speed was too great. His grasp broke and his body was cast away to the dark.

Grief overcame him and he wept.

Ashto watched as *Endale* rushed again, rounding the starlit path he had shown her. When he saw that *Mellithion* was abandoned and alone he came to him and said, "What now, Guardian? Is not your charge to protect *Endale*? Why do you tarry here?"

Mellithion lamented, "I cannot match her speed. Do you see the life that she makes, the life that she is. I am barren and without the favor of the gods."

"But you are a part of her," *Ashto* consoled, "and she will remember ere the end."

Endale had traveled the entire ring of the *Ashto's* teaching, and she was now approaching *Mellithion*. She cried out for him, and he for her.

"Come with me, *Mellithion*, for there are stories beyond dreams on the rounding path of the Sun, and from the depths of nighttime forever has joined me. It is here, in this ring, ever beginning, ever ending. Come with me, *Tifli*."[7]

For a moment, it seemed to *Ashto*, that *Mellithion's* armor glinted as if was gold once again. "I will come. I will come with you. But tell me, what have you seen, what have you learned."

"I have seen forever," she cried, as she laid hold of the moon and puller him into her embrace. "I will not see it again without you."

iii.
OF AGYAR THE PURIFIER

The tale of *Agyar* the Purifier is an extraordinarily complex and long tale concerning the relationships and intimate connections between love and war, and violence and sex. The Itonalya god *Agyar and* his lust for conflict and strife eventually evolved into the Greek god of war, Ares, or later the Roman's Mars. According to Dr. Astrid Finnley, *Agyar's* footprints trek through the Egyptian tales of Set and Anhur, the ancient Chinese

---

[7] The moon, or *Mellithion*.

deity, Chiyou, the Mesopotamian's Belus, and the Norse god Odin, among many others.

Agyar first appears in the Lay of *Melea* as a great warship crossing the sea of night to the shores of *Endale*. Like *Endale's* other Siblings, *Agyar* is captivated by her beauty and pledges his undying loyalty. In token of his affection, *Agyar* gifts the earth with three kinds of fire: one to be used as a weapon to burn, one to purify, one for love. *Agyar* shows her the power of fire by burning her. Great swathes of desert appear upon her body. Next, in places where *Endale's* forests were too thick and pestilence bred, *Agyar* set them on fire. After the fires died, the land burst with green shoots and new trees from out of the ashes. Lastly, *Agyar* set himself on fire. *Endale* entranced by the sight of him, longed to mingle her third gift, her flames of love, with his. It was then that *Mellithion* discovered *Agyar's* presence.

Mellithion becomes flame himself through some hidden gift of *Thi* and parts the lovers with awesome violence and sadness. He eventually stabs his sword of fire through the *Agyar's* war ship and sinks the god's fire down into the deep ocean of night. *Endale,* waking as if from a dream, returns to *Mellithion* and wraps him with her flames.[8] The battle is long, and it is told through twenty-seven *Itonalya* parables. But the battle is not just fought between *Mellithion* and *Agyar*. *Endale* uses *Agyar's* gifts against herself to learn the nature of desire, love, hatred and war. *Mellithion* fights against his desire to kill and to love simultaneously. In the end, the tale of *Agyar* examines the nature of war and its intimate connection to our most gentle intentions.

---

[8] When sighting a red moon (or the glinting red of Mars) in the sky, *Itonalya* will often say: *melagyar diluthia,* which means, simply, *the moon is at war and either love or blood is near.* The saying has also come to mean: love and war are the same thing, both will purify the soul.

iv.
OF UNLIFSO THE MESSENGER

Unlifso's place in the Lay of *Melea* is another long, complex and tortuous tale. A favorite character of immortal poets and painters, *Unlifso* was said to be the seed to the immortal race as well as the inspiration to the deific drama that brought on the events culminating in Loche Newirth's prophetic writing.

Unlifso was the nearest and dearest to the sun god, *Dellithion*. He served as *Dellithion's* primary herald and was responsible for the of passing of messages. Most importantly, *Unlifso* was the first to bridge between the realms of mortals and the divine. He was known as a trickster as well as the god that peeled back the veil of truth. The tale of *Unlifso* in the Lay of *Melea* deals closely with *Unlifso* as the first to trespass into the world of mortals against the Old Law of mighty *Thi*.

By the time *Unlifso* came to educate *Endale, Endale* had borne children: beasts and birds, crawlers and swimmers, and those she loved more than all the others—those she called *Ithea* (humans or mortals). *Unlifso* appeared on *Endale* as a man wearing a circlet with two silver wings upon his brow. As a man he did not remember that he was *Unlifso* the god, nor did he have any memory of his place among the Court of *Dellithion* or the greater *Oläthion*. Instead, he only felt the delicate brevity of life and an overwhelming sense of wanting to experience everything he could without a care for the consequences. *Endale*, knowing a god had crossed over into her consciousness, became mortal, too. Unlike *Unlifso, Endale* knew that she was herself a god. She also knew that *Unlifso* was breaking the Old Law. The two met beside a great river and became friends. Like *Agyar's* tale, the journey of *Endale* and *Unlifso's* story unfolds into series of parables dealing with innocence and experience, boundaries, transgression, greed and ambition while the two traveled together to the nearest city, and, in a very short time, *Unlifso* became a leader of men. At first his aims were good for the city folk. His enthusiasm, his ability to communicate and his big ideas brought him wealth, fame and loyal subjects. But as time passed his desire for more blinded him and his greed led to rampant corruption and unrest. Perhaps the greatest of *Unlifso's* sins was his unchecked influence. His actions and words inspired others to behave in similar ways so they might benefit as he did. Even *Endale* fell prey to his persuasive character, and each time she acted with her corrupt heart to fill her greed, her mortal body paid the price. *Unlifso's* voice became the inner voice of illness and *Endale*, without knowing it, suffered great injury.[9]

Deserts appeared on the earth. There was great famine and plague. Amid all the chaos, *Endale* agreed to marry Unlifso.

Mellithion in the meantime watched *Unlifso* bewitch his beloved *Endale* and her children, and it enraged him to the point of helplessness, for he could do nothing as a god—he did not know how to become an *Ithea*. From the sky he watched forests burn, smoke rise from cities, waters blacken from poisons, and he knew *Endale* would not survive if *Unlifso's* godlike powers on the earth were not stopped.

Mellithion cried out to mighty *Thi* for aid through what the *Itonalya* call the *Tengstre*.[10] He pleaded with the One to make him mortal so that he could defend his beloved.

When *Thi* learned that its Law was being broken, it granted *Endale's* guardian *Mellithion* his wish, and more. *Mellithion* dropped to the earth as rain—he then rose up as an immortal man. The first *Itonalya*.

Mellithion's coming to earth is told with a series of songs that examine the pain of immortality, the love he has for *Endale* and her children, and the fear of oblivion.

At length, *Mellithion* challenges *Unlifso* to a duel for the

---

[9] The Messenger's voice to the *Itonalya* is not always negative. *Unlifso* is known as a trickster, certainly, but he is also a purveyor of truth, and to hear his voice is considered a blessing. In the end, *Unlifso* provides potentialities both good and bad—the meanings of his messages are for the *Itonalya* to decipher.

[10] The *Tengstre* or the Long Cry of *Mellithion* is a 9000 plus word *elean* (prayer) that strikes at the heart of the immortal condition.

control of the city and the hand of *Endale*. In response to the challenge, *Unlifso*, sends one hundred of his most dangerous knights to kill *Mellithion*. They fail. *Mellithion* fills a horse drawn cart with their heads and rides them to *Unlifso's* door. The next day the two meet before the people of the city.

Before the fight, *Mellithion* tells a story to the audience about how they have been deceived by a god and how *Unlifso* had corrupted their hearts and minds as well as the lands and waters where they must continue to live. *Unlifso* then dies at the hand of the first *Itonalya*.

Endale, as if waking from out of a trance, returns to the arms of *Mellithion*. The two mend the wounds *Unlifso* had inflicted, and they live blissfully together for many years. Eventually, the mortal body of *Endale* dies of old age leaving *Mellithion* alone on the earth.

Unlifso bridged back to the realm of the gods. He sent messages to the Siblings and the *Oläthion* about how he managed to become a part of *Endale's* story. He then showed them how they, too, could go and join with *Thi's* coveted jewel. From that point on, *Endale's* lands filled with countless gods.

Thi, enraged, pulled *Unlifso* close to its side and burned him with its light and fire as punishment. To *Mellithion, Thi* sent aid. Over the long years, *Itonalya* dropped down into *Endale* with the rain and together they built a city called *Wyn Avuqua* and they remained loyal to *Thi's* charge.

v.

OF SHIVTIRIS THE KILLER

Unlifso had now provided the *Oläthion* a kind of key to *Endale's* door. Gods came in droves; and through her children, *Endale's* education continued.

Shivtiris was the darkest and most mysterious of all of *Endale's* nearest siblings. Other human myths would borrow elements of the *Itonalya's Shivtiris* and rename her Hades, Set and Lucifer (among others). Immortals would later name *Shivtiris* the *Cymachkena*, their version of the devil.

Using *Unlifso's* enthusiasm and powerful skill of communication along with *Agyar's* weapons of fire, *Shivtiris* taught the children of *Endale* suffering through the horrors of war, famine, plague and abject fear. The god's tale in the Lay of *Melea* is long and written in simple, almost child like couplets. The singsong rhythm juxtaposed to the bloody and graphic suffering of *Endale's* children is both chilling and beautiful. Her name, *Shivtiris*, means house of fear, and it is indicative of what she wanted *Endale* to become, as well as what she believed to be the greatest and most telling element of the human story: suffering.

The story in brief:

Unlike other gods, *Shivtiris* had some sense that she was not of the earth. She knew that within her a godlike power brooded.[11] She presented herself to the leaders of mortals as a sorcerer and lit within them a fear of scarcity, jealousy and pride. It was not long before bloody wars, starvation and sickness ravaged the body of *Endale*. But worse, *Shivtiris'* influence led the *Ithea* to create the chaos of war and illness in their own hearts and minds which prevented them from finding peace. *Mellithion* sent his *Orathom Wis* to settle disputes, teach patience and to care for the sick. Ultimately, *Mellithion* forced Shivtiris out of her Queenship and killed her mortal body. Some time later, *Shivtiris* bridged again, this time as a man called *Cyaenth* who bred the same pestilence as before. Again *Mellithion* hunted and killed the god. It was said that *Shivtiris* would never relent and would continue to return until *Endale* was dead.

The moral of *Shivtiris'* story for the *Itonalya* suggests that hardship and chaos will forever tangle themselves in the affairs of the earth, whether through the work of the *Cymachkena* or

---

[11] *Shivtiris* or the *Cymachkena* is perhaps the only recorded god to have bridged into the mortal realm more than once. *Shivtiris* became seemingly ever present among the *Ithea*. (Until, of course, the end of the Newirth War.)

humankind alone.

Perhaps the most exciting part of *Shivtiris'* story for both the *Ithea* and the *Itonalya* is how Loche Newirth and his cast of mythical characters have now defeated the enemy of *Endale* once and for all. At the end of New Earth War The *Itonalya*, George Eversman, son of *Yafarra* Queen of *Wyn Avuqua* took the head of the immortal *Shivtiris* on earth, Nicholas Cythe—and thus, cast the god into oblivion forever. The Newirth Mythology has now put an end to the Devil's reign of terror over humankind.

vi.
OF CERVALSO THE SEEKER

When the god *Cervalso*[12] (his name meaning both the promise of truth and lies) crossed into *Endale* he did not bring great calamity or cataclysm. He did not appear as a warlord or a seer or an *Unlifsian* disciple. Rather, *Cervalso* came into the company of the *Ithea* as a simple man seeking the answers to questions never before asked. He prodded humankind to think about death. He opened dialogue concerning the meaning of one's existence and it if there was any reason for it. He even questioned the existence of gods. *Cervalso* sought peace, and he openly confronted those *Ithea* that practiced the destructive lessons of *Agyar* and *Unlifso*. But he did this through diplomatic and philosophical methods.

When *Mellithion* discovered that *Cervalso* was a god, and came to send him back across the gulf, *Cervalso* could not understand why anyone would want to murder him. He was frightened and asked *Mellithion* to spare his life. For *Mellithion,* the request opposed his sacred charge, but something about *Cervalso* and his gifts of peace and thoughtful insight to the children of *Endale* stayed his hand. *Mellithion* told *Cervalso* that

---

[12] *Cervalso* and his presence in *Itonalya* lore represents the unknown, cloudy or misty visions and the uncertainty of existence. He was later interpreted by the Greeks and Romans as the god Neptune or Poseidon, the ruler of the vast and endless seas.

if he harmed the earth or the *Ithea* he would return and kill him.

Cervalso then built a school and he gathered students to study the stars, math, poetry, history and philosophy. *Mellithion* and the *Orathom Wis* kept watch upon *Cervalso* and his doings, and over time found that exceptions could be made to those gods whose deeds were virtuous to the children of *Endale*.

In the Lay of *Melea, Cervalso* taught *Mellithion* wisdom, mercy and foresight. *Cervalso's* teachings provided the *Itonalya* the power to grant a *Godrethion* grace upon *Endale* for their good works.[13]

vii.
OF RESSCA THE MAGICIAN

As recorded in the *Toele*, the god *Ressca* was said to have fallen out of the sky and was caught by the splayed, finger like branches of the tallest tree in *Wyn Avuqua*. He was a boy of fourteen years. Elders from each of the *Wyn Avuquain* households surrounded the tree intent on killing the trespassing *Godrethion*, but the fantastic manner of the god's entrance into *Endale* as well as his ill luck in terms of a place for a god to land caused the Elders to pause in wonder. The Minister of Wings proposed that the young *Godrethion* should be kept alive and questioned so that they may learn whether he was sent by *Thi* as some sort of omen. The Elders agreed.

Ressca was taken into the House of Wings, where he lived

---

[13] *Cervalsian* beliefs were often an area of heated debate when it came to whether a god was given grace to exist on earth against the Old Law. There was a faction of *Itonalya* fundamentalists that held fast to the Old Law and they would suffer no *Godrethion* life on *Endale*, good works or no. The movement called themselves the *Gacervals* and they rose out of the *Wyn Avuquain* household of *Shartiris* shortly after the city was founded. The beliefs and hard-lined judgements of this group were dangerous, and over time they built a reputation on savagery and willing ignorance. Over time the movement fell into disfavor among the majority of *Itonalya*—but their influence was never completely extinguished from *Itonalya* history or training, for the *Itonalya*, gods were to be sent back into the void regardless of their gifts to humankind. But it was deemed that those who loved *Endale* and her children would let a god live whose gifts would propel humankind to peace, healing and prosperity.

among his sworn enemies—but he knew only their kindness and curiosity.

Ressca quickly became of great interest to the entire city for it was rumored that the god's presence was a signal of the end of their slavery, and that the long burden (the guardianship of *Endale* and *Ithea*) would soon be over. Soon the reward of afterlife to immortals would be granted and the *Itonalya* would be free.

But this was not so. However, there was a lesson to be learned from this god from the sky.[14]

When Lord *Mellithion* returned to the city and was told that a god was living within the walls, he was eager to meet him. The Lay of *Melea* tells of *Mellithion's* appraisal of *Ressca* over nearly a hundred or more extremely complex verses. In short, young *Ressca* was described as possessing characteristics from each of *Dellithion's* Court that came before him. He had the command and size of *Chalshaf,* the thoughtful patience of *Ashto,* the quick temper and fire of *Agyar,* the enthusiasm and attractiveness of *Unlifso*, the thoughtful philosophies of *Cervalso*, and lastly, the dark melancholy of *Shivtiris*. But with all of these attributes, *Ressca* carried with him a great sense of humor and profound sadness, and the two emotions would often flow through him shifting from one to the other, just as the weather would change from sun to rain. In his darkest moments he found laughter. In deep contemplation he was quick to point out the meaninglessness of it all with great jibes and jokes. If he was filled with joy and wonder one moment, then tears would rise and he would sob deeply. *Ressca* seemed to have a firm hold on the power of living in the present moment, and other times he would lament the oncoming shadow of death that would end the sensations, emotions and experiences of his delicate and brief existence on earth.

---

[14] Elements of *Ressca* and the tales of his adventures on *Endale* evolved into many other sky god characters for the *Ithea* over the centuries. Traces of *Ressca* can be found the Greek's Uranus, the Roman's Caelus, the Egyptian goddess Hathor and the Sumerian god Enlil, among others.

The *Itonalya* named him the Magician not because he practiced sorcery or magic as we might understand it, rather, it was how he conjured the potency of human emotions within the city's populace that got him the title; for his power was, to the immortals, magic. *Ressca's* presence among them stirred a zeal and lust for life within them.

Mellithion spent each day of that year with *Ressca,* trying to decipher *Thi's* reason for sending the boy, if there was one at all. When the leaves began to fall and the chill of winter blew down from the North, *Ressca* became ill. All the *Wyn Avuquain* crafts of healing did nothing to improve *Ressca's* health. During his final days, *Mellithion* explained to *Ressca* the nature of their relationship; how *Ressca* was a god living in a city of immortals, and the immortals were charged with eliminating gods upon earth; how *Ressca* fell from the sky; how *Ressca's* passionate influence had changed the insight of the *Itonalya;* how he would be missed. In answer to these issues *Ressca* started to laugh and said he did not believe any of his wild tales save one. He did agree that he was different from all the people he had met in the city. When *Mellithion* asked how, *Ressca* told him that he felt as if he alone was the only one with hope. The young god then died.

Mellithion took the lesson from *Ressca* out into the world of *Endale's* children, the *Ithea,* and he exhibited great emotion, and a passion for living for the rest of his days. *Ressca's* magic was the delivery of hope to *Endale.*

The House of *Shartiris* adopted and wrote the *Resscian* principles. In the years that followed, *Itonalya* would celebrate *Ressca's* lessons and his life by gathering around the very tree that snatched him out of the sky (the tree they named the Hope Tree) and there beneath its great boughs they would share poetry and songs of great sorrow and joy. To this day, when the winter ends and spring begins, *Itonalya,* where ever they are in the world, will gather around the tallest tree they can find and celebrate *Yaressca* (*Elliqui*: the shape of hope within the spirit).

viii.
OF FENOR THE LOVER
AND MELLITHION'S RETURN TO THE SKY

The lessons of the god *Fenor* dominate nearly one-third of the Lay of *Melea's* conclusion, and they examine the beauty, power and tragedy of *Itonalya* perceptions on romantic love. The tale itself is broken into five parts.

The first deals with *Mellithion's* centuries-long loneliness, his reflections on life's meaning and his unrequited love for *Endale*. Since the moment he looked upon *Endale* from his place in the sky, *Mellithion* loved her, and his desire never wavered even as he walked the earth as the *Wyn Avuquain* king of immortals. He pleaded each night for her to come to him—to rise from out of the soil and become flesh and blood, or *Godrethion*, or mortal or immortal—it did not matter to him. She did not, or could not answer. Over uncounted centuries *Mellithion* remained alone and did not take a wife, nor did he love another. A series of songs describe these long years and the mechanisms by which he coped as he sought to find peace as a solitary being. However, the verses are rapt in a delicate uncertainty and a hopeful yearning for something more than self discovery and self reliance. The section's themes seem astonishingly ahead of their time. They provide a remarkable view into the immortal state of mind, and they explore the importance of an individual's emotional, psychological and social well-being as the highest and most noble of aims.[15]

The point of view moves to the god *Fenor* in the second part. It tells of *Fenor's* bridging to the earth, and her desire to find

---

[15] According to George Eversman and other sources, the opening seventy-one verses of the *Lay of Melea's, Fenor the Lover* contain the fundamental principles of *Itonalya* philosophy and the meditations on *time endurance* that are the core of *Itonalya* curriculum. Time endurance is described through what the Silent Author (in the voice of *Mellithion*) names as the three sisters: Patience, Action and Outcome. Through the first section of *Fenor the Lover, Mellithion* meets these allegorical sisters and learns the slow lesson that "time will inevitably tell," and how slow thoughtful action creates the most peaceful outcomes.

and win the love of *Mellithion* in order to stop the *Itonalya* from killing *Godrethion* on earth. Unlike others of her kind, *Fenor* had the gift of self knowledge, for even as a mortal woman, she knew of her divine origin. She also knew, as did all the *Oläthion, Mellithion's* greatest want and deepest desire: *Endale.* Therefore, *Fenor*, (*Elliqui:* peace), bridged as she imagined *Endale* would appear: a beautiful maiden with hair the color of soil and eyes as green as young shoots of leaves. Her hoped-for outcome, of course, would be to dazzle the immortal guardian and through him create a kind of peace which would enable other gods to cross into the mortal realm, unfettered by the Old Law. Several verses tell of her perilous journey to *Wyn Avuqua* from across the great sea, to her arrival and the small cottage she built for herself an arrow's shot from the walls of the great city.

One day, when *Mellithion* was walking beside the lake, *Fenor* presented herself to him. *Mellithion*, entranced by her beauty, ignored that she was *Godrethion* and the intense *Rathinalya,* and asked her name and how she came across the sea. She replied, "I came for thee, for I heard you calling,"[16] She then told him her name was *Endale* and that their time together had come. The end of part two details *Mellithion's* joy, his overwhelming devotion and how his long suffering becomes nothing more than a fleeting memory. It also tells of how *Fenor* reciprocates his love and shrewdly manipulates his manner and character away from his sworn duty and identity. She even presents a kind of antidote to the effects of *Rathinalya* in the form of a fermented grain drink called *Anqua,*[17] so that he, too, could feel as a god does on earth.

In the third part, the point of view shifts back to *Mellithion* and how he is fooled. He blissfully accepts the hand

---

[16] The *Fenor* quote, "I came for thee, for I heard you calling," is a common courting phrase that has been used between immortals and their lovers for thousands of years. Though in the tale *Fenor the Lover,* the line is used to deceive *Mellithion* (posing as *Endale*). Immortals have redefined the phrase to represent the power of manifesting a future love that will remake one's world.

[17] *Anqua* (*Elliqui:* god water). Scotch. Whiskey.

he has pined for his entire existence. He is drunk from both drink and love. The two meet in secret for the laws of *Wyn Avuqua* would forbid their union.

Slowly, *Fenor* (as *Endale*) convinces the guardian that quarter should be given to bridging *Godrethion*. Eventually, she influences *Mellithion* to pronounce that the long burden of the *Itonalya* is over because *Thi* has sent *Endale* to the king's side. The *Wyn Avuquain Templar* argued the contrary. They claimed that while the *Rathinalya* existed there could be no peace.

Interestingly, the voice of the true *Endale* makes its entrance in this third section. Interspersed throughout are verses that describe some dramatic environmental event. For example, prior to the telling of *Mellithion's* bliss, there are terrible storms. While he is drunk, there are floods. During his nights with *Fenor*, the poetry depicts powerful winds that topple and uproot trees. With each of *Fenor's* manipulative pursuits, the earth responds with anger and violence.

But *Mellithion* is blind to all but *Fenor's* affections and does not recognize *Endale's* jealousy nor her fury at *Fenor's* deceptive devices. Over the course of a year (or "A blink of the Eye of *Thi*," as the *Itonalya* say)[18], great numbers of *Godrethion* bleed into the world. For the immortals, the torture of *Rathinalya* seems ever present. Still *Mellithion* sips at his goblet of *Anqua* and rejoices in the arms of his beloved *Endale*.

On a morning in mid summer, a lightening storm sets the forest on fire. The flames quickly ignite the surrounding hills. Before dusk, the sky is blood red, choking with ash and smoke. *Mellithion* rushes to fetch his *Endale* from her stone cottage and bring her into the safety of the city, but when he arrives, she is not there. Her unwonted absence troubles him. He calls her name. He searches the cottage for her. He waits fearfully beside the door, watching the world burn. Turning back inside he searches for something that would point to her whereabouts—a sign, a

---

[18] "The blink of the Eye of *Thi*" is an *Itonalya* phrase that can mean a single year or a single century.

note, a clue. In moments he finds a bundle of letters wrapped in cloth. In moments his heart breaks. The letters are a passionate correspondence between two lovers. His lady's hand he recognizes. The other hand he does not. In moments, his faith and love is scorched and burned to ash.

With the letters of her betrayal in hand he goes out to stand beneath the scorched sky. There, he hears the wailing cries of the true *Endale:* thunder. She laments. Her booming, oppressive, terrifying bellows clatters across the lake. He sees her fingertips as bolts of lightening slashing wounds in the land and sky. He watches her rage overhead.

He is suddenly aware of her—aware of what he had missed all along. *Endale*, the earth, tried to show him, but he could not know. His aberration and faults are now woefully apparent and grief lays hold of his heart. He turns back to the stone cottage, enters inside and cries out, *"Endale! Endale!* Why won't you come?" He falls to his knees and weeps as the forest fire devours the surrounding fields—the cottage—his body.

In the fifth and final section, the point of view shifts again, but this time to *Endale*. For the first time in the Lay of *Melea*, we learn how *Endale* has finally chosen *Mellithion* as her love. Though she could not find a way to bridge into a mortal body, she tries to speak to *Mellithion* through the wind, the rains and the rushing of streams. Sunsets of ruby fire and cloudless climes she sends to him. Countless attempts to reach his heart as he walked through foggy mornings, through the songs of birds- among the hum of insects. And when she sees *Fenor* deceive him, love him, and take him away, the *Endale* tears at her own body. She becomes storm and landslide.

Finally, *Endale's* wrath sets the land on fire. As it burns she feels certain that he will hear her. But she is mistaken. And when she beholds him standing beneath the sky, broken and lost from *Fenor's* betrayal, she tries to weep—but she cannot. Her anger grows. She watches helplessly as the fire sweeps over the fields and engulfs the stone cottage with her love trapped inside. On the air are his cries for her, *"Endale! Endale!* Why won't you come?"

Revenge fills her heart and she seeks for *Fenor.* With little effort she finds her. The *Godrethion* woman is kneeling beside the lake. She is overcome with sorrow and grief. *Endale* sees that *Fenor's* beloved, the man with which she betrayed *Mellithion,* has drowned as he fled the flames. Suddenly, *Fenor* looks to the sky and senses that *Endale's* presence, and she trembles with fear.

"You have drowned my one true love," Fenor cries to *Endale.*

"You have sent my love to the fire," Endale tells the god.

"I do not want to stay here any longer," Fenor says. "The pain is too great. If you let me depart, you may have my body. You may go to *Mellithion*— you may finally know love."

So saying *Endale* falls upon *Fenor* and casts the trespassing god back into the void. The body of the woman falls, into the water. When it emerges, *Endale* tastes the smoke on the air and the sweet of cool water on her tongue. Mud squishes between her toes. Fire roars in her ears. She has bridged.

Not far from the beach is the smoldering cottage and she runs to it. The fire has destroyed all but the stacked stones. As she enters, she finds *Mellithion's* body. He is burned badly, but he is not slain. Somehow the flames did not take him, and already the rejuvenating powers of his immortal blood are restoring him. *Endale* rushes to his side, lifts his head and tells him, "I came for thee for I heard you calling. It is me, it is your *Endale.*"

At first, *Mellithion* smiles, as if he were waking from a pleasant dream. He touches her face and stares into her green eyes. "You are here. Is it you?" he asks her.

"It is me. Finally we are together," she tells him.

Then *Mellithion's* eyes turn to flame. "No. You are not my beloved. You are not she. Be gone! I am *Endale's* defender. You are no longer welcome here. Be gone unfaithful wretch!"

"No," she protests. "You were deceived by the *Godrethion, Fenor.* But she has departed, and I, *Endale,* have crossed to you." *Mellithion* listens, but he does not believe. He lifts a dagger from beside him and cuts *Endale's* throat. She falls and her blood spills out into the ash and soil.

Mellithion, the moon god, stands. *Itonalya* from his court arrive. He commands them to uphold the Old Law and suffer no *Godrethion* to live upon *Endale*. They rejoice at his words. But *Mellithion* stares down at the body of the woman he once loved and cries.

Then, from where her blood entered into the earth, young sprouts of vines emerge and whorl up. They spiral and coil. Tiny leaves of an almost incandescent green appear, burgeoning from the shoots. Never before has *Mellithion* seen such a thing. He crouches down, removes a leaf and touches it to his lips. Its flavor and scent send a chill through his entire frame. Health and vigor return to him with great speed.[19] Again, a revelation alights within his confusion and grief: the woman he has slain was indeed the earth—the woman was truly his beloved *Endale*. Again, he has failed himself.

Mellithion draws his sword and falls upon the blade. The sword enters into his flesh, but his body will not die.

In frustration he roars, "Ithic veli agtig!"[20] He removes the sword from the wound and throws it to the ground. The *Itonalya* marvel at his fury and they rush to comfort their king. *Mellithion* pushes them back. He leans down and lifts the body of *Endale* into his arms and rushes out of the stone walls.

"I will return to my throne above," he shouts to his followers. "I cannot live here without her. We were not made for this life. She and I will dance amid the stars once more. We will encircle each other until *Thi* joins us forever."

With that, *Mellithion* runs into the raging inferno that is

---

[19] Many *Itonalya* have speculated that the Lake Woman known as Lornensha was somehow able to cultivate this plant that emanated from the spilled blood of *Endale*. We are hopeful that the Heron Atheneums will give us more information on what seems to be the very plant that is associated with Lornensha, Geraldine of Leaves, William Greenhame and Albion Ravistelle's Melgia Gene.

[20] *Elliqui:* why does my death delay. This is a common *Itonalya* phrase often used to express one's surrender to the burden and tedium of the immortal curse of long life and long suffering. To our knowledge, *Mellithion's* utterance of the phrase in the Lay of Melea is the phrase's debut.

the tree-line. His body and the body of *Endale* incinerate into a white pillar of flame.

A year later, and each that followed, a meadow of white flowers with golden centers mark the spot where *Mellithion* and *Endale* entered the flames. The *Itonalya* call the flower *Deliavu* (*Elliqui*: day's eye—daisy).

ix.
THE COURT OF DELLITHION
SKY CHARTS

The Court of Dellithion

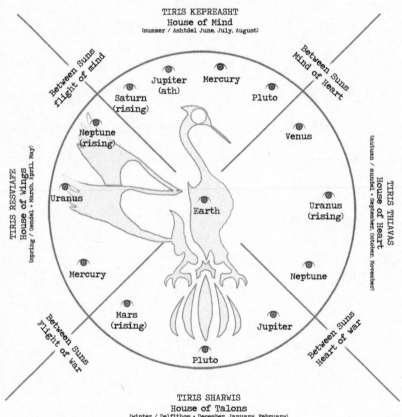

TIRIS KEPREASHT
House of Mind
(summer / Ashtdel June, July, August)

Between Suns
flight of mind

Between Suns
Mind of Heart

Jupiter
(ath)

Mercury

Saturn
(rising)

Pluto

Neptune
(rising)

Venus

TIRIS RESVIAFE
House of Wings
(spring / Gendel • March, April, May)

Uranus

Earth

Uranus
(rising)

TIRIS THIAVAS
House of Heart
(autumn / Sundel • September, October, November)

Mercury

Neptune

Mars
(rising)

Jupiter

Between Suns
Flight of war

Between Suns
Heart of war

Pluto

TIRIS SHARWIS
House of Talons
(winter / Delfithom • December, January, February)

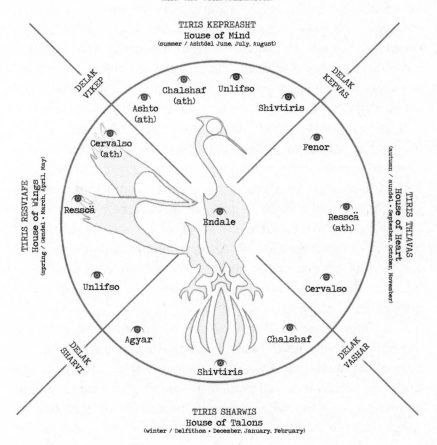

DELLITHION'S SKY
and the constellations

TIRIS KEPREASHT
House of Mind
(summer / Ashtdel June, July, August)

TIRIS SHARWIS
House of Talons
(winter / Delfithom • December, January, February)

APPENDIX III.
THE GAME OF SHTAN

shifel pleitonalya oi on
The immortal body is one together

Humans have been somewhat aware of universal oneness or the unified nature of being for over 6000 years. The *Itonalya* perspective on these truths is far older. Simply, the idea of immortals divided is against nature. *Itonalya* versus *Itonalya* is sacrilege. The above dictum is applied and practiced in *Itonalya* debate, civil strife and war, and even in gaming. That does not mean there are not disagreements between individuals or groups. It means only that to achieve well being, the immortal must eventually discover a wider perspective and find solutions that will lead to growth, and ultimately, prosperity and peace.

The game of *Shtan* represents this particular trait of immortal culture through the game's object. Players of *Shtan* do not battle against each other; instead they compete against the *godsight (shtan)*. It is not a game of black versus white. It is a game of *Itonalya* against *Godrethion*. *Shtan* was modeled after both the *Itonalya* mission on earth, to eliminate bridging gods, and the proverb that immortals must share a universal oneness of being in order to survive. *Shifel pleitonalya oi on* (the immortal body is one together).

Shtan is believed to have originated out of *Wyn Avuqua* sometime around 1500 BCE. Through *omvide* travel, *Itonalya* shared the game all over the ancient world and, over the centuries, it has evolved into different forms. *Shtan's* pieces, representing the four *Wyn Avuquain* households of head (mind), wings, heart and talons, transformed to mirror the character and environment of the adopting culture. The influence of *shtan* on Eastern strategy games like igo or go, xiangqi, janggi and shogi all seem to have culminated in the game chaturanga, the earliest version of chess. Chaturanga is thought to have come out of India (c. 280-550). Chaturanga's pieces, like its predecessor, were divided into four groups: infantry, calvary, elephants and chariotry. Around the middle of the fifteenth century in Europe, the seed of *shtan* sprouted once again, and the pieces assumed the shapes of the powerful houses of that culture, the royalty (king and queen), the church (bishop), the fortified landscapes (castles) and the military (knights and pawns). This child of *shtan*, chess, standardized its rules in the nineteenth century and they have remained the same (except for some technical and procedural changes) to this day.

RULES OF SHTAN:

Shtan is a two player game. One player plays the white and red/white pieces, and the other plays the black and the red/black pieces. Each player moves for both their *Itonalya* army (black or white), and then each player moves for both their *Godrethion* army (red/white and red/black). Each army consists of eight pieces at the beginning of the game: four pyramids, one head, one heart, one wings, one talons.

The game is played on a *shtan* board, consisting of 96 squares, alternately white and black. At the start of the game, the game pieces are positioned as follows:

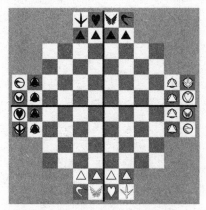

The icons with circles represent the *Godrethion*
armies of red/black and red/white.

(Photo courtesy of Graham Cremo)

MOVEMENT OF THE PIECES

TALONS

Talons, like the rook in Chess, moves in a straight line, horizontally or vertically. There is not limit to the amount of squares it can move. Talons cannot jump other pieces. (Photos courtesy of Graham Cremo.)

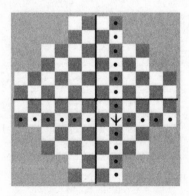

HEART

Similar to the bishop in chess, the heart moves in a straight diagonal line, and may not jump over pieces. (Photos courtesy of Graham Cremo.)

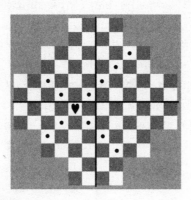

HEAD

The head can move in any direction, unlimited spaces, diagonally and horizontally. The head cannot jump pieces. The head eventually evolved into the queen in chess. (Photos courtesy of Graham Cremo.)

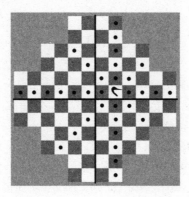

PYRAMID

Pyramids in *Shtan* move very similarly as pawns do in the game of Chess. Pyramids can only move one square at a time, and only in a straight line—forward only. Pawns can only attack and capture one square diagonally in front of their position. However, when a pyramid crosses its respective forward meridian, it promotes and is able to move and capture in any direction, one square only—as the king in Chess. When a pyramid passes the meridian the piece is turned to reveal its *godsight* eye embossed on the piece's underside. This allows the opponent to know that the pyramid has promoted. (Photos courtesy of Graham Cremo.)

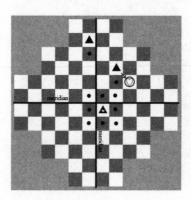

THE GODRETHION ARMIES

The Godrethion pieces are traditionally red and accented with black or white. Each player is in control of a *Godrethion* army, as well as, it is said, a god (via the roll of the dice or the four sided spinning top similar to a Dreidel). The player playing the black pieces moves the red/black pieces. The player playing the white pieces moves the red/white pieces. Again, this is not a game of black versus white, or *Itonalya* against *Itonalya*. Players stay aligned with the *Itonalya* mission of eliminating gods on earth. Therefore, black pieces do not capture white pieces, or vise versa. Black pieces capture only *Godrethion* red/white. White pieces capture only *Godrethion* red/black. Red/black capture white— red/white captures black. *Godrethion* armies move by a roll of the four sided die. This die represents the *godsight* (*shtan*) playing at the table. The number of the roll determines the piece to be moved. 1: head, 2: wings, 3: heart, 4: talons. The player controlling their respective *Godrethion* army may choose to either move the rolled number or a pyramid at each turn. *Godrethion* armies do not capture their opponent's *Godrethion*. When a number is rolled and there is no piece available on the board that matches the number, a pyramid may be moved instead. If there is no pyramid or corresponding die numbered piece, the turn is passed. The dice must be rolled before any *Godrethion* move, whether pieces are available or not. The roll allows the *godsight* to be a player. When a *Godrethion* army is completely captured, the game is over. The player with the most black or white pieces on the board wins.

ORDER OF MOVES:

Black moves first. White moves next. Third, *Godrethion* red/ black move by a roll of the dice, or by the moving of a pyramid. (There is a 1 in 4 chance that the die will provide a 2 to allow wings a move by jumping the pyramid line. Typically, however, pyramids are the first to advance, allowing space for the back-line pieces to move.) Fourth, *Godrethion* red/white rolls and moves—then the rotation begins with black again. This order of moves continues until the game is won or there is a stalemate or draw.

OBJECT OF THE GAME

The object of Shtan is for one player (white or black) to eliminate as many if not all of their opponent's (white or black) pieces from the board using their respective *Godrethion* (red/white, red/black) pieces. A winner is determined by which opponent has the most black or white pieces left on the board when either *Godrethion* army is completely eliminated, or when a stalemate is determined.

APPENDIX IV.
MISCELLANEOUS TRANSLATIONS AND TERMS

Here follows a translated version of Albion Ravistelle's song that appeared in *Leaves of Fire*.

i.

ALBION RAVISTELLE'S SONG

Nye thi so zjoy goshem
    Thi nugosht bensis ensis
    Mel hamtik, del hamtik, enthu
    Sisg ag
    Orathom ethe
    Lithion talgeth
        Thi fafe wis
        Thi fafe wis
    A Wyn Avuqua
    Endale che
    Thi col orathom
    Tiris liflarin thi avusht
    Lithion nuk te lirych
        Orathom thi geth
        Fethe thi geth
            Ithic veli agtig
            Ithic veli agtig

In sorrow I sing these words (this tale)
    For my birth began my torture
    Countless moons, countless suns, years,

Without end.
Rest is robbed of me.
The gods forbid me.
　　　But we hold the doors.
　　　Yes, we hold the path.
Oh, Wyn Avuqua
The pearl of Earth
Our only paradise
I see your towers in flame
The hand of God bears the torch
　　　We want only rest
　　　We want to go home
　　　　　Why does my death delay?
　　　　　Why does my death delay?

ii.
ANGLO SAXON TRANSLATION

Here follows a translation of Etheldred's words to Loche Newirth when the two met beside the *omvide Mellithion* in the year 1010 AD. (From *The Shape of Rain*.)

Aér gé fyr heonan, léasscéaweras, on land *Itonalya*.

Ne seah ic wídan feorh under heofones hwealf, sceaðona ic nát hwylc. Sé moncynnes. Godes andsacan þé þú hér tó lócast. Godes féond, *Orathom Wis!* Á mæg god wyrcan wunder æfter wundre. Weoroda raéswan, Géata léode, umborwesende, winedrihten.

Sægde sé þe cúþe, frumsceaft Gode, swutol sang scopes feorran reccan.

Ere you are far hence, deceiving spies, in the land of the Immortals!

*I have not seen in my whole life under heaven's vault,
some enemy I know not what. He, mankind." He looks at Julia,
"God's adversary which you see here. God's foe, Immortal." He
looks at Edwin, "And then, God can always work wonder after
wonder. The leader of the legions, of the Great People, being but
a child, friend and Lord."*

*He spoke who knew how, the origin of God, the sweet
song of the poet to narrate from afar."*

iii.
ENCRIS

Sources indicate that *Elliqui's* Original Mode (its telepathic
quality) was *stolen* or *cut* from *Itonalya* thought over a
succession of centuries. This disconnect was named *Encris*. Like
the Babel myth, the *Itonalya* confusion of tongues story is said to
have occurred because of an *Itonalya* rebellion against the creator
Thi. Thi, who would not gift the *Itonalya* an afterlife. After
several millennia as guardians to the earth and its mortal
inhabitants, the *Itonalya* grew proud and rebelled. In retribution,
Thi slowly removed the Original Mode of *Elliqui*, their true
connection to existence, the stars and Earth. Eventually, *Thi*
destroyed their great realm. When the spoken/written language
first appeared is difficult to know for sure, but we do know that
not long after the fall of *Wyn Avuqua*, the Original Mode was
completely lost from the minds and hearts of the Immortals. It is
also important to note that the earliest *Elliqui* scribes and
speakers were considered heretics and preachers of a false faith.
Encris is the first of many *Itonalya* tragedies.

iv.
GAVRESS LINNASISG

Gavress Linnasisg is the *Itonalya* funeral ritual for the fallen which includes the reciting of the poem *Linnasisg* (meaning, the ending of the light), followed by the release of the slain immortal body (or head) into the sea, lake or nearest body of water. It is believed that the ritual will allow the slain immortal the chance of an afterlife if the mighty *Thi* were to ever allow such a gift to an *Itonalya*. The litany and the water ceremony are regarded as a solemn, meaningful and respectful act to the fallen. There is also some humor included within. While the depth and weight of a fallen immortal demands pensive sorrow, the futility of nothing beyond resounds in the strangely playful ending lines of the poem:

> *There's a head in the bag.*
> *There's a head in the bag.*
> *The head is my head.*
> *It is my head in the bag.*

The *Elliqui* word *Gavress* (spirit sack) sets the tone that the body is only a sack—and it can be emptied. *Gavress Linnasisg* proclaims to all immortals that existence bears no more relevance on the universe than what can be placed into a bag and inevitably swallowed by the ocean. There is nothing beyond.

Regrettably, the moving and comical poem is extraordinarily long, and limited space prevents placing it here.

v.

RATHINALYA

The *Rathinalya* (life circle) is the physical sensation an immortal feels when a god is near by. It has been said to cause gooseflesh and extreme chills. Its affect prompts an *Itonalya* to end it (which typically leads to the death of the trespassing *Godrethion*). The severity depends upon the strength of the *Godrethion* and its intentions. The most powerful *Rathinalya* ever recorded was that of the son of Loche Newirth, Edwin, when, for a short time, *Thi* had bridged into the little boy.

Another curious aspect to the *Rathinalya* is that it provides an *Itonalya* with an inherent and advanced dexterity.

APPENDIX V.
OF LOCHE NEWIRTH'S POETRY

Collected here is a small sample of Loche Newirth's verse. Though Dr. Newirth is known predominantly for his supernatural work, *The Journal*, he preferred writing poetry. While the affect of his poetry pales in comparison to the enigmatic history-shifting narrative that was dedicated to Dr. Marcus Rearden, these writings contain the groundwork and seeds to many of The Journal's themes. Death, rebirth, the struggle of the artist, mythology, innocence lost, marriage, fatherhood and elements of Newirth's vocation as a psychologist can be traced through the poems.

SONNETS

THE GRID[21]

I live between two graveyards, down below
The circling crows. Plots dotted with grey-green
Stones, as symmetric as a sonnet, know
That order in necropolis is king.
I sometimes see slumped shapes surround a new
Dark rectangle in the grass. The uniform
Black huddle then breaks, milling slowly through
The yard and back to the paved paths. The swarm
Of crows flies over their stern lines. My wife
Arranged these flowers on my desk. Red
Round petals drop on this page as I write—
On column, form and ledger, parched and dead.

---

[21] William Greenhame recites the opening stanza to The Grid in The Journal (*The Invasion of Heaven*, chapter IV, Mirrors.)

We've built our lives here, out of stone, amid
The graves we dig. To survive is to break down the grid.

THE STUDENT

So long I've sailed upon Posideon's sea
And may Prometheus in Hades burn
For what he's given me: firelight to see
The azimuth grey and aged from which I learn
And cannot turn, enraged. Why must the sails
Go ever on? Why must they fill and breathe?
And leave an innocence that rips and ails
At every sight upon Posideon's sea?
Can I return? Divert my ship to shore?
Delay awhile upon some secret isle
Where I may raise my oars, to watch her soar?
My vulture's vengeful flight to Titan's trial.
May she devour the light and bring me peace.
And may his pain and my sweet youth increase.

LOST ALL AGE

It's when I said I could do anything:
Sail the sky water, suck the apple wine
From mythic seas. These words don't mean a thing.
When the crows circled overhead and I
Saw our reflection in and through the pane—
What does it matter these words I sing? Kate's kiss-
Lips red as blood, soft as the black pupil stain,
Grave in her eyes when she said, "I will." This
Means nothing. When I tried to angle all
Those words to life I found that I should've said:
It's nothing baby, sing, sweet baby doll,
And we will carpe diem 'til we're dead.
If I lost all age anything could be on this page.
It's easier that way, dance instead of rage.

ASLEEP

I watch you on your hands and blackened knees,
Your frame curved like an egg in the grass, planting
Our garden. Your warm fingers seed down through

Cool slender holes in the turned earth. Sweat gleams
Between your shoulder blades and you're singing,
While I fall to sleep, dreaming. I dream you
Laid me down in a basket by a stream,
A wicker boat among the reeds, and let
Your fingertips slide my craft out toward
The current- you let go. All that I've seen
All I've done, age I've lost and won, all spent
In rhyme and song I saw along the shore,
Shoot sunward. You have sown a dreamer's seed.
Don't wake me 'til I make the river bleed.

AWAKE

Now, as I stand beside the stream, returned
To where I was set free, an older man
Now, I wade through the reeds to open my
Veins— to let my blood speak for me. Returned
To have the final word. With blade in hand,
The cold edge glimmering, tracing a raw line
Across my skin, I will do now what my
Art could not: bleed, breathe— for all my life I
Believed it could be done. Believed. I feel
The breeze on closed eyes, the taste of red wine
On waking lips as your warm fingers slide
Along my wrist, on wounds you cannot heal—
I wake with your eyes smiling into mine,
Face to face with the dream that is my life.

> All that I've seen
> All that I've done
> Age I've Lost and won
> All spent in rhyme and song
> I saw along the shore
> Shoot sunward—
> You have sown a dreamer's seed
> Don't wake me until
> > I make the river bleed.

STOP WATCH

Was there a single moment that has made
A man of me? One second, Katie flung
Me kisses— left my pale lips Kool-Aid stained,

The next, my mind began to tick, my tongue
To taste and time tip toed through me. Hours tolled
Across green school yards. Thieving bells. Bells that
Taught the eyes to watch days fade, and the heart
To feel years die. And all the rest was rush.
That single moment clicked like gears behind
Her face. Now, hands and numbers circle fast;
I stop to watch my past. Oh Katie, find
Me while I don't believe the past is past.
A single moment I saw fade to black
The moment I learned I could not go back.

LYRICS

THE SLANT OF THE SUN

There's something about
A wing-snapped bird
Alone in the dust—
A black cat on the grass.
   There's something about
   A grey eyed girl
   Alone in the back—
   Not a friend in the class.
There's something about
The brown of booze
Before a broken man—
His brief case right beside.
   There's something about
   A spider's web
   Across an open gate—
   Mom calls the kids inside.
            It's the slant of the sun, I know.
            The shifting of the Earth
            In her wide, soft bed.
            Come every September
            She nods her head,
            And the stars shake loose
            And the shadows stretch out
            And I notice that
            There's something about
Empty wheel chairs
Outside the sliding glass doors—
The laughter in the park.

There's something about
A child's eyes
The closet door ajar—
And it is getting dark.
There's something about
The moon, the sea,
And the civilizations
Uncovered by the tide.

There's something about
A will to carry on,
When a wing is cracked
    And the cat is on the lawn.

THE CONS OF SHADE (a lullaby)

May the message of a little lily
Under wooden sidewalks on an afternoon
Wrapped with raindrops,
Speak to you.

Crowded under footsteps over
Lily's head, watching passers-by
Curse the sky, Those grey clouds
Make them cry-

She's reaching up.
Reaching up to you.
And she says:

When will you learn this life has just begun
I'm happy in the shade
But I'd like to see the sun.
I've got potato bugs- come for tea to see me
At least they dig the dark
Cause now it's all we've got
We've got to learn, got to learn
To dig the dark.

Her neighbors are potato bugs
Sifting through the murk and mud
Loving the cool damp shadow, black
Deep down below.

Their lives are trapped in blindness
And they're quick to remind us

That the dark is just a place
That we learn to outgrow.

They're reaching up.
Reaching up—

LEAVES ON STONES

When you said you'd rather burn
I barely listened.
Talk of death seems so far away.
Nothing more than a wisp
Of atmosphere.
Sucked vapor, like words disappear.

I said I'd prefer a stone at my head,
A chiseled name.
Let my bones shoot like stems
From beneath the sod,
From there I'll reach
Through the simple plot of God.
   But let's not talk of that,
   Bones and smoke and belief—
   Let's put it away, out of reach,
   And once more into the breech.
But fire I thought: I'd be untraced
Nameless and naked.
My one precious possession transformed
To ash, and free to fly.
No lies, no façade.
I become the simple plot of God.
   Leaves on stones
Footsteps stepping over bones.
Every life leaves a trail.
Mouths of words
Tongues are flying like startled birds.
Every life leaves a tale.
   Don't forget.
   Forget there's an end.
Don't forget
   The time we have left.

THE OLD IN

I've placed a fountain in my corner of career.
It chokes and gurgles a mechanized groan.
There's a chi that's said to stream-rush rooms
And turn attempting to achievement.

I've stopped watching TV in the evening,
For it's sure to strike me down with disease,
But a pill of ease is offered if I will
Accept dizziness, headaches and slurred speech.
Out with the old— in with the new
Too many years gone by to not to
Little did I know all the different ways to go.
But I don't know. . .
I don't know.
I've started reading my wife's happy books
Left above the toilet, at the bedside— kitchen table.
They say some law is attracting them to me
Like sunshine fingering into corner shadows.

I've begun a regimen of vitamins,
Little pellets, gold as sun-lit water that will pump
My heart-blood, skin and bones with youth.
For like food, my potency— is breaking down.
It's alright,
I'm just weary to my bones.
You think I would have learned by now.
That nothing new ever stays,
Just as it arrives it runs away.
Nothing good comes from running.
If I remake, recreate, keep myself remade,
Maybe in the end I can say:
The more I changed,
The more I stayed the same.

THE REASON

Teetering upon a step ladder
The sky blue drips down my raised arm
Over my head.
Reaching high,
I am making the ceiling disappear—
Making a home for clouds, winds,
And flight.
I wonder if this faint hue of paint (the color of all above, hot July afternoon),
The delicate, airy, transparent wisp of it
Can fool my little boy
Into thinking that he might be able to see
The drifting constellations just beyond the
Painted layer of firmament,
As he lies upon his back,
Staring up from his pillow.
I hope he considers the possibility that
I may have painted the universe for him too,
Upon the hidden 2x4 rafters above—
Just an extra stretch to the plywood beneath the roof
Where planets, spiral arms and twinkling myths
Wait to be discovered.
But even as the reach of my brush heaps puffy cumulous into the clear,
And trails out vapors of cirrus that tangle up in the corners,
I see that I am slowly becoming covered with sky
As I create it,
And space seems slightly complex.
For this sky,
Streaks of it lining my arms,
In my hair,
Upon my cheeks,
Falls as fast as I can raise it.
And I can see right through it.
I'll try to tell him about this one day.
The reason I erased his ceiling.

APPENDIX VII.
ELLIQUI

The *Elliqui* word *Itonalya* means *immortal*. But when the word is broken into parts, the etymological depth it reveals reinforces and mirrors the culture's long, enigmatic past and rich legacy. The word is old. When it debuted is difficult to trace, though we do know that the earliest *Itonalya* tomes used the term as far back as forth century BCE.[22]

Itonalya is constructed of many words and meanings all from its *Elliqui* root word, *itonel.*

itonel, *(ē•tōo̅•něl'), adj, n.*- forever, eternal
itonalya, *(ēt•tōo̅•năl•yä), n.* immortal
    it, *(ĭt), v.* revive
    ito, *(ēt•tōo̅), adj.* - again / ever
    to, *(tōo̅), v.* - age
    nel, *(něl), n. adj.* - more
    a, *(ă), v.* - encircle
    al, *(ăl), n.* ring.
    ya, *(yä), n.* - delicate, fragile
    alya, *(ăl• yä), n.* - life

It is also hypothesized that like many *Elliqui* words, the word *itonel* influenced the Latin word *aeternālis,* and later the Old French, *eternytie,* until finally, in English, *eternal* (about 1380).

Though scholars have translated *Itonalya* to mean *immortal*, I suppose if we wanted something more accurate, an attempt might read like this: r*evive forever more to the fragile ring of life that encircles age.*

Hence the *Itonalya* blessing and curse.

---

[22] The history of *Elliqui* and its transition from its Original Mode to spoken and oral traditions is still being researched. *See VIII. On Elliqui.*

Here are the first stones of the *Elliqui* avalanche to come. With the Heron Atheneum at Upper Priest Lake, Idaho, unearthed, and professor Finnley's team working tirelessly, I anticipate addenda and corrections to the lexicon below.

Photo courtesy of Graham Cremo, ©2018
Tomes of the Heron Atheneum

Photo courtesy of Graham Cremo, 2018
Elliqui alphabet book

ON TRANSLATION, PRONUNCIATION, SPELLING AND USE OF ELLIQUI

"There was no need for language for our hearts knew love, and fear was not yet made."
—The Silent Author
From the Toele.

True *Elliqui* in its Original Mode, was a language based in thought.[23] It was, to the best of our ability to define, a kind of telepathy. The *Itonalya* called communication *verceress,* meaning communing, or conversing in thought and feeling. *Elliqui* itself translates as *the language of thought.* For several millennia, immortals practiced the art and could commune with not only each other, but with the stars, and the source of their love, the earth. They could, of course, speak and understand many other languages of humankind, but the gift of true *Elliqui* provided immortals meaning and a hope for their long lives—the language was the music of their paradisiacal earthbound existence.

When the rebellion began against *Thi* and the earth began to fall silent,[24] the Original Mode began to fade. Each year that passed, *Elliqui's* potency lessened until, not long after the fall of *Wyn Avuqua* in 1010 AD, the stars, the Earth and the voices of their kin fell silent.

According to Dr. Loche Newirth's writings,[25] three figures shaped the foundation of written and oral *Elliqui*: a great blue heron, a First Born sage named Belzaare, and a mysterious immortal called The Silent Author. When the rebellion against *Thi* began, and it was clear that the Original Mode of *Elliqui* was dying, it is said that the language was sung to the *Itonalya,* Belzaare of *Vastiris* by a great blue heron. Belzaare took the bird's gift of song and began the arduous and forbidden task of recreating the sounds and ordering them into words. Thought

---

[23] The written and oral version of *Elliqui* that follow possess only elements of the Original Mode. *Elliqui* means, simply, *thought language.* Spoken, *Elliqui* is powerful, and can be dangerous. The *Toele's* teachings tell us that the words are magical in nature and should be treated with the utmost respect and caution.

[24] The Original Mode of *Elliqui* took thousands of years to finally silence. As of the writing of this, there is no clear timeline on its decline. It is hoped that we will learn more about this tragedy through what we find at *Wyn Avuqua.*

[25] Dr. Newirth's writings influenced, of course, the *Toele* and other texts at *Wyn Avuqua.*

impossible at first, and later an abominable sin,[26] Belzaare constructed the basis for what many scholars have called the *sound of light*. Many years later, another *Itonalya* known only as the Silent Author, drew the corresponding runes and characters to Belzaare's sounds.

Oral and written *Elliqui* are obvious departures from the Original Mode, but when used correctly, the pathways to the ancient's *verceress* are opened. This all that remains of the Original Mode. And it was hoped then as it is now, that by preserving what remains of *Elliqui*, we might again regain our true connectivity with each other, the earth and the Hereafter. Or, as Queen Yafarra, daughter of Althemis Falruthia of *Vastiris*, "*Elliqui* is the path that will enable us to speak to the earth once more. *Elliqui* is magic.

i.

PRONUNCIATION

The following is a key to *Elliqui* pronunciation. There are several differences between the sounds and how they are written. The reasons for this are multifold, but suffice it to say that when telepathy meets oral speech, sounds represent a vibration in the psychosomatic connection as well as separate emotions and responses. The Silent Author has written several documents

---

[26] The early oral and written forms (new *Elliqui*) were not peacefully received by the First Born *Itonalya*. For nearly a thousand years the efforts of Belzarre and others were rejected by those that regarded *new Elliqui* as heretical to the Old Law. The discrepancy gave rise to a militant group of Old Law zealots that were determined to put down and destroy what they called, "the miscreant voice." Disciples of the new forms were hunted, tortured and killed—written manuscripts were burned—and for the first time in *Itonalya* history, immortals fought against immortals. It was King Althemis Falruthia of *Vastiris* that fought to preserve the efforts of the Belzaare and the Silent Author. His dream of universal acceptance of the new *Elliqui* among the *Itonalya* sparked the Sibling War. The war would take his life. Claiming his mantle, Queen Yafarra finally prevailed, and in the early years of the 4th Century BCE, the new *Elliqui* was embraced by the culture. The flailing Original Mode was said to have fallen completely silent sometime around 1010 AD after the fall of *Wyn Avuqua*. Some believe that remnants of old *Elliqui* still exist in blessed individuals.

demonstrating the extrasensory nature of the sounds and their relation to shape in the telepathic continuum. What follows is a phonic structure. Perhaps by outlining these phonic characters and setting them back into the tongues of humankind, we may find a way to rekindle the original flame of language that was once silent but communicative beyond words themselves.

CONSONANTS: TONES I-IV

C : ∫ℐ

C has the value of *k* as well as the value of *s*. *C* followed by *y* should be pronounced as a long *i*: *Cy (sī)*. There is no *Elliqui* character for the English letter *c*, therefore *k* is used. It is thought that early translators determined a telepathic distinction with words containing the hard consonant sound of *k/c*. These distinctions are subtle and vary on the tone of following vowels, where the k/c sound forms in the mouth, and its particular stress in the word. Therefore, my transcriptions attempt to follow organizational foundation of the early translators by separating the *k* rune into the two English characters of *c* and *k* to further enhance the sound's extrasensory properties. *see Y.*

CH : ⵟ

This digraph sound is a single rune in *Elliqui*. The sound has the value of *church, chatter, crutch*. see **SH, TH.**

G : ⌐

Elliqui's g is predominantly akin to the English sound in *gain, giggle, hug*. However, there is one important distinction. For words that signify *beginnings*, or *newness (gen, gendel)*, early translators used the English g to function as the sound of *j*.

GZ : ⊦⅄

This is not a naturally occurring English digraph, nor is there a single *Elliqui* rune for the sound. Early English translators chose to represent the sound using *gz,* again, likely to mark a particular shift in the Original Mode. The *Elliqui* sound is a trigraph and is similar to the ending of *age* or *bridge.* The pronunciation might be best demonstrated by taking the digraph *sh* and replacing the *s* sound with the *z* sound and ending with an elongated *j.* Curiously, this sound appears in *Elliqui* words that convey *children* or *youth.*

J : ʃ

With the exceptions above, *j* functions as it does in English: *joy, adjoin. see* **G.**

K : ʃ

The *Elliqui k* rune functions as the English hard consonants of *c* and *k.* Again, it is worth noting the shifting of this sound's usage when translated to English. *see* **C, Y** *and* **S.**

Q : ⊣

Q, or in English characters *qu,* functions as the *kw* sound as in *quiet, question.*

R : ⊣

R trills when followed by the vowel sounds *ä* and *ĕ. Rathinalya,* for example. In all other positions it remains *r* as in *rain, far, sorrow.*

S : ⅄

The Elliqui sound of *s* is the same as it is in English. *C* when followed by the vowel sound of *ĭ* and *ĕ* the English character shifts to *c. see Y.*

SH : 𝆄

This digraph sound is a single rune in *Elliqui*. The sound has the value of *shout, share, Rush. see **CH, TH.***

TH : 𝆓

This digraph sound is a single rune in *Elliqui*. The sound has the value of *the, there, breath.* see ***CH, SH.***

W : 𝆗

The Elliqui sound of *w* functions similarly as it does in English save that there is slightly more emphasis on the blowing of air as the consonant leaves the mouth. It has been suggested that the English equivalent should include a silent *h* to accentuate the character's breathy aspect, though it never caught on.

X : 𝆙

In some cases, early translators use an English *x* to represent the paired *Elliqui* sound of *k* and *s*.

Y : 𝆒

has the *Elliqui* and English equivalent of *y* as in *yard* or *Yafarra*. However, English transcriptions often use the character in place of the *Elliqui* vowel *ī*, most often following the letter *c*: *Cy* or *sī*. This is particularly anomalous for both English consonants, when translated to *Elliqui* sounds, to change from their original sound to another when paired. It is thought that this pairing is linked directly to a telepathic marker designating evil or dark purpose. Further, the shifting from harder consonant sounds *y* and *k* to lighter long *i* and soft *s* denotes a kind of disguise in of itself. A deception. An *Elliquist* should be wary when using such a pairing. Perhaps in clairvoyant opposition to the *cy* pairing is the combination of *c* and the vowel sound of *ĕ*. *C* followed by the sound *ĕ* shifts the *c/k sound* to *s* as in *cer* and *cerwis*. Interestingly enough, these two letters together in an *Elliqui* word summon truth and power. Why early translators did not simply use the English *s* has been the subject of many debates, and has spurred research into the Original Mode of *Elliqui's* telepathic foundation.

Z : λ

functions as z in English except when connected to *g* or *j*. *see* **GZ.**

VOWELS TONES V

Elliqui's vowel sounds share many of the same complexities of English, each having variables in softness and mode. The vowels are the essence of what Belzaare calls the *Thavelle*. The *Thavelle* is the 'art of language' that *Elliqui* uses to transmit feeling. Vowels by their very nature are the sound of the body and the hum of the spirit. Or, as Dr. Astrid Finnley has written, "When the *Elliquist* masters a forceful annunciation of these tones, the connection of spirit and Earth are again, one."

Each sound corresponds to an *Elliqui* character. There is no single rune for any *Elliqui* vowel.

A : ϛ ϛ ϛ ϛ̇

The sound of *a*, to us, is really the beginning of our learning of English: our *A, B, C*'s. It is important to note that no order exists for the Elliqui tone structure, but rather an overall continuum of sound. *A* at the end of the word is often pronounced long as in *way*.

pat —	ă
pay —	ā
care, air -	âr
father, **song** -	ä

E : ໄ } ໆ

E like *a* is similar in its complexity, for example, *e* at the end of a word will function as the long *a*: away or the schwa *ə* as in *item*. The silent *e* does not exist in *Elliqui*.

pet -	ĕ
bee -	ē
item -	ə

I : ໖ ໄ

I is often pronounced *ē* following another vowel or at the end of a word.

| pit - | ĭ |
| pie - | ī |

O :

O in its many manifestations is the primary hum in the continuum. It functions as the focus of the spirit. There are several variations of *o*, more so than any other vowel:

pot -	ô
toe -	ō
noise -	oi
took -	ŏ

boot -   oō
out -   ow

U : ~C≋C

U has several varied properties in telepathic modes. *U* is often used for the English translation of oō sounds.

cut -   ŭ
urge -   ûr

ii.
USING THE ELLIQUI

The Quadrivium of Elliqui:

The Original Mode's foundational principles were identified by The Silent Author and Belzaare as four

Reason
Intention
Entheos
Simplicity

The Silent Author and Belzaare taught these four principles for the successful *verceress*: a specific reason to pass information; a clear intention; a passionate or enthusiastic desire to be understood; and finally, breaking the message down to its most basic meaning—simplify.

WRITING

Each *Elliqui* letter represents a sound. It is important to note that when writing an *Elliqui* word one must use the correct *phonic* letter: that is, the letter that corresponds with the pronunciation key, not the English translated character.

For example when writing the word:
farewell - *galinna*, one must use these letters: (*gā•lē´•nə),* in correspondence with the *Elliqui* characters for correct *Elliqui* spelling. *Elliqui* tone characters apply to the pronunciation, not the English spelling.

TENSES

The original mode in which *Elliqui* was communed did not allow for the idea of time, past, present or future. For the true *Elliquist,* these constructs would not need to be defined, they would simply be felt. Even the Silent Author suggested that it was impossible to generate words that communicated time. Past, present and future in language is often marked by additions to verbs. Like all true *Elliqui* a telepathic marker made tense obvious. After much thought however, the Silent Author found in his own *verceress* a mode in which past, present and future could be written, and even spoken. He constructed three words in order to communicate tense: *olo* (ō´•lō), *nye (*nī), and *uta (oo´•tə).* These words begin a sentence or utterance when tense is necessary.

Olo: past. *Olo* is not connected to the *Elliqui* verb itself, but instead determines that the action or event et cetera, is in the past, much like *was* or the *ed* at the end of a word. With the presence of *olo,* the *Elliqui* word for *eat* would now function as *ate.*

Nye: present. *Nye* is seldom used in *Elliqui* for all *Elliqui* words are present tense. However, *nye* can function as *is* in English. The translation of *nye* is *now,* and can be used as that meaning elsewhere in a sentence. *Nye* at the beginning of a sentence is effective for urgency, but not always necessary.

Uta: future. *Uta* translates as *the time to come,* or *the time ahead.*

Technically it functions as future thought or manifestation, for example, *when* the snow falls, or *someday I will* journey far. It also communicates the idea of *yet*, as in: I've *not yet* journeyed far.

SENTENCE STRUCTURE

Basic sentence structure is similar to the ease of *verceress* for the ancients. True *Elliqui* was wordless, though there was often, according to Belzaare and the Silent Author, an etiquette for proper communing. Written and spoken *Elliqui* reflects the original modes:

Simply, *Elliqui* translated to English is always (for the highest potency), *noun, verb, adjective*. When tense is needed: *tense, noun, verb, adjective*. It is important to understand, however, that emotional subtleties can exist as one's ability to *verceress* strengthens. Belzaare instructs that the emphasis of emotion is on word placement, and only by following this pattern can *Elliqui* retrieve a telepathic marker.

The pattern to learn is this: TNVA: an acronym for *tense, noun, verb, adjective*.

TRANSLATING ENGLISH TO ELLIQUI

To write or speak the equivalent of *Elliqui* from English, one must reduce the English phrase to its simplest, or rather, telepathic form.

Let us use an example for translation.

"The Horn of Wyn Avuqua echoed and the green of spring came."

Here we see a fairly complex sentence in English, however, we can reduce it to its telepathic form by merely communicating its essence. There are two parts to the sentence:

"The Horn of Wyn Avuqua echoed ~ the green of spring came."

This connecting character (~) allows the full idea to emerge.

Remember, TNVA.

Tense = echoed (echo is past) *olo*
Noun = the Horn
Verb = echo
Adjective = of *Wyn Avuqua*
~
T = came (past tense)
N = spring
V = came
A = green

So an *Elliqui*/English version might be:

"In the past, the Horn echo *Wyn Avuqua* ~ spring came green."

In *Elliqui:*

Olo shewu sheshu Wyn Avuqua~ gendel veli lemheth

PREFIXES

Prefixes or performatives in *Elliqui* alter the words to which they are affixed.

go : reversal, negative
ple : all
agn : not

NOTES ON SEMANTICS

For the *Elliquist*, success in communication is based on the speaker's (writer's) individual creativity and the listener's (reader's) ability to understand conveyance. In other words, not all written or oral *Elliqui* will be immediately understood, and translating can cause confusion. For example, one *Elliquist* may write, "I eat green food." Another *Elliquist*, if they are not careful might translate the utterance as, "Green food eats me." Tricky to be sure. This is where a sense of communing comes in to play.

In many languages, contrastive intonation plays a vital role in conveyance and understanding. For example:

I told the story. (It was *me* that told it, not *Loche*.)
I *told* the story. (I *told* it, I did not *sing* it.)
I told *the* story. (The *important* one, not the *other*.)
I told the *story*. (Not the *facts*.)

It is important to note, the Original Mode did not suffer the tedium and subtlety of contrastive intonation, nor did it have to endure the difficulties of semantics overall. As to who told the story, which story it was, how it was told, why, where, and quite possibly, the story's content in its entirety—these aspects could be could be conveyed by one and understood by another using the Original Mode with a focused glance. The spoken and written forms were intended to function as closely to the Original Mode as possible, but they too often fall short. And it is no wonder that such primitive mediums of tongue and pen prevent the language from ascending to the telepathic power of its former glory. The quadrivium: reason, the simplicity of structure, the power of intention and focused entheos are the four elements the Silent

Author and Belzaare have continually invoked as the bridge back to what was— simpler days— easier words. The way home.

Of course such open communication begs questions such as these: Was there individual thought? Could one withhold information? Was there a sense of autonomy?

As noted in the *Toele* and in other documents uncovered by Professor Astrid Finnley, Original Mode *Elliquists* were said to have both individual and altruistic hearts and intentions. There was no instinct to harm or hinder another that could speak true *Elliqui*. Many have remarked that true *Elliqui* was simply complete empathy.

It is hoped that the Original Mode may one day be returned to us. In the meantime, we can only speculate.

If the above grammatical rules are followed for both speaking and writing the language, the translation gap narrows. What's more, a good *Elliquist* will be able to get the "feeling" from the words and be able to place them in a proper order without reversing the initial meaning altogether. This skill, of course, is paramount to becoming a great *Elliquist*. Finally, creativity with the words and speaking simply is yet another element to speaking and writing well. Compound sentences can be difficult to translate. Reducing intention to its essence will prove the *Elliqui* more true.

iii.
THE WRITTEN ELLIQUI
TONES i THROUGH iv

	tone i		
ꟼ	: ch	F	: g
ꟼ	: k	F	: j
⊓	: th	⟟	: sh

	tone ii		
ↆ	: b	ɏ	: p
ꟼ	: d	ↆ	: t
ↆ	: kw/Q		

	tone iii		
Ꮞ	: m	⟩	: s
Ⱶ	: n	⟍	: z
⅃	: r		

	tone iv		
F	: f	⊓	: w
F	: h	ⱴ	: l
F	: v	ⱴ	: y

	tone vi (vowels)					
a	Ϛ : ä	e	Ϡ : ē	i	ꙅ : ī	o
	Ϛ : ă		Ϡ : ĕ		Ϋ : ĭ	
	Ϛ : ā		Ϡ : ə			
	Ϛ : âr					

β : ō   ϒ : ô   u   ᴄ : ŭ

β : ŏ   β : ōō   ᴂᴄ : ûr

β : oi

iv.
THE ELLIQUI LEXICONS:
ENGLISH TO ELLIQUI
ELLIQUI TO ENGLISH

Compiled by Dr. Astrid Finnely, with acknowledgement to Belzaare Lord of Air
Edited by Michael B. Koep, 1996.

PRONUNCIATION KEY

Vowels:

pat —	ă
pay —	ā
care, **air** -	âr
father, song -	ä
pet -	ĕ
bee -	ē
pit -	ĭ
pie -	ī
pot -	ô
toe -	ō
noise -	oy
took -	ŏ
boot -	o͞o
out -	ow
cut -	ŭ
urge -	ûr
about, **item**	
edible, gall**op**-	ə
butt**er** -	ər
consonants:	
ck -	long k
re**g**ime -	zj
so**ng**, hu**ng**-	ng

ENGLISH TO ELLIQUI

• A

abide - enbar, *(ĕń•bär). v.*
above - visu, *(vĕ•soō), adj.*
absolute - sosisg, *(sō• sĭs•gə), adj.*
abyss - dehul, *(dĕ•hoōl), n.*
abundant - tunefore, *(tyoōn•fōr•rā). adj.*
again - ito, *(ēt•toō), adj. see ever*
age - to, *(toō), v.*
agony - gosht, *(gäsht), adj.*
ahead - fo, *(fō), adj.*
air - el, *(ĕl) n.* aare, *(ār), n.*
alabaster - delvi. *(dĕl•vĕ́), adj.*
alike - naf, *(nāf), adj.*
alive - thebre, *(thĕ•brĕ), adj.*
all- ple, *(plĕ), prefix.*
all - plecom, *(plĕ•kōḿ), adj.*
alone - on, *(ōn), adj.*
always - eforé, *(ĕ•fōŕ•ā), adj.*
ahead - fo, *(fō), adj.*
ancient - willo, *(wĭĺ• ō), adj.*
anger - lamt, *(lămt), adj.*
arm - nooj, *(noōj), n.*
armor - resta, *(rĕst•ä), n, v.*
army - gionli. *(jē•äń•lĭ), n.*
arrow - ren, *(rĕn), n.*
art - thave, *(thä́•vā), n, v.*
atheneum, library - sotir, *(sō•tĭr), n.*
asleep - fithom, *(fĭ•thôm), adj.*
awake - efa, *(ĕf•ā), v, adj. (wake)*
aunt - mojel, *(mō´•jĕl), n.*
autumn - aundel, *(ä•oōn•dĕĺ), n.*
axe - netm, *(nĕt•m), n.*

• B

backward - revsul, *(rĕv́•soōl), adj.*
bag - rot, *(rät), n.*
balance - jequa, *(jĕ́•kwä), n, v.*
bane - brun, *(broōn), n.*
bare - opuv, *(ōp•əv), adj.*
bathe - chana, *(chä•nä), v.*
battle - glach, *(glăsh), n, v.*
bay - jor, *(jōr), n.*
be - gal, *(gāl), v.*

beam - strique *(strē•kwä), n, v.*
beauty- iful - yavule, *(yăv´•oō• lĕ), n, adj.*
bed - ra, *(rä), n.*
begin - gensis, *(jĕń•sĭs), v.*
behind - lak, *(lāk), adj.*
believe - se, *(sē), v.*
beloved - minle, *(mĭn•lā), n, adj.*
between - ak *(āk), adj.*
beyond - thom, *(thäm), adj.*
bird - iqua, *(ĕ́•kwä), n.*
birth - ensis, *(ĕn•sis) n. v.*
black - aver, *(ă•vĕr), n, adj.*
blade - nen, *(nĕn), n.*
blind - zix *(zĭks), n, v, adj.*
blood - dilith, *(dĭĺ•ĭth), n.*
blossom - pufta, *(poōf•tə), n.*
blue - skia, *(skē•ə), adj, n.*
body - fela, *(fĕl´ä´), n*
bone - biln, *(bĭln), n.*
book - tunow, *(toō•nōẃ), n.*
bow - arch, *(ärsh), n.*
branch - rych, *(rīsh), n.*
bread - ta, *(tā), n.*
break - ayr, *(âr), v.*
breathe - liva, *(lēvə), v.*
breeze - olwu, *(ōĺ•woō), n.*
bring - ne, *(nĕ), v.*
broken - val, *(văl), adj*
brother - teavoy, *(tē´•əv•oi), n.*
burn - scoli, *(skōl • ē), v.*

• C

cage - pronin, *(prō´•nĭn), n.*
cake - haljk, *(hăĺ´•jĭk), n.*
cast - koldav, *(kōl´•dăv), v.*
cat - stat, *(stät), n.*
catch - vete, *(vĕ•tē´), v*
cathedral - tircaris, *(tĭr•kâr´•ĭs), n.*
cave - hul, *(hoōl), n.*
celebrate - yul, *(yoōl), v*
chamber - tir, *(tĭr), n. - room, chamber*
chain - lek, *(lĕk), n.*
chalice - chelar, *(chĕ•lär´), n.*
challenge - dunori, *(dŭn´•ō•rē), n, v.*
change - hapan, *(hăp • ăn), n, v.*
charm - find, *(fĭnd), n, v.*
child - gzia, *(zjēä), n.*
circle - rathin, *(räth´•ĭn), n, v.*
city - nost, *(näst), n.*
claw - shar, *(shär), n, v.*

clay - dale, *(dăl´•ā), n.*
cloth - gahath, *(gä• äth), n.*
cloud - pufte, *(poōf•tā), n, v.*
cold, - bur, *(bər), adj.*
color - felbi, *(fĕl•bē), n, v.*
come - veli, *(vĕ•lē´), n.*
comfort, comforable- aath, *(ä• äth), n. v.*
    adj.
complete - the *(thā), adj. v.*
command - loka, *(lōk´•ä), n, v.*
commune - verceress, *(vĕr•sĕr•ĕss), v, n.*
cosmos - cary, *(kâry´), n.*
conscience - ur, *(oōr), n.*
council - olath, *(ōl•äth), n.*
count - tik, *(tēk), n, v.*
country - mryav, *(mrē•ăv´), n.*
course - wey, *(wĕy), n.*
craft - thav, *(thäv), v.*
creation - ion, *(ē´•ən), n.*
crescent moon - archtifli, *(ärsh•tĭf•lē),n.*
crow - caw, *(käw), n.*
crown - rathche, *(räth´•chə), n, v.*
cry - stre, *(strĕ), n, v.*
cup - lar, *(lär), n.*

• D

dagger - nenul, *(nĕn´•ûl), n.*
dance - flarin, *(flä´•rĭn), v.*
danger - zish, *(zĭsh), n.*
dark - avik, *(ăv•ēk´), n, adj.*
daughter - gzafe, *(zjä•fē), n.*
dawn - delna, *(dĕl´•nə), n, v.*
day - deli, *(dĕl´•ē), n.*
dead - ith, *(ĭth), n. adj.*
death - ithic, *(ĭth´•ĭk), n.*
death mask - ithicsazj, *(ĭth´•ic• säzj), n.*
deception - valso,*(văl´•sō),*
    n,v.
deep - de, *(dĕ), adj.*
defend - shawis, *(shä´•wīs), v.*
delicate - ya, *(yä), n.*
desire - iyuv, *(ēy•ŭv´), n, v.*
destiny - pathe, *(päth´•ā), n.*
different - agnaf, ag, *(äg´ • năf), adj.*
disappear - clesh, *(clēsh), v.*
discord - jas, *(jäs), n*
distant - milu, *(mĭ´l´• yoō), adj.*
dog - ruf, *(rŭf), n.*
doom - eth, *(ĕth), n. adj.*
down - yut, *(yoōt), adj.*
dragon - machkena, *(mă•kē´•nä), n.*

dream - orathom, *(ōr•ā•thôm´), n*
drink - slus, *(sloōs), n, v.*
dry - desh, *(dēch), adj*
dusk - delav, *(dĕ´•läv), n.*
dust - sis, *(sĭs), n*

• E

early - na, *(nə), adj.*
Earth - ae, *(āə), n. Earth*
earth - endale, *(ĕn•dăl´•ā), n.*
east - rav, *(rāv), n*
eat - cram, *(krăm), v.*
echo - sheshu, *(shĕ´•shə), n.*
empty - gobreth, *(gō´•brĕth), v, adj.*
encircle - a, *(ă), v.*
end - sisg, *(sĭs•gə), adj, n. v.*
enemy - gosong, *(gō•säng), n.*
enter - velini, *(vĕ•lē•nē), v.*
escape - othayr, *(ōth´•âr), v, adj, n.*
eternal - itonel, *(ē•toō•nĕl´), adj, n.*
evening - avidel, *(äv´•ĭ•dĕl), n, adj.*
ever - ito, *(ēt•toō), adv.*
every- kom, *(kōḿ), adj.*
evil - cy, *(sī), adj, v.*
eye - avu, *(ăv•oō´), n.*

• F

face - sazj, *(säzj), n.*
fade - lav, *(läv), v.*
fair - yavule, *(yăv´•oō• lĕ), n, adj.*
faith - ful - irito, *(ĭr´•ĭt•oō), n, v.*
fall - fallen - tuma, *(toō´•mä), v. n.*
fall (season) - aundel, *(än•dĕl), n*
family - diloy, *(dĭl´•oi), n.*
far - ham, *(häm), adj.*
farewell - gallinna, *(gäl•lē´•nə), n. adj.*
fate - pathe, *(päth´•ā), n.*
father - ata, *(ät´•ä), n.*
fast - za, *(zā), adj.*
feather - fae, *(fā), n.*
fear - shivcy, *(shĭv´-sī), n. v.*
feast - oicram, *(ōy´• krăm), n, v.*
female - fea, *(fē•ə), n. adj.*
fire - li, *(lē), n, v. see light*
fish - unwa, *(oōn´•wä), n.*
flame - liflarin, *(lē• flä´•rĭn), n.*
flesh - shifel, *(shĭv•fĕl´), n.*
flower - sire, *(sī•rē), n.*
fly - vi, *(vē), v.*

follow - lakveli, *(lāk• vě•lē ′)*, v.
fool, foolish - usag, *(oōs ′•äg)*, n. adj.
forbidden - talgeth, *(tălg• gēth)* v.
forever - itonel, *(ē•toō•něl ′)*, adj, n.
forget - kor, *(kōr)*, v.
forgive - menoth, *(měn• ōth ′)*, v.
forest - tuneald, *(tyoōn•ăld)*, n.
fortune - alyoth, *(ăl•yōth)*
front - galak, *(gāl•āk ′)*, adj.
fragile - ya, *(yä)*, n.
free - oth, *(ōth)*, v, adj.
friend - song, *(säng)*, n.
fulfilled - breth, *(brěth)*, adj. *(full)*
future - uta, *(oō ′•tə)*, n. tense

• G

garment - galt *(gält)*, n.
gift - lif, *(līf)*, n, v.
give - lifoth, *(līf•ōth)*, v.
gleam - stre, *(strē)*, adj.
go - gal, (gāl), v.
goblet - chelar, *(chě•lär ′)*, n.
God - Thi, *(thē)*, n.
god - an, *(än)*, n.
god(s) - thion, *(thē ′•ən)*
godsight, the game of godsight- shtan,
        (shtän), n. - godsight,
gold - omdel, *(ōm ′• děl)*, n.
good - we, *(wě)*, adj, n.
goodbye - gallinna, *(gäl•lē ′•nə)*, n. adj.
grace - cris, *(krĭs)*, n. adj.
greed - fward, *(fwärd)*, n.
green - lemheth, *(lěm•hěth ′)* adj.
grey - kelyi, *(kěl ′•yē)*, adj.
grief - gos, *(gäs)*, n.
grow, grown - asht, *(äsht)*, v. adj.
guard - wis, *(wīs)*, n.

• H

hair - tel, *(těl)*, n.
hand - nuk, *(nŭk)*, n.
happy - sing, *(sēng)*, adj.
harp - lane, *(lāne)*, n.
hard - omt, *(ōmt)*, adj.
haste - tig, *(tēg)*, adj, n.
hate - cyavu, *(sī ′• äv•oō)*, n, v.
head, mind - kep, *(kěp)*, n.
hear - vibre, *(vē•brā ′)*, v.
heart - vas, *(väs)*, n.
heed - aarn, *(ärn)*, v.

here - nyet, *(nī ′•ět)*, n, adj.
hello - lain, *(lā ′•ĭn)*, interjection
hidden - ild, *(ĭld)*, adj.
hide - zixilb, *(zĭks•ĭlb ′)*,v.
hill - lol, *(lōl)*, n.
history - delmilu, *(děl•mĭl ′•yoō)*, n.
hold - te, *(tē)*, n, v.
holy - caris, *(kâr ′•ĭs)*, adj. *(sacred)*
holy place - tircaris, *(tĭr•kâr ′•ĭs)*, n
hope - yar, *(yâr)*, n, v.
horn - shewu, *(shě ′•woō)*, n.
horse - hirim, *(hēr ′•ĭm)*, n.
hot - sli, *(slē)*, adj.
house - tiris, *(tĭr ′•ĭs)*, n.
human - ea, *(ēä)*, n, adj.
home - fethe, *(fěth ′• ā)*, n.

• I

I - thi, *(thē)*, n.
ice - crik, *(krīk)*, n.
illuminate - lim, *(lēm)*, v, adj.
illusion - mont, *(mänt)*, n.
immortal - itonalya, *(ē•toō•năl•yə)*, n,
        adj.
in - ni, *(nĭ)*, prep, n.

• J

jagged - razar, *(räz•är)*, adj.
jewel - che, *(chə)*, n.
join - ning, *(nēng)*, v.
journey - lonwayro, *(län•wěy ′•rō)*, n, v.
joy - ad, *(ăd)*, adj, n.

• K

key - iris, *(ī ′•rĭs)*, n.
kill - ithicne, *(ĭth ′•ĭk•ně)*, v.
kin - hoy, *(hoi)*, n.
kind - lome, *(lōm ′•ā)*, adj.
king - chal, *(chăl)*, n.
kiss - usht, *(oōsht)*, v, n.
knight - cerwis, *(sěr ′• wīs)*, n
know - ustu, *(oōst ′•oō)*, v.
knowledge - ustuse, *(oōst ′•oō•sē)*, n.

• L

labour, (toil) - gawk, *(gawk), v, n.*
lady - feasht, *(fē•äsht), n, adj.*
lake - fethequa, *(fĕth'• ä • kwä), n.*
lament - goshem, *(gōsh•ĕm'), n.*
lamp - hili, *(hī•lē), n.*
language - ele, *(ĕl•ĭ), n.*
large - chad, *(chäd), adj.*
last - sisge, *(sĭs•gā), adj..*
late - avdem, *(ăv'•dĕm), adj.*
laugh - gugad, *(goō'•găd), n, v*
law - nit, *(nĭt), n.*
lay - ster, *(stĕr), v.*
lead - fogal, *(fō'•gāl), v.*
leaf - falio, *(fäl'•ēō), n.*
leap - vide, *(vēd'•ə), v.*
learn - ustu, *(oōs'•toō), v.*
left - ap, *(ăp), adj. - left*
leg - tooj, *(toōj), n.*
library, atheneum - sotir, *(sō•tĭr), n.*
lie (untruth) - valso, *(văl'•sō), n, v.*
life - alya, *(ăl•yə), n,*
light - linna, *(lē'•nə), n. also, li (lē), n.*
listen - vibre, *(vē•brā'), v.*
lock - siri, *(sĭ•rĭ'), n.*
lonely - ono, *(ōn'•ō), adj.*
long - teng, *(tĕng), adj.*
look - avume, *(ăv•oō'•mā), v.*
lord - teasht, *(tē•äsht), n, adj.*
lost - gon, *(gōn), adj. n.*
love - thia, *(thē'•ä), n.*
loyal - dre, *(drā), n.*
lute - *lane, (lāne), n.*

• M

magic - envelliqua, *(ĕn•vĕ'•lē•kwä), n.*
magician - envelliquist, *(ĕn•vēl'•i•kwĭst)*
make - thav, *(thäv), v.*
male - teav, *(tē'•əv), n, adj*
man - teav, *(tē'•əv), n, adj*
many - tune, *(tyoōn), adj.*
march - densca, *(dĕns'•kā), v.*
marry - wetoi *(wĕy'• toō • oi), v.*
master - anfogal, *(äwn'•fō•gāl), n.*
me - thi, *(thē), n.*
meaning - fa, *(fä), n. (purpose).*
meet - roft, *(rôft), v.*
melody - teshuna, *(tĕshl•oō'•nə), n.*
memory - menic, *(mĕn•ēk'), n.*

merry - sing, *(sēng), adj.*
mind, head - kep, *(kĕp), n.*
mock - legu, *(lĕg'• oō), v.*
mood - thamf, *(thämf), n.*
moon - mel, *(mĕl), n.*
moon - tifli, *informal (tĭf•lē), n. slang.*
moon, sibling - Mellithion,
   (mĕ•lē•thē•ən) n.
moonchild - melgia, *(mĕl•zjēə'), n.*
moonlight - melinna, *(mĕ•lē'•nə), n.*
more - nel, *(nĕl), n. adj.*
morning - delna, *(dĕl'•nə), n, v.*
mortal - alyeth, *(ăl•yə•ĕth), n, adj.*
mortal/human - ithea, *(ĭth • ēä'), n.*
mother - afa, *(äf•ä), n.*
mouth - tho, *(thō), n.*
move - dech, *(dēch), v.*
music - teshlore, *(tĕsh•lō•rā'), n.*
myth - toele, *(toō'• ĕ•lā), n. (see story)*

• N

naked - ivopuv, *(ĭv•ōp'•əv), adj.*
name - soom, *(soōm), n, v.*
neck - flet, *(flĕt), n.*
necklace - fletche, *(flĕt'•chə), n*
need - iyuv, *(ēy•ŭv'), n, v*
* negative/reversal - go, *(gō), prefix.*
new - gen, *(jĕn), adj.*
newborn - thur, *(thoōr), adj.*
night - avidel, *(äv'•ĭ•dĕl), n, adj.*
no - ag, *(äg), n.*
noble - eus, *(ē'•ŭs), adj, n.*
noise - shek, *(shĕk), n.*
north - yuth, *(yŭth), n.*
nose - zle, *(zlĕ), n.*
*not - agn, *(ägn), prefix.*
now - nye, *(nī), n, tense*

• O

oath - irisong, *(ĭr'•ĭ•sông), n.*
old - aun, *(ä•oōn), adj.*
omen - uv, *(oōv), n.*
One, *(The One)* - thi, *(thē), n.*
one, on, *(ōn), adj.*
only - col, *(cōl), adj.*
orange - maksa *(mäk'•sä), adj.*
orc - ulk, *(ŭlk), n.*
order - olath, *(ōl'•äth), n.*
out - noa, *(nō'•ə), prep, n.*

• P

pace - toojsca, *(toōj´•scä)*, v.
page - now, *(nōẃ)*, n.
pain - nugosht, *(nŭ•gäsht)*, n. adj.
pale - bles, *(blĕs)*, adj.
parent - shaf, *(shäf)*, n.
path - fafe, *(fāf)*, n.
peace - fenor, *(fĕ´•nōr)*, n, adj.
peril - zish, *(zĭsh)*, n.
pipe - toke, *(tōk)*, n.
poem - eleavu, *(ĕl´•ĭ•ă•voō)*, n.
possess - imemi, *(ī´•mē•mī)*, v.
pour - tuqua, *(toō´•kwä)*, v.
power - certhia, *(sĕr•thē´•ä)*, n.
prayer - elean, *(ĕl´•ĭ•äwn)*, n.
promise - so, *(sō)*, n.
protect - shawis, *(shä´•wĭs)*, v.
pure - end, *(ĕńd)*. adj.
purple - skiamak, *(skē•ə•mäk)*, adj, n.
purpose - fa, *(fä)*, n.
pyramid - omvide, - *(ōm´•vēd´•ə)*, n.

• Q

quake - trimer, *(trĭ•mĕr)*, v.
quarrel - thiagon, *(thēä´•gōn)* n,
   v.
queen - chalfea, *(chăl•fēə´)*, n.
quest - resasht, *(rĕs•äsht´)*, n, v.
quiet - agshe, *(äg´• shĕ)*, n.
quiver - rente, *(rĕn•tē´)*, n.

• R

rage - lamt, *(lămt)*, adj, n.
rain - alyaqua, *(äl•yə•kwä)*, n, v.
reach - lum, *(loōm)*, v.
realm - mryav, *(mrē•ăv´)*, n.
rear - lak, *(lāk)*, adj.
red - mak, *(mäk)*, adj.
refuse - agiyuv, *(äg´•ēy•ŭv)*, n, v.
rejoice - adule, *(ăd•yoōl´)*, v.
remember - nemenic, *(nĕ•mĕn´•ēk)*, v.
repeat - shu, *(shə)*, v.
reveal - lifsht, *(līf•sht)*, v.
* reversal/negative - go, *(gō)*, prefix.
revive - it, *(ĭt)*, v. revive

ring - al, *(ăl)*, n.
right - e. *(ēy)*, adj.
right - wecer, *(wĕ•sĕr)*, adj, n.
rise - ath, *(äth)*, adj.
river - ven, *(vēn)*, n.
road - fafe, *(fāf)*, n.
rose - stora, *(stōr´•ä)*, n.
room - tir, *(tĭr)*, n. - room, chamber
root - qualum, *(kwä•loōm´)*, n, v.
round - rathe, *(răth•ē´)*, adj.
rule - lor, *(lōr)*, v, n.
run - dechtig, *(dēch´•tēg)*, v.
rush - tig, *(tēg)*, adj, n.

• S

sack - gav, *(gäv)*, n.
sacred - caris, *(kâr´•ĭs)*, adj.
safe - nesh, *(nĕsh)*, adj
same - naf, *(nāf)*, adj.
sea - miluqua, *(mĭ´l• yoō•kwä)*, n.
scepter - sha, *(shä)*, n.
seed - sis, *(sīs)*, n., hame, *(hām)*, n.
season - enthu, *(ĕn• thoō)*, n
secret - ildcer, *(ĭld•sĕr´)*, n.
see - avusht, *(ăv•oō´•sht)*, v.
serpent - machkena, *(mä•kē´•nä)*, n.
shadow - avika, *(ăvēk´•ä)*, n, adj.
shape - ka, *(kä)*, n.
share - jifoth, *(jīf´• ōth)*, v.
sharp - gidj, *(gĭdj)*, adj.
shield - wital, *(wī´•tăl)*, n.
short - ul, *(ŭl)*, adj.
shout - goog, *(goōg)*, v.
sibling - thion, *(thē´•ən)*, n.
sight - sh, *(sh)*, n.
silent - agshe, *(äg´• shĕ)*, n.
sing - zjoy, *(zjoi)*, v.
singer - kazjoy, *(kä•zjoi)*, n.
single - on, *(ōn)*, adj
sister - feavoy, *(fē´•əv•oi)* n
sit, seat - ter, *(tĕr)*, v, n.
shelter - is, *(ĭs)*, n.
skill - icne, *(ĭk´•nĕ)*, adj.
skin - iv, *(ĭv)*, n.
sky - wyn, *(wĭn)*, n.
sliver/splinter - doo• gĭdj *(doō• gĭdj)* n.
slay - ithicne, *(ĭth´•ĭk•nĕ)*, v.
sleep - fithom, *(fĭ•thôm)*, adj, v. *(asleep)*
slow - agtig, *(äg´•tēg)*, adj.
small - sa, *(sä)*, adj.
snow - criktuma, *(krīk•toō´•mä)*, v.n.

soft - fta, *(ftä), adj. - soft*

soil - dale, *(dăl´•ā), n.*

son - gzate, *(zjä•tē), n.*

song - joy, *(joi), n.*

sorcerer - envElliquist, *(ĕn•vĕ´•lē•kwĭst), n.*

soul - tha, *(thä), n.*

sound - she, *(shĕ), n.*

south - ruth, *(rŭth), n. adj.*

speak - ver, *(vĕr), v*

spear - nensha, *(nĕn´•shä), n.*

spider - ros, (rōs), n.

spirit - ress, *(rĕs),n.*

spring - gendel, *(jĕn•dĕl), n.*

staff - neld, *(nĕld), n.*

stalwart - ken, *(kĕn), n.*

standard - telf, *(tĕlf), n.*

star - anon, *(ə•nôn), n.*

stare - avqui, *(ăv•kwē)*

starlight - anonli, , *(ə•nôn´•lē), n.*

steel - enbiln, *(ĕń• bĭln), n.*

still - heta, *(hē•tə), adj.*

stone - om, *(ōm), n.*

stop - ni, *(nēt), v.*

storm - geshle, *(gĕsh´•lə), n.*

stream - saven, *(sä•vēn´), n.*

strength - greg, *(grĕg), n.*

suffer (ing) - nth, *(ənth), n. v.*

story - elefa, *(ĕlĕ´•fä), n. (see myth)*

summer - ashtdel, *(äsht´•dĕl), n.*

sun - del, *(dĕl), n.*

sun, god - Dellithion, *(dĕl•lē´•thē•ən) n.*

sunlight - delinna, *(dĕ•lē´•nə), n.*

sunrise - delinnath, *(dĕl•ēn´•əth), n, v.*

sunset - delav, *(dĕ´•läv), n.*

surround - a, *(ă), v.*

sweet - nyth, *(nīth), adj.*

swift - za, *(zā), adj.*

swim - yathe, *(yäth´•ə), v.*

sword - tengnen, *(tĕng´•nĕn), n.*

• T

take - ethe, *(ĕth´•ē), v.*

tale - elefa, *(ĕlĕ´•fä), n. (see myth)*

talk - ver, *(vĕr), v*

tall - tle, *(tlĕ), adj.*

taste - nyea, *(nyē´•ə), v, n.*

teach/teacher - lifthia *(līf• thē´•ä), v. n.*

tear - avuqua, *(ăv•ōō•kwä´), n.*

teeth - nibs, *(nĭbs), n.*

templar - tircan, *(tĭr•käwn´), n.*

temple - tircaris, *(tĭr•kâr´•ĭs), n.*

terror - shivcy, *(shĭv´-sī), n.*

thank (s), thankyou - miva, *(mī•vä), adj. n.*

thick -dwok, *(dwōk), adj.*

thin - wok, *(wōk), adj.*

thing - jelth, *(jĕlth), n.*

think - quin, *(kwēn), v.*

thirsty, thirst - iyuvqua, *(ēy´•ŭv•kwä), n, adj.*

thought - qui, *(kwē), n.*

throne - chalter, *(chăl•tĕr´), n.*

tie - gob, *(gäb), v.*

time - delthu, *(dĕl´•thoō), n.*

together - hoy, *(hoi), adj.*

tongue - nya, *(nyə), n.*

trap - valsild, *(văl•sĭld´), n, v.*

tree - ald, *(ăld), n.*

true - cer, *(cĕr), adj, n.*

truth - dre, *(drä), n.*

turn - thu, *(thoō), n*

• U

up - yn, *(yĭn), adj*

uncle - nats, *(năts), n.*

unknown - ale, *(ăl•ā), n, adj.*

universe - cary, *(kârē´), n.*

user - ist, *(ĭst), v.*

• V

vanish - clesh, *(klēsh), v.*

victory - tala, *(tăl´•ā), n.*

vine - wev, *(wĕv), n.*

vision - ora, *(ōr•ā´), n.*

voice - nyashe, *(nyə´•shĕ), n, v.*

• W

wake - efa, *(ĕf•ā), v.*

walk - sca, *(scä), v.*

wall - talg, *(tălg), n.*

wand - wigler, *(wĭg´•lĕr), n.*

want - geth, *(gĕth), v.*

war - agyar, *(äg´•yâr), n, v.*

wash - chana, *(chä•nä), v.*

water - qua, *(kwä), n.*

weave - gath, *(gäth), v.*

wedding - misli, *(mēs•lē)*, *n.*
we - atha, *(āth•ā´)*
weep - stre, *(strē)*, *n, v.*
welcome - adnyet, *(ăd•nī´•ĕt)*, *n,v, adj.*
west - yav, *(yāv)*, *adj, n*
wet - qual, *(kwäl)*, *adj.*
wheel -cien, *(kēn)*, *n.*
whisper - thesht, *(thēsht)*, *n, v.*
wind - volwu, *(võl•woō)*, *n.*
wine - twiv, *(twēf)*, *n.*
wing - vifae, *(vē•fā´)*, *n.*
winter - delfithom, *(dĕl• fí•thôm)*,*n.*
wise - hama, *(häm´ə)*, *n, adj.*
wizard - envelliquist, *(ĕn•vĕ´•lē•kwĭst)*, *n.*
whole - breth, *(brĕth)*, *adj.*
woman - fea, *(fē•ə)*, *n. adj.*
wood - dug, *(doōg)*, *n.*
word - so, *(sõ)*, *n.*
world - kre, *(krā)*, *n.*
wrath - lamt, *(lămt)*, *adj, n.*
write - selpa, *(sĕl•pā)*, *v.*

• Y

yellow - saf, (săf), *adj, n.*
yes - lit, *(līt)*, *adv.*
you - a, *(ä)*, *n*
young - fer, *(fĕr•ä)*, *adj, n.*

ELLIQUI TO ENGLISH

.A ς ς ς ς̇

a, *(ä) pronoun. - you*
a, *(ă), v. - encircle, surround,*
aare, *(ār), n.* el, *(ĕl) n - air*
aarn, *(ärn), v. - heed*
aath, *(ä· äth), n. v. adj.- comfort,*
    comfortable
ae, *(āə), n. - Earth*
ad, *(ăd), adj, n. - joy*
adnyet, *(ăd•nī´•ĕt), n,v, adj. - welcome*
adule, *(ăd•yoōl´), n, adj. - rejoice*
afa, *(äf•ä), n. - mother*
ag, *(äg), n. - no*
agiyuv, *(äg´•ēy•ŭv), n, v. - refuse*
* agn, *(ägn), prefix. - not*
agnaf, *(äg´• nāf), adj - different*
agshe, *(äg´• shĕ), n.- silent, quiet*
agtig, *(äg´•tēg), adj. - slow*
agyar, *(äg´•yâr), n, v. - war*
ak, *(āk), adj. - between*
al, *(ăl), n. - ring.*
ale, *(ăl•ā), n, adj. - unknown*
ald, *(ăld), n. - tree*
alya, *(ăl•yə), n, adj.- life*
Ithea, *(ăl•yə•ĕth), n, adj. - mortal*
alyaqua, *(ăl•yə•kwä), n, v. - rain*
alyoth, *(ăl•yōth) - fortune*
an, *(än), n. - God*
anfogal, *(äwn´•fō•gāl), n. - master*
anon, *(ə•nôn), n. - star*
anonli, *(ə•nôn´•lē), n. - starlight*
ap, *(ăp), adj. - left*
arch, *(ärsh), n. - bow*
archtifli, *(ärsh•tĭf•lē), n. - crescent moon*
asht, *(äsht), adj. - grow, grown*
ashtdel, *(ăsht´•dĕl), n. - summer*
ata, *(ät´•ä), n. - father*
ath, *(äth), adj. - rise*
atha, *(āth•ā´), - we*
aundel, *(ä•oōn•dĕl), n. - autumn, fall*
avdem, *(ăv´•dĕm), adj. - late*
aver, *(ă•vĕr), n, adj. - black*
avidel, *(äv´•ĭ•dĕl), n, adj. - evening, night*
avik, *(ăv•ēk´), n, adj. - dark*
avika, *(ăvēk´•ä), n, adj. - shadow*

avqui, *(ăv•kwē) - stare*
avu, *(ăv•oō´), n. - eye*
avume, *(ăv•oō´•mā), v. - look*
avuqua, *(ăv•oō•kwä´), n. - tear*
avusht, *(ăv•oō´•sht), v. - see*
ayr, *(âr) - break*

.B ↳

biln, *(bĭln), n. - bone*
bles, *(blĕs), adj. - pale*
breth, *(brĕth), adj. - whole, fulfilled*
brun, *(broōn), n. - bane*
bur, *(bər), adj. - cold*

.C ⌘⍭

caw, *(käw), n. - crow*
cary, *(kâr•ē´), n. - cosmos, universe*
caris, *(kâr´•ĭs), adj. - sacred, holy*
cer, *(sĕr), adj. n. - true, truth*
certhia, *(sĕr•thē´•ä), n. - power*
cerwis, *(sĕr´• wīs), n - knight*
CH words see below
cien, *(kēn), n. - wheel*
clesh, *(klēsh), v. - disappear*
col, *(kōl), adj. - only*
cram, *(krăm), v. - eat*
crik, *(krīk), n. - ice*
cris, *(krĭs), n. adj. - grace*
criktuma, *(krīk•toō´•mä), v.n. snow*
cy, *(sī), adj, v. - evil*
cyavu, *(sī´• ăv•oō), n, v. - hate*

· CH ⍦

chad, *(chäd), adj. - large*
chal, *(chăl), n. - king*
chalfea, *(chăl•fēə´), n. - queen*
chalter, *(chăl•tĕr´), n. - throne*
chana, *(chä´•nä), v. - bathe, wash*
che, *(chə), n - jewel*
chelar, *(chĕ•lär´), n. -chalice, goblet*

· D ♌

dale, *(dăl´•ā),* n. - *soil, clay*
de, *(dĕ),* adj. *- deep*
dech, *(dēch),* v. *- move*
desh, *(dēch),* adj- *dry*
dechtig, *(dēch´•tēg),* v. *- run*
dehul, *(dĕ•hool),* n. *- abyss, deep cavern.*
del, *(dĕl),* n. *- sun*
delav, *(dĕ´•läv),* n. *- dusk*
delfithom, *(dĕl• fĭ•thôm),*n. *- winter*
deli, *(dĕl•ē),* n. *- day*
delmilu, *(dĕl•mĭl´•yoō),* n. *- history*
delna, *(dĕl´•nə),* n, v. *- dawn, morning*
delthu, *(dĕl´•thoō),* n. *- time*
delvi. *(dĕl•vĕ´),* adj. *- alabaster*
densca, *(dĕns´•kā),* v *- march*
dilith, *(dĭl´•īth),* n. *- blood*
diloy, *(dĭl´•oi),* n. *- family*
dre, *(drā),* n. *- truth/loyalty*
dug, *(doōg),* n. *- wood*
dugidj,*(doō• gĭdj)* n. *- splinter, sliver*
dunori, *(dŭn´•ō•rē),* n, v. *- challenge*
dwok, *(dwōk),* adj. *- thick*

· E ♌ ♉ ♉

e. *(ēy),* adj *- right*
ea, *(ēä),* n, adj. *- human, man*
efa, *(ĕf•ā),* v. *- wake-awake*
eforé, *(ĕ•fŏr´•ā),* adj. *- always*
el, *(ĕl)* n. aare, *(ār),* n. *- air*
ele, *(ĕl•ĭ),* n. *- language*
elean, *(ĕl´•ĭ•äwn),* n. *- prayer*
eleavu, *(ĕl´•ĭ•ă•voō),* n. *- poetry*
elefa, *(ĕlĕ´•fä),* n. *- tale, story*
Elliqui, *(ĕl´• lē•kwē),* n.- *oral, written language of Itonalya*
enbar, *(ĕń•bär).* v *- abide*
end, *(ĕńd).* adj.- *pure*
enbiln, *(ĕń• bĭln),* n. *- steel*
endale, en, *(ĕn• dăl´•ā),* n. *- earth*
ensis, *(ĕn•sis)* - *birth*
enthu, *(ĕn• thoō),* n *- season*
envelliqua, *(ĕn•vĕ´•lē•kwä),* n. *- magic*
eth, *(ĕth),* n. adj. *- doom*
ethe, *(ĕth´•ē),* v. *- take*
eus, *(ē´•ŭs),* adj, n. *- noble*

· F Ͱ

fa, *(fä),* n. *- meaning, purpose*
fae, *(fā),* n. *- feather*
fafe, *(fāf),* n. *- path, road*
falio, *(fäl´•ēō),* n. *- leaf*
fea, *(fē•ə),* n. adj. *- female, woman*
feasht, *(fē•äsht),* n, adj. *- lady*
feavoy, *(fē´•əv•oi),* n *- sister*
felbi, *(fĕl•bē),* n, v. *- color*
fela, *(fĕl• ä´),* n. *- body*
fenor, *(fē´•nōr),* n. adj. *- peace*
fera, *(fĕr•ä),* adj, n. *- young*
fta, *(ftä),* adj. *- soft*
fethe, *(fĕth• ā),*n. *- home*
fethequa, *(fĕth´• ā • kwä),* n. *- lake*
find, *(fīnd),* n, v. *- charm*
fithom, *(fĭ•thôm),* adj, v. *- asleep, sleep*
flarin, *(flä´•rĭn),* v. *- dance*
flet, *(flĕt),* n. *- neck*
fletche, *(flĕt´•chə),* n *- necklace*
fo, *(fō),* adj. *- ahead*
fogal, *(fō´•gāl),* v. *- lead*
fward, *(fwärd),* n. *- greed*

· G Ͱ ͷ

gal, *(gāl),* v. *- go, be*
gallinna, *(gäl•lē´•nə),* n. adj.- *farewell*
gahath, *(gä• äth),* n. *- cloth*
galak, *(gāl•āk´),* adj. *- front*
galt *(gält),* n. *garment*
gav, *(gäv),* n. *- sack*
gawk, *(gawk),* v, n. *- labour, toil*
gen, *(jĕn),* adj. *- new*
gendel, *(jĕn•dĕl),* n. *- spring*
gensis, *(jĕń•sĭs),* v. *- begin*
geshle, *(gĕsh´•lə),* n. *- storm*
geth, *(gēth),* v. *- want*
gidj, *(gĭdj),* adj. *- sharp*
gionli, *(jē•äń•lĭ),* n. *- army*
glach, *(glăsh),* n, v. *- battle*
go, *(gō),* prefix. *- reversal/negative*
gob, *(gäb),* v. *- tie*
gobreth, *(gō´•brĕth),* v, adj. *- empty*
gon, *(gōn),* adj. n. *- lost*
goog, *(goōg),* v. *- shout*
gosong, *(gō•säng),* n. *- enemy*
gos, *(gäs),* n. *- grief*
goshem, *(gōsh•ĕm´),* n. *- lament*

gosht, *(găsht), adj - agony*
goth, *(găth), v. - weave, pall*
greg, *(grĕg), n. - strength*
gugad, *(goō´•găd), n, v. - laugh*
gzafe, *(zjä•fē), n. - daughter*
gzate, *(zjä•tē), n. - son*
gzia, *(zjēä), n. - child*

• H ⊦

haljk, *(hăl´ •jĭk), n. - cake*
ham, *(häm), adj. - far*
hama, *(häm´ə), n, adj. - wise*
hame, *(hām), n. - seed (see sis)*
hapan, *(hăp • ăn), n, v. - change*
heta, *(hē•tə), adj. - still*
hili, *(hī•lē), n. - lamp*
hirim, *(hēr´•ĭm), n. - horse*
hoy, *(hoi), n. - kin, together*
hul, *(hoōl), n. - cave*

• I 8Ɣ

ild, *(ĭld), adj. - hidden*
ildcer, *(ĭld•sĕr´), n. - secret*
imemi, *(ī´•mē•mī), v. - possess*
ion, *(ē´•ən), n. - creation*
iqua, *(ḗ•kwä), n. - bird*
iris, *(ī´•rĭs), n. - key*
irisong, *(ĭr´•ĭ•sông), n. - oath*
irito, *(ĭr´•ĭt•oō), n, v. - faith, faithful*
is, *(ĭs), n. - shelter*
ist, *(ĭst), n. - user*
it, *(ĭt), v. revive*
ith, *(ĭth), n. adj. - dead*
ithea, *(ĭth • ēä´), n, - mortal man*
ithic, *(ĭth´•ĭk), n. - death*
ithicne, *(ĭth´•ĭc•nĕ), v. - slay, kill*
ithicsazj, *(ĭth´•ic•säzj), n. - death mask*
ito, *(ēt•toō), adj. - again / ever*
itonalya, *(ē•toō•năl•yə), n, adj. immortal*
itonel, *(ē•toō•nĕl´), adj, n.- forever,*
                    eternal
iv, *(ĭv), n. - skin*
ivopuv, *(ĭv•ōp´•əv), adj. - naked*
iyuv, *(ēy•ŭv´), n, v. - desire, need*
iyuvqua, *(ēy´•ŭv•kwä), n, adj. thirst*

• J ʃ̃

jas, *(jās), n. - discord*
janu, *(jăn•yoō), n. - door*
jelth, *(jĕlth), n. - thing*
jequa, *(jḗ•kwä), n, v. - balance*
jifoth, *(jīf´•ōth), v. - share*
jor, *(jōr), n. - bay*
joy, *(jōy), n. - song*

• K ʃ

ka, *(kä), n. - shape*
kazjoy, *(kä•zjoi), n. - singer*
kelyi, *(kĕl´•yē), adj. - grey*
kep, *(kĕp), n. - head*
ken, *(kĕn), n. - stalwart*
kom, *(kóm), adj. - every*
koldav, *(kōl´•dăv), v. - cast*
kor, *(kōr), v. - forget*
kre, *(krā), n. - world*

• L ⇂⇂

lain, *(lā´•ĭn) - hello*
lak, *(lāk), adj. - behind, rear*
lakveli, *(lāk• vĕ•lē´), v. - follow*
lamt, *(lămt), adj. - anger, wrath, rage*
lane, *(lāne), n. - lute, harp*
lar, *(lär), n. -cup*
lav, *(läv), v. - fade*
legu, *(lĕg´• oō), v. - mock*
lek, *(lĕk), n. - chain*
lemheth, *(lĕm•hĕth´) adj. - green*
li, *(lē), n, v. - fire, light*
lif, *(lĭf), n, v. - gift*
liflarin, *(lē• flä´•rĭn), n. - flame*
lifoth, *(lĭf•ōth), v. - give*
lifsht, *(lĭf•sht), v. - reveal*
lifthia, *(lĭf• thē´•ä), n, v. teach, teacher.*
lim, *(lēm), v, adj. - illuminate*
linna, *(lē´•nə), n. - light*
lit, *(lĭt), adv. - yes*
liva, *(lēvə), v. - breathe*
loka, *(lōk´•ä), n, v. - command*
lol, *(lōl), n - hill*
lome, *(lōm´•ä), adj. - kind*
lonwayro, *(län•wĕy´•rō), n, v. journey*
lor, *(lōr), v, n - rule*

lum, *(loōm), v. - reach*

• M ᛰ

machkena, *(mă•kē´•nä), n. - dragon,
        serpent*
mak, *(mäk), adj. - red*
maksa, *(mäk´•să), adj. - orange*
mel, *(mĕl), n. - moon*
melgia, *(mĕl•zjēə´), n. - moonchild*
melinna, *(mĕ•lē´•nə), n. - moonlight*
menic, *(mĕn•ēk´), n. - memory*
menoth, *(mĕn• ōth´), v. - forgive*
milu, *(mĭ´l• yoō), adj. - distant*
miluqua, *(mĭ´l• yoō•kwä), n. sea, ocean*
minle, *(mĭn•lā), n, adj. - beloved*
misli, *(mēs•lē), n. - wedding*
miva, *(mī•vā), adj. n. - thank you*
mojel, *(mō´•jĕl), n. -aunt*
mont, *(mänt), n. - illusion*
mryav, *(mrē•ăv´), n. - realm, country*

• N ᛉ

na, *(nə), adj. - early*
naf, *(nāf), adj. - same, alike, akin*
nats, *(năts), n. - uncle*
ne, *(nĕ), v. - bring*
nel, *(nĕl), n. adj. - more*
neld, *(nĕld), n. - staff*
nemenic, *(nĕ•mĕn´•ēk), v. - remember*
nen, *(nĕn), n. - blade*
nenul, *(nĕn´•ûl), n. - dagger*
nensha, *(nĕn´•shä), n. - spear*
nesh, *(nĕsh), adj. - safe*
netm, *(nĕt•m), n - axe*
nit, *(nēt), v. - stop*
ni, *(nĭ), prep, n. - in*
nibs, *(nĭbs), n. - teeth*
ning, *(nēng), v. - join*
nit, *(nĭt), n. - law*
noa, *(nō´•ə), prep, n. - out*
nooj, *(noōj), n. - arm*
nost, *(näst), n. - city*
nth, nth, *(ənth), n. v. - suffer, suffering*
nugosht, *(nŭ•gäsht), adj. - pain*
nuk, *(nŭk), n. - hand*
nya, *(nyə), n. - tongue*
nyashe, *(nyə´•shĕ), n, v. - voice*
nye, *(nĭ), n, tense - now*

nyea, *(nyē´•ə), v, n. - taste*
nyet, *(nī´•ĕt), n, adj. - here*
nyth, *(nīth), adj.- sweet*

• O ᛒ ᛏ ᛉ ᛏ ᛟ

oicram, *(ōy´• krăm), n, v. - feast*
olath, *(ōl•äth), n. - order, council*
olwu, *(ōl´•woō), n - breeze*
om, *(ōm), n. - stone*
omt, *(ōmt), adj. - hard*
omdel, *(ōm´• dĕl), n - gold*
omvide, *(ōm´•vēd´•ə), n.- pyramid*
on, *(ōn), adj. - alone, one, single*
ono, *(ōn´•ō), adj. - lonely*
opuv, *(ōp•əv), adj. - bare*
ora, *(ōr•ā´), n. - vision*
orathom, *(ōr•ā•thôm´), n - dream*
oth, *(ōth), v, adj. - free*
othayr, *(ōth´•âr), v, adj, n. - escape*

• P ᛏ

pathe, *(päth´•ā), n. - destiny, fate*
ple, *(plĕ), prefix. - all*
plecom, *(plĕ•kōḿ), adj. - all*
pronin, *(prō´•nĭn), n. - cage*
pufta, *(poōf´•tə), n. - blossom*
pufte, *(poōf•tā), n, v. - cloud*

• Q ᚴ

qua, *(kwä), n - water*
qual, *(kwäl), adj. - wet*
qualum, *(kwä•loōm´), n, v. - root*
qui, *(kwē), n. - thought*
quin, *(kwēn), v. - think*

• R ᚴ

ra, *(rä), n. - bed*
rathche, *(räth´•chə), n, v. -crown*
rathin, *(räth´•ĭn), n, v. - circle*
rav, *(rāv), n - east*
razar, *(răz•är), adj. - jagged*

ren, *(rĕn)*, n. - *arrow*
rente, *(rĕn•tē′)*, n. - *quiver*
ress, *(rĕs)*, n. - *spirit*
resasht, *(rĕs •äsht′)*, n, v. - *quest,*
resta, *(rĕst•ä)*, n, v. - *armor*
revsul, *(rĕv•sool)*, adj. - *backward*
roft, *(rôft)*, v. - *meet*
ros, *(rōs)*, n. - *spider*
rot, *(rät)*, n. *bag*
ruf, *(rŭf)*, n. - *dog*
ruth, *(rŭth)*, n. adj. - *south*
rych, *(rīsh)*, n. - *branch*

• S ♆

sa, *(sä)*, adj. - *small*
saf, *(săf)*, adj, n. - *yellow*
saven, *(sä•vēn′)*, n. - *stream*
sazj, *(säzj)*, n. - *face*
sca, *(scä)*, v. - *walk*
scoli, *(skōl′ • ē)*, v. - *burn*
se, *(sē)*, v. - *believe*
selpa, *(sĕl•pä)*, v. - *write*
SH words, see below
sing, *(sēng)*, adj. - *happy, merry*
sis, *(sīs)*, n. - *seed*
sire, *(sī•rē)*, n. - *flower*
siri, *(sĭ•rĭ′)*, n. - *lock*
sis, *(sĭs)*, n. - *dust*
sisg, *(sĭs•gə)*, adj, n. v. - *end*
sisge, *(sĭs•gä)*, adj. - *last*
skia, *(skē•ə)*, adj, n. - *blue*
skiamak, *(skē•ə•mäk)*, adj, n. *purple*
sli, *(slē)*, adj. - *hot, heat*
slus, *(sloos)*, n, v. - *drink*
so, *(sō)*, n. - *word, promise*
sotir, *(sō•tĭr)*, n. - *atheneum, library*
song, *(säng)*, n. - *friend*
soom, *(soom)*, n, v. - *name*
sosisg, *(sō• sĭs•gə)*, adj. *absolute*
stat, *(stät)*, n. - *cat*
ster, *(stĕr)*, v. - *lay*
stre, *(strē)*, adj. - *gleam*
stre, *(strĕ)*, n, v. - *cry, weep*
stora, *(stōr′•ä)*, n. - *rose*
strique *(strē•kwä)*, n, v. - *beam*

• SH ☥

sha, *(shä)*, n. *scepter*

shaf, *(shäf)*, n. - *parent*
shar, *(shär)*, n, v. - *claw, talon*
shawis, *(shä′•wīs)* - v. *defend, protect*
she, *(shĕ)*, n. - *sound*
shek, *(shĕk)*, n. - *noise*
sheree, *(shĕr•ē)*, n. - *oneness, unity*
sheshu, *(shĕ′•shə)*, n. - *echo*
shewu, *(shĕ′•oo)*, n. - *horn*
shifel, *(shĭv•fĕl′)*, n. - *flesh*
shivcy, *(shĭv′-sī)*, n. v. - *fear, terror*
sht, *(sht)*, n. - *sight*
shtan, *(shtän)*, n. - *godsight,*
the game of Shtan
shu, *(shə)*, v. - *repeat*

• T ⚼

ta, *(tä)*, n. - *bread*
tala, *(tăl′•ä)*, n. - *victory*
talg, *(tălg)*, n. - *wall*
talgeth *(tăl′•gēth)* v. - *forbidden*
te, *(tē)*, n, v. - *hold*
teasht, *(tē•äsht′)*, n, adj. - *lord*
teav, *(tē′•əv)*, n, adj - *male, man*
teavoy, *(tē′•əv•oi)*, n. - *brother*
tel, *(tĕl)*, n. - *hair*
telf, *(tĕlf)*, n - *standard*
teng, *(tĕng)*, adj. - *long*
tengnen, *(tĕng′•nĕn)*, n. - *sword*
ter, *(tĕr)*, v. - *sit*
teshlore, *(tĕsh′•lō•rä′)*, n. - *music*
teshuna, *(tĕshl•oo′•nə)*, n. - *melody*
TH words, see below
tifli, *(tĭf′•lē)*, n. - *moon*
tig, *(tēg)*, adj. - *haste, rush*
tik, *(tēk)*, n, v. - *count*
tir, *(tĭr)*, n. - *room, chamber*
tircaris, *(tĭr•kâr′•ĭs)*, n. - *temple,*
cathedral, holy place
tircan, *(tĭr•käwn′)*, n. - *templar, temple*
minister
tiris, *(tĭr′•ĭs)*, n - *house*
tle, *(tlĕ)*, adj. - *tall*
toke, *(tōk)*, n. - *pipe*
to, *(too)*, v. - *age*
tooj, *(tooj)*, n. - *leg*
toojsca, *(tooj′•scä)*, v. - *pace*
toele, *(too′• ĕ•lä)*,n. *ancient story, myth*
trimer, *(trĭ′•mĕr)*, v. - *quake*
tuma, *(too′•mä)*, v. n. - *fall, fallen*
tune, *(tyoon)*, adj. - *many*

tuneald, *(tyoōn´•ăld), n.* - *forest*
tunefore, *(tyoōn´•fōr•rā). adj. abundant*
tunow, *(too͞•nōw´), n.* - *book*
tuqua, *(too͞´•kwä), v.* - *pour*
twiv, *(twēf), n.* - *wine*

. TH ᚦ

thamf, *(thämf), n.* - *mood*
tha, *(thä), n.* - *soul*
the, *(thā), adj. v.* - *complete*
thave, *(thä´•vā), n, v.* - *art, craft*
thebre, *(thē´•brĕ), adj.* - *alive*
thesht, *(thēsht), n, v.* - *whisper*
Thi, *(thē), n.* - *God*
thi, *(thē), n.* - *I, me, The One*
thia, *(thē´•ä), n.* - *love*
thiagon, *(thēä´•gōn), n, v* - *quarrel, fight*
thion, *(thē´•ən), n.* - *sibling, gods*
tho, *(thō), n.* - *mouth*
thom, *(thäm), adj.* - *beyond*
thu, *(thoo͞), n* - *turn*
thur, *(thoo͞), adj.* - *newborn*

. U ᚢ

ul, *(ŭl), adj* - *short*
ulk, *(ŭlk), n.* - *enemy*
unwa, *(oōn´•wä), n. fish*
ur, *(oōr), n.* - *conscience*
usag, *(oōs´•äg), n. adj.* - *fool, foolish*
usht, *(oōsht), v, n.* - *kiss*
ustu, *(oōs´•too͞), v.* - *know, learn*
ustuse, *(oōst´•oō•sē), n. knowledge*
uta, *(oō´•tə), n. tense* - *future*
uv, *(oōv), n.- omen*

. V ᚡ

val, *(văl), adj* - *broken*
valsild, *(văl´•sĭld), n, v.* - *trap*
valso, *(văl´•sō), n, v.* - *lie, untruth,*
vas, *(väs), n.* - *heart*
veli, *(vĕ•lē´), n.* - *come*
velini, *(vĕ•lē´•nē), v.* - *enter*
ven, *(vēn), n.* - *river*
ver, *(vĕr), v* - *speak*

verceress, *(vĕr´•sĕr•ĕss), v, n. commune*
vete, *(vĕ•tē´), v.* - *catch*
vifae, *(vē•fā´), n.* - *wing*
vi, *(vē), v.* - *fly*
vibre, *(vē•brä´), v.* - *hear, listen*
vide, *(vēd´•ə), v.* - *leap*
visu, *(vē´•soō), adj.* - *above*
volwu, *(vōl´•woō), n.* - *wind*

. W ᚹ

we, *(wĕ), adj, n.* - *good*
wecer, *(wĕ´•cĕr), adj, n.* - *right*
wetoi, *(wĕy´• too͞ • oi), v.* - *marry*
wev, *(wĕv), n.* - *vine*
wey, *(wĕy), n.* - *course*
wigler, *(wĭg´•lĕr), n.* - *wand*
wis, *(wīs), n.* - *guard*
wital, *(wī´•tăl), n.* - *shield*
willo, *(wĭl´•ō), adj.* - *ancient*
wok, *(wōk), adj.* - *thin*
wyn, *(wĭn), n.* - *sky*

. Y ᛁ

ya, *(yä), n.* - *delicate, fragile*
yar, *(yâr), n, v.* - *hope*
yathe, *(yäth´•ə), v.* - *swim*
yav, *(yāv), adj, n.* - *west*
yavule, *(yăv´•oō• lĕ), n, adj.* - *beauty,*
          beautiful
yn, *(yĭn), adj* - *up*
yul, *(yoōl), v.* - *celebrate*
yut, *(yoōt), adj.* - *down*
yuth, *(yŭth), adj, n.* - *north*

. Z ᛉ

za, *(zā), adj.* - *fast, swift*
zish, *(zĭsh), n.* - *peril, danger*
zix, *(zīks), n, v, adj.* - *blind*
zixilb, *(zīks•ĭlb´), v.* - *hide*
zjoy, *(zjoi), v.* - *sing*
zle, *(zlĕ), n.* - *nose*

Acknowledgments

It has taken well over twenty years to arrive at this page. I am grateful to these dear and amazing people for helping me along the path.

My parents, Kenneth and Diana Koep. Stan, Jo Lynn and Mel. Bob, Bobbi , Bean and Nic, Eric and Laurie Wilson (*Olive* and *Ondo*), Scott Clarkson *(caw minle*—for your love of this story and helping me to sharpen it) and Dani, Prue and Jude, Mark Rakes (Markr), Cristopher Lucas (Captain), Cary Beare *(Belzaare)*, Tami and Barb Clarkson, Tom Brunner, David and Lisa VanHersett, Steve Gibbs, Jeff Hagman, Joe and Sara Linch, Andrea Brockmeyer, Margaret Hurlocker, Mary Starkey, Dan Spaulding, Jason Williamson (Bag Man), Michael Roberts, Monte Thompson, Harvey Pepper, Tyler Davis, Elizabeth Stokes, Adam Graves, Toby Reynolds, Karolyn Rogers, Calvin *(Vincale)*, Majorie and Brynn Langley, Michelle, Kyler and Taryn John, Blair Williams, Anthony Nelson, Paul and Shannon Irwin, Greg and Jillian Rowley, Glenn Case, Russ Abrams, Dennis Davaz, Jane Mauser and Rory Mcleod, Darin Schaffer, Neal Plazas, Daryl Lewis *(The Magic of an Ordinary Man)*. Manito (climbing pyramids and then moving to the Azores), The Heren Sindaril and The Rubbish. All at the Cd'A Arts and Culture Alliance, The 315 Greenbriar Inn, The Well Read Moose, Elkins Resort and The Iron Horse. Lisa Koep and Geri and Walter Perkins.

It was a privilege to have drafts of this book red-inked and pencil-scratched by two exacting and thoughtful editors. Thank you to Professor Michael Herzog for listening to me talk about this story for the better part of two decades, and for continuing to teach me how to write it. And to Allison McCready *(Luminaare)*—who has been there for all three—thank you for your incredible eye, tireless imagination and your nurturing spirit for the story and all those that live inside it.

I offer my deepest gratitude to Mark Lax, Andreas John and all at Will Dreamly Arts Publishing for their love, support and enthusiasm (and countless other inspirations and memories) over the course of this journey. Here's to the adventures to come.

To Sheree Jerome *(Deliavu)* for the joy and light you have brought to my world—what wonders ahead.

And to my son Michael Scott *(Lemthia)* for the endless stream of questions, the sword fights in between paragraphs and the patience you've shown your dear old Dad.

⟊⟊⟊⟊ ⟊⟊⟊⟊⟊⟊ ⟊⟊⟊⟊⟊ ⟊⟊ ⟊⟊⟊⟊⟊⟊⟊⟊

thia alyoth thave ni tunefore

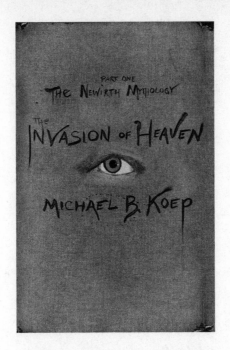

Part One: The Invasion of Heaven
Trade Paperback ISBN # 978-09893935-1-5
Hardcover ISBN # 978-0-9893935-0-8

Part Two: Leaves of Fire
Trade Paperback ISBN # 978-0-9893935-4-6
Hardcover ISBN # 978-9893935-8-4